DARKHAND SEVENTY-TWO

CHILDREN OF A LOST GOD

WORKBOOK PRESS LLC
187 E Warm Springs Rd,
Suite B285, Las Vegas, NV 89119, USA

Website: https://workbookpress.com/
Hotline: 1-888-818-4856
Email: admin@workbookpress.com

Ordering Information:
Quantity sales. Special discounts are available on quantity purchases by corporations, associations, and others.
For details, contact the publisher at the address above.

ISBN-13:   978-1-953839-23-7 (Paperback Version)
                978-1-953839-24-4 (Digital Version)

REV. DATE: 29/09/2020

CONTENTS

DEDICATION

To Tommie Pearl who birthed and raised me, Nancy who kept me out of trouble and Verdna Mae who gave me her vision. My three wonderful mothers who loved me and although two have since departed, I love them none the least.

PROLOGUE

The GOD, who met Moses on the mountaintop, wrote ten commandments on stone tablets for the Hebrew people to follow. Maybe he wrote them using Moses' fingers, maybe his own. But they got wrote, awesome concepts chiseled in slabs of rock these people could carry wherever they went. And for whole bunches of folks that became that. Chosen people, chosen rules. The Ten Commandments, nuf said.

But GOD had been very busy long before Moses' time. GOD don't wait around for nobody. In fact, Biblical scholars point to similarities between Hittite and Egyptian documents as actual inspiration for Moses' set. And those long predated the Hebrew exodus from Egypt. So if GOD inspired Moses ...you get my meaning?

Moses was, after all, a Prince of Egypt and learned Egyptian mysticism from the priests who trained him from childhood. That's the logic point.

However, some folks (probably most folks) won't be too happy if we pursue that point too far, cause they prefer their religion black and white, no thirty-one flavors of gray. And that's the problem, cause unless you trying to brand Moses a copycat, it still don't rule out GOD bringing inspiration to those earlier Hittites and Egyptians and whosoever else (trust me, it's a long list).

Amazing how many opinionated folks argue GOD had only one name and one chosen people around this whole wide world, but still believe GOD made everything and thus everyone just kept the rules secret from most of the everyones. Go Figure!

Ya'll call them Chosen Ones? Arrogant Ones maybe a better title. Yes of course, your point is who among mortal men can know the purpose of GOD?

But secret from everybody but one tiny, little group? Only they know? Around the whole world? God not talking to anybody but them! Hmmm, and it's only written in their book? Okay, if you insist so ...sounds like it's so.

But, back to the purpose of this writing. Now the original stone tablets carved on the mountain whether by GOD or by Moses at the instruction of

GOD, did not survive Moses' wrath against the depravity of the Hebrews who had succumbed to wicked temptations in his absence. It's what happens when you leave your stuff behind and go walkabout. It get tempted by this or that Devil and be giving your stuff away to any Tom, Dick or Larry that comes along. You show up unexpected an find everybody having it with your stuff, right there in front of you. It be sluts 'n nuts, kissin' 'n dissin' …an you the one they dissin'.

But Moses wasn't the kind of guy you wanna cheat on. He'd gone toe to toe with Pharaoh and near drowned his ass. He was, after all, rep'in the Lord. And it ain't like they wasn't warned. Only a few months before was all that ten plagues and drowning in the Red Sea stuff. So they had examples everywhere that you don't play with the Lord. And it's not like GOD was mean about it. Not really. After giving them everything --manna, freedom, no more pyramid building-- pretty much all these folks needed do was take Saturday off and worship only the "One GOD" and they were too lazy and slothful to even stick with that. Kinda like "I be home fo' ten" promises from our own children. But back to our story…

In his absence, Moses' Hebrew children had devolved to stages of drunkenness, lewdness and bestiality that woulda made Columbus proud. And (The big "No-No") even constructed a graven image of the pagan God Baal—son of EL—something Columbus wouldn't even do (and he would do most anything). Moses was definitely not pleased and he let them all know it.

Though near eighty years old, Moses still a formidable figure (rocking them movie star looks). He still hitting it with wifie, plus a couple handmaidens on the side and didn't appreciate nobody trying to help out ('specially hard as Baal be hittin' that thing). Standing tall above the crocked flock upon the fog-shrouded, rocky massif where GOD lived, he braced his people for their failings, called them all kinds of names that began with "Mutha".

And it worked. The Hebrews soon snapped out of the spell they had been under and like naughty toddlers, caught red-handed in a cookie jar, they again felt the presence of their unseen deity and his most loyal servant. But, too late! Moses erupted in a fit of rage and smashed the tablets to bits. All the while so doing, his thunderous voice resounded with such might it set fear in the hearts of all who heard its gathering crescendo, chastising the weakness and wickedness of all before him, prophesying doom and oblivion and when it got down to prophesying, Moses was the champ. And they could forget about that Promised Land legacy thing, too …at least for the next forty years.

His predictions quickly came to pass as Moses directed the destruction of all those involved in the debauchery and blasphemy. "Cut 'em up! Burn 'em up! Mess 'em up!" And one third of all the Hebrews --the wicked third-- were slaughtered, done away with, shitcanned.

But a Wildman's work is never done. Next, Moses was ordered by GOD to carve a second set of tablets and to build them a storage container (possibly so he wouldn't be tempted to smash anything else). So he did, to specifications possibly given by GOD, but which, just so happens, were similar to mystical Egyptian containers …that Moses had maybe seen before.?!.

Maybe for GOD's favor or simply Moses' flavor or maybe cause Moses was an overachiever and that's how he rolled. Regardless, Moses the worker bee, did as commanded and much more. He used the finest Shittim wood, carved by GOD's own hands from Shittah trees, which we'll call by its Anglo name Acacia (to reduce accidents of speech) …know I don't need to spell that Shittim out for you Shittahs.

And, in keeping with his habit of overindulgence, he covered the insides and out with the finest gold, worked by craftsmen. And this weren't no ordinary gold. This gold GOD dropped from the heavens for his Chosen People to work into this greatest creation and it must truly have been a work of art cause people still talking and writing about it, at least some people are. Inside its golden confines he placed the new tablets along with other secret materials and devices that we don't know much about BECAUSE THEY'RE SECRET!

Two golden loops on each side permitted acacia wood poles to be passed through for bearing the container by a couple lucky or unlucky (however, you see it) fellows. Its lid –aka, the mercy seat-- was also covered around and about with gold and topped by two golden angels who faced each other from opposite ends of the lid or so the story goes. The angel's wings curved forward, pointing at each other and forming the throne of GOD. A gleaming treasure that became the Ark of the Covenant kept sorta by the Children of Israel …but sorta not really.

This thing had a mind of its own. You touch it you die unless it allows you to touch it which you won't know unless you don't die. It didn't take prisoners. The contents were not even to be accessed by those perverse children into whose care it had been entrusted. In fact the priests always covered the Ark so that it was never visible by the common people.

Possibly GOD had designed within the Ark an ability, a restlessness to wander in search of a better crowd, if it didn't love the ones it was with. Mayhap the periodic flights of disobedience --the debauchery and backsliding-- did not portray these current Chosen People as responsible couriers for the task at hand. Like, maybe it found them low and untrustworthy (but you didn't hear it from me).

Not only was this Ark powerful and beautiful, but also willful! But in the absence of any others considered more worthy, it would hang with the old crowd a while. Chosen they may once have been, but GOD's new message to these erratic people appears to be: "Ya'll best get it together!"

In any case, Moses included other secret documents in the Ark that he wrote in an ancient Egyptian script known only to a few high Egyptian priests and even fewer Hebrews. He then pronounced all these writings and the Ark as sacrosanct, viewable by no man except on "Special Occasions". But the concept of what constituted "Special Occasions" became lost in the transliterations of time, as language evolved over years of regional influences to reflect less of Egyptian and more of Canaan attributes. Not saying it was so much a downhill slide ...but it did get deeper.

Started out good. Moses successor, Joshua consulted the Ark's contents to develop strategies he employed during the Hebrew invasion of Canaan. First, he conquered Jericho —using spies and subterfuge to gain the advantage-- then, he destroyed the Bethelites at the Battle of Ai. Marching behind the mighty Ark, he couldn't lose.

Joshua not only discerned battle strategies, he also gained strategic insights from his consultations. He wisely formed alliances with Canaanite peoples, such as those in the town of Gibeon —a key crossroad on the central mountain ridge of Canaan-- when such provided more advantage than simple conquest. So it wasn't always about pillaging and killing. However, it's always about time...

Joshua eventually defeated thirty-one Canaanite states. Josh was a beast. But alas, not forever. He died of old age before he could conquer all of Canaan. That feat would remain for his descendant to fulfill ...it's still remaining.

Time. The greatest equalizer. Over time these lessons fell out of general knowledge, their ritual out of flavor. Superstitions prevailed which concluded that no man should know the majesty and power of GOD, whatever that meant and for many, it meant anything unknown and for the ignorant that's quite a lot. Even high Levite priests of the Temple were eventually forbidden to look inside the Ark or to approach it more than once per year and then for ceremonial purposes only. Still can't look inside, can't learn no lessons. But that's alright cause it's outta sight.

For the superstitious, the Ark became more a symbol than an instrument. These traditions remained much the same for more than seven hundred years and over that time Israelite opinions hardened against ancient traditions surrounding a thing seldom, if ever, seen by more than a handful of their number. Even their leadership no longer sought to employ the Ark's powers during their conflicts.

Less than two hundred years from the Ark's creation, the Israelite King Saul dissed the Ark (thinking he all that), too impatient to seek its counsel or employ its superior powers. Result, Saul defeated on Mount Gilboa by the Philistines (who wisely employed their tech). Brought low by his unadvised keeping his own counsel, Saul went the way of many a fool. Unfortunate for Saul, very unfortunate for his troops …who unfortunately followed him to oblivion!

Saul's stupidity spelled disaster for his people. Very bad! But the good news, he also wrote his own doom on Gilboa, so he would never be messing up any people's lives again. Ancient leaders, you see, often assumed a greater share of the risk from poor performance owing to poor leadership skills; a condition unfortunately lost to posterity as most present day despots choose to remain well to the rear, well outside the combat zone (surrounded by their fawning legions of heroic advisors).

They so far removed from anywhere near harm's way (most unfortunate for their troops) these "Lords of Ruin" usually survive the inept decision-making that began the conflict in the first place and which sends so many of their warriors down Oblivion's Pathway. But I digress…

In truth, the Israelites did not totally abandon the Ark's traditions. Even King David counseled his people: "Let us bring the Ark of our God back to us, for we did not inquire of it during the reign of Saul."

Alas, even David's courage waned and he too became fearful of using the Ark's power, asking himself: "How can I ever bring the Ark of God to me?" Eventually, he left the Ark outside Jerusalem …out of sight, out of mind!

However, his son Solomon had a different idea and built the sacred "Holy of Holies" to house the Ark in Jerusalem. Solomon had a lotta women, so we know he had balls. But, he also had a lotta wisdom and would split you in half to prove it.

But, alas, the period of belief in GOD's Ark passed. After Solomon came kings of lesser qualities. Weak kings like Ahab and Jehoshaphat caused the Ark to again seek a more worthy host with which to abide and before it faded from historical mention, the Ark of the Covenant was twice lost to the Philistines (who decided it bad luck after coming down with all variety of maladies, including boils and rats and returned it both times) until the Ark became lost forever during the invasion by Nebuchadnezzar's Babylonian forces that destroyed Jerusalem around 586 BC. Figure the Ark concurred with its relocation, cause the Jews repeatedly fell back into their pagan ways, seeking protection of other Gods from time to time since Moses wasn't around to fix that itch.

Baal was the pagan God of storms. So if there came a severe drought, they'd call for help from Baal, which was very troubling to the devout worshippers of GOD Yahweh since Baal expected his subjects to do a lot of balling, literally. "Yo Baal, if we make it with our sisters and throw in a couple goats, will you make it rain? Really? Bring them babes on!"

The Ark's power to bring misfortune on those for whom it was not intended, was never fully unleashed upon Nebuchadnezzar the Great and his crowd (at least nothing like those suffered by the Philistines) because Nebuchadnezzar brought along most of the Jews with the Ark. Then again, Nebuchadnezzar became crazy and deranged for around seven years, so there continued to be some misfortune involved with misappropriating such a powerful, mystical force. Some attribute his troubles to the Ark debating the terms and conditions of its capture, though he did live around eighty-four years, so maybe a kinda love-hate thing. Still, his illness brought back the lesson from stories told by Philistines --whom Nebuchadnezzar had also conquered-- and when his next two successors lasted only a relatively few years, a change was mandated …time for you to go!

The Ark they considered a hazard not worth risking and after burying away in a secret location, all records of its existence in Babylon were expunged. Only by word of mouth spread its legend through the centuries …legends which tended to be incomplete.

Legend urged that inside the Ark Moses placed cryptic timetables given by GOD for safekeeping until such a time when mankind was no longer in his infant state. Legends of these, passed from father to son and teacher to student, made no mention its proper name. Only of a mysterious golden box …and the bad things that greeted those it met.

The legends all hinted at its majestic beauty and awesome power. Tall tales, some suggested, though others swore their truth. But none of these surmised a secret coded text within its words of sacred worship from Moses' to his almighty GOD …coded text whose succinct translation amounts to: "HE IS COMING!"

CHAPTER ONE

Behind him. A tiny sound, hardly a whisper above the background sea songs. Barely above a wisp, soft as a gentle breeze. Somethings were going on fer sure. He came instantly alert, not out of fear of danger, more like foreboding, as in "what's this about?"

The bed clothes lifted only a second or so, then liquid, soft skin slid up against his own, answering the question completely. No questions the somethings poking into his back. Her Twins. He recalled a time these were his favorites.

His confusion instantly clarified as was her purpose. She definitely came with a purpose. Also, definitely naked, definitely nipples erect and obviously up to no good, unless you into that sorta thing. Turns out he for sure is…

Her soft moans echoed in his memory long hours after her departure. It had been almost forever since their times before. But the gift she gave him he well appreciated. He didn't quite understand the motivation. Then, what man ever truly knows women? True, he definitely appreciated the innovation and most especially the time she spent …although it kinda felt like goodbye.

"JP O'Rourke! Knew that I recognized you! Know that picture too! That's a nice picture. Pretty girl. Beautiful!" He looked up into the intruder's eyes, not startled, just interrupted. Without a second thought JP handed the photo to the other who gave it an appreciative glance before handing it back. "Tina never looked better."

"Yeah, it was taken only a couple weeks ago. Stephanie gave it to me. I stopped by but Tina wasn't in. Nobody's seen her lately. Steph's plenty worried, even though it's not her first time going walkabout." His tone he managed to keep level, even keeled and non-accusing. It in no way reflected true feelings as he continued; "But Steph's determined to find her even though maybe she don't wanna be found. Made me take her picture to show it around; like I'm Columbo or Shaft or somebody."

"She mad at me! I got bad luck with women these days, hee hee." The other's chuckle mimicked hyena neck farts. Luckily, Mo-Mo's clown phase lasted only moments before changing subjects. "S'how goes it?"

"Every day starts good!" A quick smile he didn't feel to cover the frown growing. Why'd he say that? He never said that particular thing. That had been Tony's thing …while Tony still was a thing.

Lately, none of his days started, parted or ended good. It's really bad when you come out looking to skin a snake and get struck. One thing definite for sure, this day wouldn't be no parts of good as long as Carlos Morano cluttered his space. Can you say stifling?

Still, he never once coughed up "doucebag", "jerkoff" or "asshole"! Not even once, though the feeling filled him. He did faux civil while Carlos continued unawares.

"Man, I ain't seen you in quite a while, since the time I threw my last party in Cali."

"Yup, it's been a while. That was a nice affair. How you been?"

"Can't complain, can't complain. Say, she never told me. How'd you two meet any way?"

Small talk. He hadn't come here for that. He came to kill a man. At least eventually. Probably. Probably the same man with the same intentions towards him. It had been a mistake to have that picture out for anyone to see. Especially people with beady little eyes that see most everything. But truth be told, it had called to him, ordered its getaway from that stuffy hideout inside his pocket.

Now came another calling. The implanted suggestion took greater hold. Couldn't shut it down. Suddenly his mind shifted fully in reverse until it recaptured that first time …their very first time together.

He bathed in the ethereal light shimmering outward from dark brown, leaning towards black pupils whose hypnotic glow threatened to steal away every part of him were he not careful. But it was too much. His failing strength lost its power to turn away as she began to possess his soul …only a matter of time, it was going down!

Tweeting gay refrains in timed resonance to the hammering rhythm of his heart, pairs of red-breasted robins mocked his inability from treetop vantages high above his struggling self. Yet he heard only the musical notes singing from pouting lips so sinfully scribed that God himself must have loathed at their creation. Every word she spoke lured him further astray from his own resolve, who's tiny, forlorn voice cried out for help. It was definitely going down!

But somehow he regained himself. Women didn't take him, he took them! He ain't going out like that without a fight! "Take a deep breath and hold it!" The commanding image of a former sensei interceded.

It required herculean fortitude, and no small measure of deep, meditative breathing, But somehow he found again his balance, steeling his will against her wonderful witchcraft and wonderful he truly felt. Wonderful just being near her. But she could never take control. Can't let her! Can't never let a woman punk him, rag him out. He vowed to take care less she ensnare him totally in some future trial. Although the prospect seemed not such a bad thing …even kinda wonderful.

Now he sought to reverse the spell, leaning forward to nearly dwarf her five foot-six inch height, as well as blocking sunlight streaming down into those oval-shaped spellcasters of hers, now partly hooded against its blinding effects. At least now she could appreciably inspect the cut of pectoral muscles seeming about to leap from the tight confines of the gold-colored spandex tee that was already busy holding back impressive biceps and triceps at the corners. Physicality, the best way to woman's heart, he knew …after gold and jewels that is.

Despite her aloof nature, he knew she found him impressive. He had chosen this particular outfit for that specific purpose. Its gold sheen set off his medium-brown shade like no other color, imparting a Greek God kind of look, kind of anyway, from the suntanned Greeks that is, on the "black hand" side. He liked it, was certain she'd have no choice finding his physical appearance overwhelming. He had already seen the evidence. He'd truly enjoyed the way she tended to shrink back whenever he leaned in on her like this. Ruefully, he recalled that what he had not known until much later, his cologne was nearly as overpowering and a definite detriment. God, she hated the smell of Polo cologne. However, back then, ignorance being bliss; he had stayed with his game plan …emphasis on ignorance.

"You really wanna go up against me Missy?"

"I might be enticed to give it a try." She answered him, her own shirt's front side being stressed by her own impressive array and she knew, there was no doubt …he found her setup impressive also.

"And you don't feel the slightest out-gunned?"

"Smaller frame, bigger brain!" Came her quick answer. Backing down and playing punk were for other people and her daddy didn't raise no punks nor pussies, at least not in the figurative sense. She felt comfortable in this game of chicken or shit with this Chicken Shit.

"Fine then, you go first!"

"No, no! It's your honor. I insist."

"Don't say I didn't warn you Little Sugar."

"I won't."

"Now don't cry a lot after this butt-whippin' Miss Thing. A little wailing is acceptable, but you know how you girlies are about that sort of thing. Just please don't go on and on, that's embarrassing."

"I'll try." Condescending males. Her favorite. She had a thing for powerful, proactive women unjustly wronged by vengeful, unthinking (aka, stupid) men. Joan of Arc and Hypatia of Alexandria went high on her list beside Harriet Tubman and Sojourner Truth. He knew those things about her, thought he knew everything and now played her intense competitiveness against her natural dislike for male superegos to get her riled up.

Problem was he had two problems. One, she also knew that he knew those things about her, and two, his game was weak. He could hit them pretty far, not bad for a seventeen-year old black kid from West Philly, but not all that. And his putter wasn't butter, it was toast.

She did like his look though, especially those wonderful soft-brown eyes that hid under lashes she wished belonged to her. She had a thing for men with beautiful eyes. She also had a thing for men like her father. And it was daddy who warned that: "People lose their temper first, their pride second and their cash after that!" Daddy had also taught her a few other things, like guns and golf. And daddy had game. She merely walked to her tee and to his astonishment, calmly let loose a powerful swing. "Whap!"

Her daddy had also taught her that hate presented a weakness. So she did not hate those men back when for being stupid. Past was past and beyond remedy. Besides, suddenly finding themselves stupid must have been tough enough to take. Most of history's she-male haters had developed one problem or other over strong women who liked to speak their minds. That was a problem for their ignorant ways during those backward times.

But this guy was not them. Despite his bluster, he didn't have any of those moronic tendencies, so she did not hate him for being a man. He'd had nothing to do with what went down a hundred years prior or definitely anything further beyond that. So she didn't hate him for being male. If he stayed around long enough she'd invent new reasons to hate him for, but at the moment she just hoped he'd take his butt-whippin' …like a man.

Back to reality. Their high school golf match faded away. Inwardly he winced at the reminder. All-in-all, any lesson learned was to be joyously received. Besides, most inner city kids thought scoring a hole-in-one meant getting your date to put out. "Oh well," he remarked, "what doesn't kill us makes for entertainment!"

Outwardly, he simply smiled at the other. "It's a long story. Suffice to say it was pretty good back then. Till it went, bad."

But the other man had already stopped listening as he leaned in to wave over a bartender to bring another round. For John Paul O'Rourke --of the Philadelphia by way of North Carolina O'Rourke clan-- this was definitely an undesired result of his ill-advised pictorial review, as was the trip down memory lane. Still, memories are as memories do and he'd been in wayback mode lots lately and now his memory had sailed its next reflections even further back in time to a time when he learned things whose utility he had no idea how useful they would one day become. Confused yet? It gets clearer, I promise.

"What up Ty?"

"Every day starts good, JP!" His friend Tyrone Sims could say things like that because he was rich, at least that's what everybody thought since he never wore the same clothes more than once every couple-three weeks. Tyrone also owned at least two pairs of Chuck Taylor sneakers that they knew of, although the scoop was he had another pair of black hi-tops that had got a little torn and he wouldn't wear 'em anymore. That was significant cause nobody else had more than one pair of the famous Converse All-Stars, if they even had that. They might have some off-branded "Rinks" (short for Rinky Dinks) that they'd put on the shelf. But Chucks were state of the art for basketball shoes back then. All the "A" game ballers like Wilt "The Stilt", Bill Russell and the Big "O" wore them, even gave them away as trophies to lucky kids after a few games. But for most normal folks, Chucks you wore 'til they all but fell off.

Kids today would never understand since a single pair of the Air Jordan's they prefer cost more than a dozen of the old Chucks. But actually owning two, maybe three pair of Chucks? That was pretty rich for a thirteen-year old black kid in High Point, North Carolina. At least it was back in the 1960s. If you had a pair of white tops as well as the usual black tops, you were considered the rage. That's how you got girls…

Tyrone's other favorite saying: "A wide mouth gits a narrow behind whupped!" wasn't original. He'd picked that one up from a classmate named Vernon who lived across town and didn't hang with JP's crew, though he did attend the same school. There weren't a lot of schools available for "Colored" kids back then when black folks were "Colored". Had a few elementary schools here and there, but only one high school for the whole city and surrounding communities out twenty-five miles or so. So while he took his daily, two-mile trek to A.J. Griffin Elementary from the north side and kids like Vernon walked about the same from the east side, kids attending William Penn High could be bussed all the way from Trinity, twenty miles away. Of course at least they had a bus…

Regardless the difficulties, they all got to go to school and learn intellectual things, like the three Rs and lifesaving things like: "A wide mouth gits a narrow behind whupped!" That was important, education promised them all a future as Tyrone found out when he got educated to the practical application of that saying after Vernon threatened to shove his own set of Chuck Taylors so far up Tyrone's butt only a doctor could retrieve them. He only hinted that it wasn't no proctologist. But if he meant ENT, that would really be bad.

In fact we all received a crucial lesson that day, since a near death experience often provides the best education. We quickly learned the hazard of cracking jokes about a guy's buck teeth sister when the guy was nearby, especially a prematurely huge guy like Vernon with a reputation for knocking people out.

The lesson taught that funny is as seen through the eyes of the beholder and few behold with the same vision. Vernon possessed a zero tolerance and a sense of humor only slightly higher cause his daddy was bigger than him and didn't ever take no gruff, especially off Vernon. So it was very unwise to joke about anything related to Vernon or about anyone related to Vernon. He came out in a mood.

But nothing ever happened. Tyrone really liked Vernon's sister and everybody knew it, including Vernon. He just wasn't gonna let anybody call her names, even the rich kid. So Tyrone apologized and the whole matter ended quickly. He went back to breathing regularly and Vernon went back to his old boisterous, though jovial ways: "Hey Rebound, gimmee have a sip o' dat Nehi! Hey Chauncey, I got next. Ya heah? When ah gits dat ball ah'm gone be spankin' dat ass, spankin'!"

Three years later Tyrone actually began dating Vernon's sister, who had grown out of any stigma from the buck teeth, thanks partly to the significantly more impressive bra size she had grown into. Obviously, three pairs of Chucks did indeed help a guy get girls. While an impressive bra size? Well, it helped a girl get all sorts of things…

Tyrone also had enough Banlon knit shirts to supply the high school football team or so it seemed to JP and his friends, cause he wore a different style and color each day; even sporting JP's personal favorite, gold mist, in long and short sleeves. Totally unlike Stinker who wore the same clothes pretty much every day except Sundays (when he got to wear his only suit to church). Stinker's manner of dress had nothing to do with slovenly habits or anything like that; Sundays he even shined the faded brown Brogan boots that all other days were usually concealed within gobs of mud and streaks of dirt.

But the best thing about Stinker, he never really stank; even on the warmest days when they all reeked a few musty odors from sweating out games of baseball and basketball in the hundred degree heat and high humidity famous in that corner of the South. Even then his odors never climbed any higher than the rest of them, at least that was how they all saw it; nothing a little dip in the pool at Washington Terrace Park wouldn't fix. Besides, his mama washed the shirt and jeans promptly each night, hanging them to dry in time for the next day's adventures. But you wear the same stuff day after day; you'll get a rep quick enough. Don't believe it, ask an orthodox Jewish man.

Don't matter. Whether others achieved similar notoriety or not that's how Stinker got tagged. But at least he had something, cause even though Stinker lived at the opposite end of the economic ladder from Tyrone (with the rest spread somewhere in between) there were lots of folks out there in much worse shape. Besides, it was nothing he had caused and no condition he would soon be able to remedy, unless he somehow suddenly grew a foot taller and developed an outside jump shot.

In those days, economic positioning was usually inversely based on the number of siblings within families. More mouths to feed, less money for nice new sneakers, Lee jeans and Sunday suits. Actually, that rule kind of runs the same way these days too…

Of course, those days there weren't as many distractions to remind you how poor you were. No such things as PlayStation or X-Box, not even Nintendo. Modern day kids looking back to then see them the Dark Ages and in a sense they right cause dark people were treated pretty poorly back then. Sort of like today's dark people …only more so.

Anyway, wasn't all so bad. Back then, kids stayed outside nearly all day every day and they found stuff to do. Climbing trees and shooting marbles and racing bikes were all considered sports but looking down on yourself was not. You didn't own a new bike? So what? It'd get rusty sitting out in the rain anyway, might even get stolen. Your daddy drive a Ford? Big deal. Who really wants a Cadillac? All those knobs and switches are way too confusing and since you were "Colored", you couldn't get served at McDonalds anyway or any of the other white eateries (Colored eateries were normally called the family kitchen), so it didn't matter how much money you had or how light your skin; if there was any shade in it, you were stuck outside with the rest of the "Coloreds" …of course Change was on the horizon. Lotta folks wouldn't live to see it, but it had started peeking over.

Boycotts had turned downtown into ghost town and sit-ins that began over in Greensboro were making the local Woolworths and Five and Dime stores even more apprehensive as Jim Crow ran headlong into Dollar Bill. It seemed white men hated the idea of income deflation much more than racial integration. They much rather be in the black than the red …of course they weren't all financial geniuses.

Ol' Jim Crow had been around since slavery and didn't go quietly. Not his way. Riot police squads with attack dogs, attack firemen with high pressure hoses and "good ol' boys with nothing better to do (aka, crackers). That was Jim Crow's way. But the heroes fighting to rid themselves of racism just braced for impact and sloshed through the muck and mire.

Of course, none of JP's crew was ever allowed to participate in marches and the like alongside parents who braved the slings and arrows of jeering white crowds. So most of them never even appreciated the strength and bravery or the courage it took to do what they did, not until years later. It took a lot and once they understood, they were all very proud of those homegrown heroes. JP's father being only one on their block to participate…

JP and friends generally limited their exploits to adventures they were permitted to explore. Nobody wanted to chance that nighttime beating, the one you got once daddy got home for his evening meal that came complete with a briefing about what you had done and where. It didn't matter your economic status back then. You mess up, papa would whup!

They didn't get spankings. Spankings were what kids on TV got. They either got beatings or whippings. Either way, these tended to come at night and involved a twenty to thirty-inch switch (a thin branch cut from a young tree and lethal with whip-like characteristics in its ability to cut whelps into tender flesh) or daddy's leather belt (whose properties included arcane sound effects from the deadly cowhide slicing through night air to contact bare skin in a way most unappreciated by its receiver). "Zoooosh! Whap! Zap! Plap! Owweee!!!"

Whether called beatings or whippings these were most unappreciated by both whipper and whippee. No firm or fast rules governed what you called which when; however, although parents hated giving them as much as kids hated receiving them, disobeying that day's "orders of the day" was a definite way to get papa wanting to whup. Though by far not the only. Back then, neighbors would tell on you as soon as they found you out doing something wrong --even though you had logical reasoning why-- like breaking into Washington Terrace Park's concessions to steal ice cream in the wintertime since the park closed 'til spring and it would only get old and stale. So what the harm?

Of course the real harm came to their backsides! For reals! They learned quickly that doing such seemingly harmless deeds was seldom a good idea …especially with so large a group.

It wasn't huge, their crew and its numbers varied only slightly, depending on who got stuck babysitting or on some other chores thought up by thoughtful parents. Normally their roving group of thrill seekers consisted of five, sometimes as many as six, but sometimes only four. However, multiply that number by the amount of tattle telling siblings (upset that they didn't get to share) and the chances of a major newsbreak increased by an order of magnitude.

Although about as mischievous as any fledgling teens, they really weren't bad kids. Normally, just young lads out to learn what they could about what they could. Mostly poor, but never in spirit and with that condition much the status quo, they were quite happy with the way things were. Neither were they a gang. They didn't go out looking to hurt other people or defend some perceived territory. It was not even a formal gathering, just a get together, when you got together. And there was little drama. They were too poor to afford drama. There was just life and living it in all its forms and twists.

That's not to say everyday went along smoothly. Inevitably there would come the occasional fist fight just because somebody needed a blowout every now and then, especially after recently getting your butt whipped by a parent for complaining about the food or lack thereof or the fact that the two-bedroom, one-bath house you lived in was getting kinda crowded since the twins came in or some neighbor caught you doing something you shouldn't have been doing. You know, normal stuff.

Usually, in their group, blowouts started with Larry Denton, who they called Skeeter. Skeeter had the smallest body and the biggest mouth. He barely touched five feet tall, with a mouth almighty and not just because the size of his lips (not quite big as Satchmo's but close). He also had the largest family, up to nine by last count, though nobody really knew as none of them were ever invited inside. Which was okay by them cause Skeeter also had the meanest dad. Pissed cause all them kids his wife kept making while he making with her.

By their estimates, Skeeter got three times the beatings the rest of them combined. Then again, Skeeter was always into something. It had been his idea to break into the park concessions and another time to let all the air out of their principal's tires and (his most brilliant) that they simultaneously jump off the top of the park building's second-story railing to see who'd land first. That's also when he broke his ankle and cleaned out the last of his family's savings. So maybe those beatings were justified. But hard feelings didn't last long, the day after or the day or two after that. Soon it was back to best buds. Life was too short those days for drama …sorta like today, but back then they took the time to know it.

Not just his fashion lineup, they thought Tyrone rich cause his house had air conditioning and a garage made for two. But he also had other means. Occasionally, he even treated them all to an RC cola or a Nehi orange soda, which was JP's favorite. They thought Stinker poor because his house didn't even spell air conditioning, let alone have any, and he could barely afford the twelve cents to buy his own self a Royal Crown cola and it didn't matter because they didn't discuss financial status more than complementing buddies on the new this or that they got when and if they got it. They didn't steal from each other or hate because one had more or less, not that they didn't dream about those niceties. It's just that they left the drama on the soap operas all their mother's watched. Those that still had mothers…

"Every day starts good!" he remembered. A smile turned grin parted his dark lips that he quickly closed fully to preclude some unseen observer from thinking him daffy. But how could he ever forget this tidbit of wisdom obtained at an early age from his neighborhood chum Tyrone. As sayings go, it wasn't the most erudite, actually more simplistic than deep. But it meant a lot. Didn't it?

"Hmm, nope!" he decided in silent argument with himself in this noisy, crowded place. "Couldn't be true, if every day don't end good …and they don't!"

At least his argument so far stayed silent, though threatening to spill out his snarling lips. But logically, how could the day after a tragedy start good? Who says it's good just cause you wake up? Suppose you don't wanna wake up cause your reason for living has just died?

Then the memory machine faltered, surged, sputtered before replaying another image, another friend. Another favorite expression that still stuck with him, but much more significantly. Tony Hellerman's last words had urged: "Don't hurt nuthin' ya might need later!"

But Tony definitely had hurt something back then in '71 in a place none of them wanted to be and he hurt it bad. The memory smoldered, then erupted from the depths of dark recesses. Blazing. Parts of his best friend lay scattered all about the smoking ruin of his shattered hooch. The biggest part that remained intact was much too little, much too ravaged by a Viet Cong rocket. It had no chance. There weren't enough clamps and gauzes and blood pumps in all of Vietnam to stop all the hemorrhaging …from all the places it hemorrhaged.

He tried vainly to pimp slap the memory back into its hideout. No lesson learned there that would be useful here this night, except maybe to duck and cover when attacked by rockets. But not much else. Maybe other things from his past still totally applicable, but probably not that.

And then some of the other things decided they'd help out his ancient history misery. Suddenly, replay after miserable replay danced across his vision to help further screw up his day. "Hey, why the heck not! Pile on all you bitches!"

Mom! At an even earlier age came his first experience with people and events screwing up his day. It happened right after God went walkabout, out lunchin' somewhere instead of on watch like he supposed to be, as JP used to beg him to be when he knelt to pray: "Please God, watch over my mother and father and Aunt Maude..."

But when it hit the fan, there was nobody home. Maybe God was on siesta and his angels on lockdown. Whichever. There was no warning, no call to the firehouse, not even a helping hand to pull his mother out of the all-consuming blaze that ended her stay among the living and with him. Then again, maybe it hadn't…

The Boogeyman. He couldn't call it, couldn't figure out what it was. But for many years following her untimely demise, he got nightly visits from some strange entity, spectre , ghost or something. His childself proclaimed it the boogeyman, always praying the thing would boogey on away! But some guys just can't be that lucky. At least not some guys like him, cause his came and came back. His adult mentality later revisited and rationalized it must have been her. Cause that's what adult mentalities do, revisit and rationalize.

Whatever it was it never hurt him, only came out from his closet at night to visit. He never saw it, just felt a presence, heard slight whispering sounds in the moments before his tired, prepubescent body lost its fight to stay on this side and drifted away to Never-Never Land.

By the time of his teens it no longer bothered him, either that or simply no longer bothered to visit. That reason he had yet to figure out. But his rational self once again surmised it might have been ashamed of all those nocturnal emissions, aka, wet dreams, teenaged boys are prone to having. Typical of a mom. Regardless, it stopped, not returning until after God once again turned his back, once again countersigning his punishment and he didn't know why.

Just like Job, Satan attacked him through his family. It had to be him cause God ain't that petty, though he does have rules that you can't break or he'll allow Satan to come get you …or yours.

But, unless you counted that time stealing ice cream, JP hadn't even done anything evil yet. Didn't they even give you a grace period, like til you're sixteen or something? But they took away his father to the place they take fathers of young boys who don't obey rules and just like Job, he never knew what rules. What he had done to deserve such revenge?

It was tough (at least according to his speech writers in preacher's clothing), God's got so many of them, rules that is and though his teenage self could never figure out which one, he knew it had been his own fault that God took another "walkabout" right before Satan sent his minions --hiding under white hoods-- to lynch his defiant father. God don't like to be around when Satan's minions came to collect their due, he figured. Whether he did or didn't, results were the same. He'd lost two parents as proof. He also had lost his ability to pray.

"Now I lay me down to sleep and pray the Lord my soul to keep?" What was that all about? How could that even mean anything when everybody close to him was either dead or dying out? Aunt Maude would be next, he just knew it. Anyway, that's when she sent him to live with his uncle Charles and Charles' war time buddy, named Shiro, in Philly and sure enough, the next time he saw her face it had gone over to the land of forever slumber. Why? He didn't know. But God had sent Aunt Maude away because of him …that much he knew.

Of course he never really lived with Charles, who spent near all his life chasing down interstates in his eighteen wheeler. But at least there was Shiro. Probably a good thing since West Philly ain't no place to raise kids without somebody to do the raising 'em!

Shiro and Charles met on a hill in Italy during World War Deuce, as Charles called that conflict. Him and Shiro he called the Jig 'n the Jap connection. Bragging about its awesomeness and synergistic energy. First they wiped a shit ton o' superior racers outta this life (again, Charles' description) then began a lifelong friendship. Didn't quite make up for his brother, but then what could? His fantasy was to find out they'd all died at each other's hands after learning they were all screwing each other's wives. Just a fantasy, but wonderful!

Charles was ever the gregarious one. He could also exhibit a dangerous side. In fact, when stories swirled concerning disappearances of former klansturds (he'd never think of them as persons), some would suspect Charles, wondering out loud had he passed through that suspected area. Many hoped he had played the role of avenging angel. "Someone needed to!"

He never admitted to things like that. About World War Two battles however, he said plenty. Shiro never spoke about any of his battles except when necessary to make some point or other, not even those that haunted his dreams …the kami!

Worked out fine. Charles had only a sister in North Carolina he'd occasionally drop in on, when passing by, otherwise hardly remembered. There was a nephew there also, but nobody special enough to concern about. Charles a busy man, all business. While Shiro had lost all his family to a fire in the concentration camp where the government he fought for had locked up his loved ones …while he fought for it!

Our government called them internment camps. But the Japanese-American people robbed of their homes, businesses and freedom could call a spade a spade, especially when those were handed to them to build the fenced-in internment hovels they were ordered to move into. They weren't always appreciative of their opportunities in these prisons, meaning lack thereof. Then again, neither were they appreciative upon learning that other prisoners, like captured Nazis only needed to move into their Prisoner of War homes. No labor required. Plus, dinner served in real restaurants, by real waitresses …while Japanese-American sons fought Nazis still tryna murder our government!

What also worked out fine was his upbringing by Shiro, though it took a minute to fully appreciate. Only thing real different, Shiro never applied corporal punishment which JP would have preferred to the mental hurdles he had to leap. Starting out, he hated this new arrangement. Shiro don't catch up to him that dreary Tuesday, he back in sunny Carolina by Thursday, maybe even Wednesday. He had two thumbs, only needed one at a time.

But you get caught, you put back into basic training! Shiro never took prisoners, not in war (after coming across the remains of friends who had been captured by the animals called Nazis), and not on the mean streets of Philadelphia. To JP it was unfair, none of this his fault. All the constant lessons, physical as well as metaphysical, all the never pleasing this stranger now ruling him. It was enough to drive him crazy. As in crazy enough to chance hopping a freight, at the very least a truck, crazy! Caught! Back to LOD, the lesson of the day. God he hated LOD! "What do you mean failures must teach us, not bury us?"

It was just more drama in his young life when he didn't want or maybe even deserve drama. But drama it was and from then on it followed wherever he went, causing this scene or that tragedy and now had followed him here or maybe he had followed it. Regardless, drama now played out on this local stage and he hated drama. So now he focused on another aphorism …to help maintain his bearings.

"Heavenly rewards belong in Heaven." Often quoted, though hardly a catch phrase, its earthy logic reached a firm grip out to straighten his chin and refocus him in a different direction, away towards the golden jewel brilliantly outshining all others this night, in this place. Its message? Who knew? But as heavenly rewards go, she'd definitely be a step up from Morano. But alas, there was that rational self-thingy again, chiding, taunting, reminding: "She look good, don't she? But that ain't now for you! Now get with the program! Fool!"

But the rebuke fizzled and faded away, unnecessary. His wiser half had simply used her image as distraction to free his lesser half from the claustrophobic grip of Pudgy the Whale-like Intruder after staring hard at the Legion's organization chart didn't help. Not like he knew any of them anyway. Didn't matter. Equally, it mattered little how wonderful in appearance that womanly visage projecting across the bar and yes, she definitely looked good (at least to anyone with a pulse). But, this night, womanly appearances were secondary. The earth logic tutelage said it all. It was time to get with the program, for he had not come here for her ... but for him.

No Illusions. Not the slightest suspicion that this man's desires boded well for him. Not a problem. He had similar intent. Truly, the evil gleam beaming from Carlos, more feeling than seeing, but definitely there. O'Rourke had a sixth sense about these things or was it seventh? Whichever. He could feel the angst even though the man's real intentions --and any claws, fangs or switchblades-- he kept well-caged, hidden behind that Cheshire cat smile ...beware a smile to beguile.

But instinctively he knew, regardless the number. From their first meeting, that time in Laguna Beach, his intuition had shifted instantly from pleasant and carefree to edgy and paranoid –his sixth, seventh or whatever sense-- pealed incessant, lamenting tones to outdo any chime of good tidings. That first time seemed so long ago now. Back then, Tina was still... he concentrated to wipe out the thought. It would do no good to take that train; its heading followed the wrong track. Nerve endings cried out in anguish, every feeling ominous and foreboding, none hopeful or heartening –the Job Syndrome revisited-- but he successfully wiped away thoughts of her. Though not of him.

"Keep your friends close, but your enemies closer." Another aphorism. One more direct and to the point. But was this really an enemy? His inquiring mind desperately wanted to know. Why not just ask? Definitely direct and to the point, though maybe with fatal outcome. But the question sought escape past the gates of his lips. Who are you really? Villain be thy name? Snake in the grass? Some seemed to think so. Perhaps, perhaps not. Danger or dancer? Which was it and why couldn't he sort it out? Too close to the subject? Maybe. Deceased loved ones have the tendency to cause such quandary …and he had too many of those.

Deceased? There came those negatives again. There was yet no proof of that. Why even consider such? Conjecture be damned! Still no evidence; certainly, nothing approaching proof. She could still be alive. She could! How could he quit on her …again?

More useless feelings, more drama. Try as he did, the thoughts of her came back to plague. If he weren't careful, self-doubt would become his calling card; his world locked forever in cycles of illusion-delusion. He needed focus. Perhaps he had swung a bit off-target, again. Perhaps, but somehow he felt sure. He couldn't explain it to a psychiatrist about to lock him up in an asylum, and definitely not to those square heads at DIA, but two things he felt sure. He felt sure she was still alive, no matter how hard the pangs of doubt pealed, but even more sure this guy was involved whatever her fate. The feelings said danger and dancer. Those self-same instincts had kept him alive in Vietnam when so many others did not make it back. So many others who had turned left or right or went up or went down or just turned around and it was the wrong move for them at that time. Fate had been waiting. Just like Job, it took friends and family, but not he …at least not yet.

Now those same, life-preserving instincts warned him not to trust this man whose integrity so many admired. Not that he was much on trusting, but this guy's presence embarked him on the path of Doubting Thomas. Might look like a duck and quack, but duck or cluck! He still didn't believe it! Unfortunately, he was one of the few…

His DIA handlers. Now they had a different view entirely. Theirs seemed one side of an illicit love tryst with the man. Curious since those purveyors of "hypocrisy-run-amuck" didn't love anybody. But every look they took, each investigation they ran, unearthed only his good side. Defense Intelligence Agency? Now there truly was an oxymoron if he ever saw one, the emphasis on moron. The cynic in him wondered, "What the hell were they looking at?"

His own brand of investigation came away differently. Of course he had conducted his almost totally within the confines of his own mind, aka, putting two and two together during a fast-track trek along street

"Moronic". Though not totally. He had other resources. Still, numbers have meaning with people who can count …at least they should.

He remembered her unease their last meeting. Its lasting but a moment that sprinted capriciously away into the evening's blackness, then returned as delight. The vision of her dark beauty and wanton passion flooded in on him like an ocean of sibilant sound and movement. Dark locks of hair entangled and engulfed and dark fire from even darker eyes captured his soul while other dark areas captured his essence on a bliss-filled night of passion he could never forget. It had been long in coming, too long since their time before and too brief. Had he known she might never come again he would have made it last even longer, held her even closer. Such is the wisdom of hindsight. But now this wiser him heeded the warning issued by her roommate only one day before this.

Hate is a powerful motivator and Tina's roommate, Stephanie, hated the man like a plague, which is only fair since she possessed significant knowledge of his history (that she termed his-phony). Also only fair, JP acknowledged, is that, normally, though hate is powerful it is also a poor motivator and, that being the case, Stephanie should need to travel far to convince him. But the reality is that it took only a short trip. He caught up, can't get loose!

For her, there are no illusions where this guy is concerned. Illusional or delusional, who can tell which it is? But to her there is no doubt!

"Carlos' eyes never smile. He like a Beastie Boy."

"Beastie Boy? The musical group?"

"The beasts that's wildin'! I don't trust him! Something wrong in there," she argued, half-shouting, double-tapping her temple for effect. "Tina wouldn't listen, until…"

Maybe it was the hatred in him. Maybe there was a hatred he had never before acknowledged. Him, who had never before hated anyone, not even his father's murderers. Oh he didn't like what they did. But it was more the institution. Jim Crow he definitely despised and sure, he find those murdering douchebags, he definitely decree 'em all fish flakes. But the institution to him was distinctly different; not a person, but a thing; a loathsome thing and thus intolerable. It was the system that gave aid and comfort to rabid animals like those who murdered his father. It was the Jim Crow system that murdered many like his father. It was Jim Crow that rewarded subhuman thoughts and acts …and that abhorrent thing he hated most vehemently.

And he didn't need the fuel of hate to burn. Such abhorrent things he would always strive to destroy out of necessity. It was all a matter of intolerance towards such things. Such abhorrent, intolerable things that are a bane on mankind and should never be tolerated and he would never tolerate such. But he would never spend every day hating people just for hate's sake either. He had killed men, destroyed others beyond repair, but he had done so out of duty, never out of hate. Why start now?

Hatred. What a hateful word and so totally against his nature. Hatred, he considered too deep an emotion to hold very close or very long. Stephanie, on the other hand, had a different take. Stephanie did drama; she did it in stages from one to ten. She could and did hate, liberally. With her it was often flavor of the week. But that is a Stephanie thing.

He took her angst into account and determined not to sink to her level. One needed approach these things with at least a modicum of dispassion. Nope, he wouldn't hate or let hate rule his thinking. But he still wouldn't trust Carlos Morano. Not as far as he could throw his chubby butt (and that wouldn't be very far these days). But it wasn't out of hatred.

Dislike. Now there's a better word, not nearly as deep or as final as hatred, but what a powerful way to get a point across. Not too persnickety, not too condemning, just right. He'd just dislike the man. Yeah, that would do. Even after their little "love-in", just moments prior, he was having none of any emotion to do with him other than dislike covered by artful deceit.

It was enough to endure the first time, but again it replayed, refreshing the experience; a stifling scene that crawled through his mind's eye at a snail's pace, agonizing and long. The torrid memory was only somewhat relieved by the man's reaction to his announced travel itinerary. His revelation that he would soon be heading down to Miami had caused Morano to brighten as if that particular news were very welcome indeed. In fact, in hindsight, it actually seemed the man had only been waiting, himself enduring their proximity, until able to uncover a bit of Intel he required for the next stage in this game of Cat and Mouse.

It seemed so. Perhaps it was merely his mind playing tricks in the music-filled atmosphere of perfumed bodies jostling past his swivel seat in their haste towards the dance floor or the rest rooms, both being seriously powerful motivators. Perhaps it was the hilarious argument two seats down on his right: "I tell you it don't matter what the judge say, a man got the right to beat them kids' butts! That's why they so bad today! Hell, the judge ain't gotta raise 'em! He don't live with 'em! I whip them asses myself, they act up around me!"

Yeah, perhaps his timing did suffer from spending too much time playing nosey neighbor, eavesdropping grown folks conversations. However, the more he reflected it definitely did seem like Morano had excused himself mere moments after securing that tidbit. Then again, the plump rump had wobbled back to his lovely quartette across the bar, indicating perhaps his motivation, validating definitely his good taste …not saying much for them.

But one such lovely would have been reason enough for most men. So maybe his imagination. However, he knew instinctively it was neither the booze, the babes nor the bull. It was the Morano.

He had stood on JP's left, smiling his poisonous smile up into his face and talking his poisonous talk into his ear until he learned what he wanted to learn. Then gone in a flash went the Beastie Boy, back to the bar's other side, to spread his tentacles possessively around four beauties seated there. Gone away had this Beastie Boy, reminding him of the time they first met in a California penthouse, those same tentacles then possessively wrapped around another woman, a woman he intended to marry, a woman who had once been married to John Paul O'Rourke. He hadn't much liked Beastie Boy then and even less now. What had she seen in him?

But that wasn't quite fair. Though some might consider his shape leaning toward stodgy (JP being one of them); truth, the guy wasn't all that bad looking. If you into guys. How you characterize him? Up to the beholder. You out looking for an extra for your movie set in Juárez, prob'ly pass him right by. You wanna intro him to your Ex, he could be your guy! "Handsome? Attractive? Maybe", he considered, "maybe in a clinical sense …if you're in a clinic."

He refused the option of totally falling in love with the guy. But honesty had always been a major component of him and forced the admission that this man's looks were far removed from the classic "Beaner" profile coming out of Hollywood. Not that he got problems with classic Beaner" profiles. Besides, it ain't him profiling them …that's more a government thing now that they had to let go the Japanese-Americans.

More than that, though his heritage said Mexican, his appearance said anything but. No swarthy features, no traces of Indio; not that there is anything wrong with looking Indio, but his hairstyle and facial structure pronounced him more Ricky Martin than Ricky Gonzales and, despite the plus-sized package he toted, there was a semblance of style to his bearing.

Some might term it as class, his sense of style (somebody other than JP O'Rourke that is). But it was definitely a something-something he oozed and he knew how to make it work for him. He had oozed it again just before leaving, this Mister-Smiling-Fellow-Cheshire-Cat, when he casually "reached across the aisle" and invited his nemesis to a visit upon his arrival in Florida.

"Man, I got a party that's gonna be happening in Miami next week. You outta come out 'n have a good time." He hesitated a second before nodding towards the green-eyed, peaches and cream-colored beauty across the bar filling not just O'Rourke's but every man's eyes in the joint, even in this subdued lighting. Possibly he appreciated the lust, possibly he only perceived in his adversary an escapist technique to endure distasteful company. Either way, he then added… "Val gonna be there."

O'Rourke felt like parodying Gomer Pyle: "Surprise! Surprise! Surprise!" But merely smiled. He could smell setup even through expensive cologne …eau de toilet!

Claustrophobia then took a left turn and strolled quickly away in the form of one Carlos Morano and his shitwater. It took a few moments, but his blood pressure soon sufficiently subsided with the distasteful one's departure. He could breathe again. But what exactly was so bad, he couldn't say. It wasn't like the guy was trying to steal his wallet? And he probably would never have met her had it not been for him. But then again, did he really have a need for her if not for him? With bad guy gone bye-bye, he could take a few moments for reflection; only so far it all seemed to reflect back. Then again, on second thought, he did achieve some success …at least he hoped that's what you call it.

It was uncharacteristic for one seldom given to self-deprecating pats on the back, but O'Rourke sacrificed one moment to vanity. This evening actually working out better than he could have anticipated. He had wondered a bit at how the man might react to news of his intention to visit friends in the Magic City; not worried, just wondered, more curiosity than concern. Another's reaction however, that lingered still fresh in his memory, left no doubt.

Of the two, it was Morano's reaction that he found the most surprising. It's like he read O'Rourke's mind. "Oh you need an alibi? Ka Bam! Here's two, pick one!"

He didn't gloat, at least not much. Julia Child had been a spy for heaven sake. This ain't rocket science but his handler treated him like an idiot, like he just a soft spy (don't blow stuff up). He could barely keep the glee from hopping a ride on his text to the DIA. "In your face turkey!"

And it ain't like he don't know what's what. These guys recruited him in a locker room after a wrestling tournament! Who does that? They flew to Cali from Washington, DC to talk him into flying to Washington, DC. Literally, who does that?

When they came for him he knew even then. They don't come out like that unless they got their shit together. So it's a problem turning these guys down when they already decided to recruit you even before they approached you. "If you can't be a gun fighter, how 'bout a staff officer? Not that either? Gun shy an' can't manage people? Ooh kay, then janitor! Either way you in bitch! Or you out …permanently!"

Peterson hated his plan, but Morano just enabled it. So the only problem? Peterson! Which means ain't no problem! It's just a six inch conflict, the six inches between that jarhead's ears! Now, if it was the six inches between his legs, that would be a problem!

So the fact that he had totally labeled any Miami investigation downright useless and a waste of precious time. Nonstarter! All the arguments dropped away. He got no cover? Now he got cover. Showing up a second time, in a second place? Uh uh, issue resolved! Morano dating his Ex? Could care less, he offered an exchange. I'm from the Swap a Ho tribe! Problem over!

Peterson did have a good point though about eventually someone putting clues together, if he not smart. "Once they put together two and two, then they'll put four into you! Double tap to the chest, then the head for good measure."

But such was to be expected. Colonel Peterson, his not-so-bosom buddy had never showed anything other than contempt where he was concerned. Not that this recent news should delight the jarhead, but perhaps it would somewhat appease. Obviously, there's a considerable loss of face when the irresistible force roadgrades the immovable object! He agreed to this trip only after realizing O'Rourke's "hell or high water" intention to go there regardless …but at least he kinda did agree!

The condition that he dally there (Peterson's words) no more than two days, both understood as meaningless posturing. O'Rourke would take it under advisement. Volunteers are quite a bit tougher to control than died-in-the-wool staff members. He would stay as long as he sensed a connection. DIA may have talked him into working for them, but stubborn is as stubborn does …though he hadn't entirely gone off the reservation.

CHAPTER TWO

"Two!" The slim-waisted, spirited referee thumbed his left arm skyward; the one with the green wristlet, then emphatically extended the adjacent index finger, impetuously signaling tilt points for the ebon-hued wrestler. Next he demonstrably dove to the mat, landing in an exaggerated pushup position, his powerfully built physique held scant inches from the dark blue surface. Bulging arms, chest and shoulders, swelled the nylon, black and white striped shirt; further defining the tautness of the power-lifter frame and emphasizing the trimness of his narrow lower-half in the black jeans.

He positioned his perfect form in a manner intended to titillate. Coupled with the staged seriousness of his alert, attentive stare, it provided just the effect he desired. More than a few female spectators swept as many glances along his rigid flanks as they tossed to the two struggling combatants for whom they'd originally come to see. He understood perfectly the entertainment side of this sport. It was his main motivator for working part time as a referee. The pay was not all that attractive but supplementing his income as a referee both supported his weight-lifting hobby and helped get him dates.

Mild applause rose from scattered remnants of a once respectably sized crowd of avid fans. There were not as many left, now. Fewer, still interested in this outcome. But, as most wrestling fans are avid, they would do. More than two thousand devotees had crowded into the Southern California high school gymnasium and witnessed portions of the two-day affair. Now, however, in the final bouts, scarcely two hundred remained. Many of those other folks had left soon after their favorites were eliminated, taking those now, not so favorites along …"Sure it's nice, but it's high school!".

O'Rourke concerned himself with none of this. He was locked in monumental combat with the guy most of the crowd favored. He didn't bother to look at the score. Still ahead, but if he peeked at the boxes marked "VISITOR" and "HOME" to see how much, he would also see the time left and then he'd be counting minutes, even seconds. Besides, he knew he could tell how good the score was by the way the crowd cheered. Since they were cheering loud and steady, the score was close and that was not good, not for him. But as long as the "VISITOR" side was higher than the "HOME" side, they'd still be mixing prayers with their cheers …his desire, move them down on bended knee with those prayers.

In truth the spectators' cheering and shouts didn't bother him, much. He didn't pay attention to the words, only their intensity. The sound resonated in a rising, falling crescendo of people yelling for his doom or shouting instructions to his opponent. They may as well have been speaking ancient Greek or classic Vulcan for all their benefit. He didn't listen. In fact, once battle was joined, no wrestler ever paid much attention, if any, to those outside the mat's periphery. These sounds all mixed together in a furious cacophony to fill every corner of the rectangular building and reverberate off the raftered ceiling in unintelligible mass. But that didn't stop onlookers from venting their frustrations or their advice. Fan, after all, is shortened from fanatic.

Even though nearly all these fans were rooters for the opposition, he needed to use them. He needed to channel their raucous noise into his resolve. He felt the physical force of the waves of sound and sought to use their strength to re-generate energy within himself, to bolster his fading reserves. He attempted to use their pitch, their malevolence in a manner similar to a reverse-PSYOPS device. Then, rather than deflating emotions as Psychological Operations are intended, these screaming fanatics would see their energies instead reinvigorate their enemy …and just piss off ev'rybody!

He actually began to feel the warmth rising inside, strengthening him. Their taunts --intended to help the other—were not heard so much as felt and their negativity pleased the antagonist within him. In his mind he was ever the anti-hero, the loner. He was Nat Love, aka., Deadwood Dick --the Wild West outlaw with the heart of gold-- in a shootout at sundown with their man …a man he hated.

Well, not totally hated, just disliked intensely for now. It had to be that way. Howard Jaso was nobody to take lightly. According to the Los Angeles Times, Jaso has been one of the country's best "Freestyle" wrestlers the last two years and he was just twenty-one years old. O'Rourke was kicking a million-something, "hard-in-the-ass", as his friend Sylvia lately liked to say.

She knew the truth even though he would not freely acknowledge questions of a chronological nature. Sylvia called him an old lady because of his evasive maneuvers and she never let him forget that his years were advancing.

"Ooooh, another gray hair!" another cute little expression of hers lately. One she would often coo with almond shaped, opalescent eyes blinking their message of feigned innocence, all the while her svelte woman form rhythmically swayed a wonderfully seductive message of its own.

"An' she wonders why I ain't proposed", he thought. "She's up there in the stands prob'ly wonderin' what th' hell an' old sucker like me is doin' rassling --as she calls it when she's mad at me-- with a guy half my age."

Truth be known, he did not consider a young kid's entry into the world valid reason for an older person to step off, particularly when that older person retained viability. Chuckling, he recalled the old adage: "I may not be as good as I once was, but I'm as good once as I ever was!"

Those thoughts quickly soared through his conscious and he was again forced to focus on Jaso who had succeeded in getting off his back and back to his feet. His demeanor reflected that of a slightly annoyed padrone recovering from an insignificant trip …over an insignificant peon.

"This is gonna be tougher than I thought", winced O'Rourke. "Oh well! If I don't win, won't be many witnesses!" his sense of humor chortled. Perhaps it was his sense of irony reacting to the less-than-half-full gym.

International Freestyle wrestling could never hope to match football or basketball for spectator appeal—not in this country. No matter, it suited him. In fact he loved it. His problem was that he also loved many other life's aspects, especially including women, parties, women, boating, women, vacations, women, and on and on. Now the numbing in his biceps reminded, in no uncertain terms, how much the parties and the other distractions had cheated in on his workout time. Too late to wish for the dedication he'd left with the Marine Corps team.

Circling warily to his right, O'Rourke blocked Jaso's attempted leg tackle then suddenly drove off his right foot in a blinding ankle-pick maneuver, head lowered, fingers clutching, teeth clenched. At least he thought it was blinding. His opponent --though seemly surprised-- managed a panther-like leap sideways in time to escape.

Recovering, the man appeared somewhat pleased with his performance. It was at this time he chose to make his second major mistake of the day. He smiled. Not much. Just sort of a confident, "I got'cha" type grin to the coffee colored opponent wearing the all black singlet and black shoes.

Back was Jaso's customary sneer. It had been replaced, for a time, with a genuinely worried expression, while he fought to get off his back. Still, he hadn't panicked. O'Rourke had to give him that. But one thing he hoped to never give him again was another moment to feel satisfied and with that, to sneer. This was more than just another good match between two very good past champions (one much more recent than the other). This was a grudge match. However, only one of them appreciated that aspect.

When Howie Jaso found out who he would face in the tournament's finals he had at first chuckled and then laughed, very heartily. So relieved he would not have to risk a third straight loss to Chris Sandslowski he couldn't help it. He laughed. He would wrestle for the Southern Cal Regional, eighty-two kilo championship against an old man! He laughed! Trouble was he did so within earshot of O'Rourke.

Before Jaso began entertaining, O'Rourke's main concern was resting his fatigued body in order to give his opponent a good match. But after, thoughts of survival became secondary. Now he really wanted to punish this guy.

"Man, I can't believe this crap! Somebody tell me this ain't true!" Howie's rich voice had blared in strident tones. "Yo! Pat! Why they do this? I gotta wrestle Grandpa Jones? You got's to be kidding!"

On and on he had guffawed, playing to a group of confident admirers or anyone else proceeding by the Seeding Charts taped to the gym's interior wall near the locker room entrance. "Tell ya'll what. I gonna give him at least one point, cause it ain't nice to disrespect yo' elders. Haw, haw, haw!"

Howie and two of his fellows were bent over holding their sides, at his humor. They had recently exited the men's locker room door near the refreshment stand and spied the pairings that so tickled his ribs.

He was dressed in a white-trimmed-with-red singlet, which was now covered by a red-trimmed-with-white warm-up jacket. White wrestling shoes and socks completed the ensemble. His boys were attired in street clothes, having lost out in earlier matches. Several females of the beautiful body persuasion soon swelled their number, complete with their own swelling proportions. They also joined in Howie's revelry …so fun, Howie was such a clown!

But clowning has no place in serious sport. O'Rourke's Irish was up. He was seething from the slight. They were still smirking. These people didn't even know him, nobody did. His work had kept him too busy to enter a tourney in several years. But there was a time he'd been well thought of …at one time in his past.

It was the price he paid to achieve success. Until recently, he just simply had no time for sport, not with all the travel his job had formerly involved. But now that the company had evolved into a streamlined and well-oiled machine with a surplus of qualified staff, he could afford the time for conditioning workouts and travel to local tournaments. In fact, the additional down time had begun to grate on him. Work had become his whole purpose. He had become so used to minimal rest between flights over the past dozen years that the change to an easier schedule seemed sudden, foreign and conflicting. He missed the constant pressure, the feel of being needed. Purpose fueled by necessity demanded that he do something to alleviate the boredom infiltrating and inundating.

First he found a steady woman. Not on purpose. But she was the kind of accident every man wishes to crash into. Luckily, both were on bicycles when it happened. But even running into someone this beautiful and vibrant was not enough for someone who had unbeknownst even to himself become an action junkie …bout time to start a YouTube channel.

Now he understood why the death rates were so seriously high for men who retired early from high-pressure positions. They thrived on the stress. And his business was high stress; high pressure all the way that up until recently never seemed to stop. He needed that release.

So it was back to the daily gym workouts. Then came volunteer dojo work teaching the Fullerton YMCA's martial arts class. But his first time as Sensei did not come about by accident. Somehow Miles owed somebody a favor and had talked JP into paying it back as part of a payback that could never be fully paid back. Regardless --typical of Miles Watson's interventions—the benefits were shared equally amongst all involved.

For JP, those benefits centered around the two dozen, bright-eyed gazes awaiting his every instruction that their straining, sweating bodies attempted mightily to follow. His own, lithe body came alive, prancing erect and proud around the small room with the padding hung loosely from its colorful walls. His black, Chinese slippers might have drawn a disapproving look from Shiro, but their rubber soles provided additional traction on the slippery mats used here. Besides, Sylvia liked the way they dressed up his Gi. After all, this was Southern California, not West Philly. Style was everything here …sorta like there too, just more so.

Speaking of Sylvia, there was her recent hinting that a more permanent relationship would also be a stylish thing, even though she had always played down the marriage question. Pressure came in many formats.

He had considered the subject but had never popped the question. In fact they both had danced around it. It was the "not-so-small" matter of commitment. Both loved each other, that much was true. But they also loved their freedom. Besides, though she barely in her late thirties, he was now officially ancient. Getting kinda late for childrearing. Besides, they already spent nearly all their available time together. No benefit even from taxes. The only way he saw their relationship improving was in its status …and who needed status?

And, that question of settling down invariably came up when they were with other couples and the subject of kids and biological clocks also pushed their way into the back 'n forth. Others saw in them what they desired to see, not necessarily what they needed to see.

It was actually a no brainer to him. Both had tried marriage briefly at an early age and decided that once was an experience for a lifetime. That constituted the gist of their informal arrangement. Nothing was cataloged or transcribed. It simply just fell into place that way.

Besides, every man ain't Daddy material. He getting a bit long in the tooth for the rigors of fatherhood; taking junior or missy to the park to shag fly balls or run pass routes or shoot jumpers from the top of the key …or God forgive, teaching her about boys!

What he told none, he even kinda liked the idea of parenthood, having a child to raise and teach twenty-four/seven and he knew that Sylvia loved the idea. Children are precious. So he would not dream of harming a kid, physically or mentally, neither in sport nor in life.

But contrary to his norm --his love of kids and his abiding respect for another wrestler-- he really wanted to hurt this kid, to embarrass this overconfident big mouth and quiet his hysterically giggling followers. What did Sylvia call it, Revanche? Yeah that was it, he remembered. Except that he could never get the accent the way she did, with her pidgin mixture of Africanized French, Spanish patois and Southern English, flavored with a Louisiana drawl.

But no matter, thoughts of revenge and retaliation now immersed him, churned fiercely through him and focused on simplistic measures of proper compensation. In wrestling terms a shutout and a pin or at least one of those would compensate nicely. He did not need a pound of flesh on this mat, just to pound this guy's flesh into the mat …but easy don't come as easy as go.

Jaso had every reason to feel confident. Sandslowski was the only man on the whole west coast --and one of the few in the world-- to beat him the last two years. Jaso led the powerful wrestling squad from Cal State University at Bakersfield. Sandslowski led their biggest rivals from Cal State Fullerton. Both were on the U.S. team and pointing for the up-coming Olympic Trials. This tourney was one of the regional qualifiers.

At one hundred-eighty-point-five pounds he was unquestionably one of the most potent wrestling machines ever. His moves came almost without thought. His tremendous quickness and power were near legend. Lately, only Sandslowski's exceptional prowess had consistently prevailed over him. And even those were always close decisions. In two years, the few other losses --to other world ranked foes-- he always quickly avenged. But it had become a popular --whispered out of his earshot-- rumor that Sandslowski owned his mind and that the mere mention of his name would cause Jaso "to take the apple", a much used wrestling epithet meaning "to choke".

Jaso knew of the rumor. A concerned friend whispered it to him one day while they practiced "take downs" in their college team's wrestling room. He had nearly destroyed the well-meaning, informer, bouncing him unmercifully, again and again off the practice mat.

Deep inside he acknowledged how closely that speculation mirrored his own concerns. He had vowed to conquer the demon, even denying his girlfriend's considerable warmth to stay hungry. But now his revenge had to await some other day. Sandslowski had injured a shoulder and lost a close match in the semis to this ancient, tired assed spade. He hated that spade for blocking his chance. Now he would have to teach him a lesson about interfering…

Jaso hadn't seen the match --embroiled in a tough semifinal of his own across the gym-- but he was confident that Sandslowski's loss came because of the injury. His self-assured hubris conceived no other rational condition.

"No way this guy could down the Sandman", he'd made his friends aware. "I'm gonna beat his ta'yah'd ass like a new toy drum on Christmas Day." His friends who had seen the match all agreed with him, in spirit.

But they were slightly uneasy with the ease in which the chiseled black guy had seemed to handle Sandman …of course the old guy was a lot fresher then.

O'Rourke couldn't know exactly what Jaso's thoughts were. But had he, he would surely have agreed. The initial adrenaline rush had worn off. Now deep down --but barely hidden under his cool visage-- his butt was seriously dragging. He had thought he was in good shape and in truth he was. Sort of. All those three-mile-a-day runs to lose the sixteen pounds he had to get off to make weight, had to add up to something. But, like a rude awakening, wrestling has a way of separating boys from men …his boy just needed to stay on the man side.

Internalizing the agony each breath brought and the growing fatigue, he tried to suck it up, get it back together. He had tried a quick pin with the soufflé. It almost worked. But the semifinal with Sandslowski took too much out of him. His ribs ached from that man mountain's "gut wrench" around his abdomen. His jaw had been nearly crushed by a "cross face" from a fist of steel and his left knee was taking a powder and didn't have much feeling left. Two fingers --the pinky and ring-- on his left hand were clamped together with white, medical tape for support, after both had been jammed as he landed wrong when Sandslowski literally threw him off the mat …up against the scorer's table.

He recalled that flight, with glaring clarity. It would probably return later in life as nightmares. His travel through the air for what seemed a longer period than it actually had been allowed time for his awareness to consider one noteworthy thought: "this is really gonna hurt!"

And boy did it ever and still did. He was a mess. But at least he was a mess in the finals. Sandslowski had been relegated to wrestling in the Consolations , the Consies" for third place. So O'Rourke's pain did not seem so great, until now. He wondered what Creole-spiced phrases Sylvia would pipe out to emphasize her displeasure with the entire process. Of one thing he was sure, it wouldn't be her favorite --"Laissez le bon temps roulee"-- because there weren't any good times rolling just then. Maybe she'd simply resort to an old street slang description she tended to use whenever he pissed her off. "Dumb Ass!"

Jaso had gotten off his back and back to his feet so easily that O'Rourke almost "took the apple" himself. After all, he was an old man, a tired old man, wrestling a young lion. He was not even supposed to be in the "Open" division of this tournament. Unfortunately --part of him reasoned-- there were too few participants in the "Master" division reserved for seniors over thirty-five. So his choices were to either wrestle in the "Open" division or to go home. He had not wanted to go home, at least not then. But this was "for-real" work and now he was "for-real" hurting.

There was hardly anyone over thirty in this division. Most intelligent guys over thirty had sown their wild oats and moved on to endeavors better suited to their age and levels of maturity. This was not like professional sports where men with names like Bonds and Greztky (and Brady) grew old enjoying playing the same games they had first loved as children. Freestyle wrestling did not pay the rent. He was a Greybeard challenging youngsters. Nobody, not even Sylvia, expected him to win this match. She actually thought that he should have his head examined for even entering the tournament, let alone entering the final match nursing ribs that refused to let him breathe. To her it seemed such an easy choice for him to make, "just give in, and let's call it a day".

But John Paul O'Rourke was never one who sought the comforts of taking the easy way out. He could be stubborn as they came and twice as ornery. Tired was one thing; pussy whipped was something totally different. He tried to mentally expunge his fatigue. He was not about to give up. He screamed to himself that this guy was gonna have to prove just how much lion he was. New tactic. In his mind he changed the guy's name to Scar, the Lion King wannabee!

The whistle's shrill was a welcome sound to his ears. As the two grapplers broke apart to move from the "out-of-bounds" back to the mat center, O'Rourke's painfully burning sinews screamed back at him. In unison, their chorus rang out, nearly drowning out his will to succeed. The feeling of pending doom grew overwhelmingly.

"Lache pas la patate!" Sylvia's Creole accented voice somehow pierced the gloom descending on him.

"Yeah, I ain't gonna give up", he mentally responded, wondering if she really felt he had a chance. His heavily heaving lungs were not totally convinced, neither were most of the spectators. Up by only two points and the other guy was coming on. This all could only lead to one conclusion. Just then Jaso sneered.

It was bold, arrogant and very nearly daunting. It reminded O'Rourke of that scene forty minutes earlier. When good old Scar pronounced his, "Ahh'm th' baddist mu'tha alive", declaration including how quickly he would destroy "Uncle Sam the Spade". It reminded him the look–eyes squinty, right side mouth turned up—seemingly expecting him to fold.

"Arrogant sum' bitch", O'Rourke's tired mind thought. But suddenly he felt less tired. A bit more refreshed. The sneer burned into his mental mechanism. It also ended any conscious considerations concerning pain or thoughts of going quietly …of course those would still be considerations.

New tactic. He still needed to take it to this guy --his strategy embraced offense-- but it would have to be administered in baby steps. If he sought the quick kill he would waste precious energy. Scar was nobody's flake. However, if he concerned himself with maintaining his lead --only concentrated on defense-- he also would not achieve success.

Minor successes. That was how he had to approach this conflict, not so much in terms of overall success or failure, not of winning or losing, but of minor accomplishments. "Sochin Bassai Sho. Use tranquil force to remove an obstruction".

He would not seek to take the man down. He would seek instead to move him this way or the other. Once he was successful at instigating the desired movement, he would then attempt to capture an available body part, perhaps a leg or ankle or an arm to move about or lock up in some way. He would always seek offense. Even if his opponent attacked, he would seek to redirect the force, to use this attack for his own purposes. Taking baby steps was key, but all these baby steps had to happen smoothly and in rapid sequence.

He disdained the idea of awaiting attack. Focus on countering attacks was for other folk, more patient and much more structured. Some wrestlers specialized in that strategy. Some were very successful in that approach. However, in order for one such as he to achieve ultimate success, gotta be offensive minded. He could not throw caution to the winds but commit to aggressive action that would give this opponent little pause to plan his attack. The plan was to keep him reacting.

"Wrestle your way!" He always advised the kids he coached. He followed the wisdom of Miyamoto Musashi, a seventeenth century Japanese samurai and philosopher, who wrote that, "If you consciously try to thwart opponents, you are already late".

Circling warily to his right, feinting with his arms towards Scar's legs, he got just the reaction he wanted. Scar hopped back a bit then shot in for a "single leg tackle" of his own. O'Rourke waited until the arms looped around his right thigh. Then, moving with blinding speed, scooped his right palm against the inside Scar's right thigh and lifted, simultaneously pivoting towards him. Grasping around the thigh's outer side with his left hand, he levered Scar over and onto his back.

This time there would be no escape. Scar-Howie let go of O'Rourke's leg and attempted to get back to his stomach. But O'Rourke had already shifted to a more secure hold. As his opponent's back struck the dark, blue mat; he instantly threw an irresistible, "Reverse-Half Nelson" under and around his neck, simultaneously locking the left arm in a granite like armbar.

Howie turned as hard as he could, away from the other, straining for all he was worth, fighting the rising panic as well as the vise like choke hold around his neck. It was too much. The harder he pulled to get away the tighter the hold seemed to get.

"Looks like bad times at Black Rock", he thought. "Gwen wasn't gonna like him getting pinned. But like that guy Walsh said, 'a new love you can get; but not a new neck'. or something like that."

Almost as an after-thought, his mind's eye observed the referee scurry around in his showboat style, pretentiously seeking a better view. Since there was obviously only one good angle from which to view how closely both of his shoulders were to the mat, Howie wondered, "a better view of what?" Probably "a better view of who" would have been a more appropriate thought.

"Roger the Rabbit", as he was appropriately nicknamed --and not just because of his movement around the mat-- raised his left arm horizontally and waited. It was all just a matter of time. Soon he would raise the arm high into the air above his head to signal the "Fall" and amble over to check out that cute, little redhead wearing the tight fitting, low cut sweater.

He had alternated between officiating the animated grappling and admiring the periwinkle blue crisscross design unsuccessfully struggled to hide the shape of her jutting tatas (his thoughts). He seriously desired to subject them to further exploration and totally agreeable to treating her to a private view of the "six-pack" he worked so hard to maintain.

He balanced on his toes and on one arm in a lowered, pushup position. The other arm was held just above the mat surface, ready to end this apparently one-sided contest as soon as the down wrestler's second shoulder blade touched the mat. Rock hard and bulging muscles held him steady, evidently positioned to see all and make his judgment. Every now and then he would scuttle over to another vantage point and lock up again. He knew how much all the cuties in the stands would appreciate the view and he appreciated people who appreciated viewing his physique, especially when they had big tits.

Rabbit Roger's view of Howie's situation was shared by everyone else in the gymnasium. That is, everyone excepting one, very luscious looking redhead, sporting two well-proportioned objects of more than one male spectator's desire.

"Come on Howie, get up!" She urged on her hero, her lover, in a shrill, notably concerned voice, which carried well above the crowd's hushed murmur around the gym.

"Come on babe, you can do it! He's nothing!" She became even more agitated, jumping to her petite feet, stomping them on the bleachers.

"He's hurting him, he's hurting him!" She screamed, green eyes flaring, beginning to tear; ruby red colored, pouting lips pleading. The tears began to wet her cheeks, then her chin; simultaneously a nasal drip crept languidly from the left nostril of her button nose. "He can't breathe!"

Rabbit's hand had already started its ascent but immediately froze in mid air. His ears missed little, neither did his shifty, coal black, darting eyes , especially from such succulent beauty as hers. Instead of raising his hand in agreement or slapping the mat, signaling the fall and ending the contest, he changed his mind. The other official --the side judge-- still had his arm raised and only waited for Roger to confirm the pin. Instead, to the amazement of most and the consternation of the side judge, he reached out and slapped O'Rourke's right arm. "You're choking him! Let go, Blue! I said let go!"

O'Rourke was slow to realize what was happening. He was using his last strength, desperately seeking the pin. "What the hell was this guy talking about?"

That was the beauty of Half-Nelsons. You turn away, you're turning into the crook of the opponent's elbow and you choke (a little), you turn in towards the opponent and both your shoulder blades touch the mat simultaneously and you're pinned.

"What the deal?" Why the hell this happening? It was a perfectly legal move. O'Rourke's mind had turned zombie like. Everything appeared to his eyes through a bluish haze. It reminded him of that time when he had dropped a tab of Yellow Sunshine to escape the realities of a world he no longer wished to witness nor cared to survive. Whatever happened immediately during that LSD trip he could not remember, he only remembered that he would never do something that stupid again.

Now, reality flooded in again, snapping his focus back to the here and now. He realized that he was the "blue" wrestler, having been assigned the blue elastic band to wear around his ankle. Jaso wore the red band. He just could not rationalize what crime he had committed.

At first confused, his temper flared, he resisted. Then, glaring hard at "Roger, the Rabbit" turned Rabid; he let go the Nelson. Though not before giving one last, bone-bruising squeeze. Almost immediately, despite the grogginess, Jaso forced his way back to his stomach and then to his knees. "He was really pissed off now, he would show this sucker."

But before Jaso could get to his feet; O'Rourke, still tight against his right side, chopped his right arm out from under him. He had kept the armbar locked around the left and drove it down, simultaneously with the arm chop. Howie's face bit into the Neolite surface for a split second before being turned once more back to stare at the ceiling; back once more to stare at that stupid placard some jerk had placed there; the stupid placard with the equally stupid words: "IF YOU'RE READING THIS SIGN YOU'RE ABOUT TO GET STUCK".

O'Rourke had jammed in a double arm bar and quickly pried the man over. Some call them the "Bensalem Bars", named after a High School in Pennsylvania. He wasn't trying to give Scar Howie any chance to recover and maybe get back into the match. But, almost too pooped to throw them in and there's nearly two minutes to go.

Scar Howie was having his worst day ever. "Who the hell is this old mu'tha sucker? Where the hell had he come from, why had he come here today and how could he kick the living crap out of the two best wrestlers on the west coast?"

Now Howie was in a shit storm. He lay seconds away from being pinned. But the one dominant characteristic of shit is its unpleasant tendency to stink up everyone in the vicinity. Suddenly the match itself got shitty....

Howie's nose began to bleed. Not a lot, wasn't like he coughed up blood or anything and he still stubbornly fought to escape the pin. "Tweet"

Again he was saved when the referee called "Time Out" and directed him to his corner for treatment, while waiving over a mat crew to swipe up any blood or mucous staining the wrestling surface. O'Rourke was at once, both grateful for the rest and furious that he still needed to complete this match.

Consternation flew at light speed to all corners of his befuddled brain, invoking accusations that either this ref was a friend of Jaso or motivated by something else. Came a concluding thought "maybe it's race".

In Jaso's corner two of his friends brought out a first aid kit and proceeded to stem the trickle of blood. In O'Rourke's corner there was only his warm-up clothing draped over the two, obligatory plastic chairs. He began to feel outnumbered again, backed into a corner. An old feeling began swelling up inside him, the feeling that "THEY" would not let him win. That "THEY" would do their worst to cheat him, just like "THEY" tried to belittle and cheat all minorities, especially blacks. "THEY" were the collective whiteys who specialized in that sort of thing. The thoughts of "THEY" ganging up to beat up on him began to motivate him. He knelt on the mat's edge in front of the plastic chairs and tried to revitalize his weary frame with several, slow deep breaths of the warm atmosphere and started to seethe about "THEY".

He needed to calm. Problem with seeing racism everywhere (even though perhaps it is), you limit the discussion. Even hint there's some form of prejudice and you devolve scholarly process into WWE SmackDown, at the very least "hit and hit back"!

"Time!" Called the ref, motioning both men back to the center. O'Rourke still seethed, but had managed to garner some measure of composure. His dark eyes held nothing but enmity for the other. Their centers radiated deep pools of vehement fury. The evil took hold of him, rushing out from its hiding place, welling up from deep within to excoriate all vestiges of weakness. The pain, which had so sapped his earlier resolve, was now suppressed. Nothing motivated him quite the same as blatant prejudice.

This was by far, not his first experience with prejudicial situations. He chose not to seek them or to label questionable occurrences as prejudice or to wonder why these things happened to him. Instead, he strived to overcome them, to patiently force his way past the situation with strength, talent and intellect.

His Sensei had admonished him to treat each challenge as just that, a challenge and an opportunity to succeed. But blatant prejudice --fueled by unfounded hatred, fear, or mistrust—brought out the worst of him. He could, at times, become reduced to an extremely violent force of nature, losing all composure, capable of unnatural physical acts. That time had come. No matter how leaden his arms felt, he needed to "suck it up". He must not surrender to these pigs … racist or not.

CHAPTER THREE

"Well, what do you think Gen 'er Sir? Pretty much everything our analysis showed?" Sitting mid way up the bleachers, nearly in the center of the Gym's left side, three men in dark suits watched the proceedings with mixed emotions and views. Just a touch on the portly side –his thick shape akin to a tree trunk—he spoke his words to the elder statesman sitting in their middle. He was pleased that his group's analysis seemed accurate, even though this did not represent his group's actual choice.

His was the task of researching prospective talent for their agency. Their massively compiled digital personnel files could be tailored to mission specific scenarios for whatever purpose and contributed significantly to any such decision. Unfortunately, this decision had not quite worked out that way.

One other of their trio was even more displeased. He was the youngest of them, sitting on the right flank. Typing hard at his iPhone, he seldom ever even looked towards the mat. Though he did occasionally peruse spectators sitting near them. Security always a concern. His crewcut though was normally tilted downward into the display of the device in his hands. He despised having to sit out something so boring to him as a wrestling match. He neither understood its nuances nor strategies. Rather, to his thinking the sport had none that mattered.

He would much rather be pounding keys back at his workstation in the Software Integration Laboratory. He was seldom comfortable outside the SIL and never comfortable around these macho type assholes strutting around in their tight little uniforms. But Captains don't argue when Generals order and his General had ordered him to get on an airplane.

Still, he did not have to actually watch the match. He amused himself surfing the web for some interesting software articles. The Association of Shareware Professionals was always trying to get software engineers worldwide to join their ranks. He would peruse the ASP site, perhaps even download some neat new shareware. The General and the Colonel could watch the muscle heads, he decided. One day soon he might kiss this life goodbye and try his luck as a civilian "Geek". If things didn't quickly change, that day might come sooner than later.

The third one --the senior man in their midst-- was swept up in memories of a time long past and a youth ill spent. Included in those memories was a chapter, much of which, he'd like to forget. The part he wanted always to remember included seventy-six courageous soldiers and a stalwart Marine aviator. The part he dearly wished he could forget centered on those seventy-six members of his platoon placed in harm's way by the least capable of them …their leader.

"Yes, I believe your assessment was accurate, Pete." The tall, slender man with the graying temples replied to his middle-aged, companion. The shorter, but more powerfully built man relaxed a bit. He had never been onboard with his boss concerning this stratagem, but he would never produce a lackluster effort regardless where his true desires lay. He played the cards he was dealt.

Benjamin Peterson was both a student of history and a thorough researcher. Though, unknown to him, his Commanding General already knew a great deal about their current subject. Their paths had crossed long before. But he would save that personal history for some other revealing…

"Ah thank we ought a base 'dis decision own mo'ren a wrassling match, suh"; interjected the man on the right wing. This one was reed-thin and coiffed with short-length, blondish hairs that closely imitated a wire brush on top, before tapering down smoothly above his ears and nape. He was obviously much younger than the others, as well as less tactful. "Ah mean, when he was in th' Mo'rines 'n all..."

"That's Ma' Rines Thompson, Ma' Rines, and it's wrest'ling, not wrassling!"

"Yessuh!" responded the youngster. He loved to get the Colonel's goat and what better way than to put down his beloved Corps. The younger man carried on, "hey Colonel, did you know that the marble for the Tomb of the Unknowns was quarried in Marble, Colorado? That's the same place they got the marble for the Lincoln memorial an' prob'ly the original Block Head".

Noting that Thompson was seemingly, totally engrossed in his handheld all the while spewing out his laconic spiel, the Colonel ignored his attempt to bait him into some meaningless, meandering discourse. Thompson sported an acerbic wit that he purposefully used to ride those unfortunate souls gone afoul of his temper. He nearly always created some measure of outrage in his boss. But at this moment the Colonel was only slightly miffed by his companion. He was more engaged by the black wrestler's current approach to his situation.

They came seeking a solution to a problem. Maybe this was it. Maybe not. What he had hoped for was an operative with a Billy Badass attitude, who could take orders, at least up to the point those orders became unworkable. Usually, their recruits would have years of training, including fieldwork with seasoned team leaders. A by-the-book, basic operator skill set packages extensive leadership qualities and decision-making abilities. A high degree of intelligence is a substantial asset, but not the most sought after, neither is extreme courage. Often times, the best operative will achieve more success by evasion than confrontation.

Agent operative types that Peterson favored all possessed superior decision-making skills. Those types were more liable to avoid any situation which could potentially become violent. What most bothered him about O'Rourke's military record was its implication of a tendency toward irrational imbalance. DoD already has plenty of gunfighters. But they are ineffective without eyes and brains directing them to appropriate targets. Not from nothing, the decision wasn't really up to him…

Major General Millard Burton was impeccably attired in a dark brown pinstriped three-piece suit. Of the three his dress was by far the most "GQ". Image and ego go hand in hand and he had carefully groomed one to satisfy the other. He was neither flashy nor Spartan; cut from a conservative cloth. But the filigreed gold and black tie and matching kerchief were a present from his wife and they mated well with the crisply ironed white shirt.

Pinned halfway down at the tie's center was an emblem of a high kicking, Army Mule –its tail straight up—across the letter "A". His West Point credentials. On his left lapel was pinned a small Silver Star ribbon, a memory from a South Vietnam firefight that had cost him two of his platoon Sergeants, four of his Privates and six months in the 27th Surgical Hospital at Chu Lai.

As Burton lay in a hospital bed, more dead than alive, recovering from a large dose of shrapnel and the loss of his spleen, the medal was pinned to his left breast, by some now, forgotten, silhouette in Army Green. He never wore the pin as a symbol of his heroism or even for the camaraderie it tended to enable in certain sectors. Instead, he wore it to remind himself of that horrible day and of the hell on earth he had blundered into.

Satanic hell spawned memories were burned into his psyche by the same sulfur-laden brimstone that totally burned out of him the arrogance, the fervor and the unwavering faith in his God, his country and his ability to overcome the little, yellow, commie bastards who dared to defy the might of the right. It seemed funny to him that his medals didn't have the same effect, not even the Purple Heart. Perhaps because there were so many of them. But that single, solitary lapel pin served to remind him of a most unfair aspect of life …its selection process.

Peering at the pin's reflection in his dressing mirror always served to level him. It served to remind him of a headstrong, young, first lieutenant who had rushed his platoon headlong into a Viet Cong ambush and somehow survived it …when so many others did not. It also reminded him that it was on that same battlefield, or because of it, that he first met John Paul O'Rourke.

Burton had suffered in silence for thirty some years; his penance for surviving an Asian Waterloo. He had neither told anyone of his remorse nor confided his mistake that still haunted him nor of his morbid fascination with the Silver Star pin. Otherwise he would most likely have ended his career enduring endless sessions on a Psychiatrist's couch, instead of rising to a General Officer's billet. Logic motivated his every movement. Logic murmured that though one could not reclaim the past, one could right the wrong, one could assuage the debt by slaying the dragon. However, though logic and honor demanded that he slay all dragons. He was here to charm a dragon slayer.

To the General –though perhaps not the two men he sat with-- O'Rourke's current performance could not have been more satisfactory. None of them had envisioned he would make it this far in this tournament. Given his years, that was asking a bit much. But their assessment of his readiness was not contingent upon him actually winning, just his physical conditioning and mental ability. They had been surprised to find him competing in the "Open" division, though not surprised with his heart. But a weary body leeches away at even the strongest heart. It takes a strong will to maintain them both. They intended to find out if his was a will or a won't!

The stocky, older man still held a reservation. But his young companion had not been the least apprehensive. The knowledge that Jaso had a huge ego, easily stroked by the right sort, made it a no-brainer that they could assess O'Rourke's temper and resolve. But he had still held his confidence in check. It mattered little to him whether the black guy quit or just got his ass kicked. He just needed a way for them to assess his capacity. Still, he was a bit concerned when the black man began to tire so early in the match. He did not desire to have to do this again. Unless this guy's true nature showed through, the General might need more convincing.

Thompson sensed the same apprehension and for the same reason in the Colonel and –true to his nature-- derided his superior's unease. "Damn Colonel, ya'll ain't got no worry," his east Texas drawl tauntingly whispered across to the other's burning ear. No response, but he felt better all the same.

It had been Thompson's assigned task to make an assessment of the opponent's capability. There had been no prior thought of this necessity, because not one of them had even considered the possibility of O'Rourke's performance being this impressive. The others could not even understand their leader's burning desire to see the drama in person. Send the field jockeys. A video woulda been digitally fed back to headquarters shortly upon the conclusion. But for some reason unknown to either of them, they were hustled here to personally measure him …oh well, when duty calls.

The reality, he loved it. Ever the opportunist –whether for a chance to fart on the Marine's parade or to enhance his own standing with the boss—he was always up for either. Now came an opportunity for him to achieve both.

At first he had sided with the Colonel. But only in the privacy of the Colonel's office, agreeing that this was no time for amateur sleuth hour. Leave the safety of the nation in the hands of the professional. Constraints be dammed! They both agreed, they needed a man who could hit the ground running. They already had the right man selected …til he got de-selected!

It did not take him long. Almost immediately Thompson spied an opportunity, an enabling opportunity. He instantly produced a minor stratagem --insidiously derived and timed-- that goaded the self-assured wrestler into launching his spiel, describing how this "one-sided" victory would be handily won …just as O'Rourke happened within earshot.

Thompson had a master's degree in rousing rabble. He could get under anyone's skin. His inference suggested that a certain little redhead's interest had been stirred by a certain big black man. It was not much. Just barely a whisper. But it was timed as the handsome black man walked past. It was masterfully presented to no one in particular, but well within earshot of her jealous boyfriend. Just enough to arouse the hubris, to set him off, as was his wont.

Ever the analyst, his observation had revealed the man's insecurity. He had even demonstrated an earlier example, which Thompson had filed away, as was his wont. Jaso took the proffered bait with the alacrity of a hungry striped bass: hook, line and sinker. It was just simply irresistible.

But Howie had his own motivations. This would not be the first old black man she had admired, after all she was totally in love with Denzel, plus a couple other stars, which he sorta understood, they're stars. But she even considered her cousin's BF sexy and he drove a truck!

Jaso bit hard, then lashed out verbally, first to put the conspirator in his place, then to impress upon his friends how losers never got the girls, just the "beat down".

He began loudly, too loudly, berating her once again about her wandering eye. He verbally reminded her about the last guy he had to "straighten out" for just touching her and stated that this new fellow would not look so pretty after he had wiped the mat with him.

Ignoring her protestations to the contrary, he called her names not intended for endearment, continuing even after the humiliated woman had paced quickly out of proximity to his tirade and again he predicted a serious beat down. True to his prediction, a beatdown cometh!

Politely shaking hands with Jaso and Sandslowski, he graciously accepted his first place medal, posed with them for the obligatory press pictures and then stepped down from the top step on the ceremony stand. Though the losers offered winning smiles, neither truly wished his conversation nor he theirs. These were top athletes, closely equaled in skills and power, either one could have won this tournament. So there was no sense of happiness from simply placing in the top three. The sense of failure was like a weight on their hearts. But while their hearts were heavy and leaden, their minds seethed …especially the one who suddenly couldn't locate his girlfriend, who, according to friends, was last seen drying her tears on the shoulders of a dark haired man wearing a referee's outfit …as they walked toward his car.

For O'Rourke however, there was a deep feeling of warmth and a supreme sense of accomplishment. This was the best thing to happen in quite some time. He felt truly wonderful. Maybe he wasn't totally over the hill after all. Maybe tonight at dinner he would pop that question. Maybe. But for now he was intent only upon a quick shower and more of those succulent kisses Sylvia had rained upon him a few minutes before.

She demonstrated remarkable ability to start his juices flowing again. It was the first time she had acted romantic towards him since the last time Tina had visited and for some time now he had thought she never would seek him romantically again, transfiguring the relationship to platonic status. It was tough figuring women. Maybe he should settle down with her.

Thoughts of her suddenly filled him completely. She was beautiful, bright, loving, giving and everything else a man could desire in a woman. She cooked like a gourmet chef, played a mean game of Bid Whist and handled Jack Daniels better than any six Marines …and then there was that walk thing.

She had a natural, unpretentious --though provocative-- gait that would elicit a stage nine hard-on from ninety percent of the straight male population (the other ten percent are clearly blind). Her musical voice cast power akin to a siren's call. Her seductive charms could single-handedly negate the pernicious effects of male menopause.

Despite his concurrence, that man once burned is twice shy, deep inside he rationalized that only a mendacious, philandering fool would risk losing such a woman. His fear was not growing old alone, just losing someone special. Why not pop that question?

These thoughts and some fond remembrances caused an uncontrollable swelling, which he at first felt uncomfortable with, then relished in. Heading toward the locker room, he managed to venture a slight smile toward a few admirers, even as some insensate, but particularly cruel memory process conjured up a wraith-like image of Tina's eyes and lips, where moments before had been Sylvia's. The sudden, overwhelming apparition engendered in his heart feelings other than light and warm and in his face feelings other than happy and smiling. Not that he shouldn't smile, a couple of youngsters even wanted his autograph, if that wasn't worth laughing at, he couldn't think what was. Besides, she'd been incommunicado for two weeks now, probably off to some exotic location, with some exotic love interest. No matter, tonight with Sylvia would surely help him forget. No work tomorrow. He was definitely planning to do a job on her this night, all of this night. But, alas, forces had transpired to frame for him a new vocation…

"Excellent match Captain. I am Colonel Peterson, USMC and this is Major General Burton, Army. Might we speak privately?"

"I am not in the Marines anymore now Colonel, so Mr. O'Rourke will do nicely." A twinge of bitterness at Peterson's remark. It was amazing how they all wanted to claim you if you did something good. Just don't screw up! It brought back memories of the old days. Not the good old days, just the old days. He felt the only good thing about them is that they were old and gone. Unfortunately, they had gone taking a lot of good people with them. Still, he wondered why a Marine Colonel accompanied an Army two-star …and what they wanted with him.

Peterson was slightly miffed at O'Rourke's remarks, as well. But he was thoroughly pleased his ploy had succeeded. He had warned the General of O'Rourke's irascible temperament. Now he had been proved out. "No slight intended Capt—I mean Mr. O'Rourke. I merely..."

"Yeah, I know Colonel. You merely wanted to find out where my head was at if you'll excuse my colloquialism. You wished to know whether I still identified with the Crotch or not. Believe me when I say I definitely do not. Not even remotely!"

Jarhead brass hated when people called their service the Marine Crotch. O'Rourke wasn't about to care, but despite this victory, inside he quickly felt insensate stirrings of foreboding. He sensed an ill will blowing in. Some game was afoot and had drafted him into the play!

Burton, sensing that Peterson would succeed only in alienating their selectee, took the reins from him. Besides, nobody still alive called his Army the Marine Crotch! Emphasis on, "still alive"! "Mr. O'Rourke, please excuse my exec. We have no intention of reminding you of past events you wish to forget. However, as he stated, we do desire your immediate attention on a somewhat, sticky matter.'"

"Sticky matters are out of my jurisdiction, gentlemen. Unless this is some plot to recover that Viet Cong officer's pistol I sort' a borrowed. Really, it was just lying there begging for a home." He joked, though not really feeling very funny. He knew Sylvia could have her impatient moments and was probably even now wondering what's keeping him.

In fact --after her scintillating kiss-- she more than likely had assumed he would be rushing to get her home behind closed doors. Her fingers probably even now fought her inclination to tap dance that iPhone, blast him for his tardiness, good naturedly of course. Unknown to him, he needed not worry; her time was currently being kept by another.

"O'Rourke, we did not come all the way out to Los Angeles to escape the snow," interjected Peterson. "We are from the DIA and we have a serious problem to discuss with you!"

"You guys always got problems you can't fix," retorted O'Rourke. "What's the matter now Colonel, lost your Chesty Puller teddy bear?"

"Look you…"

"That will do Colonel, you too Captain, excuse me, Mister O'Rourke. This area is not secure and I would like to talk to you as soon as possible. Your nation has need of your services. I can assure you the matter covers a situation, most grave."

Something about the man elicited O'Rourke's respect. His demeanor and bearing reflected that of his sensei, whose remains now rested in a vase which rested on the mantle above his living room fireplace. Even without his uniform, he had a commanding presence that was …well, commanding.

Despite his earlier protestation to the contrary, O'Rourke's inner self stiffened to rapt attention at the General's softly spoken words. This was a man used to giving orders; orders, which would always be obeyed as orders from on high always were. Sort of like a commandment from God …or at least from Moses or somebody similar.

Often dreaming of becoming one –in an earlier life-- he had once wondered which criteria were used to select a General. There weren't that many of them around and they were usually holding down very important positions, so he had figured that there had to be some serious criteria used to select the few that were. He had just wondered what those criteria entailed. But that was then. He no longer dreamed those dreams, no more concerns of making flag rank. It was "yo ho ho, a bottle of rum and a private life for he!"

Maybe he was not certain about the criteria used to screen other candidates, but this guy definitely fit his model of the perfect General Officer. There just seemed something impressive that kind of captivated. Another one who qualified beyond qualifications was his personal hero, Colin Powell. These two were not alone; there were many others. Some, like Hannibal, lived in antiquity. But not so many that the selection formula did not seem in need some serious tweaking now and again. He could remember a few brass douche bags in U.S. uniforms who had greatly contributed to the aid and comfort given to North Vietnam and the Viet Cong. Those he would have loved to discover in his M-16 sights.

But that would never have been this man. Even through the steel, O'Rourke could feel the compassion bleeding out of his visage. He could tell that this General had earned his spurs by leading from the front and that that was why he was here today.

Consequently, he impressed one who was not easily impressed. Whatever this issue was, the General's presence proved how important it was to him and proved just how valuable he considered John O'Rourke to its resolution. He recalled a reading that depicted great leaders as those who choose people to lead who they perceived as having the potential to become great.

History indicates some leaders were great in spite of the people they chose. But had they chose better, they may have accomplished even more. How far could Bonaparte have gone? Or Alexander the Great? Or JC (Julius Caesar)? How far could any of these notable leaders have gone had they chosen their subordinates more advisedly? Like if Napoleon Bonaparte had not relied on his indolent Marshal Emmanuel, Marquis de Grouchy, he instead of the Duke of Wellington may have been the victor at the battle of Waterloo …but only hindsight is 20-20.

Just as Abraham Lincoln agonized for so long before replacing George McClellan with Ulysses Grant, the political ramifications of flushing out deadbeats proves prickly at best. Lincoln's case is even more classic. He did not get up the courage to fire the pathetically miscast General until McClellan ran against him for President. The ultimate cost of Lincoln's hesitation was, as always, in lives lost. Politics has killed more men than all the battles ever fought. Probably as many died due to ill-management as to ill-temper.

Both Grouchy and McClellan were selected more for who they knew, rather than their capabilities or what leadership skills they possessed. Even after the extent of their ineptitude was widely apparent, there was more concern given to the consequences of their removal rather than to the numbers of loyal troops led into unnecessary slaughter. Kind of makes one ask, "weren't there any available Ambassadorships around?"

Marshal Grouchy was such a late riser, that he could never get started early enough to catch up with and destroy the Prussian force which ultimately came to Wellington's aid and proved Napoleon's downfall. That was one time the Marshal should have remained to the rear so as not to slow the army down.

On the other hand, McClellan was all about organization and training –tireless organizing and endless training—while he languished in his armchair rocker preparing for some eventual battle, somewhere in the future, eventually. He proved to be as diligent preparing routes for retreat as he did for attack. The problem was, he prepared both before the attack. Kind of made O'Rourke wonder if McClellan was Piscean. Though he was nonplussed upon learning that the man was born Sagittarian.

Still, ultimately it's their boss' fault. So, blame the Napoleons, the Lincolns and the Alexanders. After all, it was Napoleon's hubris which convinced him that he was a better Admiral than those leading his navy and a better God than the deity ruling Russia's winter. In the end, Wellington was just a better General, as Nelson was a better Admiral.

And men like Lincoln –who have serious problems fighting wars because they do not want to hurt anybody—need to stay the hell out of positions that call for decisions which might involve war. They want everybody to come out in their finery for a few rounds, follow the Marquis of Queensberry rules, bloody a nose or two, then to kiss and make up. The refined and genteel McClellan was cut from such cloth, one reason why Lincoln was comfortable with him. But also one reason he was not effective, why so many lives were ground up before his departure. Fortunately, Lincoln finally came to realize that war is a violent, messy business.

If you play by the rules, everybody is going to want to play. The more violent, the less people will want to engage in it. The more mess, the less fun they can have bringing out their wives and sweethearts to picnic from a nearby hill overlooking the battle. Grant understood this aspect and made his war as bloody as it could be. Grant was not looking to be friends or to be neat, he was looking to kill something. That was his leadership style and it was effective…

Leadership is an art form. Leadership styles make for successes or failures. Successful leaders need to have the ability to employ the style necessary for maximum effectiveness and to know when and how to apply it. His mentor had preached that one must never seek to fight, but must seek to end the fight unsought.

Burton did not appear an overly bloodthirsty type. But neither did he seem the type who embraced the armchair brand of leadership, pointing in a direction for his people to move and hoping for success, while he decorated his office to impress. Perhaps that was the formula for Generalship. Perhaps those choosing leaders should seek out types capable of ensuring success by contributing their sweat --leading by example-- showing, not telling.

This General seemed to fit. While he might not be bloodthirsty, you would not want to go to war against his type. This kind of guy had the strength and the courage to pick you up after he had knocked you down. And that knock down would have had just cause. And he would knock you down again if need be. O'Rourke was certain of that.

Still, he doubted that such a man would leave his high-powered environs simply to recruit a Gun Fighter. So whatever services he required were probably for something a lot more subtle. Maybe he just needed his skills in the cockpit. Maybe this would turn into some heroic, Cloak 'n Dagger mystery. Yeah, right! Still, part of him ached for a less predictable assignment than bus driver for corporate assholes …regardless of the fact that his was a sky bus.

But he wanted nothing to do with causing violent death for anyone, anywhere. He could make a few exceptions for people like those SOBs who had brought about 9-1-1. But even they were not truly his enemy. They were people to be concerned about, for sure. But as enemies go, we have lost far more people at the hands of or due to the actions of the North Koreans and the Chinese. What makes them special? If we aren't Pimp Slapping those other bad guys for giving weapons to our enemies or shooting up our unarmed recon craft, why go after a few misguided Middle-Easterners?

He had long before decided that our current White House Administration was playing the same, nearly identical bullshit games that past Administrations had employed. Like Lincoln, they want to fight a war without hurting anybody.

He figured that they first should invoke Shiro's philosophy and not seek the fight. Negotiations are often a nice way of showing that the other guy is important enough for you to break bread with. Looking down one's nose and declaring the whole world a terrorist and an enemy was how we got drawn into Vietnam. We either need to find a better way to include these people in decisions concerning them or to find a way to obviate the need for such talks. I.E., blow them off the face of the earth.

Sometimes an immoveable object has no choice but to move. It might not get run over, but it might not survive the encounter either. In this example, Peterson's portrayal as the immoveable object failed a hopeless encounter with the irresistible force of his boss, General Burton, who favored giving his less-than-willing recruit a fairly wide open field on which to play this game where none of them knew exactly where to play. Intel pointed to the Caribbean, but with no specifics for certain. Could even have been South America, hell it could be Timbuktu. Stubborn nearly to the end, Peterson reluctantly chose to move off his unmovable position. "Just be careful you don't tip the Government's hand…"

"What hand?" JP had tempted to retort. To his thinking they had more of a foot than a hand. You wouldn't want to play it in AC or Vegas. At least he had a hunch he wanted to play, DIA only had a computer that played safe odds. After all the misses they'd had lately, they should realize those odds had played out…

Stephanie didn't care for Morano and neither did he. He might again be chasing ghosts, but that sixth sense, that claustrophobic sensation said differently. Shiro, his friend and mentor had always reminded him: "The wise man measures each situation then trusts his instincts."

It had to be more than the fact that Tina was about to marry the guy. It couldn't just be a jealous reaction, this knot that grew in the pit of his stomach whenever that man came near and nearly caused expulsion of any and all remnants of his most recent meal. No, he refused to believe it the result of simple jealousy, this knot that simultaneously twisted his guts while demanding: "Why you even speaking to this crud? Kill him!"

Thoughts of death and destruction filled him; morbid visions found purchase where before grew splendor. Morano, on the other hand, seemed happy with the whole thing; like he wanted to play long lost buddies recently reunited. "Wow, JP. That'll be excellent! C'mon down. You don't get to Florida much, right? Gonna be your best time!"

He seemed so happy, even enthusiastic. This seemed to be working out just fine. At least it did until Stephanie's words caught back up and O'Rourke remembered to be very cautious about getting what he wished for. He could recall the serious, no nonsense look in her dark, almond-shaped eyes, seductively beguiling even to one not normally attracted to plus-sized women. But she had those skills when she needed to play on them. Even when she didn't. Though it had not been one of her vamping moments, his mind's eye resurrected a time before when it had: "Heard about you from my girlfriend, wanna find out for myself."

She could pull off the occasional Mae West routine, notably with a Queen Latifa flavor, when motivated and obviously something about him motivated her. Tina had once intimated that something about every man motivated her. But either way, not that last time …she was all business.

She intended her look neither seductive nor beguiling. She intended it to portray just how serious she considered this subject. Accordingly, he mental-erased Morano's pat on the back; replacing it with her tutelage: "Carlos is very vindictive. If it take a year, he'll pay you back."

He could ignore her advice at his peril. Here was no fool to be taken lightly. She knew him almost as well as Tina or so she intimated. This man had his quirks, but he did not overly display them. That much O'Rourke already knew. What was yet unknown, whether a further indication more here than met the eye? Or just her desire to poke a man in the eye? Required a closer look. Hell! Most times, if one don't look closely, one won't never notice the hidden intrigue. So he did …intend to look closer that is.

Morano did not cover himself with gaudy jewelry. No rings adorned his chubby fingers. No chains of gold or platinum hung from his neck. Not even a single diamond studded the rose gold-colored watch attached to his right wrist, although O'Rourke could tell it was well made and pretty expensive; the Patek Phillipe brand name a dead giveaway. Its retail price could probably support a small family for a year …rent included. This man had his pride, but any hubris was subdued, understated, near imperceptible except by those in the know. His nature was sort of "Yeah, I'm well-heeled, so what's the big deal?"

He could hang with the jet set. The story being that, unlike most, his was kept parked nearby at the ready. Flamboyance was a trend he performed well. Foppish, almost metrosexual by some standards, but he did not tend towards extravagant bouts of braggadocio or flashy displays of vanity. You knew him rich by his bearing and philanthropy, not by his self-aggrandizing promotion.

Here was the self-made man, among America's finest. Pulled hisself up by his own bootstraps one rung at a time 'til he'd climbed the ladder of success and stood at its pinnacle. Hard work his mantra, suffering and perseverance the two conditions most prominent to his life experience. Here was the man mothers wanted their daughters to wed. Here was honesty and upstanding integrity with foresight far beyond mortal men's. Here he is ladies and quite the catch. Anytime he want, he can make paper rain…

He could be found rubbing elbows with Hollywood royalty one moment, breaking ground on a new childcare facility for underprivileged families the next. Attributed to him were superlatives intended for captains of industry and heroes of epic scale, a dragon slayer who fought the corrupt and gave hope to the downtrodden, a man of Spanish heritage whose choice of English as his preferred language pronounced to all that he was, above all, about business …and the business world loved him because of his love for business.

O'Rourke didn't just rely on the whims of an emotional woman. He had studied the man for more than a moment and decided with the business world that Morano truly knew the deal, how to play the game. More than that, he believed if his Intel was as accurate as he believed it to be, the SED (money speak for squeeze every dollar) crowd had nothing on this man and that was saying something given the level of cutthroat SED practiced by most businesses, being that most businesses practice the SED brand of economics.

It's the SEDers who fight against raising things like capital gains taxes and minimum wages while championing mega-salaries for corporate boards and their lawyers. They also do a great job maximizing the taking of your money while producing at minimal outlay (often resulting in minimal quality). If that's not working well enough they'll have their hired guns in the political corps write laws to get what's left.

Rumor suggested that hidden in Morano's closet were more than a few politicos, so O'Rourke could appreciate the more subtle aspects of Mister Bootstraps over there even if he had no intention of ever appreciating the man inside the suit. Even without the Tina connection it was nothing about his own story not playing out quite so silver spoon, rags to riches. The fact that the closest he'd ever been to a silver spoon was the one his friend Mickey used to have, before it was mentally flushed from his psyche and ceremoniously dropped into a Viet Cong punji pit. You know, the ones they smear with human excrement to make your wounds fester after you step them through your booted foot. Yeah, them. Down the shit hole beside all the other booby traps life planted over there.

Another memory. Another friend. Another tragedy. This night some gleeful daydream gremlin must have been having tremendous joy at the twists and turns it subjected him to, though this memory at least had its positives. Truth be told, silver spoons aren't always all they're cracked up to be and the life of leisure had proved so unlike some epic life of Riley, his friend had been only too happy to dump it. The consequences of such a life had very nearly pulled Mickey down an even deadlier hole, so it was just as well that he flushed them …along with their curse.

Curses. Sometimes they don't seem to start out that way. But the day he put aside all vestiges of the heir apparent, of the one and only, aka, stopped parading around like a shithead, asshole, sonofabitch (his words). On that day he began climbing out of his own little hellhole into the light and a less conflicted life. On that day, he had slipped all remaining tentacles clutching at his ankles from a spectral dominatrix once his mother.

But he made it. Kicking free, he extricated from entangling filaments clinging at his physical self that sought retention of her power over his will and it was oh so retro. She wasn't even around and she was still around. Even after providential intercession had cleaved her physical form from this world into the afterlife, still she sought to control the one thing in life she had strived hardest to control. Him.

It took a while, that seemed like a forever. But he defeated her. With assistance from his father and his best friend, he was able to do it. With mighty slashes from a mental battle axe, he had finally severed the cord stretching from deep down in the netherworld where her essence now resided. Finally, the little boy inside him felt free of her overbearing counsel until the boy was no more. That day he became whole. He became a man.

It had never been a question of want, at least not his. Reserved primarily for scions of the upper crust, she had tempted his taste buds with samples of how life could be at the very top. The price she insisted as minimal, of no consequence. It was about her wants for him and for him it was about needs. She wanted complete control and he needed to please her to keep her love. The difference was, she would never admit it. In fact, shoot her full of truth serum and ask the question of what she genuinely wanted for her son. The answer would have been: "Ever and always". Ask what that meant you'd get a repeat, she was that conditioned to her beliefs and not even drugs could make her admit a guilt.

"See it my way and you'll always see it right!" That was her want for every situation for every moment, for everything. Perhaps delusional in her own way, but truthfully, she only wanted the best for him and for anyone in her circle and she always knew exactly what's best for all of them and rationalized they should always acknowledge that reality by doing things the right way which was her way and how she say. Her rationality.

However, life's lessons eventually proved her logic flawed, revealing it had far overstayed its usefulness. So down the old bladder relief tube (aka, the pisser) he flushed this ritual of the silver spoons where logic assessed should reside all useless things...

Munching the finest of caviars and sipping the best of champagnes while trekking their way up velvet-swathed rungs on the ladder of success was a nonstarter for most Marines riding high-speed death machines. These adrenaline junkies usually required a totally different skill set. Communist MIGs and Triple-A gunners would little be impressed by a pedigree. Gomer never ranked targets by the size of your daddy's job.

Pedigree, smedigree. Such inane objectives suited neither of them, although it took Mickey a bit longer to come to that understanding. But now, life seemed so much simpler for both, at least as far as spoons were concerned. Having never owned one, some might attribute O'Rourke's path as less conflicted since --though real world—such pie-in-the-sky constructs often have little hold on reality. Definitely none in the world of flying targets.

In truth, the world of rags and riches touches many. O'Rourke, though he never possessed vast riches, well understood the rags aspect. That factor he admitted facetiously, cause along his own way up his own ladder (no caviar or velvet covers), he had acquired champagne tastes to some extent. They came along with a beer pocketbook unfortunately, but undaunted, he never restricted his choices solely to beer. For him, a more likely selection on the "Choice Lever" would be: "Less Champagne".

So he just tried to live as well as he could within his meager means. He learned early on that as long as one didn't shoot for the moon and miss, one could do well with such a strategy. More than that, as long as one didn't wish for the moon, one wouldn't miss it in the first place...

Honed on many a battlefield and foreign shore --namely in bar discussions worldwide-- this philosophy achieved the status of core value. Reinforced by many, both saint and sinner, soldier and Marine.

As they tipped their cups to those no longer able to tip with them, a wise friend once schooled him: "We owe it to the brothers no longer here to do it up right once we get back to th' world! We got's ta do it fer them and us! But we got's ta do it easy. Now, we can go out and party like paupers every night in some hole in the wall; a beer here, a shot there, no chance to buy any for the girls even if they low life enough ta show through in them kinda places. We can do it like that, or we can visit the finest spots for one night here and there and act like kings. We'll look rich and famous and the girls will love us. Tips, best drinks, shots all around. Don't need to drink the beer in life, just have to settle for less champagne! What's it gonna be?"

He never forgot this lesson instructed with such sartorial eloquence, though could not recall from which old friend's lips that pearl of wisdom had flowed. Such is the nature of bar schooling. It was enough that he had learned the lesson, not everyone did …then again, not everyone needed to.

Morano, it seemed, was one no longer needing worry over such trivialities. If he ordered beer, it was because he wanted beer. Not that he settled. The world was his oyster. He was the cat's meow. These all seemed nice, all these admirable qualities. However O'Rourke wasted little time admiring the purr-fect aspect of this man's life. It was sufficient to know that he had them and that was that.

There would probably be some model of stretch limo idling outside, he knew, a bodyguard or two on board, probably one on the inside. Inconspicuous. Hanging in the cut. None would ever discover that fact from its owner bragging about it. Seemingly, he was far from highbrow, just a down-to-earth fellow of the mean streets who just happened to make it big. But that was for another to conjecture. O'Rourke only focused on that something warning him to caution. All was not as it seemed and that was what motivated him.

From memory leaped the cautioning tale that a snake is always a snake. Some hiss and rattle and threaten with gestures back and forth. Others simply strike. Those are the ones you should most worry. The fearful ones who wave about, jaws agape; hissing and tails rattling are asking you to please leave. "Don't make me do this! You're not my type and too big to eat! Don't make me kill you …cause I know I'm next!"

You should thank God for those. Flash 'em a smile, step carefully around and wave bye. Maybe a double chest tap with a peace sign. Cause they're not trying to start nothing unnecessary. It's those others that lie in wait until you're not paying attention, or your back is turned, that you need to fear. It's those vipers that just want to hurt something, that strike from camouflaged concealment to deliver a deadly dose of neurotoxin against which you have two chances …slim and none. "Die bitch! Now it's me and you, soon it only gonna be me…"

There was the complication in O'Rourke's path. He anticipated that any threat this man posed would also be subtle and understated, until the hammer fell. Here was the viper to worry him. Here was the "strike you in the back" type. The thought resurfaced. It came more frequently these last couple days. Why not kill him first? "…Kill or be killed" is Marine Corps doctrine.

But it was not really a serious thought. This fellow might still be the link to Tina. He may be the link to the stolen government secrets also, which would be a plus. But a plus was only an additional benefit, not the primary. She came first. Either her safe return or revenge against her killer. Everything else fell into secondary status…

Now that Morano had gone away, O'Rourke began to breathe a little easier. The choking sensation subsided. Future threats not the least bit concerning. His calming was nearly completed and his pressure had just about returned to normal when Valerie suddenly eased into the space on his left that Morano had recently vacated. If you want to call it space, between him and the woman whose African braids hung well down her back and whom he had crowned Princess Braidy with her three-inch long nails she liked to "clop" impatiently against the bar top whenever her drink was late and whom had slid her chair closer towards him after Carlos departure. He figured she must have an internal clock since he noticed no wristwatch on the arched wrist whose long fingers soon began clacking those annoying nails seemingly seconds after depositing her empty highball glass. He had noticed her movement, hadn't yet figured out a motive, but kinda figured it had something to do with free drinks. Maybe it was about free men, he was sitting alone after all. So maybe …God, he hoped not.

But Valerie fixed everything. In truth, "eased" was not quite accurate, "squeezed" was a more appropriate description of her entry which did not go unnoticed and was "mostly" appreciated …in his case, "definitely" appreciated.

To O'Rourke, the softness of a beautiful woman's breasts sliding against his arm is nearly always welcome, regardless their poor choice of company. But even that negativity was not sufficient to swerve his gaze across to where that bad company, named Morano, now stood. She had a quality that imparted a definite separation factor. If one such as this admired you, who cared whoever else she admired. Her kind of beauty and bearing came not every day.

Still, her role here he could not overstate. A slim goodie for certain, in that 'middy-mini-speed-kills-so-let's-go-slow' outfit. Set here by God for the benefit of all mankind she was doing a great job. At least for all men of his kind. Maybe a woman like this couldn't turn a gay man straight, but even that kind of guy would probably wonder why.

But she was only a venue, only a way into her boss. The thought occurred, what was he to her? Maybe he was her venue into a salary bonus: "Hey Val, treat this guy nice. Ah see you get a little more in your check."

At first he had envisioned them a singing group, branding them Ice Girls. But, it was only in jest, merely a defensive mechanism, a mind trick to keep any nice thoughts concerning them at arm's length, especially any of a lascivious nature and definitely especially after they'd all turned down every guy who dared ask for a dance. Eventually though the ice melted, either that or their master gave his permission, and they settled in to partying with the crowd. It was then he relented and admitted that she and her girlfriends were all beautiful people, even the big-haired twins with all the makeup. Even them.

He didn't know if everything came natural, but they all had that symmetry thing down to a science. Like boobies and booties in perfect harmony. No top heavies here. God musta been having a good day when he made them …OMG, not to mention them twerking skills!

But his success, and perhaps his survival, depended on keeping all unknowns as suspects in this game of cops and robbers. No time to let the little head take charge. All were guilty by association, guilty until proven innocent, no matter how desirable in appearance. None of them could be trusted, maybe appreciated, but never trusted. Truth be told, he did appreciate her …and in that he was by far not the only one.

Her passage had been charted. The heavens had been opened and the entire host had descended exalting, "Hosanna, Hosanna!" Here truly was an angel from above. Everyone nearby was instantly in better mood now that she chose to visit this corner of God's earth … at least almost everyone.

Evidently her holiness had stepped inside the comfort zone of an instantly hostile Braidy, who had initially toyed with ideas of bedding down this handsome stranger before one of the others got him. All the best got taken rather quickly around here, especially if they had something going on, like a nice business …and maybe a nice car.

She briefly glared at the interloper's back before angrily tossing her head up and left to fling the braids within millimeters of Valerie's ear, then went back to her conversation with the man and woman down the bar on her left side, as if O'Rourke had represented only a passing fancy. She'd watched them dance, their energy said volumes. Now hope faded entirely, this was a lost cause …even if he did have that Denzel look going for him or maybe was it Will.

"High yeller heifer! I should'a slid her side th' head, squeezing in on me like that!" She remarked to no one in particular, before flashing her ruby red nails for a refill.

If Valerie noticed the near flailing or heard the retort, she did not let on. Instead she impishly nudged JP with her elbow, demanding his attention …as if he had not taken sufficient notice of her arrival.

"Forgot all about me!" It was both a statement and a challenge. Her large eyes shone warm and impish in the soft-yellow glow, punctuating the tossing down of her gauntlet. Their sparkling, greenish orbs radiated waves of subtle energy, enervating him momentarily and rendering him temporarily unable to respond, his breathing apparatus in stasis. Before he could recover she punched him lightly on the shoulder, her musical laughter filling their small area. "I knew you would!"

"Never!" he finally replied. "Well at least never again!"

"Silver tongued devil! Bet you say that to all us girls, like Ms Heifer behind me. Know she tryin' ta be in love at dat!"

"First I heard!"

"Don't even try to play innocent. Bet you think that stuff works 'cross the nation! Know them Cali girls easy. Just fall all over themselves tryin' to get some. You did say you're from Cali, right?"

"You got me darlin', guilty as charged."

"Originally?"

"Like a famous man once said, no matter where you go, there you are."

"Will Rogers?"

"Buckaroo Banzai."

"Oh yeah, forgot about him. Guess now I understand your definition of famous," she quipped, treating him to a second punch on his shoulder.

"Owww!" he retorted. "Okay, so what if Buckaroo was quoting Confucius? But I first heard it from the Buckaroo! An', then I kinda read about, how Mr. C wrote it first…"

His words trailed off into an empty place, their exchange leaving him somewhat deflated. Her breath had a buttery quality backed by a hint of alcohol. He figured her for the casual sipper role. Never getting too deep into whichever libations she chose on whichever occasion, keeping ahead of the buzz so she'd never be caught from behind. Speaking of which, hers was rather nicely sculpted and reacting to which, his brown eyes slid down to surreptitiously survey that aspect of her loveliness …hoping to avoid being caught.

The view was fulfilling. But he felt less than motivated. He did not want to play this game. She might be on Morano's payroll, but everything about her seemed genuine. That sixth sense again, maybe seventh or something. He wondered if she knew he was being the wise ass to keep her at arm's length. Women have those additional senses. A cat's got nine lives, a woman has nine senses. They can tell a man's temperature while predicting his future. "He hot and definitely gonna get some…"

He wondered if she had caught onto his game the way men always wonder about women. He wondered if she knew that this part of his plan had absolutely no chance of working, unless she helped. Part of him wanted her to …the other part did not.

"Please, say something to piss me off. Tell me how you do 'special stuff' for Morano. Oh, no! Please don't say it! Don't say it's you and Morano! Damn! I knew it! I hate you too!"

Back to reality. Recovering himself, he refused to look at her for a few moments, focusing instead on the prize, reminding himself she is a tool, just a tool. Even should he walk in on her performing feats of daring on the man's totally naked form it made no difference. He just needed to use her without her knowing she'd been used, at least not while he was doing the using. Either way, this cookie was sharp. He would need to be watchful…

Turned out, he needed to practice his watching a bit harder. Surreptitiously, another cookie, equally sharp, now watched him intently, satisfied so far with this part of the plan. He was less satisfied with other aspects, but time would tell. Some might call it genocide, but he had another view. There were just too many people in the world to be maintained. Either we cull some of this rapacious horde or the whole house of cards will collapse in on itself. Better some now than all a bit later, but what to do and how best to do it?

There was a time the answer to this question had driven him night and day. Lately it tended to leave his days untouched, but was still a bother. He could watch the world slowly wobble feebly about under the growing weight of this maggot horde that sucked all other life dry or he could be the hero who did something about it. But what? There were others with the same objective. Some wanted to use nuclear bombs or biological or chemical agents to cleanse Mother Earth, but he would never. Those would only make a bad situation worse. More pollution was certainly not the answer. So he still tossed and turned in his bed at night, seeking his eureka moment. As it turned out, his solution found him…

CHAPTER FOUR

Casually licking the creamy gelato before it could drip down the cone onto his fingers, he meandered from one street to the next in the warm sunlight, following no particular route but generally headed north, sightseeing his way back towards his hotel. The stickiness on his right hand suggested those attempts had not all been successful, but good enough to preclude creamy mango discoloration of his shorts and sneakers.

This southern end of Miami Beach sported myriad storefronts advertising flavors galore, some colored hot pink and promising every conceivable flavor of gelato (to which he could greedily attest), others sporting pastel green fronts boasting twelve flavors of buffalo wings plus cheese fries and onion rings. He had yet to try any of those, but the day was still young. Still other stores promised sex games and toys inside sufficient to satisfy even the kinkiest sailor home from a six-month cruise with no port calls. Strip tease acts, peep shows, lap dances and the like were inside for one and for all who possessed the price of a drink, plus the extras. It was those extras wherein the pricey nature of this business revolved.

Men could spend this month's groceries and rent in just a relative few moments to experience the sensation of a beautiful woman's body pressed up to his. Even though usually forbidden to actually touch the seductive, writhing female flesh with their hands, some men nonetheless often seek these experiences, these sensations, all these things they miss at home … at a premium.

The Miami set did not call it "Lap Dancing", here they named it "Friction Dancing" and positioned sleazy looking men –sleazy clearly being in the eye of the beholder-- seemingly on every corner he passed, waving vibrantly emblazoned fliers that invited the reader to join in the fun at all sorts of events from strip clubs to the upcoming video award show. Apparel stores proudly displayed T-shirts of every color printed with statements intended to graphically inform the reader that its wearer wanted sex, did not want sex, had never had sex, often had sex, witnessed parents having sex, wanted you to go have sex with yourself, had large breasts, had a large penis, wanted you to imitate a Hoover vacuum on their penis, and on and on, ad nauseam. Silk screening run amok…

These he passed without a second glance. However, the nearly nude women strolling blithely along the Miami Beach avenues he trod were a definite attraction, remindful of his own beachfront back home in Cali and amazing him the success of porn shops with such outstanding competition.

T-backs and dental floss bikinis, tight waists and nipples to the ready; the quality and quantity were both first rate. Also first rate was the quality of its white sand beaches and the clear, aquamarine waters that lapped up onto them. This quality they didn't have in Cali, with its deep blue Pacific. The waters and sands also filled with scantily clad females. With such freebees on display, O'Rourke could never fully appreciate the need for the soft porn, but then realized he may have been a bit old fashion, preferring to find real women one could touch …who had not recently been touched.

The qualities of its feminine treats typically high order, equally far up the scale was Florida's unfortunate propensity for tropical storms and hurricanes and, most unfortunately, the South Beach area garnered a significant share of those. Other than that, he decided that he really liked this location. At least this landscape never shook its residents from their beauty rest, threatening to slide into the ocean. He especially appreciated their art deco designed buildings –cubic forms and zigzag patterns painted nearly every color of the light spectrum-- though some of the vivid facades displayed onerous signs of crumbling concrete and mildewed woods. But otherwise this place was not so bad. It was hard to beat the scenic settings. However, his business here concerned scenes not typically normal tourist pursuits.

This visit to the Sunshine State included an invitation from his nemesis, Carlos Morano, and he determined to take full advantage. The idea struck him that Morano may yet be unaware that they were nemeses, but he doubted. His senses told him volumes that the other man's lips had not. He had come here hoping to validate one way or the other, but that might not work out.

He had landed at Miami International on a beautiful, warm Wednesday that displayed a full measure of promise. Unfortunately, this Wednesday happened to fall on the day before the predicted arrival of a tropical storm that some weather maven's computer had decided to name Eris. Just the fact that this storm had been assigned a name indicated a reason for concern. But name notwithstanding, nothing in this day's presentation indicated any untoward performances by the gods of wind and sea. Billowy clouds and bright sunshine competed for their share of acclaim in a brilliant, blue sky that both used as a backdrop.

Then one cloud image reminded him of something or was it someone. Regardless, his resolve hardened. Weather be damned this was business and he a businessman …or so he now chose to believe. Some might term him an operator, just like in the spy books where the hero ventures out into the torrent to seal the doom of wicked perpetrators of misery. His mind's eye could perceive a wry smile crease Peterson's ugly maw with the realization that their man was now fully immersed in their cause. They had him and he knew it, might as well admit it …and now he did.

Leaving the airport he had driven east, then south on I-95 to the Rickenbacker Causeway where he crossed Biscayne Bay to Virginia Key. He wanted a look at the back side of Morano's digs on Fisher Island. However, from over a mile away, there was less to see than he hoped from the small, tree-lined park area along the northern side of the causeway –a few white sandstone high rise buildings, each topped by Spanish-tiled roofs, rising above the southwestern end-- but he had already conceived a semblance of a plan that the view across the bay helped cement.

Its sunlit grandeur was actually fairly impressive. In the restricted view produced by the small pair of binoculars he had purchased, each condo unit's balcony appeared to come complete with its own hanging plants of some type –maybe Boston ferns and Pothos, maybe not—spilling green blankets down the white walls. Behind these, towering above and beyond --anchored into Miami Beach proper-- rose colorful skyscrapers whose residents commanded the most spectacular views of the mainland Miami skyline, its splendorous, skyscraping roof tops reaching high in competition for boasting rights and coloring each night sky with eclectic light scenes. But the Fisher Island folk had nothing to gripe about. He could appreciate that their views must also be quite extraordinary.

Reversing course, he drove back over the causeway to Brickell Avenue, getting turned around a few times in the unfamiliar cross streets among the concrete, steel and glass canyons before finding his desired heading, north up Biscayne Boulevard. He almost did not make it. Anxious parking attendants seemed eager to steal his rental whenever he stopped near the doors of some hotel, condo high-rise or corporate office, all of which contributed to the skyline, none of which had been listed on his map. But somehow he survived the turns and twists and one-way streets to nowhere.

It had been years since his only other trip to Miami. However, other than the downtown, he figured he knew his way around, somewhat. It's not a very large area and north is still north, even this far south. Still, he played the part of the typical, first-time tourist, gawking at the American Airlines

Arena where the Heat play basketball against the NBA's best up and down its magnificent court. Not this week though. The huge steel and glass round house had been decked out in its splendor for the Video Music Awards set for that Sunday. Still pointed north he made the mistake of stopping too long at the Bayside Marketplace, incurring raucous horn blasts and dirty looks from the traffic behind him. Further up the road he followed a sign announcing I-195 East over the Julia Tuttle Causeway onto Miami Beach, blue-green water warmly beckoning on both sides in subtle intimation that the perpetually cooler California variety could never pass the muster. But he took no time out to enjoy its liquid delight, speeding along in the light traffic. Passing the giant Mount Sinai Medical Center, he hoped there would be no need for its services …at least not for him.

Collins Avenue south was the proper direction, but he chose north --noting the many boats from pissant to mega-yacht size tied up at private docks and small marinas along both sides of Indian Creek to his left. According to Stephanie, Morano had recently sold his estate on Indian Creek Island when Tina pooh-poohed the eight bedroom place as much too large and ostentatious. Indian Creek is famous for its top ten rating in the listing of America's highest income locations, its ultra-exclusive golf course and also for its security, boasting approximately half as many police as residents. O'Rourke just wanted a look see --still putting two and two together—still curious about the mercurial nature of a man Valerie had described as "rock steady" and unswerving, while Stephanie came off totally opposite.

But almost to Bal Harbour, the idiocy of his intentions weighed in. He turned around, heading back south. This wasn't a game where he who had the most toys would win. So what if this guy had snatched the brass ring. None of those riches would bring back Tina, or in his case, lack of riches. But suddenly she had come back, at least her essence. It was another one of their discussions where he fell on the losing side, this one concerning his religion or lack thereof:

"You don't wanna believe in Jesus? So don't. Believe how you wanna. That's the beauty of freedom. You don't gotta do anything you don't wanna!" She could be so confident when she felt in the right.

"So you're saying ignore all those people on the right killing all those people on the left just cause they don't believe in what those people on the right believe? It's alright when they say: 'They ain't right so they gotta go?' That what you're saying?"

"Just act like they aren't even in the room."

"What if they're blowing up the room?"

"Freedom means free to believe and be free from doubt and especially from fear. If you live in fear, you're not free, you're in bondage. The prison of your own making. Get free! Fight the fear!"

"But they're blowing up the room!"

"They can't kill your spirit! Can't stop your ideals. Ignore them. They'll go away."

"I have got to start drinking what you're drinking!" Tina's outlook on life simply amazed him. She had the ability to break complex things down into their most basic components and reorder their sequence before putting them back together in a more manageable form, more manageable for her, that is. He only got bigger headaches. "Simplicity, thy name is Tina!"

"You'd do well to remember that!" Her flashing stare drove down deep into his soul, searing all remembrance of the point he meant to make, all vestiges of the reason they even began this particular journey down religion's path.

But that discussion or argument or heated debate, whatever, had been a long time back. Well before she had given up her Catholicism. It flushed from her body in the stream of amniotic fluids washing away the last remnants of the fetus that was to grow into her baby. It was more than a mere miscarriage in so many ways (including justice) this one had stripped away so much that had once been hers, including her love for him. In a poisonous issue of evil most foul, she lost her baby, her husband and her God all at the same time.

But then she came back. Years and wisdom reoriented her somewhat and rekindled something that had truly only waned, never extinguished. Still, this resurrected version of her was not the same girl to whom he had hoped to return after fighting the good fight in Southeast Asia. Much more complicated, still undesirous of a return to either religion or to him, at least not permanently, and now comes this latest tragedy, leaving him once again with only mysteries.

The wolves who took her? The predators who robbed him one time more? He wanted them dearly. He did not hate them, but he wanted them dearly. Hate is too deep an emotion for one such as he and all his young life he had been counseled against falling into its trap.

Hate claims victims on both sides of the lines drawn between guilty and innocent, good and bad. It claims and consumes. So he worked hard not to hate, all the easier since he still could not picture her corpse. Some inner sense: sixth, seventh, whatever (he never understood it well enough), but whatever its identity, it comforted his anguish in similar fashion to when she first took off and went walkabout, when she had first been spirited away by confusion, now it was by others. But regardless, he still felt her existence. She was not dead, not to him. Now he just had to get her back, maybe not to him. Those days were probably best left in the past. But he had to get her safe. Somehow he still felt a debt that he owed to her. Maybe he always would…

"I ain't no atheist. Prob'ly not even a decent agnostic. It's not like I don't believe in God. I just don't believe in ya'll saints 'n sinners, tip the preacher kinda guy. Hell I don't even believe that God is a guy, though maybe and I don't care. I'm just not sanctimonious enough to need an idol to worship that looks like me, dresses like me or eats the same food as me. I'm definitely not sanctimonious enough to wanna kill people who ain't like me jus' because they ain't!"

It actually worked. She bit hook, line and bait to the gills. The fact that she carried a cross and a little, black book and he never would, not a problem …until it became a problem.

Yeah, he recalled, those were the days. Back when he could talk a fine hunny outta her draws quicker'n spilt milk. Of course, it was all talk. Didn't make many plans back them days. Def wasn't planning this fine hunny to stick around, at least for not long as she did, until she didn't …didn't plan that neither.

But, far as higher power goes, of course, only an idiot could look up into the night sky and question that. Any rational being must admit there's higher powers at work. Now the specific kinda higher powers? That's where the discussion gets sideways.

Driving southbound, his curiosity slowly, stubbornly abated. Finally he acknowledged the glimmer of common sense waiving casually for attention from the recesses. Even more reluctantly, he listened to its message that this course was fruitless, that he must stick to the rules and that the rules demand he leave unnecessary things until the necessary things are all done. He blamed his ludicrous curiosity on an evil-eyed witch named "Jealousy", humorously deciding that once you've seen one ten thousand square foot mansion you've seen them all.

Southbound thoroughfares were nearly bumper-to-bumper as anxious drivers headed either for the causeway or the happy hour. Horns blared all about as impatience made the rounds. He noticed that drivers tended to communicate extensively with their aural signaling devices in this Miami area. Other than the lack of accompanying one-finger salutes, it was kind of like being back in New York. But he finally made it through the stop and go traffic to the section where Collins turned into a two-way headed into South Beach. High-rise hotels, condos and apartment buildings filled the landscape, then shops and stores, then beach. There he checked into his hotel, opened without unpacking his suitcase and changed into swim trunks and a short-sleeved, pullover shirt. Next he headed across the street out to the beach proper, still collecting his bearings, getting a feel for this place he had seldom been. What better way to get the tropical flavor than a trip along the sand?

The gentle, green Atlantic waters rolling into the shores of Magic City denied any existence of trouble on the way. A female lifeguard urged him to get into the water right now and not wait until the next day. She obviously didn't trust the peace to last, but insisted that: "Even though we're in the wash, we're well used to storms here. There'll be little disruption in people's routines."

He took her words at face value. She did not appear to be a meteorologist, but seemed to know what she was talking about, so he gave her the benefit of the doubt. She had a gregarious personality and seemed thrilled that someone would actually rather talk with her than frolic and swim in the warm sea or check out the sunbathers lying all around on blankets, bikini tops unsnapped in the back to benefit tanning. She provided him all sorts of local trivia that he worked into the plan forming in the back of his mind. It didn't seem as crazy …back there.

Hands stuffed casually into the pockets of her mid-thigh length, plaid shorts, she almost perfectly matched the profile in his head of the typical middle-aged Caucasian south Florida female. Not that he spent much time profiling middle-aged Caucasian south Florida females, but she typified many of the ones he'd met before in travels place to place.

Her light brown, freckled skin looked as if too many days in the Miami sun had introduced wrinkle patterns around the corners of her smiling eyes. Slightly loose flaps at the backs of her small arms and especially her thin, knobby knees agreed that her days were far from few. But otherwise she appeared the picture of health and evidenced a youthfulness that belied her advancing years; a picture degraded not the least by erect nipples prominently presenting in the centered outlines of both breasts. Impressively, these forced their shapes through both the white T-shirt and the one-piece swimsuit underneath.

Not that he was a gawker looking for such things (even though these were quite obviously intended for looking at) but he did notice and noticed her noticing him noticing, seemingly appreciating him appreciating, even though his noticing glance constituted only the merest once over. Obviously she did not miss much sent her way. He suspected she did not miss many opportunities to swim in the surf either. The overall taut appearance of her indicated some hidden quality, some inner strength. "Yeah, I can save a life! Wanna try me? Go try an' drown. Ain't gonna happen!"

Her confident manner confirmed that the pectoral muscles holding each breast up had no need for support or augmentation. In fact she seemed the type woman who would punch out any suggesting so. Her voice was clear and carried an almost melodious component as she unapologetically explained to him that the water was not nearly as clear as usual due to the coming storm, as if to say, "It is what it is". But he was glad she never once uttered that overly used cliché. Her manner intimated a wholeness that had no need to rely on such worn sayings.

Looking down on him from her slanted roof lifeguard shack – brightly colored turquoise, pink and green-- she matter-of-factly described for him things about Miami Beach that he, a lowly tourist could not possibly know, which he did not. She pointed to the close-in, off-shore reefs whose submerged darkness he could just make out. At least he thought he could make them out in the gathering overcast coming in from the east, further obscuring the ocean. There seemed to be something out there, whether it was underwater reefs, schools of fish or shadows from clouds he could not tell. But he never let on and if she noticed, she never let on; she kept right on talking, emphasizing the types of fish that came in close there because the water was so clean. Conversely, she complained about the seemingly endless film crews that evidently could not make a movie without some part of her beach as a backdrop, pointing out the set just across the wide sand where a crew currently had begun dismantling equipment and preparing to leave. He hoped she didn't mistake him for one of them just because he now lived in Southern California, a slip of the tongue, that admission since he often responded, "North Carolina", to people inquiring where he was from.

The trivia continued with facts about the more than two hundred art deco lifeguard shacks protecting the entire length of the beach, all about their many different designs ranging from square and rectangle with sloping or wavy roofs to round mimics of bird feeders to slick banana peel surfboard towers and all painted in a panoply of exotic colors to elicit jealousy from a rainbow. The early problems with ventilation and blind spots, she berated (because the lifeguards had not been consulted), and more—and tall tales (he figured) about celebrities being caught making out with friends under the portable, bright blue cabanas, some of which just then were being collapsed and stacked on a flatbed truck by young men. She also pointed him south, in the direction of a night spot where one of the biggest VMA parties was scheduled this evening …and he was already invited, though he failed to mention that.

That spot –at the southern tip of Miami Beach—is part of a large entertainment complex on Ocean Drive, its prestigious nightclub sitting next door to several sky scraping high-rise apartment buildings --whose altitudes are not their only lofty component—and MacArthur Channel leading into Biscayne Bay. Guests can absorb music-filled, South Beach flavor from mid-day through the wee hours, inside on the fenced-in sand and outside down to the water. Valerie had warned him about that aspect, suggesting that he wear attire appropriate for a younger, more adventurous crowd. "Something that won't show the beer stains", was the way she coquettishly put it in that way she had of telling him things that she had no intention of ever verbally telling him things. Sometimes you got to be with it to get it…

She also warned that outside seating meant sitting or lounging on deck chairs and bamboo beds under lush, palm trees and hanging pots of fern and ivy, surrounded by Tee Pee cabanas. So his clothing choice ought to be sand proof, too. She indicated that afternoon and evening wear differed only slightly with the latter period accessorized by a lesser number of designer sunshades …but not necessarily so.

The lot was already packed when O'Rourke arrived just after nine PM. He parked a block north, along the curb on Ocean Drive. His hotel was only five blocks north. Normally, he would have hoofed the short distance. But one never knew when he might need to make a quick getaway. He joked to himself that such was especially important if the lady was in an impatient mood.

He decided not to take advantage of the VIP parking for the same reason, not because he wanted to give the man's intelligence apparatus a bit of a challenge. It was not much of a challenge, more a stumbling block than a hurdle. But that gnawing sense of claustrophobia was on him, just like the one where somebody locks you in a closet. He had to get out. Rather, in this case he had to not get in…

His first impression of the atmosphere could have been summed up with one word, hedonistic. The babes from "Racks Unlimited" were in full display. Summing up the definition of hedonism as "Pleasure being the highest good" or in an ethical formulation, that "Whatever causes pleasure is right"; in his equation equaled this place. Racks Unlimited indeed! As an example of understatement, that was putting it mildly, bring on the RU gals!

True to the hedonistic philosophy of pleasure, squealing, bikini-clad females –capriciously undulating to syncopated hip-hop rhythms-- gamboled all about, thrusting their lithe, glistening flesh up against indulgent males. These later sporting the latest beach wear fashions, topped by various styles of headgear. No entourage of Dionysus: Greek god of wine, pleasure and festivity could have better played their role. They were as festive as any he had yet witnessed. Nobody twerking at this moment, but just a matter of time.

Patriotic symbols appeared the rage. Women in red, white and blue bikini bras sprayed men wearing "stars and stripes" inspired body paint --in lieu of shirts-- with beers from agitated bottles, then, licked them clean nearly of each drop, no matter where those drops seemingly rested. White cushions on the bamboo beds could scarcely be seen under the group grope, with PG-slash-nearly R-rated, sex exhibitions being demonstrated onboard, while many of the white tee pees appeared filled to near overflowing with less exhibitory pleasure seekers.

The sudden slipping of a soft arm inside his nearly startled him, breaking him instantly from the revelry. Smiling up into his deep brown eyes focused Valerie's grayish-green set. He could have sworn they had been leaning more towards hazel the last time they met, perhaps it was the ambient light, perhaps it was her mood swings. Now her breath smelled of gum, Doublemint or Juicy Fruit maybe, he could not tell which. No telltale chewing, so the culprit had been evacuated, possibly unceremoniously dumped somewhere close by. For a moment they stayed that way --unmoving, not speaking, just staring. It was as if a magic genie had snapped her fingers to freeze time all around them or at the least to freeze their awareness of those things whirling by outside their immediate sphere. Then the moment passed and they could again breathe. That was when he realized he was tightly holding her right hand in his left …a bit too tightly.

"Ooph, I-I'm sorry!" he stuttered, embarrassment flooding through him like a high tide over sandy shores.

"It's fine. It's really good. I mean I'm glad you could make it down, down to here, uh, Miami." She was having difficulty focusing herself. There was no ploy in either of them, not in these moments. Their reactions were genuine. It was as if some inner trepidation motivated both in similar fashion.

"We're at the Tiki Bar over here. Carlos will be glad to see you." she lied, though not entirely certain that she was lying. Not entirely certain of anything where these two were concerned. What she was certain of was that things went very deep between them. She had never asked Carlos since their chance first meeting three days now gone by. Or was it chance? She wondered. Her antennae radiated a warning. Or was it some delicious sensation of anticipation? Again, she simply was not certain…

"Get you a drink?" she asked. "I'm sort of the official, unofficial hostess. How 'bout something tropical?"

"What? No JD? Woman where go thy senses? Sure, surprise me," he laughed.

"Be right back kind sir." She disappeared. At least she hoped (at least partly) that she had gotten out of sight quickly enough that he could not watch her walk away. If he made any stupid remark about this stupid outfit she had on, she'd go ballistic. It was Carlos' stupid idea. He wanted her just so for his clients, about whom she cared little, if at all. She was only concerned with the one, even though, technically he was not really a client. Maybe an old friend, maybe a rival, she just hoped he was the way he seemed.

"Please be sane," she almost pleaded. She could not take another disappointment like her last. She shuddered remembering the man who tried to cut through the small talk on their first date by regaling her with snippets from his past accomplishments, aka, concupiscent conquests by Terique. He may as well have termed it the "Big Dick Principle by Mister Hot For Your Twat". Once, while holding her hand in his, he accidentally (she felt accidentally on purpose) brushed her fingertips across his crotch as he swiveled his seat around to face hers. Perhaps it had been an innocent accident, perhaps a ploy to stir a sensation in a demonstration of his capability. Either way, she was not impressed. Though his imagination seemed endless (endless in that he never shut it off), the sensation rapidly induced in her could most be described as the dry heaves.

She had to admit though, Terique did seem well-versed and knowledgeable (at least in things that pleased Terique) and he was rather good looking, so there had been that attraction. But even looks only go so far. In Terique's case they went as far as his mouth; until he had to actually speak. Then it was over and done in a heartbeat.

Once past the "Hi, how ya doing" stuff, Terique became "the man without a course", rudderless and foundering with no hope of rescue. He delivered that message early and in no uncertain terms when he related that in his experience a woman knew whether or not she wanted to sleep with a man (his mannerism said screw) from the first time she met him. They had yet to be seated, had barely sipped their cocktails and dinner (at least for her) was already ruined. He then followed up this initial revelation by questioning point-blank whether she wanted to sleep with him (again his mannerism indicated that he actually meant to say screw). It had taken two months to synchronize their busy schedules and here was her reward?

Headed back with the surprise drink, once again she grimaced as her playback machine coolly revisited that nightmarish evening with mama's wonder boy. Recalling the awesome spectacle, she remembered six and one half feet of solid muscle, chiseled by elder gods who had unfortunately forgotten that a man's most necessary sexual organ was located between his ears. They had got it somewhat good, just not quite right.

It was through saddened, but wizened eyes that she had told Terique that she considered him a good friend. Then standing up, smoothed her dress and left him sitting alone at that piano bar to try his tired line on the next woman to mistakenly sit near him. Preferably --for his sake-- a woman plagued with low self-esteem.

But this man? Yeah, this man she felt that way about. This John O'Rourke character with the smiling eyes gave no evidence of teeth sharp enough to recreate scenes in her psyche from Red Riding Hood versus the Wolf. Nothing in him seemed to suggest, "The better to eat you with my dear!"

She ruefully admitted that, in this man's case, "Terique-the-Freak" (as she took to calling that nightmare at sometimes, Mister Not-Quite-Right, at others) had been correct, just not that night. Convincing herself further about their dissimilarities, she recalled how Terique's name had at first put her off, how her first inclination to his invitation had been to just say no, thinking: "Had to be a mama's boy! What kind of mother names her son Terique unless she gonna spoil him rotten?"

She felt her initial inclination valid, proven beyond the shadow of doubt. Conversely however, Terique had only been close to the truth. Still, she concurred that sometimes, maybe most times, a woman knew and in this case, yes indeed she already knew that she wanted him. She was thrilled to see him again, especially after he had relaxed his near-crushing grip. Then came the fervent prayer, "Jus' please Dear God don't let his mouth mess this up!"

She had imagined his cool, dark eyes on her hips as they moved in practiced, rhythmic swaying, timidly summoning him to follow her through the throng to the bar. She had hoped he wouldn't watch nearly as much as she hoped he would. What she failed to notice, so preoccupied with not tripping with him watching, was the fact that he was not watching…

It sported a thatched roof and was presently surrounded on three sides by laughing customers sitting on tall stools. The backside was walled in and stuffed full enough of top shelf libations to satisfy the most discerning tastes. She waded in and back away from the tiki bar before any wayward hands could fondle her flanks or any drunken comments could hurl her way suggesting this or that kind of snack.

Her last trip in this direction actually required unplanned travel around to the backside to pin up a piece of thin, silken fabric threatening to desert the outfit and revealing more about her than she desired JP to know on a first date. Her eyes had fallen on his entrance about the same time one of Carlos' acquaintance's fingers had fallen across her top. The cherry-faced, chubby lawyer in the cherry and cream cabana shirt had apologized endlessly, begging her forgiveness for the accident and brightening quickly following her promise she would. What he didn't hear as she ducked out of sight to address this near undressing was her promise that any repeat accident would be his last. But now, at least, she felt comfortable in the outfit Morano had procured for one of the other girls who decided to pull a last minute no show. So it's up to good ol' Valerie, gal Friday. She was still hating both the outfit and the girl until he arrived, then she hated herself for wearing it. But JP liked it, so it must be okay. Then suddenly things weren't okay. She had lost him. No, there he was. How'd he get over there?

Morano had his back to their approach, but pivoted rapidly seconds before O'Rourke's fingers could tap his muscular shoulder, as if some inner sense beckoned, almost as if he suspected in him the desire to direct a swift kick into his rear quarters. This time he ignored O'Rourke's outstretched hand, instead clapping him on his left shoulder with one hand while possessively reaching out and clutching Valerie's narrow waist as she arrived moments later. A sign of possession?

"Well hello again JP!" His speech was a tiny bit slurred, but only just. O'Rourke could tell that the entire group around the bar was feeling no pain, some demonstrably expressing that fact via telltale, odiferous methods. Libations flowed from all corners as the overworked bartender struggled mightily to keep up with requests. What he could not tell was Valerie's feeling towards the near bear hug. Her face a mask, whatever she felt she internalized, exhibiting neither an accepting smile, a disapproving frown, not even a more acceptable back pedal …more acceptable to O'Rourke, that is.

Stylish as usual, Morano wore white-on-white; a white linen, short-sleeved Guayabera shirt over white seersucker pants and white leather loafers sans socks. No clothes hound or slave to fashion, O'Rourke only knew these things because he had seen a similar white linen shirt --with its patch pockets in front and tiny, vertical pleats in back-- hanging on a manikin in a Miami Airport shop. The pants he definitely knew, that part was easy; he had a few pair similar to those at home. He was happy he had resisted the temptation to buy the shirt though. Local flavor be damned, there was enough confusion in this case. Moreover, he shunned the thought that he had tastes similar to this man even though quite obviously he did …though which is the copycat?

He let the thought evaporate, admonishing himself these digressions. He had to stop thinking catty or he could end up being pussy. Morano seemed in good spirits, though, as did most everyone else in this place. But shadowy pockets in the torch-lit illumination sufficiently masked his features to hide the presence of any incongruent displays of discord, aka, the smile that hides the frown.

"So, you enjoyin' yo' self?"

"Seems like a happenin' joint. How you been Carlos?"

Again he was speaking only to himself. Morano had already turned to converse with some other. This occurrence confirmed what O'Rourke had suspected the first time Morano had displayed this particular trait. It was no accident. He was as much an asshole as Stephanie had said. Maybe even more so. But it mattered not; he was relieved that he no longer needed to make small talk with someone he'd rather not talk to. He turned also and there was Valerie, looking extremely fetching and perhaps a bit impatient, holding two, large drinks in her hands.

"One Mojito, delivered as ordered sir." Handing him the cocktail, virtually filled with some kind of green plants, she genuflected in mock portrayal of servile obedience, bringing a wide smile to his face. "Hope you don't mind plastic."

"Glad to see you made it back alive," he chided her, though not even realizing until Morano's little game ended that she had quietly slipped away --out of the man's embrace—and around to his back. Then he chided his own self again, taking mental note of how nonobservant he had become when around Morano. She could easily have slit his throat, if she wanted. He needed to fix that short fall; otherwise he could be in for a big fall...

He sidestepped her comment about the plastic, not desiring to appear vain or unmanly. Truth was he hated his drinks served in plastic. Not only was it a conservation issue, it also went back to a redneck bar he and Tina had visited a couple times in Pensacola. They were always served their cocktails in plastic cups. He thought it strange, but nearly everyone near them was drinking beer out of bottles. So he did not realize the slight until their second visit when they noticed that other patron's mixed drinks came in stylish cocktail glasses, while theirs were served in clear, plastic cups. They never visited that particular bar again ...they didn't pay for that second set of drinks either, taking both the hint and the drinks. Here was different though; everybody was served the same clear, plastic glasses. It made sense on the sand. But he still didn't care for the plastic.

While he contemplated the subject, Valerie's mind had spent barely a few seconds concerned with plastic cups. Her pet peeves came a bit more opaque, actually quite a bit, obsidian even. Her favorite, meaning the one she most hated, had made its entrance and her eyes had changed from greenish to pitch black, nearly matching its shade. Taking note, O'Rourke hoped she never had cause to direct those death beams in his direction.

"Some men can't understand sign language, let alone English", Valerie muttered, rolling her eyes. He worried for a moment that she had read his mind or something and would eventually turn to face him, until she continued, "That guy works for Carlos."

She did not point her finger, just nodded in the direction of a slight, rather smallish man whose dark complexion blended perfectly with the black suit, shirt and shoes he wore, although the suit seemed a bit out of place surrounded by so many scantily clad revelers.

"If he tells me one more time that I remind him of Halle Berry! Ooooh…"

"What does he do?" He asked in a manner that suggested it was okay not to discuss him, though in fact he already suspected the man's profession. It spoke for itself in his detached, casual but purposeful demeanor, almost as if he intended to remain hidden in plain sight. Muscle. Up to now O'Rourke had only met some of Morano's female associates. He wondered if this was one of the people who had tried tailing him that night in DC. But that did not seem likely. Paranoid rich men usually kept their personal guards close by.

"Bodyguard mostly," she confirmed. "He usually stays well out of sight. Outdoors, while he's indoors. But down here, with all the gang bangers and kidnappers they stay real close to the man."

"They?"

"Yeah, there's another, a huge white guy, that's his partner. Seldom see one without the other. Like Mutt 'n Jeff. The other guy's much bigger, but this one's much scarier. Ugly features, kinda dangerous lookin' eyes. Evil. I hate him. Always making little snide comments when Carlos isn't around. Like 'bout how my clothes fit or my hair or…"

"Or about how you're Halle's twin," joked O'Rourke, channeling her angst away to wither outside their immediate vicinity. "You know, I think I see the resemblance, especially around the eyes …even though hers are brown."

"Oh yeah? Which Halle we talkin' about?"

"Which Halle?"

"Yeah which one? The plain Halle in 'Gothika' or the plain-skinny Halle in 'Monster's Ball' or how 'bout th' Halle with the nice T's in 'Boomerang'?"

"An' th' booming booty? Nah, I was thinking about 'Jinx' in 'Die Another Day'. All wet 'n wild 'n everything. She was too hot!"

"Accepted! And you really lucked out Mister!" she chortled, jabbing her sharp, left elbow into the bruised ribs on his right side whose signaled groan nearly forced his lips to vocalize their pain. The jab seemed to symbolize possession, title or ownership. As if to say, "Stay away females. He's mine! See how I control him? He step wrong, I steer him straight back into line. Can't do that to a man less you own th' man."

A memory assailed suddenly. He had a demonstrative woman on his hands. Obviously not a shrinking violet, this woman liked to get physical with her interactions. Her manner, one of command and control, spoke in a way that emphasized familiarity in no uncertain terms. He was in for a hell of a ride, he realized …and not necessarily in a good way.

He'd already had leave. Met Tina in Honolulu for a wonderful vacation. Everything seemed awesome, for a minute. Couple months later it seemed to hit the fan. Wifie unhappy. Stresses from protesters against the war. Hate seething against all things military, the baby killers!

Why wouldn't he come home? Save her from the crazy. Help her understand his role. How many kids did he bomb today? Then their friend Shiro passed and it got crazier. She loved Shiro, nearly as much as he did. Why wouldn't he come home, at least for Shiro? Why didn't he at least cry?

How to explain his sensei's teachings in a way she'd not consider cold and distant. Same thing with his final instructions. Shiro would be taken care of by his fellow vets, ceremony, salutes, twenty-one guns, the whole nine yards. Then his cremated remains would be stored until JP came back and claimed them. He'd make the decision to keep him or give him to rest beside the old soldiers at a later time. Way too tough a decision at this moment. But everything is good to go. But everything was not good to go …by a long shot!

Soon after, that's when he got notification she had decided to leave him! Guess you could say he went total bender. Didn't wanna talk about it, gripe about it. Nothing about it. Total funk! Funkier, he even stopped the hygiene routine. Talking smellow fellow. The new age Stinker!

It dominated his consciousness! The radio played it, the record players blared it. It came from everywhere! Chi-Lites, crooning their "Coldest Day of My Life" hit song during the coldest time in his life: "I remember, signs of springtime, there were birds, music everywhere..."

They played it in the shops where he stopped to perform his other role as Maintenance Officer to discuss maintenance issues and he hated it! Every verse reminding of her! "...and it couldn't be much worse, down below..."

Down below is where the song was dragging him. That's when Mickey had enough. Airflow in Phantoms is front to back. The odor coming outta that front cockpit stank to high, holy heaven. He focusing on his radar's B-scope, tryna concentrate on possible targets, shoot them down before they get shot and the smell bringing tears to his eyes! Bad enough when the pilot been stuffing beans, but at least that'll blow away in a while! Man, we talking ripe!

So, he convinced a couple huge Marines to dump their favorite pilot into the showers with a couple bars of Ivory soap, daring him to exit until both the soap and the stench were totally gone! Only cost a couple gallons of Irish Whiskey from the Class VI store ...and well worth it!

New memory. This one of another young woman from another time and place; also beautiful, also precocious, also physical in her approach to interactions. They had met on a charter to Vancouver, he and that other violet no less shrinking. That one also liked owning things. However, that one liked owning things more than she liked things ...or at least, as much!

She owned her own company and her own Lear Jet. Her air suggested she owned nearly all that she surveyed. But even queens are subject to the laws of nature. As in, you don't have to go up, but you definitely have to come down. She learned this lesson the hard way during a takeoff from Long Beach Airport, very nearly learning that sometimes you come down and never rise again ...the lesson goes, "takeoffs are optional, landings are mandatory!"

The jet had sucked up eleven pounds of California Brown Pelican – its pouch filled with Pacific Shrimp-- and needed a new starboard engine before it would ever again be airworthy. That had been only a part of the problem, the main issue had been her. She had ordered her pilot to takeoff despite his warning that the port engine had a few hiccups and should be overhauled. Following departure of its right side cousin's thrust, it barely provided sufficient power on its own to swing them back around for landing, nearly forcing an emergency touchdown on the San Diego Freeway and possible disaster.

So she optioned to Miles High Charter Service in the interim. Miles High is where he works. She liked owning things of value and, even though unable to possess the air service, since Miles has his own loot, no need of hers. After a time she came to value one of its pilots named John Paul O'Rourke. Girl loved her trophies. She also tended towards poking men in the ribs when the mood suited and demonstrated this tendency quite often …quite used to her moods being suited by men.

That memory faded to be replaced by one featuring a pair of young lions in wrestling gear which flashed up from repressed cobwebs to remind of the damage done a relatively few days before. Just the thought of sharp elbows tested his courage. He may have won that war, but those battles had left marks which would be a long time reminding that trophies have less significance for men his age; old men who no longer heal all that quickly …or all that well.

"But at least you didn't say 'Nisi' from 'B.A.P.S.'!" Valerie kept talking, oblivious to his discomfort. Digging into another rib, she laughed again. Her straight, white teeth flashed, eased, then appeared once again and held on for a while. "You know, with the gold tooth! I don't think I coulda handled that!"

"Nope. Definitely not a Nisi or a BAP!" He did not add that one of her girlfriends from the American Legion --the one with the right front canine (whose gold appeared press-on) probably could have passed for the blonde-haired Nisi. Inwardly, he smiled to himself. This girl definitely knew her Halle Berry movies. He guessed it was true what they say that "One must get to know your enemy."

Valerie eschewed his offer to find a place to sit. She pointed out that all the outdoors spots were taken, unless one wanted to compete with guys spraying each other and their neighbors with beer or doing carrier quals, diving onto the padded lawn chairs in headfirst slides. Indoors was too noisy, so communication would be hit-or-miss at best. No! She preferred to remain standing, often leaning against the bole of a palm tree behind the Tiki Bar. Worked for him. He preferred to be where he could keep an eye on his "host", aka, Mister Morano.

They talked it seemed for hours, inventing and reinventing new methods to save the whales, the ozone layer, as well as all the people dying of disease. She had a clear, though simplistic vision of what the world should be like –no hunger or poverty or war or any other bad thing—and he found himself thoroughly enjoying her engaging wit. He told himself that she was right about many of the positions she took on world issues and she was definitely right about them finding their own space in which to talk. This time was much too precious to waste dodging drunken idiots or shouting through one hundred-forty decibel acid rock compositions in the keys of Def Leopard and Grateful Dead.

Her laughter had a musical quality, like the tinkling of harmonious wind chimes in the evening breeze. Even the way she occasionally punched his arm or chest during a hearty guffaw was sensualistic in its message. He loved to listen to her melody and loved the way her visage glowed in the flickering light provided mostly by small bonfires and torches. But he still kept one eye on his "host", idly wondering just what constituted hosting …in this instance.

CHAPTER FIVE

William Barnett was living the life of Riley. He had never had it so good. Roda was more loving now than even their college days. She kissed him off to work and greeted his arrival with a beautiful, often passionate smile. Sex with her husband seemed like a drug for her. He smiled broadly at the thought. She even cooked gourmet meals and even more than that she wanted to adopt a child. William thanked his lucky stars and his benevolent benefactor.

Thanks to his assistance the Barnett's now owned the four bedroom, Washington, DC townhouse they had dreamed about. Well, mainly she had dreamed about. But it was a spectacular find, just off Rhode Island and North Capital Avenues. Its gift to them both a wonderful home in an exclusive part of town as well as a never ending "honey doo" improvement project, the latest requiring each room's repainting in slightly different color schemes to match recent decorating suggestions in a popular home and garden magazine. And his honey was going all out to doo it up. But now at least she drove others crazy…

She hovered like a mother hen over the painters to ensure that her granite counter tops and hardwood floors survived unblemished and that the exposed, red brick walls retained their immaculate appearance sans splatter spots. She was having none of that. She had fallen madly in love with the place from their first viewing, inside and out, but especially with the treed park's expansive vista that extended out from their backyard framed like some Norman Rockwell painting by huge bay picture windows in their kitchen nook and master bedroom. Not only beautiful, its sight freed her from the onerous claustrophobic feeling their other locations had instilled.

As he watched his wife sitting demurely at a table, occasionally making small talk with other party goers, he was again amazed by her. She had not uttered a discouraging word in months now, neither bitching about events at home nor down here on vacation. It had been a wonderful two weeks. Both were well tanned and she had not complained once about the reservations screw up that resulted in their having to fly down in coach. In fact she did not even complain about the Junior Suite that Carlos' people had booked them into even though it was supposed to be a full suite and she seemed to have no problem with the double beds in their tiny suite.

She just suggested they try them both out, alternating from night to night, a double whammy that would also give the maids pause to wonder.

It had been over two years but it seemed like yesterday to him that he came to meet this man. Actually it was Roda who lucked up on him. She was always meeting influential people that way. Barnett supposed that with her it was a gift. He deigned to not believe that her gift had been presented to many others in orgasmic tribute as was circulated in scuttlebutt stories around the water fountain. He decided instead that the wagging tongues belonged to the envious …he hoped the wagging tongues belonged to the envious.

In truth, at the time he met Carlos Morano, he was at Wit's end and Destitute's door. He worried that the Repo man would soon come knocking. He was going into the toilet with Roda's hand firmly controlling the flusher. It was not enough. It was never enough. Nothing pleased her. From the time he made Captain, she began her caterwauling under the title of "More".

"More, more, more! Give me more!" A singsong message that only he could discern, but could never curtail. Once he satisfied her demands for new furniture, came additional pleadings for additional things. She had barely just filled the brand new Broyhill dining hutch with their wedding china and settled her beautiful, round bottom into the buttery smooth leather sofa before complaining that the threadbare carpet needed replacing or she wanted the new electronic kitchen appliances or her car was too old or whatever and so it continued.

The bottom line, he stayed one paycheck ahead of the Repo man, hating to see the mail come, not only because of the volume of bills, but equally disconcerting were the hateful advertisements for everything from new shoes to swimming pools. Roda's preferential eyes always missed the voluminous bills, but fell with unerring accuracy like a Doberman after fresh steak on the mail ads. Then would come the endless suggestions that their walls needed painting or something needed replacing "before it fell apart" or she would bring home a new Versace that was "just perfect for her" and "on sale". He wished she were as adept at picking out Powerball Lottery numbers as she was clothing sales. It got to the point he cringed anytime he opened the door to their townhouse. She was forever complaining that it was too small or too old or too far from cultural centers, it never seemed to cease.

The tightening in his throat always began after he exited Interstate-395 south onto Franconia Road, headed east. The huge Springfield Mall on his right loomed like a threatening animal ready to pounce in sadistic frenzy upon his last few meager earnings each time he drove past. The few times its presence appeared peaceful and contented he envisioned that an earlier visit by Roda had already fed its capacious appetite. Turning south onto Beulah Street the tightening grew to throttling proportions. Several strip malls filled with upscale shops lined the two-lane road, standing ready to pacify fervent consumers. He worried that she would one day bring home an entire wardrobe change and put him so far in a hole he would never be able to climb out. That day came, however the change was not to hers, but to his wardrobe, and it would change his attire forever. That was the day she brought Carlos Morano to their home.

"Oh! Hi honey!" she sparkled. He instantly became even more guarded, fearing the worse. "I want to introduce you to Mister Carlos Morano." She seemed extremely pleased with herself, as if finding the goose who laid the golden eggs. "Carlos, this is my husband, Bill."

Barnett had wondered at the site of the silver, Mercedes-Benz, stretch limousine idling in the parking lot just across from their door. Its smoke-colored windows hid any occupants who may have been inside and its length laid claim to the two nose-to-nose spaces where their arrogant neighbor with the landscaping business normally parked his truck and trailer. But at least the presence of its sleek, refined and polished metal temporarily spared their tiny community the eyesore of a beat-up, old Ford flatbed and trailer full of lawnmowers.

He anticipated Phil March stewing from having his treasured spot absconded and even tempted to lodge a verbal complaint with this Morano guy. But it was not his doing, so he actually relished any upcoming confrontation. March was a big guy who bullied his way through the world, so most people would backwater when his roar was heard. Barnett was one of those who had done so on a few occasions. March topped his nearly six-foot height by at least four inches and carried thirty more pounds to back it up. So Barnett assumed a non-interventionist strategy. But he would applaud someone else employing a more provocative role … like whoever sat in the limo's front seats.

"Oh, hello, how are you?" He wondered why Roda's Jeep was not parked in its spot.

"Very good, Mister, I mean Colonel Barnett, isn't it?"

"Well, it's actually Lieutenant Colonel, (Promotable). I've been nominated by the President and confirmed by the Senate, but I'm not due for promotion until next year. The Air Force doesn't like Frocking unless it's really critical to the job."

"Uh, Frocking means you get the rank without the pay, right?" Carlos was both curious about the practice, as well as smoodging his "recruit to be". He had decided the importance of this acquisition critical to his plans and thus worth a little extra time. Also, he had acquired extensive background on the hapless Air Force officer and his beautiful, whore of a wife whose ample appetites were dragging him into quagmire. He could neither have described their predicament more appropriately nor predicted the ultimate degree of difficulty in landing such a catch. But he knew a good opportunity when he saw one...

Their meeting was not by chance. A Carlos' henchman had slashed all four tires on her Jeep Cherokee SUV. Then, his limo just happened to be parked a few spots away outside the health club which she dutifully attended on a daily basis, determined that no sag or bulge would ever flaw her perfect physicality. He himself had given a few moments exercise on a workout machine adjacent the one she pulled, pushed and sweated against and exited the club in time to catch the conclusion of her vehement volley upon a red faced, youthful policeman whose ears still rang with charges of police corruption or incompetence or both which enabled the daring daylight deed at such a busy shopping center.

The tirade over, he stepped in to gallantly offer his assistance; quickly manufacturing a flatbed tow truck to cart away her molested steed, while its owner retrieved some of her calm sipping Louis Roederer Cristal champagne and sampling smoked salmon, pate and Beluga Caviar in the luxurious, air-conditioned interior of his Benz. He tempted to offer her dinner at his favorite Cajun restaurant not far from her health spa, but decided not to chance appearing other than "helpful".

On the ride down to her home the pair chatted in the limo's rear compartment like famous fast friends. Remarking on that day's latest political scandals, an upcoming opera at the Kennedy Center, some ridiculous fashion changes being championed by a well-known designer, even the irrepressible rush hour snarls that eventually forced them to eschew I-395 and, instead detour through Linconia side streets down to Burke and through Springfield over to her South Alexandria home. The winding detour lengthened her transit time from its normally twenty minutes to over one hour before they turned into the driveway connecting her condo parking lot. She felt slightly self-conscious about inviting him inside the small abode, but considered sending him on his way without so much as an offer to refresh himself, bad form.

His complimentary mannerisms assuaged her fears, but she could imagine the size home someone of his means must possess. Still, his comments praising the beauty of her flower garden --its hibiscus plants sprouting Eye of the Storm, Fifth Dimension and Dragon's Breath blooms, with artful interposition of orange Tiger Lilies and Hydrangea-- made her cheeks blush. She worked hard to maintain the health and appearance of the narrow garden bordering the condo's front, its small porch and walkway. Chinese Hydrangea vine, hoisted large, cream-colored flowers up ten foot high trellis attached to the front walls adjacent either side of the door giving the appearance that within one might find a manmade Garden of Eden.

"Did you know that its specific name is Philadelphicum? That means 'of Philadelphia' in botanical Latin."

"Oh, I didn't know that" responded Roda. She knew of course, having studied nearly every detail --even the most minute—applicable to her favorite plants. But she knew even better how to stroke a man, especially an important man who liked to show he knew important things, even when they weren't all that important. She had made it her business to stroke men's egos to get what she wanted. As with most little girls, it began with her father. Nothing major, just doing errands or playing roles for daddy. Daddy's darling posing coquettishly for an Easter picture, daddy's little girl bringing his morning cup of coffee and paper, daddy's baby marrying without love before she embarrassed him with an out of wedlock pregnancy.

She had stroked many men's egos to future her goals. Whether that ego was found between their ears or their legs, she had stroked them. As a result she was about to become the wife of a full Colonel and that was no small potatoes. It wasn't the Flag rank she craved, but that might come later. If not, she wanted to ensure her husband a place at the corporate dinner table …the one where they seated the "Fat Cats".

She thanked her lucky stars over and over again once Morano had ushered her into his limo. This day had quickly evolved from terrible to very promising. He handled everything as if he owned the entire operation –from tow truck to policemen-- soothing her frazzled nerves in the process. Then she discovered that his firm did a substantial portion of its business with the DoD, through prime contractors such as the

Lockheeds and Boeings. He dearly wanted to expand, but had not yet found the opportunity. "What a wonderful opportunity for all involved," she had thought, while eagerly informing her newest hero of her husband's position as a new Project Manager in the Pentagon.

Now Morano sat comfortably in her living room sipping a mint julep while making small talk about her horticultural skills. It seemed that providence had dropped this fat cat in her lap. For the opportunity to expand his business, he would most certainly express grateful generosity. She was certain that she could steer Bill in the right direction. If his stubborn side became a hindrance, she would just have to deal with that situation when the time came. After all, she had been dealing with men for quite some time, first as Daddy's little precious, sitting on his lap excitedly relating that day's adventures at school.

"Oh and here's my report card. I got all A's, except for just one B!" she had chortled, hugging him tightly as she deposited the report in his hands. "Uh, Daddy, can I have some money to buy a present for my friend, she's my favorite? Uh, father, can I have a new car, mine doesn't run too good? Dad, can I?"

Yes, she had learned at an early age to handle men. Her skills were honed to such a fine degree; she controlled them even while they thought they were handling her. She knew that Bill would eventually accept whatever decision she made as his own, perhaps not at first, but eventually. She could be very persuasive…

Their new benefactor (their potential new benefactor, she reminded herself) desired to sell software products direct to the government. He needed a liaison. What was the harm in that? It was American as apple pie. They passed the time kibitzing over trivia tidbits, waiting for her husband's return. Morano seemed to thoroughly enjoy himself; in no hurry to leave and she was delighted, certain that there would be a significant finder's fee for the person that enabled such a feat. She planned to fulfill that role…

The living room was not very large, barely sixteen feet wide by eighteen long. The "L"-shaped, sectional sofa's love seat functioned as a divider between living room and dining room. She hated the confined appearance, but was proud of the quality furniture throughout their home, walls adorned with expensive paintings and tabletops holding fine oriental pieces sited throughout. She tempted to offer her guest a guided tour, but realized this matchbox would barely fulfill the role of guest bungalow in his world of the upper crust. But in Northern Virginia, property rates ran ridiculously expensive and Bill steadfastly refused her father's offer to buy them a larger house. Pride played a significant part, along with the stipulation that the house's location must be a bit further north …like in New Jersey.

For once she agreed with her husband. Her father had gotten stubborn and codgedy in his advancing years. Not only was he demanding of their location, but of their status. He wanted a grandchild from his only daughter, intimating that otherwise his legacy might be passed through her half-brother's bastard progeny. She doubted the old codger would actually leave her high and dry, but there was no telling with him these days. It was not as easy to slip into his arms or sit daintily on his lap anymore to get her way. These days another's coquettish charms fulfilled that role, helping stem the loneliness. Pushing seventy; he deserved happiness in his golden years. No! She did not begrudge his happiness, only his choices. Even younger than his daughter's thirty-eight years, the new wife's delectability grade was easily on par if not greater …and she could still have kids.

The one truth Roda had never revealed to him was her sterility, that her ability to deliver children had become forever obstructed by a tubal ligation procedure at a small hospital on Oahu seldom frequented by haolies, as native Hawaiians call white people (and pretty much anyone else not born there).

Her earlier miscarriage sent a signal to her that some women were not cut out to bear children and she refused to die proving wrong that premise, as had her mother. So Daddy could forget about her bearing him anything other than the enmity rising since his marriage to that waitress from an Atlantic City casino. To Roda, this micro-mini wearing, mousy little bimbo was just a hooker with an agenda, snagging her poor father at a weak moment, selling sex for security. More than that, the bitch even bore him a son, the one thing her mother (rest her soul) had denied him as her body succumbed to bearing their only child.

He doted on his daughter, would gladly have accepted a grandson from his "baby girl", but either way he wanted his line to continue and had always wanted that son. Roda could read the tea leaves. She had no chance with that golddigger on board. It would be better that she plan not to depend on "Daddy". There were other paths to riches…

"I actually have those same types of hibiscus plants around my Florida home." Carlos remarked, pulling her attention back into the present. "I hope you don't have the same problems we got with midges. Man those little guys really make you work."

She smiled her brightest smile yet. He was so very much like her she could have kissed him. Nothing like most men, whose eyes seldom found hers; locked instead on the other attributes. She began rattling off organic pest control techniques nearly as fast as her lips could move, citing types of alcohol sprays and citrus oils and times for use; as well, she warned of expensive formulas which never worked and was about to grab literature to prove her point. It was at that moment her perplexed husband opened the door and their world turned.

CHAPTER SIX

"Let's go inside", she cooed in that seductive, coquettish voice that he had taken notice of before. He decided that this was her mechanism when she wanted to dissuade any counter argument. It worked pretty good too. At least it had yet to fail with him, a fact for which he had also taken notice.

She led him inside the nightclub past a small, oval-shaped bar with high sides and a dreadlocked bartender and around to an unoccupied, secluded section where they nestled side-by-side into deeply-piled cushions whose white-colored fabric contrasted sharply with the surrounding, rich, dark wood frames and rails. The other indoor customers sat on opposite sides of the tall bar just behind them and astride approaches to the rear and side entrances where their views of the outside area activities were less impeded.

Valerie was sipping easily on a tall concoction that she informed him was called a "Miami Vice", constructed with the combined ingredients of rum punch and piña colada. The tiny, little moans escaping her lips whenever they sipped its frothy, red and cream-colored mixture through the long straw indicated that she seemed to really like it.

In between sips, the pair speculated a little on the state of world affairs --but not so deeply as to sour their mood—and delved a bit into each other's backgrounds, again just a skosh, little chance of hitting tripwires. Then they came to pet peeves. He had already found out that she disliked at least one of Morano's other employees and decided that where there's smoke, fire can't be far behind. Curiosity taking hold, he steered the conversation where he needed it to go. "So how did you get into the baby-sitting business?"

"Good question", she replied. "This job does sometimes seem to have a lot of that! Well, it's kind of a long story, but I'll tell it anyway." Again her elbow found his ribs –now she worked his left side-- but this jab was gentle, meant to convey tenderness as well as a jovial quality. Again the picture of Cecelia Garrett rose from the back reaches to fix him with her leering, all-knowing grin. At least her snooty air suggested that it was all-knowing...

Cecelia had worn that same "shit-eating" grin the evening he last saw her, when she turned at his door and waved backhanded in the manner of a Frenchman who had just lost at a meaningless game of Chemin de fer; as if to indicate, "c'est le vis".

It was the last time he saw her, but not even close to the last time she saw him. She saw to having him followed. Saw to discrediting his stock with any female she considered him even remotely interested in and generally sought to make his life a living hell. All because he refused to play her game, to be her lap dog, her sport …her stud service.

Cecelia refused to accept that any man could refuse her. It was not enough that he had enjoyed spending time with her. She needed to possess him, to place him at her beck and call, a trophy. Then when he refused her offer of possession –lucrative though it were—she tried strong arm tactics that eventually drove him away from her forever. So far away that he now refused to even mention her name.

But eventually she found acceptance in the knowledge that --for men like him-- freedom was the only woman he would ever allow possession of his soul. She learned these things while researching his background to find his one weakness which she could exploit. In the end, she learned enough to understand that Death would possess him before she ever would. She was vindictive, spiteful, capricious and vain, all those things. But still, to her, this had only been a game. She enjoyed games. Especially where handsome men were involved. But she was neither a monster nor a murderer. She let him go.

"I had just started working for Ferguson Software," Valerie continued, her mood somewhat subdued. "Been there less than two months when the ownership changed. Old man Ferguson had had a stroke that left him paralyzed on the left side of his body. That was the month before I started. The wife blamed it on his previous Executive Assistant. Something about mixing up his medications. The Director of Operations hired me temporarily until either the old man came back or his wife decided on the company's disposition."

At this mentioning of the word "wife", Valerie rolled her eyes for emphasis before continuing. "Anyway, Mister Ferguson couldn't operate the company no more. He was never coming back and his brand new, barely legal, just outta puberty, little teenaged beauty queen wasn't about ta be running anything other than a few 'Z's o' cocaine up her nose."

From the way Valerie went on about the former owner's bride, JP could taste her bitterness and dislike. He took another sip of the Mojito, trying to find an area where only the liquid would find its way into his mouth, but again the chopped up mint got into his teeth. He figured the bartender must have popped as much fresh mint as he had ice cubes into the blender. Every sip garnered him a mouthful of mint leaves that he tried to chew and swallow without them turning his teeth green from the specks lining them. This was definitely his last Mojito for a while. He was determined to refrain from any future experiments with South Beach drink concoctions.

"Anyway", she continued. "Ferguson developed its own line of software packages that big companies like Boeing and Lockheed-Martin use to run airplane and missile navigation systems. After the boss got sick, Carlos bought the whole show --lock, stock and barrel—for a song. I mean we talkin' a steal. Rumor was that the wife was already doin' some Latin lover on the side, so it looked suspicious when a Latino bought her husband's business out from under a couple other big hitters who had more money and who really wanted Ferguson. I mean, the company was small, but it's a diamond in th' rough. Y' know what I'm saying?"

She paused long enough for his nod, then plunged on. "So now girlie is livin' large, old man is barely able ta get aroun', an' Carlos got hisself a nice business."

"He ever do this type of work before?"

"Hell no! He had a few business properties in Cali –Taco stands and coin-operated laundries an' stuff; but never any hardware development or software firms. Now he got guys from the Pentagon kissin' his ass; Congressmen givin' him special favors, you name it. Man he can really play a crowd!"

Then she gave JP an especially evil stare and spat, "an' he got jerkoffs like those two leg breakers out there takin' care o' any special stuff he might need done!"

Had he been the object of that ire, JP would have felt extremely uncomfortable. He guessed that this woman had an extreme "mad on" when it came to Morano's bodyguards. Evidently that hate went seriously deep and was the impetus which prompted her to unload as she had. But, so far, everything she had revealed was either public record or innuendo, flavored by her own flair for overstatement. There was more, he knew. He wanted to hear more, but anxiety --a nagging, gripping fear-- crept into the forefront of his consciousness; worrying him like an old lady on Prozac that Valerie's angst might push her mouth so far beyond the control of her reason that out might unconsciously spill some forbidden, company secret to the unknown stranger. Once that occurred she might withdraw from him totally, after the fervor died down and realization and subsequent terror hit her. The desire for more inside scoop tantalized him like candy before a six-year old, but he rationalized that the time had come to set this train back onto a less radical slope; a slope less difficult to surmount.

"Special stuff? Leg breakers? You startin' to make me wonder if I'm in jeopardy just sittin' here trying to keep my hands to myself!" he rejoined, mimicking a man grasping for her breasts.

"Ha!" she laughed. "Nah, they only take care o' things he needs. I take care o' guys wit' grabby paws my own way!" Then she mimicked a woman dropping the hammer on a pistol pointed at his groin.

"Ouch!" JP reacted, snatching back his hands to cover his groin, protectively. "I give!"

Then they both laughed and settled back into the couch to enjoy the music piped through nearby speakers. No one interrupted their time together. Other people drifted by, making their way to and from the restrooms –excitedly chit-chattering about this hunky guy or that—but none of them decided to move their party to the spacious, oval seat that seemed designed specifically to promote large chat sessions; "group gropes" and the like. None threatened their enjoyable isolation.

Now that Valerie's mood had brightened once again, the subject had ventured to more eclectic Miami features, such as sightseeing tours and day trips to the Bahamas and celebrity homes on some of Biscayne Bay's most notable manmade islands, namely Star and the Venetians.

"Yeah, I took a jet ski tour around all those celebrity mansions a couple years ago," he told her.

"You know, I've never done that. How'd you like it?" The curiosity in her eyes appeared as genuine as the apprehension in her voice, as if she really cared whether he actually enjoyed the surroundings of her hometown.

"It was kinda neat, lots of backyards and mansions. Few folks, though. Guess they don't come out much when there's strange aquanuts gawking from Sea-Doos just off their dock. But there's all kinds 'a yachts at those docks, a few more riding by and some neat bridges that look like somebody trucked 'em over from Venice and even an isolated island you can picnic on, really relaxing. The water is not as clear as I'd have liked, kind of a murky light green, but not too bad."

"See anything exciting?"

"Riding fast was fun; even going slow was neat with all there is to see. But I get a little paranoid riding over murky waters in small boats."

"So does that mean you didn't see anything exciting?"

"Well, mostly it was just like riding a sightseeing bus. The guide led us, pointed out stuff, 'Shack lives here, Puffy over there, Gloria around that bend.' Then he lets us do our own thing for a little while and I get separated from the group. I look up and they're gone. I'm kinda chillin' out by myself when a bottle-nosed dolphin swims up from underneath my wave runner. I mean it just appeared, right beside me. First I thought it was a shark. Man I was 'bout to pump out a capital 'J' in Jet Ski, crack that throttle and see how fast Sharkey could swim through a cloud o' toxic shit!"

At this Valerie chuckled, "Ohhh, chemical warfare! What a Chickenshit!"

"Damn Skippy! I ever tell you 'bout my first experience with sharks? Anyway, Home Boy don't play around with Jaws!" Another image. Great whites tearing huge chunks of meat from a whale carcass and him much too close for his comfort zone. At least, he later decided they were great whites. At the time his main focus concerned whether these huge, voracious beasts would mistake his cockleshell of a boat for the blue plate special.

Fast forward to a new vision. Once had been a local man who swam in the murky green water off his Miami dock every day for twenty years at the same time in the same location, until one fateful day he became the main course for a bull shark that also swam there every day. It simply waited for the time it had a desire for this clumsy meal that showed up at predictable intervals, splashing along the surface, ringing that dinner bell. "Come on over, I'm not very tasty, but I am easy…"

Lesson learned? Bad habits can kill. Bad habits, coupled with bad water and bad animals that frequent bad, aka, murky water, can kill even faster.

His distrust of things hidden and unknown she might never understand.

In truth, even he could not fathom this phobia he considered childishly irrational. Whatever the descriptor, somewhere his childhood self-acquired an overdeveloped fear of dark, insensate places. Places whose only purpose was to entrap and envelope to an extent there was little chance of escape, where he'd be unable even to sense his surroundings. Such places that tested the limits of his courage. If he could see it he'd be less afraid, even confident of it. But he couldn't sell that point of honor even to his own self. What kind of master spy fears the boogeyman?

She required several more minutes to recover from her giggles. Spasms overtook her attempts at communications each time the image reasserted of his feet kicking the water to add speed to the jet boat's flight, Flipper's bottle-nosed snout playfully nipping at his heels.

"Morano certainly knows lots of people." They walked back outside to rejoin the party under the swaying palm fronds. The group on Morano's side had grown since their interlude, though he still sat cloistered with the same man as before. JP suddenly wished he had not convinced Valerie to have dinner with him, but luckily she first wanted to make sure her boss no longer had need of her services. At least her loyalty allowed him more time for observation.

"He's a regular PT Barnum. Always a circus when he's around." Valerie had already introduced O'Rourke to a few dozen friends of Morano, although the way she said "friends" sounded somewhat off color. Now she pointed out a few more.

It was fairly easy to discern where Morano's group began. Those were the older, more inhibited partygoers to the southern side of the club area. The youngsters on the other side displayed no such inhibitions – gyrating wildly to the bouncing beat, singing loudly along with the Reggae lyrics. JP turned down two invitations to partake in their dancing. Valerie appeared not to notice …though she made no move to leave him to check with Morano.

"That guy there, I call him the Air Force guy. Kind of my own memory trick that helps me keep track o' all the important people Carlos works with. Name's Bill Barnett, some kind of Project Manager for the Pentagon. I just call him Air Force guy. He's down as a guest of Carlos. That's his Ho--, er, his wife Roda sitting over there."

"Seems the quiet type." He stepped around her snide comment, understanding at once some underlying animosity. But she was determined to clear up any misinterpretation on his part.

"She quiet alright. She keep everything on the Lo-Lo. He's a Colonel or something like that and got there because of her. You might say he got the duty because of her booty."

"Doin' the troops, huh!"

"Only the important ones. Carlos does background checks on anybody he does business with. Ol' Billy over there used to fly jets for the Air Force. Now he's involved with the Space Program. It's hush-hush, real Down-Low classified. But whatever it is, he's on top cause she's on bottom. One joke goin' 'round is that she was actually under the desk on her knees when Bill popped in to see his boss and she paused until he left, then went right back to saluting and he never knew. Talk about dunce!"

"Gives new meaning to the term, kneeling at the altar!" he stated matter-of-factly, envisioning the event. "Love a girl who doesn't dribble on her blue dress."

She lightly punched JP's shoulder, giggling. "I guess she kept everything tongue in cheek."

"You are so bad!" he chortled, smiling down into her lovely eyes, fighting to keep his focus on them and not further down to the burgundy bikini top which did little to stifle the full nature of the bountiful goodness enclosed therein. His smile also veiled a happiness with her choice of his undamaged shoulder versus his bruised ribs.

She protested his statement –a pout to the ruby-painted lips-- bent on making her point. "I hear she did half the Big Whigs in Hawaii and was working her way around the Pentagon." Valerie paused a full two seconds for effect before completing her statement, "till her ass got caught."

At her mention of the word, he leaned back to openly leer up and down at the green, ankle-length sarong. Flecked with reddish streaks, its effect kind of reminded him of the Bob Hope movies where Dorothy Lamour's trademark outfit always made Bob's heart go bing-bong, prompting his zany attempts to steal her away from Bing Crosby. "Ummm-uh! Well I can see your ass ain't been caught. It's still all there!"

"Gimmee that glass! That's the last drink you get tonight Mister O'Rourke!" She snatched his drink and pretended about to throw it into his still leering face. "I'm gonna get you for that one!"

"Unless I get you first!"

"Ooooh! You so nasty!" She feigned annoyance, thoroughly enjoying the innuendo.

O'Rourke appreciated the 411 report. But now he was paying closer attention to Barnett than the smut history of his wife. Although he could easily see how she would be a hit around the Puzzle Palace, even during these days where officers were summarily drummed out of the services for adultery and sexual impropriety. A hard dick still made for a soft head. Besides, with her there was relative security. She, being married to a brother officer was least likely to talk, not like some precocious intern out to impress her friends. This game was all about tit for tat. As long as her husband's career advanced, one thing was certain; afterwards, this married woman would definitely clean her blue dress.

Barnett and Carlos were now sitting alone at a table away from most of the crowd, quietly discussing something they obviously wanted to keep private. O'Rourke decided the time was ripe for a slight change of course. Valerie had also grown quiet, following his gaze with her own.

"You don't even want to go over there," she whispered. The red lips inches from his right ear, her left leg seductively rubbing against his right. "Here, finish your drink and let's go somewhere else."

"My sentiments exactly. I was just thinking of wishing my host a good night. Now, I am definitely ready to go," he smiled, ignoring the cocktail outstretched in her hand.

"Then let's!"

"First I want to say goodnight."

"He's very busy right now. It wouldn't be a good idea," she started, at the same time realizing the fruitlessness of her plea. Perhaps it was the set of his square jaw, but she saw in him a grim determination that would not easily be swayed, that for some reason he would have his way. He reminded her of her younger brother who had exhibited that same dogged determination when he joined the SEALs. Still, she had to try…

"You see those two shadows over to Carlos' right? Those are his brute squad. That's what I call 'em. They can be very bad news. I saw them nearly kill a man who just wanted to talk to Carlos about some trivial, B-S thing. They nearly tore him a new asshole."

O'Rourke turned to look at her. She must have been a military brat or had some other kind of relationship to the military. Not every civilian new about such things as tearing somebody a new ass. He appreciated her even more.

"Well, I am his guest. So it's probably not a problem."

"Not a problem if you just leave either. He won't be offended." Again the drink was lifted into his sightlines.

"You know you never did introduce me to those friends of yours." Again he ignored the offer.

"That's 'cause they aren't My Friends!" She emphasized "My", simultaneously rolling her eyes. "Little Heifer over there is acting real good since she got hurt in a car accident." Again she paused for emphasis. "His boss was driving. The story is that her car had broken down over near Andrews Airbase an' the kindhearted General was giving her a ride. Yeah, right. He gave her a ride alright."

"I take it you don't like her very much." He stated the obvious, just to state the obvious.

"Damn Skippy! When I first met her she looked down her nose at me so far I felt like a midget."

"Vertically challenged person," he corrected, just to keep her going. He had decided that maybe a little more smutt-411 would help after all. He was new to this spy business, working it out as he went along.

"S'cuse my French, but damn all that politically-correct bullshit! That bitch treated me like I wasn't shit in a outhouse! I hate everything about her an' she can kiss my ass if she don't like it!"

"Ohhh-kayyy!" he demurred. "We'll not touch that subject again. How about football? What about those Eagles?"

"Yeah, you better change the subject!" She punched him again, a bit harder this time. "Don't get wussie. I'm not buggin'. I just don't like the bitch. Him I can take. He's harmless. She's the bad actor! But I got her back."

"Don't tell me. You made their reservations!" It was an accusation, not a question. She had rang his phone with the "good news" that Carlos had reserved a suite for him on Fisher Island. JP figured a similar courtesy had been extended the Barnetts. All fine and dandy, except Morano would not be the one making reservations, his assistant would.

While impressed with the chance to hang out with the rich and famous, he begged off, having already booked a room at a hotel on South Beach. It was one of a pair owned by the same group; the largest one being directly next door from where they now stood. But he had decided on the other near Fifth and Ocean. It was smaller and provided a more direct route to the marina where he had rented the Zodiac boat.

The place was far from glitzy or ultra-elegant, as far as those things go, not even what one would normally consider as regal. But it had sort of a genuine, atmosphere, not frumpy or overstated, no soaring atrium nor gargantuan chandeliers hanging from vaulted ceilings a mile high nor opulent statuary posing in imposing mime. Just kind of just right enough. He liked its feel as much as its location. This would suit him well, perhaps very well.

Besides, as tempting as it was to be closer to the subject of all this spying, he still wanted as little contact with the man as possible. "Plus," he had joked to Valerie, "Oprah already sold her multi-million dollar villa down there, so it can't be all that good!"

Joking aside, he had to be cautious about too much contact. He could only pay this string out just so far without reaching the bitter end. He remembered George's humor about how the bitter end of an anchor line is when a sailor has forgotten to tie it to a cleat and the last thing he sees, after dropping anchor, is the bitter end of his line going over into Davy Jones' Locker. But in his case, it could be him going down to the ocean depths tied to an anchor. So best to keep a little distance.

He made out the evil gleam in her eyes. A vitriolic tightening in their corners suggested Valerie had enjoyed putting the woman and her "shit for brains" husband in one of the smaller suites, the corners of her mouth rose as she related how she had even requested double beds as a further dagger. He decided this was definitely a woman whose good side would be good to find and good to stay on. But while O'Rourke appreciated her vindictiveness, he figured that she knew that this small act of defiance probably did not cause much of an inconvenience. Fisher Island had over two hundred acres of sumptuous luxury and none of its facilities rated below four stars. But, like most women, she did not take kindly to high-handed, bourgeois treatment —especially from another female. So any little negative nuance she could interject meant happiness for her. She was definitely hating. He again determined to try and never piss her off. However, for her boss he planned a different kind of pissing contest, one emphasizing accuracy, as well as distance.

Her persuasive talent fell far short of the mark on this occasion. He remained determined to break in on Morano's little caucus. Desperation edged her voice, imparting a somewhat tinny quality. "He's in conference mode. See the big guy facing out, standing watch? See that look on his face? That means, 'No interruptions!' Even I stay away when he puts on the hard sell. That Colonel must not be cooperating just yet. You don't want to go…"

"I'll be right back," he told her, stepping briskly away before her hands could grab an arm, his waist, any part of him to impede. The protest in her voice faded, replaced instead by hopeful suggestion.

"Watch out for Tim…" she started. But he was gone too quickly and the music too loud.

Four or five steps before his route of travel brought him to Morano's table, he was suddenly faced with a large example of human flesh blocking his path and blocking out much of the available light. He halted abruptly before passively uttering, "Excuse me."

"Mister Morano is busy," came the low, rumbling reply from his confronter, who stood his ground, glowering in menacing display. Fully a head taller and much broader, he wore a light blue, two-piece suit that must have required a quantity of wool to denude an entire flock of sheep. The white Stacy Adams on his huge feet sank so deep in the hard-packed sand, O'Rourke wondered at how the man had moved over to block him so quickly. But blocking was one thing, stopping was something else.

"I'm his guest and I'm just stopping by to thank him before I leave." His voice was deep, but carried no threatening timbre, unlike the ominous mass of flesh barring his way.

The gargantuan creature slowly shook his head side to side. "As I just told you, Mister Morano is busy. I will give him your message."

"You're certain I can't speak with him?" Whatever he decided to do, it needed to be done very quickly. This guy was no slouch, possessing speed and power. Looking at him, it was amazing that he could even get out of his own way. Just shaking that gargantuan head side to side must have required enough energy to shove a car. Shoving it out of his way was going to require a whole lot more…

O'Rourke's demeanor remained quiescent, but steadfast, somewhat akin to the parish priest attempting to dissuade a confessor about to rob a bank. He studied the huge head, its elongated, peanut-shaped cranium indented at the frontal-parietal junction, raised higher at the rear and sloping forward in a manner indicating it had never reshaped after squeezing through his mother's pelvic bones. O'Rourke imagined that the sensation of birthing a giant must have been quite stimulating to her also.

O'Rourke's demeanor may have remained quiescent, akin to the parish priest, but inside his brain raced furiously in search of a solution. There were quite a few choices that did not require bloodletting or subsequent body parts cleanup, the most promising titled, "Walking away". But his stubborn side was up. The wisdom of the priest became intertwined with the vision of a woman's charred corpse until messages countermanded, leaving only his stubborn side and one lingering, priest-like appeal that intoned its subliminal message only to his ears, "Are you sure my son?"

But he was not a priest and his calm only for display. He would show neither weakness nor anger, but his weakness was his anger and his anger needed an outlet. Out of his peripheral vision he could see that the other bodyguard had not left his seat two tables away, nursing his drink, while either feigning or truly being uninterested. It was logical after all; his partner's bulk would frighten away most interlopers. Those ape-like features would do the rest.

He made his decision. O'Rourke had a few seconds in which he would only be faced by one of them. He had to get this show moving …so he moved.

Cloud to ground lightning strikes travel around sixty thousand miles in a second and are nearly impossible to dodge. He was not quite that fast, he reminded himself; meaning his strikes were not nearly that effective. But then again, he only had a few feet to go.

Lightning strikes are measured in milliseconds. He willed himself to flow as does the lightning, instantaneous from start to stop. Not awaiting any uttered reply from this human shield's British accent, flowing outward with electric effect.

The massive head again shook–first to his left, then his right-- but its return right was instantly curtailed by a powerful backhand blasting into the left temple with near lethal force. The monster never felt the blow that sent shockwaves reverberating through his trigeminal ganglia, shutting down all motor functions to curtail any sense of place, time or consciousness. Temporarily, it even obstructed the flow of blood at the bifurcation of his temporal artery, causing instant blindness. So his eyes would never have witnessed what came next even were his recording mechanisms still functioning …which they were not.

So massive his tremendous bulk, small mountains had often cast envious glances at him. Of course that was all before. Now they cowered out of fear for the forces capable of felling such an immovable monolith. He did not reel backwards or sideways as would many men hit with such overwhelming force. Instead he just dropped silently to his knees, before falling face forward onto the sand.

Morano was startled by the hand that suddenly appeared as if out of nowhere. He was not used to being interrupted while conducting business. His eyes flew to the bulk lying face down --which he recognized as one of his men—next seeking out his other guard, already on his feet headed their way and then back to O'Rourke's outstretched hand. Realization flooding in brought back a repressed memory. A threat passed through stern lips, a tightened grip choking off his air supply. It all came flooding back, Vietnam's hot and sticky monsoon. Wet and sweat! But here there was no real danger for him, his fear dispelled. "Uh, hey yo JP what's up? You okay?"

"Yeah! Just tripped over somebody. Anyway, I gotta go Carlos. Nice time. But it's been a long day. I'm a little tired. Thanks for the invite."

"Sure man, anytime. Come out to my place on Fisher Island tomorrow night. Val'll get you th' address an' clear it with security. Gonna be some fine honeys. You'll enjoy yourself and we'll be at the VMAs this weekend. Get your tux ready for the after parties."

"I'll do that."

Morano turned back to the man seated on his right, as if nothing untoward had transpired, totally ignoring O'Rourke's outstretched hand, as well as his unconscious employee. Maybe it was their choice of drinks, maybe it was just something in the air, but neither man seemed in tune with their surroundings …at least most of their surroundings.

Oblivious to the fallen bodyguard or to any of the banter between Carlos and JP, the other focused on his blonde beauty now perched on the arm of a wooden beach chair near one of the half dozen or so tee pees, chatting with a couple of the guys wearing red, white and blue grease paint on their bare chests. He half worried that she had designs on slipping into the tee pee and slipping off a little something, maybe even enticing her chosen partner to slip a little something into her little something. He had heard the rumors circulating around Hickam and now around the Pentagon, but chose not to confront her. He hated the idea of her sharing what rightly belonged to him, but confrontation was more her style than his. He just hoped that the rumor mill was off target and now, just as then, he left well enough alone. He sincerely hoped that on this night he had not left her alone too long…

Roda's face exuded that certain glow that he had not seen much of since their college days. Her round bottom bounced up and down on the painted white wood to the cadence of Lynryd Skynyrd's Sweet Home Alabama. He fervently hoped that was the extent of her bottom bouncing with those guys.

But she seemed to be having a good time, he decided, happy that so far this trip was going well, at least where she was involved. Unfortunately, Carlos was being even pushier than before. He wanted access to DoD information to make his company more competitive. He was beginning to be less entertaining and more annoying. But only a little. He ran a first class organization and really knew how to say thank you. So some annoying things could be overlooked.

But now Barnett wished the man would say thank you by allowing him to rescue his wife from any sudden impulse that might lead her down an untoward path. It was not like these tee pee dimensions provided adequate space for a full-fledged romp –barely six feet diameter and maybe seven feet tall-- but with a bit of imagination anything was possible. Another thought chided his ungratefulness. He chalked his angst up to work pressures. He was glad that he let Carlos talk him into taking this break. He certainly needed to get away. But he felt guilty that he should have stayed. There had been some sort of espionage attempt while he was away. But then, he couldn't be everywhere.

Still, as Morano resumed his tirade outlining the shortcomings of the Freedom of Information Act, he wished to be somewhere else. Circumventing FOIA seemed the primary focus of his every conversation with Morano and he was getting bored with the whole subject. Carlos hated the bureaucratic red tape characteristic of every government agency, but FOIA really torqued his jaws.

"Whoom!" It sounded something like the shockwave created by his Eagle screaming through the sound barrier as heard by poor unfortunate earthbound captives, though his accelerating F-15 would never notice the thunderclap trailing farther and farther behind. Momentarily startled, Barnett's vision flicked over then back to his voluptuous mate stirring hopes that the man would give up their conversation and at least walk over to see about his insentient employee lying face down. Not to be. He merely nodded to the other, the black one, as if to say, "Handle it", then turned back to his unfortunate captive and continued yammering ...tirelessly.

But this Colonel's ears were tired; tired of the constant haranguing and battering by Morano's incessant probing for more favored positioning on upcoming contracts. He'd grown more than a little tired of this glib, smooth-voiced manipulator, how he steered each subject around to business matters from no matter which direction they started. It might begin with a comment about baseball but before long would swing to the similarities between a power pitcher's optimum release point and cryptologic timing sequences. Fastballs became software engineering in this man's jaded spectrum.

A mention of the latest in scoreboard designs might be followed by an inquiry into NATO key cards, meaning a general spilling of the proverbial beans. It came to a tipping point where Barnett's patience waned nearly to the point of incivility, perhaps justifiably so. It seemed a one-way street, this route they drove, since Morano's ears never seemed to hear his put-off responses. Dearly, Barnett's normally compliant tongue longed to generate a put-off response more easily interpreted by the man's dysfunctional mechanisms, something sporting another kind of off ...like "Fuck-Off!"

It was coming. As much as he tried to hold back, this thing was about to blow. Enough is enough and too much stinks! It had been forming for some months now with this constant bothering. Even as he bit holes in his tongue to retain the retort, it fought for final escape. To his own self it sounded out and sounded so good he contemplated that his subconscious must somehow have practiced shouting it. He could hear the words ring out clear and strong. "Get your chubby ass out of my way, I'm more concerned with who's grabbing my woman's tits right now and wondering if you ever been one of them!"

But somehow he managed to choke them down, these words of no uncertain meaning, still maintaining that silly look of pretended interest even though he had little if any. Final escape. What a gloriously conflicting idea. Such were reserved for final encounters. The ones ending with, "I never want to see your ass again!'"

Carlos wouldn't be the first, just the most recent acquaintance ousted from his inner circle. Of those, not one was of special consideration, primarily just a few rumormongers bent on spreading poison for reasons of their own. He understood that rumor often stems from jealousy and revenge, not fact, so lost friends like those were no loss at all.

A couple he had even witnessed hitting on Roda. They get a couple drinks in them and want to chase every skirt within eyesight. He knew the type. Guys who struck out, struck back out of pettiness. He had heard the jokes when others didn't realize he passed near.

"Ya hear 'bout Barnett's ol' lady? She jus' did a three-sixty on Colonel Adams. I mean round th' world! Bet them big jugs tossin' all about was a sight ta see!" It went on from there, "Heard she likes 'Sex on the beach', followed by a 'Slow screw up against the wall' with an 'Alabama Slammer'! And fo' drinks she'll have Champagne! HarHarHar!"

Final it had been with them and final it probably would be in this case. But was that wise? Then came a hard edge. He glanced over to the man seated across from him. Stirrings of distaste, bordering on hatred, climbed inside. Morano had a reputation for trysts. If he knew for sure she had been one of them he vowed that he definitely would make their parting final, conviction welling inside. Final, finis, over and done with. He still had some integrity left that Roda hadn't leeched away. He refused to work with anyone he knew for certain had violated trust. They couldn't pay him enough money. Logic contended that if he could not trust a man, how could he trust that man's product? It would be illogical to do so.

The whole damn thing was illogical, if she had laid down under his Air Force bosses to further her husband's position, why not then this super rich fellow now browbeating him for national secrets to further his corporate position? If he knew for anything other than rumor or speculation, he would break all ties with them both. That they were both whorish and despicable, Barnett would no longer doubt nor that by his own inaction --his own advantaging through their escapades-- he would no doubt have proved just as whorish. Of that he had even less doubt.

But the point remained moot. He could never knowingly seek such confirmation about her chastity. He doted on her, needed her. Still, neither would he knowingly surrender information detrimental to his nation's security. That he would never do. Others might justify such breeches of trust with whimsical stories about how the data should be available to all or trips down "Who's it gonna hurt?" alley. But not him. There is no right in wrong! If Morano wanted to sell something, it would need to pass the smell test. He was never buying something inferior simply to make a buck or meet a milestone schedule. He'd seen too much evidence of those sweetheart deals coming back to bite our country in the butt. In fact, had one such occasion occurred four months earlier, he might never have been…

Trepidation shivered inside his core, shaking severely his wiry frame. His first visit to the U.S.S. Arizona had grown more ominous the closer the ferry approached. The beautiful, bright sunny day with scarcely a wandering cloud in the whole length of a deep blue sky seemed so much cooler than a nearby bank's outdoor sign alternating from eighty-two degrees Fahrenheit to twenty-seven-point-seven Celsius. His knees even buckled noticeably as he stepped onto the memorial's platform, so much so several tourists reached to steady him before he tumbled from gangplank to water landing.

Down below within the bowels of the sunken wreck rested his grandfather's remains along with well over eleven hundred other kids barely out of high school. Down below they all lay inside a huge coffin of rusting steel that proved inadequate for the rigors thrust upon it. Many just like his paternal ancestor, leaving behind widows swelling with burgeoning life they would never get to know...

Unapologetically, Barnett's jaded vision perceived this national shrine as a piece of shit in which men such as his nineteen-year old grandfather should never have been subjected to serve. Where others envisioned gallantry and pride, he saw reason for derision, contending that never had so large a beast been so easily dispatched by so small a foe since the biblical David slew the Philistine giant Goliath with a single stone hurled by his tiny frame from his even tinier sling. In this case it took a single five hundred-pound Japanese bomb to sink over thirty-one thousand tons of armored warship. David never had a better day…

Although some debate the explosion and subsequent destruction as crew failure, where someone must have forgot to close a hatch exposing ammunition, et cetera. Barnett suspected the actual failure as someone forgetting to check the type of armor the contractor used. It's always so much easier to blame the young kids manning the device than the old farts who designed and built it …especially when the kids were all destroyed with the evidence.

Wasn't gonna happen on his watch! No falling asleep at the switch, no backstroking into incompetence. No one would die at the fault of his program. Neither did Morano have enough money nor Roda enough pussy. Though neither seemed aware of that fact and even if they did and it did not stop them from trying to gain advantage, they'd still fail. He was that determined. Morano always wanted more and she always wanted Morano to get what he wanted so she could get what she wanted and it never seemed to end; but it wasn't just about them, it was about his integrity and his country and they would both be damned before he would give in. They had their stubborn side as did he. But both theirs sucked hard at hind tit because neither seemed inclined to read the slogan emblazoned above his office door that co-opted as his modus operandi: "Unfair advantage begins with superior workmanship!"

"What's the best strategy for this? How are Hewlett-Packard and Boeing proceeding on that? Did you remember to stop by the tailor's and get measured for your new dress blues?" That latter came from her, nagging as usual that newer was better. Apparently both considered the term "unfair advantage" to mean underhanded and closed to anyone else and any response short of total acquiescence totally unfair …at least from one such as him.

But beyond a few advantages of timely notification and perhaps a tidbit of opinion (short of a suggestion) he refused to provide Morano anything unintended for all. Carlos would get his information a bit early, saving a few logistical and engineering costs for last minute acquisitions and fabrications and thus helping lower bidding costs, but he'd still need to produce the better quality widget or no git it.

Unfair advantage begins with superior workmanship, meaning: "Nobody else has a chance if yours is best". The phrase was his own coinage. Morano may not appreciate it, but then he had two other choices to win the bid …slim and none.

Too late to intercept, the smaller bodyguard had moved quickly to brace O'Rourke, but reluctantly checked his action with a look from Morano. Instead he bent to tend to his fallen compatriot, barely even noticing as the attacker walked away. None of the other patrons seemed aware of the activity either, although some wondered how much the sprawling behemoth in that pale blue suit had drank, joking out loud that it must have been gallons, judging by his size.

"Damn man! You certainly don't take no for an answer", Valerie laughed after he had returned to where she still stood. Her heart had just returned to its normal rhythm. She could not believe her eyes even after Carlos' bodyguard's body lay inert on the sandy ground. Then, the nervy man had the gall to strike up a conversation while the other bodyguard came at him. "What a pair of balls", she had thought. Borrowing a page from his book, now she was just happy that "He" had made it back alive…

"He was talkin' 'bout your mother. I couldn't let it go out like that."

"Spare me your Irish charm Mister O'Rourke. I'm not one of those bleeding heart, liberal, wimp sisters who always hatin' on anybody ain't PC. I do my own shopping, on my own and I can put the toilet seat down myself!"

"Oh Gee! My kinda woman. So you're okay if I sometimes forget my non-violent side."

"It's okay with me as long as I'm never on the receiving end."

"I don't beat women, unless they wanna be spanked and then I usually tickle first, less they in a hurry."

"In that case you can forget your feminine side also. Just come right on over big boy!"

"Vat," he feigned surprise --mimicking his superstar former-Governor—"you don't like und Gurlie Man?"

"So where we going tonight?" she asked. Simultaneously she hit him on his other shoulder this time. He decided that in a previous life she must have been an ambidextrous, two-fisted puncher.

"How 'bout your place?"

"Yours is closer and less crowded." She gave him a knowing look, followed by her own leer.

"Sounds like a bet."

CHAPTER SEVEN

They sat in a dark green Jeep Cherokee three cars behind his. He had assumed it would not take much for them to figure out which was his car. Obviously, he was correct in his assumption. He was not certain why or how, but somehow they had. Thanks to Sylvia's love of action movies, he had seen too many lately where the bad guys always seemed to know exactly where the good guys parked their cars, their horses or their secret hideouts. Luckily for him he did not own a horse. They'll shoot your horse …what they'd do to a black guy in a Dodge convertible he hoped never to know.

Whether Valerie noticed them or not, he was uncertain. But as he bent to open the car door, suddenly she grabbed his arm, pulled his face toward hers and kissed his cheek. It was just a tiny peck. But it said many things all at once. He stopped abruptly, feeling her mood swing. Straightening up, he looked down at her impish smile that found its way up past the freckled nose and into her dancing eyes, transforming the face absolutely cherubic.

"Rain check! Okay?" she inquired in a coquettish manner that drove away any ambivalence for this aspect of his strategy. He no longer felt any qualms about using her to get to Morano then dumping her along the way. He would still use her if he could. But dumping was no longer a part of his equation. She was the type of woman that filled men's dreams with fondness. He determined that –providing along the way she did not come to hate him entirely—he would much enjoy a long term relationship with Ms Valerie Lewis of the greenish, leaning-toward-gray, eyes.

Joking that she was more hungry than horny, Valerie directed JP to a local Crab Shack –local to North Miami, anyway-- where both decided on barbequed Dungeness crab for dinner. He was amazed at how well she could put it away for such a slender-built lady. She also demonstrated great skill and dexterity, expertly extracting every bit of the tender meat in between bites of corn on the cob and sips of Budweiser, licking her fingers at every turn to clean away drips of butter or barbeque rub. He was not even close to her match in this contest and surrendered shortly after she belched upon happily downing her second crab cluster. It was not very loud, but it was noticeable.

"I give! If you're gonna fire off neck farts to prove your superiority,

I have not only lost, I've been resoundly whupped in a most humbling manner."

"Oooppss, sorry." she giggled in that musical style of hers. "Mama always said that a belch is a compliment to the cook, but it's not too nice for a date."

"Hmm, maybe. But how you know I didn't give my recipe to the chef, huh? How you know? If he's using my recipe, then I think that makes belching, farting and sucking your gums acceptable for our date! Hmmm?"

"Wait a minute now; I didn't say nothing about farting. Just belching!" She shook her head as she laid down the law on this issue. She really was a very pretty young woman and fun to be with. It was just too bad that she worked for his archenemy. That was another of his definitions for Morano the villain, his public enemy. A couple of that enemy's henchmen were probably at this moment sitting just outside in their vehicle. He figured they had to be in his employ. Their presence weighed heavily in his acquiescence to Valerie's decision-making process concerning food versus frolic? Too many prying eyes, so food won hands down.

O'Rourke's dilemma was certain; if he tried to lose them, suspicions could rise a notch, not that the ever-paranoid little Chicano was not already suspicious. He had to wonder why Tina's ex-husband had suddenly showed up in DC right after Tina had suddenly turned up missing or dead. He probably would not tie commercial pilot John O'Rourke's sudden appearance in with any government investigation. But given the current score, government zero, bad guys five (or was it six), if Morano did become suspicious, O'Rourke's would become the next body burned to a crisp inside the flaming wreckage of his car.

Yeah, that's what they did to black guys in Dodge convertibles. Roasted and toasted, just like they did to black girls in Ford Explorers. Then the government investigators would have another mystery, a second charbroiled corpse whose mouth had been mangled to such an extent that dental records would help little. Maybe some smidgen of remaining DNA would identify his Native American, mixed with African, mixed with European roots. But that only threw his remains into the midst of the melting pot with many other black Americans. He'd only be another mystery…

No! Better live Zero than dead Hero. He'd continue to play out this string as if Tina maybe went walkabout. Wouldn't be her first…

"Carlos likes to keep his enemies closer". It was something Valerie had uttered in jest while they danced at the American Legion that had bolstered his current strategy. She meant the quip for the man who had spent much time chewing Morano's ear. But he took the lesson. If this guy wanted close, O'Rourke was determined to give him all the close he could stand.

"Carlos invited me to some kinda pre-VMA party tomorrow night at his place on Fisher Island. You gonna be there?" He asked, knowing the answer, but hoping against it.

"I'll be the one with the sad face from no love!" She drawled out love as if it were some physical, painful thing. Then smiled and said, "Boy, he must think you're special".

"I have that effect on some people."

"You're having that effect on me now." she cooed, sliding the instep of her sandaled foot up his leg. She was being naughty again. He noticed that when they were either alone or semi-secluded, she was ever the prim and proper representative of Anasazi Enterprises. But out in a public area she let her light shine, vamping and titillating; always teasing with the promise of pleasing. Was it just for show, this act of the "You can hit its?"

Apparently the showplace was her stage. Her, "Your place or mine speech", had gone only as far as the passenger door of his rental car. Once inside she had become almost reticent, seeming to shrivel up in anticipation of something untoward about to come. She seemed to him relieved when he announced that they were being followed. He had verified the accuracy of his supposition with a few turns down a few side streets before moving back onto Biscayne Boulevard.

"Yup!" Definitely got a friend back there. Prob'ly just wanna see you get home safe."

"Probably one of your old girlfriends saw you creeping out back there and wanna holla at you. "Hey JP, wasn't tonight my night?"

She'd seemed to become more energetic almost instantly with the news. Perhaps the thought of their being followed put her back into her "on stage" mentality or maybe she just liked to be chased.

"Carlos often have you followed? Is that part of the employee benefits program?"

"I never noticed before. He is a bit of a worrier, though."

"With his kind of green I'd prob'ly be th' same. Never know who's trying to make a score. This place on Fisher Island, is this his only house?" He had to be tactful asking questions she might consider too personal or company confidential. She report her suspicions, he end up toasted. He was too new to this game to know whether she really liked him or was merely following orders to play nice …or keep tabs. He suspected it was a bit of both. But which one got the biggest play? He'd soon find out which…

"Doin' a little spying on our own, are we? Sounds a little James Bondish, Mister O'Rourke." Oops, he'd obviously stepped a bit too far. "Am I supposed to play the role of the villain girl who sleeps with the hero out of curiosity then succumbs to his sexual prowess and converts to his dickish religion? Is that it, Mister O'Rourke? A little dinner and some boom-boom? How's it happen? She scream out her boss' closest secrets at the height of climax? 'Th-the nuclear w-weapons are down the hall behind th' door m-marked Oh-oh-oh-ORGASM!'"

Her faked stuttering sounded theatrical, more melodramatic than accusing. He hoped it was all in jest. "Tell me Mister O'Rourke, why the probing questions? You tryin' to get to know me or Carlos? Which one of us turns you on the most?"

Obviously, he had not been tactful enough. What would Bond do? Forget that! What will work? Not even a man as gifted as James Bond could figure out the mysteries enshrouding feminine duplicity, though Bond never once seemed to try and figure them out. He just took them all to bed as if to say, "Well at least I figured that much out!"

"Momma always said the best way to a woman's heart is though her family or her career. Get her talking about either one, if not both, and she'll never see your fangs …until it's too late."

"Yeah, bring momma into the conversation. Why Mister O'Rourke, is nothing sacred? You'd impose the momma strategy just to get a little trim?" She rolled her eyes mockingly, filling him with the hope that at least this part of his ploy had worked. But she still used his surname, so all seemed not fixed.

"Yeah, momma gave the best advice. Daddy just said, 'There they are son. Cute, ain't they? Now go get 'em. Make me proud!'"

"I see," she smirked, "So you took your strategy from mommy? What you take from daddy other than 'hit it an' quit it'?"

"His insatiable curiosity about where his favorite woman be spending her nights."

"Favorite woman, Mister O'Rourke? Are we feeling just a bit much of the rum?"

"You brought the drinks! Nah, I just wondered if he was really that big time or just playing the part of some little piker trying to act all big and stuff. You know, 'Glad to be' versus 'Want to be'?"

"Oh no! He has a place down in Grenada also. That's usually where he spends his winters. He doesn't like the cold. If he has to fly to DC in January for a meeting, he already pissed and they better look out! I was there once. It's very nice, sits way up overlooking the sea."

At least that strategy worked, he decided. No matter how pissed they are at their husband or their boss, women don't like anybody else to put them down. She'd shot his postulate down as quick as if it had never been ventured.

"Guess now you gonna brag about how he fly you down first class, getting champagne service an' all." O'Rourke felt a bit braver, though still keeping his questions as short and unobtrusive as possible. He knew he had reached borderline. He had to discern its location before trampling on or over it. Humor usually worked, but nothing worked all the time and funny ain't funny to a pissed off honey.

"Lear Jet!" Her terse statement indicated disdain. Humor seemed to have failed. He may have asked one question too many or maybe put down her fella one time too many. He still didn't trust that she did not sleep with Morano. His nostrils had detected the man's stench that first meeting. They detected the same stench left on everything touched by the man … even Tina.

Perhaps she had sensed the same. Regardless, something had seemed to rile her mood. She pulled on her short-sleeved, dark-green shirt as if to punish his arrogance by denying his sustenance. But if so it didn't work the way she planned…

Appreciatively, he'd noted that although its midriff length successfully covered the bikini top, it had no chance of disguising those ample proportions, meaning those protruding ones that probed deep into his genitalia-arousal device and whose gaping cleavage --stretching its vee neck in a manner most enjoyable-- was only one of the dead giveaways.

Fortunately, neither could it hide the fact that the amplitude of those proportions had increased significantly as she seemed about to hyperventilate. Bad sign. He needed to get the personal out and the personality back into this conversation.

"Good! Maybe I can get him to give me a job," he laughed, bringing a quick smile to her lips.

"Oh, that's right you're a pilot!" The relief in her eyes shone even through the night's blackness which was being ineffectively interrupted by shrouded lamps atop poles every half block or so. The extra illumination coming from trailing automobiles also lent their support, as did those approaching. One set of trailing lights lent more than others. Just the thought of someone peeking over his shoulder sent minor chills of anguish reverberating throughout his frame. He wondered whether his cover was blown. His first impulse was to lash out, to push them away or slash fingers across their eyes. This claustrophobic feeling suffocating him at the moment increased exponentially each time the tailing lights moved closer. He hated that feeling…

It had started raining harder then. He'd switched on the wipers and thought about trying to lose his tail in the diminished visibility, but decided it probably better not to do anything to provoke response. Morano would wonder why the guy he was having followed was looking over his shoulder. He would possibly find another's paranoia threatening --his own extreme and unreasonable suspicion would increase, perhaps beyond recall—then he might up the ante, initiating some preemptive violence or something and then all this 007 wannabee's haphazardly derived scheming would be out the window. So he stifled the rising feeling of confinement and drove on, mostly in silence.

A little night music on the radio served to keep the mood warm through her schizophrenia and his claustrophobia. They'd chatted sparsely then, saying little other than her spoken directions and his acknowledgements. Tall, dark palms and short, squat ferns sped by until they turned back towards Biscayne Bay onto Seventy-Ninth street and then into the restaurant's parking lot. The tailing vehicle kept driving by as if trying to appear another harmless driver headed over the JFK Causeway perhaps to North Bay Village. Regardless, JP figured they'd go u-ie, long before crossing over the bay.

The Crab Shack was one large party, resplendent with wall and ceiling displays of school paraphernalia representing every grade and level, plus sports icons and various examples of uniformed military dress, as well as the usual and obligatory beer display ads and other liquid enticements. Their booth table in a rear corner gave easy view of the entrance, ratcheting down his schisms to acceptable levels and allowing him to again enjoy Valerie's company, including her ribald series of blonde jokes.

"A blonde and a brunette were sharing a bus seat and the blonde couldn't help but notice how pretty and beautiful the other's skin was. So she asked her what made her skin so soft and beautiful. 'Once a week I fill the bathtub with milk and just soak in it,' the brunette replied. So the blonde went to a farm and asked the farmer for a lot of milk. 'How much you want', asked the farmer? 'Well, quite a lot,' she replied, 'because I'm going to soak in it.' He asked, 'you want it Pasteurized?' To which she responded, 'No ...just up to my boobs.'"

He chuckled. "Past your eyes, huh. Cute." But she wasn't nearly finished.

"Why did the blond climb on the bar roof?" she asked, sipping on her Jack Daniels before chasing it with a slurp of beer.

"Don't know, you tell me coach."

"She heard that drinks were on the house." He laughed loud and hearty. She really had this thing for blondes or maybe it was just a certain blonde. But he decided to play along.

"I got one."

"Shoot."

"What do blondes and noodles have in common?"

"Hmmm," she said. "That's a new one. What is it?"

"They both wiggle when you eat 'em."

Valerie was into her second round of bright, cheerful laughter when the musical notes of her cellular phone clamored for her attention. She expertly fished the device from her small, black bag. Excusing herself –the phone to her ear—she then headed towards the front exit. He opened the small, towelette package delivered with his meal and wiped the barbeque powders from his fingers before removing the plastic bib that their bubbly waitress had ceremonially tied around his neck.

Whether attributable to clairvoyance or precognition, he had already called for their waitress –who again inquired how much he had enjoyed the meal—and paid their tab by the time Valerie returned. He could not discern whether she took any notice of that fact, not even bothering to sit down.

"I need to leave JP." Her face revealed frustration, perhaps hidden anguish. He quickly rose and followed her swaying hips to the door, smiling a goodbye to the teenaged hostess sporting the "freckles run amok" look and headed to the rental. He tempted to beg her indulgence while searching for a tracking device planted on the undercarriage, but decided to take the chance. He wasn't running from them. That was a bit too dramatic and he had experienced enough drama for one evening, hoping there would be no more. Still, that nagging germ of a thought filtered back up into his consciousness: "Sometimes they killed your car …sometimes they killed your car with you in it".

She was extremely reserved on the drive to her home in Miami Shores. Luckily for both of them it was a short distance, which was one of the reasons they had chosen that particular restaurant. Within minutes he turned off Tenth Avenue onto Ninety-second Street and then soon into the driveway of the single-story, three-bedroom, ranch-style home. In a less reticent moment she had given him the low-down, so he didn't need to guess at its hidden features, except maybe if he'd ever get invited inside to see for himself.

Seemed a nice enough place. The area was well lit, with several driveway edge lights marking its periphery and twin ornamental lamps adjacent both sides of the white doorway all beaming their brilliance into the late night blackness.

Shoulders slumped for a second or so; she seemed to gather herself for whatever challenge lay in wait beyond the closed entrance. Without a word she leaned over and kissed him softly on his right cheek, then rested her head against his shoulder, as if deriving additional strength from its broad measure. He did not speak either, feeling she needed other than words. Feeling his words would have been inadequate at any measure. She stirred, looked into his eyes and gathered her belongings –just the black bag and an umbrella.

"See you tomorrow?" she asked in a tiny, girlish voice, which instantly wrenched from him a deep emotional desire to lock her in a fierce, protective embrace so that whichever bad thing threatened could never get close. Inside him the quandary raged intense. Part of him definitely hoped to see her again; the other part hated the idea that if he did she would see him at his worst.

His plan was formulated and ready to fly; which was an apropos assessment, as he had come up with it on the fly, so to speak. He dreaded the execution. It was going to be an ugly occasion. But if it worked, the outcome could be well worth the embarrassment, maybe. But her somberness captured his heart this night. He would let the devil take the morrow, tomorrow she might hate him, but he could see that tonight she needed a friend.

"You all right? Can I help?" Inside he knew the answer before the words escaped his attempt to recall them. She had issues that she could not, did not desire to share with strangers. Stubborn is as stubborn does…

"I'm alright," she murmured. "Just a little tired I guess. I better go."

"Hope it wasn't that last blonde joke," he chided. "I don't have skills in that department."

She thought back to the joke and giggled again. "If I didn't want to hear all the crap from his crew tomorrow, I'd invite you in."

"Invite me in where?" The temerity of his question, coupled to a leering grin, he hoped would put her in a better mood since the mellow music had not seemed to work. She appeared so bothered by something or someone, perhaps nothing within his power could work. He did not speculate on whoever was at the other end of that phone call. It was her business, not his. He just hoped to lighten her doldrums for a few moments.

She punched his arm, a portion of her spark and her spunk returned. Then she kissed him again. This one was full on the mouth, hot, wet and passionate; all the adjectives. It lasted for a significant time and tasted wonderful to him, even with the barbeque flavoring. Her darting tongue sought, found and danced with his to create a pantomimed, musical score of their own making. The vibrant ardor of her passion permeated every crevasse and nook of the car's interior. The sounds of meeting lips were accompanied by slight, low-ranging moans which escaped from her throat to greet his alert ears, sending a purposeful signal to his groin that resulted in a significant reaction in that region. He was certain now that he knew exactly what "invite you in", meant. But curiosity remained an interested component within his nature…

"Hmmm. So you keep everythin' lo-lo 'til the boss leaves town? He goin' anywhere, anytime soon?"

"Aren't we the curious one, Mister Bond?"

This time he did not even blink, prepared for this inevitable suspicious reaction to his line of questioning. "Not su-wave or de-boner enough ta even attempt ta hang wit' JB, I'm just checking the weather. You know, is the coast clear? I mean, I wouldn't want to step on any toes or anything. Catch somebody on th' downlow!"

"Don't you mean su-ave and debonair?"

"I said it, I meant it." The statement came out emphatically and humorously and his dazzling smile cut through the dark compartment, warming her in ways she would not begin to admit, even to herself.

"Teach Sunday School with that mouth? Bet you be a whizz befo' a pastor!"

"Could be worse. Haven't had to resort ta hittin' up Playboy videos, thou I know porno got lotsa venues. But I been exploring a softer side of porn lately, meaning I mainly survive on Facebook friend suggestions from half-nude Brazilian babes. So I'm far from sanctified."

No heart emoji for him! He was a bold one when he wanted to be, she decided. Now if only he did not say something totally inane and blow it; some crack about the size of his crank or an eight-inch tongue and breathes through his ears. One of those comments right now would be especially detrimental to their future.

She gave the chance, praying a little that he would not succumb to some innate obsession fueled by braggadocio influenced by testosterone. So far, so good. Maybe she would keep him. Maybe. But she was as yet unsure. "And to whose toes are you referring Mister?"

"I believe his name begins with a 'C' and he appears very protective of his property."

"Maybe so, but I belong to no man. Him boss, me peon, that's all. He might worry about me a little, but I pick my own poison. Are you poison, Mister Bond?" She genuinely wondered whether or no. Times like these could be so tricky, this getting to know one another stage, this feeling out period, which this night meant literally …the only figurative part being around her figure.

Her girlfriends gave these type adventures acronyms they could text or Twitter or Facebook without the whole world picking up on their exploits. Her girlfriend Sarah called it, "snuggling-not-humping" or SNH. It was appropriate. However, for her own self, it meant more than just a "grope and poke".

She had grown much more serious about relationships with men and their worth these last few years. For her, encounters like these amounted to "phased-erectile assessments" or PEA; as in, start slowly, move gradually; then, once you've reached this advanced level of relationship, if all that heavy petting doesn't get an appropriate amount of rise out of both her and him, might as well go home to a cold shower. Especially when a cold shower was her intention in the first place; since that's normally what it was, since most times she would be checking the territory for actions yet to come.

But it wouldn't matter. It would be time to close camp. If it wasn't a happening thing, just cut your losses and say your goodbyes. That way, no one invested a significant amount of time. No one got significantly hurt and no one could brag about a one-night-stand, while the other griped about a crappy lay. She definitely wanted to avoid that latter part. Indeed, she had an agenda and it was easy, cause her name ain't Cookie so there would be no nookie, not ever on the first date …but this date it wasn't so easy.

Her active mind searching, she wondered what acronym a man such as he would give this act of engagement they were now engaged in; probably something to do with tittie-teasing or crotch-diving or something along those lines. However, something about him pronounced him a different sort. The warning in her ear clanged alarm about a different hazard to be feared. Not once had he bragged about licking his eyelids or anything like that. Not like so many other guys who tended towards lewd and crude. Men!

Women, on the other hand, tended to have a different goal. Women went about conducting clinical trials and measurements for the ultimate purpose of determining an acceptable mate with whom to perpetuate the species. She saw that as a higher purpose …with kinky benefits.

One last sizzling kiss and then she'd be gone. Leaving him to ponder just how far he wanted to take this. But it didn't happen at once. Something held her here longer than the warning klaxon deemed necessary. She dawdled a bit more before dashing. Actually, it was quite a bit. Actually it was another forty minutes or so, maybe longer. It just seemed to be a bit before a dash. But then she did, leaving only the sweet scent of her perfume behind to keep his company …and reignite his memory.

He could still see the ardor in her eyes, but there was something else. A look that measured his cut and corners for any bestial desire to slash notches into his chambered sex-gun after succoring her sweetness, amidst promises of forever devotion, then scoundrelly casting adrift the plundered treasure. But he had told her correctly. He was John O'Rourke, not James Bond. What he didn't say was, while he may be quite capable of bedding every woman who indicated an interest in him, as are most virile males, he was also very sensitive to leading women on, making them believe he would commit to some long-term romance just for the sake of one night's romance.

She wouldn't have heard him anyway, he presumed. Women categorize such dribble as meaningless lines of conquest. Still, he never had endorsed the "hit it and quit it", gunslinger mode of sexual endeavor where every woman qualified only in the "one night stand" category. If women indicated a desire for a brief tryst, he could accommodate. But he didn't lead them on. If they wanted more, they could take the train and ride it as long as it went …but there'd be no promises.

After Tina divorced him, he had locked away that portion of his heart which looked for some permanent status in relationships. He'd done a mental download of all things love and about love. But it was only the mental, he still had basic needs. He still needed the comfort and succor of women, was still affixed by their beauty and bearing and all those feminine mystique things. In fact, that topic had been a point of contention between him and Sylvia for some time now and was heatedly discussed the night that he left on this trip.

All Sylvia knew was that he had headed back east and that Tina was back east. Since he could neither reveal the nature of his visit nor the length of his stay, she had assumed the worst, despite all his assurances. The worst, being him and the ex-wife hooking back up permanently. He was not sure exactly what the DIA pencil neck who drove her home that day had revealed to her, but whatever it was she did not seem happy. JP felt an ill premonition that the guy was trying his luck at playing Jodie or Back

Door Charlie. But Sylvia is her own woman. He had no claims on her. So her choices were for her to decide and no one else, especially not one so reticent about permanent status.

Her vision confused and conflicted. Legs sinfully scribed by a heavenly Michelangelo stood wide apart, arms at akimbo, knuckles digging into her trim waist and a very unappreciative scowl across her cream-colored face. Even with the anger, her beautiful features had tugged at his heart that night. He'd hated himself for leaving nearly as much as she had hated him for leaving …and there was no doubt she was hating.

"Stay with us", they called out to him. Shapely thighs, swathed in charcoal fibers that so proudly accented her black and white checkered minidress pleaded their message. "Please stay with us!" But those were alone in their pleading. Dark eyes peeking from under even darker hair and above pouting lips painted succulent ruby sent a different message. These said: "We don't care where you go, you can go to Hell!"

The lights were there again when he backed out of her driveway. They had taken no precautions to disguise the fact that he was being followed. He wondered if they were the same people who tracked him through Virginia and Maryland. This time, it appeared, they were determined that he would not give them the slip. He was too disinterested and too tired to even try. The rain had ceased, so visibility was restored to normal levels. He would allow them to follow him back to his hotel. He toyed with the idea of awakening early to slip out, then deciding to table such a move for a more essential need. He would continue with his present innocuous, non-offensive level of operation.

Actually, innocuous and non-offensive were descriptions he shared only with himself. His suggestion to the General and his staff that Carlos Morano was as good a place as any to begin his search was greeted with less than lukewarm enthusiasm. They all considered the prospect too remote to have validity. Their investigation had brought out nothing but normal, entrepreneurial indicators surrounding the man –how he did business, his business partners, known associates and the like—the results of their delving were as vanilla as Ben & Jerry's original ice cream. To DIA, his Anasazi Enterprises three-part mission statement –emphasizing product quality and commitment to the community over economic reward-- brought visions of mom's apple pie. Their take revealed too many things right about this man for him to be wrong, with the exception of him being the wrong choice. Adding to that, he had too many powerful connections to chance unsupportable allegations.

But those were their opinions. After speaking with Stephanie and getting chased through Northern Virginia by somebody bent on knowing his whereabouts, his opinion ran a one-eighty out of phase, as in totally reversed and he was especially sensitive to subject matter related to that dude. All he knew were the clues buzzing inside him, telling him things. Not quite voices, for that would make him half crazy (answering them would cover the second half). But the sensations were irresistible. They signaled (some might say "signified") there was something wrong, so maybe it was. Did it have to not be so just because he believed it was? Regardless what they thought, it was a signal and sometimes you need to observe what the signals are saying. He recalled what they said the first time they met when Morano was with Tina and clinging possessively to signal the message: "She mine now, be-atch!"

But the last time he saw her she was ambivalent about him, her fiancé. Totally different attitude, like "Carlos who?" That and Stephanie's misgivings were enough for JP, notwithstanding the fact that his antennae now radiated warnings whenever Morano came near or whenever his name surfaced or whenever he thought about him with Tina. But it wasn't as simple as mere jealousy or possession, of hating to see what once was his with somebody else. That was totally unlike him, at least he thought it was. There was just something about this specific somebody else that just didn't set right and he just couldn't put a finger on it...

Besides, he was scarcely one to signify or play the dozens; firing insults back and forth about somebody's shoe size: "Damn, I hate to see the size of your crank with them little thangs! Then again, I guess you never seen it either!" Or tales of somebody's momma's adventures as star of the buck-a-throw, fuck-a-ho, red light district.

Serious misgivings motivated him. Whereas motivation entailed the only issue motivating the DIA. It smacked home in all three men, Thompson's matter-of-fact insinuation that just maybe O'Rourke's distrust was totally a product of his jealousy. There in the back of his mind, even General Burton shadowed such doubts. Any man could be thus motivated at the loss of one so treasured. There was no mistaking his feelings for his Ex. She may have divorced him, but he had never quite let her go, couldn't ever break free. Then again, that was the motivation they'd used to snare him...

Having seen her pictured from a dozen angles, Thompson could well understand the emotion. He would have hated any man sleeping with his wife, Ex or not. That O'Rourke's emotions were totally opposite, he would never believe. He knew that this guy had loved her as much, if not more, than anyone he had ever met. In fact still loved her, even though she might be toasted and roasted. Thompson knew all this. He did not understand the emotion so well as to embrace it as a goal in life, but at least he knew of it.

It was not that he did not understand how a man could still love someone who had used his heart like a springboard, somersaulting off into the waiting arms of another or how he could in fact love the very ground she walked upon, his love went so deep. Unfortunately, he understood those things all too well. The image of ex-girlfriend Doris dining on Brazilian organ steak was ever on his mind. What, he could not understand was how a man would not harbor a hate for anyone who had replaced his affection in her heart. In his own case, Thompson deeply desired to nuke the entire adult male population of Brazil or at the very least bombard them with enough radiation to make their hair fall out …and their organ steaks shrivel. "That would teach Doris!"

No! Thompson decided that O'Rourke was full of shit! Not a team player. He was the General's choice, not the staff's and he was wrong for the job they needed him to do. But, he was the General's choice, so he was in as long as the General said so. But the staff did not have to like it. O'Rourke might have signed on, but not only did he not play by the team rules, he had designed his own mission, focused his interest on Morano's organization and limited his involvement to that end no matter the alternative areas hypothesized in their briefing.

Not that these were necessarily all bad things, considering they had no definite leads on the bad guys' actual identities, not even a definitive frame of reference. Were these al Qaida, Russian Mafia, Yakuza, Sureños, Martians? Who the hell knew these days? Everybody was into everything or at least branching out into everything these days. It was easy for the Press to surmise al Qaida for every hit and run, bang-bang shoot 'em up where military assets were targeted. But the Press gets paid for sensationalism; reality is a term they see only for fake-real TV shows disguised as genuine.

Actually, when all other explanations seem implausible, al Qaida is usually top of the military's chart also. Their people come in a variety of colors and nationalities. So the Press might prove correct. But DIA had not yet settled on that walk just yet. To this point, the bad guys were ghosts; shadow figures that had done a drive-by, hit and run, smash and grab and then disappeared off the face of the earth; out of sound and sight …oh yeah, and a murder.

But it was the principle. If this retired, retarded, whatever, ex-Marine got to make his own taskings, he was going to screw everything up and maybe get all their dicks stuck in a ringer. Thompson decided that there was only one way to save the day …he flushed away the image of Doris' tongue curving lovingly around a dark, Brazilian penis and made a call.

CHAPTER EIGHT

Sun gods. Gotta love how twenty-first century folks bend down and worship same as their centuries ago ancestors. Yup, there goes God on his golden chariot, flying cross the sky to keep them warm and grow their crops. Gee, ain't God a swell guy?

Not so much for him. Religion to him equals just another form of enslavement, especially if you female. Problem is, females often got a different take…

O'Rourke had chaffed at Thompson's accusation. Took a little doing, but he ignored the urge to smack the skinny, little brat silly. Wasn't the Christian thing, as Aunt Maude would have put it. Though even one as full of the gospel as she might still have threatened to snatch a knot in that jerk, a truly noteworthy feat he himself had only heard of, never witnessed. As far as he knew, she never did actually snatch any knots in anybody. He was certain he'd have heard about something so wonderous.

However, what he had witnessed would have amazed many. What wonders she could have accomplished while beating the black off this Air Force pinhead or in this case, beating the blonde off. "Whap, bap, slap!" Maude really knew her business. Himself, he momentarily reveled in the pleasant feeling this thought radiated throughout his being. Saddened, he wished she were still around to radiate even more…

As far as him doing the job himself; it was only a minor urge, but boy did the sensation feel great. Violence does have its uses, sometimes for the good. He actually did not care the slightest what this nerdish, anemic-looking paleface thought. This was one of the "Indians", as his father, Henry had called hostile subordinates. Fully embracing Henry's counsel, JP was only about dealing with the "Chiefs".

"Religion has felled more trees than Paul Bunyan." He remembered also his mentor Shiro's words. They reminded that life is nothing but a pyramid scheme. Everyone tries to climb atop the shoulders of others to succeed. They use nearly every trick and tactic until they reach the pinnacle where there can only be one and they're pissed to find God ain't about to move over. Thompson seemed one of those having this problem …big time.

Still, he could understand the man's position. It was a natural conclusion. In fact, he would possibly conclude the same, were he on the outside of this issue. However, he was unfortunately not outside this issue. He was caught up in its vortex, being pulled down in the midst of the scrum.

Tina had been his soul mate, his lover. But that was then. Over these long years he had accepted the fact that she would never, could never be his again. Not in the same way. She would only come to him when she needed and then be off again to her world outside his. If she could find happiness with another he would wish her well.

But then she had come to him once again. Briefly, for sure, but she had come to cling to him, to love with him. There was a message in there somewhere. Perhaps her only message had been one of goodbye, perhaps. But to him it told of uncertainty and then there was her "other". There was something about this quirky, little man --other than those odd idiosyncrasies-- that bugged him as well.

It was not just the fact that he was strange. Strange just means different and he was one to know, because he was also considered different, sometimes very different. What actually it was that bugged him about the man he could not place a finger. It was more subliminal than physical.

So he did not blanch in the face of DIA opinion to the contrary --not only because people his complexion never really do that, turn pale that is—but mainly because his expectations barely left the ground, as far as government bureaucracies are concerned.

They did their research, easily discovering that –at the time of the theft-- Morano was on a junket, off to Alaska with that state's junior Senator and a few other politicians for some undisclosed business affair or another. They even delved into Morano's past dealings, finding not so much a parking ticket to blemish. But their truths did not sway him. Truth be told, neither did his argument sway them: "That's why it's called 'Planning' when you plan to do something. You know, like in advance!"

It was frustrating all around, but he was loath to abandon his point, though neither did he rant or rave. "Focus and articulate", had urged Shiro. "Inflammatory references only create division. If it is not division you are looking for, do not use inflammatory references."

Despite hot, passionate emotions and a naturally combative desire, O'Rourke remembered his mentor's sage advice and complied. Even when confronted by these latest examples of stubborn, one track-mindedness, he stayed the course. Tempted though he was, not once did he raise his voice or fault Thompson's inbred appearance to the relationship between his father and sister-mamma. The suggestion that Peterson pull his block head out his hambone ass so he could see what's what, remained well down in his lower levels, never once even burping to freedom.

Never did he suggest any of those things that bade passage to revelation. Instead, he quietly explained his rationale and then offered his services to help them by doing exactly that which he had suggested needed doing ... in other words, "my way or the highway".

Again the General sided with him, although his reluctance showed more noticeably this time and again his decision thoroughly confused and perturbed his subordinates. They left the meeting in his office still shaking their heads; mentally shaking their heads, that is, out of deference to his superior rank. But both Peterson and Thompson believed that he was playing this operation a little too loose and fast. In operational terms they labeled this type decision-making, as "cowboy", indicating that he was shooting from the hip. But when one has the biggest gun, it is not always necessary to aim carefully in order to do a great deal of damage and in this decision; Burton's was the biggest gun.

Burton bade O'Rourke to sit with him a while after the other men had left. Despite some misgivings, he had decided to put his personal touch on this operation; the urges winning out. He casually lit his pipe --this one a fine-grained, Tonino Facono, Corsican briar—blowing a few wreaths into the acoustic tiled ceiling above his polished, mahogany desk. Then, taking in his newly recruited charge he began to tell a tale of long ago.

"John, you don't remember me, I take after my father. He didn't age well either." He paused to smile and to slowly puff another ring into the air, this one encircling his gray hair like a wreath that seemed reluctant to dissipate. "But when I was a shave tail, wet-behind-the-ears, First Lieutenant in front of a rifle platoon in South Vietnam, I almost stopped aging altogether. My platoon was ambushed, thanks to their dumbassed, bound for glory leader and shot near to pieces. We were all gonna die and it was my fault. We were backed against some hill number that I don't remember, with a few hundred VC about to overrun us, when four of the prettiest birds I have ever seen, swooped down and made Charlie go away. They actually made him go all the way, to hell!"

JP had waited outside the emetic operating room for hours. Large fans replacing a failed air conditioning system blew odorous samples of ensanguined, disinfectant agents to mix with noxious vapors emanating from his own petroleum soaked, Nomex flight suit each time the double doors were opened by a medical staff person racing in or out. There were several operations going on simultaneously within the confines. Typically, Mickey's was not the only casualty this day, just the only one which mattered most to his pilot. He maintained vigil, refusing food, conversation and attempts to disarm him, awaiting the surgeon's outcome. He absent-mindedly twirled his forty-five caliber cannon, occasionally field stripping it, reassembling, then reloading and twirling it again. Although many nervous glances they cast in his direction, it seemed no one dare voice displeasure.

Every now and again he would jump to his feet as some medical staffer scurried out the doors. His insides almost pinball mimicry as major parts of him jangled with nervous twitches that originated from deeply rooted forebodings of despair. He tried to ignore the fatigue and focus on things around him, for each time he closed his eyes the same gaunt spectre reappeared, its bony white, finger pointing accusingly directly at him. In his heart the sense of failure exerted a nearly overpowering influence on his emotions, but he stalwartly refused to break down even as eerily voiced cries of "failure, failure, failure", rang in his fruitlessly evading ears. How many times had he nearly killed them?

Used to be a forest down there. Nothing but green surrounding green, far as eyes see. Now it's more like desert spotted with a few trees here 'n there. Agent Orange is a stone killer. Yeah, his mind' s eye exaggerated a little, but not much more'n a little.

At least up where he roamed nobody was calling him mi dang. Pronounced Me Dang means black folk down there. Up here might as well call him Ma, the Vietnamese word for Phantom. He liked that. Maybe a little tame and gender wrong, but suited his emotion, "Ma whipping yo ass, rice picker!"

Wasn't like he hated rice nor people who harvested or made it their staple. He was more a southern fried chicken fan. He kinda went his own way, like with most life choices.

Beaucoup dien cau dau or boocoo dinky dau for crazy head, yeah they could call him that and they probably be right. He definitely wasn't who most considered traditional. Didn't much care. His strive was only to be best.

Simple. He hated bullies. Bullies of any type, whether wife-beating husbands, big kids picking on little kids and even big countries picking on smaller, weaker ones. So they had him at beginning.

Didn't bother him that he'd never even met someone from either Vietnams, north or south. The bigger kid from the north was beating up the littler kid in the south, sign him up!

Ah, but politics was (and still is) an unknowable, senseless entity. It made no sense and never will! Now a days cyber bullies some of the worst!

However, reality trumps even political...

The AN/APQ-72 Fire Control Radar in the F-4B Phantom's AERO-One Able System had an advertised capability to detect a target at two hundred miles in SEARCH mode and to lock onto and automatically track a target at over fifty miles, but both those abilities are seriously degraded by ground clutter return from trees and mountains and from atmospherics ---such as clouds, dust, precipitation, children's birthday balloons, et cetera. So ranges of less than one hundred miles in SEARCH, and less than forty miles in TRACK, are more the norm. The other problem with radar is its propensity to alert the guys on the other end of its presence.

O'Rourke's consciousness was drawn into the round, phosphorescent display just below his forward windscreen. Its B-scan resembled a horizontal line that painted pictures of the forward sky with every back and forth sweep of the radar antenna. His active imagination detected a role change. He was puzzled by the Communist's actions. What was this guy doing up there? He had the sinking suspicion, whatever the reason; he would not be altogether appreciative.

Neither hunter nor hunted could yet see the other and possibly only one knew his assigned, role. But, as the large Marine jet closed the distance, there appeared little doubt to which side victory had been decreed. The only problem was they weren't certain the bad guys on the other side understood this. Mickey wasn't even sure he could withstand the waiting. He felt uneasy. A dryness in his throat and queasiness in his stomach held sway where before had been elation and satisfaction. He had already found and locked onto the target, his scope presentation had changed to show vertical and horizontal lines that intersected at the target's location and a small circle surrounding the location to depict the optimum firing angles for the AIM-7 Sparrow missiles they carried. Somewhat satisfied he could now sit back as an observer while JP finished the job. But, as he looked down at the screen to watch the automatic tracking presentation, then up and outside at the sky to check for other dangers, the dryness in his throat threatened to choke him.

No more bravado—only apprehension. Mickey was no coward. He just reacted differently towards the various roles they played in their assigned game of aerial combat. The fleeting sensations of power engendered in him during air-to-ground assaults disappeared completely in air-to-air engagements. Moreover, timorousness embraced him, usurping his resolve. Possibly it was the uniqueness, where death may only be microseconds away.

Up here, amongst the sky lords, the hunter is never positive whether someone else thought him as the prey. Up here there manifested the tiny, inner voice of fear.

Contrary to his voiced displeasure with bombing missions, deep inside he understood that the dangers there existed primarily during the bombing run on a known target. On the other hand, dogfights were very different and constantly evolving affairs. He appreciated that these feelings in him were counter to most fighter jock mentalities. Perhaps those contributed to the Marine Corps' decision to refuse his candidacy for the front seat job … every backseater is a front seat wannabe.

Somehow, some lowlife determined that he, Michael Watson, Stanford graduate, was better suited for a backup role and had him kicked to the curb! Total quandary within the high-strung, sandy-haired youth. Nothing to do with eyesight. His could challenge bald eagle vision. So wasn't that!

Other than with a conniving girlfriend, he'd never been secondary. But now not a main player, just a backup where forces beyond his ability to control would mollify. How they know the feelings and deep down terrors that persisted? How they figure that inevitability would ever prevail? Who they interview that dropped the dime 'bout mamma …not Lindsey?

Sure his tendency toward caution did not wholly overawe the fatalistic fascination for the inevitable holding held sway within. But death was never his major concern. Rather, the possibility of being maimed or dismembered was ever the nightmarish doom haunting his psyche's nether regions. But if Death was to happen, he wanted to witness it fully, to see it coming.

That he did not seek Death, nor consciously sway from its path --only from the path of its more cruel sisters—was a powerful force within his mentality. They should understand such. He relished life, not longevity, never old age. Shouldn't they see these things empowering?

Took a bit. Challenging a bit. But eventually not an issue. Also empowering was a tremendous faith in his pilot.

O'Rourke always marveled at the implanted efficiency of his weapons platform. It could destroy hostiles beyond his vision while emitting spurious signals to confuse an enemy seeking to destroy him. Though old and nearly outdated, it remained a very effective tool when employed correctly. Now it exemplified this with deadly purpose.

Relative to the U.S. fighter, a glance at his scope revealed the target's position, speed and altitude. He noted it remained at twelve o'clock, slightly lower altitude, soaring leisurely along, undaunted by the impending doom.

"Cool!" He thought. "Just maybe Charlie won't run before we get in range." He alternated watching both sky and scope—making minor course changes at Mickey's suggestion. Even on such a clear day –only wisps of cloud cover down below ten thousand feet-- their prey was still outside visual range. MIG-21s are so small and sleek they usually on you before you got the visual. But even though beyond their eyesight, they knew where he was and figured they knew what he was.

Uncle Ho no longer sent his old stuff south. MIG-17s did not tangle well with the mighty Phantoms. He would rely on his best, the Mach 2, Mikoyan-Gurevich developed MIG-21, NATO codenamed "Fishbed". Their only question was why he was? Uncle Ho liked to keep his fighters inside North Vietnam where they received coverage from NVA ground control radar systems and ZSU-23 Anti-Aircraft Artillery. Phantom Flyers feared Xa Thu more than the MIG. That was wise considering the ground to air gunners had bagged far more Phantoms, by an order of magnitude.

The first thing Marine fighter jocks learned when they landed "In Country", well before their first orientation flight, was that if you dive below ten thousand feet after a MIG up north of the Demilitarized Zone you will most likely be introduced to commie triple-A waiting to swat you like a fly.

That "G" band growl from your Threat Warning Receiver would come moments before parts that make your aircraft fly began shredding all around you. Some smart aleck squadron mate (probably your sponsor) would describe it in a manner akin to Aesop's Fables meet Major Henry Livingston Junior, maybe something like: "there you are in the sky with your galloping beast, been boring holes all day or an hour at least, when out to the north comes a target to treasure, you spring to the dance and you challenge his measure; you got this chump buggered, right dead in your site, make him soon one dead duckie, fo' he know 'bout the fight. 'Bout to pickle your missile, 'bout to fi-yar him up. Kill a commie for mommie, sho as Skippy's a pup. But then what to your wondering ear should you hear, but a threat warning growl, Zoo twenty-three, loud an' clear? And alas and alack, oh me and oh my, you're a prisoner of war boy, just too dumb ta know why!"

The speed and flight profile he flew confirmed that this was more than likely a MIG-21, one of the deadliest, most purposeful fighter planes ever designed and a handful for any U.S. aircraft. So why was he rolling south like he was out for a Sunday drive? One other possibility and, another reason Uncle Ho shepherded his flock, was to reduce the temptation for defection.

O'Rourke began to wonder whether he was about to take a pot shot at a guy trying to change sides at the dinner table. Maybe it's a good thing, by rules, he couldn't shoot 'til he could see the whites of those slanted eyes.

The rules of engagement, a.k.a., how to fight a war with your left arm and right leg tied behind you, forbade American fighter pilots from firing their beyond visual range missiles until they could visually identify the target. As with most Vietnam-era rules mandated by the staff weenies in the "Puzzle Palace", these particular ROE greatly evened up the playing field to the benefit of communist MIGs. In truth these rules resulted from limitations within the Identification Friend or Foe circuitry carried in fighters as well as in the EC-121 Warning Star which had tragically caused a couple of U.S. aircraft to be shot down by other U.S. aircraft. But instead of fixing the technical and operational problems with the IFF devices, the Pentagon Wonder Boys simply reverted back to strategies employed in every air war up to and including Korea. See 'em before you shoot 'em! Get in close! Of course that's where the lighter, smaller craft have more of an edge. Grrr-eat Wonder Boys! Final conclusion, advantage MIG!

The range had decreased to ten miles; O'Rourke's jet was now at twelve thousand feet and heading on a bearing of three-two-zero towards the MIG. "Tally-Ho Mick. I see him. Eleven O'clock high!" He banked slightly right, setting up to take the head-on shot at the MIG's port-forward quarter, hopefully before the Communist's noticed them creeping into picture frame.

This should be a sweet shot, slightly upwards, from his lower elevation, the reflected radar energy would guide his Sparrows without any clutter return from the jungle below and really fuk up this guy's whole day.

The Sidewinder is a much better close in dogfighting missile, but he did not have one aboard, this beginning as a strike mission, fulla iron bombs. So he cautiously sought to ensure that he optimized his flight profile and stayed well inside his radar guided missile's parameters.

The HUD's symbology showed a circle with notched cross hairs that he maneuvered to keep the MIG's image within. No snap shots. Play it cautious, Just a tad bit more right rudder.

Time. He reached his left hand out to his Armament Panel, flipping on the MISSILE PWR switch, sending continuous wave RF energy from the AN/APA-157 system out the AN/APQ-72's nutating antenna's spinning feedhorn to reflect off the target and back to the seeker head in his forward, portside Sparrow missile. The Communist's reaction was unmistakable. Mere seconds after the CW energy began radiating; the elevation indicators on their dual scopes dropped sharply and the "B" sweep beam indicators swung to the left. The antenna's angle and error signal resolvers nearly overdrove the radar's mechanical limiters to follow the twisting, diving MIG's direction.

"There he goes JP! He knows we're up here!" Yelled Mickey, excitedly.

"Stay with him Mick!" Replied O'Rourke as he shoved forward the dual throttles, simultaneously tweaking the joystick down and a little left, hot on the pursuit. Responding instantly, his sleek craft picked up speed in the shallow dive, devouring distance to its target. Abruptly, Mickey's radar presentation began to chatter, spasmodically bouncing green, phosphorescent light onto his visor. A red light marked "AOJ" for Angle on Jam, began to intermittently flash, alarming the somewhat morbid Mickey. But only a little. He was cool …they made a great team.

"He's jamming JP, AOJ's on, but we still got him!

"Nearly there Mickey, hang tuff!"

"We still got him!" Absently repeated Mickey, as his radar system's agility caused rapid, automatic frequency shifts through its operating frequencies in the I and J bands. The pseudo-random changes in frequency effectively extended the radar system's radiated power over its full operating bandwidth, while it actually used only a relatively narrow instantaneous bandwidth at any one time. In effect these features significantly reduced the capability of the MIG's jamming system, forcing the jammer to deal with a much wider spectrum, diluting its power.

To the young RIO, impressive though these features were, they were less so than the fact that their adversary was now headed in the opposite direction. He felt much better now that the MIG had turned and was running towards Cambodia. His apprehension lessened slightly. He always felt better when the enemy ran. The fact that usually they made it back to North Vietnamese airspace before the American's got within range did not matter as much to him. The spectre of his charred form, his skin held on by the few remaining strings of green flight suit – discolored and wreathed by rising black smoke-- again reared its ugly face to him. It usually haunted his dreams, but lately had been a more frequent daylight visitor. He hated the vision which always sought to steal his resolve, his manhood, to turn him into a sobbing child. But that was old him.

Junior grade Mickey had always felt uncomfortable feelings of helplessness with all the variables with which erudite dogfighters are forced to contend, slicing through the azure skies as he struggled to hold onto the radarscope's two, shiny metal handles while being bounced around by the maneuvering jet. Understandable. Supposed the missile missed and the MIG got behind them. Momentarily came back at him and he shuddered involuntarily all the while maintaining watch of the scope and of the outside sky. He consoled himself that shit like that seldom happened to anyone anymore. Especially flying this kinda jet, with this kinda guy!. "Suck it up Watson!"

Mickey's desires were never farther apart from O'Rourke's. While Mickey hated air-to-air combat, O'Rourke preferred it to the ground support role. Too many people down there throwing stuff up at you. Below ten thousand feet you had the ZSU-23s, below three thousand or so you had tiny, little folk carrying old muskets and older bows and arrows. Shit flew from everywhere. Airedales called it Indian Country.

He'd much rather take his chances up high against MIGs and SA-2 missiles. You could see them coming and react accordingly, usually, but who could see a bullet? Even if they used tracer rounds you would still only see the tracers, not the four or five inert rounds in between. To the VC and NVA, didn't matter a bit. They just out to kill something!

"Missile's hot Mickey! We gonna ram thirty-five thousand dollars' worth of Sparrow up his ass!" His voice expressed none of the excitement that coursed in rampant streams throughout his being. He was home free ...he hoped.

The speeding MIG dove sharply, jinking left and right and shot low over the trees --under four thousand feet above ground level where the American radar would lose some effectiveness—headed home. Both Phantom Phlyers knew now that this guy definitely not trying to defect. Mickey's scope presented new information as the AERO-1 Able tracking devices adjusted automatically—revealing much to the two airmen.

"He's picking up speed JP!"

"On him Mick! Going supersonic!" O'Rourke fire walled his throttles, simultaneously he selected the Wing Stores Jettison switch and punched the button, dumping the empty bomb racks and both three hundred-seventy gallon wing tanks, that were also now empty. Free of the useless drag, the Phantom leaped friskily after its quarry—anxious for reward, filled with the bloodlust. Both men watched with a detached sense of awareness as their aircraft gobbled the distance between itself and the MIG. The wolf after the rabbit, but this rabbit also carried fangs and the Phantom Phlyers knew well their nature. They also knew those tools of death would be little use to a fleeing adversary.

All at once his radio crackled to life, bringing a disgruntled curse from O'Rourke's lips, nearly drowning out the call sign as it was urgently repeated. "Come in Magic-Two, over!"

"Now what!" He muttered. "Don't tell me the Air Force wants in again!" He was determined this time it was no dice. They had a habit of calling off Marines to sub their Barrier Combat Air Patrol or BARCAP guys. "Yeah, this is Magic-Two go ahead Bunkhouse!" He felt something bad was about to happen. Flycatcher was seldom that formal.

"Get the hell outta there, JP! You got big trouble! Bandits, two o'clock! No IFF, definitely unfriendly!"

"How many and how far?"

"Three, bearing one seven-five, angels zero-niner, forty miles and closing fast. Break a port one-eighty and push it!" Yelled the Flycatcher. His attempted calm was startled away by his shouting, imploring the Phantom to speed away from certain death. "Gun it JP! Balls to the wall! Vector one-eight-zero!"

"Damn! When it rains it just wets everything!" Cursed the pilot. "What you think Mick, do we oughta shit 'n git or do we got time?"

"Up to you John," responded a surprisingly calm Mickey Watson. Though unable to use his radar to find the new players without breaking the lock on their initial target, his eyes automatically began scanning the sky off their right-forward wing for tiny dots, which would signify danger or impending disaster. He could not see the Gomers, but that told him little. It was six to one and a half dozen to the other. "What the hell, they can't eat us!"

JP grinned beneath his oxygen mask and rammed the throttles over the ramps to maximum power. The big jet rocketed forward, its speed passing Mach two, a silver blur to observant earth dwellers. Sitting stop two, roaring fireballs both men alternated watching their scopes and the starboard sky. Ahead their target was but a tiny dot against the horizon. Now less than forty miles away, up around nine thousand feet AGL were three uninvited interlopers. O'Rourke found himself straining ears as well as eyes. No matter that, at his present speed, impossible to hear the approaching enemy. Impossible to hear his own engines. Back to reality, he thought, "this is gonna be close."

O'Rourke waited until the "Missile Ready" light illuminated, indicating the portside-forward weapon had locked onto its target, then grasped the joystick tightly with his right hand—index finger poised. "Musta been a setup and I walked us right into it!"

Hard eyes like steel flints. He grinned a second time, this one a decidedly unfriendly smile which evidenced that his "Evil" had indeed returned and predicted ..."well, they may yet regret that!"

"Six miles to target John, can't miss!" Mickey sounded almost absent-minded as he droned his monotone speech. O'Rourke grinned again. If they lived through this he'd never let his RIO live it down. If they lived. He pulled the trigger, felt the aircraft lurch and watched a fire-breathing projectile speed away, in seconds out of sight. Five seconds, became ten. He sweated—a cold aching sweat—fifteen seconds! Seemed like forever.

The major negative of the Sparrow missile, is its semi-active homing capability, thus its reliance on the aircraft's radar to illuminate and provide steering vectors to the target. In this case, O'Rourke and Watson had no choice but to keep their radar locked on the target, which meant keeping their aircraft pointed at the fleeing MIG, which was now fleeing in the direction of its onrushing mates.

"Do it baby!" JP's silent prayers paralleled Mickey's as both men fervently hoped their toils had not been in vain. But when the silent variety did not suffice, out from his downward curved lips spat a snarled, "Come on baby!"

Answering O'Rourke's voiced appeal, a brilliant, orange-hued ball of flames erupted. It there marked the last known, earthly position of one North Vietnamese flown, Chinese supplied, Soviet-built, MIG-21 aircraft.

Death's bony finger --in one impetuous, implacable slash-- had ripped a loving husband and father, a budding poet and warrior from this life into an eternity of non¬existence. So quickly was this accomplished that Death scarcely had time to admire its handy work before determining that this latest charge should not make such a harrowing journey alone. There were others within opportune proximity and though most were unenthused with the idea of sating the immediate desires of Death, ain't always their choice when they line up.

Maybe one JP O'Rourke had been picked for first in that line, but he wasn't having it. Perhaps some later time, but now ain't that time. No time to gloat either. Gotta jet!

He never gave second thought to his kill, only how to boogie outta the immediate area. The glory of the event, along with other such nonessential trivia, must wait. Suddenly, however, he felt maddeningly reckless. Why run and risk a missile up the butt? Inverting the Phantom, he dove for the trees, his decided direction, toward the onrushing MIGs. A quiet thought percolated, no brag, just conviction, kind of a warrior's rote that went, "Yea, though I walk through the valley of the shadow of death, I will fear no evil …cause I'm the baddest mutha fucka in the valley!"

"What you doing JP? They less than fifteen miles away." Mickey had remained calm until now, but standard practice called for standing a Phantom on its tail and blasting into the upper stratosphere where they held most of the advantages. Down low the MIGs could....

"Pick a good one Mick!"

Mickey killed his morbid imagination, hoping the enemy would not inflict similar afflictions on his body. Deciding to close his mouth and let partner do his thing, Mickey locked his radar onto the center dot. After all JP was driving this bus and JP never acted without thinking objectively

...at least most of the time.

O'Rourke's active mind could picture three communist fighter pilots salivating as he drove towards their greater number above the lush, blue-green veldt four thousand feet below. He knew their eagerness to splatter him all over the landscape, to kill him. He felt Death's bony touch at his shoulder, ice cold chilling deep into his bowels. He only wished to change all their minds. He'd give Death an alternative...

"Fox two!" The right forward missile launcher's electrical squib fired, ejecting five hundred pounds of missile from its semi-recessed, fuselage cavity into the air stream where the rocket motor fired sending twelve feet of death down range.

His imagination went active with the rocket motor on his messenger of death. He could sense the sleek missile's seeker locking onto the reflected RF energy, could feel the fins moving up and down to steer the Sparrow's business end directly into MIG central. Nothing in his demeanor evidenced a trapped or cornered quarry. Rather, his was the determined mindset of the hunter. The one thought which kept replaying in his mind was an age-old adage, "when engaging in a game of Fuk-Fuk, one must ensure he brings the biggest dick!"

Maneuvering to keep his radar's energy on the target, he felt like the last time he rode the Cyclone at Coney Island; now bouncing around, now weightless, breath now coming in gasps. Like, yowsers! He had to concentrate on his breathing to ensure he did not hold his breath. A large plume erupted in the sky at their twelve o'clock level position. The remaining two blips diverged and dove even closer to the carpet in case more missiles were headed their way. "Boo-La, Boo-La! Got him Mick! Now let's get the hell outta here!"

He chopped both throttles with his left hand, pushing hard forward and left on the joystick in his right, while simultaneously kicking in the left rudder pedal, going inverted before leveling his rudders and jerking hard back into his stomach. His eyes watched the ground coming up at him while his prayers hoped none of the trees below were very tall. At their speed this was going to be close, that is if his plane held together.

Half-praying to the Gods of McDonnell-Douglas, half-listening to the groaning protests vibrating out from the airframe that they had designed, that he was overstressing, he forced twenty-five tons of aircraft into a gut wrenching Split-S maneuver at nearly one thousand miles an hour.

Air pressure and centrifugal forces collectively threatened to tear the flaperons and spoilers from the wings and the stabilators from the tail, with both groaning wings nearly agreeing to chaperon their escape. But true testament to the builder's craft, it held together and eventually pulled out of the inverted dive with room to spare above the reaching trees.

A glance at the compass rose confirmed the Heading had changed towards due south —no cares for precise measurements bothered him— one-eighty, one –eighty-five, two-zero-zero, it did not matter to him as long as it was away from the bad guys. Hard to see the damned thing anyway when pulling heavy Gs.

Throttles were full forward again, over the ramp into afterburner. His left hand snaked out, first finger punching the red button, firing squibs that jettisoned all external stores. He absently hoped they might land on one of the Gomers down below shooting their triple-A up at him. But he was going much too fast for pajama-suiters aiming through iron sights. Besides, his embarrassed-self remembered, they didn't have anything left to jettison. Those external stores were long gone! The aircraft was as slick as F-4Bs could get. He hoped that would be slick enough.

Gravitational forces helped increase his energy; the airspeed again exceeded Mach 2 as he brought the stick back forcing a climb at forty-five degrees. Extremely high gravity forces concaved O'Rourke's face—hollowing his eye sockets—while pulling life-sustaining blood from his brain downward toward his legs. Gray images blurring, he fought to stay awake. Grunting out hard exhales to tighten his stomach and abdomen muscles to help stem the blood drain. Fighting to survive he literally willed his brain back from the stupor. His anti-G suit inflated rigidly, helping in its part to force the blood back toward his head, countering the relentless, downward pull. He became dizzy, his eyes fuzzy, losing their focus --seemingly for minutes or was it hours—but actually only momentarily. Straining greatly, he fought back the tempting urge to sleep.

Looming ominous in his steadily sharpening mental focus were imagined pictures of the two remaining communist airplanes. At first wondering what the hell he was doing, then veering away before the expected Sparrow or Sidewinder arrived with another deadly purpose, each pilot was now most assuredly in chase. They could not know that he was out of missiles, but with his ass end to them, they need not care.

He was at first perplexed at being still alive, half expecting the shock of an exploding Atoll missile any moment, ripping him from this reality into a questionable afterlife. His tanks were bordering on poverty, but he kept the throttles maxed out. Climbing through thirty thousand feet AGL, he wondered how close the MIGs were behind and just how far a Soviet-built Atoll could fly and how accurate. He had been briefed once on their capabilities –along with a host of other Soviet weaponry, tactics and doctrine-- but could not recall any of the details at this moment. Hopefully he was already outside the infrared missiles' envelope.

All slicked outside, now that every bit of ordnance was used up and the empty bomb racks blown off the underwing stations, his sky stead's speed indicator was pushing Mach two-point-five, over sixteen hundred miles per hour. The hurricane winds flowing over and about his canopy's exterior were completely silent as their sound was left far in his rear for those trailing to possibly hear. Not even the sounds caused by various cockpit vibrations in the space immediately surrounding him could be heard. This last part not due to their exceeding the speed of sound, but to the thunderous thumping of his own heartbeat as its energy nervously pounded against the inside of his chest as if fighting to come out and see for itself how closely behind were those who trailed him.

"If they did not get him soon they could forget it," he thought. Still looking up and out at the three rearview mirrors positioned just slightly ahead inside the canopy at the ten and two o'clock positions. He could not see them, but he knew the Gomers fer sure pissed that their game o' "Fox and Hounds" had failed. And that's how games sometimes go. Sometimes the Fox gotta win, tuff titty says the kitty …milk still good!

Nose up at a forty-degree angle, both afterburners blazing, the Marine Phantom climbed, and kept climbing—streaking breathlessly through a cloudless sky to over sixty thousand feet before he leveled off. Now all sounds external to their cockpits –like engine noises, exploding missiles that missed and communistic curses—were well behind them and could never catch up at this speed. But two pairs of eyes still stared up at twin sets of rear-facing mirrors, while two minds mirrored each other in silent prayer. "Go baby!"

Mickey, stifling a rising feeling of horror, observed the fuel flow meter on his forward instrument panel pick up speed as twin J-79's insatiably gulped the high octane JP-5 kerosene faster than he thought possible. "We down to 'bout three hundred gallons JP. Pretty soon you gonna be the only JP in this thang! I think you best slow this ol' horse down or we won't be riding th' range much longer! Less there's a handy tanker nearby." He meekly added.

"If those bad guys catch us, we'll need more than a filling station, Mick!" O'Rourke was already thumbing his radio. "What about it Bunkhouse? Do I still got nasties on my tail? Over!"

"You got more guts than a prairie dog in heat, Sky Juggie. But don't fret the bad guys. BARCAP will intercept in two. Over!"

"Thanks Bunkhouse. Throttling down."

"Anytime you Jugheads need a hand. Take care JP!"

"Been nice flying Flycatcher Airways! Later buddy." O'Rourke checked his gauges for the third time in as many minutes, fuel level readings being at premium. "Ever try to land one of these things empty Mick?"

"Good thing I got on brown pants JP! That last guy didn't want to quit. He scared the blue shits outta me. Anyway, I got one hand on the ol' face curtain and the other on my Teddy. If this thing so much as sputters, me'n T-Bear be punching out in no time!"

"Don't leave me Mick! You know how I hate drafts. You really got a teddy bear?" Despite their jokes, both knew that, aerodynamically, Phantoms fly somewhat similar to twenty-five ton rocks, figure about one foot down for every one and a half feet forward. Without the twin blowtorches lit…. well, they'd have to leave their cockpits very quickly and there'd be little choice in their picking spots to drop the iron bird. Air refueling was a non-starter, as no tankers were close enough. He could have diverted to Da Nang, but the feeling of invincibility ingrained in all fighter pilots had returned and he was being stubborn… again.

"Hey Mick, you know how far a Phantom can glide?"

"Yeah, half the distance to the nearest landing field!" Mickey's voice did not sound very enthusiastic and came over the intercom at a much lower timbre than usual. He realized his pilot was only attempting to cheer him up, but visions of bailing out over some VC controlled area or of being injured by the force of the ejection, left him humorless.

While O'Rourke nursed his dwindling fuel supply—flying as economically as possible—Mickey glanced at the two, black and yellow striped, rubberized loops above his head. Taking one last sector scan for weather or traffic, he thumbed the radar antenna to zero degrees elevation angle, unlatched the radar antenna hand control and slid it back into the stowed position. He was taking no unnecessary chances with his legs. His radar would still provide some coverage. But if it came down to ejecting, he would only have to pop out. Too many RIO's were still limping around after busting a kneecap during a hasty egress.

The hand control was responsible for more crippled, back seat flyers than the Count de Sade's leg machine. He wanted no part of it. It was designed to automatically retract and stow upon initiation of the ejection sequence, but design was one thing, actuality was another thing entirely.

Low hanging clouds obscured their view forward. Mickey ran down the pre-landing checklist to ensure he would be ready for landing or punching out, whichever was de rigueur. He became so engrossed with his chores, he very nearly did eject when O'Rourke dropped full flaperons as they crossed over Landing Zone Charlie Brown, just north of Chu Lai. The sudden rumble of interrupted airflow took him very much by surprise.

Lower now, they could make out the hilly terrain north of the base, many hilltops sprouted artillery pieces pointing west and north. Army soldiers manning them, growing larger as the altitude decreased. Passing under their left wing, the greenish-blue surface of the South China Sea – foam crested waves speeding towards shore-- told them they were nearly home. Ten minutes later the weary pilot nosed his sputtering jet (it really was not sputtering, but they felt that it was) up to a revetment, set the parking brake, shut down the engines, gathered his wits and climbed slowly out. Walking off the flight line towards the Operations Shack, he turned to look at his resting steed and the horde of techs and mechs scrambling around and inside it, popping open panels here, repacking the drogue chute there, swinging open the massive radome to unveil its huge electronics package within and performing the thousand and one tasks necessary to ready their charge for its next mission. He reflected the fact that these young men who made this complicated beast work so well, were the only reason he still existed in this life. "I gotta get them a couple kegs a beer!" He decided.

He mentally saluted them while blowing an affectionate kiss to the jet. "Git somethin' special fo' my baby, too!"

Back outside the ER. He regained himself enough to again hate himself. Some guys fuk up a wet dream! His F-4 was probably never gonna fly again, just like his RIO was probably never gonna walk again and here he go Scott free, only things hurt are his feelings!

It was not until the doctor walked proudly out to inform him of his success that O'Rourke felt cause for relief. The joy flooded throughout him and he silently thanked God for giving them both the strength to succeed. But then the news of his friend's sacrifice brought sobering to his thoughts as realization's arrival flushed out joy's temporary hold. It was his belief that one man's actions bring about reactions that affect other men. All fingers pointed back to him. Everything that happened was his fault. His screw up! He earned his partner a shiny new Purple Heart medallion …in exchange for a foot.

Him they gave the Navy Cross for heroism. Something about selfless devotion and bringing back a crippled aircraft with a crippled companion aboard rings all sorts of bells for the rank and file. A brief visit from the local Navy shrink assured him that none of the earlier misfortunes contributed to this latest casualty. That these things and many more happen during war. Life sucks!

O'Rourke did not believe any of it. But he eventually accepted his Karma. His fate was to live a charmed life devoid of close friends. Close friends would either be killed or crippled or divorce you. So he decided not to accept any other close friendships, ever!

Returning to Thailand, he got a new airplane with a new RIO and finished out the majority of his tour without killing or maiming anyone on his side of the fence. A minor incident concerning the couple Migs he and Mickey shot down somewhere close to the Cambodian border drew some heat. But those things happen.

Mickey finished his tour in Vietnam on that same hospital bed, eventually being evacuated stateside to recuperate at the Balboa Naval Hospital in San Diego. In ten months he was already walking with the prosthesis, though he'd never again jump into his fighter plane. Then --shortly after receiving medical clearance-- resigned his commission on the advice of some very influential people searching for just the right sort of war hero to mold into a prime, political candidate. They need not have bothered to concern themselves.

Mickey had no need of king makers. The influence of his missing foot provided its own persuasive impetus. Any ideas of future military activities for him had been curtailed by Communist fire. Additionally, any pre-war political agenda had also been destroyed in the air above Southwest Asia. Not included on the casualty list though, that supreme sensation of dancing above the clouds. He had become forever molded.

He knew his hero flyer status was done for good. However, nothing the Cong nor the NVA had thrown at him could dissuade his desire to cruise the heavens. There at Da Nang's hospital that O'Rourke and Mickey decided that flying was too much a way of life to end so soon.

CHAPTER NINE

Miles High Executive Charter Service was an instant success. It was not unlike many fairy tales ...on the surface. Mickey's father --relieved at his son's easy acceptance of the missing appendage-- poured tremendous sums and energies into the venture. He became their backer and the third partner ...although not a silent one.

With his father's influence as a most important commodity (their capability being the most important commodity) Mickey soon lost himself in the company and it was wonderful! He and JP put in long hours making the three-way partnership into one of Southern California's most exclusive charter companies. Their reputations --aided by an impressive array of medals-- made them very much in demand, indeed.

Miles Watson, II, heir to resplendent wealth and servile philanthropy, found the company more than a business venture --it was almost a fetish. Here-to-fore, his money had always worked for him. Other than stocks and bonds, he had had no real interest in investment. Preferring the life of a philanthropic patron of the arts, he served on the boards of a few regional charitable foundations funding wars on cancer and muscular dystrophy and so on, as well as the Los Angeles Philharmonic Association, regularly supporting concerts at the Hollywood Bowl. But those duties were, by and large, predominately figurehead. Now he was working for his money and the feeling was finer than he would ever have believed.

Whenever the intrepid pair took off for their flights to far corners of the western states, Miles bubbled over with a pride he had never before known. The company gave him an outlet such as no other before and brought him nearer his son than he had ever been, a son who had become more a man than anyone had thought possible ...once freed from a woman's bondage.

Miles --the only child of a patrician California real estate mogul-- learned quickly, firsthand, the perils of matrimony by arrangement. His bride --Eleanor Adams Braithwaite-- was the haughty, beautiful brat of his parent's closest friends. Their marriage was arranged by those friends — particularly those respective mothers-- who saw in them the perfect couple.

Almost from their beginning, he cursed his parents for ever having had such friends. He was totally unappreciative of their talents at matchmaking and hoped they experienced in death what he was forced to experience while living ...a much too literal hell.

He had done his best --repeatedly striving to love her-- to make her love him. But her overbearing arrogance and capricious nature were insurmountable ...nearly as insurmountable as her vivacious body.

For years following their disastrous honeymoon, he would continuingly admonish his instincts for not picking out her true nature in time. She had thrilled him, enticed him, impassioned him, then eschewed him ...refusing his advances more often than not.

After much trial and tribulation, Miles finally surrendered. He submitted to her adamant demands for separate bedrooms and eventually he came to prefer this desolate arrangement. He also, eventually, preferred the company of streetwalkers to that of his own, lovely spouse.

Always, he searched for something or someone, never identifying exactly what it was for which he searched. Cheap booze, cheap trinkets and cheap hotel rooms --for the cheap whores he frequented-- became commonplace with the troubled man. Eventually, he took a mistress.

Miles always regretted his inability to enforce his marital rights. To command and dominate the arrogant bitch, taking her at his leisure instead of hers. But he was never very good at those things. She seemed bred for conflict. He most regretted his ineptness when Michael was born ...end result of one of her arduous moments.\

He wished the moment could have lasted longer. But it didn't. He was as powerless to rend control over his son's rearing, as he was to rest authority over his own household from the oppressive matriarch.

Unable to cope and shunning the suicide suggested by his malevolent better half, Miles directed all his frustrations towards his young mistress. She wasn't beautiful or voluptuous or even overly intelligent. But she was submissive and willing. She accepted his vicious punishments, sexual humiliations and verbal abuses without balking. When he was in a bad way she accepted that this was his way of keeping his sanity. She allowed him to experience the power, the thrust and the fervor of manhood denied him in his own house ...and she loved him, deeply.

Miles maintained this pace for over two years. Always he turned to the woman and always she turned away. Then, he would seek out Jazzy, as he nicknamed Jazmine. After a time, he no longer beat on her --he even began to love her also ...in a way.

Their nondescript relationship might have continued for a much longer period if Eleanor hadn't seen fit to intervene. She ended the illicit affair in a somewhat unique fashion for women engaged in unbeknownst rivalry ...she died.

The call came from Mickey, their only child. His mama named him Michael, like the archangel and did not appreciate when his friends nicknamed him Mickey, he wasn't a mouse or a gangster. She appreciated even less his father's adoption of the sobriquet ...so naturally he only called him that.

She didn't tolerate it in her presence. Actually she'd long gone past tolerating most things from him. But Michael, she would never let go. He was her treasure and as long as he toed her line she would endure nearly every infantile transgression. As long as he never let his harlots nor stains in his undershorts remain overnight. His reputation, as well as, hygiene must remain above reproach, especially any of his breath that ever contacted any parts of her!

Mama got big plans for her big boy and they didn't include nothing bout being, smelling nor acting filthy. It was much too late for his father, if she had to occasionally utter that repulsive word. But at least she profited from his finances and, at least on one occasion, his seed.

He started hating every time the phone rang. It was either somebody selling crypto currency or car warranties. He could do their pitch from memory.

"Surprise, surprise do we got something you sure ta need." First few times he'd given 'em time to stutter their broken English spiel (since most of the tellers sounded Filipino). But nowadays his patience lasted barely past their announcement of the product. "We gonna give you an all expenses cruise to Honolulu ...click!"

Patience was never his virtue. Probably why he had so few friends lately. He barely frequented friendly acquaintances and seldom even those. He barely even knew his son. He belonged to wifie and it would take a act of Congress to get him back, until Mickey got free of the monkey ...and became a Marine!

It was a first. A thing he did entirely on his own. Katie bar the door! Too late, the Mickey is out the barn and never coming back! How'd she lose control like this? She hated this new Mickey ...Michael!

Mickey grew up a sucker for women's suggestions. And true enough, the suggestion came from Eleanor's chief rival, one Lindsey Cranston, who luxuriated in sharing. She shared him with his mother. Their secret pact to build a man out of their little boy …but she also shared the boy with another.

Lindsey was so sensationally alluring she caused upheavals within his young heart. Luxuriously long blonde locks, body built by Michelangelo, beauty by the score, she was all that plus a bag of chips! And her skillset? Let's just say her advancement in years dwarfed impressively her advancement in life …especially the more lascivious areas of life.

Men didn't get rid of Lindsey. Lindsey got rid of them. But she really didn't know what to with her Ex. He'd made starting quarterback and those aren't easy to come by, especially one so good at making her cum! Mickey she liked lot's, sort of. A future with him would set her in good stead with her love interest with wild shopping sprees …unfortunately, that prospect was ended on one wild night.

Doesn't pay to travel one stud muffin's love marks over to another guy's bed. They really don't appreciate that sorta visitation. Mickey didn't appreciate it at all, especially its location! He visited a recruiter the very next day! Pissed on girlfriend and momma in one fell swoop! Erased girlfriend from memory. But he did remember momma…

Driving east on Interstate Ten, Eleanor rattled on busily belaboring the, already battered, ears of a close friend over the phone when her blasé' attitude became terminated for all time by an all too untimely death under the misdirected wheels of a six thousand pound Rolls Royce. Her death --while not wished upon her by Miles-- stirred very few tears from anyone and was untimely only because she had yet to get her point across. In all fairness, it could be easily considered droll that her closest companions' only appreciable dilemma resulted from their argument whether or not the death could still be considered chic once they discovered that the Rolls was from an off-vintage year.

Few mourners graced Eleanor's funeral —not even her Audubon Society cronies-- it was simply not the in thing that year. Many of them equivocated that it simply was poorly timed. They faulted her philandering husband's insouciance that the funeral was held on the same day as their annual Pelagic Trip to Santa Barbara. This further emphasized his lack of appreciation for their work charting habitat and habits of the Northern Fulmar, the Black-vented Sooty and the Pink-footed shearwaters, among others. Seated on wooden benches around the jouncing deck, roughing it, while eating boxed lunches on their way to the island, each lamented her passing while passing bottles of vintage wines.

However, a few of those sufficiently moved to attend, recalled those tears which had been stored and refused exit previously. There was genuine wetness upon the cheeks of more than one of the few present …especially, Miles.

His slender frame remained hunched during the entire proceedings and his haggard, hollow-eyed visage left little doubt of his continued, though puzzling, love for the departed one. He never saw Jazzy again, except to explain and make certain her welfare. His love for her was never more than an extension of his love for his wife. But neither Miles nor Mickey was left unduly shaken by her death.

Though both resented her domination and its overbearing blight, both loved her none-the-less. And it took some getting used to, this newfound freedom. They could sense an uncovering of their innate desires. There seemed to be a general lessening of previous tensions they had not previously recognized. An air of contentment proliferated their bereaved household …but it was so sad that she had to die just so they might know happiness.

O'Rourke did not say anything —especially anything about the interiors of government buildings being non-smoking areas-- but at least he now understood why this man looked so familiar. Somewhere within the cobwebs his face claimed a position of significance, younger and less time-ravaged, but just as prominent in relation to the steel-gray eyes, high cheek bones and determined chin. Despite his protestation to the contrary, the General was still a youthful, handsome man of years who could still turn a pretty woman's head. Nothing weak or anemic here and nobody you'd pick first to challenge in battle. But O'Rourke had met hundreds of people during a war whose distasteful events had been purposefully merged and relegated into shadowy visions haunting the recesses at the edge of his memory. He still could not place him, but gave only token, cursory effort, for he instinctively knew the job would soon be done for him.

The man had seen his share of combat and in more than one theater, this he could see from the rows of ribbons on the General's jacket hanging on a coat rack behind and to the right of his desk. Also immediately behind the General's desk —hanging on the white-painted wall above the mahogany credenza—O'Rourke observed a large painting of a nineteenth century, "Buffalo" Soldier staring sternly out towards the viewer, as if ready to leapt to whatever task was at hand. On his dark blue, blouse sleeves were gold Sergeant-Major chevrons, three up and three down. Belted around his waist above the light-blue trousers hung a black-leather holster holding his Army Colt, forty-five caliber pistol against his right hip and a scabbard with saber against his left. Covering much of the matted, shaggy hair, his silver-grey campaign hat pinned up in the front revealing the crossed rifles and insignia of the Tenth Cavalry. On the credenza itself were miniature replicas of Bradley Infantry Fighting Vehicles and Abrams Main Battle Tanks.

Burton noticed and explained, "A present from my men. You see I once commanded a squadron of the Tenth Cavalry at Fort Hood, in Texas", he added the state in case the other man had never heard of its location. "Buffalo Soldiers come in all colors these days."

He seemed to feel the need to clarify his every position, as if O'Rourke might become offended by some unintentional slight. But it was he and not O'Rourke who had concerns about their roles in race relations. O'Rourke had already classified him as color-illiterate, meaning that while he would not pick a man based on color –except for special circumstances-- he was unaware that too many of his picks all tended to be of one color. Color-illiterates were trainable. While they were not always harmless –that also depended on the circumstances—they were just not the enemy …usually.

But since Burton did not know any of this –or, more importantly, how his recruit felt about all this-- he thus took no chance that he might accidentally step on some sensitivity, like the other's sensitivity with the DIA's hiring practices. His illiteracy did not allow him to consider the fact that too much side-stepping made for too little progress. But a nagging sensation tugged at his attention mechanism to warn that he was boring his guest, so he abandoned the remainder of his trip through, the land of "Me like Black People" and proceeded.

"Anyway John, I found out later it was your flight that had saved me and my men. Then you saved me again a bit later when they finally considered me strong enough for surgery. Only problem was, I needed more Type-B Positive than the hospital had in stock. In fact they were short of everything after my platoon hit town and we weren't the only grunts needing fixing. Lucky for me they got a pint out of a pilot who happened to be hanging around. Type-O, the universal donor. You saved me twice without knowing it either time. But we did meet. In fact we spoke a few times in the hospital when I shared a room with your RIO. Mickey, wasn't it? So, for that I will always be grateful."

"Goes under the heading of doing your job, General, nothing special." Now he had an iota of understanding of at least one aspect of this man's steadfast determination to recruit him. Trust. Not just blood brothers, his relationship to Tina was apparently another. But to him it all still made little sense for these career professionals to go "off the reservation", as it were. He was neither trained nor of like experience and was little interested in retrieving some stolen secrets which did not matter to anyone outside of Homeland Security. Plus, he wanted no part of another's hero worship. All that being said forever and without end, for Tina he would endure Hell itself…

Focusing his steel gray eyes on O'Rourke, Burton understood that very same thing. But within him he still felt a need to fully explain his rationale. It was as if he were back to the rank of Lieutenant presenting his ideas for the approval of his Captain.

"JP, I needed a universal donor back then and I need a universal donor now. I need you to donate your efforts even though doing so might bring you harm. I hate to pay back all I owe to you in this manner. But believe me, not only does your country have need of your services, but our situation is so dire, I doubt that any Federal agency will be spending much time investigating your wife's death. In fact some people believe she must have messed up, leaked information about her route and schedule." He tread lightly on this subject, even though he knew O'Rourke had probably considered that same possibility. It was a natural assumption. "I am giving you carte blanche to follow the trail where it leads and prosecute anyway you feel necessary. Needless to say, I'd rather you kept what I have just said between us. Doesn't look good, a director being motivated by emotion."

Colonel Young in his parting address: "Yeah, we all know you believe it's your war. Go out in yo' fast jets 'n shoot down Commie Migs 'fo they shoot down you! But th' ground pounder don't care shit bout yo' trophies, yo' high'n th' sky cartwheeling or who you fukked over at Mamasan's pussy parlor las' night or any night! He jus' tryna git home alive ta fuk his own an dependin' on you ta see dat he do! He kin git it frum them or us! Either way he KIA! Am I makin' myself clear Marines? NVA, Charlie or goddamn USA bombs dropped wrong! Either way, he KIA! You make sure it's never USA! We protect what's ours an kill ev'rything else! Got it? Pay fukking attention!"

Thirty-one thousand feet over patch marked earth that once was solid jungle that raspy voice floated back into his thoughts. What a way for big daddy to make it easier to go to war …it was war, but it wasn't easy.

"Oh God please don't let me fuk up an' kill the wrong kid!"

"Buddha Three! Here we go, take second lead!"

End of the commiserations, time to do the do! He followed the two birds diving below. Death was coming for somebodies. Just hoped it was the right bodies!

Happened soon after his favorite Radar Intercept Officer returned from burying his mother. He actually missed the exuberate shrieks screaming out the back cockpit! "Bammo! Crispy critters!"

This day, not so much. Maybe cause they'd been at it so much. Concentrated ground fire erupted suddenly, seeking him out, seeking to terminate his stay on earth. His F-4 Phantom fighter-bomber dove in low over lush, green elephant grass leading into a triple canopied forest in support of an VNMC battalion. Behind him came others. There had to be a full NVA division down there, bent on a mammoth offensive and they had to help stop them. Otherwise a bunch of those Thủy Quân Lục Chiến, the TQLC, might not make it home. Not if their air support punked out. Their Americanized title was Republic of Vietnam Marine Corps or VNMC. Though some called them the "Very Nearly Marine Corps". But to JP, these were Marines and with a battalion going against a division, they were outnumbered by a lot.

So they kept going, he and his Airedales, these Phantom Phlyers as they were famously known, at least famous to those who depended on them. They kept hammering at the bad guys with nape and snake on one sortie, cluster bombs and frags, the next. So far, no one in his flight of four had suffered a single casualty, just a few minor taps to the chin.

Four birds under his command. Pilots in the front seats, RIOs in the back. Death at their fingertips. Eight crewmen, his men, under his orders and he remembered every one of their names and their faces; he even remembered the perfume on their wives letters, the couple that had wives. It's a hell of a thing to hold someone's life in your hands. You say turn left and he dies, you say kill and he dies trying. He hoped he never caused any such thing. He hoped he would have no need to explain to those wives or mothers or girlfriends …what had happened.

Jellied gasoline erupted from napalm canisters and ignited to sear human flesh from bones. Those not immolated or suffocated by the nape were shredded on the next pass by five hundred pound snake-eye high explosives or the hundreds of grenade-sized submunitions ejected from each cluster bomb canister. All of it raining death and destruction on the heads of lurking NVA troops and armor, sending the message: "You trying to hide from this shit? Son, ain't no hidin' from this shit!"

And there truly was no way to hide from that terrible onslaught. He remembered it like it was yesterday, because in a sense it was. He would never forget the things he did, the things he had been forced to do in the name of God and country. But there was no way to change what he did to men sent to do similar to him by other men. Somebody is always being sent by someone else to do things like that. He remembered hearing their screams, even though there was no way he could have heard the voices of dying men on the ground from inside a roaring jet fighter, twin afterburners shooting it high in the sky like a Roman candle. But he heard their voices…

In between the Phantom passes came A-6 Intruders with their mammoth bomb loads and AH-1G Huey Cobras dispersing withering volleys of air-to-ground rockets, seven point–six-two machine gun rounds and forty millimeter high explosive grenades into Uncle Hồ's Bộ đội, the North Vietnamese Army. Even B-52s joined in to surprise the Bộ đội, who could neither hear nor see nor even suspect their presence, until steel rain from thirty thousand feet began suddenly exploding the very ground occupied by these green suited regulars. Sheltered only by a thin canopy of jungle and pith cover campaign hats, the once proud army died in horrendous numbers. But still they came.

Staccato burps from twenty millimeter gun pods, hung under the centerline of each Phantom, joined with Cobra guns to serenade the enemy below in deadly imitation of the NVA's triple-A firing up at them, supplanted the singsong "Caca Dau," "Caca Dau," "Caca Dau" with its American Marine translation: "Pow, Pow, blam, blam, boom, boom for 'I'll Kill You,' 'I'll Kill You,' 'I'll Kill You'". Not quite the same ol' song, but definitely a hit!

Eventually, the combination of merciless air strikes and determined ground thunder by South Vietnamese grunts sent the NVA Bộ đội heading for the hills. But not before their vehemence had vented a thundering argument of its own.

His jet took more hits that day over Quang Tri Province than all his previous air-ground actions combined. Most, small arms stuff --nothing major-- a patch here and there and back into the air. It might have become almost mechanical, except for the killing and the being killed. Distance-wise, wasn't too bad. From their base in Nam Phong, Thailand (where bad Marines get exiled for being bad) it took less than an hour flying the two hundred-seventy miles due east to drop bomb loads, fire off Zunis and blast twenty mike-mikes into the jungle-shrouded targets. Reward came by way of secondary explosions mushrooming up when their ordnance found a tank or truck or ammo dump. Of course then there was another hundred miles southeast to Da Nang to rearm for another run on the way back.

"This is the third. Three times the charm JP". He remembered Mickey's worried voice over the intercom as they taxied to Nam Phong's runway. He remembered his only response, a double-click on the mike switch. Both were dead tired and badly needing rest, but so did all the other crews, not to mention those Marines down on the ground. His flight crews had been keeping the pressure on since sunup with their last flight figuring to land well after sundown. If necessary, tomorrow would be a repeat. But the ground pounders didn't get to go back to a decent bed, after a decent meal.

"Charlie-Lima-Delta, firing smoke markers now! That's the target! Bombs on target! Good job Marines!" Secondaries were good, but the best reward came from shouts of approval over the radio waves.

His crews did a masterful job, never attacking the same way twice, ever mindful of inducing bad karma by adopting bad habits. But Mickey's premonition was a bit hasty. Sortie three was a piece of cake. It was the return trip, sortie number four which became their Waterloo. He wasn't about to forget it either…

Dusk approached. Almost too dark to see the smoke markings pointing out the NVA positions. He had just pulled out of a dive after releasing four Mark-82 five hundred pound bombs and it was a good thing too. Had that explosive triple-A caught him on the dive, he might never had gained control enough to pull out. Headfirst is not the way he ever wanted to land. "What, me kiss the ground? Hell no! I don't wanna go!"

Shuddering from several, proximity-fused, twenty-three millimeter anti-aircraft artillery bursts spewing destruction and death into its aluminum skin, his shiny silver eagle no longer portrayed the invincible war bird, very nearly falling out of the sky altogether. He worked madly on the control stick and rudder pedals to break out of the searching death while his fellows sought to reciprocate in the form of three diving, twisting birds of prey raining their own brand of death and destruction on the hated enemy.

He felt relieved that he had restored some measure of control over the wobbling goose and then a shriek tore through the headphones that very nearly ruptured his eardrums. It came from the backseat where Mickey lived. He grimaced; at least he hoped his RIO was still alive; there had been no response to his repeated calls. Following that inhuman scream had come total silence.

But all he could do was hold on and hope. He could do nothing else as the backseat is totally isolated in flight; there is little view and barely enough room for a pussy cat to crawl through between cockpits. Which they had always considered justified since they weren't allowed to play with pussy in F-4s anyway. Regardless, his hands were full just keeping the big fighter-bomber in the air. Left hand coaxed the throttles while right yanked, jerked and skillfully worked the joystick.

Clusters of gauges aiming black needles into the regions of red numbers weren't a lotta help. Neither the flashing red warning lights nor the high pitched alarms blaring doom and gloom. Just one assessment. The shit had hit the fan …and it was very bad!

One high explosive burst had cracked several wing spars, another severed a control cable, while a third turned Mickey Watson's left foot into a pulpy, bloodied mass of raw meat. But he knew none of these things until much later. At the time his only certainty, that both aircraft and best friend were in sad shape …both writhing in pain.

"Two systems we need you to study. The first is called STREAMLINE, the other, TRON GOD." Oh God, he had awakened from a nightmare into a horror movie. How did Peterson get inside his Phantom? Since when did an F-4 hold three? And then he recovered his wits sufficiently enough to remember his situation and settled in to try and make heads or tails of the man's lecture. It seemed life had all of a sudden become full of those things. Lectures that is…

"It is not overly important that you acquire in depth knowledge about STREAMLINE, only to understand its relationship to our dilemma. Suffice to say that all classified documentation is now transmitted using the STREAMLINE encryption algorithm. Moreover, all hardcopy is also encrypted and written to data disks for transport between sites."

"I'm guessing that was the stuff stolen by the bad guys, right?"

Peterson's patient look was shared only with his boss. After O'Rourke's question drifted away, he continued his spiel as if having never been disrupted. "Now TRON GOD, Mister O'Rourke began life as a short-range, point defense missile system to be carried aboard P-3 Orion Aircraft. Unfortunately, we do not believe whoever stole its secrets will necessarily employ it so. You see, what goes down, also goes up. They could sell it to terrorists or rogue nations who might hold the entire aviation world hostage. Imagine if they installed one of these things on a boat and fired on a few airliners transiting the Pacific. We'd be picking up bodies by the gross without a clue who did the deed. But this is a two-edged sword…"

To O'Rourke, Peterson's monotone sounded similar to the countless lectures given by tired, overworked night school professors who would much rather be at home sipping a dry martini than trying to coax some level of interest out of student minions attempting to remain somewhat alert after their eight and nine hour day jobs. The somnolent effect so much reminded him of that produced by his Accounting 101 professor, that he very nearly dozed through much of it, just as he had in that class back in the Spring semester of 1973. The professor with the thick Indian or Pakistani (none of the students could discern which) accent never seemed miffed by the view of fully half his class nodding away in tune to his vocal cadence. But somehow he instinctively knew better than try that technique on the Jarhead, so he persevered through its tedium, at least he did not need to first decipher the language and then the meaning …though still, it was barely less challenging.

"…you see, its initial purpose was to bombard launching missiles and shallow-depth submarines with high energy, positively charged ions," continued Peterson, looking very much the Jarhead in his Summer Service "Charlie" Uniform. Creases on the short-sleeved, summer tropical shirt and green gabardine trousers appeared sharp enough to cut flesh. Stuck snugly under his trousers' khaki-colored, web belt, his garrison cap, informally called a "pisscutter" or front to back --also green gabardine—displayed its black, eagle-globe-and-anchor insignia prominently.

"…in effect, it would rain down upon the enemy. But its effectiveness and enhancements in its effective range caused defense specialists to plan for its employment in protecting missile silos and some major cities.

Techniques and technology enhancements to reduce attenuation due to atmospherics, especially water absorption, have transformed this into a truly awesome weapon. We can't let it out to turn our world into chaos."

He used a notebook computer on the General's conference table to display dozens of artist renderings and schematic diagrams. O'Rourke felt his frontal lobes about to explode from all the data points being absorbed or perhaps to implode from all those points still attempting entry as the Colonel droned on ad nauseam. The classification of the meeting was Top Secret --equivalent to the interim clearance he had been given through the General's authority—so he could not write down any relevant notes that would be meaningful. Every noteworthy detail could only be scribed into his mental notebook. Luckily they had fed him between the morning and afternoon sessions. So he had sufficient energy to withstand much of the verbal onslaught.

But his own sixth sense --maybe the seventh, he was not certain—kept nagging at him, intimating that these guys were not telling him everything. It struck him that their actual concern was not somebody blasting airplanes from the friendly skies. They had bigger fish to fry. Their main concern had to be something else entirely. It took a lot more to hit a jet flying high and fast than a relatively slow submarine. Guidance systems were the big bitch, that's why the most effective missiles have their own onboard radar. Close up is much more accurate than far away. Plus, there are already a whole bunch of rogue states possessing the capability to shoot down airplanes. But that was his take …him, the amateur.

"These plans are encrypted in an optical disc storage media format which cannot be easily copied or downloaded." Peterson could put an insomniac to sleep. "In fact the encrypted portion is transparent to users. You could actually load it into your DVD player, as long as it's capable of reading DVD-18 media. That's double sided with a double layer on both sides and you can watch the movie, as long as you don't mind listening to a Chief Warrant Officer from the Tennessee National Guard narrating the instructional video for the operation and maintenance of the AN/MLQ-40(V)3 PROPHET Countermeasures System."

To O'Rourke's blank stare, he merely smiled before continuing, "PROPHET captures radio frequencies from five hundred hertz up to two gigahertz and DFs, err, direction finds to the source, but is not classified except for theater-specific, time and location stuff. Most individuals or organizations engaged in software piracy won't be attracted to a Chief Warrant Officer giving instructions for raising antenna masts and parking

Humvees on hilltops."

"Unless it's a female Chief Warrant Officer," joked O'Rourke, instantly wishing he had kept the quip to himself. The image of a shapely model fading, a CWO's silver bar with twin black rectangles pinned to her camouflage bikini.

"It's really quite amazing," interjected Burton, ignoring the witticism. "It remakes the classified data into what appears to be an unclassified presentation. You can't even detect the encrypted information because of the manner in which it is sequenced. Numbered and cataloged data discs are used for high level briefings where necessary, they are carried by special courier and are considered much lower on the security risk ladder than encrypted transmissions..."

"And several orders of magnitude lower than regular hard copy firmware." Peterson said, grabbing back the reins. After all this was his briefing. "I mean with these you gotta have very special equipment just to detect there is an underlying algorithm, then you'll need the one of a kind embedded cipher code which was created simultaneously with the encrypted data device and even then you'll need special conversion software to read the data you extract. It's quite a few steps more involved than standard DVD-18. You see the algorithm is burned in a randomized pattern on each side and on each layer of the media as instructed by the encrypted editing software and that encrypted pattern is contained in the cipher key, so only significant players need apply."

Again Burton interceded. He had also become bored with Peterson's agonizingly long spiel. So he made one nearly as agonizingly long. "You're probably wondering why the big deal since most information these days travels across the internet or satellites, at the very least copied on USB thumb drives? Well, included with these DVDs is both the foundation algorithm, as well as Level One command modules. These were provided to demonstrate the capability to our allies. They would allow the user to read all STEAMLINE data encoded anywhere on any media, when paired with the appropriate command modules. So satellite and phone transmissions indeed are included, otherwise only password protection would stop a determined adversary."

"And passwords can be cracked by dedicated programs you can buy off the internet." Peterson's turn again. "The bottom line is Level One command modules mean just that, Top level White House, State Department and DoD only. Naturally, succeedingly higher numbers mean correspondingly lower level access. It's all controlled by modularized computer algorithms provided on need to know basis. No more low level clerks with an agenda downloading communiqués between heads of state. No more Walker Spy Rings and no more Wikileaks. That's the intent. When those thieves took those coded discs (after they killed your wife, he didn't say, though O'Rourke heard his thoughts say it) they knew exactly what they were after, so we suspect they know all about the transparent code. Our guess is…"

"My guess is that you want it back?" interrupted O'Rourke. In his mind they still had the wrong man to accomplish this job. His knowledge of computers could be typed on a single sheet of notebook paper, single-sided, double-spaced. But at least now he had a little more insight to their real headache. They did not want the crooks to have their top secret software. They probably could care less how many planes got shot down as long as nobody could read their cute little message traffic. This potentially could have even greater impact than the Walker Spy Ring that lasted between 1967 and 1985.

O'Rourke often wondered how many lives were lost to that traitor's greedy madness. But one thing was certain, the men killed aboard the USS Pueblo were the direct result of the Soviets sending their North Korean henchmen to attack and steal its crypto gear for which John "Slime Ball" Walker had already provided the decoding keylists and operation manuals. Also obvious, Walker's contribution enabled the Soviets to eavesdrop not only on incoming Naval message traffic, but everything that had been transmitted years prior. Suspicious ship sinkings, like the submarine USS Scorpion might also be part of Walker's work. But O'Rourke mainly wondered why Walker and his gang were still in the land of the living. Obviously, high treason carries a different penalty these days when playing these games grown men play.

All major players routinely copy every bit of transmitted information from all the other major players. Intel satellites, spy ships and planes, even ground intercept sites spend their days and nights pulling in all they could find. The Pueblo was such a ship and loaded with crypto gear, a soft target full of hardware that proved too tempting for the Soviets to ignore once they got those controlling keylists and those were primarily just naval communications.

With STEAMLINE the potential was endless. Once collected, all they needed were the correct crypto sequences and voila, the keys to the kingdom. Not just national security, one nation could blackmail another over more personal issues. "Hey, yo Mister President, remember that time you said you didn't authorize Victor Krinkoski's assassination back in March 07? You sure you wanna stick to that story?"

He could envision panic to the extreme. This STREAMLINE stuff could open the door to all the crap either coming or already out of the White House, the State Department, DoD, everybody. They'd need the crypto keys in those command algorithms to make it all go, but greed is a significant motivator. You never know when the next John Walker will show up.

Besides, just acquiring the basic capability would surely enable some low-level discovery. "Every journey begins with the first step", JP remembered. But that wasn't everything. A little birdie whispered to him that they had bigger issues …and weren't about to say.

"We either want it back or destroyed and if it is destroyed, we'll need verification, so you tell us where and when, we'll verify."

"Aye aye!" His words to the affirmative clashed with his thoughts. They didn't have to say more; neither did his little, imaginary feathered friend. The lie was evident. He'd go out and do their bidding. He'd search for their MacGuffin, their Fool's Gold. But he'd make no promises beyond that. They had the wrong guy to send out with so obvious a lie. Didn't they read his history, his aversion to bullshit? Didn't they see the incredulous look on his face or the huge question mark floating just above his head? It had to be there for any to view …didn't it?

Peterson had no need to read O'Rourke's mind. He already agreed this the wrong man for this job. That the man suspected they were withholding information did not faze him all that much. He himself had developed their story. Good news. Nobody ever trusted the Government, that was small potatoes. The big issue, the one that riled him beyond measure: they could not possibly prepare him in time to do any good.

While not dangerous, meaning he knew better than to use the DVD tray for a cup holder (as one Peterson's new hires once did) he still was not quite harmless. Peterson remembered how the "seventies something" little, white-haired grandmother also became extremely aggravated by this intrusion to her daily routine, blaming the Chinese, the procurement system, design flaws, even the weather when the tray eventually broke under the weight of a sixteen ounce Cinnamon Café Latte with double cream. He cringed, reflecting on the limited-use people available for hire these days, thankful that she had never been his choice …just like someone else.

No. Begrudgingly, he admitted that was not a fair comparison. O'Rourke's skills were decidedly more advanced. Not that he had a Facebook or Twitter page or anything. Still, he had no real training in subterfuge –not counting panty raids—and his computer literacy measured closer to elementary students in first year computer lab. He barely knew his way around basic "Windows". How was he ever going to manage all they needed him to?

"One other thing, not only is the program classified, its name is also "Black", meaning…"

"Yeah, I know. Can't say th' name to anybody that isn't 'Read On' th' program, but since I won't know who is, 'Read On', I can't say th' name at all, so I might as well forget th' name. I'll just call it Project X."

"Better yet, don't call it Project anything. People start digging with the slightest hint. They can't help it. Mention 'Aurora' and ten thousand ufologists run out to Groom Lake, Nevada with their night vision goggles and spend weeks scanning the skies for hypersonic Air Force jets.

Just like you were briefed in sear school, don't give out anything, don't skirt around the subject, don't even lie about its features or attributes; just deny, deny, deny. If they can crack the algorithm they get two highly classified programs for the price of one and America will be a dozen times more vulnerable."

"Colonel, I'm a confirmed bachelor. Trust me. Telling people a whole bunch of nothing about anything they want to hear is second nature." He remembered the lesson of Survival, Evasion, Resistance, and Escape (SERE) School. They pronounced it sear and it was indeed quite severe. You want to low-crawl through the muck and mire of snake-infested swamps, exist for a week or so on what you can catch, then get captured by evil-intentioned enlisted men (who totally hate officers) and legally tortured, all in the name of making it harder for the enemy; IF they capture you? Anyway, that was SERE.

Not one to romanticize places and situations merely because he'd survived them; he never wanted to even recall that place. But its lessons, he'd never forget. This last joke had no more chance of success than the others. Even as it slipped past his lips, he had realized it had no chance: "Cause this Jarhead has absolutely no sense of humor."

Meanwhile, inside the Jarhead ran a continuous loop soundtrack playing and replaying the tune which he had first heard at the start of this crazy mission, "What the hell have we gotten ourselves into?"

A variation parroted that they needed a more serious-minded operative. Sending this carefree, "I give a damn about procedures" person out on this mission was all wrong. How could he explain anything to him that he would listen to? How could he impress upon him even the minimum security requirements for this mission, like the need to secure the notebook computer, at all times.

"Not just sometimes, all times! Don't leave it out for the maid to play with! Don't lose it in the airport. Yes it uses fingerprint coding! No it is not booby trapped! It has to fly in airplanes, remember (idiot)! Secure it at all times (you low life scumbag) …and please don't use a common login password, like your dog's or your girlfriend's name (jeez)!" It was impossible! But he had his marching orders so he marched…

"The good thing about these disks is we can send updates as popular movies. Embassies around the world could upload the latest version, then entertain guests with prereleases months before the commercial release, even prior to the theatrical viewing if need be. All safe and secure, provided the originals aren't handed to the ambassador's kids. They need to show off? Just burn them their own copy.

"Except, it'll be HD without the odd head silhouette popping up occasionally to block the view," chimed in the General. "Sans the classified, of course."

"Yeah, they'll know it wasn't copied using some video camera in a theater, like a lotta bootlegs," asserted Peterson, jumping back in to reclaim the spotlight in this high level game of "you can't have it, I stole it".

True, he had to admit, it all sounded like a good way to transfer classified material around. Had to be better than sending guys carrying black bags that begged to be hijacked or whichever method currently in use. Then he remembered Tina's fate and suddenly realized this too had its flaws.

Her liquid beauty stood for a moment before him, daring him to blink, then vanished back to the netherworld once he did, back to the shadows it now inhabited, leaving the memory to chafe and grate. She who had been his Galatea, the beautiful statue brought to life by beneficent gods in response to Pygmalion's prayers. Except that he had not carved her image from stone as had the mythological Greek. He had merely prayed to someday win her heart, then rejoiced when he did; his own fairy tale come true …until fate interfered.

Bottom line, bad guys were always gonna want to steal these secret things. If they did, they'd not only be able to intercept traffic sent by our side, they could modify our stuff and use to transmit their stuff. Imagine every terrorist cell possesses its very own, unbreakable, encrypted cell phones and computer networks. You think NSA is crazy now. Then they'd really commence to hair pulling.

He resisted the temptation to quip how he could really use this to secure his Facebook and Twitter. Wouldn't have mattered, he knew. Like they would have picked him for this soirée if he had any of those things...

Still, it did seem kinda humorous, in a way reminding him his fascination for the ghostly spectre who snuck out of his closet at night. Every night without fail it came to rearrange some aspect of his bedroom, waiting patiently until certain he had lost his nightly fight and finally surrendered to the welcoming arms of slumber. Its prank would escape discovery until he was back with the world, for only he could see. No amount of reasoning could convince his stubborn self otherwise, just as no amount of convincing ever got through to his doubting family.

The riskiest part of this operation, the need to scan any suspected DVD for the STREAMLINE signature. But not a lot of choice. Would not be at all funny their agent returns from his mission carrying a collection of greatest hits from Sonny and Cher or parodies of Sonny and Cher by Weird Al Yankovic. Would not be the first time such had occurred, but still wouldn't be funny. Even worse, if he initiate overt measures aimed at the wrong site, the wrong company or simply just on the wrong day. Overt, in this case, meaning use of deadly force by a strike team or smart weapon launched from a targeting aircraft, as the situation required …or both if available.

He'd need to be absolutely certain. They ain't even trying to resurrect the type of negative publicity generated when a one hundred seventy-two foot, B-2 Spirit bomber --unheard and unseen— inadvertently delivered its payload onto the wrong target in Belgrade, Sarajevo.

Oh it was a super achievement, so they did celebrate that all five, two thousand pound bombs hit the designated target. They owed that much to their evil-twin selves and danced joyous jigs at the accuracy of their weapon systems … for a minute.

However, it was their professional backsides that took the whuppin' for using erroneous intel that marked the Chinese Embassy as a weapons procurement facility. After much brow-beating, ass-chewing and the like, they all made mental notes to be much more circumspect regarding CIA-developed information. Don't trust, verify!

Only one viable method to validate whether suspected DVDs contain the STREAMLINE algorithm, their agent needs to load them onto a capable reader. And therein lay part deux of their problem. If the bad guys captured the agent, they might also capture the method of determining which DVD's were truly valuable and which were some reality TV show, aka, worthless trash … so DIA installed countermeasures.

DIA itself doesn't condone "Mission Impossible" approaches to counterespionage (they're DIA, not CIA). Accordingly, this particular reader would only give unauthorized thieves a horrendous, smelly sensation as it slowly cooked itself, along with the entire laptop computer. They had not lied to O'Rourke (at least not about that part), it would not explode, just sort of self-format, wiping out every bit and byte of memory on the hard drive, processor and motherboard. The smell they added as their way of announcing just how shitty a job the thieves had done. In less than typical government humor, it was partly insult, partly friendly way of saying "better luck next time, this time no kaboom."

Dry. Albeit humor is as atypical as common sense in most government organizations. In fact, typical of this monolithic behemoth comprising the Defense Intelligence Agency; its commander, Major General Burton, knew nothing of this particular feature. Perhaps he should have inquired.

Perhaps reasons such as those explained the reason his boss had so far neglected to recommend his third star, though not necessarily. They call that five-sided place across the river the "puzzle palace" for a reason. This one he'd never know until the Secretary of Defense decides to tell him … if ever he does.

Whatever the reason, Pentagon politics may have held up his promotion to Lieutenant General, but his need to clean house came from another direction entirely. True, what they say, the boss is last to know … don't be around if he finds out!

Burton still didn't know that his troubles were more than few. Subordinates deem it unnecessary he be made aware of such things as equipment variations? Problematical. But a couple of them deeming it mission critical that he have as little operational knowledge of this mission as possible, barely more than his reluctant agent. His agent, not theirs! Major problem! Obviously, they wanted both gone ...and it wasn't like they hadn't tried.

This was all happening too fast, even for an established campaigner like Peterson. Only a few days prior they'd flown out to Southern California to watch this man win a wrestling tournament not one of them ever suspected him capable of winning. But win he did, immediately lifting him to the top of the General's list. Sure, he beat up on two of the men considered the best America had to offer. But this mission needed more than just brains and brawn. Why couldn't his boss get that point? Sure he was a Marine and yeah, being a small service, Marines are bred to have a greater variety of skills to manage all their additional duties. Normally he would have felt greater comfort with such a fellow. In fact, normally he would probably be the one touting his fellow warrior's skills to the boss.

Why not this time? He refused to chalk it up as racial bias. The Army Ranger his team had selected was just as black; though, even more capable, to his eyes,. Guy even had a Dominican heritage. No, it wasn't the race, it was the man himself. He just wasn't the someone this mission needed. Sure the General saw their selection process as rigid, monolithic, unyielding and the rest. But it truly was not. Why that man could not see, he did not know.

Patiently explaining his issues to his commander, Peterson finally gave up. This was getting him nowhere. It was like wrestling with a cloud, impossible to grab or corner. He had patiently expounded point after point to his commander who had just as patiently listened, then apparently ignored. Peterson was certain this was so even though his General's lips actually moved when they stated that he had weighed the ramifications against the potential benefit. So basically, his dual-hatted position as acting Deputy CG and Chief of Staff meant little or nothing to this Commanding General. Neither his positions nor his experienced counsel mattered. There was no potential benefit here, only a potential for detriment.

Unfortunately, so focused on the potential for operational hazard was Peterson, he neglected to consider the potential detriment to his career. Balefully despising his leader's decision, he unfortunately forgot the first rule of military lore, again!

An old experienced, campaigner who had survived and even flourished in Pentagon politics, Peterson's consternation led him to do something he had not done since a wet-behind-the-ears Second Lieutenant unhappy with his first combat assignment. He vented his frustrations to a subordinate. That previous confidant was his Rifle Platoon's Gunnery Sergeant, who promptly chewed him out –superior or no—for conduct unbecoming a Marine officer (calling him by first names rhyming with punk-assed, weak-kneed, tittysucker and such) and probably saved his career with earthy counsel, such as his first rule stated simply: "If you can't be part of the solution, don't be part of the problem!"

There are many types of authority on a battlefield. There is the legal authority of a commander, given him by another commander. Then there is the actual authority of a leader, given him by the men he leads, men believing he gives them the best chance to emerge from that battlefield alive …this Gunnery Sergeant was the latter.

Instantly realizing his mistake --that particular point of fact made known to his reddening ears-- he became obeisant, paying rapt attention to the skinny, cigar-chomping, clean-shaven, teen-lookalike standing ground before him, hurling epithet upon thunderous epithet with the force and fire of Zeus from atop Mount Olympus. Mid-way through his second tour in Vietnam, he only appeared young. But this Gunny had already lived a lifetime in this place and any brand new "Butter Bar" had best pay him attention …if they ever dreamed of turning those gold slivers to silver.

Peterson had listened and learned and had never repeated such a faux pas, until one fateful day stupidity again claimed him and he erupted into a twenty minute rant in his office, again in front of a subordinate. But this time the subordinate was no eighteen-year veteran, salty Marine NCO looking out for his Corps --which included his boss-- but a social climbing, parasitic Air Force Captain looking to weed out any obstacle above him on that social ladder, especially his boss.

Thompson's demeanor during the Colonel's tirade evidenced a decidedly dichroic nature, filtered to appear supportive; totally depending on one's angle of view. Small sounds emanated from closed lips, which this man might attribute as supportive and encouraging, but from which an objective observer would not interpret as accord. The reality, indeed there was no accord.

In actuality, his mannerisms contrasted directly his intentions. "Say nothing which means anything" someone famous was once quoted. Maybe Emily Dickinson, he couldn't remember. What it matter less you dicking them or at the least trying? He had no care.

He only knew everything was all dicked up! His purpose for knocking at the Exec's door at that faithful moment could be construed as purposeful, even parasitic. But, truth is, he had no purpose, except what lies with opportunity and therein his only purpose. It was in keeping with the seamier side of his nature that had gained significant momentum since his last turn in the Air Force promotion barrel.

He had become forever scarred by the selection process for Majors. First he blamed his failure on the fact that he was "wingless" in an organization run by aviators, bitterly complaining these things to his girlfriend Doris … just before she left for Brazil. "They'ahs only a few slots left after them damned flyboys are finished taking care o' they'ah buddies!"

Following her unconvincing attempt to convince him that she agreed that he was getting the shaft, he expanded his logical diatribe to include his lack of an advanced degree as the deciding factor. His summation was simple: "The Air Force only rewards those pissant, pencil necks that spend majority of they'ah working hours studying up for or applying to advanced courses 'cause dat's the only way they know how ta measure performance! While they wasting our tax dollars ah'm holding the fort, not shootin' th' shit in bullshit classes where th' only goal ta pass mediocre, dream world tests. They got no homework ta do! No papers to write. No need ta actually learn anythin' meaningful! Nuthin! Jus' figger what they need fo' th' test!"

Doris' demeanor remained unconvincing that she was convinced. He needed more, so next he included favoritism to minorities as an essential component to his being passed over since he knew personally that one of the guys recently promoted was black. Specifically, he specified blacks and women, especially blacks who were women, intimating that the problem had become exacerbated by recent trends permitting women to fly combat air. More Zoomies slotted ahead of him…

The fact that black officers –including males and females-- represented only about seven percent of the total officer corps did nothing to discourage his angst. Neither did the knowledge that only one of their total count has achieved rank to Lieutenant General in recent history. These facts he omitted from his tirade. But experiencing a clairvoyant moment, Doris had anticipated that argument and done a bit of her own homework study.

Her evaluation of his synopsis revealed what he had suspected all along; that she considered his summation flawed his attitude poor and his rationale irrational. She further reminded him --just in case he had missed the fact during whatever cursory examination he had performed-- that perhaps his lackluster qualities might also be apparent to those in his chain of command, up to and including the selection board at the Air Force Military Personnel Center. Her concluding statement she aimed even lower, citing that only a "closet bigot" could stand before her using the promotion of one man to justify evidence of favoritism. Only one individual, not one percent of the Air Force generals, one man! Then she had left to catch her airplane ...for Brazil.

But he still felt that there was an unannounced recruitment effort afoot which had stymied his promotion opportunities and that his career was destined to end at captain. One more pass over would do the job just as certain as if he had mooned the Chief's wife. He decided that Doris' childhood as an Air Force brat and whose closest friend had been black, had "colored" her judgment ...that and her allegiance to the "Sisterhood".

Instead of heeding her advice, he had become more predatory, no longer the conniving jokester, now just the conniving. His measured approach to life now parodied that of the Great Lakes Lamprey which survives by latching onto the unawares fishes swimming past and sucking them dry, in their turn. Here in Peterson he saw such an opportunity. Here was his chance to literally kill two birds with one stone. It was too tempting an opportunity to resist.

First step, he needed to instate a controlling mechanism. In order to play this thing his way, he needed ensure all operational mandates flowed through his scrutiny. Especially necessary when saddled with a guy who gives the term "Maverick" a bad name. Wouldn't do to let him out the barn too early. He had just the vehicle in mind.

Step two, he initiated measures intended to reduce, perhaps even eliminate, compromise hazards to the mission's success. Namely, that none ever suspected which puppet master's fingers truly pulled the strings. So for the tasking orders, he used his knowledge of computerized methods and human tendencies to surreptitiously generate the appropriate edicts out of the Colonel's mailbox.

He did not concern himself that close inspection would vindicate the Marine. If this mission ended in failure, namely, if they were unable to reacquire the stolen data before it could be compromised, the resulting blame on Peterson's head would obviate desire in all but the most dedicated or loyal to render aid. He couldn't see this square-headed jarhead having any of those in his lonely, little corner. Moreover, if things indeed went bad, the broad-brush strokes of incrimination could taint the lily-white motives of any exercising such poor judgment.

"Why'd you give those task orders?"

"Following orders! Boss say jump, I ask 'how high'!" Glowing with self-righteous confirmation, he initiated the taskers…

CHAPTER TEN

Eris, the storm's computer-selected name, closed quickly on South Florida's east coast. None was one hundred percent certain exactly where it would achieve landfall, but forecasters –citing computer models developed for exactly this purpose—predicted a path north of Miami, somewhere in Broward. Television shows on channels four and six were all preempted by officials from Miami-Dade and Broward counties –including respective Cuban-American Mayors—advising their constituents how to best prepare for and deal with the incoming storm. They even opted out "Good Morning America" in favor of local coverage. Juicy tidbits like move your boat to a safer area, bring outside furniture in --pets too-- and lower the water in pools but not too much (or its shell might get bounded out of the ground) and many other nuggets of enlightenment. None of these things mattered much to him. But having never experienced a hurricane directly, he absorbed the lessons …though not necessarily all of them.

He ventured out into the early afternoon rain showers, presumably to shop for a few essentials –a couple bottles of water, a two-liter bottle of coke to accompany the fifth of Jack Daniels he had purchased the day before (in case a power failure derailed the hotel's machine dispensers) and various chips, salsa dips and a bag of nuts, just in case. Provisioned for Mother Nature's coming attractions, also meaning too cheap to pay the hotel mini bar prices, he decided to grab lunch in the form of a cheeseburger at the Hard Rock Café in the Bayside Marketplace.

Service was excellent thanks to the relatively few tourists. Most anybody around seemed to prefer watching the marine workers outside moving boats into leeward areas and tying in more line to keep them there. O'Rourke had opted for drier environs, spending a relatively few minutes learning those ropes …eschewing the wet look.

The café's staff actually outnumbered its customers. Even so he knew that at least one of the customers was not there for the food. Later, a half-pound of juicy beef and all the fixings downed, he was fortified for the trip back to his hotel, but suddenly decided on another side trip. Curiosity combined with his natural vindictiveness to direct the little convertible into a left turn off the Macarthur Causeway onto Star Island, where many of Miami's elite kept homes.

The guard politely inquired as to his purpose for the visit, then raised a questioning eye at the answer. "Sightseeing? On a day like today?" his vacuous expression seemed to ask, though his mouth never did, instead he merely raised the liftgate and waved this wayward stargazer through, though not before instructing that he was not allowed to trespass on the residents' property.

O'Rourke could feel the guard's perplexity, but more than that, he could feel the chagrin in whomever it was who had been shadowing him since he left the party that previous evening. They had not followed him over the bridge leading to the island, so one thing he felt certain, they obviously wanted to remain inconspicuous and probably would not want to follow him past the video security cameras at the guard shack. A chuckle of mirth bubbled up from his throat. That was something anyway. He felt the satisfaction of a minor victory.

He was only the tiniest bit interested in this manmade island with its racetrack-shaped drive and its collection of some of America's most famous. Although he would not mind meeting some of them –definitely the Daddy Twins, "Shack" and "Puff"-- but he was not star struck by any means and the acquisition of mega-millions would never be his goal. So their money did not impress him …their incredible performance skills were another thing.

One of these homes had been used in the movie Scarface. The idea of living alone in a ten thousand square foot palace, cloistered behind giant walls and huge, steel gates left him as cold as its marbled floors probably left all their owners. This place –though swathed in obvious opulence and beauty—seemed literally, deserted. Not one other person could be seen other than a crew of Latinos piling into a flatbed truck, leaving one of the homes they had been repairing before the storm hit. He decided that tomorrow they'd need to return and repair the repairs. He had his look and also left.

Soon, back inside the safety –and relative luxury—of his boutique hotel, half wondering how its art deco styled front would appear the next time he walked through it. He poured himself a coke, broke out a bag of chips and settled in for a while on the soft bed covers, fingers working the television remote. He skipped past movies, game shows and shopping channels to those more important for his mission. Every local channel was filled with reports of the storm. News reporters and meteorological forecasters interspersed their discourse between the official announcements and pronouncements. Predictions came with all sorts of serious looks of gloom and doom. There were none of the frivolous quips and jokes about family matters or airline security goofs that flavored most morning news programs. Only formalized versions of someone's idea of appropriate conduct in the face of possible disaster came forward on the stoic visages.

As downpours go, this current storm was living up to predictions that it would be a true gully washer. Even the pigeons were trying to get in out of its blast. In his estimation, they had more sense than the surfers he watched excitedly paddling through heightening ocean crests and the TV crews out filming their juvenile madness. Obvious to him, the pigeons' motivations were totally at odds with the youthful adventurers who refused to get in out of the pelting rain, patiently waiting for that one big wave. In fact, several pigeons --pitifully huddling close against his hotel window-- looked in at him as if to say, "Can you believe these fools?"

No longer a tropical depression, the storm hit land with winds clocking eighty-five miles an hour. Sixty-foot tall Fichus trees were blown down. Power was knocked out in many areas. As powerful wind and storm surge began to wreak havoc all across the Miami area, falling trees killed several people. Too late for those, the Director of the National Hurricane Center came on television explaining the forecasted storm track and potential effects on people and property. He worried that the storm could cross the narrowest part of Florida, emerge still power-filled into the warm Gulf waters and become a full-fledged hurricane of category three or above. All officials urged people from Florida City to Vero Beach to stay home or head to shelters if living in low lying areas –especially those idiots scouring the surf for missing boards in the category one storm. The frowning image of the screen said it all. Three men had already died in Broward County because of the effects of this storm and these fools were wandering the shoreline to find surfboards swept away by the wind.

The ludicrous demonstrations continued. Newsies of both genders demonstrated the storm's power for their viewers by stepping from protected places into the teeth of the wind –raingear whipping about, bodies bent against the force seeking to launch them-- their microphones picking up and transmitting the roaring, whooshing sounds of God's fury unleashed. All the while --as lightning crackled and struck nearby-- they pleaded with the general listening public to remain indoors, preferably at home –reminding them also to avoid stepping into puddles, because those might be hiding downed power lines capable of electrocuting the unwary.

Though O'Rourke had seldom appreciated these shiny-faced, pretentious zealots from the press, he had to grudgingly admit to himself that they provided outstanding service to the public this day –at their own peril. In Vietnam their inflammatory type of one-sided reporting did often offer great service and comfort to the enemy, including playing a death knell to the career of one obscure Phantom driver named O'Rourke. But here they made significant contribution.

Moisture from the Gulf of Mexico was sucked into eastern Florida to intensify the southern edge as it passed over Homestead, AFB, though nothing like the Category 5 Andrew, one day removed from thirteen years prior. Homestead appeared struck by the wrath of God after Andrew rolled through.

But Eris had a few tricks to play. A tractor-trailer truck was blown over onto its side --very nearly blown entirely off a huge flyway overpass-- hanging precariously nearly one hundred feet above the lower roadway for hours. Power lines were down all over especially around Deerfield Beach --even though the northern part of the storm was considerably drier and of lesser intensity than the southern half—and would remain down until the wind force subsided sufficiently below the thirty-five mile-per-hour safety threshold established to protect power linesmen. Eventually the truck's weight, along with the storm force, overcame and collapsed one section of the flyway --which toppled onto the road below—pinning a car and crushing its unwary driver.

O'Rourke could appreciate that a storm's size could never measure the scale of the tragedy it caused. There were several families for which it had already rung the full measure. He felt their pain without knowing any of them.

But the news folk and others manning emergency stations or trying for home were not the only people out braving this storm. While many were out serving the public's interests, some were out for no good. One opportunistically inclined, male felon was apprehended by police in Key Biscayne for breaking and entering a business. His was the misfortune to be exiting the jewelry store at the very moment that Eris's eighty-five mile an hour winds subsided long enough for the foggy mists and wind-driven rains to clear enough for other people –emerging from sheltered locations-- to see him running for his car and alert police. His fortunes went even further south as the wind and rain came back with full fury just as the officers held him --pressed face first-- on the waterlogged pavement.

JP lounged on the pillow-top comforter, but felt anything but comfort. The glass of coke on the night table to his left still fizzled slightly, though he ignored it entirely. Still weighing his options while watching the TV, he got to his feet. It had become a pattern, his rising every ten or fifteen minutes to make the same, identical circuit around his small room. Not that the room was tiny, it was just nothing Miles or Mickey would have chosen. But then they owned hotels that dwarfed this one.

For O'Rourke's purpose though, this was not a bad choice. For one, his name was O'Rourke, not Watson. This place —the advertisement termed it a suite-- was mainly a studio, a spacious bedroom with an adjacent sitting area and kitchenette. A narrow hall led past the closet and bathroom to the entrance, whose door led out to an inside balcony that overlooked the plant-filled greenery of the courtyard dining area of the ground floor restaurant.

It took only one stride for him to reach and glance out his side window into the alleyway between his hotel and that next door. The mid-length curtains he kept open, despite the close proximity permitting people next door the ability to see inside, should they desire to look. The possibility that his across-the-alley neighbor might be on the Dirty-Tricks Detail seemed a little too farfetched, paranoid even. He had considered closing those curtains for increased privacy, ultimately deciding against shutting out all outside view.

The voyeur in him gave small consideration that this need perhaps evolved from some self-repressed, loathsome distrust that news people on the boob-tube might fail to report cows or witches on bicycles flying past. This was not Kansas, but he definitely was not in Cali anymore, either. But the curtains guarding his patio door he kept closed. Reaching these to peer outside took only two more strides, but their position enabled anyone on the second-level of the garage to peek. Only a fool would choose the unprotected upper level, but at least one of the bad guys was stationed underneath on the ground …in these horizontal rains it wasn't much better.

O'Rourke felt not the slightest pity for the man braving these elements just to keep up his assigned surveillance. His only concerns were the best options to circumvent that coverage. The last resort had to be a direct encounter, possibly resulting in termination. But it was one of the options he considered viable if necessary to preclude the worst of this night's possible outcomes, discovery or capture were definitely two to be avoided …and then there was that death thing. It had a special significance in that it was so, final.

But the bad guys and any death or destruction they might bring were not what really bothered him. It was this whole setup. The question kept repeating, playing back in his mind that he'd seen this play before in a similar scenario starring a couple very prominent actors. Maybe theirs had not included a hurricane, but again, there the good guys had to help government bureaucrats get back stolen devices capable of deciphering any and all computerized programs. He could not remember how it turned out…

He wondered whether life now imitated art, reflecting that bureaucrats --being not the sharpest tools in the shed—seldom encountered original thought, often parroting others' successes for their own purposes, adopting known formulas from paths blazed by entrepreneurs, just as the British copied strategies first used by the biblical warriors Joshua and Saul to defeat the Germans in World War Two. Even the U.S. Army spends time and dollars on computerized simulations, training M-1 tankers to fight the decisive battle of "73 Easting"–expunging Iraqi armor over and over again-- fifteen years after Desert Storm. As Mickey often remarked, after Christians, Bureaucrats are the ultimate copycats. They probably consider themselves inspired …in which case inspiration becomes triumph.

The details floated around and about, tantalizingly close to his grasp and accessible, though he had yet to put them into a useable format. Something about all this did not feel right to him. Warning bells were jangling their ominous tone, but his brain was still on lockdown. Tina's helpless image kept flooding out his ability to rationalize new and challenging information, sending him scurrying back to defensive mode …her defense.

Eventually the feeling reoriented itself, shaping back into a more recognizable form. Vietnam flashbacks inserted "crispy critters" formed by smoldering heaps that he had helped create out of once vibrant creatures –human, fauna and flora— and twisted metallic wreckages turning to rust in the highly humid environment. The whole countryside was laid to waste at his urging. Dead were everywhere. Dead friends he barely knew. Dead enemies he never knew. Dead everything and everyone. He had caused all this destruction and simply walked away without a scratch. He had vowed to never again be a part of such and now here he was again playing again the part of Death's servant.

Keeping up with the local news channels, more segments reporting the police apprehending an individual, he continued his routine. He was not interested in joining the hapless man sprawled helpless on the pavement – gasping from the knee force from two of Miami's heftiest policemen on his back-- so his approach would need to be entirely different. He could forget about any support from the DIA. He had already been warned against just such an overt move. His mission was to be strictly surveillance. If Peterson found out about this escapade, he would probably call the cops himself.

A slight chuckle as he recalled his most recent parting shot to the Colonel. Best described as most recent because they tended to occur frequently, like at every parting. The salt-n-pepper crew cut came back into his vision.

"We've done a thorough background check on Mister Morano and his operation down to the number of times he changes his underwear. Our best people. He's clean and not just due to the number of undie changes and yeah, it's boxers, not briefs." He paused a bit to let this bit of irreverent humor seep in, then continued when even that elicited not the slightest chuckle. "He's also very well thought of by some very influential folk around this town. We have no reason to suspect him of any wrongdoing. Are you certain your accusation isn't personal? Him shtupping the ex-wife and all!" Peterson's words came flat, without inflection or apology.

It was a challenge. This crew cut, hippie-hating jarhead had just told him he was a lying sack of shit more pissed off about Tina getting laid than her getting dead! He even used his limited version of humor to punctuate the decree. O'Rourke paused a few heartbeats for consideration. He may have been right, but he was only partly right and not about which knife cut deepest.

True, he had never stopped loving Tina. But he wasn't Taliban or something. Nothing in him would ever wish her harm no matter how many people she slept with. He loved her unconditionally and that was that. Some people can't truly appreciate just exactly what love means.

He allowed his pause to extend a few more beats while flushing any semblance of emotion from his voice before speaking. He especially needed to clear out any desires to describe in full detail the man's questionable ancestry. His mother's propensity to mate with sailors of the shit-faced condition and all. Only way she could get laid. He even flushed away the tiny smile attempting to turn the corners of his mouth. When he spoke, his words rang clear and strong, no wavering here…

"A guy walks into a bar, sits down and asks the bartender for a glass of 1910 scotch. The bartender looks at his stock, but can't find any 1910 scotch. He finds a bottle of 1909 scotch and figures it'll do just fine. After all, what's in a year? He pours the guy a shot and walks away. The guy sips it and spits it out, 'Shit! This ain't 1910 scotch. This is 1909 scotch. I hate that shit! Gimmee 1910 or I'm outta here!'

Startled, the bartender rushes back and apologizes, 'Sorry sir, my mistake. I know we have some 1910 scotch. Must be in the cellar. I'll be right back!'

He rushes down into the cellar and searches but still can't find any 1910 scotch. He only finds some 1911 scotch. But now he's wiser. 'Guy musta read the label. I'll show him!'

He puts the bottle in a brown, paper bag and climbs back upstairs. Now he pours the impatient guy a shot and delivers it. The guy barely even sips it before again, spitting the liquid onto the wood floor, 'Damn! This is 1911 scotch! What kinda place you runnin' here?'

Now the bartender is truly amazed. But he also is worried. His reputation is in jeopardy. His few customers are starting to wonder out loud about their own drink pedigrees. 'Oh no! Sorry sir! I musta grabbed the wrong bottle. It's a little dark down there. I'll find you that 1910 if it takes all night!' Back down to the cellar he goes thinking, 'Wow! This guy is good!'

This time he turns on all the lights, pulls bottles and cases off the shelves and at last finds a bottle of 1910 scotch. Proudly, he dusts it off; then rushes back to the guy to pour him a shot. 'This is on the house, sir.'

The guy cautiously sips the brew, then relaxes and sits satisfied back into his chair. 'Ahhhh, 1910 scotch. None better.'

Meanwhile, an old drunk at the end of the bar is also amazed, thinking, 'This guy is good.' He gets up, goes to the back of the bar with his glass and pees into it. Bringing the glass back to the guy he slurs, 'Here buddy. Try this.'

The guy takes the glass and takes a sip. Wrinkling his mouth in disgust, he spits it onto the floor beside the other deposits and yells, 'This tastes like piss!'

The old drunk confirms, 'Yeah! Now tell me how old I am!'"

The other chuckles, "Cute! So what's your point?"

O'Rourke looks him in his eyes with a steely glance or as steely as brown eyes can. "Point is, experts sometimes ain't got the sense they was born with."

"You're saying Morano isn't what he's cracked up to be?"

"I'm saying take a sniff before you drink th' piss!" That said, he turned and left the Colonel fuming at his desk.

Back to reality, he wondered if the man still fumed or if he'd ever get the point. If not, it would be in keeping. The middle name of the Defense Intelligence Agency is only slightly less oxymoronic as it is when placed in Central Intelligence Agency. DIA did not quite approach CIA's level of dogmatic ritual and obeisance; however, also being an inside the beltway organization, they too had their moments. O'Rourke knew one thing for certain; they'd never appreciate this deviation from authority. Deviation hell! He wasn't just upping the ante on his own, he was going all in.

The DIA had convinced themselves the culprits worked for some Arabic terrorist cell, maybe some Baader-Meinhof or Red Army Faction spinoff that had gravitated to al Qaida after the Soviet Union's collapse deprived them of reliable funding. Now these rabid post-WWII throwbacks had aligned with another group out to control the world. Their ideological calls to nature were not quite synched, one being of God-less conviction. However, anarchy is its own religion. So they would march to the beat of a different drummer as long as the rhythm extolled doom for common foes …such as the western military.

Typical of military in this post-911 era, DIA saw al Qaida behind ever tree. It made sense, sure. They had video imagery and phone intercepts verifying some kind of "White" al Qaida cell operating in Pakistan that had even recruited some Americans into the group. However, there was nothing about their intentions or current missions outside Afghanistan and Pakistan. No Caribbean links, no American operations, no planned attacks outside the region.

DIA took these indicators or lack of indicators, to indicate they had yet to discover indicators of the real plot. Indicators were that they needed to keep looking until they found the link to the al Qaida bad guys as indicated in their Intel as stipulated by the factors factored in, scripted and altered by their worldview of terrorism. Everybody knows this is how it is and that is that …as so indicated.

His worldview however, originated on the Piedmont of 1950s North Carolina, forever altered by terrorism lawfully conspired under the wide-sweeping practices of Jim Crow racism. His worldview constructed a different vision of what a bad guy looked like, normally, more resembling a Timothy McVeigh, than a Timothy al Sheik. However, in this case, his more resembled a Timothy El Morano.

Televised updates kept coming. All events scheduled in conjunction with the VMA award show were either cancelled or postponed. That meant no celebrity parties for the rich and beautiful. Even the Moonman balloon figure and the Hotel MTV sign were removed from their locations in front of the Surf Hotel. Though uncertain about how much the warm Florida waters would swell the storm's power, none desired to provide more debris for its winds to fling, reminding that later on this night, he might end up as flung debris...

Friends faces flew across his shuttered eyes. He didn't immediately open them, but wondered how this would affect them. Sylvia, Mickey, maybe a few more, like his karate kids. How would they receive the news of his doom? Would they experience regret or hate that he had not the decency even to leave a note of goodbye? Then the images vanished and he reopened his eyes to the television. There would be no notes...

This storm had more tricks than Houdini. It had begun its acclaim for notice first as Tropical Depression Twelve just that Tuesday; on Wednesday it was named Tropical Storm Eris and pronounced a possible threat to land. Then, a relatively few hours later the name was changed to Hurricane Eris just prior to its slamming into South Florida. Even then it managed another surprise, changing from due west --heading directly for Broward County-- to south-southwest into Miami-Dade. Even more surprising, the Channel Seven broadcast was interrupted when hit by Eris's eye-wall and its self-proclaimed newsplex lost total power for fifteen minutes or so.

As nature's fury played games of havoc with mankind's toys, Jane Addams provided appropriate backdrop for this present condition. From O'Rourke's memory her poignant verse sprang to remind him that the reality of failure is in not trying: "What after all has maintained the human race on this old globe despite all the calamities of nature and all the tragic failings of mankind, if not faith in new possibilities and courage to advocate them."

Mother Nature had more games in waiting and kept them coming, but then so did the news folk. The TV view now showed what appeared to be a forest growing out of several streets as fichus and palm trees had been knocked over by the fierce winds. Their shallow root balls gave insufficient support in the face of this hurricane force. Jane Addams had obviously been hero worshipping people such as these braving the elements this night. They were in abundance, though severely outgunned.

Reporters turned their camera lenses to capture efforts of local road crews to clear some street blockages. Excavator tractors crunched the trees into kindling, scooped up the debris and deposited it all into dump truck beds, clearing the roadways. But the sneaky, resilient storm lasted much longer and hit much harder than predicted. That was unfortunate. Even more unfortunate were its next victims –further north and west, up the gulf coast —who would fare far worst.

But he never witnessed any of those reports. A different motivation now possessed him, for the information he sought was not being televised. The luminescent hands inched closer to twenty-five minutes past ten. He was further behind schedule than he had hoped. But it could not be helped, not if he wanted to keep his accomplishment secret.

One other good thing about this place, lobby security made entry a tougher prospect for non-residents. So they probably wouldn't try and keep tabs on him that way. But they'd be somewhere about. This he knew.

This time he went looking for them. Not that they were all that difficult to fish out from normal comers and goers, cause those folk usually attempted to get to shelter as quickly as possible. That and the fact that there weren't a whole lot of them…

More than likely, his two watch bowsers themselves had to be weighing the necessity for risking their lives in this wrath from God. Then again, some folks are just dedicated like that. In this example, dedicated was spelled: S-U-C-K-E-R and they weren't the only ones …nor were they first on that list.

Sucker number one, aka him, John O'Rourke, El Stupido (one of several new categories he now perfectly matched, dumbass stubborn mule head another) now left his room to check out the view forward. A dozen other hotel guests also stood or sat in the compact-sized, second floor lobby through whose wide plate glass front they hoped to see some spectacular happening worthy of one day enthralling the grand kids.

The counter behind them seemed as abandoned as the street below. Only subdued lighting gave any indication that someone might possibly have remained on duty rather than sprinting homeward to ensure safety of family. But it was sufficient to permit safe negotiation around furniture and furnishings while permitting them a better view outside at rivulets of liquid sky savaging swaying palms that bent low in silent resistance.

Back-dropped by a nearly pitch black ocean, wild wave fronts broke fiercely against the white sand. His imagination saw their line moving higher and higher, tsunami-style. Anyone could see that this thing hungered for a taste of human flesh, this killer off its leash. Anyone could see or so he thought. His view evidently was not shared with at least one of his lobby mates.

He could blame it on the drinking. Drug and alcohol consumption have been known to cause nyctalopia or night blindness, along with other things such as impaired judgment (even worse in his case as he had yet to taste a drop). Plus, the area power outages assured even lesser illumination outside --of the artificial variety-- street lights being especially hard hit. So maybe their outside view was more limited than normal.

Whatever the reason, several guests chatted about the advisability of a stroll outside or even up on the rooftop terrace where the hotel's pool and Jacuzzi were located. They seemed especially intrigued by the latter site, the sole exception being its comfort rating as all lounge chairs had been brought inside, so no place good to sit for these dating website newly mets. Still, its intrigue held some quality …for some.

"C'mon Cathy! Hey Bret, grab Yvonne! Let's go skinny dip!"

"Ted you crazy! Free Willy on th' ceilie? Ah right, let's go baby, I'm in!"

"What you say Kat? Vonnie? Know ya'll first dating so gotta be feelin' freaky! Wanna go slippy dippy?"

"Theodore! I'm not about to sit my naked behind on the cement. There's no chairs out there or towels!"

"Ditto for me guys! I do freaky, but not filthy! No telling what's been blowin' across that pool deck and in case your drunk ass doesn't remember, bad things can get into the parts of girls ya'll like most. Some of them can get around to ya'll!"

"Shit! I clean forgot about clitty litter! Yeah, she right Teddy. I got no need fo' VDs, HPVs, HIVs and any other kinds of alphabet crud. Can't take no chance with the STDs and you know I'm gonna be hittin' that tonight!"

Their muffled conversations both confused and confounded him.

Could they really mean such madness? He had no idea their drugs of choice, chemical or liquid, but that nyctalopia must have been a bitch!

The murmurs gained volume as discussions took flight. While he said nothing to motivate them either way, every part of him wondered what idiot gene pool spawned these people who gave first consideration to comfort while deliberating the merits of sitting outside in the open, seventy feet above street level, during a hurricane.

Were these the Deathstalker types he'd viewed jumping out of his TV screen to wrestle voracious crocodiles and Great White sharks? Was taking potluck in a hurricane all that different? Should he remind them their folly? Would death stalking, thrill seekers listen even if he did?

No Sylvia present, but even still his tongue refused release of the suggestion stirring at its base. This reluctance was so unlike him. A single remark should do it, just a little innocuous accounting on the dangerous tendency of hurricane force winds to sweep unwary bodies over and off rooftops.

Funny. Before meeting Sylvia he spent as much time deleting matches on singles websites as picking them. She unattractive? Delete. Posing with animals? Delete. Only one "above the neck" photo? Hell, if she scared to show more, what I'm looking for? Delete! Delete!

Didn't matter that they probably wouldn't want him either. Tuff titty! He wasn't going out like that!

Then came the collision. They took to calling it The Crash! But, hey! You gonna run into something, please God make it something like Sylvia! Besides, no cuts, breaks or bruises. What's not to like? It was on!

He'd have married on the spot. That is, if he hadn't already sworn off hitching up to wild things!

Couldn't tell her about this, that's fer sure. Seemed perfectly sane and self-explanatory to him, but --more-than-likely-- Miss "Heal the World" would once again condemn his morbid sense of reality as she usually did whenever his discourse ranted against stupid people doing stupid things. His sense of sane she interpreted just the opposite, preferring the soft-pedal approach to his more blatant, "in your face style". Her words.

He might just be able to convince these people otherwise, but would she consider the beneficence in that? No way. All he need employ is this simple embellishment, this low-detail narrative on the effects of high speed wind gusts launching people bent on getting high while up high. Namely, one could quickly travel from the high to the low places resulting in instantaneous trajectory termination.

A mouthful, sure, but nothing overly blatant or in your face the way he saw. Thrill seekers and death stalkers came in all shapes, sizes and affirmations. Even she would have to agree he had an affinity with people who volunteered to risk life and limb. Not that his particular brand of myopia would matter much to people who'd never dodged death as an occupation. Not that combat necessarily made one visionary.

In truth, the only pictures he remembered from war tended towards horrific displays of barbaric intensity rendered in black and white images chosen for endless viewing by some merciless deity. From the recesses of his mind sprang monstrous depictions rendered as mute, still frames frozen for all time and, according to his shrink, it was a similar scenario for too many others unfortunate enough to be acquainted with war. Played across personal video screens, one scene follows another in ponderous procession; bleak and dismal, an amateurishly recreated film noir.

Water drops. Drip, drip, dripping wet from the faucet. Hated those two. Reminds how lazy he gotta be to put up with something he can't stand.

Simple wrench, maybe a screwdriver. Zip, zap! Done son! Completo finito! No mo' bother. But it's still dripping.

Now a days, VA calls it PTSD, a type of depression. Kinda like sadness, but doesn't go away. Not really. Guess they oughta know, they gave it to him …at least somebody in uniform did!

"Man! Depression sux! Robs character, initiative, everything!" When he close his eyes real tight he can make it go away for a bit. Comes back though, sometimes worse. Turns out a bit ain't shit! Neither is a shitter…

Even his memory of the man came in gray scale. The face would forever claim a back corner with other evils that had imperiled his life. Most prominent of bony thin, acerbic features --parading in the guise of a hapless Lieutenant-Commander unable even to find clothes that fit-- the hollow eyes seemed to suggest a myopic blindness to such endearing character traits as humility, generosity and devotion. This fellow –for whom there did not exit sunshine weak enough to tan under without burning his pale skin away-- obviously had never spent a single night with any of those alluring creatures and probably few with anything that could be identified as alluring.

His stare bored straight through patients as if they were not there. Word was leaked, this was a hit man, a hired gun. He was a Pentagon target shooter sent in to dispose of difficult cases period. The brass did not concern themselves with his appearance or even how he accomplished his tasks, only that he accomplish them efficiently and effectively and leave no blood trails. They care, because they didn't plan on inviting him to socials, not even the Navy Ball. They didn't even need to give him an agenda or marching orders. He would accomplish their purposes without so much as a surreptitious phone call. It was in his nature, which was why they used him, which was why his role as Naval Officer was only a temporary respite from real world challenges.

Men of his profession could only be tolerated for limited periods before becoming a liability, also. Too soon he would know burial locations of too many skeletons. He must never be given the chance to bite the hand of the masters. Even without direct orders from the queen, a bee might sting.

Ultimately, his chance of climbing the rungs of power, about the same as this patient of being shitcanned by the Marines, on reverse day! He'd never go high up the scales for sure. Equally, this man had even less chance. His masters were confident their ace could accomplish that goal, with jail time a bonus…

His unsympathetic nature, omniscient ability and sour disposition fit the task nicely; he possessed a God Complex. He already knew for certain the man was criminal, not victim. A few tests to validate, no need to verify, just to confirm and it was off to Leavenworth for the long course in military schooling. He'd done the same several times before. His expertise at courts martials always sealed the deal. The judges loved his no-nonsense demeanor.

But it was real chicken versus egg. Few peers could recall whether his nature had soured before or after realization had kicked in. Whether or not, nothing in him was going to help John O'Rourke. It's lucky there were others who did…

Yeah, combat don't necessarily make one visionary, but this useless recalcitrant in his outsized sailor suit had neither skills nor experience to draw upon for treating combat casualties of the mind. For O'Rourke, recalcitrant being the nicest of several descriptors he picked out, "douche bag" another.

Scuttlebutt proclaimed him and his skill set exactly what the doctor ordered, as far as the brass were concerned that is. O'Rourke could never be certain of that. However, he was very certain that Doctor Darkside's poor technique only entrenched the black and white maelstrom, making the monstrous images worse before they got better and they didn't get better due to any treatment at the hands of this sharp-nosed, near-albino with an agenda.

He came with only one purpose. This undisciplined man had violated trust. Not only violated, gone off the reservation. Shit'n poop! Loopty loop! You ordered to do a certain job, fly a certain sortie, be willing to die a certain death, goddammit do it! It's why you get the big bucks ...such as they are.

But no! He decided to fight his own war. Chased a commie MIG into Cambodia, way off the legal landscape, way outside the established boundaries. Coulda escalated an already ticklish situation, especially since the press already on th' story an' tellin' th' whole world!

Don't matter it's a stupid rule that causes a lot more dead troops. Don't make one bit'o difference if he ain't the first. Rules are rules! He going down! Simple as that! Fun fact, gonna be wonderful!

O'Rourke would never forget Lieutenant-Commander Pale Face whose full nickname included "Asswipe-cuntface-cocksuckin-muthafuckin-sonofabitch". There were others...

Flying a Phantom is simultaneously both exhilarating and scary. You always wonder if this gonna be your last flight and worry that it will, but look forward to leaping into the sky anyway. It's truly a drug and he the junkie. But like anything to do with drugs, it ain't good to let them ride you, at least don't let the control freaks know ...problem is, he let them know!

Military control heads cater to their similarity with chess players, except on an even larger scale. Missions and operations all about moving men and machines. They move a piece on their chessboard that represents a brigade, a company or a single squad, don't matter if it's a zillion miles away, it best move! It don't move? It's a problem ...if it's you, you the problem!

If you a problem, it's back to the game zone where they much rather play taps over your corpse than deal with your attitude. "Shut it bout th' ways we tryna git ya killed an' maybe we promote ya. Die in combat, we give ya medals. Embarrass us, we lock you up an' report you died in combat!!!"

It's complicated when tryna deal with shadows. You never know where they coming from or consist of, just that they ain't never really got your back until you become one with them ...in the shadows!

Basically it's like, no easy ways out! In O'Rourke's case, the "out" way was about the worst way. They took away the only thing he had left ...his double afterburner hot rod!

Withdrawal was the worst. Flying F-4s was like a drug to him. He had a sweet tooth and daddy loved his candy. When they barred him from the cockpit he got to a point where life no longer mattered either.

He felt emaciated, drained and totally helpless. Gone went wife and mistress and he'd only half-heartedly attempted to get both back. He'd never been that kind of fighter to hold onto something that don't want him.

The double whammy! Losing both his consorts, was too much even for him. He withdrew into his turtle shell and stayed there. It took Mickey to lure him out, club foot and all ...right after he got him a bath!.

Not totally destitute. He did own the house in Philly that Shiro willed him. He had a few savings from the joint account his runaway wife had barely touched. Plus, a couple other odds 'n ends, mostly odds.

But most financial experts would assess John Paul O'Rourke's finances as minimal at best. He really needed to start a job search and soon and find one even sooner. The question of how soon? Wasn't no one close enough to break him out of his funk and tell him: "Stop sulking, start looking".

Problem of breaking him out of his malaise? Again, nobody close enough to help. They took away his wife, his only real friend Tony and his mentor Shiro. Oh yeah, and his jet plane.

Not like they care! No such animals as PTSD, Agent Orange or any of the quite a few other calamities calling plague on Vietnam vets. Vietnam vets the only living war heroes who more often got blamed for losing the war they weren't allowed to win than celebrated like the heroes they truly were. Over fifty-eight thousand paid the ultimate death price. But it was hundreds of thousands more who continued paying the costs to "soldier on" after you no longer a soldier. Not talking physical wounds as much as the unseen mental tortures. Admittedly they all bad …just seldom read about a paraplegic soldier popping a hot one into his temple!

"Say you got nightmares while awake from visions o' mangled corpses prancing just behind your eyelids, open or closed? Sure you not imagining? We got couple other guys comin' in here talkin' that same smack! Sounds like ya'll attended th' same coach! Come back when you got somethin' real! Oh, you do? Got a little trichlorophenoxyacetic acid mixed with dichlorophenoxyacetic acid and glyphosate on ya? Well, not only is that a hellova mouthful; exposure during the euphemistically titled 'Operation Ranch Hand' never ever happened! That was simply a "thought experiment" intended to force the VC out of the elephant grass and into the open where we could find him! Ya say that's the chemical warfare strategy most know as 'Agent Orange'? Well buddy ain't no such animal! So we tempted ta give you compensation fo' yo' creativity if nothing else! But son, yo' real problem, you a slacker! You can't take responsibility for your own failures in life. Always tryna git U. S. Government handouts, alla money we spent feedin', clothin' 'n housin' ya ungrateful ass in wherever th' fuk place we mailed ya to an' when! Embarrassing! The state our military has become after we state ya'll no longer military! Useless when ya no longer useful! Hate ya'll!"

They'd never let him stay. Forget that word spelled R-E-T-I-R-E! He'd be lucky they even let him keep the memories. Once a Marine, always a Marine? Nope! Not no more him! Oh, he still caught the dream, now and again. Except now more nightmare…

"I'ma goddamn, America-lovin' member of Uncle Sam's killer-elite force, the one of a kind, genuine United States Marine Corps! Don't say corpse you shitbag! We ain't dead yet! We th' Corps and it's pronounced "core", cause we th' center of the best there is! Make no mistake, we ain't no fake! Not even dat tub 'o lard currently occupying our nation's presidential palace can get dat wrong ....an his dumbass done screwed up ev'rything else! Yeah, kno I'm old an' discharged, but once in, in fer ever! It's a way of life, a way of living. God, country, Marines! Don't git twisted, family's there too! On point! Jus' sayin'!"

It came back at least weekly. Him sporting the graybeard look, steppin' out in a bowler hat and cane. Sharp as a tack and rich beyond measure! Spending that major general retirement pay! But alas, the troubles you earn as a child haunt you as an adult! Too bad children seldom get that picture…

People who'd practiced at war saw scenes every time they closed their eyes for rest or sleep or just for whatever. Spectral visions rose from bodies torn and burned beyond recognition, friends and enemies killed alike, leaving those who survived in a constant struggle to retain at least a sliver of remembrance of names and faces. The most they achieved were those black and whites, for the most part. On the other hand, images for those who visited conflict only through the resources of CNN or the evening news came crisp and sharp with myriad colorings; at the very least, filtered through rose-colored glasses. Sylvia belonged to this latter crowd.

Women are wondrous creatures, but oh so confusing. She loved him dearly and hated everything about him just as much. Even those occasions when he soft-pedaled it, tried it her way, she would instead hear thesis and support on the science of non-aerodynamic capability, aka, that shit don't fly! Whatever, the subject!

He say red, she see blue. Substituted in place of what he intended as well-meaning, neatly-constructed argument, her disapproving side would insert some humorless, emotionless rote indicative of a Star Trek revival featuring Mister Spock.

They say opposites attract. However, it sometimes paused him in wonder how someone so supposedly compatible one moment, could harbor such intense differences the next. He figured maybe God had cursed him a little for going on that dating website. Meeting a woman on dating websites is like a blind date, except you can't blame your friends. You picked her you suffer!

Had to admit, though, God wanna curse him with a woman as fine as Syl, curse him every day! He wasn't looking for marriage, just companionship …and this companion sailed an awesome ship!

Of course, can't tell her about everything. Not even his concerns about these kids heading up to the hotel rooftop pool during a hurricane. From deep within her mindset would generate vivid pictures supplanting his cautionary suggestions with hurtling, shrieking bodies executed high arcing parabolic vectors up into the thinner atmospheric regions until the lifting winds subsided sufficiently for gravity to again overtake.

There, they would parody some Wile E. Coyote scene from a Road Runner cartoon. They would hover momentarily. Up would raise a sign displaying the word "HELP!" A split-second later, their bodies would descend, accelerating rapidly as they screamed their hatred at the one responsible for the roof party, until they realized that individually they were all responsible. They would achieve this realization just before going, splat!

She would appreciate none of these thoughts, not one, no matter that they originated within her idea of him, not from him. Neither would she appreciate her recreation's stoic reminder that the probability of fatality figured to factor very high …even though none of this was what he had said.

Eventually though, rational consideration outdueled ludicrous and the collaboration soon agreed with other hotel guests to pool stashes of liquor and snacks for adventure in a less challenging location. Hurricane parties remained in vogue this evening, however it was thankful that suicide parties were not …well not for everyone.

The howl outside came in waves that increased to levels near shrieking before dropping near to nothingness only to rise again as Mother Nature had her way. However, although he was far less impressed with their change (just the thought bordered insanity) O'Rourke refrained from copying the TV man and casting a disapproving look. People living in glass houses should never throw stones. Instead he scanned the parked cars for sign

There! Both men were smokers, at least one a chain-smoker. The flare of a cigarette lighter from a dark interior caused his head to swivel immediately towards a Jeep Cherokee parked across the street on the east side of Ocean Drive. It looked similar in model and color to the one following him the previous evening, though they all looked similar at night in the rain. Didn't matter. He already knew what he already knew … he was not alone.

He headed back to his room. The other had initially set up surveillance in the underground garage behind the hotel affording excellent view of the rear exit, as well as the private balcony outside his quarry's room. But even with the powerful area torrent, visibility was still relatively good, so evidently he had decided to find a spot that exhibited a less drenching quality.

Illuminated by small flood lamps —some which reached light beams high into the boughs of thirty-foot palm trees to drive away any menacing shadows-- the entire right side of the hotel area could be easily covered by a single pair of eyes, much too easily for him. The whole block dark, but unfortunately, this hotel had plenty of power. He cursed that reality along with the fact that the left side had no ground-level exits at all, unless one first tunneled through the bar area then the adjacent restaurant out to Fifth Street.

The slender, boutique structure was all very tastefully contrived and its lighting, actually subdued. But desiring pitch-black shadows, O'Rourke cursed any and all illumination provided by colored arc lamps or neon signs throughout the area. Though it could have been more challenging…

Luckily this was a low level structure, one of the reasons he had chosen it. That and the fact that it was easy walking distance from places he might need to get to or away from. No part of his planning lay in cement. It was all fluid. Meaning it was all a work in progress. But the hotel's sides only climbed five stories --not like some others nearby whose top floors appeared to disappear into the lowering night sky-- and as fortune favors the prepared mind, he was unconcerned with finding his way past the surveillance. He'd grab a rope and rappel from the roof if necessary.

Still, it would not be an easy task. Once the rain began sheeting, the man in the rear apparently decided to move his watch location from underneath the first level garage. The force of wind and rain blowing directly in off the ocean and down the alley --that separated the adjacent hotels-- rammed through the tunnel-like garage structure with unerring aim, finding its victim huddled miserably between the parked cars. Eventually he wised up and moved. Now he was holed up somewhere O'Rourke could not see him. But he was definitely somewhere close by …O'Rourke could feel him.

In another life, he would like to have discussed the logic of working for an employer too cheap to provide his employees sufficient facilities for the tasks assigned to them, like another vehicle in which to ride out the rear guard. But that was their problem. His was circumventing those obviously dedicated and deluded individuals.

To his reckoning, the nervous, twitchy man might have found a way into the --normally locked-- back door on the right side of the hotel, almost directly beneath O'Rourke's balcony. He figured the man probably stayed inside there, mostly, then occasionally headed back outside, braving the hurricane force winds when it came time for another puff. Every now and again a hacking cough exploded into the night air from below.

"Nails!" O'Rourke reflected, "He's close, real close." He speculated again how little capacity the chain-smoking man's lungs retained, thus his quandary over the nickname. "Nails" fit to a tee. The guy was obviously pounding another one into his coffin with each deep puff. Still there was that other idiosyncrasy, that one he had noticed first. He nearly chose to stay with it. But he appreciated the location assistance more. A humorous anecdote flirted across his brow that he could drop a can of gasoline on the guy as he lit up. But gas was missing among his suite's amenities, so he moved past the absurd options to those with a greater chance of success.

"Dink, de-dink, de-dink! Dink, de-dink, de-dink!" Its chime shook him out of the deep contemplation. Sylvia. He let it go to voice mail. He had little time for socializing and none for playing kissy-kissy. She sometimes required long distance love-making to get her through the nights they slept alone. The dichotomy concerning bridges is which ones to cross and which to burn. Her beautiful eyes, smoldering and dark stared accusingly into his. He hoped she'd understand he couldn't help her out this night. The thought came that someone else might …oh well, her life, her decision.

Back to his immediate problem. O'Rourke's preemptory reconnoiter the previous evening gave a look at the enemy's surveillance procedures. Lots of people on the street and in the hotel restaurant made sneaking out to watch the watchers an easier task. Tonight they seemed much the same, apparently only adjustments for the weather. There were at least four men operating in shifts. His scrutiny had only detected four. Two Cubans on days, their rapid-fire Spanish a dead give-away. The day crew now replaced, he was left with Nails –as he had more appropriately nicknamed the backdoor chain-smoker, though Twitchy or even Hacker would also have sufficed—and Arnold, the big white guy.

His observation of Nails' mannerisms revealed an evidently nervous habit of jerking his left shoulder, as well as that nasty smoker's cough. He appeared to become even more nervous the longer he went without lighting up. That fact spoke nothing about his competence as a warrior, but said volumes about his alert status. Still, the occurrence of the cough appeared at random intervals, apparently unpredictable.

Nails' location options were limited by the wind-driven rain bludgeoning Miami Beach. His choices along the length of the small street running between the hotel rear and stores backing up from Collins Avenue were all very wet and threatening. He was probably even now cursing the Miami Beach architects who left little spare space unfilled in their quest to maximize economic potential. Essentially a back alley, the street sported nothing akin to any sidewalk widening its area. The backsides of storefronts facing Collins nearly touched the curb.

So the opportunity to spy a fast moving individual crossing tiny Ocean Court where it intersected the curb at Fifth Street would rest with fortune or fate. Only the garage that serviced the stores, two hotels and an apartment building offered any semblance of cover and decent visibility. But a half-block long, its straight-through design --wide enough for two-way traffic as well as parked cars on either side—acted like a wind tunnel. So the torrent barely even slowed down until it hit the storefronts across the other side of Collins Avenue. O'Rourke decided there was very little chance that Nails would venture back across just for sake of the odd viewing. If he did, things might get dicey.

The other man on the night crew he had named Arnold for a reason. Not just because he plodded around, his bearing and gait very similar to the silver screen muscleman; but because he was also almost as big. This Arnold also smoked, but looked to be otherwise fit. So if it came down to a choice for confrontation, there was no doubt with which one he would rather argue.

He seriously weighed his options, knowing full well that anything less translated as juvenile, even infantile; definitely less than warranted. These people were obviously serious about their business and whatever their ultimate reason, something bad could occur should he provoke them unnecessarily. One bad move could result in an outcome from which he might not come out. The sensible side of him wanted a review of this "Out of Hell and Into Damnation" strategy. Just to relook alternatives, checks and balances and the like. Not necessarily for revision, more like reconfirming what had already been confirmed. Even though, there did exist an alternative or two.

Reason cautioned that he could always just play out the string, stay in his room like a good little boy. But he hated that idea. The irascible side of him hated it even more. He had already made up his mind that he was going out tonight, reason be damned. Neither Mother Nature nor these bad guys would dissuade him without serious argument. Whatever their temperament, they'd be in luck. Tonight he was in perfect mood for an argument. But that was for later. Now was for rest.

"Who are you?" The voice emanated from out of the dream state.

"I am a son of God."

"Are you certain of this?"

"Yes!" Conviction filled his every fiber. He sat cross-legged on the bare wood flooring, its highly polished surface reflecting rays from a small incandescent ceiling lamp. The soft, yellow glow cast all around his form imparting a golden quality to the brown hue of the naked flesh, flesh whose monolithic position never changed, with the exception of a rhythmic rising and falling of broad shoulders timed to slow, deep intake of the tropical air, its content heavy with moisture in the ninety percent humidity.

Meditation. They say it shapes your brain. Some devoted practioners can even defy physical laws: levitate, survive underwater long time periods, even lightning strikes. He had heard about such things. Never really thought about them much. Still, the concept he stored deep in the dark corners. For now. His mind unfocused, navigating through the myriad places it desired, his form like a flowing wraith soaring through sunlit skies past green meadows, tall forests and deep rivers.

His form bent forward slightly at the waist, elbows resting against muscular thighs. The center of his forehead balanced easily against the tips of both index fingers, channeling the focus through his Ajna chakra, his mind's eye. The manner was similar to that taught him an age ago by his Aunt Maude, but not the purpose. Both that age and Aunt Maude were long gone. Her teaching centered on a reverence for the Christian God; however his current purpose centered on an entirely new religion ...the worship of self.

She had taught him to hold his hands together in this manner while he prayed. But its position displayed more than simply a reverence for all things greater than he, of equal motivation was an intuitive understanding of its benefit to channeling, focusing energies and thoughts.

While he would never feel an urge to vocalize endless chantings like his Buddhist and Hindu friends (at least they seemed endless), there was something to that focusing the mind's eye part of the dance. He had come to appreciate the sense of clarity he sometimes achieved; those times he chose to slow down enough to seek clarity, that is. Surrounded by enemies and questionable friends, this seemed to be one of those times ...when clarity was exactly what was needed.

The deep breath he held to a count of four before allowing its pent-up gases to slip easily out flared nostrils, until almost all gone. Then squeezing hard his diaphragm he forced nearly all the remainder to reluctant freedom, totally purging all vestiges of waste gas and clearing the way for a fresh replacement. Normally he would hold this empty-lung state for a two-count, but this night he counted four before reversing the flow and refilling.

In this manner he believed would also come fresh thought, with every new breath. When the process imparted a slight dizzying he chided himself, thinking: "Too long away!"

"Bow your head and pray." Aunt Maude's determined soprano ordered his prepubescent self, then bowed her own head and quoted the same grace she usually said prior to the meals the two of them shared together. "Father in Heaven we ask in Jesus' name that you bless this food, our family and friends…"

His father Henry said grace pretty much the same way, though he'd usually add a wrinkle or two somewhere along the line, mixing in something about weather or work or finding work, those few times when he joined them. He, being head of house and all, automatically assumed those duties whenever available. Maude insisted on that rule, although Henry would have been just as comfortable following his older sister's lead, especially those times he wasn't quite as available as she thought he was, like after a night out with friends. "It's morning, get up, come to th' table and say grace!"

"Take a deep breath and hold it," commanded Shiro's soft baritone to his adolescent pupil. Their images merged, intertwining; their voices becoming one, the messages the same and then they left him once again. Neither Henry, Maude not even the indomitable Shiro now remained to cajole or command. But their lessons he retained …at least some of them.

Eventually the effort eased, ceasing to be so burdensome and dizzying and he no longer needed concentrate on the breathing aspect. Now his mind's eye could wander freely through the inner realms as it chose. Now he could relax enough to permit it free travel as the rest of him came along for the ride, not as controller, but as witness.

It was never the easiest of accomplishments. A popular tune became stuck in his head and looped around endlessly. It finally lessened only to be replaced by the jingle from some commercial he had heard far too much recently. It was never easy. But, "Patience defeats even the hardiest of foes".

He remembered that lesson, also, concentrating to cleanse it before it began its own loop. Too late. The benefit of patience, exasperatingly explained again for the zillionth time by a sensei nearly at the end of his came full circle to haunt, then taunt much in the way he had so done himself. To this day, he still wondered whether his teacher ever suspected his pupil's gaming with these pretended lapses of recall. "Shiro, how do you focus on nothingness? How can one create a blank slate within his mind?"

Ruefully, he finally decided that Shiro knew exactly his childish prank, painfully remembering all those extra fingertip and knuckle pushups innocuously slipped in at the end of training sessions. Looking back, those seemed to have been the sessions during which he had interjected some smart aleck prank. Why he had not seen the negative result back then, only heaven knows. Shiro had a way of refocusing his students, whether they perceived that side of the equation or not. His older and wiser self could now appreciate that the lesson paid off "The wisest man seeks first to learn control of himself, not others."

No chants, only the sound of his breathing exercises escaped the pursed lips. Even that he no longer acknowledged. That part of him he put on automatic as he did the monitoring of all other common sounds on a night filled with repetitive blowings and rumblings and other things unimportant for now. Thoughts he focused on nothing in particular, allowing misty vapors to rise within and swirl around and around until their soft, silken touches eventually receded and their wet, tender kisses ceased; the taste of each ebbing, then suddenly spiriting, wistfully away; until clarity found its way inside.

The plan he had concocted came full central to a thought mechanism no longer cluttered with useless dribble. There would be time for pleasant reflection later, if he lived. If not, maybe there would be time in the next existence in heaven, hell or reincarnation. Come what may, now he was ready. He rose, dressed quickly and prepared to leave. He would need all his focus for what came next …and most of his luck.

"This is what we do. Don't judge, don't hate. This is how we do what we do!" He could see them, hear them, sense their call to arms. Visions of men packing the trunks of cars with explosives and scraps of sharp metals intended for the soft flesh of women and children shopping in a faraway street bazaar. The thought chf Tina flitted across his mind. A picture of her ruthlessly murdered carcass littering the Washington Mall, blown to charred ruin because she could not be controlled, just like those women shopping with their kids in that far off bazaar. "Don't hate us, this is what we do!"

He would not judge them or hate them. He understood them; they were only fulfilling their nature. Some are meant to be lambs, some wolves.

Nature tends for lambs to be slaughtered by wolves. No need to hate the wolves. Of course there is no need to live in the wolves' neighborhood either. But once you lambs get tired of the constant moving and the inevitable wolves following, there might be a need to develop appropriate countermeasures.

Sheepdogs work okay for a time. They live to drive off wolves, reducing the numbers of lambs taken for the slaughter. But even the presence of powerful Sheepdogs will never totally subvert the wolves' nature. After all, wolves love to be wolves. They're good at it and they're gonna get some lamb every now and then. The Sheepdogs may drive them off again and again, but the wolves will eventually succeed. They just bide their time. It's their nature.

Back to him came that last night, the only time she opened up the real, her true feelings. Like her Ex the one with the best kno on her Next! Just how crazy are things inside her head right now? He didn't ask her. Maybe he shoulda.

"Money. Money don't change you it just shows what you really are. That's Carlos. The money just smokescreen he hide behind."

An oldie, but supergoodie, Isaac Hayes "Walk on by" playing the background. How does Isaac know these times to show up? Like it's perfect timing ...if you need rewinding!

"...and I start to cry each time we meet."

"...I just can't get over losin' you, so if I seem broken and blue..."

He didn't pry, just did his sounding board routine. She wanna talk, he got the ear. She wanna convo? Maybe then he'd give advice, maybe not. It's a far leap jumping into somebody else game. They could end up hating you for it!

Tina's smile fading into the past, he made his plans. Her murderers were just outside his grasp. All he needed do was snatch them up. He did not hate them, but had no interest in changing their true selves. They were wolves, predators; by definition only interested in predation, capturing and eating others. That is what they do. Modifying such behavior is what social workers do. Social work was for others not such as him. People like him, instead sought results modification. Specifically, he hoped to help these wolves experience different results and new sensations, the sensation of the slaughtered ones. Though no easy task, it's a learning experience, meant to be delivered by a learned individual.

Marines are cut from similar cloth as wolves. They don't like to wait patiently for the wolves to attack. They also have very sharp teeth and tend to practice more violent forms of countermeasure than sheepdogs. Given a choice, they prefer to take the lesson to the enemy and they're very good at giving lessons.

Teaching new sensations really is an experience best delivered by a learned individual in the proper environment employing a personal touch. Whether "learned individual" fit as a proper description, was a maybe, maybe not. Regardless, John Paul O'Rourke intended to deliver his lesson, in person. All he needed do was first find them…

"Hmmm, so killing is your thing, huh? Well, try this on for size! Slap! Wham! Kapow! Crunch! Next!"

Piercing brown eyes scoured the liquid air through narrow slits as he searched for signs of their spy. Only a little rain fell and that only came sporadically. No sign of the chain smoker. If Nails was stupid enough to brave this night's fury, he might never see another night. O'Rourke had already made his decision. His vow to destroy any blocking his path was irrevocable. Maybe Tina was gone, maybe not. Everyone seemed certain of her demise, though he still held out a glimmer of hope. Maybe stubbornness, but he still could not envision her existence as ended.

Perhaps a ruse of nature, this feeling, this modicum of hope retained in the shadow world of his soul, but within that corner might possibly lay the last vestiges of his humanity. All outside had become cold and barren, a tumultuous wasteland devoid of mercies. Thoughts of her doom instilled greater fury. Those who crossed paths with him had better not cross paths with him. Mercy would not become him this night. Staff Sergeant Haynes voice came back to him, flat, raspy and hard, "Kill or be killed …maggot!"

He ran through his plan as he dressed. The rain now surged back full throttle. Arnold was out front, nice and dry in their vehicle, Nails bringing up the rear and fighting a face full of liquid sunshine coming at eighty miles an hour every time he peered around a corner. The chances seemed in his favor. Swarthy and reed thin, Nails was a man who apparently hated to get wet, a fact confirmed by muttered curses leeching out into the roiling air, so he probably would not devote much surveillance to the one other door at the hotel's rear. At least that was the hope.

Down at the hotel's right rear and used exclusively by employees, that door seemed his best way out, much preferred to jumping down from his balcony for a battle with whoever stood below. Tough to fight with a broken ankle. Besides, there probably weren't many of the night shift who'd be going out anytime soon this night. Another hope. The time was wasting; he had already decided to take the chance…

Appreciating the power and majesty of Her Royal Highness --aka, Mom Nature-- O'Rourke chuckled to himself that the backdoor duty guy, whose Spanish-flavored curses he had overheard , should have selected more appropriate clothing instead of the short-sleeved, tropical shirt and cotton slacks. He could have been Dominican or even Puerto Rican, not that either mattered, but Florida during a hurricane demanded a whole new dress code and that wasn't it. In this case, what was okay for Wednesday, really sucked on Thursday.

By now the fabrics were no doubt plastered to his skin, mimicking the appearance of a sad sack who had inadvertently tripped and fell into a swimming pool. Balding on top, the jet-black hair –at the back and sides of his dark pate-- alternated from hanging like a wet blanket dripping rainwater down his slight shoulders, to flailing about like an unfurled sail as new wind gusts found their way to him. Regardless from wherever he had originated, O'Rourke's impression was that he sure did not seem much a hand at anticipation and preparation …or at heeding predictions.

Another series of coughs racked his skinny frame even as he struggled to shield the flame flickering out from the disposable lighter in his hand. He concentrated on connecting the fire to the tip of his cigarette, backing deeper inside the little niche. Here the winds calmed, so much easier for his skin-on-bones frame to deal with than the aerial flood blasting the periphery. Intending to perform his duty, while surviving the night, realization overcame dedication. A spasm of violent coughs shook the night. This would not do. He improvised.

Bent low, still hacking like there'd be no tomorrow, he ducked head first into the boiling winds with their liquid offering and made his way around to the front of the hotel. Waving angrily at his partner –sitting warm and dry—he quickly ran across Ocean Avenue and jumped into the vehicle beside the perplexed other and that was that. Though their argument was heated it was also short. There was no way he would risk his life and limb on the off chance their mark decided tonight was perfect for a stroll …or a swim.

Hearing the receding sounds, O'Rourke raced to the side window in time to catch a glimpse of fleeting shadow, then out the door to the lobby in time to witness Nails' return to join Arnold. He waited for the other to take up the rear surveillance, but neither left the vehicle. It seemed nobody wanted to play. Back in his room, he turned off his computer and left, taking one last look at the satellite map image downloaded over the internet. Carlos Morano's home featured prominently in the center. Just off the golf course. He wondered why a man who detested the game seemed conditioned to owning homes on golf courses. Perhaps for his guests; perhaps for the prestige; still, curious…

He left the television playing --in case Nails returned to his post-- but turned the lights off as an afterthought, then walked out to the rear stairwell and proceeded down. It took very little time as no one seemed interested in venturing out on this back corner of the hotel. In short time he had scooted out the rear kitchen entrance and out into the storm-swept night.

Casting a series of glances up and down Ocean Court and spying nothing suspicious, he strolled casually out of the building, keeping close along the near side until he reached Fifth, then crossing over, headed towards his destination at a manageable trot. Feeling much relieved, he did not quite throw caution to the wind, remembering the old adage that people often find their destiny on the road they took to avoid their destiny.

He had timed his leaving more or less to coincide with the arrival of the eye wall as broadcast on the TV news. The winds still sounded a bit like ghosts and goblins roaming about on Halloween, but at least they no longer screamed like banshees hell bent for innocent blood. Maintaining a steady pace, on he ran the nine blocks through sideways blowing rain to the Miami Beach Marina. Almost there …five blocks to go.

CHAPTER ELEVEN

The Zodiac's engine pushed his small boat easily out past the marina's seawall into the Government Cut, where waters of the mighty Atlantic rushed in to merge with those of Biscayne Bay at the entrance to Miami Harbor. There, with a definite and definitive finality, ended any resemblance to any terms defined as easy. Here in Eris's eye much of the chop had subsided, especially with the tide running out. But it was still pretty rough. Nothing to be sneered at. He quickly decided against attempting to steer through the Cut, out into the Atlantic's thundering fury, to access Morano's side of the island by shortest distance.

Just twenty-four hours past, this entire waterfront had been lit so brightly he could have read the daily newspaper sitting on a dockside bench. Throngs of people paraded sidewalks along the wharf down to the Atlantic edge and into open air restaurants and Tiki Bars ornamented with Polynesian gods of sacrifice or fire or whatever.

From cars parked nearby in the lots or boats docked next door in the marina, they came from far and wide and sipped their Mojitos, slurped their drafts and tossed their shots all the while scheming, all the while scamming that next sexual rendezvous with opposite, sometimes same, sex opportunities. In the glare of brightly lit dance floors they gyrated in tune to the beat of Rock, R&B, Hip-Hop, Jazz and Reggae. All of which came well-spiced with Latin or African-Caribbean flavor and they appreciated it all. Even O'Rourke had sampled some of that.

However, that was twenty-four hours past. Now, only a relatively few dour offerings from outside lamps lit tiny patches in this commercial area. All gasoline feeds and most outside electricity had been shut down. No sense feeding this thing more utilities to wreck. What a difference a day makes...

Laying his maps on the dining table, he had charted his best course with the Atlantic's thundering fury a major consideration. He also decided against chancing one of the beaches, their greater exposure increasing odds of discovery by xenophobic residents needing only look out a window to catch a glimpse of a large, dark fellow dressed in black sneaking onto their secluded zone. They might simply be checking on the storm's progress, wondering whether to bail and head to a shelter or something, and experience the new wonder of this obvious party-crasher flopping out of his boat onto their seashore. It was dark, but not that dark, with all the shore-edge lighting, not nearly dark enough. He would not chance such a random encounter bringing out the guys with guns, his plan called for ingress by way of the marina.

This manmade island –first owned by a former slave named Dana A. Dorsey—appeared as having the shape of a westward-pointing, alpine ski boot. Morano's villa sat near the southwestern-facing side of the toe or as O'Rourke saw it, under the toe. So luckily, its closest approaches lay in somewhat, protected, waters. The marina entrance was almost halfway to the heel, facing Virginia Key to its south. An extra measure of protection, though he would still have to chug through Fisherman's Channel and face ocean-sized waves traveling across the widest expanse of the bay where it intersected the island. Hopefully those were not now being lashed into furious momentum by Eris' eighty-five mile per hour circular flow. Otherwise, negotiating them without being slung across and pounded into the rocks on Dodge Island, could prove extremely tricky. He could soon experience what it was like cresting ten-foot breakers in a twelve-foot, rubberized dinghy …maybe higher.

The adventurist component of his character leaped to that thought and toyed with the idea of slashing out into the dark ocean waters where the waves probably topped twenty feet --leaping from wave top to wave top-- surmounting each crest with the powerful thrust of his outboard for a joy-filled, purposeful transit to his destination. Its seductive message sought to smother the disdainful, warning cries that such action was sheer folly. But fool's errand or not, the beaches facing Virginia Key were much closer to his objective. Two ways to get there. Time was premium if he were to succeed. Shorter distance meant less time. Better to ride than walk. No way by car. The idea was both challenging as well as tempting. The sneering voice remained with him. "Why you such a pussy?"

The villa's location had been confirmed. Without land transportation he had only two ways to get there. Three, had the normal ferry remained in operation. But tonight his choices were limited to directions. Either left to the southeast or right to the west. There was a chance no one now guarded the ferry landing, which was closest of all. But that was too crazy. Had the option still presented, he would rather have tried to sneak aboard the closely guarded ferry while its well-heeled patrons drove their expensive gas-guzzlers onboard.

Eventually though, daydreaming resumed its hiding place, rational reason prevailed and he angled the outboard's tiller left, turning the Zodiac right, heading it into the ship channel. Unnecessarily chancing the ocean would be sheer folly and his was an already momentous task this evening. In the back of his mind he hoped no one would notice that his hotel's rear kitchen door had been left unlocked or the small ditty bag, holding his spare clothing, tied to the dock. But he tabled those concerns to come again later. If later came…

Once across the Cut, O'Rourke headed west, past the giant cranes along the shore of Dodge Island, their anti-collision lights blinking brightly through the swirl to chastise his decision to run without navigation lights lit. He ignored their coded message, certain that he would be the only fool chancing these waters this night. Conditions were fairly clear under the dark sky, but no moon shone through the thick clouds, so he was navigating entirely by the unfamiliar light sources on the adjacent shores. As he proceeded past their gargantuan arms, the giant cranes along the eastern shore of Dodge Island –which the day before were scooping cargo containers from oceanic freighters—loomed over as if determining what he intended in these stormy waters. "You want the hookup now or do we wait and pick your lifeless corpse up in the morning?"

Heading around Fisher Island's northwestern tip, he steered southeast and hugged the rocky coast. He again felt the slap of powerful waves hitting his face. But the clear lens goggles he wore kept the burning salt from tearing his eyes, though it still did its best to choke away his breath.

The aviator in him would definitely have preferred to use the high ground of the heavens to fulfill this mission downgraded to seafarer tactics. Still, his experiences with George back in Barnegat Bay helped him a good deal, so he did have a few skills. However, he really was no sailor and hoped he would not really "screw the pooch" this night where visibility came and went, more often going with the combination of rain squalls and wave spray thundering past. Every bounce of the bow sent sheaths of spray skyward only to be driven into his face by swirling winds. It seemed every nearby breaker had only one purpose in life, to find its way to his seat in the boat's stern.

However, he grimly clung to the tiller and kept the throttle turned halfway to batter through inky hammers, nearly impossible to see before their arrival. He drove as much by feel as by sight. Ahead were a few lights still shining from downtown to steer by, to the right were the cranes on Dodge Island. But everything to his left appeared dark with the exception of some windows high up in the high rises. But even these seemed dim and far off.

Looming high above, seemingly stoic and aloof, the nearby high rise apartment buildings totally ignored his foolhardiness in this barely minimal storm, their remaining outside lighting amongst the few indications of life. Eighty-five mile an hour winds made only minor impression to steel and glass enclosures designed to easily withstand twice that force. These could withstand wooden beams hurled from miles away and were nearly impervious to this lesser of nature's hurricanes. Though they'd generate not one ounce of pity for any others out on such a night. Then, none of them had ever needed sail to sea in the midst of one.

The high-rises may have been impervious to minor hurricanes, but the electric grid was another thing. Few windows lit up to cast a bit more illumination into the shadows. Evidently power outages restricted most nearby buildings to emergency lighting. Then again, this did constitute what South Floridians consider the off season. He figured many snowbird owners and renters wait a bit later to make their way south from European, Canadian and upper U.S. homes. He knew a few retired officers and NCOs who poopooed cold weather locations during winter and could afford to have a second home in a warmer location, especially a few unlucky ones formerly stationed forever above the Arctic Circle. He also knew of many seasonal business owners who closed up shop in the Northeastern shore towns after Labor Day and, their coffers full of summer loot, headed south to fund other ventures or simply to relax and frolic.

The less adventuresome would start arriving after hurricane season. Obviously, Carlos didn't figure in that crowd, though permanent residency in a state like Florida --where the taxes are sustained by high tourism taxes—had to be a lot more attractive than Cali. He wondered if Morano used his dual-residency status to submit absentee ballots from both locales. If that didn't make one feel the power…

But he'd witnessed no Snowbirds yet transforming the roads into stop and go nightmares or signaling their arrival with lights blazing from high rises. Nothing but gloom and doom. Normally they lit the sky, in fact, joined forces with the multicolored spectrum of downtown Miami to illuminate this entire side of South Beach so well the sidewalk along Governors Cut needed no other. Not this night. Unfortunately, on this night downtown obviously had power issues also.

He carried the small, waterproof GPS --that normally performed as his cell phone-- to chart his way through the area, but he needed to slow down to use it properly, a concession he was loathe to make. Time was precious. He had a party to attend, didn't want to be late.

Soon Eris's backside would arrive. He didn't want to be late on that either. A small boat on the water when her second strike fell would become a submarine under the water. Still, pounding through five foot breakers in a Zodiac was a two-handed proposition –lots of fun, but you needed to hold on with one and steer with the other-- so he was not one hundred percent certain if he read the glowing display correctly and was actually rounding Fisher Island or if he had made the turn too tight in this night's weather and now headed directly into a rocky shoreline or if he'd sailed out too far and now headed on a course bending past Virginia Key and out into the Atlantic or dozens other negativisms. Those little islands all looked alike on the small screen. They appeared so much less an issue when he installed them from his laptop …go figure.

He tried to ignore those worries. Still, as memory served well, the Nav systems in his vehicles were much simpler and even they sometimes led him astray, once leading him to Freddie's Taco Tico in El Segundo rather than the trendy Fred's Place, seafood restaurant in Westwood. He'd never forget those lessons. He doubted his date would either. Totally different style of dress…

Other meaningful lessons he learned that night were never drive without watching where he was being led and never ever get into an argument with a woman while he was doing anything mechanical. Had he been operating a woodchipper he'd most likely have lost his arm or at least a hand. It had proved a very frustrating evening. Sylvia's nonsensical solutions to resolving the plight of starving kids in Africa still made his head weary with fatigue. Her normally pacifist state eroded very quickly wherever tortured children were involved and never gave slightest consideration to his argument that we didn't have enough Army, Navy, Air Force or Marines to police every country everywhere there was cruelty being inflicted upon children, including our own. It was doubtful anyone could convince her that dropping nuclear bombs on warlords who were barely more than gang leaders was probably counterproductive at the least and definitely of questionable economic and ecologic sense.

But this time he figured he headed on the correct course. He had memorized the layout and had even driven around through South Miami and crossed over Rickenbacker Causeway onto Virginia Key to get a different perspective for his binocular view. There he could see his objective and felt better about his chances. Of course that had occurred before he knew anything about hurricanes or this new quartet of followers now dogging his trail. Both of those events now contributed to his unease…

Standing on the northern beach where the Navy once trained its black and brown sailors, away from the "white only" beaches used by the "white only" sailors, he studied the small island from under the gnarly boughs of shading pine trees waving in the gentle breeze. He thought it ironic that the only Miami-area beach --to allow Blacks and Hispanics-- would possibly aid one to destroy the other. Things were very different from 1945. Things tonight were very different from yesterday...

Details look very different when standing on a beach half a mile away during daylight than when bouncing across windswept waves in the dark, nary a star or glimmer of moonlight to steer by. The small flashlight was not much help. Its beam on the plastic chart map produced nearly as much glare as useful illumination. He used it only sparingly as it destroyed much of his night vision, reminding him that he should have bought a red lens.

The waypoints he'd plotted in his GPS receiver he hoped kept him far enough from the rocky shoreline, but not so far he'd miss the marina entrance all together. So far these did seem to jibe with the map as well as he could read them, the map he taped to the starboard gunwale (aka, buoyancy tube), the GPS (aka, cell phone) currently hung from a strap on his right wrist. He needed to balance his elbow against the buoyancy tube, then lift the device to scan its plot, then quickly clutch back into the handhold strap before the bucking bronco launched him out into a watery gravesite, all the while keeping the throttle nearly wide open. No speedometer, he couldn't tell how fast he traveled, only that he traveled nearly as fast as this thing could in these conditions, the twenty horsepower motor screaming out its war song. It all worked pretty well. But the light could have been better.

Some illumination did arrive from Miami skyscrapers, across the bay. But these did little in way of help, mainly just washing out his night vision so it was practically useless for finding details in dark places. Hindsight now punished him for not preparing better. Night vision devices were not difficult to acquire ...if you considered acquiring them.

The Greek goddess Eris is sister to Ares and his constant companion. He may claim the title as god of war, but this goddess of discord brought about the Trojan War on her own. This night Eris evolved into the goddess of wicked winds and roiling seas and though easing her furious assault, was by no means done. Powerful waves from the mighty Atlantic shot his craft in through the breakwater with a force sufficient to reduce the outboard to secondary status.

If he slammed into some billionaire's big dick substitute it could ruin his whole evening. He break an arm trying to ward off one of those big boys and it's trip over. Of course if his little boat inflicted damage, portraying the mouse that scored, well DIA would love that on the expense report. He could envision the written print: "Zodiac's outboard propeller chewed into a three hundred-foot ship belonging to the Prince of Mega Land and seriously damaged the custom, million dollar gelcoat. Repair Costs: Sixty Thousand Dollars for normal people, eighty thou for Government!"

But the nightmare remained in the world of his imagination. He encountered no untoward resistance and tied both stern and bow lines to pilings supporting the gas dock. Prudence directing his decisions, he docked at the end furthest from the Dockmaster's hut. Prudence was joined by the elation he felt at not having drowned during this harebrained, ill-prepared, ridiculous scheme. Then again, there was always the return trip. So best not be too happy.

This night was young. There would be plenty of opportunities to screw up somewhere, harebrained or not. He was not actually, totally unprepared, just mostly unprepared --doing things he'd never done in a place he'd never been-- and he mostly understood the risks …and that they were many.

A thought trickled to the forefront that even given these formidable challenges it was not as if he was old and out of shape and incapable. Then the reality chided that actually he was kinda old. Still, his stubborn side argued that if not all that young and capable; at least he was pretty much in good shape. Then came the reminder "…for someone your age".

But he did not come totally without preparation. This was not his first time in a Zodiac either, although two times out did not qualify him an expert by any means. Actually, one of the kids he had tutored way back a while had bugged him until he finally came out for a ride one spring afternoon. The kid had failed to mention that his boat was more a dingy than an actual sea going vessel.

All sorts of apprehensions invoked his daydreams as they chugged out through the breakwater at Long Beach Harbor. Looking back towards the Queen Mary, moored majestically at port, he had fervently wished they had one of those.

His main memory of the event was that they were too far out to sea in a boat that was too small. At least too small for him to be comfortable in.

He was happier than a sixteen-year-old virgin on prom night, once they got back to shore. It did not help that the pimply-faced, little smart ass had purposely drove them up close to where a couple sharks were tearing apart a California Sea Lion carcass. While he was not certain which kind of sharks, he was certain that each one was larger than the fourteen-footer he rode in. But the main thing he remembered was that he had never seen so much blood …not since Tony Hellerman.

Tying the long painter line in the bow to a piling, he changed his mind about the stern and tied it off with a dock line left for customers with thirsty fuel tanks. He hoped that these veterans of a thousand such storms would again survive and not tumble onto his rented craft or blow away out to sea, taking his only way back with it. He oriented his bearings. Morano's beachfront villa was only a few blocks, as the planners here had seen fit to build. His list of alternatives was not extensive, so he put the game ball into play using the more direct route.

He was dressed in a black scuba suit, both for its waterproofing and its night camouflage qualities. On his feet were cross trainer styled, black sneakers. He carried nothing else excepting the cellular telephone and its "Bluetooth" headset. When not in use, these clipped securely to the belt at his waist and were --unlike the wet suit-- both waterproof. Peterson's assurance of its waterproofing bragged that he could even send text messages while immersed. Worry about losing it to Davy Jones' Locker? It floats. Can't find it at night? Tap the sender on the Bluetooth, the display will light up. You dropped it? It's shock proof, can almost use it for a sledgehammer. This was Superphone.

No key identifying his hotel. This he stashed under a nearby flowerpot outside his door. No identification. Just a little currency in case he needed bribe a cop or pay a cab ride. He was pretty much all in, win or don't go home. The Zodiac had been rented the day before by Norman Charles, according to the fake ID provided by Peterson …even though Peterson didn't provide it for this.

If stopped by police or some security patrol, Norman Charles would then employ his invented excuse of thrill seeking in the face of Eris's fury. If that didn't work, John Paul O'Rourke would portray Norman Lewis Charles in jail.

"Driver's license? In my wallet, in the car. Didn't want to chance losing them in the rough waves. Why am I here? Man this th' bomb! Am I retarded? Officer, you're violating my civil rights." Razor-thin? Sure.

Even after the fourth rehearsal it still was less than convincing, so he hoped excuses would not be required among this night's adventures. He hoped the bowsers on his tail never got wind either.

License. She opened her azure eyes, reddened by too much scotch, and found "J" staring at her in the dark. He immediately bent to her full lips and singed her soul with another of those wonderfully warm, deep, wet kisses. Only a momentary puzzled look had passed his dark eyes.

But he showed no real compunction. Nothing he did suggested that any concerns other than the act of making love to her drove the man. He made her feel special ...very special.

He strode atop the world with her, attentive and secure. Only she mattered. Only she concerned him. She could feel his heart's rapid beat and it was only for her. He softly bit her ear and reached both hands down to cup her bottom, plunging his stiffness faster and faster down her "Tunnel of No Love", as she had nicknamed her pussy, "that furry little, cute creature that couldn't", as Tony had named it.

Suddenly the tiny room's walls began to reverberate from a strange, rumbling sound unfamiliar to her. Focusing as she could, she sought to pin it down, to discern its point of origin, its location …to name it. It was gone before she could. But then, there it was again. "What was...? No! It couldn't be!" She mentally exclaimed. "It couldn't be!" But the truth was undeniable. It was her. She was moaning. She, who had not even considered such a thing in years, was moaning uncontrollably!

Some long ago forgotten reflex forced her to clamp short fingernails, newly painted deep red, deep into his muscled back, while her love starved loins arched, straining ever upwards to meet his own impassioned thrusts. She was cumming! Mary, Mother of God forgive her, but she was CUMMING! No longer a moaner, she became a screamer. She just might have to change his name to Mister J!

The sound started from deep within her throat, from deep within the very fabric of her being. It took a long time before it finally came out --to her seemed forever-- but come it did and when it did it surged into the dark room's space, into every crevice. It bounded off the ceiling and walls and into ears totally enraptured by its intensity and its temporal timbre.

She clung wildly to his muscular frame, feeling his passion, reveling in the hot ejaculation spewing so deeply, so purposefully into her. She nearly throttled him, striving to become one with him, to pull him down into her.... all the way down into her.

The wave crested and slowly she sank beneath his panting form, still clinging but less rigidly now. She peered up into his face only to be rewarded by a stinging drop of perspiration from his brow. She barely noticed it. Almost cow-eyed, like a schoolgirl on her first date, she stared up at him. In truth, it was her first time in a long time …her first time in a long time making real love, that is.

When he attempted to roll off her, to relieve her of his bulk, she refused him, holding even tighter with arms and those sinuous legs he had earlier complemented her about as she sat perched on a barstool in that black dress, "that dangerous, black dress", as the saleslady at Le Petite's had described. A memory stirred, she had bought it to wear for Tony. May as well have wrung out the dinner bell. "Come git sum guys! Ho fer let! No cash required!"

Since he never even came home, Tony never got the chance to see and be compromised by its damnable witchery. Instead it brought her here to get laid by some innocent soul it grabbed off the street. She was such a Ho! But seemed such a short time ago she wasn't. But now she is. First time, but isn't that enough? How many pickups gets you into the Ho club?

Once a wife no longer concerned about wifing things or dressing for hubby things and rather be with most any other guy, doesn't that at least constitute first step? Speaking of which…

"Damn! What did she step into this time?" Another scintillating kiss! Playing games of tongue twister, swapping spit, intertwining tongues, hoping this night never ends. "Lord, been so long!"

Eyes tight shut, she promised herself, if Tony ever come back home, he could have his whores. He could have their master suite, she'd gladly take the room downstairs. All she wanted was an occasional night like this... occasionally.

Desire moved her. They were moving purposely against each other again. It was like she felt this time might never come again, that she might never again have love. She came quickly and then again and still another before he reached orgasm and then came even more fiercely with him, screaming out her love call as the room awoke with harsh, startling light.

The door had been thrust open and in it stood two people. Panic mingled with long sought out satisfaction as she recognized the lipstick-smeared face. Both she and her lover sat straight up, but otherwise said nor did anything. No scrambling to cover themselves. No demanding the intruders about face and scurry out of this room already occupied. Can't they take a hint and take their fukking elsewhere, as there's already serious fukking going on up in here!

Man and woman in doorway faced man and woman in bed. Somebody should say something!

"What th' hell is goin' on!" Finally yelled the disheveled man in the doorway. "What th' hell you doin' here? Who th' hell is this, this niggah?" He stammered. "Get yo' ass outta here!" He yelled, his face double scarlet from his companion's lipstick and his own blood steaming angrily through straining vessels …not to mention that complexion issue.

But she merely stared. Stared right into the dark eyes of the livid man standing twenty feet across the room from her. Stared right past the half, undressed honey blonde at his side. Stared right into the alcohol-reddened, now furious eyes of her husband.

"Jeannie!" He exclaimed. Instantly enraged. "Bitch! Cheatin' ass bitch!"

She neither called his name nor cringed from his ire nor spit at his whore nor anything. Just stared into his eyes. She remembered how they once were. Not as they were now, blood red and deadly. But how they used to be. Sadly, she recalled those brooding, puppy dog eyes that had so enthralled her, so many years before. These days they were always less brooding and often more threatening. Especially from the boozing since his baby brother died. She took no notice of the disheveled clothes nor the lipstick prints around his mouth, which was now curled in a vicious snarl.

The eyes held her. They accused her. They told her she was his and only his. They said what the heck was she doing in bed with this spade? Who the heck did she think she was? Didn't she know that he was her husband? Her lord and master? They acknowledged no guilt of their own.

They had done no wrong.

Her silence angered him even more. "Bitch I kill you!" The words came simultaneously with his motion. Simultaneously at the note of "you", he expertly grabbed for the thirty-eight caliber Colt revolver in his left side shoulder holster and fired two rapid shots, further disturbing the night's stillness. But his alcohol-dulled reflexes were not nearly up to par with those of the man in whose direction the bullets he launched.

Diving to the floor on the bed's opposite side, pulling both woman and covers with him, he caused both shots to instead bury themselves into the headboard's simulated wood façade, which had obviously been hung there just for such an inevitability by some fashion designer wannabe. What other purpose could so useless an item fulfill other than bad guy distracter and bad bullet catcher?

But, neither those concerned at the moment. He had to move fast or both of them were about to die! He did not pause or look back to see that both projectiles had crashed violently into the veneer instead of between his and the woman's eyes as they had been intended. That they had found no flesh was only temporary respite.

In nearly the same motion he had reached up to the small night table beside the bed and pulled her tiny purse down to him, opening it with a flick of his fingers at the simple catch and dumping its contents on the floor.

Tony took his time now. It did not matter to him which of them died first. His second shot had really been intended to tear deeply into his sluttish wife's left side breast. Those perfectly proportioned globes that had recently been positioned underneath and naked up against someone else. It did not matter whom else, just someone else. It did not matter that he was here to do the same thing with someone other than she. To him it was simple. Men were allowed. Men are different than women and that is that …besides, men don't give birth to horrid, little things having absolutely zero chance at a full life!

Tony was sure of his rights. Gonna kill both of them and no one would convict him. He was gonna kill the bitch and the nigger. These next bullets would not miss.

He roughly shoved away the woman still clinging to his left arm and took six quick steps to come around the bed's end and into sight with Jeanie's pink nipple. He pulled the trigger but the bullet broke a window high and to the extreme right of his target. "How could that be?" He tried to reason. Then, through a rapidly encircling fog, he noticed that his body had been wrenched violently around and to the right and against the adjacent wall. "That makes sense", he slowly perceived. "You turn to the right, you shoot to the right."

Then, as he tried to collect his thoughts to rationalize, to reason as to why he would do such an asinine thing, his body's strength started to fail and as he began to slide slowly downward, he continued to rationalize. He was expert with a pistol. He would never turn to the right without reason to shoot someone directly in front of him. Not without good reason.

As he slid down the wall to rest upon his knees on the carpeted floor, he peered down and noticed something warm, dark and sticky pooling around them. The realization came to him. It was sort of a rude awakening that overthrew all other concerns, penetrating the senselessness and uncovering the cloak of numbness.

Uncovered, suddenly mind numbing pain washed through him like a tidal wave and nearly choked him. Then it was gone again. But blood from the severed artery sucking into the hole in his right lung did choke him. He coughed several times and died, all the while mentally berating the half asleep, half-drunk night clerk asshole, who must have given him the wrong key again …at least he needn't worry about it ever happening a third time.

"Ca-Ca-Cauk sucka!" He coughed as the gurgling in his lung reached his throat and shut down his wind for good. His last thoughts were of his poor little brother's handicapped existence. Who would care for him now? Would he ever appreciate big bro's sacrifices, refusing to ever chance such a child of his own? Would he even understand such a thing?

He died never seeing and only momentarily feeling the effects from two nine millimeter, copper-jacketed slugs in his chest or hearing the constant, screaming from the woman he had picked up in a nightclub less than two hours before, the same club his wife had departed ten minutes before he arrived. As the light faded his last vision was of the woman across the room, near the dresser, quietly pulling on her clothes, emotionlessly staring back . . . into now sightless eyes.

Jean Scott Braithwaite watched the life's blood pour inexorably out from her husband's torn shell. Not even a flicker disturbed her stare. No feeling touched her as she unconsciously brushed away a few wandering strands of her jet black hair. It was a darker shade than her natural color.

She had done it this way to look sexier to Tony. Maybe he would give her a baby if she could rekindle some of their earlier warmth. Though even as she sought to enhance her beauty, pangs of doubt deep inside had troubled that it was much too late. Too much bad had happened. Too many lies, half-truths and unfaithful acts had transpired. But she had to try something. Anything.

He had always told her how beautiful he considered women with jet black hair and she had heard that he was often seen in the company of black women, verified when she had surreptitiously discovered pictures he had hidden, but not too well. Alas, her doubts became justified. Her surprise found little favor. He told her she looked silly, while walking out the door to who knew where. She had forgot herself and had cursed him, even demanding to know where the hell he thought he was going and he had beat her and laughed at her plaintive crying. That had happened two months ago.

Now she stood over him and just stared while he died. No emotion. No concerns touched her. No thoughts of his death or of how close she had come to her own. Nothing. She was as cold as ice water and nearly as empty of rational thought. Neither the endless sobbing coming from the woman, still standing near the door, frozen to the spot where Tony had shoved her, nor the wailing of an approaching siren touched her consciousness. She was hardly even aware of "J's" strong hands as they helped her into the tiny mini-dress that barely contained her curvaceous bounty or of the acrid gun smoke drifting from the barrel of the pistol he had lain on the table. In fact she had not noticed the weapon at all, even though it had exploded right beside her face, its deafening report striking her with stunning ferocity.

Only a tiny entreaty, a subliminal message welling up from deep within, touched the woman's consciousness. It pulled at her, tugging gently at her persona, counseling her. She somehow listened to its message ...and somehow understood.

Gently and a little sadly he covered the partly kneeling, partly sprawling corpse and helped his date into her clothes. He had not killed a man face to face before and he had never killed any man over a woman, especially when it was that man's woman. But how was he to know? Then somewhere in the cobwebbed recesses of his memory he recalled a part of their opening conversation that had nagged at his value system ever sense. Even while they twirled the dance floor, his thoughts had repeatedly stole back to his whispered question concerning her significant other's whereabouts, attempting mightily to discern the meaning of her answer.

"Wow, you sure got my back! That rescue was right on time. I need to thank you for saving me from the big, bad wolf." his fuzzy memory displayed. "So! Your beautifulness. Do all you Virginia girls keep an old boyfriend or husband on the sideline or is the coast clear?"

"Clear as mud." She responded, impishly looking back over her shoulder into his eyes, while playfully thrusting her buttocks against his groin to mock several of the younger women dancing around the club.

He knew that she was testing him, giving him "strokes", as it was colloquially called. "Probably trying to see how much Dog I got in me," he related. He could tell that she was only joking, only mocking the other females, just playing with him, while the instant swelling in his groin only reacted to her skill. Regardless what parts of him outwardly reacted, internally he kept his cool, kept his hands to himself and just maintained his spot on the floor. No pelvic thrusts. No reaching out to grab her breasts as they did in some locations –this was not New York, after all-- not even taking hold of the undulating, tiny waist which was usually permissible … some would say, required!

But it was her reply that had piqued his curiosity more even than her dance. It was just a twinge, just a minor peculiarity that had teased, but did not overly disturb him at the time. He was well used to the vagaries and mysteries of womankind.

He had wound up at the Woodbridge, Virginia nightclub looking to air out his head a bit, nothing more, picking it off a web page, disdaining the local Fort Belvoir area clubs as being too close to the military bullshit he despised. This night he despised just about everything. Thoughts of Tina plagued his every thought, his every action. For a while the thoughts included Sylvia also, but Tina won out. Their time went back too far to be easily usurped. Now he felt that some cunningly wrought scheme, devised by some impish god creature, had mischievously altered his, already clouded, destiny.

Shellacked pine walls bordered by light green painted sheet rock at the upper side, which was dotted with Redskins pennants and neon-lit Bud Light, Fosters, Heineken and Molson signs. The restaurant area in the back was now nearly deserted. Inside the rectangular bar's center area seven hundred-fifty milliliter bottles containing Johnny Walker, J&B, Yukon Jack and Courvoisier were staged on the upper shelf of a three-foot square, four-foot tall platform built around two ceiling supports. The lower shelf stored dozens of Seagrams, Frangelico and Jack Daniels spirits. On each of the bar's eastern and northern sides stood a draft beer station with twelve taps for everything from Molson to Budweiser. Egg crate floor coverings provided safe walkways above the various wet or sticky spots for the two hard working bartenders.

Orioles' jerseys were in vogue. A few brave souls wore Red Socks or Yankees shirts. Usher's lyrics sang out to send the patrons into furious gyrating. Mick Jagger's wailings and Prince's high-pitched vocals did their best to perpetuate the frenzy.

She sat three seats down the rectangular bar from him, looking like new money, kind of unspoiled but full of value. He watched her fend off half a dozen or so would be suitors. He watched her throw down several shots of scotch over rocks... double shots. Once, while his eyes were halfway through their fourth full pass over her shape, she caught him looking and threw him a wink, followed by a knowing smile that seriously warmed his morose mood.

She looked good to him, real good, like somebody's mistress. She had on this tiny, "drop dead" black dress, a mini-dress actually, that had exactly that effect. It was certain to make every other man wish that any man she came in with would drop dead so they could take his place. She was probably waiting for the guy now. "Too bad", he had thought. Then insisting that it was not too bad for him, because he was not out looking for adventure, choosing not to approach her at all. He was definitely not looking for her kind of trouble. But, while he pretended to watch the milling throng gyrating under the multi-colored lights above the main dance floor, trouble found him, or re-found him…

The smoke eater was working overtime to ionize noxious odors in the bar air. Debbie had lost her boyfriend and came back to present him a closer view of the twin pale globes nearly spilling from the top of her low cut dress. She was obviously inebriated, too inebriated to notice his disinterest, too inebriated even to care. She persevered, pursuing her goal until her boyfriend found her again. The boyfriend who was also inebriated and who was very jealous sober, way beyond that drunk. His obvious displeasure radiated onerously from fiercely glowering dark brown eyes. He stalked through the crowd towards the pair who paid him no attention. No matter, he knew how to fix that. He would fix them both. He would fix his face and her memory. She was about to remember who she came here with, and why.

A part of his foggy mental faculties focused enough to register that the man she was standing next to seemed to be paying little attention to her. But who could tell? Good as she looked, if he wasn't paying her attention, he must be gay. So even more to hate him for.

He approached from the guy's back left side. Her thirty-four Cs were thrust up against his right shoulder. The strapless, plaid one piece dress that clung tightly to her every curve could barely contain her breasts, could not contain the twin points formed by hard nipples jutting enticingly outward. What if it was not contact with his shoulder, but with his fingers that had teased them so erect, what if his right hand had moved down from them and was right at this moment probing sensitive, moist parts of her where they should never be allowed?

At the thought, his eyes darted down to her legs, down to those long, sexy legs that he enjoyed so much, then down to one of the open toed white pumps that she had stepped her left foot out of to rub against the man's right leg. Hairs on the nape of his neck pricking, he stormed towards them. He had long ago moved past the point of bottle courage, which meant that he had also moved past the point of no return.

He had a mean streak that was only exacerbated by alcohol. His was the type of personality that should never be mixed with strong drink. And this night it had steadily been mixed with draft Budweisers chased with Kamikaze shooters. He was upset that Debbie had become unreasonably upset and was playing her stupid games this night. She was again threatening to break up with him until he proposed as he had often promised that he would. This game was so old he was getting very tired of it. She always seemed to do something stupid like this around "that time of the month", as he put it. He felt that the word lunatic was especially applicable to women, since their patterns of strange behavior seemed to coincide with phases of the moon …with Debbie it was lun-atic!.

Now, there she was again --just as that stranger with the Caribbean accent had said-- drunk on her ass, hanging all over the same guy he had pulled her away from an hour ago. He wondered for a moment how the stranger knew him and his girl. But whoever he was and whatever his connection, he definitely had hit the nail on the head and he agreed with the little midnight black Jamaican or wherever he was from. This was no respect. They had been warned. This time he was going to ensure the guy would be unable to hang on to anybody anymore. Five paces and he would be there. The half-filled bottle of Bud lifted in his hand. Almost there…

Suddenly a clear, confident contralto sang out in near music quality lyrics, "there you are, you bad boy! I can't leave you alone for a second." Nudging Debbie's arm away from the man's back, she moved against him and smiled. "Sorry miss, but my man is already taken."

With that, they walked away, arm in arm, with not even a backward glance. Pete, the boyfriend stopped, dazed and confused, momentarily, then remembering himself, grabbed Debbie's bare, left arm and dragged her away before she could even protest. All she managed was a blurted, "oh, honey".

O'Rourke did not know the name of his savior. At that moment he really did not even care. She had saved his life. Of that he felt certain. For he was certain that he would soon suffocate from the foul odor blowing out of the drunk woman at every breath. That he was about to be cold-cocked from behind was never made aware to him. He had been oblivious to the threat from the rear, but the writhing, giggling creature clinging like saran wrap to him earned more than enough of his attention. She had seemed a great catch one hour before, before she got wasted on shots of tequila, chased with beer, and before her jealous boyfriend made his presence known.

They had met when the bartender had mistakenly mixed up their drink orders. He found it hard to believe one could confuse a pale, freckled, burn don't tan, five foot seven inch tall Irish woman with a brown-skinned, six foot-two inch Black man, but it made for good conversation. They sat together at the bar and chatted about the subject for a few minutes, until the boyfriend showed up. He did not introduce himself, just angrily motioned for the woman to follow him and strode away out the nearby door.

He was just kind of glad that she was gone before he ended up wasting his time hitting on someone already encumbered. Besides, he preferred his women a bit darker. He was also kind of glad that her replacement was still around. The replacement was not very dark either, but her hair was nearly black —that had to count for something-- and those intoxicating eyes, practically smoldering. She had laughingly apologized for interrupting his fun, explaining that he looked so helpless she just could not help herself. He had gone from first liking, then hating that confused bartender to liking him again. Sometimes things can work out.

Somehow he found himself standing next to her, and then dancing with her ...close with her. Soon they found themselves casually walking out on the patio above the docked boats, absently watching the moonlit waves lapping gently against myriad hulls, surreptitiously gazing at a pair of lovers snuggled close together on a nearby craft. It made for an awkward moment, so they decided to change locations.

Back inside, they moved to the smaller, less crowded rear bar. It was to the left side of the restaurant area and permitted no smoking, so the air was decidedly cleaner than at the main bar. They appreciated its intimacy. It only sat fourteen or so, sometimes more when patrons squeezed together on another stool or two. There was only one long and one short side whose right-side top opened to allow entry. Behind it were all sorts of mirrored beer displays and more Redskins paraphernalia.

The long legged, blonde bartender wore a black and white stripped pullover shirt that draped so far down her shapely, deep-tanned thighs, near totally covering her tight, black cotton shorts and giving the impression that she wore none. Her long hair fell down in the front to tantalizingly cover part of her mascara-highlighted, hazel-colored, left eye, but was pinned up in the back, out of the way, revealing the large hoop earrings hanging from equally large ears.

Known for her stormy temper, which seldom suffered sexist fools of any sex, the ear size was a clear warning that if you didn't mean it, don't ever say it, cause she will hear it! Frequent patrons knew not to get on her bad side. She served up drinks and shots in rapid response to any of her more frequent patron's cues, all the while conducting a continuous conversation on the subject of that day with whichever patrons were interested. Tonight's subject was the owner of the Redskins and whether his purported deep pockets could buy enough quality talent to get them back to the Super Bowl. O'Rourke being a lifelong Eagles fan, he stayed far away from that discussion, less he suddenly find his drinks watered with cleaning solution. But there were plenty others with passionate opinions on every side, and they left no doubts which side was theirs.

The bartender seemed to stay center of the road in this matter. Which could not hurt her business.

She was an expert in reading body language who seldom got a complaint, but almost always got maximum tips. Whether they exhibited a nod of their head, a wink or just placing the empty glass down outside the napkin, she was quick to notice. She was never too busy or too important for her regulars. In their case, they figured that she must have either mistaken them for some others or had simply decided to adopt the two into her family of bar VIPs. Whatever the reason, whenever their glasses approached empty another drink would miraculously appear. Her operation was so smooth that, unless they were focused upon her, watching her subtle performance, patrons seldom even witnessed the occurrence. JP and his companion were focused on each other's conversation, watching each other. Occasionally they would notice a full glass in the place of an empty and marvel at her skill and joke about her seeming self-possessed intention on getting them all hopelessly intoxicated. She succeeded admirably.

Somewhere along their way to learning about each other, they decided to spend some more time on the dance floor. Everyone in the place seemed to be having a great time and they were not exceptions. She carried a permanent smile, which often broke out into a very pleasing laugh at the colorful jokes meandering around the group at the bar. On the dance floor she revealed copious amounts of energy as if it had been stored away for just this one evening. Her form was flowing, her movements practiced, as if she had studied ballet or even modern dance or maybe just grew up on Soul Train or now DWTS or something. Either way they boogied to the beat of song after song, oblivious to the evening's march through time.

The effect was nearly as intoxicating as the liquors both had consumed in large amounts. Then the D.J. sealed matters by playing one of his infrequent sets of slow, melodious tunes. They danced this time on the patio, seemingly inseparable, oblivious to any others, intent only upon the music and themselves. They kissed for such a lengthy time that it was decided they should retire to a more appropriate location before someone accused them of having sex on the dance floor.

In the beginning she had clung plaintively to him, as if he were a lifeline to her salvation. She moved with him, but somehow her movements seemed sans passion. She was going through the motions but he could not convince himself that she was enjoying the event. It was as though she had something to prove but was afraid to prove it. He remembered his earlier assessment --somebody's mistress …or wife.

But it was too late to worry about that and he could not allow this situation to remain, so he shifted gears. Thoroughly enthralling firm, young feminine flesh was his life's ambition, a hobby to be practiced at every opportunity. He would leave no stone unturned in his quest to bring sated bliss to this sultry lass.

His tongue rolled slowly over her cool flesh. His strong teeth nibbled gently at her every part, especially the nipples. He teased them erect, then sucked hard at both until the rosettes surrendered their pinkish color to a ruddy red; nearly identical to the shade of the painted lips he had first kissed an hour before.

Her body was responding but not her mind. His flashing tongue probed deeply between full lips, long devoid of the dark gloss. She was a very good kisser, expertly using the tongue, but still a bit too cold. Kind of frigid.

He next probed deeply past the two, nearly identical, birth marks which respectively adorned the inner most area of each upper thigh; past the full, blood swollen lips perched perfectly between her artfully sculpted legs; all the while caressing her from head to toe. She noticeably softened, the passion stirring. Still, she would not let go. For a moment he feared that she might scream for the whole thing to be ended, for him to leave her alone. Something was really bothering this woman... probably something terrible.

He mounted her. Slowly and with genuine gentleness, he penetrated the saliva-wet, vaginal crevasse. She trembled as he took an eternity before finally reaching her deepest point; then, just as slowly, withdrawing fully only to repetitively enter again and again. The trembles became shudders, the shudders spasms, almost rhythmic in their occurrence. Then, slight sobs rose from deep within her, animal-like noises that channeled up the long, luxurious throat to add personality to room noises, which until then consisting primarily of the harmonious sound of their movement upon bed springs.

Her initial series of orgasms were small tremors that she scarcely felt, so wrapped in her worries. He felt them though, channeled into her inner most self as he was. He sensed that she had not known passion for quite some time and would have trouble finding it now without some serious assistance ...he determined to give her all the assistance that she would need.

"Darlin' you are definitely gonna cum this evening", his braggadocio promised to himself, hoping fervently that he was right. He switched from "long poling", as he termed the slow, deep, sensuous strokes into her love canal, to what he called a "kill stroke designed to really whack a cat", his sobriquet for a woman's vagina. In her case it decidedly broke the drought. He pinned her legs back, nearly to the headboard, and hammered hard and viciously into her tenderness, withdrawing slowly, before again diving deeply and powerfully on the thrust or down stroke.

Her controlled indifference broke and ran away. She moved more intently, more purposefully against him, seeking to match his power, clinging cat-like, claws bared, to his broad back; arching ardently up to him, meeting him thrust for thrust; opening herself wider to his savage onslaught. Reveling in his masculinity, totally enthralled by his majesty, she welcomed his love.

He punished her sweetness, plundered her treasure; measuring the full depth and breadth of her; he was brutal but tender at the same time. She was strong, this beautiful woman, he did not fear to harm her. Whatever or whomever, had made her so insecure had not totally destroyed her spirit.

An uncontrollable urge began to take him faster and faster; she followed suit; both desperately seeking each other, rising higher towards utopia. There was a dualistic explosion of opposing furies and then, as they slowly drifted back, her passionate screams ringing in his ears.

Now there were another woman's screams ringing in his ears. She had ceased those screams, but his ears still heard them, his brain still amplified them. He strolled purposefully past the women and around the bed's rumpled evidence; sadly looking again to the tan covers hiding the hulking form resting against blood stained, pastel green and white wallpaper; quietly, though reflectively, laying the pistol beside the telephone, he made a phone call.

It was a good thing that she had told him. It was a real good thing that she had begun to pour her heart out to him; a good thing that she had needed someone to confide in. Good that while they rested and during their post-coital petting and "newly-found-each-other" lover's talk, she had told him about the gun. Beginning with her marital woes she had ramblingly told him almost her whole life.

A virgin at twenty-one, her husband, she never used his name, just called him "my husband", had been her first. He worked as the primary broker in her father's Tysons Corner office. They met at one of the Christmas Parties that Harold Scott held annually for his employees and soon after began courting. All the girls wanted him, so she felt lucky to get him. Holding off his advances for two years she had proudly offered herself on their wedding night only to find sex a painful and unsatisfying experience. But attempting to be a great wife, she had tried mightily to satisfy every wish of a man who could not be satisfied. Now she was determined to end it one way or the other. She would take no more beatings.

This night she had decided to spend away from their house (it had long before stopped being a home) and made a reservation at this motel. On the way she had decided to stop for a drink or two and one thing led to another. At that time she exuded how happy she was with that decision.

They both agreed that fate was mysterious with its twists and turns, but that it sometimes worked out very good. That was before they became aware how fate had prompted her to unknowingly register at the same hotel her philandering husband frequented and caused a confused desk clerk to issue electronic key cards to this same room to two separate people last named Braithwaite …that was her side of the tale. His was not nearly so sad, til now.

He had two days to kill before scheduled to fly his prestigious human cargo back to John Wayne and came into that particular nightclub only intended to wash thoughts of Sylvia's angry dismissal from his mind. Now he might be headed for a murder rap. The cops did not take kindly to black guys shooting white guys over white women. His childhood memory recalled the sad demise of Henry O'Rourke over much less an egregious situation.

She had taken the gun from the drawer in their family room where he kept it. Her intention, to kill either herself or her husband or first her husband and then herself. She was not sure what to do or how to do it. However, she carried the gun around with her anyway. Good thing. Maybe the weapon had a soul. Maybe it had decided whom it should destroy. Maybe it had decided that Tony was a worthless piece of flesh that was already devoid of humanity. Maybe it had considered any event causing the death of someone like Tony a mercy killing, to put him out of his obvious misery. Maybe it had caused them all to come here to play central roles in a necessary act.

Regardless what the reason or the purpose; whether fate, karma or just bad luck; he had killed a woman's husband in a fight over the woman, with an unregistered weapon. She had told him that too! The bottom line was that somebody had to go to jail. This much circumstance would be far too much for an ordinary policeman to easily digest. Somebody was definitely going to jail.

Scarcely had he replaced the receiver on its cradle before the barked order came, demanding he raise both hands. Complying, he turned slowly around to face the business end of a locked and loaded, nine-millimeter automatic. Behind it stood a very angry Virginia State Policeman.

His sense of humor attempted to induce a laugh by reminding him of a joke about black men in New York: "you better not have a wallet in your hand when you try to surrender".

She had come to his cell bright and early that morning. Her hair was combed up and back into its usual bun, several strands hung rebelliously down across her left ear, the lips once again spouted fresh, red coloring. She looked nearly as good as before.

"I now know why I went there with you", she admitted. "I'm sure I do." She walked to the holding cell's only chair and sat, hands in her lap, knees tightly held together, head down, eyes on the blue-flecked linoleum. "Tony wouldn't give me love, but that wasn't it. It should have been, but it wasn't."

Her voice was as calm as a still morning. She paused a few moments before continuing. "He wouldn't give me a baby. He wouldn't let me fulfill my womanhood." She said this as matter of factly as if she were directing tourists around the Woodley Park Zoo: "Oh, you want the Panda exhibit? Well, out of parking lot B, turn right onto Olmsted Walk until you pass the giraffes then turn left. If you get to the kangaroos you went too far, good day sir". No emotion cracked her countenance or her voice. There was a kind of huskiness in her throat, causing her to sound much older than her twenty-nine years, but nothing more to betray her.

He watched and listened in silence, daring not to disturb her train of thought, sensing the need for her to speak her thoughts, immediately understanding her hidden anguish. He also sensed an underlying satisfaction deep within her.

She stood up and paced across the tiny cell, holding herself tightly, not looking at him, not seeing. "I'm pregnant, I feel it. You have given me my baby. She told me. Told me she was with me. I'm sure I'm not going crazy. I'm sure I'm, we're, going to have a baby, a girl. You don't have to be responsible." Finishing she finally gathered the strength to face him. He stared into her eyes. She was serious.

"Oh God", he thought, straining not to let this feeling show, "why me?" He was still quite angry and unnerved and saddened about the life he had taken. Sure the guy was a dirtbag, an asshole and several other terms that came readily to his mind. But he had killed a man over that man's wife. He did not like the idea of ending anybody's life. Not since Vietnam had he killed and he had done that from altitude, not face to face, not watching them choke on their own blood and never over another man's woman. His senses cried out.

But she was serious. Worse yet, he believed her. Some sixth, seventh or eighth sense convinced him. He touched her arm as she stalked slowly by on one of her pacings. She stopped, timidly facing him, unsure. His arms surrounded her quickly, pulling her in to nestle in his warmth. Then her emotions flowed, shudders became sobs and the tears began . . . in earnest.

Visions flashed through his consciousness as he held her tight against the racking sobs. He did not have a kid. Almost once. He quickly buried that thought. Maybe this was a good thing. Maybe fate and his karma had teamed up and planned this all along. Maybe all that "it's a cosmic thing" dribble he had spewed forth in his younger days had come to fruition. Maybe he would leave something on this earth after all. He kissed her, softly at first, then more firmly; saying everything was okay, that all was well and good. Then she was gone.

He spent one night in the cell and was released on his own recognizance the next morning. At his arraignment hearing the court invoked the Latin phrase, "actus non facit reum nisi mens sit rea", meaning that "the act will not make a person guilty unless the mind is also guilty". Virginia had come forward into the twenty-first century, somewhat. It was now okay for African-Americans to shoot whites, especially when the whites were evil drunks who shot first. But there was still the problem of possessing an unregistered firearm. He would have to answer for that.

He was already answering somewhat, they had clipped his wings, changing him from an eagle to an aardvark. The Sheriff pulled his pilot's license until such time as the District Attorney decided whether or not to try him for possessing a weapon, possibly purchased by the man it had destroyed (obviously can't take the word of a battered wife). He would have to come back, but at least they let him go home…

They were out there somewhere, them and their backers. Right now they were probably tracking the rubber sole marks made by his sneakers or the wake left by his watercraft. He could sense them and their evil intentions, using their superior technology gone amuck. They could have come from Morano's group or maybe even al Qaida, as Peterson suspected. But just as likely, they could belong to some splinter group hiding deep inside DIA funded by some ultraconservative political policy group, some shadowy government think tank or somebody.

Rather than James Bond of the Super Spies, locked in a never ending battle to protect queen and country; we find Jimmy Boy of the Red Neck Guys, locked in a never ending battle to protect their demented idea of the American way of life, aka, "How they want it to stay like it used to be".

Where James counters endlessly any threats to the security of the free world, Jimmy Boy rails endlessly at any perceived threats to his freedom to dominate the entire world.

"What, we're no longer the majority? Aaahhhh! Ah hate these dark people! What, we can't lynch a spic or a nigger when we want? Aaahhhh! Ah hate these dark people! What, we got spics an' niggers runnin' fo' President? Well what the hell has happened to America? They're taking away my liberty. Aaahhhh! Ah hate these dark people! Damn it! We gotta do sumptin'!"

Nearly there. Jimmy Boy's cartoonish image sailed from his vision. He had carefully studied maps of the island and felt comfortable finding his way even without the GPS. Using the address Valerie provided he planned his route carefully, circumventing as many of the larger, communal areas as seemed possible. The preparations helped, but could negate only so much guess work --him having physically never been here before-- and there were a few occasions requiring his Artful Dodger skills to evade discovery, for he was not alone out, braving these diminished, but again mounting winds.

Several times he dodged passersby, who were seemingly out only for a routine, evening stroll. He wondered at the sanity of these Floridians, not to mention his own. Shattered remains of red Spanish tiles and smashed green coconuts --amongst scattered palm fronds-- littered sidewalks here and there, to remind what dangers awaited the unwary. As the eye's back wall approached –heralded by deepening pitch in the wind's whooing and hooing and increasing rain—he became even more cautious, furtively flitting from shadow to shadow across rain soaked, manicured lawns. It was not only more difficult to discern sounds of people who might be out and about, it was equally challenging to glimpse the outline of any security person taking this opportunity and stealing a cigarette break …and then there were the unidentified flying objects.

"Woof!"

"Oh shit, grandmamma!" Walking her Springer Spaniel out from behind the bole of a large tree the little, old lady seemed to come out of nowhere. The small dog's nose twitched in its excitement at meeting another living person during this nocturnal journey to find a suitable spot to christen. The rushing winds disconcerted its normally keen nose, eroding its ability to sniff out familiar --previously marked-- territory. The weathered, grandmother figure draped in a dark, rain-slicked poncho was much less thrilled. Her four-foot-nine inch frame bristled at his appearance.

"You young people should know it's very dangerous surfing in these storms", she croaked, her tiny voice barely heard over the howl, but sounding like the voice of doom to his rattled imagination. He did not respond, just kept moving. She had already formed an opinion on her own. No need to confirm or deny the accusation. Hopefully she wouldn't speed dial 9-1-1 on her cellie. But now at least he felt a bit more confident with the cover story.

The words had formed, "Sorry ma'am, I know you're right," but remained unspoken. Better to let her myopic senses think he was some teenager. No matter the color, a spoiled rich kid was more apt to ignore a scolding than acknowledge that it was either directed towards him or of any consequence to him.

She walked off in her disgust, dragging the dog straining at its leash to touch and taste this stranger. The experience left him only slightly shaken, though sweat soaked into his suit's inner layer to mimic its rain-wet exterior. Not an issue, just a reminder that he needed to be careful, especially once he arrived at his destination. Morano's villa was just up ahead somewhere on his right. He had mentally fixed the location, but the reminder again resurrected his knowledge that landmark representations on a two-dimensional map are very different in perspective and appearance to the actual structures in 3-D.

No one seemed to be conducting outside security patrols around the villa nor did there appear to be activity on the verandas about its two-story, white walled structure. But they could be sited under a sheltered overhang or in a vehicle on the street with night vision goggles for all he would be able to discern in these conditions. He took his fool's chance, made his choice and let it ride. Chances were any security was relaxed and not anticipating the threat from suicidal nuts out in this weather. Chances were also good that the meeting was still on. He could only trust that a pissed off Mother Nature had not undone that event along with all the other rearrangements she caused this night. The Mother is a female after all and females normally went well with guys named John…

It was a female that had started him on this night's journey. As they necked in his car the previous evening, she had made mention of this meeting in passing. Actually, there was a whole lot more going on other than "necking" that brought out this revelation.

His body leaned heavily across the center console, lips frolicking in endless arcs over and around the sumptuous breasts that had been bared for only him to see in the dim glow. Both were aroused now, with thoughts of culminating the adolescent tryst in a more satisfactory manner. But reason prevailed and reluctantly he relented his assault; recalling purposeful fingers from their wanton probing into the area between her quivering thighs.

Sighing softly her latest moan, Valerie sadly retracted the tips of her own fingers from their possession of him. Light from electrically stimulated, liquid crystals in the vehicle's radio display reflected her serious side as she suggested Thursday night as much better for such a fait accompli. Her intimation that such a deed was preordained –perhaps by forces beyond their ken—warmed him throughout.

He had to keep reminding himself that he was playing the role of 007, while she fulfilled that of the seduced, enemy agent. Even though he suspected that Morano had instructed her to "be nice" to him, it was extremely difficult to view any part of this beautiful creature as the enemy. She played her role well, a little too well.

It was in the midst of rearranging --the act of pulling parts of herself back into appropriate locations within her disheveled clothing—that she voiced the revelation, almost as a fervent plea. "I-I have tomorrow night off. A-all-all night. Carlos will be entertaining some people I-I don't need to help with. We c-can get together for dinner again, if you want. M-my treat!"

He gazed into eyes whose wholesome passions were scarcely diminished by the dim lighting. There seemed a rather schoolgirlish quality to her haltingly proposed suggestion that worked magical charms, loosening the suspicions decrying her motives. He fell deep inside her spell, lost for a moment outside the firmament of the heavens and the bowels of hell, needing to reassert tighter control to wind his way back onto a level plane not being tossed about by his own trepidation.

"Sounds good." He answered after a perilous time on a teeter-totter. "What's a good time for you?"

"Got any plans for tomorrow?"

"Well, I had planned to visit with an old friend. But he's Air Force and they've decided to move some aircraft out of the area with the coming storm."

"When's the last time you saw him?"

"Way back in ninety-eight. We were classmates at UC Fullerton in the late seventies, early eighties. I was the old, seasoned veteran catching up on a misplaced youth and he was the junior flip freshman charging headlong into the future. Now he's a Colonel in the Air Force JAG, err, that's the Judge Advocate General. They're the lawyers and prosecutors and such. Last time we hooked up he was out west with a team investigating for one of those witch hunts that took place in the wake of Tailhook Ninety-One."

"I heard about that. Whole bunch of oversexed, misogynistic guys running round Vegas, playing grabass with any female unwise enough to leave her room. My girlfriend Beth was a flight attendant for TWA back then. She never missed that convention. Whole bunch'a hunky stud pilots, all in one place. That's why a whole lotta women showed up. Err, well, before it went lame and got boring. Now she's with American. I don't think she attends anymore. But, wasn't Tailhook a Navy problem?"

"Started out that way, but eventually became an "all throughout the Federal Government" problem. Fallout from that scandal sent a whole bunch of careers into the crapper, civilians too. I mean it got to the point where a lot of older guys were almost afraid the press would find out they even had dicks. Some o' them prob'ly still can't get it up!"

"He-he", she giggled. "I can see that's no problem here…" Even in this light Valerie's exaggerated leer was unmistakable. During their passionate interlude, her fingers had accomplished a probing mission of their own of sorts and by her own design. Now she slid fingers downward to rekindle the relationship. Here was no young virginal maiden or lady-in-waiting. She knew her way from one end of a man to his other and wanted JP to have no doubts about that fact. That wantonly, lascivious message being sent left him no doubt that this was a woman who would meet a man halfway, perhaps even more where necessary. His own fingers conducting maneuvers of their own, the message he sent back was that more would not be necessary …unless she wished it so.

She became all a giggles for a moment, paused and giggled then again, as if unable to get past whatever humor held on to her, until finally, spoke out her message in a manner classic Mae West, mostly vamp, almost tramp. "So big boy, are you happy to see me or is that a rocket in your pocket?"

He ignored the remark —much more successfully than he had been able to ignore the fingers—and continued his tale. He needed to finish then get her back on track about this coming meeting where personal assistants were unnecessary.

"So many careers in all the services got shit canned –I mean we talking two-three hundred guys, including the Navy Secretary—there's probably a whole lot of soldiers dying in Southwest Asia right now because their commanders worry more about them behaving appropriately --in a politically correct way—than closing with the enemy. They never tailored their training for the tough road."

"Don't get me wrong, the Gun Fighters, you know, the tankers, the armored infantry an' Spec Ops guys are all a tough enough breed. But ain't no women in those units anyway. But most of the military is composed of logistics and support types. Mechs an' Techs. Lots of females in these units. These types get a little rah, rah, rah stuff in boot camp: th' bayonet training with pugle sticks an' th' hand-to-hand wrasslin' an' trippin' they euphemistically label as combat training and th' rifle range, laying rounds on target. But after that, outside their technical specialty stuff, 'bout all they get is sensitivity training an' 'how you find the PX' drills. Not how to survive in combat, but how to get along with female soldiers an' such."

Withdrawing further into her side of the car, she studied him more closely, at first unsure where he was going with this line. Perhaps he just needed to rant. She hoped he was not blaming her for the military's malaise. After all, she liked the idea of dressing up so that men would fight to undress her. But she also liked the idea that it was her choice which of those men succeeded. Then she remembered his friend.

"So your friend?"

"Oh yeah. Sorry. He was loaned out by the Air Force to hunt down a few strays that had somehow escaped all the initial persecution and fallout. His words. Anyway, some unwise Army individual had impregnated his secretary's nineteen year old daughter. Evidently the secretary had wanted El Bossos' twenty year-old son to show through for her baby girl, but the son already had a girl he liked and dissed her. Moms was crushed but determined not to let such a find get away. The kid was all-American quarterback or something like that, gonna star in the NFL one day."

"Moms keeps finding excuses for gurlie to stop by the boy's house unannounced. 'Hi, I was just in th' neighborhood' or 'Hello Colonel, I hear it's Sonny Boy's birthday' or whatever excuse she made up followin' moms' instructions. 'Wear that cute little outfit I bought you. He'll be eating outta your hand!'"

"But boy was always gone with his gurlie or out playin' ball or someplace. Miss Persistent want to wait him out. Mom says: "Wait as long as needed, I'm practically family. Colonel won't turn you away. He's the greatest!'"

"Colonel sees it different. He says: 'come on in Miss Legs-So-Long, wearing that too-short-miniskirt and that too-tight-top. You look so much more mature than that picture on your mom's desk. Have a seat. I'm lonely. Wifey died three years ago. I enjoy the conversation. Want a soda? Have a cookie. Oh, you prefer a cocktail!'"

'Soon they're taking trips to Vegas, Mexico, you name it. Hot casinos and hotter sunny beaches an' somewhere along the line, daughter decided that she'd rather experience an old bird at hand rather than a young one in the bush. Long story short, after about six months she showin'. Moms really pissed. Wrong family member impregnated baby girl. She claims sexual harassment. Claims her boss coerced her to intro baby girl and his son when he really desired baby girl for hisself."

"Did she have the baby? Boy or girl? Did she testify?" Valerie's curiosity jumped at him like a thing possessed. Her ardor had cooled somewhat. She seemed a bit standoffish. But he was too busy trying to construct a plausible cover to concern himself with her mood changes. His hands he now kept to himself. He only used his lips …and only for speech.

"Not certain about the gender. He didn't mention. But anyway, it turned out that the daughter testified in favor of the father and he got off even though his career was over. No jail time, but lots of, 'Colonel, you seem to have found your dick and are a danger to society! We don't want your kind around us. Now git to stepping!'"

CHAPTER TWELVE

Head on a swivel --eyes sweeping the grounds left, right and forward-- he made his way towards the house. His approach bold and direct. He disdained the idea of a perhaps more cautious, furtive approach, flitting from shadow to shadow, tree to tree.

The white stucco walls and his black outerwear were poor matches. For the most part, any areas of shadow had unfortunately been driven away from where he figured he needed to be and nothing attracts suspicion quite like quick, shifty movements in a lighted environment. He circled slowly just at the perimeter, where the curtain of shadow still held sway, close but not close enough.

No movement revealed itself to his scrutiny, but he still felt qualms of unease. Macabre, ghostly wraiths swirled tormentingly about above his head, briefly appearing just outside his peripheral view in the black sky, only to vanish entirely before his searching eyes could capture their fleeing form. Their message was certain, "We're watching you…"

He had anticipated this moment all the while romancing Valerie in the front seat of his little convertible. But now that he was here, the second guessing plagued steadily. From across the other side of the backyard --outside the range of a few ornamental, amber-colored lights—he could see into the house. But as he had not yet gotten close, he could only presume the subjects being discussed inside, imagination suggesting it concerned Tina's condition and whereabouts. "Ya'll be careful ya don't say nuthin' that'll tip JP to where we holdin' his ex-bitch! He gonna be real surprised when he find out we th' ones got her!"

It was just his imagination, not really real. They were speaking, but unless he took a crash course in lip-reading, this vantage point wasn't about to work. Even if one of them talked about Tina or the stolen documents or even the Easter Bunny, he was not yet ready to intercept. He had to get into position. But for a few moments more he stood where he had stopped, rooted to the spot as his eyes followed the movements of a man he considered his nemesis, as well as a douche bag.

Every fibre told him to dislike this guy as much as Stephanie did and while hate was much too deep an emotion for the most part he did. Kinda hard to feel anything but animosity for a guy who may have caused the death of somebody you still cared for. Plus, this guy had enough strangeisms to fill a book; not to mention his ofttimes, boorish mannerisms. Oh, and that urine drinking issue didn't fly at all.

Definite turnoffs all those things were. But none any more perplexing than now. Morano was putting on a show. Not quite Kabuki Theater, no garish masks and flowing costumes, but not quite sane either. O'Rourke watched a few more seconds before moving on, asking himself: "What the hell is he doin' with his hands?"

"Which is most moral? The woman who refused operation to abort the fetus killing her and save her life or the woman gored by a bull who refused an operation cause somebody might see her tits? Both of them died for their morality, but which one was most moral? Trick question, the correct answer is neither! Both were just dumbassed bitches who had too much Bible, not enough sense!"

" I can't see why you'd draw that conclusion. They were both women of faith who chose how they wanted to meet their maker. I see that as highest morality and greatest examples of human virtue."

"Cause fer both they only concerned 'bout risk-reward! I kill my kid, gonna git punished by God 'n go to hell! I show my tatas 'n God gonna punish, send me ta hell cause God made clothes fer a purpose! Adam 'n Eve found out th' hard way!"

"That's a pretty simplistic answer to a very complicated question!"

"Fuk complicated! Science 'n tech prove that the only tool we require is the six inches between our ears. Too many only focus on the six inches 'tween their legs 'n worry God gonna send 'em hellside for usin' it! What kinda simplistic dumbshit is that? On one side it's don't fuk or God gonna fuk you up, on th' other it's be fruitful 'n multiply!"

"Man you all over the place!"

"Cause they all over th' place an' it's all silly shit! Th' ones being fruitful forgot to turn off th' tap! Earth being overpopulated, they still under orders from some bronze age deity! Th' "prohibit sex" corner wanna blow up anyone gettin' blow jobs! You fuk! You die! Then there's the issue of contraception. You bad if you pre-abort by taking birth control. Again it's back to the issue of the fuk! So anyway you go, whether you give a fuk or get a fuk, you damned! Can't believe none of this shit! All about religion! Funny how when plagues happened in most corners of the world we cite nature. There's always some red algae bloom killing oceans and rivers, fish dying, frogs abandoning, insects multiplying, people starving, etc. There's places in recent times where people and animals are choked to death by sudden surging toxic gasses from this phenomenon or that, acids from volcanic magma an' whatever. Why ya'll tryna invent a god jus cause ignorant, superstitious peeps wrote about it? Maybe it's just mommy nature's way ta clean house now'n agin. I bet the folks in Hiroshima thought the same til August 45. Guess the Enola Gay gave them religion!"

He'd had it up to the gunnels, this guy's spiel, including his concept of religion on the whole. Divine command, epistemological, ontological, eschatological on and on ad nauseam. Is it too late to kick him off the guest list?

Chaco also sees them everywhere. Ten dollar names for simplistic evaluations. They answer each argument with confusing terms that throw the questioner of his game. Just another Chivato trick! But his tact is a bit more …tactful!

"Did he just call my facts right or wrong? …he best not be talking 'bout my mamma!" His was only mental jest. Carlos, not so much…

"Ugh! My brain hurts. Speak English, not this high order, hunnerd dolla verbiage crap don't nobody understand 'cept you douche bags wit' nothin' ta do but study unnecessary shit! If yo lady wasn't such a cold bitch you'd have sometin'!"

"Ah, Mijo, our friend makes a decent point."

"Yeah maybe, but who'd ever kno? Can't unnerstan, half dat shit!"

Chaco understood his cousin's distaste for the state senator's bourgeois spiel. Even he'd need a translator with a thesaurus to decipher and after a few drinks, forget it. But it was more than that. Sure the senator was being boojee. That was his nature. That's how assholes do. But Chaco's concern was Carlos. He'd come in with a stage nine mad-on!

True, Carlos never been a fan of religion and this holier-than-thou toady with his hand out definitely pushing the wrong buttons this night! But Chaco suspects his cousin has done something even appalling for him. And he been down the road a bit. Other than a bad vintage grape, not much unsettling him.

The woman's miscarriage? No-no, he corrected. Not miscarriage.

Murder! The AA folks find out it's gonna be serious. No, not alcoholics anonymous, Anti-abortion! Pro-life! Them folks send armed neo-Nazi's to hunt you down. The AA don't play!

But his humorous ploy fell on its foolish face. Didn't change the reality. Didn't change the cousin crisis. Maybe no way back for him. Maybe shudda let him go when God first called …with his family.

The scotch burned its way down his throat as he pulled hard on the glass in his hand. He realized he was becoming drunk, but it was too late, he was already at the gate, mostly through. He went with the flow.

Only about five foot, six inches tall, Morano would never qualify for the NBA. Didn't matter that some had, who stood even shorter than he, those were exceptions. Actually, some of those were exceptional exceptions.

Morano's skill was not a twenty-foot jumper or even the ability to drive the lane. However, he did have his abilities. Such as the ability to monopolize a room like few others outside some of history's most acclaimed orators. Alike a modern day Caesar or Napoleon, people rose when he approached, giving him deferential treatment, desiring his good will, his favor. Everybody wanted to be his friend …nearly everybody.

He didn't come off as bossy or know-it-all or even important. But some innate charisma, some animal magnetism, projected, radiated in all directions to overawe the common as well as the not so common folk who chanced into his presence. O'Rourke couldn't help but admire the man's ability. Men half a size taller, possessing similar wealth and even greater looks, envied him, wanted to be like Carlos. His wit and mannerisms rivaled those of a regal, as if he ruled the entire world within his survey. This evening though seemed different…

Some people possess the ability to either rise to the same level or even to a plane higher than those to whom they are conversing. As if they speak from a raised podium, they look either directly across from and often down on those they address. "You're in my world," they seem to suggest. Nothing smug or arrogant, just a superior quality others envy. Even when faced with the requirement to look up into the face of another, appearances indicate the opposite, as if the ones possessing superior height have inferior quality, manner and bearing. It's quite a trick, Morano pulled it off well. He never needed to tell you, you knew he was the man. He didn't need to shake hands because he never needed show fealty with you,

you swore allegiance to him.

That's what first threw O'Rourke back a few steps. Morano's slurred speech seemed totally out of character. He never seemed frazzled or out of control. Maybe he was just off his meds or maybe the urine fizzes were catching up to him.

That thought commenced another train of strange. Urineade? Urinojitos? O'Rourke's imagination had just gone on field day envisioning the possible combinations. Urine 'n coke? How 'bout urine shakes? Maybe using his own milk too. That had to be some sight, him self-milking, sucking it out of both tits. The possibilities were endless …Margarurinos?

"Around the world, 20 children die every minute before their fifth birthday. That's ten million kids each year, who die horribly thanks to poor health, poor facilities, poor families, you name it! Just because of poor everything!"

Carlos was still ramping up, still on his mission, wherever it was taking him. Others exalted such as God's mystery. But to him it was a sign. He saw it as God's poor attitude. God doesn't want all these babies growing up to pollute his already polluted world. So God's got a culling process chaired by the Grim Reaper. Same with Christians and their abortion prohibitions.

"Bible say suffer lil' children ta come unto me! Yeah, suffer! That's why they die in hor-horrible agony! Didn't find Jesus? Cause yo' parents suck! Are you th' antichrist? Why else you question God's love? Didn't they teach you nothin' in school? Bad parents! Bad schoolin'! That sux! You suck!"

"You think it's God at fault? You blaming God? Christ Jesus?"

"Wouldn't it be better ta die those kids 'fore birth? 'Fore they kin feel pain an' sufferin', pestilence an' starvation? Isn't that th' humane approach?" A moment his slurred speech slowed, at a loss. Where he going with this? Is he playing God? What God? Then it came rushing back. Not a lost. In his view, most those kids would be born to parents and cultures who worship religions bent on killing themselves anyway.

Everyday somebody's kid cuts the throat of a sister or brother who made the mistake of falling in love with the wrong kind of girl or guy or even worse, both. Everyday somebody's child blows up themself to get at other people's children. Every single day! World is going to hell in the ol' proverbial handbasket and bleeding heart idiots are working harder to prevent abortions than they are to prevent wars, poverty and pestilence.

"Ask yourself, why don't ya. What th' ratio o' murders outside versus inside th' womb? About abortion, is your God pissed cause you beat him to th' punch and he don't get th' pleasure? Ask yourself would a loving God do such a thing as cause millions o' babies ta perish horribly 'fore they fifth birthday? Is there really a God or are those children of a lost god?

Ask yourself! Is your God too small, your morality too vague? Are you on th' righteous path or a pathway to doom?"

Morano's ranting and raving and wild gestures reminded of a person who had lost his way. JP understood, personally, having experienced similar emotional distress. Tina could make a man that way. Possessing that same ability to make others seem less important without consciously trying to do so.

Totally reversed from the prior evening, Morano seemed a mess this night. Maybe he had found his Achilles' heel of alcohols. There's always something you can't handle, often finding out too late as the cops are slapping on handcuffs, taking you away for DUI. Whatever. He sensed that something other than just the booze exacerbated this man's morass. Maybe Tina, maybe present company included. Though, obviously, Morano had competition in his own house, this night…

"Calm down Mijo," cautioned a graying, smallish man wearing amber-tinted glasses that neatly blended with his Native American features. "Our guests will think this a fundraiser for the Democrats. Everyone here is a Libertarian, right?"

Laughter broke out across the room. The vertical blinds were open, inviting outside inspection. To his thinking, it was quite obvious that not one of the occupants of this room was overly concerned with maintaining anonymity. That made sense to him. Privacy and incognito were paramount with most of this island community's denizens. But only a fool would hide his head in the sand while a hurricane was bearing down. Besides, what idiot reporter would choose a night like this to gain a scoop on the "Who's Who?" Of course, not only reporters desired to gain advantage. Hopefully, none here considered that…

O'Rourke's view revealed only four men other than the graying Indian. The room was medium-sized, sufficient to entertain a good number of the more eclectic party-goer crowd Morano normally frequented, although its dimensions would be challenged a bit by younger, Generation-X types performing hip-hop routines to chants by Outkast or Public Enemy or moshing to the beat of Smashing Pumpkins and Megadeth. Megadeth lyrics seemed especially appropriate this night: "I am a sniper, always hit the mark. Paid assassin, working after dark. …Killing is my business and business is good."

According to Valerie, Gen-Xers were also occasional guests of the mercurial man and his peculiar style swings. She described his gyrating syncopation as something to behold. JP could imagine it truly was. Probably not this night though…

The frenetic routines devised to cope with those music genres could challenge the proportions of Carnegie Hall, let alone a single room in a private home. He could imagine its volume stuffed port to starboard and bow to stern. But currently it looked almost cavernous with the few men gathered. Its walls extended high up into the white ceiling where recessed, incandescent lighting glowed yellow and soft to light up the entire room. He was far more concerned with that lighting than with the room's capability to house rock groupies forming mosh pits.

One good aspect, no table lamps obstructed his view. All the light came directly from above, almost vertically. That also meant less light cast horizontally through the glass to the outside, where he prowled.

Indeed, prowling was an almost exact description. His every movement was short and stunted, catlike. A cat in the hunt. Rapid starts followed by even quicker stops. He sought out the smallest shadows for cover though there were not many such areas this close in. His eyes took in as much of the scene as he dared. He had already risked much. But he would need to risk even greater exposure to chance a better view.

Still, he could see the principles. Morano and friends or so he envisioned them. These few sat on cream-colored, thickly-padded leather-covered sofas and armchairs arranged comfortably around low-height, chrome-framed, glass coffee tables in the…

A thought interrupted, he did not know whether this should properly be called the salon or the patio room or maybe rich people had a whole other word to describe their things which further separated them from the little people who tended their lawns and swept their kitchens and wiped their asses. Maybe it should simply be named "The White Room". After all, it was all white –except for the furnishings. Even the flooring was white tile squares, covered here or there by brilliant Persians.

He did not care what it was called. Only that it was a place of interest for him at this moment, primarily because of one man inside it who now stood facing his guests, his back to the patio doors, oblivious to what lurked there or who. Oblivious even to the possibility. Apparently oblivious to anything and everything outside his immediate periphery.

He was engrossed, seemingly self-absorbed by some issue or other. Words formed and flew from his mouth in a constant stream. O'Rourke's ears could not discern them all over the howling winds, but his imagination envisioned their message as one filled with vehement, acrid diatribe and peppered with flowery epithets. Regardless that Stephanie's jaded depiction failed to mention any tendency for expletives excessive. Such omissions did not prevent his own imaginative inventing.

So intent on the man, he had not at first noticed the goodie locker until one of the insiders gained his feet to stumble over towards a chrome and glass sideboard set against the back wall. About medium-height, on its long flat top stood various bottled beverages and decanters of colored liquors grouped towards the center. Hors d'oeuvres and large cocktail shrimp sat to each side reminding O'Rourke's innards that they had been denied real sustenance since early that afternoon. The energy gained from a few potato chips consumed as substitute dinner was already past tense and out of consideration. Fervently, he hoped any growling sounds reverberating through his digestive tract would not out duel wind noises. The jibe worked, he forced his concentration back to surveillance mode.

The house rear presented the shape of a capital L flipped to reverse. A wrap around patio dotted with flower gardens framed the large pool and Jacuzzi. Though not Olympic-sized; the pool could work out some decent laps in its length. The observance merely in passing. Any swimming he performed this night would bode bad tidings. His main concern at the moment was not falling in.

O'Rourke had initially approached the house from the north, along the top of the "L". But now, up close and personal, the whole of the rear seemed to be made of glass. In truth, much of its two-level, Mediterranean-styled structure did permit light transmission in both directions. But it was the view from inside-out mostly concerning him.

Walls of alabaster sandstone; arched entrances with ornate, half-moon windows topping white, patio doors and covered balconies; its six thousand or so square feet had the look of a place a gazillionaire might own. But he hadn't come out to see the sights. Its presentation gave him the impression that anyone could see him coming. At this very moment, even a Barney Fife, Gomer Pyle reject, sitting nearby an inside vantage point, could look up from his TV or card game or even a book, and spot this unwise intruder. Not to mention electronic aids…

Fisher Island is two hundred-sixteen acres of prime real estate complete with marinas, upscale restaurants, an internationally acclaimed health spa, and a nine-hole golf course. He was certain that it was a great place for a visit under normal conditions –and he was probably going to need the services of a talented masseuse, and soon-- but these conditions were anything but normal. He had taken the "two if by sea" approach and snuck in for his own view of life aboard this exclusive bastion of the rich and famous (at least one perhaps infamous).

Leaving the marina, he had walked in a southwest direction past many homes which appeared dark and empty, evidently their owners finding less threatening areas of the world to visit. Coming to within eyeball distance of the address provided by Valerie, he had then circled inland --around to the backside—careful not to trip over any neighbors out to experience the majesty of Eris.

His recall mechanism resurfaced her most revealing comment on Morano's neighborhood, "Just don't ever show up with a camera. You'll see people ducking for cover all over the place while speed-dialing cell phones, calling Security. Don't think I've ever seen a more paranoid bunch of people anywhere."

Now Morano's voice and his ranting spiel carried to O'Rourke's ear fairly clearly even through the glass, though attenuated intermittently by the random intensity. Between gusts, he sounded more paranoid with every sentence. Unfortunately, Morano's back faced the room's twin, patio doors. The emanated vocalization needed first to travel out from his location to reflect off objects across the room –primarily the side walls over ten feet away—before bouncing back to encounter the mullioned glass to which O'Rourke attached his little toy. Even with the best filter and discriminator circuitry, optimized for human vocalizations, his little system could barely separate out vocal resonance from the outside gamboling by Mother Nature. Ol' Girl interjected just enough untoward influence to insert a fanciful Joker into this agent provocateur's card deck. She seemed determined to deal him a handful of troubles…

Captured sounds, received and amplified by the disposable "bug" microphones, were further scrubbed inside his PDA-slash-satphone-slash-cellie. Although his weren't as disposable as advertised, since these four were all he had with him; he guessed they figured five too many. But the mystery of these is that they must have been as much a mystery to the DIA.

Peterson had neglected even to mention the handy little toys, surprising since the one thing on which Jungle Juggie prided himself most (after being a Jughead, that is) was his thoroughness. Luckily, the Operations Menu showed both location of the little gadgets (each about the size of a dime) stuck inside the phone's back cover and detailed operation instructions. Easy even for one technologically backward as he …once you got past the keyword protection.

Atypical, in these days of built-in menus holding minimal data where operators are expected to figure most technical things out for themselves, this one held a wealth of tutorial information and suggestions. A little study and practice and he felt much less the nugget. DIA even made the password easy. "ChuLai71" he would never forget; so remindful of the last time the Government tried to get him killed.

Adhesive tape strips, of some special design no doubt, held the bugs onto smooth and most rough surfaces, according to the instructions. He hoped he would not need to find out how well its special design performed on rough applications beyond wherever "most rough surfaces" ended. Nightmarish depictions of oak tree bark and stucco-plastered walls flashed into his mind…

The Bluetooth transceiver he wore in his right ear, the left was a no show (still a bit puffy from challenging young lions in tournaments he had no business in). He still held out hope that the cauliflower condition would not prove to be a permanent reminder of pride run amuck. Wrestling he loved, but not the scars from wrestling.

Decoded audio coming through the window glass became digital signals turned back into audio sounds he could easily understand (at least he could whenever the wind died sufficiently). Linked from the micro-bugs, these streamed over to the multichannel, digital transceiver (aka, the PDA now clamped to the belt around his waist) then up to the earpiece. So he spent much of his time hunching against a tree with right hand covering the ear while left hand fiddled with PDA software buttons to achieve optimum voice reception.

Problem was, its operation still relied on the capture of sound vibrations and these were abundantly flying off that glass this troubled night. Fiddling with the tiny controls, he concentrated mightily in order not to miss some critical tidbit. He also remembered a few of Peterson's other crucial tidbits.

"Now I'm not trying to make this into a lecture."

"Too late", came the instant thought.

"Now, this is what you'll use to communicate with us." He pulled an electronic device out of his center desk drawer and continued his Intro to Intel for Dummies class, which in this case O'Rourke considered appropriate, because he was not even certain whether to consider the thing a Personal Data Assistant or smartphone, mainly due to his ignorance as to whichever golly gee whiz gimmicky nickname the marketing weenies had determined more salable this month. His only certainty was Peterson's intention to make him certain. He didn't have long to wait.

"This PDA cannot be intercepted by normal means, the signal is encrypted and in normal transmission it broadcasts to a satellite. Its transmitter operates only when keyed. So it doesn't do all that handshaking built into normal cell phones and is not as easily tracked. But you still need to be careful. Unfortunately satellites may be high in the sky or low over the horizon. So the PDA emits a radiation pattern that is nearly omnidirectional. Even though the data is masked, its RF transmission can be detected by any receiver tuned to the right frequency and thus located. If no satellite is in range, it will transmit through cellular towers. This icon indicates cellular transmission. So limit your calls when you're trying to remain covert."

"Here we go again," he thought, "back to that, bad guys behind every tree philosophy." But he took note of the icon and kept his lips firmly sealed, his thoughts private.

Now from the Colonel's mouth, a sales pitch: "It's got some nice features that you don't get from Verizon…"

"But I must caution you on using your private cell phone to talk our business at any time. If you want to call your girlfriends it's okay, as long as the conversation does not address this project. Cell phones are an extreme liability, Mister O'Rourke."

"Okay." Simple replies, that's what he needed. He'd keep it simple and objective, the object being to stifle small talk and close out this session. No questions. No snide comments, at least from his end. However, at the same time he couldn't help wondering if the same liability applied to satphone-cell phones.

He also noted how Peterson always emphasized "Mister" when addressing him. Obviously, snide commentary followed no rules of exclusivity. Everyone had their own way of saying "I hate you" and this square-headed, pompous-assed descendant of God's Marine himself (aka, Chesty Puller) was no exception. He bristled slightly at Peterson's comment about "girlfriends", but only slightly. All Jarhead Beastmeisters have their little, kiddie games to play. Might as well accept it, just as Peterson would have to accept all twelve or thirteen of the pet nicknames (depending on the situation and how he felt) JP had created for him. At this moment he favored his latest creation …Jarhead Beastmeister.

"Telecommunications interception has developed into a major industry these last few decades, you see. And it's not just Big Government or Big Business!" Peterson again paused, feeling a need for emphasis even though he could not possibly know of his student's childish devolution into a world of nickname games and vindictive responses to evil headmasters. Neither did the Colonel care; such is the nature of evil headmasters.

"It's pissant little governments, Ma and Pa storefront shops and private snoops, you name it. Every embassy or consulate from every country everywhere routinely tries to intercept any phone call that might give them an advantage whether it involves political, economic or military information. And preferably all three. We got Intel agencies running operations all over the place. NSA tries to intercept them, we try and defeat their capabilities, and the FBI tries to catch 'em. All part of the game."

"Right, no cell phone, got it!" He hoped the man understood as much. This was getting to be the lecture he had promised not to give. But Marines are a stubborn bunch…

"Back a few years ago, the entire Greek phone system was compromised by hackers. They got everything they wanted by creating software that copied messages sent to and from the cell phones of powerful businessmen and politicians. That damage is still being undone, so don't take this lightly."

"So I can't talk on the phone. No prob."

"This PDA we're providing sends point-to-point encrypted signals to certain programmed numbers. But that's no good for normal conversations with civilians. You can't talk to anyone other than this office about anything to do with this project. Calls or texts to your friends or whoever else will be subject to interception. Of course, even calls to this office will be subject to triangulation from satellites or even cellular towers when in areas out of line of sight with satellites. It's gonna switch from its primary satellite mode to cellular if that's the only means available. If we cut out the locator function the phone would drop calls instead of switching to the nearest tower in the network. So if you don't want people to locate you, turn off your phone."

He wondered why Peterson was so insisting to call him a total idiot at every turn. Obviously, anyone who had watched any episode of CSI had learned all about transmission location through a cell phone's GPS signaling or just the normal pinging back and forth. The gang seemed to solve at least one case of kidnapping each month with that navigational aid. But he bit his lip and held onto the retort forming inside his ego. He'd be the bigger man and keep the "Yes Daddy" response locked up inside…

"I just can't emphasize this enough JP…"

Oops, he slipped. No Mister O'Rourke that time. But he'd stay the bigger man and not remind him, at least not of that. "This thing got a tracking device?"

"Yes it does."

"Can you disable it? Otherwise it stays!" He'd promised to play nice, but only to himself. Besides, he never promised to be stupid.

"Now look here…!" The words stopped mid-sentence. Detecting a modicum of smug one-upmanship in the face of this stubborn enlistee, the exasperated Colonel momentarily flashed back to another exasperating moment with another stubborn man. A man he had grown up with…

Almost as if the spirit of his younger brother Ricky now possessed O'Rourke, seemingly every word he questioned, every responding sentence he uttered as a challenge. It seemed just like that last conversation all those many years before with Ricky expressing hatred, blaming his older brother for signing their mother into the rest home where she died heartbroken only a short time after.

But to him, Ricky was a typical sailor; all wet! Perhaps moving her had been a mistake. Perhaps the stress of leaving her home of forty-two years for entirely foreign surroundings had been a contributor to her death (Ricky was convinced it had indeed done so). But there were extenuating circumstances. He acknowledged that it had to have been a shock for his younger brother; to step on a boat --feeling like you possessed the world—to sally forth out into the deep blue; then returning home and finding no home …and no mother.

Listening not one moment to his older brother's plaintive cries that there had been no other choice, that there was no one else to care for the invalid old woman, that one son spent six months a year submerged in his Ohio class "Boomer" and the other spent at least fourteen hours of each day searching out bad guys seeking to destroy our nation. Ricky still would have nothing to do with the suggestion that both sons were much too busy with their chosen professions to watch her. But Ben had really tried …at least to his thinking.

Things had begun heading downhill shortly after the eighty-six year old had slipped on an ice-covered walkway and broke her hip on falling. Fiercely independent, she had had to swallow her pride and accept this blow to her freedom. Initially, he and Ricky took turns seeing to her needs, then hired home health aides to provide her twenty-four hour care. But Ricky's part had amounted to chipping in on the financial side. He was never around for the endless interviews and evaluations. He was never there when his mother called because one of the "girls" failed to show up several nights in a row or always smelled like an ash tray or even smoked in the parlor. No, those were issues best left up to the older brother.

Managing her care concerns had just about driven Ben mad. Agencies sent people over and she called for him to send them back. Most could not even speak passable English and she spoke almost no Spanish. He had even experimented with a few live-in nurses. But one was more interested in playing sexual, night games with her lover than listening for an old woman's cries for help getting to the potty.

Conducting a periodic check, he caught the woman's "stud service" about to sneak out one morning. It was not as if he considered the guy a threat to his mother, of such he did not know nor care to find out. It was the sight of his mother still lying on the floor where she had fallen, trying to get into her wheelchair, a stench of urine and feces clinging to every corner of the room. It almost broke his heart …and he almost broke the nurse's neck.

Both nurse and her boyfriend were rudely shoved from the house and ordered to never show their faces again. Then he carefully washed and dressed his mother as lovingly as any child had ever done for someone they held in high regard. After interviewing several other candidates, he finally settled on an older lady –named Agnes Maple-- who appeared far enough past her prime as to be unlikely of harboring desires for midnight liaisons or at least unlikely of having the ability to carry them out. Grandmothers don't have sex. They're grandmothers. They don't make love. They make cookies …and at least she spoke English.

Unfortunately, "Miss Marple" --as he grew to calling the aged spinster—was forever the community gossip when it came to her patient's sons and their government business. She took to eavesdropping on their phone conversations, reading letters mailed from all points of the globe to their mother and openly speculating with her few friends about what business the two men were involved in.

Just like Agatha Christie's famous, blue-eyed spinster, the frail, gray-haired woman constantly knitted, producing sweaters and mittens for nieces and nephews, who never called on the telephone nor dropped by for a visit. But two years into her stay, when she took one of her needles to the lock on Peterson's briefcase --ostensibly in search of a smoking gun of some sort—push had come to shove and she had to go. That was when he decided to move his mother to a place populated by those of her own kind and less by those out to exploit her or her family.

She never protested his decision. She never even questioned the reason her new friend had been let go and he hoped that the disappointment would soon leave her sad, brown eyes. But it never did the entire three months that she lived "in the home", as she called the hated place …and then she died.

O'Rourke could know none of these things channeling through the man's mind, only that Peterson had suddenly gone very quiet, seemingly on a hiatus. He waited for the focus to return to this time and place (before he could legitimately continue his childish behavior without appearing cantankerous and foul) and eventually it did. But suddenly this Peterson evidenced a softer, more tolerant side. There was still the purposeful Jarhead before him. Just a more mellowed out version. Where had his evil headmaster gone? Now all flavor had left the game. It required an opposing force at which to push back. He wondered exactly what kind of trip the man had taken …and why he had chosen this moment to take it.

Not the trip's length, only his reflection on its effects mattered, creating in younger brother a vehement, forever hatred of older and in older brother, a modicum of disdain for younger's flawed decision mechanism.

In retrospect it seemed eerily similar to this other man's blaming him for all things wrong since Vietnam. How could he possibly blame him for every ill inflicted by the Marine Corps? It was so like the short path taken by his brother. Neither man could see the big picture…

The similarity caused Peterson's composure to slip far enough under its normal state that formality faltered and he resorted to calling O'Rourke by his nickname, as if he were the irascible Ricky. It was an unconscious response. In his mind he pooh-poohed them both, ultimately deciding that neither had valid reason to blame him. But now he unconsciously felt an affinity for the man. He intentionally refrained from divulging details concerning the micro-bugs, hoping to dissuade JP from trying anything stupid. There he was using that nickname again. He keep this up he might deserve some of the nicknames the man was probably making up for him in his head right now. He shook himself, it was time to move out of this preoccupation and get back his focus.

"Just consider it a global surveillance network that works like a big Hoover and it sucks in huge volumes of all types of telecommunications" continued Peterson's spiel. "I mean this is a vast worldwide system. There're rooftop antennas on commercial buildings, special deals with satellite companies, taps on undersea and land cables, you name it, it's all there for a price. Then there're backdoors in switching and encryption software supposedly put there for maintenance and it all gets filtered through computer networks snooping for buzz words or code phrases that the clients are interested in. Not just phone calls either. Emails and faxes get intercepted and analyzed too and if the interested parties are too busy, they file the intercepts away for future review."

"So you're gonna disable the tracking right?" And I shouldn't contact you when I leave this building? Okay, I'm on it! I can go now, right?" O'Rourke got up to leave. Evil headmasters or no, he'd gotten the message from the start and now became thoroughly bored with the overkill. It wasn't like they were equipping him out "Q" to James Bond like.

This square head just wanted to go over a phone and a laptop. Unfortunately, he wanted to go over and over and over again. Most of it unnecessary dribble it was. Why bother with endless warnings about private cell phones? Totally unnecessary. While he appreciated the utility of redundancy, he detested the thought of carrying around pockets full of electronic gadgets that all pretty much did the same thing. Friends of his stepped out with pagers, cell phones and palm pilots clipped to their belts or stuffed inside jacket pockets, all at the same time. He had never owned more than one cell phone at a time and often left that one in his car's console storage. They want him to use this phone and take this computer? Fine. He'd take them, but he wasn't about to lug his personal stuff as well. That's definitely overkill.

Moreover, he understood the military's systematized delusions concerning security breaches. That's what systems are all about, delusions. But when Peterson associated worldwide intelligence gathering with a Hoover vacuum cleaner, he nearly laughed out loud. It brought to O'Rourke's mind that this man was about as paranoid as J. Edgar Hoover. As he rose to leave he contemplated the possibility that Peterson might see intelligence gatherers the same way J. Edgar saw Communists … everywhere.

"Not done yet," rumbled Peterson. His mannerism informed O'Rourke that he had again ruffled the Colonel's feathers. Once again he reflected that he would have to try and not do that sort of thing so much. Never knew when one might need help in a pickle. He sat back down. They were the only one's present for this final briefing session held in the Colonel's office, just across and facing the General's, but stealing away might not be as easy as it had once appeared.

As usual, closed tight were the twin entryway doors leading from the large executive suite, where the secretarial staff held court, to the outside world populated by peons and other beings of lesser worth. Presumably, it was prying eyes of curious passersby these portals shielded.

They played their little peek-a-boo games, these DIA folks. As if half the agency wasn't aware of his daily arrival. Little chance those looking up from their dank and dark dungeons aren't at least partly aware what the boss is doing. That's their method of survival in a dog-eat-dog world. The game goes on, only the names change. Regardless, shuttered closed was the entrance to this executive suite …and the exit.

Nice and large, one might describe as voluminous this entry room holding two desks made of the same polished mahogany as those hidden behind the office doors they guarded and very near as large. On opposite sides facing forward, standing guard; their placement purposeful.

A single curio closet –filled with small flags, pennants and figurines-- stood at the back of the room, stretched below two picture windows. Above it and between them hung a large plaque containing the DIA seal displaying a flaming torch stuck through a light, blue-green colored globe crossed by two red, atomic ellipses, over a dark blue background. Thirteen stars arched above the globe while a laurel wreath curved below.

Only one secretary occupied her station when O'Rourke arrived that day. He preferred to think her "on guard" since primarily she ran interference for her boss, screening visitors and calls and whatever his preferences. That is, as long as those preferences didn't require a great deal of physicality. She didn't look capable of running marathons or anything, but if the coffee pot sat close by, she would do all right …then again, she could be packin'.

A plump, robust-looking woman, she sported cherry-colored cheeks and dimples set deep in her face. Ample jowls gave the appearance that she had no neck at all. Her chin fell almost directly onto an equally ample bosom. Hairs colored silvery-gray had invaded nearly all the territory once claimed by a natural brunette, indicating advancing years and grandmotherly temperament.

He realized that grandma could just as easily become Grand-Ma-Ma pulling double-duty in her guise as mild mannered secretary to old farts dressed in green. There she stood, arms akimbo, Grand-Ma-Ma in sheep's clothing, able to leap tall desk chairs at a moment's notice, her Beretta .40 flashing up from its quick draw, thigh-holster, ready for Freddie. He could imagine her in bodyguard mode, her lightning quick hands snapping it out whenever the Colonel was threatened. Humor pronounced that scene a daily occurrence (given Peterson's ability at pissing off anyone he met) and such necessity justifying the split-hem dresses she seemed to favor. At least he hoped that was the reason this seventies-something old lady showed that much thigh. Then again, maybe seventy was the new fifty … as if he had room to talk.

But this day she had barely even looked up as he approached, concentrating on the computer monitor resting on the right side of a desk so richly polished and shiny he could nearly see himself. Pictures of her family sat on the matching credenza desk behind her. Further back, mauve brocade curtains fully drawn, permitted full sunlight on this beautiful day. She did not smile in any of the pictures he could see, neither frowning; more neutral than anything and she was not smiling this day, either. But she was pleasant, offering a cheerful "good morning sir," as she waved him to the door on her left, into Peterson's office. "Go right in."

The realization that he would be stuck in this room for hours going over endless details while being lectured –if pressed he might have said, advised-- by his nemesis was nearly too much for O'Rourke to take. Unfortunately, the realization only came afterwards. No phone calls interrupted, obviously being intercepted by the secretary. But he would have welcomed an occasional break. Peterson's breath smelled like garlic and onions. Not too heavy –as if he'd just polished off a whole calzone-- but somewhat significant, like he had just done in a South Philly bagel. O'Rourke truly wanted to get the guy a Tic-Tac or, at the very least, a mint candy, doublemint or something.

He had never been so happy to get away from anyone in his remembrance –with the exception of one other man wearing a similar uniform. Regardless of his disdain, every portion of Peterson's spiel had been absorbed --not necessarily appreciated from Mister Too-Paranoid-for-Words-- but absorbed nonetheless.

It still bugged him. Something about this entire operation still troubled. Surfing for snippets off the internet he found less than he hoped on Morano and his people. No pictures, or bios, just addresses and email addresses. Eventually he changed focus to the DIA web site to learn more about his clandestine employer. Theirs wasn't much more revealing, just propaganda and sales pitch.

Scanning through the written text, even watching their recruitment video, he was struck by one overall conclusion. DIA owned tremendous resources worldwide (and they definitely sported very nice office furniture), so even with the ex-wifey's possible involvement, why was he so important to the success of this mission? No mole should have been able to get in so deep as to circumvent all their compartmented safeguards. You got worldwide assets; bring in an asset from some other corner of your world. Something was afoot, he decided, and those feet smelled something most foul …then again, it could just be his imagination.

The smart-looking laptop computer Peterson provided hung in its bag from his shoulder. Nice and light and very thin, he did not know whether he should think of it as a laptop or a notebook. But the term laptop had applied long before some smart-leaning, next-generation-geek --locked in self-gratification mode—shrunk it down a tad and reinvented it as a notebook.   Peterson had declared it a notebook. However, since notebooks tended to come without DVD drives, he stuck with the former, happy to find a legitimate reason to oppose the Jarhead.

It was full of all sorts of neat features though, a lot more than his own personal HP. It was also faster and would only work for the owner.

Otherwise they were nearly identical. Maybe they'd let him keep it …if he lived to bring it back.

But the practical side of him doubted this as any type of perk, only a loaner, never a gift; the government being the government, after all and practically filled to the brim with bean counters. They probably had the IRS on standby, poised to take away his home, vehicles and lifesavings should he fail to bring this thing back in one piece. Even though --paranoia being a government norm-- there were measures designed-in to preclude necessity of return; namely, a strange little desktop icon that Peterson had pointedly brought to his attention.

It bore no resemblance to any thundering rain cloud --lightning flashing from its dark underside-- giving direst warning to the intended user of its purpose. It wasn't circled, stuck inside a square, nothing; just a capitalized letter P, floating in the ether between the numbers 5 and 1. Colored dark blue, the P sported a distinctive, cursive flair and represented the Philadelphia Phillies; the bright red 51 representing the number of his favorite closer …relief pitcher Brad Lidge.

To the unsuspecting it could have been a game or website. So those not in the know might have overlooked, passed it by in the hunt for more serious stuff. But a triple-mouse-click selection of this icon, while simultaneously holding down "CTRL" and "ALT" keys began a countdown at the end of which you no longer had a notebook or laptop. It was "Lights Out" …just like Brad's slider.

Just in case though, its activation also opened an instruction window warning you this computer was about to go away, giving you a chance to halt the countdown. In case you really didn't want that outcome. "Hello! As per your command, I'm about to melt into silicon goo. You know what to do. Goodbye!"

Peterson had decided against further antagonizing his "guest" with more condescending lecture (or discussion) beyond recommending O'Rourke familiarize himself with its "ReadMe" instruction on the "Start" menu. That and strongly advising he activate immediately should capture or compromise become an imminent threat. So maybe they wouldn't have the IRS seize his house …so maybe he could work something out.

But he took the lesson of most of the proffered advice, lecture or what have you. Only a fool would not. Then again, he felt less than qualified to discern fools from wise men. Until recently, he had doubted that any fool would devote resources to keep tabs on a nobody like him. However, the chase through Maryland countryside still very fresh in his memory, he now knew better. Lucky is the man who survives to recognize his mistakes...

The trick is to learn from past blunders to endure future slings and arrows. As much as he disdained the Jarhead's attitude, he'd take his lesson. Some bad someone tracking his calls could provoke especially negative consequences. If he weren't careful, such serious folks could mean no more Mister Carefree-Wise-Ass.

Accordingly, he decided to enact his own survival mechanisms, concluding that when things look strange, do strange things until things look right again. Obviously, it would be especially unwise to call any DIA switchboard exchanges from his room phone. That was what his super-duper, all-about-this'n-that satphone was for and given his revulsion with thoughts of calling in to them anyway he'd even reserve those, to like zero.

It wasn't all about rebellion. Though not capable of intercepting the message, some Gomer on phone watch maybe could get a record of numbers he had called. A computer programmed to search for government exchanges –particularly those used by intelligence agencies-- was certain to generate an alarm for people concerned about such. So he'd carry these things, but he wasn't calling nobody. He hoped text messages weren't a problem. At least they went out fast....

O'Rourke practiced diligently, becoming familiar with both devices and their features on the flight down from Washington, careful that none spied over the seatback or across the aisle on his right. Still paranoid, but he didn't overly worry. Half the world's population spent so much of their time on the phone or online; it was the other half that looked suspicious. Besides, these features weren't what he considered formidable. They fell more on the side of the improved rather than the new.

He was especially interested in the handheld PDA. This version of Smartphone looked similar to his LG. The shorter learning curve obviously why they chose it for him, though this one had been modified for DIA by a Silicon Valley firm. Secure voice, video and text messages were addressable using software switches. The menus and software-configurable keyboards looked the same; however, some of the apps routed transmissions over military satellites in encrypted format to their destination from any spot on the planet. Other than its miniature listening devices (aka, bugs), the special features included a low light, HD-video camera and a ton of RAM and storage memory that boosted all its other capabilities. He could record six hours of video at twelve mega-pixel resolution and uplink the video feed for real-time reporting, plus there was that fifteen times digital zoom. This was also a perk he'd like to keep. He had to remind himself again that this wasn't really a perk, was it?

Peterson's counsel concerned usage and possible disposal of the devices, not their condition or return. Particularly mentioned were this phone and its surveillance features; with emphasis to maintain situational awareness at all times while operating.

"Remember," his rumbling voice had stressed, "don't get so caught up when you're using these," he pointed to the cellular apparatus and its wireless accessories, "that you forget to use these", pointing to his eyes. It was back to Fighter Pilot U: "Head on a swivel. Don't get caught not looking. Watch your six. Safety is no accident. Fundamentals, fundamentals, fundamentals; blah, blah, blah ...and no fun".

No fun is right! Still, advice is a cruel temptress. Often a thing of beauty, but seldom easily engaged. Cupping both ears to enhance the audio in his right ear, O'Rourke found himself concentrating more on the snooped sounds from inside --to discern and separate voices and dialog-- from the blowing, whooshing outside that occasionally was punctuated by booming sounds of debris smashing into nearby structures. He had the maximum amount of filter dialed in, but this thing probably was not designed to operate in hurricanes. The Joker in the deck --Mom Nature-- reapplied her other intermittent aspect to his surveillance, rain.

He hoped the phone's built-in recorder functioned okay. Looked like it did, but who knew. At least it was on. Suddenly he regretted not reading further into the tutorial, might cut down on the speculative aspect, leaving him more with hope than hip. So he kept up his hoping. Murphy might be about. One never knew when Murphy would strike.

Sincerely, he hoped Murphy's Law plagued the other guys for a change. Murphy had done enough to foul up his life. But eventually he relinquished the hater side of life's choices, dialed back the hoping and merely wished Murphy would just leave him alone. Almost he gave up even that limited longing, but managed to retain some measure.

He kept some measure of hopefulness, hoping the damn thing was waterproof, as advertised. But as long as he was primarily into wishes, saw no harm in wishing the little "bugs" had video capability. Close-ups would have been a neat addition. But then again, this was DIA, not Her

Majesty's Secret Service. Later, when he text messaged the entire account to Peterson's folks --attached as an encrypted format file—perhaps he would suggest they contact "Q" for assistance.

But at least the DIA wordsmiths could analyze the audio for anything he might have lost in the stormy blow, provided there was audio to analyze. He did not fear the bad guys intercepting his text, not even the Russians. Back in the day they kept surveillance trawlers off our coasts to snoop any juicy tidbits to find. Anyone out tracking phone calls in this neck of the woods on a night like this would only find a destination designated for an AOL account …that and they would obviously be crazy, suicidal, et cetera.

Paul Mua'Dib's tale came back to him out of the deep recesses of his memory. Those huge gumbo lips savoring each spoonful of the three bowls full he devoured in the tiny Baton Rouge Creole restaurant where they settled on for dinner. He'd taken to describing in great detail one time his P-3 crew hunted a Soviet missile sub during a North Atlantic gale.

It was a killer tale that seemed to never want to end, always additional add-ins, forever circling back around through alternate paths and streams. Mua'dib famous for his rousing stories of warfare and woe, meaning woe unto the ones stuck listening to them and warfare if you piss him off by dashing off. Plus, you really can't just up and run away. Mua'Dib's not only a good sprinter for a big man, he motivated. No problem he don't finish tonight, there's always next time. Even a month later, he pick up pretty much right where he paused.

But this time O'Rourke's fault, he later regaled to Sylvia while they snuggled in for a long winter's night.

"Coulda got outta that evening with the short two-hour version (the long version is truly a scourge from the gods of long windedness). But in a moment of Jack Tongue, where the alcohol liberated too mucha my brain, by killing off too many cells (which further freed vocals to flap their gums), I stupidly commented that if the Navy Reserves did that sort of thing, chasing down actual Soviet boomers, I could imagine what full-time crews must accomplish. Of course to Paul, who considers his Reservists just as, if not, more capable than the full-time boys, that's a significant challenge!"

He recalled that she seemed convinced that bedtime stories are great for sleeping through. He still talking as she began softly snoring. Now there's a lesson fer sure! But, he was still going strong, his own imitation of Mua'Dib story hours…

"Plus, even today, Mua'Dib is so totally down on all things Russian, including everything and anybody who down with them, it's never smart to get that type of convo going. He a dog lover who even hates their wolfhounds, won't even drink Russian vodka, even if it's free. But I had opened mouth to insert foot way too fast to appreciate my error …until story hours had begun!"

'…Soviet subs targeting our cities! My moms lives in a city! Russians cut from the same Soviet cloth! How ya jump in bed wit people threatening ta nuke yo' moms?'

Yeah, I screwed th' pooch that night. Anyway, th' lesson is… err, Syl?"

"Snooooorrrrrreeeee!"

O'Rourke and Mua'Dib never served together. Just hung out sometimes when in the same town. Hard to tell where Paul lived. He really got around. Kinda like the "wherever he lay his hat he home" type of guy. Hard blue eyes that can soften at the first notes of a baby's cry, this big bull of a man whose knuckles seemed bigger than most guys fists. He truly didn't have a lot of dislikes, but the ones he had he disliked them intensely! The F community …now there's another reach.

Mua'Dib doesn't totally hate the F community. But he does barely tolerate Zoomies. He don't hate the fact that the F community consists of superfast jets while his four engine turboprop takes quite a bit longer to get anywhere. He merely points out that his bird would still beat all those to overseas deployments F-4s, F-15s, F-22s, etc., cause it don't gotta stop for gas!

Four turning 'n burning, launch into the sky to patrol for the bad guys, sometimes the good guys in harm's way. He loved the life, especially loved chasing bad guys in their deep diving subs and spy trawler surface vessels snooping off our coasts. Those top his list for pet peeves, but far from the only…

He got another pet peeve about Vets being deported for minor offenses. Typical. They beg Mexicans to come work for them, fight wars for them. Then they kick them out when they done with them!

"Ya'll done pickin'? Cool! Hit th' road! South! Not north bitches!"

To him it's same ol' shit, just another day the treatment of America's current slave market. Mua'dib takes no shit off nobody and loyal to everybody loyal to his country. "When white people cry freedom they crying about their freedom. Nobody else's."

To stir the pot, Mua'dib urges Mexicans to build a wall to keep Americans out. Of course the American government would probably invade, but then they'd owe reparations to the Mexicans. "Ain't right they tryna keep us out! Cancun needs us! Won't let us in, what they hiding?"

But eventually he gets back to his story. O'Rourke already confused, trying to follow, but seems that they've solved at least a couple social issues. Mua'dib can definitely ramble…

"Sea State 7, waves cresting thirty-forty feet, fifty-five knot winds and Ivan doing his best to stay quiet. We drop sonobouy patterns we had no hope of sustaining an' little hope of even hearing. Every time the waves they rode on dropped, they dropped and rose when the next waves came. You got dem hydrophones a thousand feet down, where dem Yankees liked to prowl. But every few seconds that sucker is getting jerked up, then slammed back down. The only sound it's hearin' is ambient noise from its own swishin' through th' water. Tough job hombre!"

"Yankee is a sub, right?"

"Yeah, a boomer. Sixteen nukes. Fast and deep divin'. Ivan learned tricks from us (aka, stole) and started makin' 'em quieter, tougher to track, tougher to find and Poseidon wasn't helping at all."

"So you're sayin' you couldn't find it?"

"Couldn't find, Him! The Soviets named their boats after guys. And no I didn't say that. It was a tough mission, but we found Him and tracked his ass 'til we left. God of the sea be damned!"

"So how'd you do it? How'd you keep on Him even with all that interference?"

At that, Paul just winked and said, "If I tell ya, I gotta kill ya!"

Sometimes he did not fully appreciate Mua'Dib's peculiar style of humor. Bad enough he took his handle from a Sci-Fi movie that he misspelled and was too embarrassed to correct.

He never again asked this big bull of a man how they'd stayed on that boat in such foul weather, either. The Navy has all sorts of tricks up their sleeves. Maybe they had one of their attack boats trailing the Soviet or maybe there was a SOSUS net nearby. Paul never specified which part of the North Atlantic they searched. Not that he had any idea the locations of the super-secret Sound Surveillance System, but supposedly its sensors were pretty long range capable.

Regardless, he doubted Muad'Dib was the killing type; maybe over getting caught with somebody's woman, but probably not over boats named after men. Besides, the interesting part that had brought back his memory walk was Mua'Dib's conviction that no self-respecting trawler captain gonna wanna be out in weather like that. Great way to visit the down under …and he wasn't talking Australia.

So hopefully he had little to fear from the Hoover community out to scoop every radiated electron from the airwaves. But for now, he had other concerns, like girding against complacency. Bad guys out around his hotel, bad guys could be out around here. In fact it made much more sense they'd be positioned to protect their employer at his home. Maybe. He just hoped they hadn't…

One other item pulled from that same drawer and handed him by the stone-faced Marine was much smaller, but much more appreciated. He thanked the man and matter-of-factly pocketed the small card sealed inside transparent plastic, barely even looking to confirm its printed information. He did not need to; it had been a part of him for so many years he knew intimately each line and symbol. But he had missed it for the time it had been absconded away and it might come in handy before this drama played out. But he stubbornly refused to display even the remotest relief in the Colonel's presence, although the warm feeling flooding throughout was difficult to mask.

Curiosity intrigued. But he held it in check, refusing to ask how DIA had been able to retrieve his pilot license from the State of Virginia. He wondered how many favors its return had cost the Federal Government. Perhaps they had played their "National Security" card. But that seemed unlikely as such an act could possibly have started tongues wagging and associated him with the very thing they all hoped to avoid …an undercover assignment.

CHAPTER THIRTEEN

"Dummies look for excuses, the enlightened mind seeks inspiration," slurred one of the men in the room. His voice sounded familiar. It could have been the same guy he had seen with Morano the previous night. It might have been him. The voice came through scratchy and distant. But he recalled the figure; angular, fairly tall guy sporting blonde hair, cut kind of close, extremely blue eyes, wide set in a square face, strong chin …not so this voice though.

Only a glimmer of greeting had passed between them, hardly more than a nod and not even one spoken word. Other than the tail end of the man's conversation, a snippet whispered into the night air as he walked up to Morano (after decking his bodyguard), he'd never heard him speak. Still, first impressions being key; his impression of the voice was anything but impressed; mid-range timbre, kind of dull and flat, lacking verve and definition. This night it reminded him of a nobody trying to be somebody, a Jimmie Stewart body with a Pee Wee Herman voice; grabbing at the high life …in an inebriated kind of way.

Its echo muffled, borderline garbled --but only partly from the growling storm noises— this voice, leaking back, sallied into his earpiece, disemboweled from human ownership, but still a physical point of fact. Its resounding pealed like from a guy encased in his cockpit wearing his mask too tight in vain effort to suck more oxygen faster, aiding recovery from a full-on binge. Like a player better prepared for sleep mode than his scheduled sortie off to see the wizard.

Its familiarity reminded of one too many pilots he'd caught swaying unsteadily up ladders into the management end of heavily armed fighter jets. "Bottle courage" they called the somewhat-accepted practice. But when overdone, it led to conditions one should refrain from even operating motor cars, let alone war machines. "Just one more sip and it'll steady my hands …burp!"

Some others used the bottle to stiffen resolve and shore up sagging spirits. Some of these also overdid it. Characterized by an apparent lack of comprehensive thought and mixed noticeably with slurred speech, it sounded like this speaker was one of those who went a bit too far, perhaps quite a bit. Indications indicated his current condition as three sheets to the wind … flapping in the breeze and feeling no pain.

If this was that same guy, what was the connection? Morano selling some new software packages to the Zoomies? Or maybe he decided on trading his Benz for a surplus F-16. There were a whole bunch of them parked on the Tucson sand inside the Davis-Monthan graveyard and they'd definitely get you around a lot quicker than a Lear.

He figured the fellow —whoever he actually turned out to be-- paraphrased some olden day's saga or maybe a once famous politician, as if those people were plentiful. Which one of these people had launched this tirade did not much matter to him. Lacking video capability on these bugs, it didn't much matter if it mattered or not. It probably did not matter to the speaker either, loaded down as he was with heavyweight liquor or to anyone else in the room for that matter. The conversation rushed right along as if this speaker had never spoken, monopolized as it was by their host.

It appeared that Morano held a fondness for the sound of his own voice this night and continued unabated as the other fellow petered out. He evidently believed everyone around him shared that affinity and never once let up.

But unfortunately, from O'Rourke's perspective, this random spiel had yet to include any useful information; nothing tangibly linking him to murder or theft or any such skullduggery. He just simply rambled in a talk that seemed to last hours, which in truth measured only in minutes, though too many of those. But O'Rourke hoped at the least for some indication of malevolence, some chink in his armor he could send back triumphantly to Peterson. He'd settle for just about anything, even a syncopated rendition of George Carlin reciting "The ten things you can't say on TV: 'Shit, piss, cunt, mutherf…'"

Another man anticipated the identical outburst. This one bore witness from a much closer perspective and in more than one way. He decided it about time to step in before the ten things you can't say were said then turned to twenty. He had already held his breath in anticipation longer than he deemed prudent.

The Carlos Morano he knew was quite capable of spewing forth a George Carlin type profanity-laced diatribe, among other things. Though he seldom ever did and never in public. But this night, such was nearly at the stage of eruption…

He knew intimately that few people ever witnessed Morano's dark side and that of those, even fewer survived the experience. "Beware smiling faces that lie", sang his mother's advice. It did not matter whether Morano was smiling or not or in which style he dressed; underneath he was always the same.

Outwardly dashing and debonair, you seldom ever need worry about him showing a violent side to his nature whether he padded along the beach in tropical wear or stepped out to serious functions in two thousand dollar Ermenegildo Zegna suits, two hundred-fifty dollar Hugo Boss Shirts and leather shoes costing more than entire cows. He loved how the lustrous wool-silk blends converted even his chubbiness to irrelevant. In either scene you'd see only the picture of a man to worship and respect. But outside the public view and given the proper motivation he would as soon claw out your eyes as look at you ...though never with his own claws.

The metamorphosis took time. Initially clothes mattered little, only his image as mover and shaker and major player. But then he found he had no such image, bringing his hubris crashing down in a dreadful heap from which his more vengeful nature screamed vociferously for release. Still, he persevered.

Gala affairs he frequented, rubbing elbows with the power elite as well as those of a more familiar, wannabee status; until he realized to the latter his lot was cast. Recognition hit hard after some members of the "in crowd" lambasted any and everything that applied to him; branding him just another example of what he hated most.

Snickers vanished quickly whenever he approached, descriptive terms they passed only to his back, never the front. But the lampooning stung no less. So much so, the perpetrators of this back-biting and belittling —who nicknamed him The Clinger-- he tempted to expunge, in a most unpleasant fashion. But, with counsel from his older, more learned cousin he embraced a new direction. They considered him a hanger-on, a bootlicker, an uninspiring phony-baloney? Well he'd show them...

He took a hiatus to give time a chance to heal, then readdressed those instincts that had kept him alive on the mean streets of East LA (cept when they killed him). Good time Charlie was put back in the box, out came his former gangster self in a mellowed version with a better wardrobe.

On his return, the backbiters found a whole new man. He'd changed his manner, never seeking introduction to anyone, regardless their status or elevation. He changed the company he kept, became known for the beautiful women in his tow and the lavish parties he threw. He seldom overtly exhibited any competitive side, but his parties were A-list and top shelf all the way and the quality of the women in his company superb.

They came in all flavors of heaven-sent succulence, classy and fashionable and fulfilling the object of many a man's wet dreams for subsequent nights and counting. He never mentioned business outside of his offices or hotel suite and refused to engage with anyone so intended in their discussion. Totally revamped were his style, his flair and his wardrobe.

They had "pooh-poohed" him as staid and ordinary in the "off-the-rack", three-piece suit worn to the coming out party of a congressman's daughter. Now they considered him upbeat and visionary. Amazing what a little change of attitude, along with a flash of cash and a little "bling" will do.

But attitude is a component of will and his will was iron clad in this effort. He would not be caught dead in blue jeans, not even during casual times. Around DC it was always suits, sometimes with ties, sometimes not. Down south, he tended to step out tropical in pure-silk, Saint Thomas pants under short-sleeved shirts weaved with colorful pictures like large, golden pineapples adorned with green leaves on black backgrounds and such. Covering his bare feet he favored black, tan or beige-colored Fisherman sandals to complete the island look. But there were a few who knew him and knew that any who swallowed his tame act did so as the bluefin attracted by the bloody, greasy chum slick that promised shiny, new treasures …including hook, line and sinker.

This night he sported tropical wear. The shirt was a white, short sleeved, pullover knit and the pants beige. But they fit the pattern. What did not quite fit was Morano's mood. He seemed impassioned by some influence; perhaps aggravated was a more accurate description. Obviously he had been drinking heavily. Maybe Mother Nature's arrival as Hurricane Eris had unnerved him or maybe her canceling out his pool party had just really pissed him off.

From his exterior observation post, O'Rourke watched for a few moments as the man took a long pull on the Corona in his hand. He remembered what Stephanie had told him, "Morano drinks his own urine" and wondered if perhaps the amber liquid in the clear bottle he raised to his lips was recycled product, aka, "essence of Carlos". He almost chuckled aloud at the thought, but refrained, maintaining a silent vigil.

Inside the house, Chaco silently swore once more to himself. At any moment he expected a series of epithets to flow like the Colorado River from his cousin's snarling lips. Too much drink in Carlos made for a lousy drunk. Usually he held himself in check, did not let the devil get into him this deep. But this evening he was distracted in the worst way possible for his kind of man ...and distraction leads to disaster.

He was about to tumble over a cliff unless caught in time; his current path headed to nowhere he needed to be going. One little set back and now all of a sudden he seemed intent to right the wrongs of the past two hundred-fifty or so years, aligning himself with dangerous people who had no honor. Chaco's powers of recall chagrined him. He should never have let things go this far.

Carlos seemed too far gone. His pregnant girlfriend lay on the floor beside him, already deceased. Somehow they'd gotten to him, poisoned him! Chaco would take care of that later. For now he would care for his cousin.

At first all appeared just business as usual. They were breaking away from any ties to narcotics or other illegal activities. Their financial picture rock solid, they cut ties with any of the old gang that wanted to stay "connected". Any threatening entanglements were eliminated in manners nearly akin to a Mexican version of the Godfather, parts one and two (though not nearly so bloody). Just like the Italian version, however, a few sacrifices were necessary. Such is the lesson of change; everyone should not make the trip. Some won't change enough to travel well...

Not so much revenge as repair. Fixing the broken parts as business dictated. And business dictated elimination of several who's continued existence proved unnecessary. Beginning with the animals who murdered Carlos and family. Those all had to go, along with Carlos' identity. A new organization, a new name for it as well as for Carlos. Chaco evolved from wolf to sheepdog. A veritable Poacher turned Gamekeeper.

What Chaco failed to recognize at the time, is that not all who seemed capable of change could hike the necessary hills and trails. Inevitably some got lost in the process; while others changed just enough to become hostile travelers rocking the boat from the inside.

Changes in Carlos now spun beyond any of their intentions. He'd become embittered, exhibiting hatred for nearly all things mainstream, as if he no longer held any optimism for the future. He became consumed, almost as if he held a death wish, as if life itself held little meaning. Then he decided to move permanently to Miami. From there it got crazier…

He now played the corporate games, wooing sneak thief power brokers from all genres; bagging a senator here, a CEO there. And those he seduced, he used as he needed. He screwed them like the putas they all were. However he portrayed himself to these chivatos, these sneaks, his focus was totally on vengeance and none knew this like the cousin who also recognized that something needed to be done about it …but just could not determine what.

Chaco had little concern for chivatos or how Carlos used and abused them. To him, these were the most ungracious form of mankind in existence. This type represented those who came in your front door --hat in hand, innocuous and fawning-- then stabbed you in the back when you turned to fetch a crust of bread to feed them. This type sought the aid of other men in times of strife, then quickly forgot (even downplayed) the significance of that aid.

Chivatos did it to the French. Only a few short years after the American Revolution had ended, they refused to assist the country whose assistance had enabled them to defeat their former masters. They even continued supplying raw materials those former masters, the British, needed to war with their former allies, the French. The French king first lost his country's fortune aiding the Americans and then his head because he lost his country's fortune aiding the Americans.

Chivatos did it to the Mexican-Americans who had fought shoulder-to-shoulder with them to achieve freedom from Mexican dictators and then again to the Native Americans who helped them defeat other Native Americans and they've done it to black Americans after every war this country ever had. Chivatos had done them all. They had no honor or conscience. It took a while, but his people soon learned to see the fangs behind those smiling faces.

Chaco wondered why it took black people so long to see the pattern. Those tear-stained eyes, those lips you knew were lying because they were moving. That plaintive plea: "Please help us fight to be free. Think of our poor women and children. Oh shit! We free now! Don't need you no more, slave! And git the hell away from our women and children!"

White men even told the blacks that they would never get a fair shake, even wrote it down in their Constitution. Ya'll lucky ta be three-fifths, niggers!

Were blacks that trusting? Could they not surmise how appeasing dishonorable people is a no-win situation? When were they going to throw off the yoke and slaughter these cabrones the way his mother's people had after they had learned the lesson? Then he remembered that they too had learned the lesson too late. A yoke is so much harder to throw off once it's lashed on.

So he watched with mixed emotions his younger cousin's mendacity towards others, the dishonesty and backstabbing, taking advantage of every advantage. Literally, he watched with mixed emotions his younger cousin's riotous rampage through life. And at times it was not pretty, nearly driving him to drink. Within a short period, the older cousin could meander between a highly amused: "HaHaHa, he did what? That boy crazy!" To a deplorably enraged: "He did what! Something wrong with him. That boy must be crazy!"

He now felt strongly opposed to his cousin for the first time in their lives. It was not his first time in opposition, but it was his first time so diametrically opposite. For several reasons he felt Carlos wrong, beginning with his resurrecting the "kill or be killed" gangland theme once employed by La Raza 18, moving their entire operation back onto a dangerous path. Carlos' world view, seemingly his main impetus, now also typified the one thing that Chaco had always cautioned against …revenge.

Willful and more headstrong than ever these past few years, Carlos had become arrogant, less inclined to listen to reason; his absolutist views denigrating the most basic of human values, bordering on anarchy. Though it remained hidden well beneath the surface, his insufferable vanity now spiraled so out of control he became easily provoked, set to make total war against any progenitor of insult to the heritage he himself eschewed. Chaco wondered if perhaps that too was just smokescreen; a mask to his true intentions. Whatever it was, nothing in his present lifestyle spoke of pride in his heritage. Not on the surface.

Carlos kept much to himself, his true feelings. Inside still beat the heart of a Chicano, impassioned and prideful; love for his people still moved him. But for reasons of his own, these days he conversed solely in English; never engaging the English-flavored Spanish or Caló so prevalent among their people that some called Spanglish. If they wanted to converse with him, it would be English or not at all. He wasn't about to be confused with some wetback Cholo who'd jumped the fence in Tijuana or swam the

Rio Grande from Juárez.

English being the language of business, Chaco understood the business motivation. It just struck him queer that Carlos now did everything Anglo-style: speech, dress, women, even the neighborhoods in which he chose to abide; nothing to remind anyone from where he came. And although the practice left some others pissed off, if that was the extent of the strangeness, Chaco would not now have strayed beyond his practice to "live and let live". But from there it just got stranger.

Seemingly, his superego had undergone a reversal in its aging process. Rather than mellowing out --seeking the comfort of grand kids, Saturday morning golf and Sunday afternoon football-- he became more hardhearted and mean spirited. Instead of settling down with women near his age group, he gamboled about with girls barely legal that he passed on to business acquaintances as tasty hand-me-downs in tit-for-tat arrangements, favor for favor.

Avaricious pursuits, vanity run amuck, all compounded by the ever growing seed of nihilistic values. He had lost himself. High probability for damnation with little possibly of redemption and in Chaco's measurement it all stemmed from one tree …evil, thy name is woman.

In his mind, none of these unseemly mannerisms had ever transpired in his relative before she arrived. She was the true motivation. Hers was the face that drove him as surely as the oxen before their master's bullwhip. Her every whim he sought to fulfill, even before she wished it. He was the tinker toy she shoved around her makeshift track, inciting whirlwind jaunts to exotic, far corners of the planet and lavish bashes thrown in expensive, posh hotels at her merest whim. Jewelry, cars, even a jet plane he procured.

Truly, hers was real beauty. Poised and polished, regal in bearing, she brought it all to the table. But paying a flight crew exorbitant amounts to repose in standby on the off chance he might decide to use their services (often meaning she might decide), well that was just plain crazy.

All these issues and others, Chaco cautioned against, but found only a deaf ear. Carlos remained smitten, at her beck and call, succumbing to her merest whim and still she denied his greatest wish. His proposals she'd rejected so many times they changed the betting pool from the date she'd submit to the date he'd take the hint.

But he never did. She shot him down in flames so frequently they called her the Red Baroness. Him they called Snoopy. If not so bloody, it would have been embarrassing. Because of her he was a hopeless case.

But Chaco did not place the blame entirely on her. She was only a woman. A man must be a man, not a chocho. Reconsidering, he slowly shook his aged head. No he did not act the part of a cunt. Worse than that, tonight he played the part of crybaby pendejo in front of strangers. Even worse, this pendejo, this asshole was unlikely to respond to taunts hurled his way in Spanish. Such a huevo, such an egghead he was.

He was as pathetic a figure as Napoleon attempting heroic deeds in order to woo his unfaithful Josephine away from her many lovers. If anything, Chaco recognized the danger his naive cousin seemed too blind to perceive. He saw the similarity, just as certain as the Pope is Catholic that Carlos might one day discover this woman's loins to be the site of his own Waterloo. It became his goal that his cousin survived to retire to his own Saint Helena. But in the blink of an eye, there came another change…

Tina's tryst with JP, ex-husband or no, was last straw for Morano. The humiliation causing hissy fits that literally sent him over a steep precipice. Visions of naked passion –the two of them writhing and straining together-- followed his plunge to rock bottom, cursing and fuming all the way down.

Double humiliation. Morano never once revealed to Chaco that most embarrassing moment in his existence. The hero, fighter jock Captain versus the dope-dealing corporal! He played the latter role of the wronged one whose memories would replay that execrable scene forever and a day!

But the lesson he learned well and never again used his C-130 aircrew position to shuttle drugs from Southeast Asia. He lucked out. The lesson taught just how lucky. Prison stared him dead in the face. But the Captain cared more about teaching the lesson than punishing the misguided enlisted man.

Probably all of South Vietnam knew the story of his straining reddening self, twisting ineffectually to escape the iron grip of her then-husband; choking pain searing his soul, sobs and tears of frustration streaming endlessly. Who knows, they might even have inducted the scene into Marine Corps lore to be recited at reunions …at least he would never forget.

Then he wrangled his way into the Captain's life, first stealing his child and then his wife. It was awesome, glorious. In the game of revenge, he had scored big time! Until the Captain took her back!

He hit hard. But he rose up stronger and, he felt, more complete. The double hatred seething from deep inside nurtured him, giving strength and purpose. He still had only conjecture as to whether she had actually slept with her ex-husband, that night she chose to stay with first mate against second mate's wishes. Well, against betrothed's wishes anyway.

Made even stronger by his spy's report, he still fumed at descriptive details such as the light illumination from sleeping quarters. Perhaps a bit too descriptive, the details of laughter and giggles and sheer joy reverberating from inside out into the night air. His suspicions had filled in him a terrible resolve. It was easy to do the math. Including the live-in maid, there's three people present and only two bedrooms had lit up. Moreover, only those in the master's bedroom were lit when the woman exited at dawn's light. This latter tidbit struck so viciously he literally blew a fuse. "I'll kill that bitch."

Truly the wronged party here, he gave her every yard of rope she needed and she hung herself with it. His tolerance had surmounted Herculean proportions, the lava overflowing a volcano's rim. These past years her visits with the Ex he had treated as de rigueur. His inner demon satisfied that she never spent the night.

In some masochistic fashion he had even enjoyed the game she played, trying to make him jealous. There was only the occasional indicator that her motivation was anything other than pay backs, a two-edged revenge at both men's transgressions. Him for some bauble or tribute he had denied her. The Ex, for seeking the services of whores he had never sought. "Beware the fury of the woman scorned, even if you never scorned her."

Now that he was the one scorned, bitter recrimination chafed deeply. He had never considered himself a "Macho Hombre" in line with stereotypical depictions of many Latino men. But as a bug, jealousy had bitten him on more than one occasion. He had done his best to hide its effect, satisfied that though Tina often joked about her other lover, she had neither evidenced any impropriety nor indicated anything more involved than the fulfillment of some inner, sadistic need to stomp on the other man's prospects for future happiness.

Concluding long ago that she still hated her Ex for past wrongdoings (evidently some inner child still motivated by cruel cravings) her vindictiveness satisfied Morano's own. He had chuckled at the irony and secretly hoped to never piss her off as much …because she really held a grudge.

He had also chuckled with the satisfaction that she hated her Ex for things she believed he had done to her, even though the poor guy had actually done nothing wrong, except piss off a powerful adversary. That wasn't very smart. Of course, that was the beauty of backstabbing. If you did it correctly it hurt so good …at least it hurt somebody good.

The Methotrexate formula fulfilled its sinister purpose. It was easy to sneak it into her chicken soup, she was so trusting. He regularly brought her the meal, often having already procured it seconds before her arrival in the college dining hall. It was always still piping hot and she always beamed her thanks at the puppy-dog like creature insisting on waiting on her as servant to the princess.

When eventually she began having complications, her Navy doctor assumed them to be from the pregnancy. Well-qualified and dedicated, this was to be his eighteenth delivery since graduation from the University of Pennsylvania and he often joked with Mrs. O'Rourke about homespun Philadelphia facts and factions, especially the Philly sound. The Delphonics, Patti LaBelle, the Intruders and other singing sensations like Harold Melvin and the Blue Notes were never far from their conversant topics. But when tests showed inconclusive, both doctor and patient's conversations became focused on what was wrong in her life that was threatening her child's.

Psychological counseling concerned the purpose of this war, her husband's role in it, his hero status and all the other myriad things that military support groups invoke to maintenance organizational members. Family health is always a sensitive and primary consideration as it enables serviceman's health for there is no one without the other. So the whole weight and mechanism of the MCAS El Toro support staff swung into motion to help this distressed woman whose Marine husband was far, far away dealing with other life and death issues. He did not need the distraction, so they didn't distract him. Believing in their own abilities, they kept her condition from him. But what none of them understood --what she kept from their knowing—was her husband's apparent complicity in the breaking of their sacred vows …that he was cheating on his wife.

Another area that the otherwise exemplary medical staff did not suspect —and thus did not test for—were the miniscule amounts of chemotherapy being regularly introduced into her body. A steady influx of ambulatory patients returning from Southeast Asia permitted only so much attention to any one individual and these represented only the tip of the iceberg, overflowing from the primary facilities at Balboa Naval Hospital down the street in San Diego. The doctor eventually admitted her, but by then it was too late.

It was not until after her body had aborted the tiny fetus that the El Toro family actually realized just how mentally depressed this woman actually had become. Then they faulted the combined complications and the war stresses as the cause. Psychological resources were also being challenged –too many battle-shocked patients, too few shrinks-- so professional aids to her damaged psyche were slow and few to come …so for these she did not wait.

She packed and moved her personal items in a record amount of time, wanting nothing else to do with any of them. Something had snapped inside her fragile psyche. None of the Marine community knew at the time, but she would not again set foot on a military base for many years … and then it was for another purpose.

One thing had become apparent to the El Toro community, that Tina O'Rourke's problems were manmade. They all assumed that man was her husband. But neither they nor she could know that the man in question was someone totally unexpected; a dark, sinister, skulking wolf in sheep's clothing pretending to be a friend. She could not know, never ever suspected, that one so selfless and seemingly deserving was actually one so venal and self-serving. She could not perceive this puppy dog man as actually a snake in the grass. While he was bad for her, she became all he ever wanted.

He truly loved this beautiful brownskin, this complicated woman with her fine lines, silken tresses and smoldering gaze. Because of her his whole world would never be the same. Because of her he had permitted his cousin to convert him from pretender into the genuine businessman he now had become.

She made him want for more. He dearly needed to prove himself to her. Struggling mightily, he earned his bachelor's degree then helped turn the small businesses his gang owned into literal goldmines. Now he had grown far beyond what he had once been.

"See how far I've come. Love me now?" But still she eschewed his grasp, treating him as perpetual friend, never the love interest. Yet still his pursuit never wavered. Possession of her became his goal and possession of her he determined to have. But she cavorted about in free spirit as some elusive sprite newly released from bondage, always just outside his reach, temptingly millimeters beyond his grasp. She would at times seek his company and at others deny him hers.

Capricious. Unbound. Wouldn't be tied down. Living for the day, dam tomorrow. Her way or the highway. Katherine Hepburn sans Spencer Tracy's steadying hand. Liz Taylor without Richard Burton. Dorothy Dandridge's Bess with no Sydney Poitier's Porgy. He called her his untamed dame, but knew deep inside the truth ...that she wasn't really his.

"What man can ever truly understand the feminine mystique?" he had wondered. "What inner need did this other's presence fulfill?" He tried to man-up, to rationalize her Ex as her "Rock", to which she occasionally returned to regain her foundation. But at times his resolve to allow her the tiny indiscretions nearly succumbed to a green-eyed monstrosity rising higher every time his henchmen transmitted back digital photos of her entering the house in Manhattan Beach.

Jealousy clawing higher in his throat had almost choked out all reason in him on several occasions, almost sending his fingers toward the speed dial. But some inner graces had dissuaded them from pressing the "SEND" key and ordering some final solution. He had stuck to the plan. As her husband he could order her to break off all relations, but as her friend, he could only sit and stir. So he had held pride in check, followed his cousin's advice and stayed his hand. There would come the day. This he knew. Deep inside, this he knew!

It got worse before better; patience waned 'til nearly exhausted, until she finally gave the answer she had withheld for so long and with it unbridled joy. His heart took to flight, his reward worthy of the wait. But then, it got worse again.

After finally deciding to agree, she had inexplicably flown suddenly, directly back to spend an entire night in her ex-husband's home. He tried as well he could, but her coolness during the phone call defeated all resolve. She neither denied that truth, nor his summation that much of that night she also spent in her ex-husband's arms. Her words: "You must believe what you must believe. I cannot help you. Gotta go, goodbye!"

"Gotta go, goodbye?" Who did she think she was? Who did she think he was? And he lost it. Lost his calm, lost his minuscule hold on comportment, lost his desire to permit her continued existence...

Surmounting the tallest peaks at Denali National Park, his growing rage eventually dwarfed even the mighty Mount McKinley or so he supposed, since he never actually got to view any of its wonders, thanks to weather. McKinley's wasn't the only cold front, though his associates didn't get a view of that side either.

Long a cherished forte, role playing this trip constituted facilitator of record not ridiculous-ranting-raconteur, the silly teller of tales. He needed retain that role, at least within earshot of these others. They needed consider him the facilitator, without purview of his step off the edge into madness.

Facilitator in Alaskan back country primarily means procuring food stuffs and stuff to keep off thirsty bloodsuckers. Mosquito repellents, head nets, Pic coils and ointments for all. Food, beverages and someone to prepare them were important considerations, but eating meals is not nearly as enjoyable while swatting away hordes of tiny critters trying to eat you.

He needed his fellows to concentrate their energies sightseeing, retaining the mellowest of moods for the proposals he next would spring. Led by a congressman and senator from America's largest state, this herd was his for the shearing and in keeping with their elevated status, he procured the best of everything money can buy. While they concentrated on vivid accounts of the park's history (being lustily portrayed by their executive tag team) none even noticed changes transforming his resemblance to Lord Foul.

A jovial atmosphere pervading the others, their Toklat River campsite rocked with glee as story after sidesplitting story filled the cool, evening air. "Then there was this old trapper named Moose Horn Davis who never hunted nothin' but moose. Wouldn't shoot rabbit, squirrel, even deer. Nuthin' but bull moose. And he always came back with the biggest moose anybody ever seen before. Never missed. Til one day he changed, went out in search of grizzly. Never did say why, he just decided all of a sudden he wanted a griz. His mind was made up and off he went to bag him the biggest grizzly he could find. Now Ol' Moose Horn is way up the Porcupine River when he comes across this thirteen-foot tall grizzly goin' at it with a female, I mean he strokin' th' stuffin' outta this sow an' all th' time she eyein' Moose Horn, not growlin', not even movin' jus' lookin' at him as if to say, 'Well, what'cha waitin' for fool?'"

"Now Moose Horn got a heart, he ain't about to interfere with true love. But this big-ass bear don't wanna quit. He goin' at it like it's th' last pussy he ever gonna get. He workin' it! Huffin' an' puffin' to beat th' band. After what seemed like hours, big fella finally git's his nut an' stands up tall an' proud as if to say, 'Tore that up didn't I bitch?'"

"That's when Moose Horn let him have it. Blam! Blam! Blam! Ol' boy died on th' spot without even a howl of surprise. Flop! Down an' done! Now Moose expects th' female to skedaddle, but just in case he jacks another round into that big ol' magnum he uses. But she just snorts at the dead bear and walks away back into th' bush. Moose Horn swears that later, when he's raftin' that big ol' carcass down river, she came out to the bank and waved at him as if to say: 'Thanks, ain't never gotta be bothered with him again!'"

He paused while their guffaws reverberated into the night, then waited an additional measure for full effect before continuing: "Just go to show, don't no female, not even a bear, appreciate gittin' laid without permission." The congressman's dry humor flowed endlessly, interspersed came park details from the senator who admirably played his role as straight man, keeping up the "Ooh-Wee" factor.

"…Denali means "The Great One or The High One, depending on your grasp of Athabascan." Established in 1917, it was originally named Mount McKinley National Park. Renamed to Denali in 1980. It's got six million acres, bigger than Massachusetts. Formerly called Mount McKinley, Denali Mountain is twenty thousand-three hundred-thirty-five feet high. First climbed by white men in 1963. Indians aren't telling when they first did…"

Apologizing repeatedly, he reminded his guests again and again that Denali (aka, McKinley) makes its own weather and that even though one can see the peak from seventy miles on a clear day, one is more likely to see a bear, a wolf or a moose than to see the mountain. Unfortunately for the politician's reputation, none of those creatures appeared during their trip either.

Even had they, Morano might have missed them anyway. So intensely did his dark eyes seethe at the vision of traitorous passion, it totally captured his imaginings. He had to steel himself before he did something insanely stupid like ordering her terminated immediately …or better yet, both of them.

While he was no longer the gangbanger he once was, he still had a host of deliberate resources. Deliberate in this case meaning, dedicated and deadly. But she was still important to him and to his plan. He kept reminding himself of this fact throughout a battle that he nearly lost to the fervor. For him, nothing before had ever been this difficult …at least nothing he could readily recall.

His tortured mind kept running the envisioned replay of them making love and assessing that this puta had taken from him his manhood, that she should no longer be either trusted or desired. Seething internally, his mood alternated between desires of sending his legions after her ex-husband O'Rourke, after her roommate Stephanie and even after her aged parents. He was very nearly overcome with vindictive desire to do something that would teach her a harsh lesson, one that would pay back totally her unfaithfulness. But somehow a voice of reason instilled in him just enough control to permit common sense to take firmer grip.

Lucky for her his cousin Chaco had been that voice of reason. But only because it reminded him of an earlier teaching that plans can always be modified as a need occurs or an opportunity presents. Now her part in their operation he reevaluated and revised. All he needed to do was modify the plan a bit and case closed…

Nearly all of the others from their old gang had long ago been captured by law organizations or killed by rivals. Two of the few remaining members, Carlos and Chaco still led (Chaco preferred to call it their old organization) and the old rules still applied. True to their code, those captured and imprisoned had never talked, never revealed confidential aspects of their organization (the lawmen preferred to call it their gang), their affiliations or their associates. But one by one the rest were somehow found out, rooted out and either destroyed or captured.

But those who transitioned were never found out. At Chaco's insistence and example, they had already begun moving from drug-related, into legitimate commercial ventures. Never planning to remain in the drug business at any measure for long, he perceptively got them out while the getting was good.

Restaurants, dry cleaning shops, information technology development and agricultural products, such as seedless grapes, formed the backbone of their company, Anasazi Enterprises, representing its three major divisions, each headed by an "OG", an "Original Gang" member, though no one of them still used the term. It too passed into history as they moved further into legitimacy, along with other changes considered for the best.

Overall leadership moved from the younger to the older cousin. It happened amicably, by mutual concurrence and almost at the outset. Still, some things change more easily than others.

Carlos was more an action leader. His style was perfect for negotiating the vagaries of street transactions and conflicts. But in order for their new business strategies to succeed, their organization needed a different type of leadership. They all recognized that the focus of their organization needed to be the good of their organization, not any one individual. In this current trend, their leadership needed forward vision, not backward hierarchical concerns.

The barrio they left behind them, along with the narcotics trade. Turf wars over market share and adversarial bouts with police forces became mainstream commodities development and commercial transactions. Corporate strategy replaced hit and run ambush tactics; daily discussion focused on financial news, stock quotes and other paradigms of investment.

Now they had need of a different style of leadership capable of creative planning and high order communicative skill sets articulating clear values and beliefs, rendering positive unifying effects for the group's future growth. Now they looked formally to one who had long provided impetus and direction from a secondary position.

As before, their structure remained loosely based. No corporate lawyer dictated organizational decisions or scrutinized intra-organizational agreements. The one law firm which represented their entire corporation consisted of a semi-retired old man --who had occasionally defended heroes like Caesar Chavez—and his divorced, middle-aged daughter, who practiced law while helping her own daughter with homework.

Insurance edicts did not weigh heavily into every decision either. They evolved some practices to maintain pace with the rest of corporate America, but did not attempt to squeeze every cent out of every dollar. They took excellent care of their workers –providing health insurance to some people who had never before heard of such a thing—so there were not a lot of frivolous lawsuits to deal with. If a worker became injured on the job, he or she was covered, "end of story". No "co-payments" or "deductibles" or any of the sort. Injured were fixed back into the closest possible condition to the original. If such was not possible, they were well compensated; provided a "Golden Parachute" to keep them comfortable for the remainder of their life and sometimes beyond.

There was seldom such a thing as workers faking injury to enact a frivolous suit. After all, though Anasazi was a legitimate corporation, its underpinnings were rooted in the bedrock of La Raza 18 and La Raza 18 began as a street gang. Its founding personnel had all come up the hard way as street hoodlums. They believed in fair play, up to a point, family values deeply ingrained in their chemistry. But, to pull them out of the friendly confines of their homespun organization, into the convoluted world of the gringo legal system would be taking the group too far afield. That was a definite "no-no" …a "no-no" which could evoke consequences of serious proportions.

But as long as the justification was legitimate --the motivation genuine-- sense of fair play dictated a degree of forbearance; that they "play the game" to a certain extent, although they would ever retain reluctance to permit conclusions specified by gringo lawyers and courts.

Their ancestors had discovered exactly how unfavorable such a proposition presented people of their ethnicity. Instead, Anasazi would decide. To their leadership, this was as it should be.

Tabulation would be made to transition all pertinent factors into monetary terms, an offer would subsequently be tendered and a period of time allotted for the complainant's acceptance. No further negotiation. Their offer might be considerably lower than a complainant's figures, but there would be fairness, even though their offer was "take or leave it". Any lawyer fees accrued by any individual foolish enough to engage one would also be left to and for the individual to dispose as Anasazi' policies mandated direct negotiations over indirect. If an employee decided to speak through a polished mouthpiece, he or she could pay for the service out of their settlement. The offer amount would never change nor would there ever be issued threats. The implication would be, take or leave! Though actually, the offer was more "do or die"!

However, pity the poor fool whose case was found unjustified, frivolous or rapacious. For the dawning of such a day would also spawn an actionable condition with significant retribution as a bi-product. Said action could range from the seriocomic –where minor rearrangements or coloring adjustments would befall the guilty one's lawn furniture—to the deadly serious, where physical rearrangements would befall the guilty one.

But these things seldom ever occurred. The only two serious applications had occurred in and been summarily adjudicated in Miami. The Miami workforce tended to be of a different "flavor" from the western folk. Still, regardless the location, Anasazi worked ever diligently to reduce the drudgery and strain of labor tasks. Its standards exceeded those of the Occupational Safety and Health Administration. Human Factors Engineers surveilled each facility for potentially dangerous conditions –air quality, equipment requiring repair or replacement, workforce training-- and the like. Despite best intentions, some OSHA standards they only met, but often that fact was attributable to the superior quality of those standards ... the few such standards not recently rescinded or reduced.

Moreover, Anasazi recruitment practices were purposely structured to weed out litigious sorts. Psychological profiles, background checks, as well as the interview session itself, contributed to these successes. Many of their workforce had family ties. Thus every workday evidenced a reunion of sorts.

They did not consider their practices revolutionary or anything as such. Their business was still about making money. But there were significant deviations from standard business practices. PERT charts and linear graphs did not fill the majority of meeting briefs. Performance at the upper echelon was a long-term measurement independent of profit margin. There was not a daily analysis of "the bottom line". Decisions were based on dialogue across the board and on consensus rather than authority and command. To their thinking, a man's superior age did not automatically endow him with superior logic.

The organizational structure they evolved to form three divisions. Two already existed as separate entities. Their next task had been to seek out a corporate name, an overarching appellation befitting such an erudite undertaking. But that task proved easier than he had at first thought. Its solution rattled haltingly off the nervous lips of a young man whose handsome, Aztec features reminded Chaco of the tiny child he had tutored in English so that he could qualify for scholarship to a private school. On this night, Chaco's heart swelled with pride when the recent Pepperdine graduate made a suggestion in perfect English that met with instant approval. Anasazi, Incorporated was born when all twelve members --constituting their central committee-- raised hands in acknowledgement and the name stood. La Raza 18 became but a memory…

Their organization was a study in diversification, but its loosely structured divisions maintained a synergistic affiliation, each division providing goods and services to others in their group. Product cost control was major focus.

Carlos "Dondi" Morales controlled their food distribution network in Southern Cali. Dondi –no one ever called him Carlos-- had been nicknamed for the comic strip character of the fifties and sixties. While still a child, the thick, wavy, raven-hair and coal-black pupils, button nose and big ears had reminded all who saw him of the cute, little boy from the Sunday funnies. His early life as an orphan also parodied the story of the character found in Italy after WWII and adopted by a GI from the Midwest, though their Dondi had been found on the streets of El Centro where his prostitute mother had died of an overdose purposely administered by her pimp boyfriend. Eventually the boyfriend's body was found having succumbed in like fashion. Fair play dictated this heartless one reap what he had sown.

Dondi grew strong under their tutelage and was also now married to the daughter of Chaco's Tio Juan and Tia Juanita Lopez. The beautiful little Chica that Chaco had once bounced on his good leg now had delivered her third son. After his jovial reminder to his cousin she had jokingly reminded that he would have serious trouble ever performing that duty again. They all laughed at the thought, given that her weight had blossomed up to two hundred-ten pounds. They had also agreed that Dondi, now equally no lightweight, liked his woman healthy.

Carlos Morano ran the software arm that also integrated and supported all the corporation's software requirements, while Chaco commanded their agricultural division. He was especially fond of the acres of grapes hanging heavy with tart and sweet fruit up and along the southern-facing hillsides in Southwestern New Mexico. Near San Vicente de la Cienega, called Silver City by the Anglos, his small Vineyards Research Facility challenged his love of astronomy for first position. They often laughed that the wines he produced were sold by Dondi's and drunk by Carlos' crew. In truth, they were all enamored by their liquid produce.

Wild and beautiful, the land was especially challenging for the growing of grapes. Water is not a plentiful resource here in these arid, dry lands. Moreover, the rocky, undulating landscape is over six thousand feet above sea level and leans towards chilly, especially after evening. So plants need to be as hardy as the terrain, as do those who busy themselves doing the growing …his facility enjoys both.

Ever the defender of those less fortunate, Chaco became a supporter of the local Gang Risk Intervention Project. He not only employed troubled youths to bring in his product, he helped get them scholarships and other funding to attend the downtown Western New Mexico University. A few of the more motivated were tasked to help in developing new, pest resistant strains, especially plants capable of withstanding the plant louse phylloxera as well as wide climatic swings which tended to kill off less hardy plants. So he and his research staff spent their days grafting and sampling produce from the various hybrids.

The match was mutually rewarding, both for the Anasazi Group as well as the small, dying on the vine, winery they had invested in. Having purchased the holdings from a disinterested owner who had inherited them from a distant relative, the ideal circumstances were supported by both tradition and history. Genetics research intrigued him, though totally confused his cousin. He had laughed so hard that his one good eye had teared beyond seeing when Carlos had asked how they were going to get seeds for the seedless grapes.

Explaining that seedless grapes are clones grown from planting vine cuttings into soil, Chaco wizened his younger relative. Stifling a following spasm of laughter, he pointed out the fact that most fruits –like apples, blueberries and cherries-- are so grown. He had learned so many of these things in his youth. It brought him back to his roots and to memories of his poor father and to that time in his life when he could see out of both eyes and walk without pain and dream all the things all kids dream –like playing football for the Rams or baseball for the Dodgers or blocking Bill Russell's shot and scoring the winning basket for the Lakers. All those things.

Back inside his reality, although a cruel fate had prevented him from accomplishing any of those lofty dreams, he now could still achieve lofty accomplishments. He was now as firmly entrenched as his hardy grape plants in the nurturing lands of his namesake, the Anasazi. Moreover, this region of the four corners –with its cloudless skies and unpolluted vistas— provided excellent views of the heavenly tapestry.

Chaco put more of their company's day-to-day operational burdens into his assistant's lap and went off to pursue the love to which even Astronomy came in second, but only just so. Working with the facilities' botanists he helped them develop larger, sweeter tasting, hardier grapes and was hard on the trail of expanding their variety and hardiness. But only during days, his nights were much influenced by the heavens.

Chaco had become convinced that the Goddess, who was Mother Earth, had guided his path from his childhood until this present day. She came to him in a vision one night as he slept. Perhaps it was only a dream, but its power clutched him and spun his slight frame around in a slow, onerous three-sixty spin that was irresistible to his every attempted countering.

The force was invisible to all but him. Its presence overwhelming, though non-threatening as it made itself known to his very fibre. A chiaroscuro of colorful shimmering luminance surrounded and engulfed him. Within he bathed in her glorious manifestation. He could sense her benevolence and her message and became totally overtaken.

"I feel you o' Mother!" he cried out, perhaps for any witness to record, perhaps only to himself in his dream state.

"I hear you! I am with you!" But later, he doubted. He wondered whether he had experienced only the vestiges of a deep dream while emerging from REM sleep and nothing more. He hoped for some additional sign, a reinforcement to assuage his doubting. But only for a moment or two, then he resolved to fulfill her call.

He had discovered petroglyphs of six-toed feet carved on rocks near a small mountain just north of his vineyard. Actually it was more a scrub brush covered foothill. The scrub consisted primarily of Mormon Tea bushes that his Mother's people had boiled into reddish-hued teas for treatment of all sorts of ailments, from stomach pains to nasal congestion. But the petroglyphs held similar appearance to some carvings he found pecked into high canyon walls inside the huge Chaco Canyon complex in the San Juan Basin northwest of Albuquerque.

Those broken, wide-strewn boulders he had struggled to climb, finally succeeded, then gazed out in awe at the wonder and splendor. Carved high into the solid rock walls, petroglyphs shaped like humanoids and four-legged animals that he perceived as his native American ancestors hunting bighorn sheep and geometric forms (possibly astronomical observations) stared down at reddish-hued, flat brick and mud mortar dwellings cleverly linked together by bricked steps and walkways and to large circular, meeting rooms called kivas. These, his people built at the sites of Chacoan great houses named Pueblo Bonito –for Beautiful Villa-- and Una Vida – for One Life—and so many others.

Chaco knew not the names given these places by his mother's ancestors, only those told to Lieutenant James H. Simpson by his Mexican guide, Carravahal, in 1849. Their Spanish titles worked well enough, often expressing particularly accurate depictions, however that given the kiva called Casa Rinconada (for house of corners) struck him as a little vague, since this largest of all the kivas shared a similar, rounded shape as its kin. Obviously, its features had changed a bit in one hundred-sixty years, perhaps quite a bit. But the matter was not their calling, neither their original names nor the ones adopted by conquistadores, just the message intended for him by The Mother. Now it seemed to him that she had directed him to this present site for a purpose.

Like a wakening flower, opening to greet the spring sunshine, into her obedient servant he transitioned. Within a short passage of time he had erected his observatory atop that small mountain (slash foothill) overlooking his vineyard and commenced to scan the skies for their offering of whatever was to come.

Unlike his ancestors, he had no need to perfectly align window cutouts with wall symbols to mark solstices and equinoxes and such. His calendar, his wristwatch, even Action News made unnecessary such measurements of the sun's passage. Good thing too, it was not a large facility, just a single-story one room affair with a bathroom off to one side. There wasn't much left over for measuring sun angles and the like. With all the gear lockers and charts and thirty-by-thirty inch photos hanging about and crammed inside, space came at a premium.

Never intended to mark planting seasons, as the ancients used their observatories, his needed no fixed points of view. Attached atop, the electric-driven, fiberglass dome could rotate three hundred-sixty degrees to align every point in the sky from horizon to zenith. Ten feet high and fifteen feet in diameter, and the closest thing to a second floor, its fat cap covered much of the little room's otherwise flat roof. Also electrically powered, its semi-door shutter would appear magical to his mother's people as it slid open upon command to expose Chaco's prize, sixteen-inch telescope to the cosmos. But then, so would nearly every one of the technologies we employ on a daily basis.

Also not huge, by any means, but its computer-controlled features and advanced Ritchey-Chrétien design enabled him to span the galaxies of time and space in a way his Puebloan ancestors could never even dream. But their collective, ancient knowledge spanned centuries; leveraging rudimentary advantages he was only beginning to appreciate.

Though these southwestern people did not build huge pyramids, their accomplishments atop Fajada Butte —rising three hundred-sixty feet above the canyon floor-- rivaled ancient Egypt's in astronomical scale. So it was good that amateurs such as he could avail of a few enhancing tools developed by modern science. It was especially good for an old cripple like himself.

The built-in GPS receiver, magnetic declination compensators and North-seeking, electronic sensors made his tasks much easier to set up. Not quite up to NASA standards, however it was well-designed and a highly capable tool. Its high-precision pointing capability coupled to an onboard celestial software library that contained over two hundred thousand space objects.

"You want to study Messier Object M32, no problem. Bang! There you go!" boasted the proud technician performing its installation. "Now you see light from that dwarf elliptical galaxy in the Constellation Andromeda, twenty-two million light years distant."

The telescope's movement –instantly accomplished using speed drive controls on horizontal and vertical axes—also controlled the dome's rotation to capture and autofollow the movement of both near and deep-space objects. It was truly a marvel. However, Chaco was not slaved to technological wonders. He still devoted a portion of many nights for just sitting outside or –when climate insisted-- inside his darkened solarium underneath the obsidian tapestry that stretched from horizon to horizon, reveling in its magnificent gloom punctuated by millions of glowing points of light that were not always clearly visible …but were always.

Out under this panoptic rendering, he let his thoughts wander where they chose, often embracing the knowledge that his ancestors had once shared the same view and felt the same awe. In a hillside just north of his land sat the mountain cave. Inside he had discovered more pictographs and petroglyphs inscribed by the ancients. Some of these depicted what he interpreted as a super nova showering earth with flaming debris out of the Orion Nebula. Of this he felt certain, the star patterns aligned. What their depiction did not made clear was whether the event had already transpired.

Modern astrophysicists have developed computer models seeking to explain evidence brought back by Apollo astronauts indicating that nearly all craters found on the moon appear to have occurred during the same geologic period, approximately three-point-nine billion years ago. One concluding theory purports that a super nova --within twenty or so light years—hurled massive amounts of debris, gases and space dust into our own developing solar system; not only bombarding the moon and earth, but providing the additional materials that greatly increased sizes of the gas giants –Jupiter and Saturn—as well as the ice giants –Uranus and Neptune-- possibly shifting the orbits of some if not all of our system's planets, especially the two gas giants, maybe even the location of our entire solar system.

Given the cave depiction, Chaco believed all these as valid possibilities.

For if a super nova could send fiery rain from Orion –across thirteen hundred light years-- why not from somewhere much closer. In his mind, it mattered not whether the Old Testament accounting of God creating earth was right or wrong. He did not judge. Such things are a matter of faith and impossible to know for certain. Plus, it kinda depends on one's concept of God.

To him, the point whether Orion Rain has already been or will be sent either by an all-powerful God or by a freak of celestial nature is moot. Somehow, the ancients knew something and this is what they conjured to tell us, their descendants. We just need to figure it out. Sounds doable. Maybe not so simple, but doable!

Then, maybe it is simple. The ancients tended their focus on future things, coming events. They predicted weather and seasons for planting seeds, growing crops. So seems logical this event has yet to come. Troubling, but would they have told us if nothing for us to do but watch it happen? Could this be their two-minute warning…?

However, Chaco was no longer a young man. Never fatalistic. But the idea of being consigned to the looney bin for his remaining years did not exactly motivate. Besides, he had no children with which to concern himself (though there were a few he cared deeply about) and these days he could seldom even climb up to visit his ancestral cave or walk far along the dirt paths of Chaco Canyon to visit the ancient ruins. So, he backburnered any concerns about a fiery cosmos.

One day perhaps he would take a helicopter to the tops of the tall buttes resembling submarine conning towers and tabletop mesas rising far above the saltbush, yucca and sumac and from this bird's eye view peer upon dizzying vertical heights where rock walls chiseled and sculpted by Mother Nature's majesty from mudstone, shale, coal, and sandstone seams alternated bands of reds, oranges, blacks and yellows piled one upon the other. Perhaps he could even land and dig up a few fossilized shark's teeth and clam shells left over from the cretaceous period when an inland sea encompassed these valleys chiseled with rincon nooks, crevices and recesses. Perhaps that constitutes a better pursuit, less confusion, fewer dead ends. Perhaps he would …though not just yet.

This prospective signaling the End of Days did little to affect his routine. There is little that one such as he could do to prevent such a coming. Besides, the Mother would endure and eventually recreate no matter how many calamities rained down to scour her surface. Her heart would barely skip a beat, at least until our sun had spent its energies and collapsed in on itself becoming a super nova that incinerated its nearby children. That would truly be the End of Days.

So he maintained his routine. Though engaged with myriad duties for most of each day, he still also managed to keep in touch with his younger cousin —for whom business was as much adventure as relationships-- who now spent most of his time either on the east coast or in the Caribbean, only occasionally back to his native Southern California. Little time Carlos devoted to nurturing old relationships, enamored mainly with those things new: like new planes, new homes and (especially) new friends.

For Chaco, the art of creation almost wholly consumed his interest and was his passion. Unfortunately, of their company's day-to-day operations, he defined his largest task as keeping a loose rein —which occasionally he had to tighten appreciably-- on an ever more irascible cousin whose egocentricities sometimes manifested in dangerous ways. Often these required direct mentorship prompting Chaco to leave his southwestern fiefdom, charter a flight out of the local Grant County Airport up to Albuquerque or down to El Paso and jump on the next available commercial flight to wherever on the planet Carlos had decided to be at that moment. Such trips were infrequent requirements, reserved for times when telecom links proved useless, but always unwelcome interruptions in the older man's schedule.

On one such occasion, a weary Chaco had hung up the phone in the midst of the raging torrent streaming from the other end, promising death and destruction in biblical proportions, just to prevent a rapaciously raving Carlos from completely annihilating his fiancé, her friends and family. A quick shower and change of clothes to rid him of the dirt and dust of that day's labors and off he flew with his friend and bodyguard.

Chaco had arrived in time, greeting his cousin's private jet as it touched down at Ronald Reagan from his trip to the land of the midnight sun. This new toy replaced his older aircraft and he loved to show it off to clients and congressmen. Actually, the sleek, new Learjet belonged to their entire corporation, but only Carlos ever used it. This was primarily because he based it in Miami, Florida; a bit too far for easy usage by the other team leaders, like Chaco and Dondi. So it became his private transport, the aircrew his private staff. But none of the others grouched about that obvious disparity. If they had a need for any shared corporate resources, they would have access …in this case, just not quite right away.

Perhaps it was his past position as their leader. You pretty much always remember the boss. Whatever the motivation, Carlos had always been treated with kid gloves. He was the youngest of their corporation's leaders and thus the most irrational at times. He was also the one most tempted by the dark side of untold wealth and riches. He spent the most, demanded even more and they tolerated his deviant ways, regardless how threatening to their community. But they kept a choke collar at close hand at all times in case this irascible puppy became rabid pit bull. More often than not, the task fell to Chaco to hold that leash, few others possessing the necessary powers of persuasion …without implementing a final solution.

On this occasion, Chaco took great pains in soothing his cousin's irrational ire down to manageable levels; something that needed face-to-face counseling, cellies would not suffice. But even though his surface temperature had apparently chilled, Chaco still did not trust his combustible relative. He decided against returning to continue one aspect of his life's work to ensure against the fall of another and kept up his coaching during the next few days they languished in Washington. He even rode with his student down to Florida, afraid that the lesson may not yet have had sufficient time for seasoning. A house of cards only needs one strong breath to blow it down.

"How many times I gotta remind you? Family is the most important thing, sobrino. Women are not family until they marry and even then they are only sustituto, surrogate family." Chaco often referred to his younger cousin as if they were uncle and nephew. It was his way of reminding the other of his greater years and experience. He sometimes also referred to him as mijo --a sobriquet, meaning son—for similar reasons.

Carlos did not trust himself to speak. He stared out the living room window to the ocean waves breaking onto the beach and then receding as quickly as they had come. Rabid thoughts of revenge and retribution bashed headlong into common sense reminders of need and purpose. Chaco had no idea of his ultimate plans, but what he said made sense for those reasons alone …this was not the time to upset the apple cart!

It saddened Chaco that his charge had gotten worse over the years. His avarice had increased but it was not his most unfavorable feature. Chaco had heard and then confirmed other rumors, such as his cousin's consistent use of urine therapy –drinking his own—as well as his propensity to contract hookers to give "Golden Showers", bathing him all over with their urine. But these were minor. These stories bothered him, but only a bit. Every man had his quirks. Even Chaco had had his own adventures with ladies of ill repute. One eventually became his mistress ...until her death from AIDS.

The fact that he never contracted the disease over the years she unknowingly carried it, he attributed to his diet of antioxidant-enriched vegetables and the gallons of citrus juices he consumed daily. He felt that the antioxidants defeated any "free radicals" seeking to bring harm to his body and to reduce his resistance to disease. But alas, his poor Chiquita —her name was Roxanne, but he preferred the other—she hated the sight of the dark greens, broccolis and yellow squashes and especially the red and black beans that he loved. Occasionally she might permit strawberries or raspberries in her breakfast cereal, but veggies were a huge "no-no" and the only juices she drank were in her Mai Tai cocktails at dinner or Mimosas at brunch.

He mourned her passing for a full year before taking another mistress, the aches and anguish tearing daily at his lonely heart. In marriage he had no interest; however she had come as close to being his wife as any would ever come. A truer love he'd never have.

This time he picked a young woman whose past profession was other than mounting strange men for cash. Consummating the relationship, however, remained in limbo until well after thorough examination proved her disease-free, out of concern that antioxidants might on occasion decide to take a day off. He had learned his lesson with so close a brush with death for the second time. He would take no more foolish chances. But she was only a temporary solution to his dilemma. He left her behind in California, along with other useless aspects of his past.

So he forgave Carlos' more sybaritic indiscretions, his dalliances with the flower of female persuasion, plus the yellow rain squalls. He was just a man being a man. But not so the more offensive examples ...even those times when he purposely looked away.

Though potentially serious and harmful, he brushed aside and accepted, even forgave some matters for concern whispered discretely in his ear. He rationalized these courses based on his total knowledge being summed up as conjecture and rumor. In cases where he had no direct evidence or concrete proof to support the allegations he would normally just issue out subtle warnings in the manner of generalized discussions. Usually these served the purpose and there would be no need of further deeds ...or so was his understanding.

Rumors involving involuntary, induced-abortions or premeditated murders were dealt with in this fashion. His approach to maintaining his corporation on an even keel he intended never to become high handed or iron fisted. But he made it clear to all that he would forever be intolerant of mindless acts of violence for whatever the purpose and that he would deal harshly with the perpetrator of such. He had no qualms about reminding everyone associated with their organization that it was he who steered this ship. Unannounced surprise visits --to intended locations and their primaries—he felt made significant impression.

And while he did not desire to bring harm to his cousin, he had no such compunction about his cousin's underlings. Ruthlessness carried its own message. The suspicious, suicide deaths of three people in Southern California, said loud and clear more than words.

One was a young chemist apparently overcome with grief over his recent divorce who dove headfirst into a vat of designer chemicals he was mixing. Investigators unsuccessfully attempted to confiscate amateur photos of his feet sticking up and out of the top-loading, polished steel container, shots of which the entrepreneurial photographer sold to a newspaper and made page one …back in the days before YouTube.

Neither did investigators learn about the witches' brew of chemicals this newly-deceased chemist once concocted to cause two unsuspecting females to abort the tiny lives growing within them, lives that had been vibrant and hale before his influence. His death note neither alluded to that occurrence nor implicated the two people who had delivered those chemicals. Had they learned of this despicable past, those investigators might think it obvious that someone else, who also knew, evidently wanted others to be aware that they knew.

But investigators saw no evidence of foul play, which sent its own message. Driving these messages home even more effectively was the ruthless manner in which the other two supposed "suicides" ended their earthly existence.

One suicide, a young woman, had worked for the UC Irvine cafeteria whose soup had masked the deadly potion from one innocent mother-to-be. Her cafeteria uniform lay neatly folded on the floor at the spot investigators found her naked corpse dangling from thin electrical wires, which took an agonizingly long time to choke out her life. Liquid eyes, black and bulging and a tongue, purple and swollen, hanging from a pale, bloodless face made her an instant celebrity with the Insider rags.

The third suicide's demise, another young man, also made the newspaper. He had owned his own landscaping company. A color picture of his entrails and viscera spewed against a white, picket fence ruined many a Sunday breakfast. The storyline indicated suspicions that he had opted to slide feet first into a powerful woodchipper to atone for unforgiveable sins. At least the note scrawled in his handwriting so indicated. Whatever those sins were, none was specifically addressed. And no one had heard his screams over the loud gasoline-powered engine. The woodchipper chewed any other evidence literally into shreds. The real evidence, however, could never truly be destroyed…

Over ten years passed between the crimes and Chaco acquiring what he considered sufficient proof of the guilty. But once known, hesitation became no more. All three "suicides" occurred on the same day, within hours of each other. In one fell swoop he sent the same powerful message to any others involved that: "Regardless how or when, crimes against the organization will be punished". It spoke for itself.

He worried that his cousin's quirks could cause self-inflicted harm and possibly bring harm to their entire organization. Not so much due to his avarice. Avarice is not necessarily a bad thing in that it may motivate ordinary men to do great things. Varying degrees of avarice had motivated them all to come as far as they had. So Carlos' avarice was more a challenge for Chaco to control, rather than a threat to be feared. Normally the younger man had the goodness of the organization at heart …just not always.

Chaco also felt a strong dislike for Carlos' two bodyguards, perceiving sinister intent in their every movement. His senses earmarked them as contributors to the harsher side of his cousin. Then, of course there was the question of whether it was his avarice or advice from his reprobate leg breakers prompting him to keep other significant secrets that Chaco knew which Carlos thought were still secret. Secrets like the Colombian Sting that very nearly started a drug war and others that Chaco found even more significant. Like his cousin's coming acquisition of a particular golden box. A golden box which, if rumor had it correct, might one day stave off the four horsemen of the apocalypse.

CHAPTER FOURTEEN

When he left the site in the Badiyat Ash-sham --northwest of Fallujah, about fifty miles from the Euphrates—Eisa had been extremely agitated and it had nothing to do with that bite from a six-inch long Wind Scorpion, that Americans call a Camel Spider due to its humped profile. Though painful, the non-poisonous arachnid's bite could not otherwise threaten him. So he decided to let it live. He had unintentionally invaded its space when reeling from the destruction. Now he was again reeling. Lowly Colonels don't just storm in to see princes, but he was on his way to do just that. He needed to find favor in the worst way. Otherwise he was about to lose his wife to that ravenous, impure pile of camel's dung named Odai Hussein. Perhaps not forever, but what man would want her after that? Odai was a pig!

Panic. Jumbled thoughts tossing about in helter-skelter mode, a death grip clutching tight the leather steering wheel, he literally flew through the desolate, arid desert in reckless abandon; down the ancient camel road his four-wheel drive SUV hurtled through steep-sided wadis, more rocky than sandy and muddy, that cut through stunted hills and high plateau stretching to the horizon in places to make travel a jolting, relentless adventure. Although the soil is fertile, there are few trees in this region so close to Syria. Good for him at this moment, less obstacles to bump into, although there were still more than enough obstacles in the form of ruts and boulders.

Not even nomadic Bedouins cultivate the sparse desert vegetation here, as hardly anything else seemed anxious to grow here. It was a prime reason the leadership chose this area. Hardly any chance anybody or anything would stumble upon their dig. Cattle wouldn't grow here; neither would sheep, goats, wheat, not even corn; hardly anything lucrative, just those damned Wind Scorpions. The Bedouins never pitched their black tents in this part of the Badiyat Ash-sham, not since their Amorite ancestors four thousand years before, in tents that looked much the same ...excepting the Land Rovers they now parked outside.

But after sixty kilometers of jouncing and bouncing and dodging death and destruction he finally made it to the highway. This section did show signs of life. Black tents dotted the landscape, goat herds and scattered crops also. Still, the multi-lane road had virtually no other traffic this time of day, bringing him straight into the heart of Baghdad, past colorful mosques and skyscraping spires and billboards and posters showing the many sides of Saddam; holding a rifle here, a child there; the defender of their faith garbed in Arab headdress, all a sham. The only thing Saddam defended was Saddam. Worse, out from Saddam's loins had spewed misogynistic crud that threatened to pollute the entire earth, starting with his wife. The thought kicked spurs to his flanks, shifting to a taller gear he drove like the wind…

Odai was asleep, as it was his custom to work during the night hours. If you called what he did work. The sun was still high when Eisa drove into Odai's brand new digs at Al Azimiyah Palace, sprawling along the eastern edge of the Tigris River. But the huge proportions and uncompromising opulence of this sandstone structure failed to exact even a token of appreciation from his hurrying form. It took several minutes of arguing before Odai's aide would agree to wake him. Such action could be extremely hazardous. But, eventually he agreed that to withhold information of this importance could ultimately be even more dangerous.

Odai could be as unpredictable as the wind. But the one constant in his psyche was the desire to please his father. Ever since he had miscalculated and murdered Saddam's personal food taster and friend back in 1988, his stock had been reduced in value below his younger brother Qusai. More than just a simple cold shoulder, Saddam had taken the habit of avoiding this rabid dog he had whelped. Perhaps even Saddam feared the eldest of his miscreant progeny…

Eisa nervously awaited his chief in the crowded library. It was stacked high with books from nearly every part of the planet. Eisa had once wondered if Odai ever read any of them or were they only accoutrements as were most of the things around him. Golden plumbing adorned the bathrooms, crystal chandeliers hung from vaulting ceilings and majestic, palatial stairways swept upwards into ever more magnificence. Multi-colorful Persian carpets lay across creamy, white marble flooring running throughout the lavishly furnished buildings on this seventeen acre compound that boasted its own streets with broad lanes (complete with traffic signals) and a wild animal zoo.

But Eisa doubted if any of these baubles mattered to this psychopathic hell spawn. Probably the only time he ever even noticed the immaculate floors --constructed from the finest European marble—was when he took out his penis to wet down whichever unlucky girl he had selected for that day's debauchery. But this day's chosen one would surely be spared once

Eisa's news became known. He had unearthed a legend and would live to tell of it when so many others had not.

The story had passed down from father to son over an eon, but only glimmers of its telling even mentioned this possibility. Since the time of its burial by the Babylonians, in what is now called the Syrian Desert, even mention of its concept had been forbidden fruit, a subject to be avoided under pain of death.

There it rested, another desert dweller, remaining undisturbed for over twenty-six hundred years until discovered by the new Babylonians. Like their ancients, these New Babylonians had also been conquerors and still harbored dreams of repeating Nebuchadnezzar's drive down into what once constituted ancient Judea. They believed fervently that it was their destiny proscribed by Allah ...regardless that their ancient kin worshipped multiple gods like Anshar and Kishar.

Since these modern era Babylonians have yet to produce such a drive only Seers possessing the gift of supernatural sight can know whether those dreams will ever prevail. But even untalented Seers, possessing few gifts and limited vision, could predict that these men would not take part. These had been members of a special team assigned to perform special tasks. Each was picked for his loyalty and trustworthiness, namely his ability to follow orders and keep his mouth closed. Most had no wives, children or close personal relationships, which made their sharing of secrets even more unlikely. But unfortunately for these men, fate had prescribed a different destiny, which --like the Ark itself—would also become intertwined with speculation and remanded to the annals of mystery. But unlike the mighty Ark of the Covenant, unearthed by these men, even the ashes of their charred corpses would remain lost to mystery in the year 1996.

The entire country seemed in turmoil. Control of much of its skies belonged to foreigners and now it appeared so too its lands. The United Nations had decreed that Iraq must open its country to another special team. This one composed of experts who would search throughout the country's facilities and even its forbidding deserts for weapons of mass destruction. Nuclear, biological and chemical munitions and materials, all fell within the definition of WMDs and the worldwide organizations were intent on ensuring themselves that Iraq neither possessed nor manufactured these.

Saddam Hussein made his own decree. He tasked a special team of Iraqi soldiers –primarily engineers-- to excavate additional underground spaces in which to hide his stores of special weapons. At risk were precursor chemicals capable of making as much as 100 tons of VX nerve agent; also aerial bombs, tactical rockets and artillery shells with a variety of chemical and biological agents. Not for the first time. During the Gulf War his people had hidden whole fighter planes under the desert sand. He had no doubts that they would successfully secret his stockpiles from the UN.

His teams scurried out, first constructing huge assemblages of camouflage netting, then driving their powered digging tools underneath and wiping away any tracks which might be visible to the American, French and even the Chinese satellites circling high above in the heavens. It took an enormous passage of time. Known satellite flyover schedules and meteorological predictions ruled their activity. Periods of heavy cloud cover were gifts granted by Allah. The team toiled as steadily as these factors permitted and accomplished much. Their leaders urged them even harder as the impatience of the outsiders grew. They became reckless as the deadline drew near.

One last dig remained. It was here in the Badiyat Ash-sham that their digging encountered a huge underground cavern. At first they worried that it was an unknown river, which would mean choosing another site and starting anew. They listened carefully for any roaring torrent, even the gurgle of a tiny stream. Only quiet and gloom greeted them. They decided that this cavern must have been a treasure chamber. One that tomb robbers must have found and emptied millennia before their coming. But then the outline of an ancient crypt was discovered in a smaller side chamber. It sat on a raised platform built of cedar wood. Its outer casing was a lead casting, heavy and ancient and dark gray in appearance.

Its top displayed a raised sculpture in bas-relief of the great seal of Nebuchadrezzar II (who is also called Nebuchadnezzar). But the Iraqi team understood none of this; neither did they understand that the symbols below the seal were ancient depictions representing warnings of dire circumstance. The symbols depicted Death.

To their thinking, these were the remains of some great leader out of antiquity. Perhaps related to those excavated near the Great Ziggurat at Ur which Mesopotamians built in 2100BCE, as homage to the moon god Nanna. It's rectangular mud brick structure (a veritable highrise to the heavens) inspired the Old Testament tale of the Tower of Babel.

But Saddam don't do Old Testament or even old Ziggurat pyramids. He'd even snugged MiG fighter jets close up to the ancient structure to deter U.S. bombers from destroying the ancient treasure while destroying his MiGs. Survival of his sleek, shiny birds a much greater concern than survival of three thousand year old temples. They don't finish in time, Saddam will do them and won't be pretty ...or survivable!

So they had neither time to admire their own handiwork nor that of their ancestors. Saddam was not a man to be kept waiting. Every man present trembled at the thought of what might happen to his self and his family should they displease their leader. They worked like ants, quickly lifting the entire construction onto a sturdy, wheeled dolly and tugging and pushing it all out to the entrance. Once outside, the engineers attached a heavy-lift sling and hoisted all up and onto the flatbed of a two and a half ton truck they'd bought from the Americans in friendlier times.

They congratulated themselves that this finding was heaven-sent leaving the schedule easily achievable. Then they took time out for a leisurely lunch, an especially unusual occurrence these past months. The meal was made a celebration for their herculean labors and their leaders spared no expense to reward them and show appreciation. No last meal could have been richer...

It was in the aftermath of their meal that the curiosity became strongest. They had stuffed themselves on delectable, spicy dishes of kubba --made from minced lamb with nuts, raisins and spices-- and a special dish called masgouf that is made from fish caught by Tigris River boatmen, roasted slowly over brushwood fires and topped with chopped onions and tomatoes. Also, they ate amber rice topped with quizi, a savory, roasted lamb stuffed with rice, pistachios and almonds. Dessert included fruits, rice pudding and baklava pastry made from honey and pistachios layered between wafer-thin, filo sheets. All was washed down --quite satisfactorily-- by cups of thick, black coffee and heavily, sweetened tea.

Their bellies settling with the heavy meal, most of the men settled themselves in the shade of their vehicles to better enjoy the moment. However, some of the engineers decided to have a better look at their find. They used cutting tools to separate the bottom from the slab sides – marveling at the ancient alchemy which had constructed such a container-- then pry bars to inch the heavy sides up enough for them to insert metal hooks underneath. Then they winched the entire top and sides up and away from the bottom. That was how Eisa found their remains. Twenty-six men had been reduced to ashes ...that simply blew away on the desert winds.

Never much of a globe trotter, Chaco hated leaving his New Mexico home for any reason. He didn't mind the occasional visit, as long as the occasion occurred only seldom and almost never desired to swap locations with a place where the average number of humans per square block dwarfed by an order of magnitude the average to be found out here in a square mile. Occasions like those were about as far from his idea of ideal as sipping one of Carlos' "special beverages" …and occasions like those he could well do without.

The hustle and bustle of people living literally atop each other left him unappreciative and unimpressed. The daily saga of angry honking car horns he could well do without, not to mention the pollution and living extremes soaring from Lilliputian to Godzilla. Places like that would never provide for him the lure of territory once roamed by the likes of Geronimo, Cochise and Pat Garrett. This land may have looked to the outsider like a mistake made by God on Monday, before he got the hang of it, but to him it was home and home is where his heart was …and he dearly hated leaving home.

He especially hated when the sole purpose for a trip was to put his cousin's feet back onto a firmer path. Gnashing his teeth until the gums ached, Chaco reflected that sometimes his younger relative was still a little, spoiled brat inside who would never survive without timely intervention. Now, once again Carlos was treading in quicksand and could be sucked under into oblivion if he continued as he was.

Wearily boarding the flight to Albuquerque, Chaco admitted to himself that though unwelcome this break would probably be good for him. As of late he had become staid, settled and unadventurous …unless secretly pirating encrypted messages constituted one's foremost definition of adventure.

Neither was he certain whether the ordeal of three takeoffs and landings for one destination constituted adventure. But it would definitely represent change to a schedule which seldom varied, lately. The quest for better grapes competed with his celestial passions, but seldom else interrupted his daily agenda Dard the fatigue was wearing on him. Shaving in the mirror that morning, he had reminded himself that his days were not very many more than his cousin's --in truth only a handful-- though few would assume so watching them stand side by side.

Deep wrinkles had turned his face craggy. His hair, more white than black, barely made an excuse for his barber's attentions anymore. But that was minor, it was just hair. Realizing his stubborn nature made him a lost cause, his barber no longer suggested enhancements --such as color treatments-- to the few hairs left over after the rest deserted. It was not hair problems plaguing him daily. Even more pronounced, thanks to an advancing arthritis eating away his hip joint, it was his limp that further signaled a difference in their vitality. Truth be told, he looked more like a father to the still youthful Carlos (who never saw an enhancement he did not like) …perhaps a grandfather.

His friends and staff --they were one and the same-- were delighted that he was taking a getaway. They did not need to know the reason, figuring any reason that got him a break was a positive thing. It was a truth he reluctantly admitted, but he did eventually admit. Days he worked with his team of adroit, independent thinkers exploring the world of genetic engineering. Nights he expanded his knowledge of the celestial heavens, his telescope reaching out to touch the face of God, merging him once again with the Cosmos in search of things he still did not know. These things were endless; he neither knew them nor knew about them. He knew not what he searched for, but he definitely knew that he was searching for something. The Mother had steered him in this direction for some reason and he chided himself for being too inadequate to find out why. So perhaps a change was just the ticket to awaken something lost in the doldrums of his routine.

The task of maintaining this planet had been assigned to all mankind, not just to one lone Cholo, as someone had once joked about his Mestizo features. All of mankind had the responsibility to husband the earth's resources, to protect its wildlife, soils and waters from pollution and destruction. While his heritage made him sensitive to this task, such huge effort needed much more than any one man could accomplish. But he could try…

Such a task had always appealed to his sense of purpose even though outsiders, relying on his physical appearance, never saw any such abilities. Amused by their own cleverness, school mate jokesters had insisted that the half of Chaco that was Indio (they pointed to the ruddy complexion, high cheekbones, black eyes and straight chin as evidence) had usurped the European half that came down the line of his father. They wondered openly whether he would one day take the warpath and hunt them down for their transgressions, dressed only in loin cloth, headdress and moccasins, wielding a tomahawk.

These slings and arrows came from Chicano youths in a manner whose blatant ignorance one might assume from gringos. They were never in fun and intended to bite deeply into one for whom life had never shown such things as fun.

But these never truly found their mark, sailing wide of target. It did not matter to him either way. He was equally proud of the dual lineages flowing from Spanish Conquistador and Native American sides. But, in truth, he felt closest to the Indio in him, the Anasazi ancestry inherited through his mother.

Her purposeful spirit rode bareback astride the unbridled stallions of the four winds. She had introduced his prepubescent self to the Earth Mother and taught him to revere nature in all its forms. She had taken him in hand on long walks out beneath the stars and patiently answered his juvenile queries about the Celestial Spirits, the Sky Gods who inhabit the Heavens and the like. And then she had gone away to live among them.

Her teachings, her spirit stayed well within him long after she departed on her journey. His father's religion made its attempt at abolishing those ingrained beliefs but failed miserably. Without the Spanish whips and firearms, he felt certain that the early Catholic priests would have been equally unsuccessful with all of his mother's people, rather than the relative few who still kept to the old traditions.

Now as he winged his way east, from the love of his life, he focused on his feeling that the Earth Mother may herself have created this respite. Perhaps he had allowed himself to become too staid, his searches too predictable. He may have become a useless prisoner, trapped by his reluctance to step beyond the confines of his comfort zone.

The pattern was as unchanging as the New Mexico hilltop where his small observatory rested and would have remained such for a longer period had not his cousin again gone "Injun Joe", as observed by his friend Pancho Martinez. To quote the Mexican truck driver --who often delivered Chaco's supplies of pesticides and fertilizer—"Carlos was crazier than an Apache on firewater" …and Pancho had firsthand experience with Carlos Morano's rages.

Pancho was short, plump and sometimes caustic. But the endearing quality of his character, his straight forth honesty, was also his most trying. Pancho called a spade a spade, occasionally to his detriment. But at least he was genuine. At least in Chaco's eyes, though quite the opposite in the view of some others.

Pancho was the only name any of their crew knew him by. No

surname. Not a Señor or a Mister or any other titular rendering. Only Chaco and Hilda knew these things. But even they were kept at arm's length in the matter of some topics. The extent of his garrulous personality ended where the subject of his family began. That subject was the only one he considered taboo, never to be discussed in mixed company. It was the one subject he neither broached nor responded to. He spent so much time in their company –sharing lunch while his truck was unloaded—the other workers joked that he was their "legal illegal". Good naturedly, the primarily Mexican-American workforce chided him for his poor English and rotund figure, even his squinty eyes.

But Pancho was proud of his heritage and made no bones about his nationality. He jokingly accused the others of selling out. He was also proud that his eighteen wheeled diesel truck complied with all U.S. highway standards and regulations and still saved his customers significantly. So they should appreciate, not denigrate. His words were more like, 'pre chate" and "den grate".

The fact that he paid neither U.S. highway taxes nor purchased the higher costing U.S. fuels (both facts which grated significantly on U.S. truckers) he ignored. But under the North American Free Trade Agreement he was not required to. So those qualifiers he left unmentioned.

Feeling neither compunction nor compassion for U.S. truckers' griping about NAFTA shortcomings; neither did he feel the necessity to incorporate politically correct terms like Native American or Original People or any other such "north of the border" terminologies when communicating with such "north of the border" peoples. This style occasionally created a few difficulties, but to him, such lengthy terms were for gringos to use. He often did, though, extend the courtesy of calling gringos "white people", when they were around, and a similar courtesy for black people, whom he called African Americans if some were within earshot ("niggers" if they were not). His sentiment was that both groups employed ethnic slurs against him and his kind …even against themselves.

So all ethnic groups he felt fair game for his flowery speech and depictions. The fact that his, as well as his compadres' blood lines also flowed back through Montezuma's Aztecs was another feature for him to ignore. Lots of their ancestors even crossed paths with Africans, in the heing and sheing capacity. But one thing he would never ignore was his hatred of Chaco's condescending cousin, whom he considered both crazy and –like Mark Twain's Injun Joe-- unequivocally evil.

To Pancho, the episode –which began as a minor snub—initially wasn't much, no big deal. To Carlos, it had been a major affront from jump street; demanding appropriate retribution (cause paybacks is a bitch and so was Carlos, when it came to paying back). To Chaco, it was a prime example why his truckdriver friend should learn to bite his tongue more often (before someone bit his ass). Regardless whether one considered its instigation major or minor, its result was nearly catastrophic.

They say, if you mess with the bull you'll get the horns. Unfortunately, Pancho never felt the compunction nor compassion to follow such commonsense rules either …until he locked horns with Carlos.

The episode initiated from Pancho's reaction to Carlos' refusal to shake his outstretched hand. The man just turned around and walked back toward the headquarters building, literally turned his back on him. Perhaps he was in a rush to get out of the hot ninety-degree sun. But could he not at least pretend to be civil? Irrepressibly, Pancho did not wait until the other man was outside hearing before firing a retort. His words flew before his brain could apply the brakes: "Dat Injun' nose so far up dat nigger bitch' ass he act like ghetto trash!"

He said it and meant it. Still, Pancho had considered his comment purely a jest, a bit of sport, all in fun; until Carlos applied his own sense of jocularity. While forklifts worked to unload the cargo, an unseen figure worked underneath the trailer. Hidden by tandem axles --each sporting twin-set tires to either side, as well as the loading dock's overhang-- no one noticed the wraith quietly cutting a shallow notch into one of the lines leading to Pancho's trailer brakes, the service brakes. The saboteur did not stop there…

Rather than hydraulic fluid, semi-trucks employ air pressure to actuate their brakes, easing coupling and uncoupling of trailers, as well as reducing systemic problems common to hydraulic systems like fluid leakage and brake fade due to fluid vaporization in hydraulic lines. Adding his own improvisation, the artful saboteur also drilled a dozen or more small holes into the inside-facing walls of both of the trailer's emergency brake reservoirs, which he patched with a rubberized sealant. For good measure, he then backed a few turns off both spring brake pushrods …this guy was both artful and motivated

Big Rig tractor trucks incorporate an emergency feature in the event air pressure to either the tractor or the trailer is lost. The feature ensures that neither unit will lose all braking capacity and become uncontrollable runaways. In normal function, both the tractor truck's parking brake and the trailer's emergency brake activate automatically when air pressure in the system drops below a certain level. Both deactivate when air pressure is sufficient, permitting normal driving operations. So theoretically, a big rig should never totally be without some sort of stopping capability …with the exception of extraordinary circumstances.

Coupled through a connector behind the tractor –called a "gladhand"-- the air brake line sits alongside the electrical cable, which provides power to the lights and any specialized features of the trailer. Gladhand connectors (also known as "palm couplings" and sometimes referred to as "pig tails") each have a flat engaging face and retaining tabs. The faces are placed together, and the units are rotated so that the tabs engage each other to hold the connectors together. Similar in design to the ones used for a similar purpose between railroad cars, this arrangement provides a secure connection, but allows the couplers to break away without damaging the equipment if they are pulled --as may happen when tractor and trailer are separated-- without first uncoupling the air lines.

Pancho dutifully inspected his gladhand and electrical connectors and then the lines leading out to the service brakes and emergency reservoirs. This was no country to lose the brakes on forty thousand pounds of eighteen-wheeler. Too many sharp curves, steep grades and rockslides made for a catastrophe just waiting to happen.

Next he performed his pre-start checks, including both tractor and trailer service brake systems. Everything looked good from where he sat. So down the long and winding road he go, hoping any catastrophe just waiting to happen would just wait and happen another day …to another guy!

Wasn't just the run of the mill for regular hazards he was concerned for, at any moment in time, added to those were people perpetually driving sub-compacts into his "no-zones" or blind spots and worse, idiots attempting suicide stunts they copied from movies such as "The Fast and the Furious", "underriding" big rigs lost their "go fast" Japanese hot rods. Professional drivers had to remain alert and focused to get through unscathed and he prided himself on always getting through.

Unfortunately, even Pancho's sharp-eyed inspection did not discover the small scalloped out section of rubber hose in the service line nor the matched-over holes in the air reservoirs. But once he started up and the lines pressurized, it was not long before the hose's interior wall pushed outside, forming a miniature balloon. It was also not long before the plugs in the emergency reservoirs began failing. The rubber sealant's compound was never designed to withstand the one hundred-twenty pounds per square inch pressure generated by the truck's air compressor and the plugged holes popped open by two's and three's.

Only minutes after he pulled out of the small parking lot and headed down US Highway One-Eighty towards Silver City, the air pressure started pressing its way to freedom. Holes opened in the emergency reservoirs, bubbling began in the service line. But all the while, the truck rolled onerously on, no warning lights nor alarms.

Turning southwest at the intersection of Highway 90, he waited patiently at a stop light, absent-mindedly perusing signs pointing to sites made famous by the escapades of local bad boy and favorite-son Billy The Kid. But he had no interest in touring the dilapidated, old jailhouse the youthful outlaw once escaped from. Soon Pancho had escaped the few traffic lights and departed Silver City for the wide open yonder.

On he sped past nearly desolate landscape, almost barren except for mesquite trees, scrub brushes and grasses that dotted the white sandscape with ubiquitous uniformity. Spreading out from both edges of the roadway the level surface traveled only a short distance before dropping precipitously down to the valley floor before flattening out again. The few homes, posted here and there, tended to appear small --of little notoriety-- but completed the desert postcard along with the backdrop of mountainous slopes squatting far off in the distant view, whose forest greens appeared dark and forbidden under a cerulean sky.

Just past the tiny village of Tyrone, the grade began climbing, gradually at first, until the four PM sun began taunting his gaze. Somewhere off to his right was Tyrone's old ghost town of Spanish Mediterranean-style mansions and businesses deserted when the price of copper plummeted in 1921.

For a moment, sun glare tricked his eyes into seeing gentlemen in tuxes accompanied by ladies dressed in elegant finery who floated over the roadside on winds generated by the speeding truck as if motioning for him to come join their frivolous cavorting. He blinked them away. He was never one to believe in ghosts, at least not gringo ghosts. The mirrored sunglasses he preferred worked their hardest but were only partly successful in defeating the glare. Squinting eye slits accommodated the rest of the sun's blinding effects, but its full-on-face orientation began to warm him appreciably. Fingers pushed the fan control to full on, urging his tractor's air conditioning to dissipate the increasing heat now inducing sweat beads along the broad forehead.

As his speed leeched steadily downward --as the pull of gravity ramped upwards—he automatically compensated with increased throttle, nearly touching the carpeted floorboards. But gravity's relentless pull reduced his speed to under fifty-five by the time his rig crested the two-mile slope. He soon had it back up to sixty-five; however, the next upgrade presented an even steeper contest, though not as lengthy. So these presented little challenge, if any. His main discomfort came from the occasional popping of his ears from the altitude changes. At the crest, his speed had dipped only to sixty. Over this hump, he again put pedal to the metal to build up momentum in time for the next incline.

The roadway surface was smooth and nearly straight having only a few, easy curves as it dipped steeply downward towards the valley below. There appeared few challenges, even at his increasing momentum. The few connecting roads presented no drunken locals about to steer their battered pickup trucks forth in a game of inebriated bumper tag and no loose steers threatened to trot out onto the roadway to get to the other side (he was not at all worried about loose chickens crossing the road).

Suddenly he spied the tail end of a National Guard convoy, just ahead, which he rapidly overtook, still pressing his speed to achieve advantage against the next hill. Yucca and pine and larch --on each side—waved as he sped past. At least he had assumed they waved, later he would muse that each could have been flashing a warning.

But the road was dry and stretched long before him. All the military trucks and Humvees kept well to the right lane while he steered into the left. Over the next crest and instantly down the decline that swept first left then right then left again, leveling off for a short distance as it passed the first entrance to a giant copper mine, then another drop, but at the bottom this time the road narrowed to form single lanes in each direction and his speed had passed eighty-five.

But he still felt unconcerned as the convoy moved too slowly to bother him before he could pass their lead Hummer and there still remained sufficient room for maneuver into the single lane before it dove underneath an old railway bridge at the bottom --rusty patches and colorful graffiti darkening its light gray paint-- and climbed steeply up the next slope. He had always lamented that the copper mine it serviced (as a conduit for their precious ore) should one day spend a few of their mega dollars to repaint the old landmark so it did not go the way of the ghost town. As huge as the nearly endless dirt mounds piled high on either side of the road, he felt the mine owners could easily afford a little paint. They had to be making money…

Pancho Martinez' first indication that something was amiss came quickly. He was in a rush to return home to Juarez and his short, plump wife, in whose blood directly flows the lineage of Mangas Coloradas – the great Apache chief and uncle of Cochise-- but first he had one more delivery, this one in Lordsburg, about another thirty miles or so.

He could see her soft face smiling through the sunshine at him. Dozens of pounds heavier, she still possessed much of the girlish beauty first enthralling his adolescent self, though Pancho often joked that his wife looked exactly like her famous ancestor –gaunt and craggy, with suntanned, leathery facial skin and all—but he truly loved every well-rounded curve and rumors had it that she was actually quite striking. He spread those rumors. He also often joked that he had helped her escape from the Reservation, evading a posse of over three thousand in the process, humorously referring to the three thousand U.S. Army troops who searched vainly for Geronimo until the Apache Chief decided to give up.

Unknown to Pancho, other less humorous objects were about to give up, for not only did the atmospheric pressure fluctuations affect his ruddy, dumbo-sized ears, but each time his rig ascended a long, steep hill –climbing high into the stratosphere—the lesser outside pressure allowed the balloon to expand further, at a greater rate. Its dark size increased --one, then two inches in diameter-- growing larger as the hose materials' integrity weakened. Each time he pushed his brake pedal, the pressure exerted even more force on the main air line. Soon the balloon pushing through the gap in its exterior wall became larger –three, then four inches wide—then it failed altogether in a loud pop that was too far back behind for Pancho to hear even had his radio not been blasting a Spanish-English hip-hop tune sung by Control Machete.

Distance as much as volume drowned out the sound of the small explosion in his airline. Spanglish rhythms pounding his ears, he took no notice. Nor had he noticed the slight drag caused by the increasing engagement of the emergency brakes as lowering pressure in the emergency tanks permitted the spring-loaded brakes to apply, at first lightly, then increasing until they began to heat up with the friction which also wore away their surface, but did not cause the sudden reduction in power which would have been instantly recognizable.

Behind his high-backed seat was the sleeper compartment whose necessity he hated. Its purpose meant another night alone; another misadventure in the land of the stumbling out of some dark, smoke-filled, alien bar at a wayside truck stop somewhere in the middle of nowhere, to practically fall into its small bed while the effects of too many Coronas conjured even greater realization that he was alone. The picture evoked heightened desires for his little two-bedroom flat in Juarez and the piquant smells of Juanita's kitchen where she toiled, a soft humming emanating from ruby lips as she stuffed the light, puffy sopaipilla bread with ground pork and asadero cheese and chile peppers. Sometimes she would substitute beef or add refried beans and chorizo sausage. His stomach, also puffy, growled with pleasure at the thought of her cooking. Then there was the envisioned sight of twin, voluminous globes spilling out of her halter top...

Anxious eyes gobbled miles of highway. Green signs with white lettering shot by, their messages lost, left in his wake. He had no intention on stopping to visit any of the scenic wonders they announced. Only those announcing diminishing miles to Lordsburg interested him. But he paid them little attention as well. Next would come the I-10 east to El Paso. He knew the route by heart and counting the miles would only prolong the drive. Instead, his memory tricking game counted "out of state" license tags on the vehicles that he passed. Especially appreciated were the "out of" country tags from Mexico and Canada. Those helped him feel less the outcast.

Yucca plants, fanning sword-shaped leaves at Mormon Tea bushes, he swept past and left in his wake along with stands of tall piñon and juniper trees. The beauty of sweeping vistas leading to far off mountains --holding up a bright blue, cloudless sky-- dominated horizon to horizon. He opened his expansive lips and popped in another roasted piñon nut, crunching the snack as he quickly scanned the instrument gauges embedded in the stone gray, plastic-wrapped dashboard of his massive cockpit.

Finding only normal indications his urgency prevailed. He had taken no notice of the drag. At first, he thought the diesel engine may have encountered a minor hiccup. So he compensated, applying more accelerator pedal. Four hundred-ten horses offered lots of compensation. He merely added throttle and away he went. Minor issues he would remand to a later time. He could fix any minor problems in a more opportune location. But for now, he was on his way, and soon for home.

The phenomenon is far away from unique in travelers. It is an especially common syndrome with airmen stationed far from home. In fact, the U.S. Navy reports that its carrier aircrews will voluntarily fly home the worst examples of aviation nightmares in order to shave their arrival time by a few hours. Airplanes once relegated to the ignominious role of "hangar queen" –their parts being swapped out to keep other aircraft flying, while the carrier was on station—are launched for the flight home with barely a backward thought. The Navy terms this condition "get-home-itis". For Pancho, this exceptional example was no exception…

Pressing to drop off this load and reach the I-10 before sundown, he had just crested a hill --headed down past the copper mine-- when the brake line hose erupted. But still, there came no obvious notification, nothing apparent manifested itself sufficiently for discovery. Slight smoking in both axles was blown aside before presenting to the National Guard drivers alongside or to his large outside mirrors. Even a more copious presentation would probably be mistaken for the twin plumes of diesel smoke pumping their steady volume out the highrise exhausts to each side of his Model 378 Peterbilt. Down the two mile slope he roared.

Accelerating over seventy-five, he allowed gravity to do much of the work in preparation for the next climb, a tactic employed by all truckers which significantly eased fuel bills. But at this speed, the probability factor for missing twice-roasted nuts was twice as high, far exceeding Pancho's pass catching abilities as attested by piñon litter at his feet. But the thick lips still posed significant threat to a great majority…

The fifty-three foot long trailer's emergency brakes had been steadily engaging for over twenty miles now and had lost much of their capability to the tremendous heat buildup. Add the proper conditions and something could go boom! Now came one of his worst nightmares.

Just as he was about to clear the lead vehicle –a sand-painted Humvee riding two soldiers wearing desert battle dress uniforms-- an elderly woman darted in from a side cutout just ahead of the oncoming hoard. Stubbornly she refused to either speed up or to move back onto the right shoulder even after his repeated horn calls and high beam flashes signaling her to move it or …well, you know!

She may have fixated on the Army National Guard convoy --rolling their usual forty-five—but hell was coming at her from a much more significant source and speed. He could almost empathize with the old dame, had she not been about to die under his wheels. Why the American

Army did not purchase trucks capable of maintaining highway speeds had always miffed Pancho. For some reason, military trucks were deemed incapable of safely climbing much past fifty, even without air conditioning (to cope with this hot southwestern climate) so they were restricted by regulation. They literally taunted other drivers into reckless methods of getting around them. On more than one occasion, he had been forced to slow to a literal crawl while stuck behind a procession of two and a half-ton (deuce and a half) and five-ton trucks and Humvees sporting forest green or desert sand camouflage colors. But that was not this nightmare…

He came up on her fast, only back a few car lengths now and Granny — driving a light gray Hyundai-- was not budging, seemingly oblivious to the huge beast blocking out all daylight from her rear view mirror. There was no other way. Traffic in the east bound lane prevented any excursion across the double-yellow lines. He could not get around her without shredding her tiny, little roadblock. So Pancho began tapping his brake pedal to gradually slow down. Except his rig did not slow down! Now he began to apply more force to the middle pedal, simultaneously downshifting from tenth gear, enabling the engine brake to aid speed reduction. The big diesel's noise volume spiked appreciably as its RPMs increased with each lowered gearing, but he was still rapidly overtaking the old woman and she still refused to move.

He watched in anguished horror as her tiny vehicle disappeared under the huge, long nose —painted in the green, white and red colors of the Mexican flag-- expecting to hear the crunching sounds and feel the thudding and thumping as his truck devoured the tiny car and its unwise driver. But even though the trailer system was severely limited by pushrods that could barely push (not to mention nearly empty air reservoirs), some measure of luck or providence provided sufficient slowing to bring the truck's mass below the Korean import's fifty miles per hour speed. Then the trailer's emergency apparatus overcame the heat and momentum and locked up all together. Forty thousand-two hundred pounds of tractor and trailer jackknifed before sliding to a screeching halt underneath the railroad bridge —blocking it entirely-- while the sixty-seven year old grandmother proceeded on her way …at still a snail's pace, albeit now with heavily soiled undergarments.

But Pancho's undergarments were fine. He was a professional after all; professionals don't easily piss themselves, though his nerves were shaken by what could have happened. Had the trailer brakes not finally locked up fully, the entire rig would likely have jackknifed fully around and slammed into the bridge abutments, taking them out, every one of them, and collapsing everything down on him. Then there would be no need for paint …or Juanita's cooking.

Jackknifes were dangerous and usually not much fun. They were also tough on snacks. He did not need to look to know that his bag of nuts had spilled its contents all over the cockpit. Talk about a mess...

Eyes closed, Pancho relived the near catastrophe, its scenes flashing as Technicolor images against the backside of his eyelids, only to be replayed again and again in sequence. He was aware of the position of his trailer –fully blocking both lanes of the highway and causing a backup which would soon stretch far from northeast to southwest—but he did not want to open his eyes. Sweat streamed even in the air conditioning. His truck could have crushed that old lady, but that was not what unnerved him. After all, he was a professional and these things happen. No! His thick fingers gripped hard at the steering wheel. What really unnerved him was the realization that this happening was no accident. Carlos!

CHAPTER FIFTEEN

Chaco woke just as the Boeing jet began its decent into Miami International. A sight seldom seen around his southwestern homestead; thick, lower level cloud formations blocked much of his view, but off in the distance to the east, his one good eye spied bright green waters emerging out of the deep blue. He reminded himself that the Bahamas was yet another earthly treasure not yet uncovered during his search for all things extraterrestrial.

Seated one row behind and across the aisle was his chauffeur and bodyguard, Alex, operating at the moment solely in the latter role. Soon that role would be co-opted with his skills behind the wheel. He preferred Alex to drive him in a rental car, rather than have Carlos send a limo. Carlos was enamored with the long, opulent vehicles, while Chaco preferred to travel in one of the large SUVs –like Denali's and Navigators-- which permitted him to sit high up where he could see over things like roadway railings and other vehicles clogging the roads. Their height reduced a portion of the handicap with which life had encumbered him. The Miami scene did the rest.

Miami's panoramic liquid scene and esthetically pleasing skyline – dominated by colorful, tall buildings-- always served to lift the heaviness weighing down his mood. He could understand Carlos' love of this place. There was actually a freedom here that California had misplaced. He felt hard-pressed to explain it. Perhaps it was the thought of so many souls lost back there. Perhaps it was past family and friends he had once known –now buried, but not totally forgotten— that created the sensation of depression.

Perhaps it was the stifling pollution still filling the atmosphere. Pollution that the politicians claimed was no longer a problem even as it continued to murder people. They had cleaned up much of the brown haze which once colored the sky. However, unseen carcinogens contributing to deaths from cancers and respiratory ailments have made Los Angeles' numbers tops in the country and still growing. Maybe that was the cause …but just maybe it was the lives taken at his behest.

The skies here appeared clearer, the sun brighter and the waters bluer than his remembrance of Southern Cali. Add a few mountains and he would consider moving his observatory here. However, Florida's highest point at less than three hundred-fifty feet would not suffice for his purposes. Britton

Hill had been appropriately named, nowhere near New Mexico's thirteen thousand-foot tall Mount Wheeler up near Taos. But then the Rockies tend to reach much higher than these east coast rock piles.

Still, moving here was possibly one of Carlos' better ideas. It was unfortunate its beauty had not worked similar magic on his cousin's countenance. Perhaps if he took the time to settle in –rather than the constant motion which kept him on the go—the South Florida flavor --mixed in with tropical island spices brought over from Cuba and the Caribbean-- could ease whatever ailed him.

Chaco wrested back from his daydream. His patience was at an all-time low and he was anxious to get to his cousin's home. He could scarcely believe the story in Rubin Martinez' report to him, but he had to, there was no one else. Of the twenty or so employees, Rubin was the sole Mexican-American on Carlos' staff at Anasazi Software and one of the few without a degree in engineering. His field of expertise was business. His official title was Director of Marketing, but he also fulfilled the role of house spy for Chaco; keeping an eye on "Carlos Things" –as they called their over watch—to ensure that the volatile leader did not go so far off the reservation they could never get him back.

Rubin's email had sat in Chaco's private mailbox a week before anyone got around to opening and inspecting its content. True to the nature of "Murphy-isms", this message had come at –perhaps not a bad time-- an unfortunate time. It came when people who should have been minding the store were feeling unmindful.

Normal traffic flow was copied to his assistant, who ensured that all the important business matters were covered. Occasionally she would even ask him for approval before resolving significant issues. But the young mother of three, who often worked out of her own living room, could discharge most details while changing the diapers of her youngest son. In actuality it was she who ran the company, and well. Her meetings with him were held mainly by cell phone or internet video link. So he seldom became aware of day-to-day exchanges until afterwards …which was exactly how he liked it.

It was his desire that only controversial or threatening issues interrupt his work in the lab or the observatory. So to her fell the burden and she responded marvelously. It had not always been that way. His first two assistants were less concerned with office management –capitalizing on business trends, fulfilling employee needs, et cetera-- than with matching their outfits to that day's mood. Their total tenure lasted less than thirty days.

Chaco needed someone motivated, someone who could "hit the ground running", as it were. He was little interested in managing daily operational requirements for his pocket-sized company and Chaco often boasted that Hilda Torres fulfilled his every need. But then he would modify his brag with a slight caveat…

She was reed thin and looking to be in poor health when she walked into his small office for the interview. If anything seemed a perfect match, it was this woman and this office. Dingy windows, dirty floors and serious need of dusting described the room's interior just as coke bottle glasses, yellow-stained teeth and disheveled clothing described her. Both were in serious need of aid. The room he had simply given up on, just as she had given up on herself.

Less than five minutes into the interview, Chaco's active mind had sized her up sufficiently for his purposes. His estimation was that she had taken his interview out of need to fulfill some government mandate to qualify for food stamps. Plus, she had evidently had a recent, close encounter with some liquid representative of the spirit world.

Her answers to questions were matter-of-fact, cursory, devoid of enthusiasm, though somewhat compelling and evidently honest. She neither avoided his eyes nor questioned his motives. Her story was told in a manner that verified all that he saw. Deserted by her drunken bum of a husband. Left with no money, two young kids and bills piling up, she had simply existed; drifting from relative to relative, staying until asked to move on. "You promised you'd look for work! You still on that bottle! You're just looking for a handout! Pack up your kids and go!"

By the time she met Chaco, her six year old kid was living with an aunt and her boyfriend in San Diego, the five year old lived with her at a cousin's in Boyle Heights. When she walked into his office –ratty, brown, tangled hair tied up in a haphazard knot-- he instinctively almost asked her to turn around at the door and come back when she was better prepared. He had had enough of plastic people only looking for a paycheck. If she did not care, then neither did he. But he gave her a few minutes, then stated flatly, "You're not what I'm looking for, goodbye!"

Without uttering a word, the vacuous woman had left the way she came –out past the stacks of wooden pallets, through the steel door of the small, dingy white building that sheltered his wine distributorship. He figured never to see her again, and did not care. His company was barely in its infancy at the time and in his own words, "All tits 'n elbows", trying to deal with local liquor stores, state licensing, et cetera. He hoped to one day move far away from Northridge, but today was not that day. So he endured.

So did Hilda. She came back to see him two days later. A different woman entirely. Her hair was combed and shiny. This time in a neat bun at the back of her strikingly curved neck –reminiscent of a Spanish Belladonna—appropriate lipstick and mascara; tiny, pear-shaped pearl earrings hanging tantalizingly from delicate ears; and a one-piece, sleeveless shift dress that cut just above her skinny knees. She even had a bit more color in her than the first time, brought out even more by the pale, pink dress and matching slippers.

The interview lasted all of fifteen minutes and he hired her then and there. She impressed him that she was ready to try. That was all he ever asked of anyone. It was the last time Chaco ever saw the dress. She arrived the next day wearing jeans, sneakers and a faded gray sweatshirt. But the face was freshly scrubbed, the hair and makeup neat and she jumped straight in with both feet. She cleaned everything up, including herself, and their relationship could not have been better.

The old building on Reseda Boulevard was now a strip mall with a women's fitness gym, a jewelry store and a Pizzeria. Actually, the building that had housed Chaco's first foray into "grapes distribution" --as his cousin Carlos always joked—collapsed in on itself, destroyed by the Northridge earthquake on January 17, 1994.

But it worked out okay for Chaco. None of his employees was even slightly injured. For although it occurred on a Monday, the seventeenth was Dr. Martin Luther King's birthday and he had given everyone the day off with pay, as he did for all-important holidays. Others around him did not fare so well. A couple buildings made soup stains out of owners and employees who ignored the holiday and opted for the cash. He always wondered whether their friends and remaining relatives would ever deign ignore the terrible lesson taught that day.

But that was all before the move to New Mexico. It was also before Hilda's kid got beat up badly by the Aunt's boyfriend –jealous that the childless woman spent too much time on the kid, not enough on him. Hilda was working and saving to afford a home for herself and her sons, but was not quite there. Southern California is a tough place to acquire property --unless one is born with a silver spoon or doesn't mind a ghetto or a barrio. But this lesson came hard, her kid almost died and she bit the bullet.

She swallowed pride and accepted her employer's offer of temporary lodgings (he had offered once before). Now she knew that he would never take advantage of the situation. Also, she could save enough to feed two kids if she did not have to spend so much of her small salary on that long bus ride from Boyle Heights --notwithstanding the fact that the trip took hours, one-way. Plus, Chaco was the gentlest man she had ever met. He would never force her unwillingly.

Others would, she knew. Her figure had begun to fill out quite nicely with the steady job and the money for lunch, even the occasional acceptance of a co-worker's offer to treat her. Offers came much more frequently than she desired. Others saw what she did not, the long dark tresses falling past a high-cheekboned face sculpted out of pure honey by a master craftsman, down to a lithe, sinfully-proportioned figure that could grace a Parisian walkway.

It took a while, but after she and the boys got settled, she began to accept the occasional date, though she made it plain that she was a mother of two and that two would do. So anyone looking for more than a friendly evening out should look elsewhere. Hilda's heart held love for only two young men …and one old.

It was her love for Chaco that prompted her to follow him all the way to the badlands of New Mexico. She admitted later that the thought of living in a wilderness --near myriad Indian reservations-- initially terrified her. Pictures of barren hills colored in reds and browns, blacks and oranges flooded her vision; nothing even remotely green or smooth, just craggy crevices that dove to unknown depths before climbing high into the stratosphere to joust at the few clouds wandering past. Ever more threatening were the envisioned packs of coyote and hordes of puma on the prowl for wayward house pets or small children to snack on. But even these seemed tame compared to the thought of Apache warriors making midnight raids on unsuspecting foreigners from California. Her fears nearly throttled her with these thoughts and many others.

But she bravely fought the fears off. Chaco's confidence was compelling. She would have followed him to the moon if he asked. He had become the mentor she never had and an uncle to her boys. He fixed her life, rescued her from the cellar and an early grave. He could fix anything

…including child molesters.

Chaco sent a couple members of La Raza 18 to pay a visit to Hilda's aunt's boyfriend and fixed his own need for retribution. Hilda never knew the real reason behind the demise of her Aunt's rabid boyfriend. Chaco never wanted her to find out that his puppy dog visage hid sharp teeth. She only knew she felt glad that the miscreant would never threaten her son again. And even the Aunt —who wailed incessantly over her loss-- had to feel at least some sense of relief that she would never need heavy makeup and dark glasses to cover the results of his tirades …at least until her next boyfriend.

Hilda also finally decided to take a boyfriend. Lonely for her family in Southern California, Hilda later began dating and eventually married Rubin Martinez. He was tall, handsome and good with the boys who were growing larger now and needed a father around to teach them football and about girls and such. It did not work out as well as hoped —both were older and too set in their ways-- but in their trying they produced her third child.

After the separation, Rubin volunteered to go east, as much to separate farther from her as to provide Chaco a set of eyes and ears in Carlos' division of their corporation. The act in itself declared that Chaco was in charge and Carlos hated it and especially hated Rubin, even though they were second cousins. The truth was, Rubin hated Carlos even more.

Sticklicious, Bootylicious, plus menage a trois that he calls "menage a twat" cause he the only guy. But even though some might call him sex fiend, he real popular with a whole lotta churchmen.

Then there's that whole "adulting" theme. "Hey watch Carlos buying ev'rybody a round! He's really all grown up now!"

"Carlos picked out his own insurance plan! Isn't he something? Hash tag, Adulting! Way to turn it up young Mister C!"

Yeah, right! They cheer Carlos up every time he wipes his own ass! It's why he believes his shit don't stink. Also why he believes he can get away with the shit he do! Rubin vowed that one day he would catch Morano in the shit. That day Morano's ass be grass, and he'd be lawnmower! Just catch him one time...

"Sex is a very necessary human interaction. You don't like to fuk? You fukked up! Ya don't wanna fuk me? Fuk you!"

"Har, har, har! Man, you 'bought ta split my gut!"

"They probably right though. I recently tried signing up for bone marrow donations, told me go home ta my rocker! Man I know guys twenty years younger can't git outta they wheelchair, but they wanna donate, no problem."

"Son, gittin' old a bitch an' no way back gonna change that! What it means taking care to stay healthy when you th' only one prechatin'?" The other smiled his most magnanimous grin. A prior boss once referred to it as a "shit eating" grin. He neither liked that description nor that boss, not after that. So that boss is no longer around after that! After him, he found Carlos Morano, who never made up descriptions about his appearance. Suited both just fine. But he had to admit it kinda was a shit eating grin he was smiling as he shoved the near headless body into the boot of his car.

Too bad. He kinda liked the guy. But orders are orders. Besides, killing is like heroin for him and he loved the high! Plus, getting old never a problem when you don't live to get old!

It happened one night during one of his infrequent visits to New Mexico. He did not come often. Did not care for the dry heat or the dust or to be bossed around. But he came with a desire. Tina had eschewed him once more and once more the vindictiveness crept back into control. There was another who had once eschewed his advances, but lately she seemed warmer, less distant, not so restrained. He decided, "I'm gonna take one more crack at that crack".

At his behest, they began the evening with dinner at a trendy restaurant named "Sagebrush". Carlos, Hilda and Rubin then spent the Friday night partying together at the Martinez' comfortable home just south of Silver City. Rubin had partied a bit too much and passed out holding onto the remains of a liter of tequila he had spent several hours enjoying; beginning with shots, until bottle-pulls seemed so much easier. But the party continued on without him. It was only a minor indiscretion --to Morano's way of thinking-- and lasted only for one night, as she later justified to her husband…

First falling back into her old bottle habits, Hilda then fell into Carlos' arms. Arms not only very willing, but greatly instrumental in this tryst; holding her resisting form tightly against his until she resisted no more. Soon the smoldering fireplace was not the only heat source in her living room. As her ardor climbed higher, so did her desire for him. Its climax came much too soon and abrupt for her wants. But then she found out about his wants.

"Damn Hilda, I didn't mean fo' this ta happen!" His back to her gave little suggestion whether there was any truth to the statement, neither did his voice. "I musta drunk too mucha dat Yak!"

Then he was gone. When she saw him the next morning, it was as if nothing had happened between them. Business as usual. He did not even acknowledge her awkward smile. Then he was gone. Back to Southern Florida's nightclubs and beaches featuring topless blondes …and redheads. She did not even have the chance to explain to him why she had succumbed so easily. How he had caught her eye years before --shortly after she started with the company—and how she had secretly fantasized about him …and her.

Her fantasies all came crashing down around her one day later, when Rubin came into their bedroom holding the empty bottle of Cognac in one hand, his suitcase in the other. "Carlos called. He left a message on the recorder. Guess he figured I'd be working too late to retrieve it before you. He said he was sorry for the other night, him not using a condom and all that. He was very civil through the whole speech. Said to make sure ol' Rube never finds out…"

With that Rubin's civilities were finished. He threw the bottle forcefully through the room's plate-glass window, shattering the glass and the outside stillness simultaneously. "Guess we won't need ta waste lotta cash on expensive trials an' lawyers an' all. You bein' a Ho' an' such! You kin keep th' house. You kin make th' payments. I'll send fo' my stuff or git it when yo' Puta ass ain't around …an' you kin fix this window too!"

It was with this last statement that he hurled the bottle, the memory of that night's opening ceremony still at the forefront of his psyche. He had opened up his home to a grinning, pattering serpent and now it was no longer his home. He grimaced inwardly at the mental picture of his cousin's flashing teeth as he held up the XO Special Rémy Martin decanter in one hand, a box of Cuban cigars in the other. "Hey Cuz! I brought the party favors. Where th' party?"

When Rubin's email arrived, she at first pretended not to notice it. She hated Rubin. Did not want to read anything he had written. He had not come to see his daughter in two years. Plus, she was mad at him for not calling the boys on their birthdays. Sure they weren't born his boys, but for a while they had been. She did not deserve or want his compassion for herself, just for the kids. Now they had only Chaco and he was always so busy he seldom made time for them anymore.

She knew she could not place blame on her friend. Her issues were with her Ex. Her complicity was acknowledged. She did after all have a fling with his cousin. Only for one night, though its intensity still lingered. But she hated him for leaving, then coming back, then making their baby –though she truly loved their little girl—then leaving permanently. It was the permanent aspect that she hated most…

So she did not even open it. She was also mad at him for being mad at her. Not very adult, but the very description of bitchiness has already obviated any conceptual identity with either rationalism or maturity. So not only did she leave it unopened, she toyed with half a thought of deleting it entirely. However, she reasoned that he would only send it again. So what was the point? That was the beauty of email. It was all just electronic reproductions of the original. But still she resisted. Then, after a week passed, when there was nothing further, she began to worry.

Normally, Rubin would have called Chaco with personal business or important communications not intended for other ears. He would have phoned Chaco directly to make this report, but had grown worried about the possibility that his calls were being intercepted and people he did not intend were listening in. He eschewed the phone entirely, instead he decided to employ other means …means he considered less easily compromised.

But the very nature of this method had its own difficulties. Chaco had become almost totally dependent on his assistant, to the point of neglect. He had complete trust in her and --excepting major business or personal issues—generally stayed out of her way. Salaries, schedules, shipment manifests –all the normal operations-- she handled with the department heads, while he stayed in the lab or the observatory. He had no desire to bother about anything else. Not even women, for the most part …not since Roxanne had died.

So he depended on Hilda to screen his calls, emails and visitors. Other than visitors, all the rest was accomplished very efficiently from her home. She seldom traveled to her cubbyhole outside his office, he seldom called her and the security detail generally dealt with visitors of the non-VIP variety. She came in only when necessary. This email was no different from the host of others mailed from business associates around the globe. Excepting her loathing of its sender…

When she finally got around to reading the text and scrutinizing the photos, she nearly panicked. Speed dial brought Chaco online, but he could not make any sense out of her speech. As luck would have it, she was in the office that day, so he only needed to drive his golf cart over from the adjacent lab building and climb a long flight of stairs set against the east-facing, outside wall. Even on days when his knee nearly refused civility, he still refused to take the elevator for such a short distance ... except during one of the infrequent rains.

Office spaces occupied the second level of the winery. The first level was basically a twenty-five foot tall open bay filled with wooden barrels and casks to one end and wine-making equipment to the other. Forklifts and other materials handling equipment –shuttling supplies and finished product from one side to the other or outside-- completed the picture permissible through large, sliding doors centered in the east and west walls.

There was no sign pointing in from the entrance road that ran up a quarter-mile from the main highway, only a mailbox with the address, 007 Tajos Verde Road. The official address was 7007, but one needed to get very close to the mailbox to spy that first digit, half as large as the others. Every one of the employees thought it added a bit of flair, a touch of verve. So they kept it.

Painted white with each side marked by a pair of handprints. It looked as if a giant had coated palms to fingertips with bright red paint and pressed them once, against each side of the building, as he struggled to lift it into this place. A small sign simply stating "Red Hand Wines" topped the eastern wall's doorway. Just inside, the one and only elevator whose one-level travel lift lead up to the offices.

The facility included two other buildings adjacent to and vectored due west from the northern end of the winery. Air travelers --or air traveling Gods—passing over on a southern track, might perceive the outlined shape to be a large red "L" emerging from green fields; from the south it appeared to symbolize the number seven, which was appropriate; seven being considered their lucky number. All three buildings were similarly adorned with white walls, Spanish tile roofs and hard packed, dirt paths leading between each other. Chaco had toyed with the idea of paving the paths, but decided instead to maintain the rustic appearance.

The crescent-shaped, twenty-eight acre ranch itself spread southwest from the main road. Its borders encompass the crests of low, reddish-clay hills, dotted with piñon pines, juniper and cottonwood trees and spots of mesquite that gave cover to the local denizens. Despite her initial fears, Hilda loved the red-headed woodpeckers that burrowed into the barrel cactus and the tiny white-breasted hummingbirds that visited her feeders daily. She grew used to the small, dark lizards flitting from tree to bush, the occasional greenish-colored skink searching for insects in the early evening and a seldom, but occasional encounter with some variety of rattlesnake. She never took time to discern which, beating a hasty retreat. Wary, but undaunted.

The central building was Chaco's home. The Hacienda, others called it, considering its nearly three thousand square-foot space splendorous. He simply referred to it as "My Place". He spent much of his time there –the little that he allotted to such times—languishing in the southern-facing solarium off the family room. That term had always struck him as ironic.

"Family room", invoked ideas that one had or planned to have a family. Chaco had neither. He planned to keep it that way. Ever since Hilda had married and moved away with the boys, this room, this entire house, had lost its luster. Its walls feeling closer, more penal than entrancing. The idea of making kids at his age or adopting and watching them leave, had no appeal. Once was enough. The hole rent from his heart remained unhealed. His housekeeper was the only other inmate, her bedroom across the main hallway from his. Occasionally she also fulfilled the role of lover. But only occasionally and only when she desired. He did not force her or seek another. Besides, he had his work.

Westernmost of the trio --at the edge of the acres of grapevines-- sat the Grapehouse --so named by staff members-- with its one-level, rectangular structure consisting of one half greenhouse and one half lab room.

Chaco simply considered it The Lab, but he let the staff employees name it as they pleased, painting bunches of purple grapes hanging from green leaves on the white, exterior walls. There indeed were a few artists among them.

White coated technicians worked its interior. Only two of these were degreed. One, an Oenologist or wine scientist, experimented with various levels of acidity and the effect on the bouquet and fruity flavor. The other, a Viticulturist, specialized in the health and development of the grapevines themselves. All the rest were local high school and college students who filled in as interns and even helped during the harvest time that grape pickers call "The Crush".

Pyrex test tubes and tumblers lined steel tables along with stainless steel Bunsen burners, an autoclave and various funnels suspended from wire supports --their short tubes attached to dull, yellow, flexible piping whose opposite ends plunged down the throats of glass or plastic decanters. Various colored liquids occupied space within many of the containers.

Here was Chaco's primary domain. Others in his employ could run everything else like they felt necessary. In this strategy he attempted to emulate the Son of God. He believed Jesus Christ as the ultimate delegator of authority: "Disciples, here are the guidelines, tell all of Mankind this message; tell them that love is the answer, now do your thing!"

Following Jesus' lead, he strived to be somewhere close behind, careful not to bite off too large a piece to chew without choking. Others virtually ruled outside. The penultimate hands off manager, he played second fiddle to the Christ's lead, never wanting to become involved unless the ship was not just sinking, but foundering, just about to go under. He worked with his department heads to develop loose organizational goals and strategies, then vacated, seldom intervening except to resolve conflicts that crossed divisional lines. That was his style of management. His attitude: "Why do both of us need to be involved?" That was why he searched carefully to find capable people with proper motivations to handle the business and they did.

Manuel controlled the Vineyards, Felipe the winery and Hilda the office. But here he held sway. He enjoyed it most when all the others had gone home for the day and he had the place to himself. In truth, there was always his personal bodyguard on hand to handle security situations, but at least there was no one else.

Through the middle of his vineyards, a small, fairly smooth path climbed west and slightly north from the Hacienda up a small slope to his observatory where his heart ruled. That was where he preferred to be any time after sunset, once the stars began peeking through the settling hues of red and orange.

Four-wheel drive, all-terrain vehicles fulfilled the transportation role. He drove himself, though Alex was normally just behind. Out here there was no problem dodging cars and trucks that suddenly appeared in his limited vision. Sometimes he would walk, but hiking presented its own set of problems for him, not the least being the thinner atmosphere in this high, hot desert environment.

He also rode his ATV around the vineyards to inspect produce, usually flanked by others in his employ. They drove in single file, along separate rows and slowly so as not to fill the air and cover their plants with the reddish dust. Any untoward appearance and they would all stop for closer inspection and consultation. The sight of even one Grape Leafhopper on the wing or settling down to a tasty feast would merit a follow-up by Manuel the Viticulturist, who also doubled as the vineyard manager. To him would fall the decision whether the situation required preventive measures, aka, pest controlling chemicals.

Their southernmost range they called "the Steak House", as it consisted of several acres sprouting thirty-inch high wooden poles staked in parallel rows, approximately two and a half meters apart. Tied to each pole was a tiny green plant (resembling a small bush) that represented the pride of their developmental efforts. The "new trees", they called this latest adaptation. These represented hundreds of hours of labor, of trial and error, sleepless nights and rivers of sweat. The new product --a low acid, higher sugar content hybrid-- should resist blight and preying insects, while producing sweet fruit for tables and for table wine …or so they all prayed.

Each line proceeded apace, as a march of stakes stretching approximately two meters in length to the next and so on. But it would be years before these "new trees" took part in "The Crush" --years of constant checks to ensure proper flow from the irrigation sprinklers, years of searches for visible evidence of blight or leafhoppers or whatever.

The honor of participating in the annual "Crush" they reserved for the veterans, campaigners of many seasons whose six-foot tall vines had withstood attacks from opportunistic birds and insects and periodic bouts with blight. The new kids would have their time …at some other time.

At harvest, the whole place filled with Spanish-speaking men and women wielding needle-nosed pruners whose curved blades made short work cutting through the fleshy wood stems. Plastic tubs colored blue or red or orange are pulled along behind the pickers who work in casual, though scripted fashion to strip the plants of their lush bounty. White grapes –requiring lower sugar content-- are picked first each season, then the red. Once filled, the baskets are unclipped to be lifted and dumped by others into a tractor-pulled, wagon whose bed lifts to the side to dump its load into hoppers. A short break is taken at the end of each long row and out of strategically situated backpacks come snacks or a thermos full of soup or the occasional cerveza.

After a few stories and jokes, it's back to work and the process continues about the same pace for three weeks in late summer, early autumn. Each morning the pickup trucks arrive full of bright-eyed, eager people –hued from light to dark brown skins-- dressed in faded blue jeans, leather work boots or Nike sneakers, head scarves of every color, dirty ball caps and full of chatty vigor ready to work. Then each evening they leave full of quiet, fatigued mounds of flesh, slumped shoulder to shoulder against each other, ready for bed.

Washed clean, much of the harvested product is loaded into the centrifugal destemmer/crusher machine --which separates out stems and grape skins at a rate approaching six tons per hour—and turned into sweet wines for storage in steel vats to ferment before being transferred into wooden barrels for aging between three and five years before sale. The remaining grape bunches get packed into crates and shipped to distributors for sale as table grapes. This annually is their busiest time by far and sleep becomes a seldom visited luxury. Chaco often dropped into his bed without even bothering to remove his clothes, fatigue seldom diminishing the smile which broadened with each day's progress. He only wished his cousin could appreciate such a wonderful connection with Mother Earth. Perhaps one day he would. But until then, Chaco would embrace the nurturing, sweet words of his mother's whispered counsel, that: "The Creator has his own timetable, man will just have to endure…"

Carlos was his biggest headache. He had become the eight hundred pound gorilla, graduating from committing acts of fraud to acts of espionage, kidnapping and murder and --even more troubling-- was preparing to step up to the "Big T" …the Treason category.

Upon learning this latter installation to his cousin's nature, Chaco's first reaction was a pressing desire to send over a few people --who specialized in the problem elimination business-- to make this problem go away; all the way to a watery hole in the Everglades. But you're not supposed to treat family that way, even though Carlos had not been as considerate; committed similar acts against his sister's unborn child, as well as a distant cousin of his mother's sister-in-law. Not quite family. But it was still a sin, was still not right.

Chaco's stomach churned each time he allowed himself to recall that unexpected, terrible sight. About to become a corpse; the bullet-riddled, coughing, gurgling remains begged forgiveness from an all-seeing God, while struggling with its last breath.

But he was not always diligent enough to perceive its approach. It sometimes snuck into his unwary consciousness to reawake his recollection in glaring clarity. Still, he did not overly chastise himself for failure to prevent the revenge killing. After all Julio had confessed to supplying Carlos' brother's habit, launching the mounting dependency that eventually fueled his death by overdose. So he understood the motivation. Retaliation was certainly a consideration …eye for an eye and all.

But Chaco never condoned the manner in which the retaliation was concluded. One simply did not toss a man out of a car and shoot him full of holes in front of his mother. Not only cruel, it was barbaric, simply not done. Only rabid animals behaved that way…

The one positive outcome –if one were to look for the positive outcome in a brother's death—was that Carlos became more motivated than ever before to pull totally away from drug trafficking. Inwardly conceding that his own arrogance had been a contributor to Roberto's overdose, he soon left the remnants of La Raza 18 to its own devices and joined his cousin in the world of legitimate corporate conventions. Although for Carlos, legitimacy often involved questionable deviation.

Chaco also knew all about Carlos' "dirty tricks squad" and of the chemical formula he had secretly fed to his sister Sonia, before he fed same to the woman who now was his fiancé. Sick, sick, sick! And now that she had disappeared, he conjectured that the woman was probably also now dead --like the two, innocent babies-- and was appreciably saddened for the harm inflicted by his relative …even though he had otherwise disapproved of her.

Chaco's value system, his beliefs --nurtured by his father's religion-- forbade abortions or any such violent acts against the innocents. His cousin's values saddened him greatly. But again, these hideous acts had been committed without his prior knowledge. He could not change the past, but he could restrain its repeat…

Once he arrived in Miami, the first thing Chaco had planned to do was visit with Rubin to get a "lay of the land", so to speak. But calls went unanswered. Rubin had also mysteriously vanished. He neither answered his cell phone nor house phone. An inquiry to Carlos was returned as a simple, "Don't know, ain't seen 'em."

Chaco began to suspect that Rubin might now reside in a hole similar to the one he had considered for Carlos. He felt sad that such a thing might be his fault, another thing, even though he did not intentionally cause its happening. He made a note to do something about the people probably responsible …perhaps all of them.

However, although Chaco despised many of his cousin's choices, some of the schemes benefited his purposes greatly. One such was the new software program developed for the government. It permitted him to pirate classified transmissions right over the internet. It was no good for data protected by daily changing COMSEC codes. But for the civilian level stuff it was evolutionary. He was only interested in recent discoveries that they had yet to make publicly available. These files were generally classified but unprotected by significant passwords, which scientists truly hate to use. It was a matter of digging up background info on their families, pets and pet names …not a problem.

Now he could snoop images right off NASA data feeds to its scientific community. Infrared, Gamma and X-Ray images of Io expelling huge plumes of gas and dust were captured from ISO --the Infrared Space Observatory—as soon as uploaded. When Hubble discovered two new Cepheids in a galaxy estimated to be one hundred million light years away, Chaco was in on the scoop and fascinated by the display of the distant stars pulsing with varying intensity.

He was also in on discussions by some scientists arguing for or against equations and formulas ventured by the community. He would love to have been able to weigh in with his own arguments. He could poke holes in arrogant assumptions of astronomers who believed they could measure the enormous distances in space from their living rooms. But he needed to remain unheard in the background since pirated software powered his capabilities. As a course, he rationalized that public dollars –relentlessly absconded from taxpayers-- had funded the development. So felt no remorse at Carlos' endeavors in that area. It was not as though anything from NASA could threaten the security of our country …was it?

Now as Chaco entered Carlos' home, he wished to quickly conclude his business and get back to his own. He experienced trepidation, but not at the thought of harm from his cousin. His friend Alexander "The Angel" Martinez topped out at six foot-seven inches, three hundred-ten pounds and –in another life-- could have qualified for the Olympic biathlon team.

Masterful with nearly every weapon in the arsenal, his bullets hit whichever target he aimed. No! Fear of manmade harm was a non-factor. What troubled Chaco was the latest series of images his automated, computerized program had snooped off the NASA transmissions while searching FTP archives. Curious goings on, very curious. Suddenly they all shut down. Something was definitely wrong in the astronomical community, indicating something was wrong in the Cosmos ...and somebody didn't want anybody to know.

Luckily, his people had developed software to automatically download this type scientific archive at first detection. Matching a prioritized algorithm, it data mined file archives from two university sites, also ghosting the download address --washing it through several dead ends-- to erase any records or histories. At first the images thrilled his one good eye ...but even a blind man could sense there was more to this than meets the eye.

Nearly the size of Pluto's moon Charon, maybe bigger, and headed in toward our sun. It would cross the orbits of the inner planets themselves. That constituted a problematic equation for earth cosmologists whose job it was to compute its incoming and outgoing trajectories, configured for gravity-induced deviances, particularly where it crossed earth's orbit. He would work to beat them.

It appeared to be a huge asteroid or comet, but hard to tell so far out —even for the living room astronomers. He and an assistant had begun comparing projected NASA trajectory data with their own estimates when they noticed the anomaly. They waited for additional feed in order to confirm their findings, but nothing further came and the original archives disappeared. Now all that followed were shots of other sectors in the cosmos, seemingly every other sector. Troubling. After much initial fanfare, NASA now seemed uninterested. Moreover, it was how abruptly that interest died which was the most troubling aspect ...right after they published their questionable findings.

He chaffed at his intuitive feelings of dread. Was The Mother trying to tell him something? According to his calculations, this space traveler did not appear to have an outgoing trajectory. What did that mean? Could his initial computations be totally wrong? Way off base? Fervently he wished it so ...the alternatives seemed about as bad as could be..

But deep inside, he believed his unsophisticated skills to be sufficient and his projections not only accurate but further substantiated by the government's actions. Just as they had continually denied the existence of UFOs, they would probably deny any coming calamity of biblical proportions ...wouldn't they?

He dearly hoped this was not the case. But, how else to explain it? He needed to be home in his observatory, not wasting time two thousand miles away. Carlos' mendacious plotting and asinine ranting was grating on his last vestiges of patience. Even though actually oriented more towards his collected possessions than money, his cousin's greed was just another indicator of his vanity and it was his vanity that most bothered Chaco.

His Mexican heritage, his lineage, formed a double-edged sword that cut one way only, one side not quite as sharp as the other. Most who knew him were left truly perplexed by the hypocrisy of his commitment to something he never otherwise showed commitment to.

He left them nearly amazed, awestruck even. After all, he neither hung their art against the walls in his home nor his office –not a Kahlo, a Rivera, not a Baray-- nor did he celebrate their cultural festivals and holidays. On the 5th of May, he'd never fly home to celebrate their people's victory over the French. Cinco de Mayo may as well have been Groundhog Day.

He'd more than likely be golfing on Dia de Los Muertos than joining in celebrations of the continuation of life after death. He'd as likely don the wooden skull masks, named calacas, and dance in honor of his deceased relatives as sew shut his own asshole. Pochos like him, those Chicanos gone totally Gringo, considered themselves too good for their own people. So why the sham playing that undercover Mexican game when he was with the Mexicans? Carlos kept them all perplexed outside his wall of confusion…

Around whitey, he acted white; nary even the odd colloquialism in his speech. Around his people, other than sipping the occasional Corona, he also acted white until somebody said so, then he acted gangster. Not like Tony Montana, screaming and yelling obscenity after threat after obscenity. He didn't do Scarface. More like Don Corleone. He'd make them an offer they couldn't refuse; either they let his goons kick their ass to teach them a valuable lesson in manners or let his goons kill them. No other choices, none.

Egocentrisms fueled by ethnocentrisms were fuel for the fires now seething within him. Any perceived slight to his heritage and though his behavior did not change, his mood could instantly degenerate to rival the basest gangland hoodlums …revenge his main objective.

They called him Chaco the Anasazi, meaning the ancient learned one, and to Carlos, his counsel was just as old. For him, Chaco's continuous message played like the band had left the building leaving behind only a snare drum. "Chee-chit-che-chee-chit-che-chee-chit-che-chee! La Raza ain't no mo'. Eighteens all blown away. Gangbangin' died long time ago, yo' sense has got ta stay!" It was oh so monotonous…

La Raza 18 was truly a long time ago. Carlos knew that. He just needed to act like he knew it. They all needed to lose that name to history as well as the attitudes that had prevailed back then. Even the ones who continued their former life of cocaine and marijuana smuggling now called themselves by another title. But it was ever an uphill fight …to rid the past from his cousin's psyche.

Much more than a haven for pastime, hoodlum gangbangers, Anasazi Enterprises represented an ancient culture whose influence spread throughout the old southwest long before the Spanish or any other European came to enslave its people, plunder its riches and pollute its beauty.

The name Anasazi came to the Pueblo People by way of the Conquistadors, so some attribute its origination to a Navaho name meaning enemy. However, in Chaco's mind, it is less important that some descendants rather be called Ancient Puebloans, instead of Anasazi. He himself proudly preferred the definition meaning "ancient ones" …the "old guys".

The importance was not in the name but in the resurrection of their rich legacy and culture, to reestablish the old ways as taught to him by his mother during their relatively few years together. Besides, the Navajo learned to weave from Ancient Puebloans and even though they may at some time have considered the Anasazi enemies, he believed there obviously must have been respect, probably some hein' and shein' too … them Navajo get around.

Both his parent's cultures stemmed from traditional living in harmonious relationship with natural forces, just as the ancients. These teachings began under his mother's tutelage and were further impressed into his psyche by his father. Unlike her though, his father mixed his Roman Catholic religion in with the legends of ancient Aztec deities from his Mexican heritage. This was nothing new for Catholics who often augmented their modified Jewish traditions with regional worship customs and standards to make them palatable in far flung regions. Although first came Jesus Christ; Chicomecoatl --the Goddess of Corn and Fertility-- and the feathered serpent Quetzalcoatl --God of Civilization and Learning--

were his father's favorite Aztec deities …when he was sober.

But not his, his focus swung in a different direction entirely. No blood-demanding demon gods for him. Though raised to the Catholic faith, he worshipped Earth Mother Goddess Awitelin Tsta --as did his own mother-- choosing to select the deity, not the entire religion. He had no need of religion on the whole, especially the Aztec version with its seventeen hundred gods and goddesses. They both confused and disgusted him with their insistence on human sacrifice. They had a god for every rock and tree. A bit too varied and definitely too bloody for his tastes and too limited in scope.

But it wasn't just these gods. He found the people who worship those types a bit too easily swayed to the dark side. The whole business was asinine. It made no sense this Bloodsport. Sacrificial death for the creation of life? Blood for the gods, who they believed demanded it? That didn't sound like godliness that sounded like deviltry…

"Ten in th' morning an' th' sky is dark. Oh that must mean th' gods want blood, right? Gotta be. Bring me a virgin! We got's ta' crush her skull at th' sacrificial pit! Oh, darn, th' rain has gone? Bring me two more. That didn't work? Bring ten children! Nobody over six! Ain't no god can resist th' blood o' them cute little innocents. I know I can't, he-he. An' throw in a couple still-beating hearts from some footballers, just in case!"

"Think that'll do it? Dagon keeps saying you're reading the signs wrong."

"Hell! Somebody go grab that sonofabitch! We'll roast his ass too! And skewer his bitch while you rip out his eyes. That'll teach them!"

"Okay, but, how can you say 'I told you so', if they're dead?'"

It was all so crazy to Chaco that too often mankind has considered the guy with the better idea as the one yelling: "Kill everybody else!" Often times, once the fervor had died and they took a good look, people found themselves actually in worship, not of a God but of another person. Names like Caesar and Hitler came readily to mind.

In his worship, Chaco the Anasazi, chose a global entity worshipped by his mother's ancestors whose homes inhabited this same area of Western New Mexico. Awitelin Tsta, the Earth Mother of the Zuni people, was the one to claim his focus. The Zuni being descendants of the Anasazi, it all came full circle.

Earth Mother Goddesses such as Awitelin Tsta appealed to him for their benevolence and nurturing nature. Rather than demanding blood from worshippers, Earth Mother Goddesses anguish over the pain caused to and by their children. Both Awitelin Tsta and Chehooit, who is held in place by seven giants to prevent her falling through space, are First Nation Goddesses; Chehooit being worshipped by the Tongvas from California's southern side. But he did not limit his appreciation only to those. Even Gaia, the mythological Earth Goddess of Greek legend, appealed to his nature. Each of these is a giver of all life on earth; each is part of a creation story, creation myth, what have you. The act of creation, fingers in the dirt, growing things, that was his love. So, whichever name be applied, the Earth Mother was Chaco's Goddess.

It was her incarnation as Awitelin Tsta –the Pueblo Zuni Earth Goddess— Chaco believed, who had breathed life back into his tattered, torn form following the accident, after it savagely hurled from his father's ancient pickup truck. Awitelin Tsta had come to his rescue in the western desert wasteland that encompassed the site of his near demise. That had to explain the miracle the wondering doctors kept shaking their heads about for days following his recovery. Perhaps they even caught a glimpse of her bending over to tenderly kiss his forehead and shake his tiny form free of the grasping clutches of Lord Death.

Using her wealth of herbs and plants and their amazingly medicinal properties, he believed her incarnation as Chehooit had saved him from that dastardly AIDS virus lurking in the veins of the lover he had so foolishly romanced. The lover whom it took, leaving him unscathed, though wiser thanks to Chehooit of the Southern California Tongva tribe.

To him, this salvation was a blessing just as much as that time his hurtling form had crashed into the elliptical, fruit of a Yucca Tree, instead of the rocky ledge behind it. The six-celled, fleshy pulp cushioned much of his velocity and saved his little life; much in the way some force of nature had shielded him from the insidious disease that destroyed his lover. In their own language Tongva means "people of the earth" and they worship the goddess Chehooit who protects and nurtures those like Chaco who are absorbed with things pulled from the ground …sometimes, even things two heartbeats from being buried in the ground.

That Mother Earth nurtured him he was certain. He likened the benefit of her embrace to that enjoyed by Antaeus –son of Poseidon and Gaia and rival of Hercules—who remained exceptionally strong as long as he remained in contact with his Mother Earth. Unfortunately for Antaeus, he was killed by Hercules, who lifted the giant out of contact with the ground and then crushed him.

Bad for Antaeus, though perhaps beneficial to him. Its lesson, he felt, to remain grounded, to always remember from whence he came. Besides, Chaco had already concluded that Antaeus --a rapacious giant who saved the skulls of his victims for building materiel-- was not a very nice person anyway and unworthy of remorse.

He remained grounded, thus assured of the Earth Mother's protection; conflict became anathema to his approach to life. He neither planned to live forever nor to build temples from human skulls nor would he battle demigods. So he felt fairly safe in his Mother's arms. He learned the lesson well; to love and appreciate and never misuse the gifts that are given you. He also learned that it was sheer folly to screw with powerful forces ...or anybody named Hercules!

Purely spiritual, his belief system needed no support from organized religion or protestation ceremonies proclaiming fealty to his chosen path. His church lived outside under the cosmos where its wonders revealed. Chaco did not ever intend to follow in the footsteps of his father's people --chasing one golden trail to another, no matter how deadly or to where they lead-- or become a Don Quixote, jousting madly with fictitious monsters in the form of windmills, but he did intend to acquire better understanding of his roots…

CHAPTER SIXTEEN

Chaco reveled in the architectural wonders dating back to the Puebloan Golden Age. His visits to ancient, Anasazi ruins at Chaco Canyon in New Mexico and Betatakin and Keet Seel in Northern Arizona had made him extremely proud. If his people could accomplish all these great deeds oh so many years ago they must have indeed been very great.

Their civilization encompassed sixty thousand square miles across the four corners region of America's southwest, before there was an America. Where Arizona, Colorado, New Mexico and Utah now meet; these sandstone dwellings were possibly their most important cities, the "Great Houses" designed to withstand harsh desert conditions so well that several are still in excellent condition centuries later.

They also were stargazers, charting movements of the stars and constellations, as well as supernovas, and other significant events transpiring in the heavens. The Anasazi were artisans, constructing their great sandstone kivas or meeting rooms to be in alignment with solstices and equinoxes. Unfortunately, they were also people of mystery who just up and disappeared, leaving archeologists who still wonder what happened to an estimated one hundred thousand people. Only left behind was evidence of their accomplishments; evidence they somehow moved one hundred million pounds of sandstone and fifty thousand trees from over sixty miles just to build the Pueblo Bonito site in Chaco Canyon and its five-story apartment houses, dams and canals.

There was a lesson to be gleaned from the ancient Puebloan message. One day they were at the pinnacle, the next they were non-existent. Perhaps their organization, their civilization, had overtaxed the natural resources. Perhaps they had become overconfident and failed to prepare for some natural calamity. It seemed obvious to him that they had overdone something. He determined that such would not become a similar fate for his organization.

It was he who had insisted they let the old gangland ways die; he who argued the fact that all, having made their money, were wealthy enough to try a saner form of enterprise …those who were left. Special emphasis he placed on the reduced numbers of their inner core. Emilio was now dead. Killed years before during a drive-by shooting that his crippled body was not quick enough to duck or outrace. Chuey Garcia was in prison for the rest of his life. Even Uncle Leonardo had passed on …though his passing came due to natural causes.

These all were in themselves signals; time to leave the drugs and the guns to the other twenty-five thousand gangs across America; leave it to them and their seven hundred thousand members who wanted to live that life. No more gangbanging for him. He wanted, more than that, he demanded legitimacy in a world that suddenly seemed rapidly degenerating.

It had happened soon after Noriega's capture by U.S. forces during Operation Just Cause. Even a blind man could see the handwriting. Their closest associate in Central America, El General had provided them safe haven in which to bring cocaine out of Columbia and stockpile it not only until a safe window opened, but when market demand caused prices to soar appropriately.

From Panama, shipments sailed or flew on to Mexico and from there by air to desert landing strips in California or Arizona or by boat up the coast to Oxnard. But with Noriega himself in jail, the serpents took permanent control of this Garden of Eden. One rapacious drug lord named Pablo Avaldos took even more than that when he killed the Scubaman.

It seemed the Colombian was sensitive to certain forms of humor, not the least of which involved anything related to his sense of taste. Barely five-foot-three inches in height; he had a temper even shorter. A simple joke, a perceived slight and things could become very bad, very quickly. Scubaman's faux pas was to openly laugh at the shape of his swimming pool, observing that it resembled a square cook pot.

From there, his sense of humor --exacerbated by a few snorts of white powder—spun even further out of control, oblivious to sharp elbow nudges from his companion. On a hilarious roll, Scubaman pointedly described how Pablo should fill the pool pot with cocaine, fire up the pool heaters and get the whole neighborhood high. He then proceeded to sneeze on his host after taking too large a snort. He never got the chance to apologize…

Neither did Carlos get an apology from the rabid beast who had cold-bloodedly murdered one of his people. He had grown to like Scubaman and had taken great pains to weed him off the heavy use of narcotics, turning him into a first rate bag man.

He had even given Connie to him, partly as a reward for services rendered, partly as punishment for Connie. She was getting a bit too big for her britches in his eyes; asking to leave his employ; even sleeping with Julio Mendes from the Hill Street Gang.

Connie had been sent to negotiate a deal with the northern gang leader and ended up in his bed. She said it was Julio's requirement for making the deal. His words she relayed matter-of-factly as: "We'll discuss it in th' morning…"

It was the only reason Carlos allowed her to live. Truth was, he expected Mendes to try and get with her. He just didn't expect her to let him. Disloyalty was not an attribute he found desirable in employees, especially those who he believed owed him their very lives. She may have considered it an act of sacrifice, but since she had made the decision without being so ordered, he had decided to teach her not to try and fly alone.

It was not enough to simply remind her that without his aid she'd become just another Icarus --plunging to her death from the heat of the sun-- or of the difficulties her sickly, old mother might experience if she lost the home he had donated them. He felt the need to demonstrate his superiority. Lord of the Dames, so to speak or, in her case, Lord of the Damned. Then he killed two birds with one stone by giving her to Scubaman, feeling as wise as Solomon.

She was good for The Scuba --as she called him-- he came out of his malaise and back into productive society, no longer just the neighborhood junkie. Now he had a woman to work for, to impress; a woman who would not accept his slovenly self. More than that, travel is less tedious for a couple and there is less chance of slipups.

Singles on the road tend to mingle, sometimes not so wisely. One minute you're picking up a stray to lay, the next you get a bit tipsy and start bragging your business to impress. Suddenly you're shot as a rival or arrested as a felon. Then they come for your boss. For a while the ploy worked better than Carlos had anticipated.

But he had never intended she witness Scubaman's head being blown off by the forty-four-magnum pistol Avaldos had suddenly produced and fired point blank. It was only her dispassionate cool that kept the megalomaniac from popping one into her as well. Scarcely had the tremendous report finished ringing in her ears before she had casually looked down upon blood spatters newly adorning the front of her cream-colored blouse and then calmly rose from her seat beside the sprawled corpse –lying nearly headless across the veranda, where the force hurled it—and asked, "Perdóneme senior, is there someplace I can wash up?"

She brought the news back to Carlos the same way, calm and objective, describing with vivid detail, even relating the sweet smell of coffee plants and the coolness under the veranda out of the warm sun. Having never visited the rancho outside Medellin, he envisioned the lush bounty of the landscape on the ten thousand acre spread and the gentleness of the local peoples who tended it for Avaldos. She described in detail the huge size and awesome picturesque beauty of the villa with its many cars and ATVs and horses all guarded by purposeful, armed men keeping watch.

There were vividly-colored parrots –eagerly accepting proffered crackers-- there was the large, blue pool --square shaped, with a nook that resembled a handle—that both she and the Scuba had found so intriguing, except he unfortunately had articulated his fascination. And then she described the thunderous blast that consumed Scubaman as if he were just another of the many useless ornamentations sited around the lavish estate.

Then and there, Carlos decided never would he trust such a callous, visceral monster. You don't just blow up and shoot important guests. That was very bad form. He came very near to sending a few of his Eighteens down to pay the man a visit, but decided against an action sure to incite a war. So he only dealt with Avaldos through Noriega, though festering with the desire to retaliate for Avaldos' affront. Noriega sometimes got a bit greedy about currency exchanges, but he was much more tolerant than the mercurial Avaldos. Noriega even assigned members from the National Department of Investigations --also known as Departamento Nacional de Investigaciones or DENI-- to escort their couriers to and from Panama City Banks. So the benefit outweighed the added cost …until Manuel was taken away.

Panama had become a center for drug money laundering and a transit point for drug trafficking to the United States and Europe. It all worked out so well until the crooks in Washington, D.C. decided that they could no longer put up with their crook in Panama and sent down their troops to do battle with his.

So now, their drug-trafficking days were behind them. They gave it over to others still willing to chance incarceration by increasingly vigilant international anti-crime organizations or death from increasingly competitive criminal partners. Then they saluted their decision as more and more of their former compatriots and rivals fell to one group or the other. They still eschewed attendance at any memorials for those who paid the ultimate penalty. Although in one case --before they were totally through with the business-- they helped one competitor pay that penalty. Carlos decided to deal one last hand …and he dealt out aces and eights.

It was simple revenge and happened soon after Scubaman's demise. Morano had made it his goal to become good friends with Pablo Avaldos' cousin Geraldo, a fact made simpler because Carlos had once met Geraldo at the Presidential Palace in Panama City and already knew much about the man, his toys, his Andean villa and especially his sexual proclivities. The younger the girls, the better he liked them and the further north they originated, even better. Noriega himself had provided the details, making him aware of that tidbit.

Geraldo and Pablo were like brothers, even shared baths as kids. Maybe he could use Geraldo to get close enough to hit Pablo. He wanted Avaldos, but not if it required an army. Unfortunately, Pablo was surrounded by layered security wherever he traveled and Geraldo had no desire to take over control from his cousin. His aspirations centered on fast things: fast cars, fast boats, fast planes and beautiful females who were also fast. Carlos tried to remain patient, but he had never been a patient man. He decided to settle for second best.

Everyone who knew him knew his less than aspiring ambitions. He was Good Time Charlie. He kept a bodyguard around more to keep away irate husbands and fathers than anything else. He provided liaison services for his cousin, nothing more, not handling money or product. If he made a few bucks on the side of a deal, a handler's fee, that was fine and to be expected. They had that agreement as long as it didn't cut too deep into the overall deal. Even then, they'd be more likely to curse each other out, then arm wrestle to determine the ultimate winner.

He just would not get greedy. Carlos couldn't find a way. These guys actually loved each other. They'd call up just to say hello and talk about nonsense things that schoolboys do. They worried over each other. It was a bit sickening, much too syrupy for Carlos tastes. They actually made each other happy. So he'd make them unhappy…

It was a variation of the ancient tale of Samson and Delilah. He could never defeat Samson head on, but Delilah could strike his weakness. DENI made the proposition of hitting him too risky in Panama. Besides, it showed poor taste to embarrass one's host. So Plan B needed to use his own tools to trip him, without tipping off the cartel and starting that war.

One can't retaliate if one doesn't know from where your enemy came … at least so went his theory.

He lived halfway up a hilly slope in Bogotá, less than a mile away from the entrance to the Universidad de Los Andes campus, even less to some of its dorms. In fact, from the Master Suite of his expansive villa he could watch University co-eds sunning themselves on the lawns and balconies of campus dorms. This front side view rated high up his list of premium sites. Higher even than that of majestic Andes Mountain peaks rising high into the heavens at his rear.

He had sharp eyes that missed little and with a pair of high-powered binoculars voyeurism achieved even greater heights. Dental floss bikinis that barely covered taught, shapely figures always signaled promising prospects. Any waving a bright smile towards his peeping Tom-self signaled the dinner bell, followed shortly by him heading to school …for takeout.

Eventually, dozens of those same co-eds wound up enjoying that view on a more personal basis with this raven-haired, dark-eyed, youthful, forty-something they found so handsome and intriguing. It did not hurt that he was also rich, well-connected and owned a downtown nightclub.

Having cousin kill cousin would have been such a rewarding feat. But even were he to instigate sufficient animosity he doubted Geraldo had the huevos to kill Pablo. Ideally they would square off with dueling pistols at forty paces and fire simultaneously. End of both. But such was unlikely. If sufficiently threatened, Pablo would probably just kill Geraldo and justify the loss as a needed condition, none the wiser. "Love you Cuz, but you gotta go!"

If Pablo killed Geraldo for the wrong reason, now that would be sweet. Revenge demands the revenged one enjoy some measure of pain extracted from the one whom the revenge is extracted. So there would be no sweet revenge unless Pablo knew that someone else had set him up to do the deed or done the deed themselves. Carlos had just that someone else…

The rising sun broke across the tops of snow-covered peaks and streamed down into wide windows on the eastern face of Geraldo's bedroom. He was the consummate collector as was reflected in the cornucopia of artifacts, hanging paintings and Louis XVI furniture pieces. A bit chilly this early in the year, his latest collection still languished seductively beneath luxurious thick-piled covers on the massive oak-wood bed. Her almond eyes blinked lazily to clear sleep still lingering within them.

"Ah Chiquita, you finally back wit' us!" He sat in a filigreed armchair whose carvings matched those of the bed's posts and headboard. She sat up at his greeting, the lavender percale top sheet falling away to expose one of her shapely breasts –its dark rosette around an alert nipple capturing hungry eyes-- immediately prompting desires to once again devour their delectable sweetness. His indigo robe –loosely tied around the waist—slid open to display dark hairs contrasted by lightly tanned skin, above and below the belted middle.

"Looks like somebody missed me!" Her musical voice titillated. "Or are you just happy to see me again?"

Geraldo glanced down to where his erection had parted the robe, aiming its fullness in her direction. "Yeah, I guess you right about that!"

He stood and paused for a moment, turning towards the sun peeking its warmth in through the plate glass, giving her time to take him all in. In another moment he planned to allow her silken thighs to do the same. But first the anticipation wrought by her view of his hard manhood --commanding and at right angles to the trim waist and taut abdominals – to stimulate her pre-copulative juices to flow. Next he strode over to the wide, patio doors facing south, towards the campus. His gaze looked across the wrought-iron table and chairs on the patio to the buildings further down the hillside. Red brick and white sandstone surrounded by brilliant greens of springtime foliage looked back up at him. Sliding closed the sheer, shoji screens; he cut off the outside view with white panels accented with Japanese kanji-characters laid in mauve-colored brush strokes forming delicate flowers. He laughed, "Don't want to entertain any voyeurs…"

But when he looked back, she was already out of the bed. Wrapping a matching robe around her shoulders, though shorter than his and more petite, she headed into the bathroom, drawing its double-doors behind her while casually tossing back a suggestion, "I'll need a minute to freshen up a bit. You might want to join me …after a while."

Now it was his turn to experience anticipation, as well as a bit of frustration. The ache in his groin had become a raging giant, which possessed him. He did not think he could wait much longer. But protocol demanded he do just that. He would know the time. If not, she would call. He knew she could not long deny herself a repeat of the previous evening's bliss. In his ears recalled the timbre of her soft moans; his back relived the clutching and clawing of sharp nails that nearly broke the skin; and his lower half chafed longingly to recreate the ardor of her passion that spurred the long legs to lock in a vise around him, urging him deeper into such suppliant succulence that now all he could envision was a return to their warmth.

He waited ten minutes that seemed to him like ten hours, but still no beckoning call issued from behind the frosted-glass bathroom doors. These also sported mauve kanji characters. However, unlike those on the patio doors spelling "Flowers and Lilies" and "Birds and Bees", these simply spelled out "Bathroom".

He could not see inside, but his active mind envisioned her nakedness luxuriating in the wide tub filled with bubbles and warm water up to the tops of her breasts. Tiny splotches left by soapy splashes on the marble surround called for him to come forth and free their fellows --still trapped within the tub's confines—to join them in the manner his passion had fulfilled on so many occasions ...with so many young vixens.

Fifteen minutes. He was growing exceedingly impatient. She was drawing this game out much longer than he anticipated. He would endure no more. Grasping the handles, he flung both doors inward, away from their obstructing what he desired to see ...and do. But there was no one in the room; the tub was filled with suds, but no female. He was growing tired of this game.

The adjacent door to the outside hallway was closed. So at first, he stalked around to his left. The shower's stream surged at full force. But again, no woman-shape evidenced. He was simultaneously perplexed and enraged. "Where was she?"

"Connie!" his snarl issued. "Bitch! Where th' fuck you go?" No answer. He turned to head back inside the bedroom. He'd grab his clothes, before continuing the search. But he didn't make it that far. His eyes widened at the scene before them. There she stood; fully dressed. On her feet, the four-inch black pumps, trimmed with the gemstones he had found so alluring the previous evening. Unfortunately, the alluring part had lost its luster. Held in her right fist was the hilt of a menacing, looking semiautomatic pistol.

Death staring full in his face from what looked to be nine-millimeters of cannon; he now reconsidered what appeared to have been poorly chosen words. If he could he would swallow them all, "bitch" included, if she let him. But somehow he doubted she would.

Memory playback recalled the moment those pumps stepped casually out of her taxi in front of a restaurant near the college, where he had decided to eat a small meal before finding a suitable playmate for the night's entertainment. The decision was instantly made, as a plaintive urging stirred in his groin, deciding: "This one would suffice nicely". She had taken barely three steps past him, before the long fingers of his right hand had wrapped their manicured nails lightly around her left wrist.

"Perdóneme, senorita. Mi yamo es Geraldo. Tu' sabe Espanol?" She appeared startled at first. But then relaxed somewhat –her eyes taking in his handsome smile and seeming innocence.

"Uh, poco, pocito." She stammered, "Just a little. Que es? Cómo puedo ayúdele? How can I help you senor?" She turned to face him as he rose, nearly matching his height in her heels.

"Forgive my intrusion, but are you a professor at el Universidad? I am supposed to meet my cousin's professor here to discuss his poor grades and how to help, how you say? Motivate him to do better? I never meet her. Is she you?" He quickly dispensed with the Spanish to ease her transition, but purposely employed simplistic diction and style to appear innocent and genuinely confused.

"Ha, ha! No I'm not," she giggled.

"Ahhh, Americano," his thoughts remained within. This little plan might work out well after all. He loved the taste of all women, but was especially fond of those from the northern hemisphere and most especially, the Americans.

Europeans were good, Canadians alright. But the American females who came south without their husbands, came with mainly one thing on their mind. Adventure. He also knew that for many, their primary concern was that they might somehow insult a member of the host nation, adding to the stereotypical "ugly American" image. Many of them would rather bend over backwards with kindness and consideration before committing such offense. He had learned to capitalize on their phobia.

It took all of twenty minutes after she had first explained that she was visiting friends in the school who were unfortunately busy preparing for finals and could not devote much time for a few days. So she was left up to her own devices until then. "Well, I would be most pleased if I could show you about our fair city. Unless, such an offer is, how you say? Offense? Offensive? I no want make you thin…"

"Oh no! It's not that I would be offended. I mean, it's not like I find you offensive. I just…"

"Ets sokay." He had her. Now to lay it on a little thicker. He kept at the broken English. "I unnerstan'. I hold you up too long. I…"

"No, no! I was just going to take a bike trip around the city. You know, along the Ciclo-Ruta, the bike paths. Along the Bogotá River, maybe stop at the shops along Avenida Caracas and Calle 80. My friends are gonna take me sightseeing on the TransMilenio buses later this week, but I don't want to just sit around 'til then. You know?"

She sounded hopeful. Hoping he would not get offended at her refusal. She became the putty out of which he would carve his next conquest. "Si! I know what you say. Why not we ride together? I know a couple great Ciclovias. Those are cycling streets. No car allowed and places to stop for Ajiaco and coconut rice."

"Ajiaco? That's the chicken soup, right?"

"Si! Chicken with potatoes, flavored with guasca and cream and capers. Bogotá Café over on Avenida Ciudad de Quito, near the river, makes the best and excellent empanadas, too!"

She laughed, "What, no roasted ants?"

"Si! No! No ants. Too salty, I never liked them!"

"Okay!" She laughed again, seemingly relieved that she would not offend. "I'm sold. Let's go!"

"We go tomorrow, okay? I don't think you like much riding in those shoes, might slip on pedals or something. Please join me for lunch. I already ordered wine." He did not need to add that her designer dress would not have fared well on a bicycle either.

Hesitantly, she sat in the offered chair. Soft winds wafted sweet smells from inside through the restaurant's open door to its outside diners. Not even the hustle of cars and buses passing in a steady stream compromised the beauty and splendor of this tree-lined setting backed by a wondrous view of the magnificent Andes Mountains, radiant with golden light from the westerning sun.

They had consumed only a small meal for this time of day. She followed his lead and ordered Morcilla cocida, a blood sausage, served over white rice with fried plantains. The mid-day meal usually fulfills the largest role for Columbians, but neither of them felt the need. Her North American norms remanded the larger role to the evening meal and he was obliging, though they had put away two full carafes of a superb, white lambrusco. Through the entire meal their conversation shifted through politics to sports and beyond. They solved quite a few of the world's problems along their way. His English also improved along that way…

By the time they resolved that South American fútbol beat out North American football for popularity, the sun had set, going on to fulfill its duties to citizens and denizens in other parts of this world. The pale moon, full and all knowing, rose halfway up to join bright stars hung across the endless tapestry of the black sky to their northeast. Night birds called their cheerful messages to mates and issued challenge to rivals. "Over here girlfriend, got a good time for ya. Don't come over here, less you want a whuppin' dudes!"

A few more words and she sat down beside him in the molded right seat of a bright yellow, quarter-million dollar Lamborghini, listening to the twelve cylinder engine's roar over the rushing wind sounds coming through the open targa roof. The Diablo's velocity eagerly chewed through the sparse traffic as its owner seemed in urgent desire to reach his home. He sensed that her agreement to a nightcap was all it took and moved like a lightning strike. She still felt a little dizzy from the speed with which he had guided her into the passenger side of the powerful vehicle that had arrived beside their roadside table as if by magic.

But those were mere memories now, replaced with the terror that comes with the realization one is coming to an abrupt end of his existence. Formerly bright and vibrant, the dead look now occupying those lovely eyes told all. His doom was upon him. A single word escaped clenched teeth. "Why?"

He never heard the reply. Neither did anyone else. He had given his housekeeper that day to attend her grandson's christening. The bodyguard's body lay in eternal slumber in the kitchen nook where she found him snacking on his last supper. There was no one to bear witness.

It ended quickly. Blood pumped through the hole in his left temple, matching an identical one where his right eye had once lived. His lifeless body slumped to the pine and cherry hardwoods decoratively interlaid in the bedroom floor. His right-hand fingers froze clutching at only air, this time seeking to grasp the handle of a Glock semi-automatic pistol stashed behind a chair near the bathroom door. The dive a bit too short …and much too slow.

"Wanna take a message?" she whispered, stashing the silenced pistol back into her pocketbook. "You tell Scubaman hello and that you're sorry that your sorry-assed cousin blew his head off. Oh yeah, and for your own edification, soccer sucks!"

Then she stepped away and walked to the door where a yellow taxi had pulled up beside the Diablo. Two hours later she lounged back in the comfortable seat of a Boeing 767 headed for Miami. There she would leave Avianca Airlines and anything else associated with Colombia. This was her last mission for Carlos Morano. He had promised and she truly hoped it the last time she would be involved with anything seedy, dirty or illegal. She was very glad that the housekeeper had left early that morning. No need to kill someone who did not even get a glimpse of her face. She also hoped she had caused Avaldos to feel a little of the anguish he had caused her. Not quite retribution, but a little payback. All she needed now was for Carlos to keep his promise …this time.

Swarthy images clouded her vision. A hated mustache, that always smelled heavy with garlic, guarded thick lips; their rough touch even less appreciated. Its jet black color perfectly matched the unruly coif dominating his regal head; but it was the dark, thick hair above his nose –creating a unibrow effect—that especially reviled her senses. It was obvious to her that the man considered this a mark of beauty, the way he ritually exercised a practiced arching of first right, then left brow in a poor man's mimicry of Groucho Marx. She wondered if such an act passed for talent in Iraq.

However, even all those negatives did not top her pet peeve concerning this pompous ass. That title she awarded to the love affair he obviously had with cologne. She couldn't tell which brand or even the aroma, but his liberal use could gag a painted horse or so she believed. Regardless, it definitely did a number on her own olfactory processes.

She knew he wanted her like a thirsty man wants to drink and while the thought in itself gave satisfaction, confirmation that she still had the power to render powerful men helpless, she had no intention of spending even one more moment in an intimate setting with this miscreant who believed modern day women deserving of punishment for crimes committed by all women throughout antiquity. She would never take another beating at his hands or any others. Life is too short.

She had said as much to Carlos, flat out refusing his orders. This one last trip and that was it. He should never make promises beyond his power to keep. "You don't own me!" Determination had flowed across the wires linking that call. She sincerely hoped her resolve would hold out. But his veiled suggestion that life could get much shorter didn't sound too promising…

CHAPTER SEVENTEEN

They sat in the den across from each other, but for a while each was left to his own devices. Neither spoke one word to the other. Instead, both just stared out at the scenery. Yesterday's brilliant blue skies were now gray and forbidding. Soon the tropical storm would land somewhere near. But neither thought much about that approaching fury. Only the conflict between them was paramount.

"Where you been Mijo? I been waiting for you." His words were soft, almost feathery, so delicate was their touch on his cousin's ears. The reply came back just as soft…

"You know, I never ever slept wit' her. Everybody thought so. But I never did." Chaco was very surprised, given Carlos rep as a ladies' man. In fact he would have bet the farm that Tina had enchanted him the same way Xochiquetzal, the Goddess of Beauty, enchanted and seduced the Cloud Serpent, Mixcoatl, the God of War, and produced Quetzalcoatl, the Feathered Serpent. Apparently, Tina had limited her involvement with him to the enchantment aspect. For the seduction component she had another in mind …she obviously did not understand that part about War.

"She been married all this time." Carlos hooded eyes never met those of his cousin's. Instead, they held to a spot on the floor near Chaco's feet. "We talking a ton o' years an' I ain't never hit it. At first, after she lost her kid and got her divorce, I thought we'd get together. But no dice. She wouldn't even drive down the street in my car. So that was that. Then I meet her again at a fund raiser for some fake wanna be closet democrat and she look jus' as good, even better than when I last seen her. I'm talking twenty-three, twenty-fo' years. She gorgeous. Can't believe she ain't let herself go. But nope. No implants, no botox, just a little hair coloring an' not a lotta makeup, either. Girl don't even got a wrinkle you kin see. My black beauty had returned."

He paused while his housekeeper-slash-cook brought in a pitcher of chilled orange juice and glasses on a tray. She smiled politely then set it on the cocktail table that divided the space between the two men seated comfortably on matching, white leather couches.

"I waited a year befo' I even called her. Little intimidated. She work fo' th' government, so wasn't no big deal to ask fo' her number. I jus' decided not to rush 'n use it. We started meetin' a few places fo' lunch, the occasional dinner. Then we started goin' round ta different events, here 'n there. Jus' fun stuff, ya know. I wasn't tryin' ta git serious. In fact her girlfriend was always wit' us. Took years ta git up the nerve an' I finally asked if she'd marry me. She left skid marks. That was the last time she'd even answer the phone for about three-fo' weeks."

Now his eyes burned brightly. Staring straight through Chaco as if fixed on the wall directly behind his head. So fierce was the stare that Chaco tempted to turn and look himself to see whatever was there. But he resisted. In his memory he recalled the picture hanging there, a man and woman sitting on a bench beside a sloped roof house under a full moon. An angelic figure hovered above the couple. Below the print, a small caption pronounced it "The Lovers" by Marc Chagall. Chaco recalled when Carlos had first introduced the painting to him a few months before. Now it seemed the message had lost its appeal.

"When she finally called me up and agreed to be my wife, I couldn't believe it. I got rid o' my other friends. Couple huneys who all about nuthin' cept flash 'n cash and it was jus' gonna be us from then on. I know I kin do it! Be exclusive.

"Remember that Ho, err, girl you use ta live wit' back in Cali? Remember how she always played th' lottery, always trying ta get lucky? But she didn't get lucky. She got AIDS, then got dead. That's how it feels to me now. I thought I got lucky. But I didn't. Then this…" his words ceased. There was no intention of further explanation. Chaco could sense he would get no more out of his cousin …voluntarily.

"You know she is Catholic Mijo. Her faith has kept her strong all these years. That's why she kept going back to visit her husband. She might have divorced him, but she never really left him." Chaco's words flowed from some unknown corner of his ken. He seemed instinctively to have finally figured out the mysterious woman's purpose. She had married for life. Even if she remarried, she would never truly be free of the first time.

"Lost th' hookup. She cheated me …an' lost it. My temper. Guess like they say, miscarriage kin make women crazy."

"Not miscarriage! Murder!" The words screamed inside Chaco. But stayed unvoiced, never revealed to the man before him transitioning through alternative realities. Sometimes, so many times lately, Carlos' meanderings gave him stomach gas on an epic scale! He can't take much more of this. That's what love does, but Carlos pushing dangerous buttons!

"You should have never stepped in between them Mijo!"

His last words hit Carlos like a thunderclap. Instantly he understood that Chaco had known the truth of his past transgressions. He had suspected Chaco might have acquired knowledge of the abortion drugs forced on his sister, but now it was apparent that he also knew all about Tina's misfortune, as well. "I-I, ah, I-I didn't…"

"No more lies Carlos." For once, Chaco did not employ the diminutive as was his norm when addressing his closest family member. "Tell me about the device."

"Rubin, right?" Days spent inside left his complexion only lightly tanned, now his face flushed with the blood pumping. Now he faced his mentor, realization flooding in to declare that the secret was known. "It's ah, ah, it's ah question mark. I got a few guys, they workin' it. Tryin' ta figure it out. They gotta move slow, cause it's kinda …dangerous. We ain't even made th' trade yet. Tryin' ta work that out too."

He thought he was alone. Outside the villa a dark shadow fell across the right rear corner of the building near a large palm which had nearly christened the intruder at its base with a heavy coconut it had just dropped. The thudding sound from the heavy fruit bounding across the wet grass sent a shiver through him. That thing had come very close to braining him. He gave a glance above to ascertain if any other palm nuts were about to depart home station. But most of the husks swaying high above remained in shadow. He decided that if they did fall he would probably be the last to know …what he did know, he wasn't quite alone.

O'Rourke had come into the back yard by way of the adjoining golf course. He had not rushed in, but remained crouched in the shadows studying the target for almost ten minutes, looking for any untoward movement or surveillance post. It was an almost impossible task but one that he knew he must at least attempt. Otherwise, life might soon begin running out of him before he could even perceive the attack. The coconut only added emphasis to this fact…

Windows and doors in the estate house were all closed and most shuttered, though only partially. Light beams playing through gave subdued illumination to the white exterior walls. Water in the pool blew about with reckless abandon, surging and frothing in tune with the wind's edicts, to splash out onto the cement deck. He studied the layout for any obvious sensor devices, admitting to himself the futility of such, but searched anyway.

Spying nothing untoward, through the swirling rain he splashed, crossing the deck's periphery towards the rightmost corner of the right side set of twin, patio doors. He figured that any inside activity might be more easily observed here based upon Valerie's description of the man's habits.

"Carlos probably gonna make me work anyway," she had informed. "Sometimes he makes me soooo mad!"

O'Rourke did not respond to her comment, almost as if he wasn't listening when the reality, his Hoover sucked in each word, every expression. In his former line of work, one lived or died based on such.

The fighter pilot in him had survived on details and observations. Operational skills are great, but don't do nearly as much if you ain't paying attention and seeing what needs to be. Both Wild Bill Hickok and Jesse James were skilled pistol men back in the day, but both died from being murdered, a single fatal gunshot in the back of the head. Obviously, somewhere in the process, each suffered a fail to his observational skill set …only takes once.

He totally focused, even to the radio DJ's warblings on this subject and that. Things were beginning to trend his way. No time to blow it by missing something pertinent or letting tongue fly. Tongue in cheek? Uh uh! Keep tongue in mouth and keep mouth shut!

He played dummy. Just continued softly massaging her scalp and treating her to light caresses about the ear, neck and bare shoulders. He did not need to say anything. She was doing fine by herself, without his urging. He mentally jotted down her words and kept up his pace. Tiny tremors reverberating up through her flesh revealed the technique was working fine.

"Mmmm," she moaned in a soft contralto that caused a reaction in him also. "D-don't get me wrong. Carlos is all right, JP. I mean, every man has his own little quirks. But be that as it may, as a boss he's pretty good. He don't verbally degrade you in public, he pays pretty good and he don't ever try to push up on the help or anything like that."

"You're saying he doesn't try to sample the staff? Is that what you're saying?" He decided that he had to at least offer minimal response.

"Exactly! I mean he's got a few really strange quirks. But what man hasn't? Besides, he's extremely rich an' he don't try 'n take advantage of it! If he did, he'd be yesterday!" She seemed to be getting defensive, as if determined to convince him that no hanky-panky had taken place. He did not know why she felt the need. But, to him it was obvious that she considered the idea of being sexually harassed by the boss to be a definite no-no. She came off totally unlike some of the more publicly prominent names on the social climbing ladder who tended to suborn criticism until after they had achieved whatever successes were available, then cried foul.

"Okay. No advantage. I understand," fingers twirling a lock of her short hair.

"Exactly! Girls are more than just a vagina with tits."

"Yeah, I know. They got legs too."

"Ooooh, take that back you clown!" She fell in with his jovial banter, thoroughly enjoying the attention he paid to the parts of her situated away from noted erogenous zones. Even with the off-colored jokes, he actually looked into her eyes as he talked. Too many men had wasted too much of their time grabbing her breasts, pinching her nipples and pawing areas around her vulva: "Kiss, kiss. Lick, lick. You wet? Good. Let's fuck!"

Those men she sent home still holding their hard, unfulfilled erections, cursing her name. In her mind, the uninformed need not apply. But this guy seemed in a hurry to go nowhere. He had been meandering about her head and shoulders for the better part of thirty minutes now while they talked. She felt very at ease with him. Even without her boss' suggestion that she should "entertain" him; she could safely say that nothing would have changed. But she could not let his comment go unchallenged. Reaching out, she pinched his nipple, "I said take that back!"

"Wow!" he followed, I guess that's good. If you say it's good!"

"It's good!" she smirked, continuing their banter and letting go her hold. He was as much a smart ass as she could be and she really enjoyed that part of his wit. She especially enjoyed inflicting that bit of pain, even more its result…

"Then I agree!" he stated more seriously. "I mean I'm not a woman. So I don't always know what women like."

"Well, we definitely don't like a boss coming onto us!" Realizing he was not getting her point, she had bristled, slightly.

"Uh, sorry, I didn't mean…"

"Just as long as the guys learn to read women's English better. No means no!" She interrupted. Now he was aware that he had pushed a button that he had not intended. But it was too late for him to tuck his tail. Besides, he did not play "Pussy" to anyone. To him it was just like wrestling on the mat. Attack! Attack! Attack!

"So what does 'Maybe' mean? Or how about, 'Oh but we just met'? All the while she's moaning and they're going at th' heavy petting, her tongue halfway down his throat, his fingers stuck deep in her crotch." This time he did not let her interrupt, continuing his spiel before she could block his attack and render it useless with one of her own. "Yeah, I know, women don't want to hear it, but men are being led around by their dicks and afraid to use them for anything other than an occasional pee. A friend of mine thinks it's part of the general 'Wussification of America' and I totally agree."

Now he was on his soapbox and had a head of steam. "Child porn, vicious rapes and the like are always bad news. Animal behavior is almost always unacceptable, too! But come on now, they tryin' ta make a Federal offense outta regular hein' an' shein' games played between willing guys 'n gals. It's like when Richard Pryor typified America as a land where it's okay to talk about killing, but not okay to speak about screwing. Go figure. Hell, guys don't know that the girl don't want him unless she tell him so! But now a days it seems she don't never tell him except through her lawyer or the cops or the EEO or somebody. An' what about the reverse? Let's face it; a whole lot of guys receive unwanted attention from women that they got ta put down."

"Is it my turn yet?" She interjected, letting him know that he could now get off his soapbox and allow her equal time.

"No. But you gonna take it anyway." His fingers continued to caress her. Now they toyed with an ear lobe.

"Ha!" she answered in agreement, before proceeding. "First, Richard didn't exactly say screwing, but I'll let you go on that. Yeah, I'm young, but I ain't that young. Second, I agree that criminalizing those types of interactions is wrong. But what about the greasy, sloppy, nasty ol' 'won't take no for an answer' kind of trash?"

"Him you have my permission to kill, anyway you want to. My preferred method involves sharp knives in the manner of Lorena Bobbitt, followed by eight to ten shots to the back of the head."

"Damn, you really mean to kill the guy!"

"It'll look like the worst case o' suicide anyone ever saw," he joked. But she could hardly tell if he was joking in seriousness or in jest. All he knew was that same joke woulda brought out the worst of Sylvia and turned on her lecture app. Consequence? That's why he no longer told those type jokes around Sylvia!

"So we agree then?"

"I agree that fat, sloppy, lazy, greasy, nasty; neck bone sucking perverts don't deserve mercy. But I also submit that criminalizing normal, everyday ordinary boyin' and girlin' is a criminal act in itself.

"Still gonna maintain status quo, huh?" she remarked, seeing that his mind was firmly entrenched on that score. "Well anyway, I better get my beauty rest. So are we still on for tomorrow or what? There might be a storm…"

"You scared of a little rain?"

"Actually, I hope it does. Then there won't be no pool party and I won't have to show up in my bikini and serve drinks 'n stuff."

"Oh! So you are the eye candy!" It was a statement, not a question as his elbow gently nudged in her ribs as payback for her earlier, "My boss don't take advantage," declarations.

"Just had to go there didn't you?" Her responding jab was both physical and somewhat painful.

"Only kidding." he winced noticeably, seeking whatever consolation she might deign give. Instead he was rewarded with another shot to the ribs. "Ow!"

"That's for trying ta get on my good side!"

"Baby, when I get on your good side, you'll swear to God it's never been that good!"

"Ooooh! You so bad!" She rewarded him this time with a generous kiss that sent shivers rushing, her tongue darting in to intertwine with his own.

"So if it blows up a gale, you don't have to work?"

"Nope. Carlos will probably just set up in the patio room and entertain in there. He won't get more'n a few diehards if it's bad, so won't need much help..."

Barcelona's soccer team was locked in a zero to zero tie with Madrid's team. He could not tell whether this was a replay of a past game or current. It really did not matter to him. He understood soccer about as well as he understood hockey, meaning he had no clue other than the observation that both proceeded back and forth with lots of defense and little scoring. Still, both drew crowds of rabid fans. Obviously, somebody appreciated their action.

From his cursory scrutiny he knew that the guys in yellow jerseys and black shorts seemed to be controlling much of the offensive play while the guys wearing red tops and black shorts kept making sufficient defensive plays to keep the ball from finding their net. He could understand how some people considered this game exciting, but it was not for him. Too much running back and forth and long kicks out of bounds or back to the other team --aka, boring-- nothing like freestyle wrestling or the NFL.

Headers and wheel kicks added excitement, but his experience indicated that he could get up from his seat, go to the kitchen, prepare a sumptuous meal, then return to his seat and consume the meal with little change to the official score. Many soccer matches came down to penalty kicks to decide a victor. That was another aspect about which he was unsure, what exactly constituted a penalty? Guys seemed to be constantly knocking other guys down with no cautions, then suddenly a slight brush between two players would beget ejection of one or other; kind of reminded him of basketball. The one other thing he did know was that outside this country soccer is football.

Apparently no one inside Morano's patio room was much interested in the game either, typical of a majority of sports bars he visited during his wilder days. ESPN playing, no sound, no one watching, no interest. He wondered if the sponsors had figured out that aspect yet. He wondered if it was relevant. But he did not wonder long. Work to do.

"Which is better? To never be born or be born into a hopelessness? To die in hunger? To kill in wars? WWJD, What Would Jesus Do?" JP couldn't believe Carlos back on that track, thought he'd concluded his circular arguments (aka, Circle Jerking) fifteen minutes before, calming down when no challengers emerged. He also couldn't believe Morano actually spelled out "WWJD" then explained it, like no other way these drunk asses would get it!

That was when he remembered to take time for a look around. If he got killed ignoring Peterson's warning, the Jarhead would never let him live it down. In a manner of speaking that is…

The wind began picking up, further confusing his reception. But he could still hear somewhat. It would have been much better if he had someone to watch his back; unfortunately he was not so fortunate, so he decided against maintaining visual observation on the participants and instead snapped off a few shots with the built-in camera, before retreating back to hide in the lee of the nearest palm tree bole, the same palm tree that nearly brained him minutes before. But being the magnanimous individual that he was, he decided that it probably did not try to hurt him on purpose.

The RF link was good for over one hundred yards, giving plenty of range for his purposes. He would upload the entire take back to DIA once he was through here. He hoped the little "stick 'em on" would keep his mike attached to the glass. So far it had.

He had to be careful. This might be Miami, but he was not Miami Vice. He suppressed the thought that it could be Miami Nice, though, if Valerie ever made good on her promise. Thoughts like those he needed to leave for less hazardous moments. As much as he might try and see a similarity to Miami Vice, he possessed none of the skill, verve or intuition of Ricardo Tubbs or Sonny Crockett (or the special effects). Added to that reality, he had limited support, no backup and not even a decent ride. No one would ever confuse his domestic Rent-a-Wreck with either of Crockett's Ferrari stallions, though he favored not the white Testarossa Pimpmobile, but the sleek, black Daytona which was actually built onto a 1980 Corvette chassis and he loved Corvettes. But he needed to refocus; tripping through "Life in the fast lanes" was beginning to make him homesick for the wonderful aroma of Martha's cooking. Now came another aroma riding the swirling breeze, one not nearly as wonderful. He sniffed. What was that?

"Marine!" No hesitation, he instantly curled into a ball rolling across from left shoulder to right hip, all the way through then back up to balance on the balls his feet. The voice shouted to him in a deep bellow that he had not heard since before Vietnam, sounding exactly like his boot camp nemesis, Staff Sergeant Haynes and it saved his life. He sensed rather than felt the whoosh of disturbed air molecules displaced by the rapidly moving object that had just missed the back of his head at the apex of its arc.

JP did not know whether he should thank his lucky stars, his kami or the one God Henry had first introduced him to those many years before. Perhaps he should just thank Sergeant Haynes for training him so hard so that he would neither freeze in dangerous situations nor pause to first study the situation.

"Now ah'm only gonna tell you Shit Maggots one mo' time," Haynes thick, down-turned lips would spit out, "dem dat wait ta' figger th' shit out or stands there peeing in dey pants ain't gonna be the next ones dat git ta knock boots wit' lil' Suzy Rottencrotch back home in Bum Fuck, Ohio. Ya git down low an' movin', then ya worry 'bout posin' fo' News-Fuckin'-Week. Ya heah?"

"Aye Aye Sir!" came the thunderous reply from seventy-six screaming voices.

Haynes voice ringing in his imagination, JP faced his enemy. The other also dressed in black clothing, but his right hand held a collapsible, tactical baton, also black. The steel shank would have rendered JP helpless, if not dead. Its full swing velocity probably could rival Eris' winds for speed and force. He was a pretty good sized guy, too, looked to be a formidable foe. JP toyed with the idea of fleeing rather than fighting his way out of this situation. But his adversary finally had a face and he had a need for action. This adventure had been anything other than adventurous. Only the "car chase" which was more like a "car follow" had generated any real excitement …until now.

The other man did not speak. "Good!" Neither wanted interruptions. That meant both considered themselves tough guys. In this most deadly version of the game of Fuk-Fuk, both thought he had the biggest pecker. Both were about to find out…

His form flowed easily as he moved to his left, away from the base of the tree he had snuck around to ambush this interloper. Deciding to stretch his legs during the storm's eye, he'd chanced upon the vision of someone scurrying away from the villa's rear patio. Out had come the steel baton from its small holster that in Iraq would have been accompanied by a Tariq nine millimeter, bringing this conclusion to an even quicker ending. No matter. Quick it still would be and he then crept around behind the man from the direction of his blind side enabled by the tree's girth. But his lightning quick strike had missed. Suspicion, based upon honed instinct, then entered his thoughts that he had an above average participant in this night's soirée …his instinct had never achieved greater accuracy.

The baton lashed out again. This time its force was swung in a shorter, tighter arc aimed at his midriff. If it connected it could easily shatter a rib or at least knock the breath from his lungs. But again it found only open air. The adversary's backward leap saved him from its fury. But he pressed his attack forward, swinging the narrow shaft back and forth, attempting to make contact with the elusive dark shape.

Totally defensive for a much longer period than he desired, inside he raged, eager to return the favor and press home his own version of attack on this sneak creep who evidently preferred to announce his arrival on nicotine-flavored winds reeked in aftershave. He'd thank him later for the tip. But he needed to first nullify that deadly stick. He moved nearer to the palm tree and awaited the next strike. But this guy was no dummy. His strikes were purposeful and controlled.

Mister No Dummy maneuvered around to force JP's back to the tree and close where there would be less room for any backwards flight. Now he had the perfect position, the quarry could only move left or right. Either way his body could not dodge as fast as a baton could swing. Confidently Mister No Dummy moved in for the kill.

A short feint toward the man's eyes from the right set up the roundhouse kick from the left. He had supreme confidence in the outcome. The natural response would prompt the interloper to duck away, directly into the power of his follow-up. That kick had downed many an adversary. One more trophy on his warrior wall of fame.

He hated Americans anyway. He hated them since attending their military schools in the nineteen-eighties, their pompous rules favoring English-speakers, as if so much more advanced than someone like him who spoke four languages. He was about to hate them even more…

Sudden pain in his groin was his first indication that his plan had not quite transpired as intended. Then he landed face first into a puddle of rainwater.

JP's patience had run its course. Eventually this guy's friends would show up, turning the advantage totally in the favor of the bad guys. The darkness degraded his ability to time the swings of that metal shaft, plus the wind and rain were kicking back up. Normally he would have moved in between strokes and blocked at the arms or wrists, then disarmed him. But all it would take was one connection and he could be in serious difficulty. So he backed closer to the tree to give his enemy a better opening.

Anticipating the double move, JP scooted low and forward onto his right side, slapping the wet soil with his forearm while simultaneously shooting out a side thrust kick. The heel dug deep into the opponent where his legs came together. JP then whipped his body over and slashed a horizontally aimed front snap kick against the other's right ankle, sending him sprawling. Instantly he was back onto his feet, pressing forward to end this contest. But instead, now his reward was the sensation of pain.

Panic filled him. He could not see. Blinded by dirty debris from the water puddle, he somehow regained his feet, even though his lower body felt as if it had been kicked by a mule. But instinctively he had held onto his baton and now lashed out blindly before him. A small glimmer of satisfaction infused him with energy. He felt the end of the metal rod contact something. It must have been the other. Wiping at his eyes with one hand, while still swinging with the other, his vision had nearly returned when suddenly the blur of a ghost appeared before him and his baton went flying through the air.

Now weaponless, he scuttled crab-like back towards the house. His only intention was to call for help. He very nearly made it to the rear glass doors, back into the spotlights. But again the wraith caught up to him and he had to resort to an active defense. Kicks and punches he threw with reckless abandon, all the while attempting to get away. But he was being hammered. He would block a right only to be hit by a left. A kick thrown would find only vacant atmosphere, then a countering blow would take his balance, sending him tumbling once more …those doors seeming farther away.

The pain in his groin had not fully subsided and greatly interfered with his ability to move as normal. He worried that it would also interfere with his ability to sleep. He need not have concerned himself with such. He managed to block a roundhouse aimed at his left temple. But it was only a setup move. Next a powerful back kick caught him in the solar plexus. Blackness overtook him and he knew no more…

CHAPTER EIGHTEEN

Soaring supreme above windswept clouds, the half-empty private jet curled gracefully southeast, heading on a trajectory intended to carry them south-southeast across Cuba's eastern edge, straight to Oranjestad. The Bahamian capital of Nassau on New Providence Island floated past on his left. Shallow depths surrounding New Providence and its adjacent island cousins exhibited a light green color that carved out a niche in the deep blue Atlantic. Too high and far to make out the six hundred-foot bridges connecting Nassau to its neighbors on Paradise Island. But he could envision the tourists beginning to wake and roll out of their hotel beds excitingly anticipating their upcoming day of frolic and shopping and banal encounters with opposite sexes. Below him, the Florida straits were overtaken and now receding. All the while, his mind was reeling, rerunning the events which had conspired to place him in this place, at this time…

He had arrived back at his room just in time. Only minutes after sneaking in through the backdoor he had left latched, but unlocked, he made his way up to his room. No other guest was out and about the lower levels. But even so, he should fit right in, dressed as he was in a tropical green, short-sleeved shirt and matching swim shorts. The sneakers and ball cap weren't even waterlogged from their ordeal, which seemed appropriate, as the cap sported a Philadelphia Eagles logo. Every sports fan knows eagles fly in all weather conditions.

Making the switch at the marina, he stowed the wet suit in the ditty bag and trashed all in a local bin, then he made like Edwin Moses – hurdling puddles and debris-- back to the hotel. No other fools or track star wannabees showed themselves…

Upon reaching the second floor he did run into a couple heading for the elevator. They yelled for him to join them on the roof as they raced past, giggling and laughing like children. It took a second or two before the overwhelmed translator in his mental cavity deciphered their speech. Words coming fast and furious from the fleeing pair, announced some sort of "After Eris" party. Tom and Katie were the names he reconciled from their jumbled, lightning-fast discourse and he decided to join them. It might prove a useful cover story just in case some math wizard put two-and-two together and ended up with one-minus O'Rourke.

No need to shower, rain had washed most of the salt away from his face, the suit had protected the rest. He just needed to grab a few party favors. But the ringing sound coming through his door put that decision on hold for the moment and subsequent conversation with the caller changed his mind entirely.

The impetus for that call sat in the back, facing forward, his chair in full recline. Eyes closed; his face showed none of the concern his assistant had intimated during the hasty phone call. She was already up out of her seat --the starboard forward chair, just behind the cockpit bulkhead-- and busing herself in the aft galley, preparing cocktails and snacks for two.

JP canted his head back and to the right for a glimpse behind, into the cabin. He had resisted that urge until Valerie left her seat. He could feel her eyes following his every movement. But that knowledge did not faze him. Actually, it emboldened one so used to occupying similar chairs in similar cockpits. He had not flown Lear Jets in his recent years –most hours of late were aboard the larger Grumman Gulfstreams. But Bombardier had done good work in this design. Nice positioning of the instruments and controls, it was also fast and maneuverable with a high rate of climb; easily sliding up to forty-five thousand feet in under thirty minutes. Not in the same league with military fighters of course, but then again, these twin Honeywell power plants did not come with afterburners. Conversely, what F-4 or even F-22 could sprint aloft with eight or so people on board? Some of them extremely shapely people.

For a moment he actually tempted to invert the craft to demonstrate this bird's full capabilities. In other words, he started to show off for a girl. But he resisted the temptation. There were at least a couple reasons why such a demonstration was a bad idea. First, the FAA people probably would not appreciate acrobatics. They did not have a lot of humor these days following 9-1-1. Second, the people in the back might get sick; especially that Air Force guy who probably never got to fly anything but a big, fat office chair and matching desk.

But that wasn't right. He mentally chided himself for the abrasive thoughts. Kinda unfair to degrade people you don't know and he didn't know this guy from Adam. He only had Valerie's opinion to measure by, well that and the guy's soft voice that some might term as wimpy. But long before (and many times before) Shiro had cautioned him about jumping to conclusions and flying off the handle and such. Two wrongs don't make a right. He mentally ratcheted down his ire one full notch, successfully focusing on his deceased mentor's sage counsel ...and chilling out.

As if rewarding this wise choice, Shiro's image flew out of the southern sun to glide just ahead, matching the speedy aircraft's course and speed. Smiling a bit of a wan smile, the mentor's elderly picture stared back silent and unmoving. His hair cut short into a crew cut, salt and pepper, more gray than white. His cheeks swelled prominently as did his forehead, reminding JP his joke to Tina once about Shiro's swelled head and her retort that big brains need room, so he should have plenty to spare. She would never allow anyone to crack jokes about Shiro. And now here he was, flying high; all tanned and healthy he looked, as if he had recently returned from the Japanese House in Fairmount Park; spending most of a day in the garden, sharing his lunch with the multicolored koi, watching the sun's passage in quiet reflection.

The image smiled again; seeming full of health and vigor; ever hiding the inner malady eating his insides, even from friends. It was the picture he left, dying peacefully without a word of his ailment, just his love. The image looked very peaceful, perhaps even approving its former pupil's discretion (though more than likely disdaining his initial journey down this rocky road). He wondered at this. Shiro had seldom expressed disapproval in uncertain terms; he tended to let you know you screwed up, though never once in the distinct manner of Staff Sergeant Haynes: "Listen up you numb nuts! One aw-shit wipes out ten attaboys!"

Shiro's manner was akin to the ripples formed by a tiny pebble dropped into still water. You knew there had been a disturbance, except you didn't feel it a threat to all mankind as if to say it wasn't good, but it wasn't so bad you'd never recover or that he would hate you or anything like that. In Shiro's world, there seemed never to exist situations so extreme as to be unrecoverable.

Then he was gone. No more glowing phantasm resembling his friend and mentor, only blue sky lay ahead. An instant later, he lay back in his Chu Lai hooch, the phantasm visiting him once again at night. Could that spectre have also come from Shiro? Even before his death? Can loved ones contact others in harm's way? Was his certainty that Tina still lived another example of this power? So many questions unanswered. How to get the answers? Another question unanswered. How indeed?

Brilliant glare from the sun --now coming out of his two o'clock-- intruded his daydream, snapping him back to the present. It too appeared alone in its heavenly presentation, supreme in its place. JP smiled back in appreciation of the wistful memory (despite his uncertainty) then turned back to his chores.

The bold Atlantic stretched its blue panoramic splendor beneath the craft and far out beyond his ocular abilities. But the color radar display reported its electronic findings as "all good". No conflicting aircraft on this heading, no weather clouds painted red or even dark blue in his current path, at least none within the one-hundred-mile radius he had selected to search. He reached up and over to adjust the translucent, green shade on the co-pilot's side. Some stubborn sunrays still managed to dodge past, streaming in from above as did glaring reflection from below …but his sunglasses handled those.

Eris' recent passage had swept any evidence of haze from this entire sector, leaving only scattered clouds slowly meandering along, pushed casually westward by slight breezes left in the storm's wake. Up from the gently, frothing waves came a gaudy, shimmering display that highlighted their temporal quiescence. Perhaps they were putting on a show just for his benefit …anticipating it would be his last.

O'Rourke stared into those azure depths. Into the bowels of the birthplace of all living things; his imagined X-rays pierced the calm, revealing fierce sharks razing terrified schools of fish. Quicker than quicksilver they shot this way and that, their voracious maws churning the transparence murky with newly liberated clouds of blood, spurring them to even greater frenzy.

As the torrid scene below evaporates --curtailing the insensate fury of the feeding ritual-- his consciousness returns to the cockpit's interior for barely a moment before he is off yet again, lapsing into another visionary sojourn. This time he is back inside his hotel suite, texting messages to Peterson over his cellie. He decided against a voice call. However, even without the benefit of an audio feed it was clear that at least one person in the DIA found agreement with the sea crests far below …that this could easily become his Waterloo.

The Colonel's text summed the trip down with Morano as just further along the road to nowhere. However, and this point he stressed, if he was to turn out right, he'd probably turn up dead.

Basically, the Jarhead assessed his chances --in this quest of his own choosing-- somewhere between slim and none, no matter how it came out. "Put it like this son (he didn't type in the word "son" but it was implied), there is little likelihood Morano did the deed. We find not a shred of evidence. However, if Morano turns out to have done the deed, there is even less likelihood of you surviving this mission. You got no backup, no help close by, no chance. So (baby) don't go."

Obviously, Peterson neither said or even implied the term "baby". But O'Rourke's sleep deprived self was experiencing brain fuzz. Still, he soldiered on…

Deleting the texts as a commonsense precaution, O'Rourke's primary response summed up as resigned, silent rejection, although he did send back a cryptic "ROGER! OUT!" He also chose to ignore the black-on-white worded disclaimer placing his future squarely upon his own shoulders …before deleting that also.

But at least DIA did not forbid him from his present course. Perhaps because they were convinced that he would ignore their orders and proceed anyway, on the one hand; on the other, they were still going in circles, chasing their tails. So why not let the bait do its own bit of fishing? Where was the harm in thinking outside the box? At least that summed his take on their take. In other words: "If I don't know shit, I make shit up!"

Then again, though he casually described the fight with a guy outside Morano's place, he had omitted any mention about trespassing or the people watching him and definitely nothing about nearly drowning on the way back when his zodiac filled with more water than its self-bailer could handle.

At least the craft hadn't totally sunk by the time he tied up back at the marina, only up to the gunnels. He reasoned that details like that seldom matter as long as you survive them and just hoped he didn't get stuck with the bill…

But he was more than ever convinced that he was on the right path, no matter what the "gee-whiz" computer simulations predicted and regardless that his spying on Morano had netted exactly zero supporting evidence. He acknowledged that the trail of blood seemed to flow between Paraguay and Barbados and that nothing tied Morano to any illicit dealings and that any of the paranoid-xenophobic denizens of Fisher Island would probably have attacked intruders the same way. He could have been anyone of several types of people they all hoped to avoid, from paparazzi to stalker, even kidnapper.

They don't call this place fantasy island for nothing! They do because of its isolated arrogance where rich folk treat the poor folk like peasants. There's always disputes, lawsuits and the like, but nothing really changes, including the salaries. So the poor stay that way.

Billy Ray always called white people "beasts". All of them definitely ain't, but some of them definitely are! But he wasn't here for social engineering and he definitely wasn't here to tangle with fifty security guards on golf carts!

But the sensations clanging within pealed near to overwhelming. When he added them all up it all made perfect sense. Add one dead fiancée (whom O'Rourke still refused to believe was dead) to one questionable linkage with one high-ranking official who just happens to have access to one classified military project, which, oh-by-the-way, just may have been recently compromised and what do you get? One Carlos Morano!

He chided himself again, this time for not taking better pictures through the glass door, rushing the shots instead of taking time. But it wasn't all him, big credit went to Mama Nature's penchant for dropping lots of wet stuff all over the glass surfaces. The distortion component was significant thanks to refracted light fuzzying the images coming through the rain splattered glass.

Unfortunately, distortion was only one problem; the other was that he knew nothing about the problem until he uploaded the files to his computer and took a better look. It looked clear enough to his naked eyes on the view screen, but cameras don't necessarily see the way people see. Then again, he wasn't spending time checking closely either …blame it on Mrs. Nature's eye wash.

The blurring defied his ability to clear the images up. He used every bit of its photographic enhancement capability, even switched to infrared, which only gave him gray shadow figures, so could do little more than verify that there were shadowy people inside the room who were eating and drinking and talking. He could make out the Air Force Guy and Morano, if he used his imagination. There was some older guy sitting here and another over there whose face and features were even more shadowed. No way to lighten them sufficiently for recognition. All he achieved was more pixilation. Maybe DIA could do better….

Okay, so he had no real knowledge that the project this Air Force Guy ran was in anyway tied to the project which had been breached --its documentation stolen—however, Valerie did mention that the man had been in some hot water. Plus, it made sense to him that if DoD had invented a super spiffy way to secure classified data, they would be using it for all classified programs. The only information Peterson would surrender concerning this Colonel William Barnett, was that his program is classified, which is typical military parlance for: "Sorry public, we can't give you the expenditure figures for Project XYZ. It's Top Secret cause you'd be really pissed if you find out!"

In retrospect, DIA only confirmed that their evaluation of Barnett came up clean. He spent lots of money, but his wife had a very rich father, so money should not be a problem for him. Plus, even Light Colonels are paid rather well in their own right. As far as this vacation, his TDY had been scheduled the month before. Now, in retrospect, he considered that maybe the DIA's iron brain knew what it was talking about. After all, it had correctly predicted his response to the news about Tina. Then it had predicted a sixty-five percent probability that he would follow his own counsel, ignoring their instructions. Perhaps their system was best. After all, they were the pros, weren't they? But despite their assurance there was still that nagging sensation…

"Miami Oceanic this is Anasazi-eight-six-one, with you at flight level four-one-zero, over!" He was out of his sojourn, back to the business at hand. They were outside radar coverage and passing beyond VHF radio range with the Air Traffic Controllers in Miami Center. It was time to fire up the HF and contact the overseas airways controllers who would chart his aircraft's progress down into the Caribbean where he would next pick up San Juan Oceanic and on to Aruba.

"Eight-six-one, this is Miami, over."

"Miami this is eight-six-one. Present position…"

"Err, excuse me pilot!"

"Huh? Wait one Miami!" So intent was he on fulfilling the necessary radio check with controllers back in Miami, he had not noticed the other man's approach. He turned to find the Air Force Guy standing in the entrance to the cockpit, what used to be called the "Cockhouse" since that section of an aircraft was once overwhelmingly populated by males. Still is mainly, though not so much these days as more representatives of the fairer sex climbed into the front seats. He was not annoyed that he had not detected his approach through the whisper-quiet cabin, just curious. "What did he want?"

Morano still appeared asleep. His last glimpse of this other man --identified by Valerie as Bill Barnett, "The Air Force Guy"—was as he casually read from a magazine while sipping the cocktail she'd handed him. This guy moved pretty quietly. He might need to remember that…

Morano had neither moved nor seemed to acknowledge in any way the drink she had carefully placed on the small table ahead of his portside seat. Now back in the galley, she prepared snacks to serve before their meal. Its aroma drifting forward reminded JP that he could do with a nice steak himself. Those breakfast eggs were wearing away…

This was the same man JP had observed sitting with Morano at the beach club and again inside his home on Fisher Island and now he was sticking his face into another man's cockpit. What was his purpose here? What's he up to?

"Eight-six-one, Miami."

"Hold one Miami." He then turned to the man climbing into the starboard cockpit seat. "Yes, can I help you?"

"I'll fly up here with you for a while and help with the nav, okay." He let go the words, but it was neither question nor request. JP felt the man's temperament. Wimpy voice and all, his mannerisms indicated he really meant, "Cause I wanna, that's why!"

JP did not answer, turning back to the radar presentation on the multi-functional display. He realized something was afoot. He would follow Shiro's guidance. Remain quiescent, a quiet pool of water.

"You up on button two?"

"Button two," he affirmed, "Miami Oceanic."

"Yeah, thanks. Err, call sign?" His fingers held a sheet of paper.

"Anasazi-eight-six-one." O'Rourke wanted to ask about the paper but held his tongue. He was not the one running this show.

"Miami Oceanic this is Anasazi-eight-six-one." The Air Force Guy read off a series of numbers representing their current position, flight level and estimated time reaching the latitude-longitude coordinates of their subsequent location. Only, none of the location information he radioed to Miami represented where they were or where they were going. Now O'Rourke could wait no longer.

"You wanna tell me what you're doing?" Another glance back proved Morano still in his seat; this wasn't quite panic time, yet. But he alerted himself for possible action just the same.

"Oh, didn't Carlos tell you? We changed the flight plan you filed. Something came up. We need to go to Grenada instead of Aruba." The man waited, evidently expecting additional protest from their surprised pilot. Instead it was his turn to be surprised.

"Okay," was all O'Rourke said. Then he glanced back outside, checking for hazards. Things now made more sense to him. Grenada is very close to Barbados. Didn't DIA suspect some connection with Barbados?

"Coffee JP?" It was Valerie. She handed him a paper cup filled three-quarters to its brim with dark, rich, steaming liquid. "Black, no sugar right?"

"Thanks V!" He took the cup, staring hard at the other man. "Is there something else?"

"Oh yeah, stay on our present heading and could you call me five minutes prior to our next check?"

"Aye aye!"

"Oh yeah, you were Navy, err, Marine, right?"

"Si! And you?" Now he had an opening that would not appear too inquisitive, just normal B-S banter between two guys getting to know each other ...measuring their dicks.

"Used to fly F-15s. Been a while. I get just enough flight hours these days to keep my wings. But I'm current." His voice seemed somehow stronger, more man in it, when he discussed flying?"

"Wanna take the wheel?" O'Rourke suddenly felt even less hostile. Though not a Marine, a fellow wing flapper, a fly-guy. So what if he wore funny-colored, blue suits? At least he wasn't a desk flinger.

But he still was not happy about the change to the flight plan he had filed, after he had verified when and where Morano wanted to go and connected all those dots in proper order to get flight clearance. Suddenly, it just turned out to be the wrong flight clearance and somebody back in "We Control the World" central was gonna be pretty pissed about this. His recently recovered license was looking less like a permanent part of his entourage. Once they lay out where everybody is supposed to be on their great big sky map of "Who's Where and When", they don't like any deviations. Change is not their friend. Plus, there's others in this game and they don't give up control lightly ..."the heck you mean they decided to go there, instead of there?"

He remembered that night at the American Legion, Morano asking him about his license. Was he planning this even back then? Probably not. After all, not even Morano knew about the hurricane. Did he?

"Naw, I'll just head to the back 'n let you kids bust ya'll rap."

At his "bust ya'll rap" mention, JP nearly busted out laughing. Nothing cracked him up more than an older mainstream white guy trying to talk street. But he merely smiled as the man gave a knowing grin and climbed out of the seat. Valerie waited for him to pass then slid her lovely frame into the space.

They'd had not much chance to talk since her phone call. She looked good; straight-legged blue jeans, white T-shirt emblazoned with a pink, Playboy bunny emblem that rode snuggly across well-endowed endowments; hair pulled back exposing opulent earrings whose round cut diamonds were set in gold mounts and surrounded by tiny emeralds. The diamonds looked to be about one-carat each; with the emeralds and the gold they had to set somebody back-a-ways.

A part of him –the curious part-- wondered what she did to get those, but decided whatever it was, it was her business. Valerie flashed a quick smile through pink lipstick, then turned her head to stare outside and below at the ocean. "Are we over the Caribbean yet?"

"Getting there. Boss likes his rest, huh?"

"He had a long night. He's really happy you could help us out at the last minute. Both his pilots are unavailable. Eris really tore up the house they share, and this is kind of an emergency."

"It's okay. Never been to Aruba. I mean Grenada, now. Actually, I've never been to either one. Sounds like a fun trip even if I gotta work to pay my fare."

"Darn! I kinda thought it was me." She wrinkled her freckled nose to demonstrate feigned sorrow, then coquettishly batted both eyes in mock seductiveness.

"You comfortable? I can turn up the heat."

Hearing his impish tone, she glanced quickly down at her nipples struggling to break through the thin fabrics of both bra and T-shirt, then busted a hearty, musical laugh whose volume caused him to join in with his own deep guffaw. "Like I said before, you are soooo bad! Mister O'Rourke!"

They communicated with small talk the rest of the way, breaking only when she went back to finish preparation and service of the meal that only the three of them ate. Morano stayed knocked out to the world, snoring gently in his reclined chair. Words made it almost to the tip of his tongue to express admiration for her choice in earrings, but never passed the firewall hastily erected. He figured he knew the deal and suddenly did not want to know.

"Maurice Bishop, this is Lear-eight-six-one. Out of one-six-zero to one-two-zero. Over." Air Force guy stayed in the back during their final. He had only come forward one other time to watch as JP gave the updated time and coordinate info to oceanic controllers in Puerto Rico.

"Lear-eight-six-one, Maurice Bishop. Descend and maintain flight level zero-eight-zero! Come left to zero-nine-zero. Cleared to runway one-zero. Wind, one nine zero."

"Roger! Zero-eight-zero left to zero-nine-zero. Cleared to runway one-zero."

The landing at Maurice Bishop International Airport went as smoothly as the rest of the flight. Turquoise water disappeared as his craft crossed the runway threshold. He followed the "Follow-Me" truck, the lighted sign at its rear insisting on his compliance and taxied the corporate jet to a spot at the west side of the terminal, then shut down both engines. Within seconds, a blue Land Rover drove up to meet them and the passengers deplaned, though not before Morano offered a subdued expression of gratitude and praise to the man sitting in the cockpit before deplaning. "Thanks JP. Nice flight."

Then he and his guest were gone. Whisked away by the two men O'Rourke had met with Morano, two days before. The Colonel winked at him before following Morano to the Land Rover. No one else said anything. In their wake, the hot Caribbean breeze flowed in to challenge the air-conditioned chill. It felt good and smelled even better, kind of like apple pie. There were no other aircraft engines turning nearby to pollute the climate with the foul odor of burning kerosene. It actually made for a nice, quiet Friday afternoon.

A slender, dark-complexioned face sporting a broad smile under angular features and pearly white teeth climbed inside and greeted JP. His manner was laid back and full of confidence. He smelled okay also. Blue letters on a white background, trimmed in red piping announced his name and pronounced him a representative of "Spice Island Air Services". His dark blue jump suit proclaimed his function as ground crew, possibly a mechanic. JP's eyes rose from the label stitched to the man's left breast pocket and found the light brown eyes affixed to his. The smile stretched even broader.

"Hallo Mister, I'm Trent. I take care o' Mister Morano's plane here in Grenada. Any difficulty?" His pronunciation said "Grey-nay-da", forcing JP to mentally correct his own pronunciation. This was not the Spanish city after all. So he flushed his tendency to say "Gran-ada". Lesson number one. Thank you very much.

"Smooth as silk Trent. I'm John O'Rourke. Call me JP. I'll be out in a minute." Completing the post-flight checks –parking brake on, switches off, engine circuit breakers out-- he wondered if he was supposed to know what they wanted him to do next. Find a room on an island full of tourists, at the last minute? He did not like the idea of spending two nights, possibly a week, bunking in the back of this small jet. Then he realized Valerie had not said her goodbye. After she had dropped the door, he lost sight of her. He guessed she must have climbed into the Rover with the others. Servants must attend their masters, after all.

"Oh well", he thought, maybe Trent could recommend a good place to stay." He actually had not accepted this task concerned about his own comfort. There is an old adage, that goes, "Once a Marine, always a Marine!" It still intimated his approach to life, even though his inner self often railed against the idea of being so associated with the organization which had tried its best to kill him or at least, to get him killed. But one might as well rail at the sun for waking them.

In keeping with the old traditions he could rough it for a few days. Push come to shove he would find some flea-bit, backwater rooming house where only native Grenadians stayed. It would probably be good, provide him better opportunity for checking up on Mister Carlos. Then came her protest "…JP! I'm waiting!"

They breezed through customs and then picked up their self-drive rental from a confident sales agent who assured them a child could navigate the distance to Prickly Bay. They left the Airport and promptly got lost. Distance was not the problem. Distance to their hotel was only about four miles, as far as he could estimate on the map they gave them, only one mile as the Tropicbird flies. It was the combination of disorientation aided by fatigue --especially for O'Rourke-- plus the requirement to drive on the left side of narrow roads ruled by legions of local daredevils.

While these action junkies seemed to come in all flavors –black, white, yellow and whatever—many careened past him jerking madly at the controls of taxis and minibuses, horns blaring. He felt himself back in Manhattan with another breed that exhibited similar tendencies to dodge their vehicles around any perceived obstructions at full speed, making the drive even more tenuous. These folk obviously considered any vehicle moving slower than light speeds to be obstructions …or so it seemed.

"Bet we made the wrong turn at that last roundabout." Her statement had the conviction that came via the clarity one gets after passing a sign that says, "Too Far". This particular sign announced their arrival in Grand Anse. Totally the wrong direction. He marveled at her gift of hindsight.

"I see, said the blind man!"

"Hush, smart ass!"

"Yes ma'am. So you wanna keep going?"

"Might as well see the sights. We're almost to Saint George's anyway and I'm hungry."

"Next time cook bigger meals." He suggested, a little hungry himself after that airborne TV dinner preceded by a few chips and pretzels.

"Hey! It's a galley, not a kitchen! And it's only got a microwave! You want steak, take me to a steakhouse!"

"Just kidding ma'am! You know I love your cooking."

"You're about to love my right cross, you don't get me some real food!"

"Roger-Dodger!" Easing the ire of hostile females demanded instant placation…

A sideways glance and he again wondered where she put it all. Slim and trim, except in a few exceptional spots –what one might consider an innocent flower of womanhood-- she looked as if the idea of pigging out had never crossed her mind, a concept foreign to say the least. But anyone witnessing her performance in Miami, with those Dungeness crabs, would attest that this girl had definite skills. He figured she must have a tapeworm or at the least a very high metabolism. Probably better for her to have the latter…

She still had a bit of a wait for dinner, though. Their adventure had only just begun. This four-door Jeep was one of the few American vehicles to be found in this land ruled by Honda and Toyota, although they had spied a Buick hearse and a Ford truck. But he decided those two not a knock on these people's tastes for cars with backward control systems. Painfully grinding another shift, his vindictiveness achieved satisfaction in the knowledge that this backward vehicle would need a new transmission before he was done torturing his way through the gears. What idiot had decided to save this as their very last rental car? Even more bizarre, why would they reserve it for Americans? Driving on the wrong side of the road was one thing, shifting left-handed quite another. Good thing it had a hardy clutch. Good thing too that the Jeep was larger than most of the Kamikazes zooming past in both directions and agile enough to do its own bit of dodging, especially those trucks and minivans whose bulk outmuscled theirs…

Grenada's countryside is magnificently arrayed with carpets of lush, green mountain fern and exotic tropical streams cascading down rocky slopes to natural pools, exactly as reported in the travel web sites he had been able to pull up on his computer using the air terminal's Wi-Fi. "Never been here before? No worry, you gonna love this place!"

Everywhere were black-coated Bananaquit Birds preening their yellow breast feathers then swooping from perches high up in the thick foliage to sample nectar-rich flowers along the roadside and grey-rumped Swifts, sporting a grey triangular band across their small rumps with underparts colored slate grey and all the remainder jet black, whirled through the atmosphere above chasing juicy insects for their mid-day meal.

Obviously, all those carpets of ferns and exotic cascading streams belonged to a different part of Grenada. This part seemed composed of high hills covered top to bottom with houses of every type and condition. The few signs he saw snuck up and flashed by before he could read them and Valerie was little help, unless one could consider her constant leaning out the left window, snapping photo after photo, to be of help. She seemed never to see a sight not of interest, whatever they were …excepting direction signs, she never saw those.

None of this particular skill set enthralled the harried pilot, turned chauffeur, who'd managed to fly them nearly sixteen hundred miles down from Florida with no problem, but could neither find the correct road to their villa in Prickly Bay nor seemingly how to make his left hand shift in coordination with his left foot. "Grrrrooooaannn! Screeech! Gaaawww!" Embarrassing!

"And another great shift oh noble one." He bit hard his lower lip to prevent his mouth from relating the exact location in which she could shove her comment and kept driving up the winding, two-lane past honking minivans headed both directions and unfamiliar sights on all sides of them. On their left, one familiar sign for Kentucky Fried Chicken and another announcing Colonel Sanders drew his eyes to a crowd gathered to watch cricket batters swing flat bats furiously and miss balls hurled at them by artful pitchers. No Hank Aarons here. Across Lagoon Road, the "SUPERFUND" nameplate atop a highrise building (what accounts for highrise in these parts) reminded again that he had not recently checked his portfolio with the hedge fund group.

They had seen all this once before on their way to visit the u-shaped lagoon comprising Morne Rouge Bay and its emerald waters separating white sand beach from Caribbean Sea. Snorkelers swam far out, nearly outside its western edge, sunbathers languished in beach towels and chaise lounges, small children raced through the surf, splashing and screeching like banshees. Centered on this seaside basin's eastern edge stood two beachside resorts. On the hills high above, lavish two and three-story homes competed to present the greatest impression. Indeed, here was a beautiful bay, but this was not the right bay. Again, they had been left out …left right out!

Road signs were a decided luxury in this part of the Island, although one did point out the Friday night Karaoke contest at one of the parks they sped past. Indeed there were many signs, too many. But nearly all advertised some commercial establishment or commodity. It seemed as if directions were considered an unnecessary feature here. It would have been nice if this vehicle had come equipped with GPS, even a compass. But the agent did not appear concerned with such features, though his thin, ebony face beamed with pride when he informed them that the Jeep came equipped with factory air conditioning and power steering. "Yeah? How 'bout automatic transmission? Oh, and while you're at it, put the steering wheel on the right side, known as the left!"

JP took several dozen jibes from Valerie for his inability to navigate while reading the tiny little map handed them by the agent. He had decided against the cell phone's navigator which would have done the job quite well. Initially it began as just a preference, soon transforming into dogged determination. His nickname she changed to "Uie", for all the U-turns. But all the while she berated him with jocular barbs whenever he turned the wrong way, she never once offered to help. It seemed her job was sightseeing, waving to passersby and snapping their pictures with her little camera, as well as hers from the distance of an arm's length. Head cocked to one side, a knowing wink and "click", self-portraits her specialty.

She had her selfies photography down pat. He figured she averaged one at her for every five shot at other subjects. Caught up! Obviously the unpaid job of navigator didn't suit her. JP just hoped she didn't have a Instagram page. Be kinda hard explaining to Sylvia why he showing up on some strange hottie's gram! Operative word here is strange". Occasionally she might point out a road sign announcing the distance to the capital, Saint George's, but that helped little since it often proved some roundabout direction. Still, they appreciated that Grenada's road signs displayed distances in miles …no conversion to kilometers necessary.

They'd have appreciated them more if one sign called out the direction and distance to their hotel, which never seemed to show up on whichever route they drove and he did stop a few times to ask directions from native Grenadians walking this way and that alongside the roads they drove, except those they had already passed at least once before. One set of bad directions would do from each one of these rapid speakers.

The people were friendly and laid back. Often their demeanor turned from distrust to smiling within the space of a few moments and when they gave him directions, those came nearly as fast. "Calabash? Hmmm, let me see. Aye t'ink you take dot road down dere." The words sounded so close together all he heard was Takedatrodowdere." Ask for a repeat, you get it back exactly the same way, and then there was the accuracy issue: "Yeah, maybe make a left, no maybe right. You see when you get dere. Oh you already been dat way? What 'bout udder. Hey Rudy, you know best way to Calabash over in Prickly Bay?"

Lilting intonation dominating the Caribbean English spoken by these locals was refreshing, but at the same time, confusing to this wandering driver, often filled with colloquialisms the American tourists needed time to decipher. The difficulties mounted…

"Dem, dey don' go dee way I say!" This was the only time they had violated their "Don't ask nobody twice rule".

It was even more embarrassing than listening to her quips. His navigational system may have been a failure, but his hearing was good as ever, intercepting the remark one old man yelled to his fellow, as both paused their labor, sweeping debris from a small restaurant parking lot. Leaning against straw brooms and chuckling to themselves, they seemed to think these Americans so daffy. After his brain caught up, that realization required another one-eighty turn. They both waved again as he drove by the third time. No clue apparent in the two brown faces that split to show pearly white teeth behind broad lips. "Thank God. At least these natives are friendly."

Then they were out of sight and the old men went back to sweeping away the debris and telling each other tall tales of other tourists who had visited from the U.S. in the past. "Man, you know dem folks drive th' wrong way all th' time but dey get a good look –HaHa!"

Had the couple heard the old man's comment, they would have agreed that he was right as rain, for their odyssey garnered stunning glimpses of the sun-splashed Caribbean through breaks in the verdant foliage or better yet, breaks in the resort hotels where the road curved close enough to the seacoast. Along the way they passed small stop and shop stores dressed in colorful, pastel yellows and greens and red roofs and offering myriad Island souvenirs and delicacies for snacking. Supermarkets and Gas stations with their own convenience shops reminded them so much of home. Different names though, not a Target, Walmart or 7-Eleven to be found (Oh thank Heaven). Ever present on the warm, gentle breezes was the delicious aromatic blending of spices.

They made another turn. Vacation homes, villas and small hotels climbed up the hilly terrain on both sides of the road; some pastel-colored, Jerrybuilt homes --supported by stilts of bamboo or concrete—that dug deep into the steep slopes angled towards the sea. Up over a hill on a winding road and suddenly it dropped propitiously towards blue ocean waves. A narrow expanse widened to unveil moored sailboats riding secure at their tethers, powerboats tied up at docks inside protected coves and bays that stretched right and left on this southern edge of the Spice Island where the Atlantic Ocean met the Caribbean Sea.

O'Rourke's new handle may have become "Uie", in deference to all the u-turns he made, but he took solace in the fact that at least she did not call him "back up" or "wrong way" or something more negative. "Uie", while not a sterling portrayal, he could live with it. They finally found the villa three hours after leaving the airport and settled in. Neither of them gave any credence to the car rental agent's assurance that the trip only required eight to ten minutes. In truth, they had decided to have lunch at a small seaside inn discovered as a result of a wrong turn. So they did not entirely fault the agent…

Besides, getting lost is half the fun of vacations. You find yourself, in more ways than you know, when you're lost. At least that was his feeling. It eventually became hers also, but not until after their meal. Prior to that she had occasionally pointed out how for everything and everybody else, the dinner bell had sounded …except for them.

They found this place rustic, but friendly and the grilled, spiny lobster perfect, as was the location. All the boats anchored offshore appeared to be on extended break or even holiday. Nothing moved to disturb the wonderful sea scene lovingly painted one pixel at a time on Mother Nature's canvass by God. Whatever you want to term them, some creator's skills --whether accidental or on purpose-- were obvious and much appreciated by the pair. Equally appreciated were the accurate directions they received from their waiter, his dark brown face beaming. "Ah, people take dis' road all de time. Den dey eat an' drink, dey watch dee sunset an on dere way."

O'Rourke felt very at ease in this place, its open-air spaces warm with tropic scents and ribald humor. People conversed about music, politics —world and local—and cricket matches, often at the tops of their lungs. But it was all in good spirits. People like these were the reason he seldom concerned himself with precise directions. Hotels don't move. They would get there eventually. Possibly after finding another gem like this one … further detours however, were unnecessary.

Furnished in soft, supple leathers and sumptuous, thick cushions, the interior sent one message, "we want your visit to last!" Its chairs and twin sofas alternated cream and chocolate leather cushions over dark brown mahogany wood frames. The flooring changed from its predominate cream coral to caramel ceramic tile in the kitchen area and to dark wood on the lanai patio, where a bottle of champagne sat cooling in an ice bucket sitting on a small square table, between twin chaise lounges. Accessible through twin patio doors --cousins of those assigned watch on the bedrooms-- the intimate sitting area looked out across Prickly Bay to the Caribbean Sea and southwest towards Venezuela.

The sun's direct rays had gone from this sector of Grenada. But there was still sufficient natural light, it would be a while longer going down. Also, subdued, incandescent lighting exuded from colorful, pastel shades that shuttered plump lamps set on end tables around the living room and wall fixtures to further warm the villa's environs. Around and alongside, were artfully placed decorative plants and tasteful paintings.

One apartment with two bedrooms. Two bedrooms! He noticed those right away, their unwelcome pairing veering off to the right side from the entrance door. So much for the romance. Good thing he didn't put in for that mega size order of those little blue pills. Might as well have numbers above the doors, then she could send him to his room in proper fashion. "Hey, Mister-Not-Gonna-Get-None, you're in 1B!"

Both sported French doors; latticed, glass-paned, double-doors whose wide openings permitted easy view of the king-sized beds beyond piled high with pillows and comforters. Beige linen curtains covered the backside of each door to extend their privacy options once closed.

Both bedrooms came equipped with private baths and --built within the ceramic splendor of each-- its own whirlpool tub, co-opting the message that obviously this was going to be all business. No need even to visit next door for a splash. Got your own.

He decided not to dwell on that subject, opting instead for a visit to the bedroom –the one she had passed up-- to settle his belongings and set up his computer; swiping his thumb against the biometric fingerprint reader. Finding no emails from Peterson, he read the two jokes from Mickey, sent a quick reply and then gave into the beckoning beach and its gentle waves.

After locking his more important belongings in the safe, he changed the blue, pullover knit and faded blue jeans he wore down from Miami for more appropriate beach clothes and left the villa, locking the door behind him. Paradise this place may be, but he meant to maintain at least a partial sense of decorum, at least where security was concerned. He had made certain all the windows and the patio doors were also locked. The bad guys knew who he was, where he was and who he was with, what they did not know was why? At least he hoped they did not know why, otherwise they would ensure he never got to know anything else.

He disliked leaving without a word to Valerie, but his senses detected some change within her after dinner during their drive over. Maybe it was the sheer volume of her meal.

He had reminded her the old adage about eyes bigger than stomach.

Regardless, she had seemed to become more withdrawn the closer they got to the hotel. Perhaps she dreaded the next evolution of a trip that required her to share an intimate space with this stranger. It reminded him of her mood swing two nights past in Miami as he drove her home. One minute high, one minute low. One word. "Strange".

He tempted to knock on her door, but the sound of the shower convinced him there was no need. She had already intimated that she might want to take a nap after her bath. He would catch up to her later. Keys were on the cocktail table if she needed to drive somewhere. Seemed like a good idea. Loose ties might enable better chances.

Their villa was part of a horseshoe-shaped enclave that represented the westernmost part of a large hotel situated along Prickly Bay, just east of the L'Anse aux Epines Peninsula on the southern Grenada coast. A holdover from the 1650 conquest, the French meaning of épine is "thorn". In Grenada the name derives from the spiked leaved Calabash trees that grow around the island. Its fruit –shaped similar to a large, green coke bottle-- they used as an ornamental gourd to decorate the rooms in area hotels. He did not see any gourds in their room, but neither did he notice any spiked trees during the drive, just a lot of green, now he needed a different shade, one more golden and liquid...

Valerie came out of the shower in her room's private bath, refreshed and ready for an evening of exploring, adventure and possibly love on the making. She had finally decided to teach this man about real women, obviously he didn't know, not yet. Probably had only been with hoochies. Two knocks on his door and a subsequent opening revealed that her aspirations were hers alone. Now she was upset to say the least. "How dare he!"

She grabbed the phone to call for service, but an incoming transmission preempted her dialing. Then she became even more miffed. It was Timothy. Carlos' number one bodyguard and pain in her side. "Yoeo! Val! This you? Timothy here! You busy?"

"Yes Timothy! I am a little busy right now. Can I help you?" Her tone hinted that she did not want to be bothered, but then she never wanted to be bothered by him. Knowledge both of them shared.

"Damn baby! Don't crucify th' bloody messenger just cause yer wanker can't last!" he smirked. She did not respond, aware that she was probably under their surveillance. She did not know why, but for some reason, Carlos seemed cautious of JP. That made his urgent call the previous evening all the more puzzling. He sounded apprehensive, afraid, even when he asked her to contact her "friend". He had an emergency. He needed a pilot. Had to fly out that morning and would pay any fee.

One moment he seemed to admire the man, the next he seemed wary of him. Why would he need help from someone he distrusted? And where were Leonard and Bernard, his two pilots? Half-asleep, in her stupor, she suggested she should call them. But he slammed that thought in an instant. His voice was near panic. She agreed and was told to pack for a week. Then she became even more apprehensive. Carlos had never once asked her to join him on one of these Caribbean jaunts. She was lucky he let her fly up to D.C. on occasion. Why the change?

Timothy's voice brought her back to the present. "Carlos wants you to show your friend the island a few days. Won't need ya all a while. Get back to you maybe Sunday. Plan on flying back Monday, Tuesday latest, 'kay?"

"Okay!" She hung up wondering which Fairy Godmother she should thank. This was going to be wonderful, simply wonderful. Three whole days, maybe. Alone on an idyllic tropical island with the hunk of a man who had set her world a kilter just two nights before. Maybe he did know about real women after all. A quote came to her, brazenly whispering subtle suggestion into her ears. It was one of Ava's favorites when describing traveling on her government job, "Getting' paid ta get laid!" But then, of course, Ava was a hoochie…

Placing the phone back in its receiver, she replaced Ava's words with a thought of her own. Carlos might be using her to appease an enemy. But why is he enemy? What had happened between these two? This is getting curiouser and curiouser Alice. She vowed to get that story out of JP by hook or crook as soon as she figured out where he had gone and then she'd smack the crap out of him for leaving her. First the sugar, then the vinegar…

Remembering Timothy's revelation over the phone, she ran to the front door and looked out. Their Jeep was still parked there. Then she sauntered to the balcony. If he knew JP was not with her, what better vantage point to observe than, "On the beach"!

He was just coming up out of the surf, swim fins in one hand, mask and snorkel in the other. Blood red trunks made her look twice to ensure his body had not been injured and now spurted crimson rivers. Even in this dimming light, to her he appeared an African God of the Hunt --perhaps Kalisa, once worshipped by the Nyoro Tribe who are still found in Uganda and the Congo next door-- although he held no struggling game nor even a bloodied sea creature in those powerful fists. But as the sinewy thighs powered his narrow waist and wide muscular shoulders up out of the surf, to stride powerfully out onto the brilliant white sand, she could perceive a god-like quality in him. Perhaps not the Ugandan-variety, introduced to her by a girlfriend from that part of Central Africa, but close enough. Certainly not some Greek, Roman or Celtic god-creature with their pale faces and stringy hair. His manner captivated her imagination in a way that sent tremors reverberating along her spine; titillating her in ways few men had in many years.

Nothing about his manner indicated any fear of meeting up with the dolphin that had chased him out of Biscayne Bay two days before. If anything it evidenced someone whom any menacing creatures below the azure surface would be wise to avoid. Inside her, it engendered an instant yearning for the succor his gentle fingers had promised in their last, their most intimate meeting.

She quickly doffed the silky-smooth robe, chosen for its vanilla bean coloring that brought out the glow of her hue. She still had not unpacked anything except for toiletries and toothbrush. But finding her next outfit took mere seconds. The robe floated through the bedroom atmosphere to land unglamorously across the bed as she traded its "open me first", loosely tied appeal for the black, two-piece, bikini that more than compensated with its own "peel me, eat me" message. Definitely too good to withhold from the Happy Hour crowd. Grabbing her room key, she sauntered on down to join him.

Happy Hour over and done with and only a few pairs of eyes at the beachside bar to appreciate her outfit —most of those overweight and over the hill-- they returned to the room and now sat on the lanai watching ruddy hues mix and mingle with fading blues; twilight colorings pronouncing this day was done, gone the sun. It was still hot though, nearly eighty degrees, encouraging frequent sips at the tall glasses neither seemed willing to put down. To the contrary, twin bowls of chips and salsa sat on the small, round table barely touched. Actually, one bowl's dimensions was easily twice the size of the other's, but both sported identical blue filigree tracings in their white porcelain.

She wore baggy, khaki shorts and a brownish tank top made even darker by beads of perspiration. He also wore khaki shorts but topped them with a black polo shirt that hid all evidence of sweat (men don't perspire), with the exception of a few beads along his forehead. Both languished in the gentle breeze, settling deep into the dark green cushions of side-by-side chaise lounges, neither speaking for some time now. He even wondered if her mood had gone sour but refused to break their silence. Then it happened naturally…

"So how you liking this place JP?" Her eyes fixed out over the bay to whatever points beyond they envisioned.

"Very nice and relaxing." He too fixated on some far-off location; somewhere over the horizon where a wizened race of people had achieved true enlightenment; a place where conflict had become unnecessary. Shangri-La or something, a utopia on earth. No conflict, no wars or avarice and hatred and petty differences. Sounded mythical, unobtainable. Still, in this place he could almost believe that condition achievable and, from what Danno, the bartender, suggested, it got even easier to consider.

"Sunday man, you make sure you got all you need Saturday. Sunday nobody do much of nothing." He told them that Sundays on Grenada were typically slow and even more laid back. Outside of restaurants and hotels, tourists generally had to fend for themselves on this island paradise where religion played a large part, as advertised by the many churches, seemingly one on every block. He even suggested a good Baptist Church for them to visit on the coming Sunday, watching in amusement as they play-acted out their mirthful disdain with his suggestion...

"Hey mon, what yer think? Us two goin' worshippin'?"

"Church? We go to church? We on a paradise island girl, what we waste go church for?"

"Oh pretty boy, it don't take all day. We still get yer dem t'ings yer cravin'!" This time she gave the knowing leer, causing an even bigger grin to split Danno's deep dark, handsome face.

"Don't I know it! Can't wait! But you don't know dem Baptists like I do. Dey get you in dere, then after service dey find excuses to keep ya. Dey got visiting choirs and dinners and stuff in dere. Dey be barbequing slabs o' ribs and potato salad and corn on dee cob and sure, dey be singing, it spectacular and dee feeling divine and don't even mention dee corn bread and collard greens and fried fish so tender you never wanna leave. But don't fall for dee okeydoke cause dat's how dey get'cha. Yeah, den it's all over an' you saved an' sanctified."

Suddenly though, the mood tightened. She was no longer giggling at his left-Jamaican-gone-Grenadian accent. It really was a pretty bad copy. Though not her impetus down into the land of the serious. A sudden revisit of a memory well past caused that…

"For a guy who don't like religion, you sure seem like you like church."

"Oh I never said I hated going to church. I just started hating some people who go just to go there, just to sit up in there all pretentious-like and hate on anybody they get the chance to look down on. Be talking like, "don't ya'll be backslidin' now."

"An' don't git me talking money! Tithing is church speech for 'send us your cash even when you can't come to our service'. It's like you don't owe us, you owe God!

"Ain't about how God made everything including your money. Obviously, God don't need it (he above cash), it's just a test to see if you love your money more'n you love him! So you best come clean with the bucks or we gonna have ta tell the rest of the congregation you a cheap, low down, you kno what you is! It's the Christian thing!"

They left Danno soon after, saying their goodnights; promising to return the next day and deciding they'd stock up before Sunday arrived. But not this night. This night on the lanai, watching ruddy hues mix and mingle with fading blues; this night would not be a night for work. Shopping for Sunday would be a tomorrow thing and Sunday they would declare their own "laid back day", as well…

"Funny about this place yo," she offered, breaking the silence. "Prickly Bay was formerly known as L'Anse Aux Epines, before that something Spanish and something Amerindian before that."

"Hmmm, what do you mean? That the names kept changing?"

'It's funny that every one of these groups that came and conquered this place, wiped out the ones that had come here before just because they had a different language or custom or God. Each one of them considered themselves the more superior because of these reasons. Ya see."

"Yeah, I get you. In reality it was their superior numbers an' weapons."

"Exactly mon!"

"So you find that condition funny?" He found the alteration of her speech pattern to be even funnier, using terms like "mon", ayebegoo and nawferme in rapid fire substitution for her norm. It didn't matter the conversation, she find a way to use these new saying.

"You okay Valerie?"

"Ya mon! Ereryting good?"

"Wanna go someplace?"

"Ya sure brudda!"

"How you doing today?"

"Ayebegoo!"

"Want more roti?"

"Nawferme!"

The peninsula in which their hotel resided, named L'Anse Aux Epines, she pronounced "Lanceapeen". Suddenly she had gone native, especially when conversing with Grenadians, at times he barely understood her. She couldn't quite keep up with the French-Creole patois of the locals, but their Pidgin English she handled quite well, all words linked and flowing in rapid fire sequence into one. He vowed to keep her away from lengthy conversations with Paul, the hotel beach bar's main bartender, who fed her too many cultural idioms and definitely too much of the local Caribe beer. Actually, they had both been drinking too much of that lager. Didn't matter for now, she still had a ways to go with this current conversation…

"I find it funny that none of them seem to admit the real reason they came and murdered those coming before."

"I'm ready! Put it on me oh princess of the beautiful eyes. Thrill me with your erudite wisdom," he jested. The Jack Daniels had not taken over, but its influence did instill a liberating effect upon his tongue, that and the vision of her lying all but unwrapped mere feet from him. He cautiously allowed that bit of hedonistic license, a bit of sexational eroticism, but no more. Loose lips sink ships and doom unwise spies…

"Greed! That's what it's all about, greed. Slavery and warfare are always about greed. Simple as that. Everything else is just an excuse."

"You don't think there are other, more principled reasons?"

"Nope. Greed!" She seemed to have a one-track mind. He agreed that many examples proved her correct. But felt there were many other cases to the contrary.

"What about the Trojan War? The Greeks fought for honor of a betrayed trust."

"Nope. Greed! They wanted their girl back. 'We own her, you can't have her. We hate thieves!' Simple greed, that's all!"

"Damn girl. You make it sound like anybody wanting their property back is as greedy as the one who stole it. So if I break in and rob a jewelry store, I'm justified because the owner is a greedy pig and so is the cop they send to lock me up and take it back? Then I get to shoot the cop cause he shudda stayed outta it. Anarchy! Thy name is truly Anarchy!"

"Not what I'm saying. Pay attention!" Obviously the Jack was getting in touch with her also. In touch with her sense of humor, cause she totally failed to get that joke. Well, he tried. She never even noticed the lightness of his tone or the jovial smile on his face. Nope! Just jumped straight back on message. "Let's use the example of the Civil War."

"Okay." Admonished, he bit his lip and let her go get out what she had to get out.

"Historians will cite every reason, every excuse for the Civil War but greed. They justify inhuman acts of barbarism on their fellow humans --blowing them up with cannons and blasting them with guns and stabbing them to death with bayonets-- for the sake of owning, torturing and committing barbaric acts on other humans for the sake of profit. They treated their dogs better than the black people they owned. Then they point to jerks like Robert E. Lee and Stonewall Jackson and pronounce them of high moral character cause though they didn't support slavery they felt compelled to defend their country, Virginia, which did. Every time I hear this crap it makes me want to puke. How you gonna support an unjust cause and consider yourself honorable. It's like that guy that blew up the Murrah Building in Oklahoma City cause he was pissed at the country. He thought he was honorable, but he was just an asshole."

"You don't remember his name?" He found that hard to believe for one who had committed such a heinous crime. But she was unrelenting.

"Who cares? He was an asshole! Same thing for the Confederates. Assholes. Most of them didn't even own slaves, couldn't afford them. They just didn't want things to change in case one day they could afford to own one. Wanna have somebody to do their work so they do better. In their case they were hopeful assholes. Probably prayed every night for God to give them the means to buy a slave."

"Like people praying to hit the lottery?"

"Hey, hold up home boy. I'm one of those people. Almost hit the pick six last week. Don't jinx me!"

"Serves me right for not knowing my audience."

"Damn skippy! Anyway, back to my point. Slavery sparked the Civil War and greed sparked slavery."

"What about power and religion? Lots of wars are a direct result of people striving for power."

"Power is just another word for greed. If I control it, I benefit from it. More money, more sex, more real estate, bigger house on a bigger hill. Anybody want mine; I hate them and kill them. I give them unflattering names and titles. I treat them as less than human, lower than beasts, lower even than the insects I crush under my feet. All for the sake of getting and keeping more of whatever there is."

"And religion? The pilgrims left Europe to escape religious persecution, just like the Jews. No money there, just get outta Dodge." She started this. He determined to get a better read on her convictions along those lines. It wasn't like she had drug him to church or something. But she had started this, he aimed to finish or at least better understand.

She began slowly, "Religion is just a way for us to get closer to our idea of God. People have written their histories and their religious stories in ways they see as befitting their worship as modified to justify whatever other conditions they seek. But then along come other people who seek to benefit from those religious histories and the rest is history. Mainly it's a history of proselytism, crusading and parading. You don't like our God; our God will kill you, through us! If you don't show our God tribute, through us, our God will take everything you got, through us! Man, I wish God would just show up one day and blow all these fake prophets off to the Hell they created for the rest of us."

She definitely had a way to put things, he decided. A fierce gleam in her green eyes confirmed her devotion to that wish. It was his turn to fetch the ice and cola. Better to go now and let her ire simmer. With irate women he had plenty of experience. He knew his place needed to be someplace else …at least for now. But stubborn was his middle name. He did not come here to wuss out.

"Interesting concept. You've really given this a lot of thought." This was the part when the hostile she-spy breaks down and confesses her every sin, including when and how she masterminded the theft of government secrets and kidnapped her archrival, the incomparable Tina. Then again, maybe not. He had a way to go where figuring out enemy she-spies was involved.

"I used to attend church when I was a kid. Even sang in the kid's choir. Wasn't much. Our parish was so poor; we weren't even supposed to have a choir. Piano upkeep alone crashed our budget, HaHa. The big guys hated on us for that. But Father Pete kept us going anyway. There was speculation he used money intended for Rome and that couldn't be good. We never knew for sure. We just kept on singing and really liked it. But I guess what we liked didn't matter. They defrocked him. Father Pete. He always did things his way. Interpretations of scripture and the like. He got away for years without any hard leanings from the big guys. But when he did a sermon on greed one Sunday and used the church as the example: enslaving natives in Africa and the Americas to dig for gold and silver and precious gems and the like. Well, when he made the comparison between the church and Judas, how they got their thirty pieces of silver for betraying the faith, he stepped out on a shaky limb and they cut it off."

"So what happened?"

"They called him to the bishop and we never saw him again. He wrote us one time. Said he loved us and that he had found a new calling. We found out later that his new calling was a return to his old. Flying. He flew as a pilot in the Korean War and he used to take some of us flying sometimes. First time I was in an airplane. After they defrocked him, he went south and flew supplies to isolated villages in Nicaragua…"

She hesitated before proceeding, as if an especially painful shadow had temporarily voided her memory. "He really loved flying, almost as much as teaching. He didn't preach. He taught from the pulpit. At least that's how he described it to us. I-I think he was Peace Corps an-and then he was killed by rebels or somebody. Back in the seventies. Who's to tell?"

"He sounds very special." He sincerely meant it. "Especially the part about teaching. We could use a few more people with knowledge in this world. Got enough idiots trying to tell us what to do. Always preaching an' all wrong. But they get on TV an' watched religiously by two or three hillbilly suckers who never finished eighth grade and they're an instant success cause it only matters that they're watched, not about what they say or do, just that somebody is picking their show to fall asleep on. Twenty-four-seven television. Gotta love it."

"Anyway, my mom and I switched right after they made him leave. I mean, if he'd been molesting little boys, most they'd have done was move him to another parish." She seemed impatient for him to silence so she could get back to her tale. But she did not rush. "All he did was tell the truth anybody past the fifth grade already knew or should have. I mean even if they missed history class, who hasn't watched Discovery Channel? So we left the haters and moved on. At least my mom did. She became a Baptist and we switched from Saturday to Sunday service. Didn't have worry about money for the choir no more, at least that part was nice, Baptists gotta have their choir or ain't no church. But I left my faith in the cockpit of Father Pete's crashed airplane, somewhere in the rain forest. It just never switched back on for me and a few years later, when my mom died, I stopped going all together. We flew over the Everglades, the Keys, out to Bimini. It was so great."

"Then he's definitely my kinda guy. A teacher who flies, err, flew. Gotta love those Airedales."

"I'm guessing that means something about flying."

"Yeah."

"Okay. He was a good flier, but he was a great teacher, at least he was to me. He had a few views that kind of stepped over the line, but that's what we loved about him. For instance he felt the Old Testament should be renamed, 'Why we did the shit we did', for all the pillaging and plundering done by the Hebrews with God's blessing …according to the Hebrews."

"You know I hate to talk religion when I'm thirsty. Be right back," he interrupted. Returning minutes later, glasses refilled with ice, he poured in generous amounts of whiskey and soda. Sunlight had deserted them, a full moon was rising over the far away edge of the gentle, silvery waters dominating nature's panorama. She winked her thanks with full knowledge it probably went unnoticed in the dim light they chose for purposes of reduced advertisement of fresh meat to anymore of the island's bloodthirsty mosquito population. It was his turn anyway.

"So your priest believed his church was built on greed. Sounds like a good reason to leave it anyway."

"He didn't fault the faith, just the fools who corrupted the faith. They definitely wanted their thirty pieces. Back in the day, you didn't tithe; they sent soldiers to hunt you down. If you complained that they were robbing you blind, they put out your eyes and left you blind and took whatever you had left, probably tapped wifey on the way out."

"Yeah, those medieval troops made an art out of that raping, pillaging and plundering routine." He wanted to keep her talking and hoped Mister Jack motivated her chatty side to something he could use. Religion wasn't it. Surely nothing bad could come from that or so he supposed. "That's why you left your church?"

"Father Pete was so right about them. That's why I left. Immoral people teaching morality and charging you for it. They say you can't get to Heaven unless you pay and if you still don't or you don't pay enough, they say you'll go to Purgatory until your family kicks in enough coin to get you out. How can you believe in a God that allows such atrocities committed by the people teaching his word? How could I? I couldn't!"

"So you don't believe there is a God?"

"I don't believe in their God." He looked into her eyes, now moist from pent up frustration, their glistening visible even in this light. He could see some of his own dysfunction in her. "I actually believe that anybody who believes in an all-powerful creator with a personality disorder is not to be trusted!"

"Yeah, I kinda got into that rut back when my mom died in a grease fire cause she couldn't get to safety cause management didn't care about their employees' safety. They worried that some of their underpaid kitchen staff might steal a few vegetables. So they forced them to march past their check point before they could leave each day."

"Back door locked and only management had the key? That's criminal!"

"Not back then. Money talks. Fire started in the front of the kitchen trapping mom and another lady in the back. Combustible construction, stuff went up. They couldn't get out."

"I'm sorry you went through that. Must have been devastating."

"Worse for my father. He kinda reacted like your mom, got closer to religion. Bible thumpers all but moved in. Prayer services twenty-four, seven. But they helped him find his balance. Me, I just got more confused."

Already sensitive, sympathetically she touched his hand, reflexively sending signals of comfort. "Guess we're both cut from the same cloth. Maybe it's a generational thing. I mean, our parents grew closer to religion while we both grew away because of the thing that made them grow closer. Kinda crazy, huh?"

"Life's crazy. The book became the word and all he talked from that time on was this biblical quote or that. But it was only a band aid. My father kept his faith only up until the time some drunk-assed rich kid ran down me and my brand-new bike with his brand new car. He wrecked my bike and me and unfortunately he wrecked his car."

"For somebody who doesn't believe in the bible, that's awful understanding of you. He almost killed you and you worry about his car?" She was more than a little confused.

"I didn't say I don't believe in the bible. I just don't believe in all the stuff they put in the bible. I don't believe the bible is infallible. I believe they put in some wrong stuff and left out some right."

"Yeah, that's why there's fifty versions. They keep trying to get it right. Father Pete intimated the same things. Although he pretty much summed it up that some of the interpretations were rather liberally applied."

"That's a nice way of spelling W-R-O-N-G!"

"So back to your father."

Unfortunate for young Master Jimmie Boy and for me; the accident, that's what they called it back then when a drunk white kid mows down a black kid with his automobile…"

"That's usually what they call it now!"

"Oh-kay. Unfortunately, it happened down the street from my house.

White kids on a drive-by through the colored neighborhood; gonna scare the darkies. That's all it was, stupid kids out joy riding. But my dad took one look at me, remembered what the white man had done to him all his life; remembered what had happened to my mom because of their cavalier attitudes towards minorities, remembered how they'd robbed him of his boxing career, remembered a whole lot of stuff he never shared with me, and he nearly killed that white boy standing over my limp form shouting that I'd wrecked his car. He beat that boy like a toy drum at Christmas. Beat him so bad the kid probably fed through a straw for months."

"What happened to your Dad?" She tried not to ask, but the curiosity overwhelmed. "Did they put him in jail?"

"Yeah, then they let their white-hooded fellows come take him away …and lynch him."

"Oh no!" Now she hated herself. Even the ghoul in her curious nature hated itself for asking the hellish question. She just had to know. She felt like smacking herself…

"Anyway, suffice to say I never came close to having any kind of faith in his religion after that. Some guys tried to tell me I was being tested like Job. I told them I had no need for a God that felt the need to torture and torment kids just to test their faith in God. Most idiotic thing I ever heard. That's one part of the bible I think they got wrong: 'You're having bad luck? Check your faith!' What kind of crap is that? Please tell me they didn't mean that!"

"Like I said. Birds of a feather."

"Oh I get you. Trust me, I get you. Of course you never said."

"Never said what?"

"Birds of a feather."

"Hmmm, when you're right, you're right. But you're wrong. I did infer."

"Stubborn to the end."

"Damn Skippy!" With that, both fell silent.

"But you know…" They both started simultaneously, stopping almost at once; her giggling, him laughing. It was a good laugh both enjoyed.

"You go first," he offered.

"Y'know, the book of Revelations says that Christ will use the 'Word of God' to kill everybody in Satan's army. He'll just utter it and kapowie! All dead. Only Satan an' his evil angels left, an' even they can't hang. Satan git his ass kicked into a deep hole; his boys all kicked into th' lake o' fire." She had lost none of her earlier zeal. The cocktail had suddenly converted her into an erudite goddess of knowledge and irony and even with the occasionally butchered phrase; she seemed far from done with this subject. "But these self-righteous assholes still runnin' 'round trying ta kill off their neighbors in th' name a God, cause evidently, they either must not believe God can do th' job wit' out them or they jus' wanna get their lumps in too. Either way, they surely don't seem to believe their own book, so why should I?"

"Yeah, good point. They all wanna be a soldier in God's army," he agreed. Now was not the time to disagree, even if he did, mostly though he didn't.

"Now, the kinds of people I never suffer are idiots, zealots and fools. You won't believe all the people in my old neighborhood wanting to fight every nonbeliever back then. I stayed well away from those nuts. Wouldn't trust 'em far as I could throw 'em…"

Her speech had spells where the slurring cleared up almost entirely; causing his suspicion that she might be faking, for some reason, though she may just be fighting the effects. Taking another small sip, she continued her current train of thought,

"…literally gonna kill 'em as Satan worshipers when their own holy book says God got it all in check. Don't even need their help, just want them to take care o' their own soul and he do the rest. Only Satan really needs help. He the one needing folks to back him up. I bet somewhere in the Koran there's a similar passage."

"Yeah, it's in one of the sutras, err suras." Now the drink affected his own speech, confusing Buddhism with Islam. But then again, he was far from the only one and perhaps that was a universal condition that created or at least contributed the problem. Confusion, that had to be a major reason so many people felt compelled to murder their neighbors in the name of their chosen deity. "Yeah, suras. I forget which one. Had a young Marine trying to teach me all about the Koran when I was almost as young. Guess I should'a remembered."

"Jus' r'member it ain't you th' problem!"

"Crazy thing is these people see the antichrist everywhere they look. Got a woman who don't kiss they ass, she antichrist; got a neighbor wit' a shotgun callin' you th' asshole an' keeps a savage dog in his yard ta keep you out? He see you th' antichrist; and lord don't ever have a black politician who becomes President, definite antichrist."

"Don't ya wanna kiss me?" Suddenly her mood became amorous, creating instant suspicion in him as to her motives. She leaned forward, expectantly, though just a little, not wishing to appear too eager.

"Nope." His flat statement caught her off guard, stinging slightly. But he did not leave the moment time to sink deeply. "Cause then your magic might steal my heart and I'll be forever under your spell."

The hurt frown quickly turned impish grin. "When I get you alone I'm gonna..."

"Err, we are alone, Genie."

"I mean when we, owww you know what I mean!"

"I know what you said."

"Well know this smarty mouth, when those goons are outta our hair, I'm gonna spank that butt like you stole somethin'!"

"Know ah'ma be likin' that." He smiled his best imitation of the Cheshire Cat to Alice.

"Oh, you..." That's when the phone tingled its diminutive chime. Unfortunately, just loud enough to bring guilt to the one ignoring its summons. But since men invariably tend to ignore guilt as well as various types of summonses, she became the one enticed to succumb ...which in this case probably made for a better outcome.

"Oh, hello Carlos..."

"THE MESSIAH IS AN INCARNATION OF MAN. NOT OF GOD. THIS INCARNATION IS A GROUP OF HUMANKIND. WHO WILL SAVE MOTHER EARTH FROM ARMAGGEDON?"

The text message displayed boldly on his cell phone, demanding attention. He checked the sender's address, already aware. Sure enough it had come from his twenty-year-old sister whose brain had become programmed by the theology courses she took at the University of Würzburg. In his opinion their study was a total waste, transforming what might have become a world-class surgeon into just another useless zombie of the religious right. The Stuttgart native quickly deleted all traces and focused back on the presenter's spiel, hesitating to wonder whether his sister might know a better way than he at this juncture…

"We believe the object will slow from its present velocity as it passes Jupiter and gets a slight redirection, but it should be traveling approximately fifty-thousand kilometers-per-hour upon impact. At present its diameter is the size of Germany. It will burn right through earth's atmosphere, heating the surrounding air around it to over ten million degrees Fahrenheit, turning it to plasma. And us…"

The speaker paused for effect, holding his audience in momentary stasis. "So the impact will produce a crater the size of the Arabian Peninsula, larger. The resulting shock wave will generate earthquakes topping magnitude twelve, equal to over one hundred teratons of TNT going off all at once. That's one million megatons if you prefer those kinds of numbers. Either way it'll decimate an area at least as large as the United States, possibly the entire Eastern Hemisphere. I want to emphasize, inside this area will be 'Wrath of God' on a biblical scale straight out of Revelations. The four horsemen cometh, the sixth seal is undone. Damage will be total. There will be nothing left. Buildings will all be flattened, lesser objects will be thrown for miles; rivers will all be gone, cut off, their waters evaporated; even mountains will crumble and seas will boil and all living things, well, there will be none left living. You might find the gold fillings from people's teeth."

Murmurs circled the assemblage, worried looks flashed about, rising panic seemed about to take flight. So far, though, no one spoke out. Anticipating. He didn't let the wait last too long. "We do not believe our combined capabilities at present could stop or deflect it. At most we would probably blast it into millions of incoming fragments, converting a single warhead into a cluster bomb the size of…"

Another pause, waiting for the full impact of his words to sink in. Most of the audience came from their nations' power elite. Ministers of this office or that, chief scientists and some military. All listened quietly without comment, but inside their heads were all churning; facts, equations, principles of meteorology, et cetera. All were Caucasian and male, either

Christian or atheist, though none was devoted to religion …with good reason.

A glowing satellite image of Earth's Eastern Hemisphere appeared on the left side screen. Uncluttered by atmospheric aberrations such as fog or clouds, it began scrolling down from a view on par with a space god to offer scarcely more than a bird's eye perspective of the tri-border swathe incorporating eastern Iran, southwestern Afghanistan and northwestern Pakistan. As the scroll began, features changed from a two-dimensional picture of flat earth --predominantly tinted by reddish-browns, spotted with shades of green and bordered by deep blue oceans-- to become mountainous slopes towering above rift valleys, stretching endless across the wide expanse. The highest slopes sported coats of white.

Thin, jagged, bright yellow-colored lines —that seemed to have been crafted on a small child's Etch A Sketch toy-- provided the sole features identifying boundaries separating the region's nations. No geographical limitations or natural dividers. No rivers, mountain edges or lakes provided rhyme or reason why on one side stood country A and on the other, countries B, C, et cetera.

But the fact that some British politician's whim had been the primary driving force to partition this region would mean less to nothing to the upcoming event. The mountains would be plowed under, ultimately merging with the valleys. Rivers and streams would fill the resulting chasm. Archeologists could anticipate years of adventurous fieldwork, spelunking brand new caverns and digging through broken ruins of former cities and towns …any who chanced to survive.

But for now the only lines of importance were a series of concentric rings forming colored circles that enclosed progressively smaller geographical areas, the largest of which enclosed western China and most of Iraq, east to west, and from Kazakhstan to Pakistan, north to south. Inside this red circle, the designers portrayed the predicted blast radius, where nearly every living thing above ground would be instantly vaporized. The middle, blue circle encompassed an area less than one sixth the red ring and represented the crater dimensions where even those things underground would stand no real chance for survival above an average one hundred feet. Both these areas were so much larger than that encircled within the smallest ring, colored white, symbolizing the actual impact area, giving obvious and ominous representation of scale. Here the predicted crater depth was over twelve hundred-fifty feet.

"Naturally the main concern for those of us outside this area is thermal coupling resulting in the heating of our atmosphere which may effectively scourge the earth's surface of all life, including the oceans. Planet recovery is on the order of one hundred years, minimum. Of course hardly any higher order life forms will be around to witness that eventuality!" He paused again, but not to permit others to comment. He merely wanted time to gauge their temperament, half expecting a few to dash for the door or begin rapid fire conversations on cell phones, but none did. After all, this wasn't for TMZ …or Sports Center.

"NASA calculates that the collision could possibly generate a force equivalent to two million megatons, if this comet impacts the earth dead on and traveling as fast as predicted. But odds are its anticipated trajectory will result in a strike angle of approximately seventy degrees, plus or minus three degrees. Almost a glancing blow. So this white circle is really an inaccurate representation of NASA's prediction. It should depict an elongated slash or gash; say between ninety to two hundred miles long. Let's just use the white circle to mark point of impact."

As if by magic, his presentation changed to elongate each of the rings forming west-oriented ovals. Now Israel, Syria and Lebanon fell inside the red periphery while much of western China dropped out.

"If we permit this predicted impact, approximately two billion people will cease to exist within minutes. They can't run far or fast enough. Possibly another billion will die in the aftermath of debris falling back to earth from the Mesosphere. The rest of us will go in the aftermath of the global firestorm and the impact winter. Doesn't leave much hope for our future."

It had been all gloom and doom up to that point, but then his audience noticed an up tempo to his mood, almost brightening. Hope gained a foothold…

"What we propose to do is slow the object down quite a bit by simultaneously exploding nuclear warheads underneath as well as behind as it enters our atmosphere. If the angles are complementary, we believe it is possible to carom it back into space, limiting and greatly reducing the area of destruction. Although the nukes may somewhat contaminate the immediate area, any destruction should be concentrated within our initial predicted CEP as shown on the map. Also, this technique should minimize the amount of superheated regolith ejected into the thermosphere for reentry around the globe. It is paramount, for our world to survive, that we eliminate the possibility of this secondary fallout."

The view had changed back to the first set of concentric rings. To the relief of the few closet Bible-thumpers in the room, Israel was safely outside the danger area. Jerusalem would be spared. That fact alone provided justification for signing onto this plan. Still, some would require a tad more convincing.

Murmurs generated in one corner spread to others, gathering momentum; questions, comments and assertions achieved a dull roar. But he was not about to allow their changing the steerage from monarchy to anarchy. America would tell these clueless bastards what they would be expected to do. When the big dog comes through, the little dogs shut their yaps and move out of the way …or so went his belief.

"Sacré bleu! What arrogance!" quietly muttered Jean-Pierre Bertrand to no one in particular. His closest neighbors sat three feet away to his right and left at the large polished table. Nicknamed JB, his patience usually ran longer than his official title as the French Minister of State, attached to the Minister of Foreign and European Affairs, responsible for European Affairs. This day, the youthful and flamboyant man's normally relaxed demeanor was decidedly opposite. Not only did he vehemently detest the idea of blowing up one half of the world to save the other half, he equally hated to be party to some half-baked American scheme. The problem was his own scientists had also come to a similar conclusion. There seemed to be no better alternative to killing one corner of the world before a giant rock killed it all. The good news centered on their belief it would be the other guy's corner that died. So he bit his tongue and kept his peace while the American, as if sensing the need for reinforcements, turned another corner.

"Now! Better news. As you are aware, comets have been credited with bringing rare minerals as well as fresh water, possibly even kickstarting life as we have evolved. We believe a significant amount of the comet's icy surface will vaporize and eventually fall to earth. Also, although there may be some damage to infrastructure, petroleum deposits won't be measurably impacted. The average depth of the region's deposits is below fifteen thousand feet. Now there will possibly occur significant surface searing. In fact, oil wells and production facilities may actually be totally destroyed, depending on how much material actually rains down from the comet as well as rebounding as regolith."

The power of suggestion ruled. Instantly, hundreds of thousands of tons of fiery debris --pulled back to earth by gravity's superior embrace-- streamed in live video feeds through most of the minds present. Clouds of superheated regolith could change any disaster scenario from regional to global. Luckily, the presenter's suggestive powers had yet to finalize the good news category…

"However, despite possibility of said damage, supplies stockpiled outside the region should suffice to meet demand for the short term until drilling can begin again. Add the reality that most of the world's zealots and troublemakers may also no longer be around anymore and we kill two birds with one stone. After things cool down we can go in and it's business as usual, even better. Not even China will want to try to impede us after our demonstration of force and will. So there will be some beneficial tradeoff and it's all in the name of saving our world."

He did not need to add what everyone was thinking, "Just not that corner of our world…"

CHAPTER NINETEEN

"It's official! We're in the crosshairs." His jowls trembled with his message. "The object is as large as the state of Oklahoma and massively dense. They're calling it the Old Man."

"The Old Man?"

"Yeah, on account of its resemblance to an old man kinda kneeling down. Anyway, Old Man's gonna hit the Earth and there isn't anything we can do to duck or shrug it by. Not Jupiter's gravity, even Saturn is out of position, neither is gonna be close enough when it crosses their orbits to change its trajectory even a bit. It's headed in towards the sun and we're in its way." At this meeting he preached to an audience of only one, but one no less important.

"Fudge! What about all these Goddamed nukes we got? We got 'em, the Russians, Brits, French! Hell even th' Chinese an' North Koreans! Why can't we launch a massive strike and take that bastard out before he even gets here?" The Director had gotten up from his plush chair and now stalked around the periphery of his huge office, ignoring its opulence and space-inspired accoutrements, ignoring even his easy acceptance of the nickname. The shuttle --poised on its liquid-fuel tank, with solid-state rocket boosters attached-- raised up on one tabletop, ready to blast into low-Earth orbit. The International Space Station floated above, dangled from the ceiling by a pair of wire tethers. But none entered the picture cast in his brown eyes. Only the glow of utter frustration and abject submission.

"Probably do more harm than good. Have a few hundred-thousand incoming comet pieces rather than just one. You ready to experience that many Hiroshima-sized nuclear blasts all at once?"

"So do we give up? Proclaim the doom of mankind? Pronounce to the "End-of-Days" adherents that their dreams are coming to fruition? Their time has come? Shit! We might as well slash our own throats now and be done with it! Once they find out, anything we try to do to reverse this coming will cause them to create even more havoc!"

"It's bad. It's unbelievable bad, I know. There will be people of all races and creeds joining to celebrate the coming end of the world. Lot of people. But there will be even more who will join arms to demand their governments do something to stay this execution. Lotta people not ready to die!"

"I dunno, there's a whole bunch'a religious nuts out there waiting for a sign of the coming apocalypse and the messiah. There's already people moving to Israel, they think to trigger the messiah's return. They decide we're working to prevent it, we may as well slit our own throats!

They both lapsed into quiet reflection. The Director walked to his windows and stared out into the dark clouds announcing a coming storm. It all seemed appropriate to him somehow. He wondered how he would tell his wife, his children …and their children.

"End of days. The Old Man cometh. Never thought it would happen in my lifetime. Thought we'd have more time. You know, time to raise our grandkids. Time to grow old or old enough. You know, I used to cringe in my bedroom at night, wondering if the Russians, the Soviets, would launch their missiles while I snored …now I lay me down to sleep!"

"Yeah, me too. We'd have all those drills in grade school, hide under our desks in preparation for atomic blasts and nuclear fallout. All the time I wondered what the good it would do. I knew the Government was just applying a band-aid to a shin splint. It wasn't gonna be any good. We'd all be dead or radiated to barely living. My parents always kept the stiff upper lip, telling me that God would never desert us. And I tried to keep faith. But I knew that if those bombs dropped, if those missiles flew, it was the end of us, at least, most of us. But with this thing, there won't be any most of us, it'll be all of us."

"You got plans? I mean, 'til the comet hits?" The Director had stopped his pacing. His eyes followed the flight of a sparrow flitting from one tree to another in search of insects. He wondered why he had never noticed such things before. It had been years since he took the time. Time. That was the luxury he had never seemed to have in this job. Time. It was always a luxury. But now, with doom bearing down on his planet at over five hundred thousand miles each hour, time was no longer a luxury.

He made up his mind to take an immediate vacation, one from which he would never return. He would spend his last days with his family. They would take the boat that never seemed to move from its berth on the Chesapeake and drive it down to Florida for an extended outing. He would make his apologies to his family --that he had never found the time to love-- and peace with his Maker with whom he had never seemed to find the time to worship. And he would cherish every remaining day … until the end.

"Okay!" He stated the word with an impish alacrity, tossing in a wink for added effect. "Now that we've given honor to God, cried in our soup and pissed in our pants, we need to address another side of the Doomsday scenario. I need you to get your people working on a couple solutions."

"Huh? I thought you said there was no way!" Puzzlement encircled his head like a merry-go-round. A half-hearted specter of Chance raised its besotted head in his clouded vision.

"What I said was, there is little chance!" reminded the corpulent harbinger of misery. It had been nearly five months since their last meeting at the Goddard Space Flight Center, during which time he had been too busy to even have lunch with his friend. They had cooperated to successfully shut down all outside access to data streams coming from Hubble, and other spaceborne systems focused on the onrushing giant. But worldwide communications had not ceased; rather, they had multiplied exponentially.

"There is a theory", he began. "You know that the French and the Russians, correction, the Soviets, were the last to conduct aboveground nuclear blasts. Well, it appears that they may have a solution."

"Well damn man! Let's hear it!" The Director was in no mood for riddles. "How on God's green earth can we fix this?"

"During one of their nuclear tests at Fangataufa Atoll in the South Pacific, a small asteroid fell into the test area. The French being the French, they exploded the device anyway, figuring it wouldn't be a good idea to let the meteorite smash it and not having a lot of time to decide, because this thing was heading right for them. As it turns out it would have been a near miss, but they didn't want to take that chance. They abandoned the countdown and just popped it off right as the meteor passed overhead. It was only about a two and a half megaton, device, but it totally vaporized that meteor. Now, we don't always get along, right? So it appears that our French-fried brethren decided not to tell us until just recently. Something about oblivion coming that brings even the most stubborn back to the fold."

He smiled a sly smile before sipping at his coffee cup. His host was gobbling every word. He did not leave him hanging for long. There was too much work to accomplish before any of them could rest, plus the fact that if this plan failed, there would come eternal rest. The thought sobering, he rumbled on…

"Of course, the Russians said they already knew. Said they had purposely detonated a nuke in the path of an incoming meteor back in sixty-six. The site was all ready to go, the rock was inbound, and the Russians, excuse me, the Soviets, were curious. So, they delayed their test until the meteor entered the atmosphere. Again, it wasn't very big, nowhere near the size of the Old Man, but neither was the nuke, about one megaton. Anyway, meteor blazing by, nearly overhead, they ignite the device and poof! No meteor, just a lot of tiny fragments. No major hits on their territory either, a few casualties, lost a house here and there. But nothing major. At least, that's their story."

"Like we could ever trust them. But damn that sounds promising. But if we do trust them, why all that nonsense before? You really had me worried." He was still worried.

"Problem is, nobody believes we can achieve that same effect in outer space. All the Sims we've run indicate, 'no workie'. We try, we die. Just create a hundred thousand mini-comets smashing into our big blue marble, total annihilation.

"When comet Shoemaker-Levy 9 smashed into Jupiter, one two-mile long fragment hit with a force around six quadrillion tons of TNT. Six hundred times every nuclear warhead we got. That's just one. Shoemaker-Levy broke into nearly two dozen fragments, pieces of rock and ice traveling at hypersonic speeds. Not what America's got, what the whole world's got. So we can't succeed by hitting this thing early. We can't divert it without turning it into cluster bombs. We need to meet it head on just as it enters our outer atmosphere when it's already being torn by gravitational shearing and cooked into a fireball by friction. To those titanic forces we'll add a billion tons of nuclear explosives and turn the whole thing into charred dust and water vapor. No humungous hole in the ground. No upwelling of molten rock to rain back and ignite the entire planet, not even a cloud of smoke and ash to cover the sun and bring on nuclear winter. The opposing forces will all but negate each other."

"You're certain you're telling me everything?"

"We've modeled the effects on supercomputers. Simulations are almost ninety percent conclusive. Of course the shock wave will destroy everything below it for some distance, say five hundred, a thousand miles. You don't want to be anywhere near."

Ninety percent? The director wondered. These people had to be smoking some serious narcotic to believe a ninety percent computer-predicted solution meant anything other than a wild-assed guess updated to add scientific on the front end. Thus WAG became SWAG, a scientific wild-assed guess. Still unproven, therefore damn near useless. He couldn't believe what he was hearing. They'd outlive the Mayan calendar prediction, but not by much, 2022 instead of 2012. It was time to start his vacation. One final fling, a few tender moments with the wife and then that last sunrise…

"Nope, we gotta hit it inside our atmosphere." His friend was still selling though nobody was buying. "Got something to do with compressibility and temperature-induced valence transition. I'll get you a physicist to explain it later. Suffice to say the combination should destabilize the comet material's atoms by inducing their outermost electrons to instantly lose all bonding abilities. It'll be cooking at over a million degrees once in our atmosphere and when those nukes go off; the theory is that all those fireballs will consume each other."

"Probably consume a whole lot more," the sage director responded. He still wasn't buying whole hog, but he could still envision that glimmer of hope. "So what more can we do from here?"

"We need your folks to tighten up our predictions on time, location and impact angle of the comet strike." Jowls set and firm, he took this moment to issue forth a phlegmy cough into his handkerchief.

"We already passed that along! It's Iraq or Iran, two years and counting! Its picking up speed, should hit around five hundred KPH until gravity from the inner planets slows it down to about a hundred. Best we can do." Chance had faded, slightly. But Hope remained, though diminished.

"No! We need you to narrow it down to seconds, by specific lat-longs, within GPS CEP.

"Now?" The Director wondered which brilliant idiot had dreamed up some new capability within his workforce that would permit them to determine the exact moment and location a hyper speed object –still two billion miles away-- would strike the Earth, two years hence. And what good would such information do? It wasn't like a few hundred yards here or there would matter.

But his State Department friend was far ahead of him. Anticipating the sense of inevitability and withdrawal, he remarked, "Within the next two years we're planning to nuke someplace above Iran!"

Shape nearly oblong, with a nip and a tuck here and there, sculpted by cosmic forces beyond the ken of mortal men. It first showed up in a Hubble wide view image. Seemed interesting, a new object for observation. But, of course, everything in the sky fits that bill.

Then came the fly by of New Horizons photographing Pluto and it's five moons. At first sight, it appeared Pluto had six. Except this new moon had disappeared in follow-up shots, proving at once that neither was it a moon, but this guy was really humming along.

To some of NASA's more impressionable troops it gave the appearance of a hatless old man kneeling on one knee, a burl pipe clenched between his teeth and its size dwarfed Hydra, Pluto's second largest moon. Its journey had begun eons before man had even acquired the ability to stand on his hind legs, long before dinosaurs dominated. Well before then it had traveled a repetitive, elliptical orbit around a giant, red star at the edge of the Orion Nebula in the region known as the Trapezium. The Orion Nebula comprises the middle "star" in the sword of Orion hanging below Orion's Belt which girds the waist of Orion the Hunter. But in a time well before recorded history, before earthmen discovered the ability to record, there was not yet a bright nebula here whose light crossed the heavens for earthmen to see.

As if on a tethered, rubber band, this traveling Old Man's mass swung in a gigantic arc, curling around the star's periphery from close in to very far away. But it never came close enough to lose its fight totally and plunge down to become one with the star nor flew far enough out to a point where velocities and mass would multiply its momentum sufficiently to break the tether. Far out, in a deserted corner of space, it would again lose its momentum and soon begin to slow enough until gravity again reigned supreme. The point of aphelion.

As it closed towards its giant master, its tail became fully displayed as radiant star fire coaxed the errant creature's icy mixture to melt and stream particles that the solar winds blew behind it like a red shimmer of gossamer majesty visible for millions of miles. Also fired by its red giant master, the creature now sported a rubicund corona of its own whose circular bloom radiated its presence for all to behold its oncoming magnificence.

However, most of its hydrogen fuel gone, the star began growing bigger and brighter, hot enough to burn helium and for a time a new source of energy reigned. Orbits of the closest planets it soon encompassed, searing those hapless worlds to lifeless cinders. The outer planets its pressure pushed out to even larger orbits, preserving their lifeforce for a time. But alas it was not to last, for though the heavier helium fed its furnace, depletion of the hydrogen weakened the red giant's gravimetric forces to a point where eventually this red giant could no longer maintain its size through the might of its waning nuclear furnace and it began to collapse back in on its core. Its awesome light, now even more tremendous, radiated over thirty thousand times brighter than the yellow star sustaining our own Sol System …that is until the massive red star suddenly went supernova.

A chain-reaction of ever-expanding eruptions began to occur, one feeding on the next, spiking energies ever higher by orders of magnitude until the star tore itself apart in a calamitous conflagration that threw stellar plasma out into space. Mega-trillions of tons of it flying ahead of the blast wave at dizzying speeds. Within a single year, the blasted material literally filled space for a trillion miles in any direction and in time far beyond even that mammoth distance.

Out of this cataclysmic chiaroscuro came the image of this deep traveler, this newly liberated Old Man. Only a God or one possessed of special capability might differentiate the exodus of this individual from all the other untold masses redirected and tossed away by the blast wave as easily as a Hercules swats a flying gnat. His monotonous cycle became forever disrupted in the star's abrupt end. Just one more of the untold trillions of projectiles fired out into the far-flung nether regions of space at speeds surpassing millions of miles per hour.

Soon the Old Man left all behind as his greater bulk retained its energy long after the shock wave's fury had dissipated. Now he again became the ultimate traveler with no discernable tether to challenge his freedom, truly alone for the first time in eons.

It had recently darted past Pluto. Pluto's current location being still fairly close to Neptune's orbit is much closer to earth than at other times. Pluto at perihelion is even closer to the sun than Neptune. But much more so than the Dog Planet, this Old Man was very dark and not very reflective. Its surface consisted mainly of black ice and dust particles. Moreover, it had no reflective polar caps like Pluto. That and the limited sunlight, which reached out this far, made it tough for earthbound sky searchers to even detect, let alone identify this Old Man.

Barring its chance photobombing New Horizon's photograph of the

Plutonian moons, it might never have achieved any notice, at least not in time. Then again, time has a way of inserting a relevance into any situation.

The Old Man's speed began to increase again. At first only slightly, then at an ever-advancing rate it hurtled straight towards an obscure, yellow star and the Old Man's ten thousand millennia of wandering about aimlessly was over. All those myriad globular clusters and glowing nebulas it passed along the trip to this place had failed to ensnare, but suddenly a new master exerted commanding pull, interjecting order and purpose to nomadic roving.

This one was nowhere near as large as the Old Man's previous master. But its timing was perfect. His momentum had decreased sufficiently and there was insufficient gravitational attraction from other large bodies close enough in this celestial neighborhood to counter the tremendous urges instilled by that distant, yellow orb. Out here, three-quarters of the way from the galactic center, the yellow sun ruled this sector alone. No other star hailed within six trillion miles. Supreme on its shimmering throne, it called to him and this Old Man surrendered in a manner akin to a new bride on her wedding night. He went as called …by his new master.

The Treaty of Versailles (1783) acknowledged the independence of the thirteen colonies of the United States and gave back to Britain several French possessions in the Caribbean Sea, including the island of Grenada in the Grenadines. Today's island country of Grenada consists largely of three islands –Grenada, Carriacou and Petit Martinique—of which Grenada Island is both the largest and home to the capital of Saint George's. After Saint Kitts and Nevis, Grenada is the second smallest nation in the Western Hemisphere and considered by many the most idyllic …although all is not necessarily ideal.

Saint George's is about one hundred air miles from Venezuela, making Grenada a prime intermediate stomping ground for drug smugglers seeking to transit their product north to the USA. Carlos Morano first came to know Grenada's benefits following the capture and conviction of Manuel Noriega. He invested in a few local businesses, but he never fully exploited the benefits of its location for narcotics transport and soon after Noriega's fall, he and his cohorts left the illicit drug trade altogether.

But he never totally left Grenada. Eventually he purchased a small, twenty-acre island just off the main island's southern shore, with the intention of one day finishing and renovating its lone structure, a faded colonial mansion built by a failed sugar baron. Its flora consisted primarily of palm trees and bougainvillea, this latter climbing freely all over the stone dwelling. There was little else, save the occasional beaching by a dying sea mammal or sea turtles burying eggs. Sugary sand there was aplenty, but hardly any sugar cane and no sugar barons to be found anywhere ... until this new lord strode its powdery beaches.

Morano's renovation program began slowly at first. He had grand ideas, including central air conditioning, water storage and power generation facilities and outbuildings for hired help who would no longer need to take daily water shuttles back and forth from homes on the main island. But these became radically altered by the arrival of Hurricane Ivan and its one-hundred-forty mile per hour winds in 2004. After Ivan, the plans changed from renovation to rebuilding those parts destroyed by wooden missiles and searing winds. Luckily, flood was never a problem thanks to the house's elevated location. But most of the roof was lost.

Morano's house was no exception, as Ivan destroyed or damaged ninety percent of Grenada's buildings, leaving parts of the three major islands appearing as if the U.S. Air Force had come back and bombed what they missed during the 1983 invasion. In truth, Ivan killed nearly as many as had the U.S. forces, in total, slaying over forty people during its seven hours stay in the area.

Eschewing the idea of repairing structures incapable of withstanding nature's fury, Morano then initiated a building project to replace all those structural components considered weak. The Department of Defense uses a similar analysis to determine weaknesses and design flaws. Its acronym "FMECA" is pronounced fa'meeka, for Failure Modes, Effects and Criticality Analysis. The idea is to pre-determine how components of an end product –in this case a house—could possibly fail and either redesign or install backups to preclude the possibilities of failures "screwing the pooch".

Seemed like a win-win solution to him. Some prefer to lump such preventive techniques into the "Waste of Time and Money" bin. But he'd always believed it better to be glad he did than wish he had.

Using such a technique, NASA could possibly have saved a couple space shuttles named Colombia and Challenger and fourteen lives. But then maybe they consider risk-reward from a different perspective, cause burdened with cost and schedule constraints, engineers often reduce risk-reward strategies to the practice of ignoring risk altogether, only seeing potential reward with their jaded eyesight ...plus, saving pennies is how you get promotions.

So, more often than not, they forgo full FMECA programs and either substitute off-the-shelf commercial products, not intended for applications such as what they have in mind, or enter full-scale production with the intention of fixing flaws at a later date; either as they are identified during usage or as scheduled during pre-programmed product improvements. The military establishment calls these "P-cubed-I" or "PIPs". In other words, as money comes available. You ask, "What if the money does not come available quickly enough to update your flawed machines?" Well, then you get apply patches, either that or to buy a whole new machine …or, in the case of Colombia and Challenger, a whole new crew!

Morano decried such planning as anile and deleterious, liking it to paltry government expenditures on education facilities versus mega sums for state-of-the-art prisons. Those he termed "The Bureau-Cats", were never out on point and seldom if ever prescient. Instead, hindsight was their mantra. Always the clean-up crew, arriving well after the nick of time was already long gone.

Probably his pet peeve was Bureau-Cats. In his view, this penny-pinching, bean-counting crowd took office in search of better opportunities for their business cohorts rather than the general public. Their loyalty was to the gods of increased profit margins and lower taxes paid by the upper crust. Social programs did not measure high on their scales. Neither did national unity.

It was the one thing that had drawn Tina to him. Certainly, was not the golddigger image suggested by Chaco. Tina could go anywhere and be welcomed. She carried the kind of package desired by every man …at least the kind with a pulse.

She preferred men with a purpose way loftier than gold collection. So, he made it his mission to always point higher, shoot for the stars. Corporate bottom lines were essential, but not the ultimate.

He would worry about corporate issues in their turn. But as for his house, Morano took his lesson from the several earthquakes he had survived in Los Angeles. It was much better to spend a little more now than later. The villa he ordered rebuilt to specs similar to those used in new constructions in South Florida …following Hurricane Andrew.

His construction crew kept the stonewalls but replaced all the exterior woods with southern pine lumber due to its superior "give" over hardwoods. Laminated and solid timbers bolted together with steel collars and couplings were sunk into the steel-reinforced concrete foundation to act as shock absorbers against Mother Nature's fury. The floors, walls and roof panels were similarly bound together to add strength. All windows and doors were impact resistant glass. Not quite bullet proof, but close. Even the generator house was double-walled, and its roof made of steel. The refinements did not come cheap, but then again, neither does replacing an entire building …or its occupants.

His teardrop shaped island sits not far from Prickly Bay, only about two miles as the crow flies or, down here, it would be as the tropic bird flies since there's no crows. Using a pair of binoculars or a small telescope he could almost see the hotel beach where his assistant and his fiancée's Ex were enjoying the afternoon sun. But their frolic was not paramount in his mind. His primary concern featured that unknown snooper outside his home the previous evening. His pulse had not settled down until his Lear Jet passed the two hundred-mile EEZ, putting them outside the U.S. Exclusive Economic Zone. Jittery to the point of terror, he kept expecting a flight of F-22s to appear off his port wing, demanding they return to Florida. He even pretended to sleep so none of the others would suspect his terror.

But now he could relax here, far from the American authorities, safe on his own island in another country; all alone with Kalliope. Although alone was not the way he had envisioned his life here. Still, he found the big, beautiful, colonial villa breathtaking even though the work was still not quite complete. Still, only a few, relatively minor details still required attending.

He remembered not to count the steel window shutters in that details figure since Tina had never approved of their look, considering them more "overkill" than necessity. Her oft-repeated expression that "sometimes less is more" still echoed within his memory cells …as did the picture of her soft-brown eyes and tender lips.

Literally awe-inspiring, her face and figure bent low to kiss him with those. Magical gifts from the heavens and she used them like weapons, those succulent attributes of hers that seemed never to age. She played with his weakness for her, even played him against himself; the effect stressing, creating a semblance of psychosis within him. On came the occasional hallucination to plague his waking moments; distorted realities leapt from dreams. Her disapproving eye he saw at nearly every decision point and, despite this fear of disappointing, he had at first stubbornly refused, doggedly resisting her powers. It almost worked.

But there was no win to this situation. Eventually he had succumbed to her vision. Just like all those other times and just like all those other times he had rationalized his weakness. It was part of the price he paid prior to her relenting and finally giving in to name to the villa. That was what he convinced himself, all the while realizing it for what it truly was …total capitulation.

His one bit of pride centered on the knowledge that this time she had to work to move him off his chosen course. Even her proclaiming his a "Schizoaffective Disorder", didn't faze him. He gave it the mental heave ho it deserved. Right down the old bladder relief tube (aka, the pisser) he flushed her plaintive arguing that his intention to bar the windows and doors all around with steel bordered on a childish phobia requiring professional aid to repair.

Tina could be a hand full when trying to get her way. If Dondi were here he'd have chimed in: "Like most women!"

However, this time she was on a mission. She demanded huge windows from which to view the wide vistas of sea and sky, accusing his tastes as draconian and his Schizoaffective Disorder totally out of control.

But he stuck to his guns. Besides, he did not at first even know what Schizoaffective meant. He figured she was just showing off her book learning. Part of him feared she described some sort of Napoleon Complex, she being a bit taller than he, especially while mounted on her four-inch pumps. Fearfully, he refrained from asking clarification, deciding instead to ignore the thought …he'd Google it later.

Because his logic he believed legit. His decision he had justified upon his fear of the windward storms. It was from windward that came the demons he most feared; demons often beginning as West African thunderstorms. From that direction came those demonic creations of Mother Nature that sprang suddenly out of foreboding cloudbanks to form tropical cyclones. It was the windward side of Kalliope that looked out into the teeth of those demons, so logic advised those be protected. He argued that he could live with only securing windows at just the back and the sides. But it was an argument with himself. Tina would have nothing to do with his concerns, barely even listening. She turned her nose upwards to the idea, pooh-poohing even the necessity. "You already put in impact proof windows. So what's the deal with metal shutters? Besides, they're ugly as hell!"

What he did not reveal to her were other, equally fearful concerns. These involved assault troops coming in off the windward beach, charging into his home. Metal shutters would not keep them out but might delay them enough for evidence to be destroyed or evasion and escape. It was like back in the Barrio days; Five-O knocking on the front door, them running out the back. But she could not know these things. He intended that she would never find out the illicit side of his nature …at least not until after the wedding, hopefully not even then.

Of course, inevitably she won again. "What else is new?" Asked Chaco's know-it-all look. The older man never voiced it, but it was still pronounced in his subtle way he had of telling what he wanted you to know with out verbally telling you anything. That was Chaco's way to pronounce him inadequate …Tina's was a bit more in your face!

So he had rejected his architect's plan even though half the villa's window closures had already been installed. Actually, Tina's observation that they made the place look like a prison helped the convincing, much more than her diagnosis of his mental state. His new instruction to the architect was to either find something esthetically pleasing or forget the whole idea. The image of a prison house he found most displeasing, as did the image of a deranged Napoleonic character out of contact with reality. Eventually, they decided to leave well-enough alone.

He walked along the half-mile long beach, heat from the sugary sand warming his sandaled toes. Occasionally an aircraft would take off or land from the airport not far away across the emerald waters that lapped gently on the shore, his shore. He reveled in the knowledge that he commanded all his eyes fell upon. But he shared the hint of glory with no one. The vision of Tina's serious brown eyes faded. He felt very sad and alone, lost without the woman who had so infused his world with ideas of love and hope all these years, then just as suddenly made his hate a living, breathing component.

Looking back up the hill at the two-story home, he could appreciate her sense of style. It wasn't all that big. He did business with people whose boats stood taller. But it spread out pretty good and really had beautiful lines.

Many of the renovations sprang from her ideas. It practically gushed from its all-green, eco-friendly features that included both solar and wind power and waste recycling. Gone was the gray stone and weathered wood eyesore that had provided young Grenadians a getaway for beach parties and sexcapades before his purchase. In its place rose a main house whose double-decker, tetrastyle porticos extended front and back. Embossed onto the frieze over the front portico were seven inches high gold letters bearing her choice for this place she named after the Greek Muse, Kalliope.

She preferred this spelling over the more modernized version. But the idea for the name itself she took from Carlos' cousin who worshipped Mother Earth all the while studying the cosmos. Kalliope was the daughter of Zeus and Mnemosyne, who was the daughter of Gaia and Uranus, Mother Earth and God of the Sky. She believed the title appropriate for a man who needed to get in touch with something more meaningful than financial wheeling and dealing.

Built in a classic tetrastyle commonly used in public buildings by ancient Greeks, as well as Etruscans, it sat beneath a low-sloped hip-roof supported front and rear by four Doric columns anchored to the upper patio which was, in turn, supported by a lower set of four of significantly thicker circumference than those on the second tier and providing a more aesthetic appeal. But all were substantially strong, adding to the overall integrity. Latticed fencing surrounded both upper and lower patios. Admittedly biased, he reflected that the whole effect was a great look.

Kalliope would never be confused with the gothic mansions dotting both sides of the Hudson River on its trek north of New York City. She would barely suffice as the get-away bungalow of a Rockefeller, Astor or Gould; nothing close to an iconic abode in the eyes of those iconic demigods. Neither did she favor some gleaming Georgian castle topped by towering spires and turrets or surrounded by lavish fountains, this place. Regardless, however bland her architecture (by some standards) her beauty still enthralled him, passionately. But it was an odd pairing, his desires for her. He had no passion for marble statuary or rooms filled with original masterpieces by long dead mad men. Any close approximation of such grandeur bore the stamp of Tina alone. However, furnishings were another matter.

He loved sumptuous couches and expensive chairs covered in the finest fabrics and skins; chairs with padding so thick you could lose yourself and handmade tables and cabinetry to fill every room. Inside Kalliope's walls they both agreed on nearly every detail, seeing nothing extraneous with hardly any of its internal flourishing and there were many. Gilt-edged ceilings in the center hall and living room danced with artistic renditions of harlequin pantomimes of every color. Massive fireplaces in the family room and living room, as well as a smaller scale in the master bedroom, were all unique and faced with the finest marbles colored shades of gray and green flecked with white and each of her six bedrooms boasted its own luxurious bath. Kalliope may not have suited the Hudson River elite, but she was far more than adequate for his tastes. She belonged on his island, not some rocky bluff in Hyde Park or Rhinebeck. She belonged here, with him. Just as Tina once had…

She had insisted on the floor-to-ceiling mullioned glass windows and the triple-wide French doors in the home's front and rear to capitalize on its east and west facing views and though they contributed significant challenges to maintaining overall integrity against tropical blows, they were well worth the effort and expense. The patios were accessible from any number of sitting rooms, bedrooms and the like, adding to their utility. They'd often breakfasted on the upper patio. Tina enjoyed --used to enjoy, he reminded—sipping her dark, rich coffee with the sunrises in the front and coladas with the sunsets at the back. Lounging on thickly padded, white patio furniture or sitting at a small table with her paper or magazine, she'd reveled in the idyllic, picturesque displays and had finally capitulated, agreeing to be his wife.

He was not certain the impetus, the thing that motivated her capitulation. Perhaps it was all those years of "begging", as Chaco's cousin Rubin Martinez alleged. Rubin had grown decidedly more embittered after that shtupping the wifey thing. But that's just the way of the world. Rubin had once diddled one of Carlos' Ex's and payback's a bitch! Besides, he hated that "wet-back, son-of-a-bitch". Hated him even more for the accusation but had to admit his assessment was probably accurate. Carlos' deepest memories seemed to merge all their previous years together into one long endless frustration for a man so in love with a woman who was not so in love. Once he put it on her though, things would be different "…bitch ah make you want me!"

But the frustrations abounded even now. He remembered how she would share his hotel suite, when they vacationed together, but never his bed. How the long legs peeking from under her elegant negligee seemed to call out for his attention, even though her lips never once called for him. How she teased and titillated him. Her every action suggested that she wanted his friendship, nothing more, until she finally said, "Yes!"

Perhaps it was her love of Kalliope. After all, not once had she even hinted at capitulation before they --actually, before she-- refurbished the house. Kalliope was her baby. Plus, she had never cheated on the house, just him. He fell into sadness once again, reflecting that even now gone, she still held him in her power. Her style, her choices of colors and fabrics were all before him …in her house.

Hating his minimalist tastes so prevalent in the Miami dwelling, here she got her way. Its interior they filled with butter-soft leathers and Persian rugs in some rooms, Berber carpets in others; gold flecked vases on polished wood or onyx tables and lots of potted plants hanging or filling up nearly every corner. On the walls they hung original paintings from modern artists and a few masters. He could have done without these latter but had no real dislike for any of these embellishments Tina demanded to have.

Its exterior walls they covered with pink stucco, trimmed all around by the soft white pine, because she said so. That memory brought forth a smile to his lightly tanned face; it did not take long for his color to return. The sun felt good as he turned up to greet its warmth before again facing Kalliope. Tina had a thing for the white on pink motif. He reflected that given her way he might end up bankrupt like the previous owner, but wished she was here to tell him what to do now…

He still needed her approval. She made him desire to please, to achieve. The decision came suddenly. He would throw a party tomorrow night; invite some of the Saint George's crowd. Several of the government ministers might show up even with this last second notice. They loved a good time. And women. Yes, lots of women. Good booze, good food and a good, local band. Yes, that would make this place less lonely…

Soft sunlight filtered through the overhead canopy of palm and calabash trees, reducing its radiant effect enough that gentle breezes pushed by the mid-day trade winds needed no assistance from fans hung above in the hut's ceiling. Beyond their location, facing across the beach bar and out into Prickly Bay, it was a different story altogether. There the sunshine lit the entire scene bright and shimmering and cooking.

Gently bobbing boats at anchor, soaring birds on wing and sunbathers on lounge chairs all shared the stage with lovely homes and cottages climbing into the hills along the periphery. Around the beach bar, a dozen others slurped at tall, cool cocktails and discussed events past, present and future. For JP and Valerie, the future included an afternoon of shopping, which he really looked forward to …not!

The chimes rang nearly a dozen times before the bartender sauntered over to answer the telephone. His casual "hallo" was followed by a few seconds of silence. Turning to the rightmost of three couples sitting at this side of his bar; he offered the handset to Valerie. "Dis fer you."

"Hello Val, what's up Love?" She stiffened measurably, instantly O'Rourke suspected the reason, "Tim". He first wondered how the man knew how to find them, then realized that he could be sitting in a boat offshore or in his car somewhere nearby, maybe he'd just called the desk to ask the maid. Obviously, the guy intended to send the message that big brother was watching. He now felt more certain than ever that Morano sent the men who had followed them two nights before. Eventually, he would need to duck them.

But now his eyes followed the progress of her lips. He was not very good at lip-reading, but casually tried to pick off any familiar words formed by the exquisite pair. His success rate remained dismal. Valerie hung up the phone. Taking a strong pull on her cocktail, she smirked at the curious man sitting beside her at the outdoor bar. "You're not going to believe this!"

CHAPTER TWENTY

Nutmeg, Grenada's chief export crop is used to make everything from jams and jellies to soaps and cosmetics, like lipstick and nail polish. Even arthritis treatments are derived from the reddish mace that surrounds the brown nut. From a distance the fruit looks almost like a peach, hanging from its leafy, green parent in a Macon, Georgia backyard. Except this distance is quite a bit south of Macon …so no peach.

Signs for Petit Boue, Mont Tout and Grand Anse rolled lazily past. He wished they had time to explore. Unfortunately, this time they had an agenda –or at least she did-- plus a timetable. So far he had followed all the right roads into Saint George's.

They drove through crowded streets lined with cars, minivans and vendors selling wares from sidewalk markets that included products derived from locally grown bananas, mangoes, cocoa, cinnamon and nutmeg. Two, three and four-story brick and plaster buildings rose on both sides; the ground floors typically engaged in some sort of business venture.

Bars, spice sellers, variety stores and insurance agents seemed dominant. Here and there, along this sidewalk or that, cooks turned over ears of corn roasting over a charcoal fire and over this way or that was an occasional sign urging the reader to "Top Up" their phone card minutes. Everything seemed primed for the customer. One could stop at a corner, jump out and be back inside your vehicle's air conditioned comfort inside two minutes, slugging down a cold one or licking at an ice cream and often there was little need to disembark in order to partake.

Seemingly, at every stop sign, youthful vendors pranced up to their Jeep with offers of all sorts of apparel, whole fruits, spices dried and jarred and sapodilla drinks. Young kids carrying huge bunches of bananas were having much success with nearly every tourist they approached. O'Rourke was the exception. In fact, not one approached him, instead opting for the softer sell on the left side. Their instinctive choice of Valerie even included a good-sized tip.

He did not blame the locals. Wearing a welcoming smile, she looked like Heaven, even dressed campy in tan-colored, khaki hiker shorts that hid much of the curvaceous legs, offering only the briefest glimpse rising above wheat-colored Timberland boots with white socks peeking over their ankle-high leather tops. A loose-fitting, pastel yellow blouse and amber-tinted Serengeti sunglasses completed the ensemble, along with the obligatory brown leather, shoulder bag. He felt she would even look great in a burlap sack …just not too loose fitting.

She had her bossy moments though, ordering him to stop so she could jump out and buy a T-shirt here or local soap there or to "hold on a second", while some vendor ran over with some trinket she waved for. Myriad things she spied as they progressed through streets not so narrow but far from wide. She seemed to want them all…

"What can I say", she chortled, pulling down her shades to peer over, winking at the same time, "I'm a soft touch."

"Seems like it."

"You disapprove!" Hers was statement, not question, only a bit acid tinged. However, the afternoon sunlight glinting from her amber lenses hid any hint of tightening around her eyes. Didn't matter.

"Nope. Just don't ah-prove. Your vacation, your choice." He was not looking in her direction to discern any mood swing. He drove on through the narrow streets towards their destination, determined not to get sidetracked to the point of getting lost again. He did not want to chance having to again listen to her pet name for him. In fact, if he never again heard the name "Uie" directed at him he would consider himself a lucky man.

The horseshoe shaped Carenage forms Saint George's natural, inner harbor and runs from Belmont, on the southern end, around to Fort George in the north. Geologists believe it was created by a volcanic eruption thousands of years before. Boaters believe its gentle, protected waters were made just for them. Dozens of boats bobbed easily at anchor and at docks, in tune with the few ripples creasing the clear, blue liquid. Schools of tiny fish dodged their larger, hungrier cousins in search of their own meal in the shallows.

Barely stirring, the breeze was light; heading out of the northeast it crossed the mountainous spine --running down the island's middle from top to bottom—before greeting Saint George's on its way down to Grand Anse and onward, possibly all the way to Venezuela. Carried in its gentle flow came fragrant offerings; aroma therapy for all to enjoy, wafting up from a multitude of spice trees and plants.

He stopped and parked on the western side of Wharf Road across from white-sided buildings with bright-red roofs on the right and quiet moorings on his left. From there she tested his stamina, taking the lead on a seemingly endless march from site to site, stopping to snap pictures or to hand him bags containing the souvenirs she purchased: bottles of exotic spiced liqueurs, handcrafted souvenirs, batik cloth sundresses, more nutmeg soaps and T-shirts emblazoned with cute, colorful quotes. He came to think himself the pack mule of this expedition. Cause he was. At other times he operated as the photographer, shooting shots of the posing female beside Colonial Period cannon at the Fort or standing arms spread wide, big smile, halfway down the length of the otherwise deserted cruise ship pier —straddling an imaginary line down its center—unfortunately with no cruise ships currently snuggled against either side. It made for an interesting shot all zoomed in but would have been better with a pair of massive boats docked, like: "Hey, look what I found!"

Thoughtfully, she led him back to drop off packages in the Jeep to give his tired frame less load to bear before "The Climb". She even purchased an ice-cold water to replenish some of the fluids he'd sweated during his labors this day. She needed him in good shape for those to come …ever the benevolent slave owner.

He was very glad that he had opted for the shorts rather than pants. It was a very warm day and perspiration became self-evident, after braving the five-minute shortcut through narrow Sendall Tunnel for the third time. Auto traffic they restricted to one-way and usually stayed to the right —headed North-- pedestrians got to pass through in both directions and usually stayed on the left side opposite the cars and minibuses. But it wasn't necessarily a fair tradeoff. Some drivers strayed a bit more to the center than the right, sometimes quite a bit more …that's where the bravery part came in.

Too many Speedy Racers seemed bent on changing the thoroughfare into a dual lane with no room for walkers. By the time they'd successfully dodged nearly every NASCAR wannabee south of Key West and reached the street level steps leading up to historic old Fort George, he was certain the worst was over. Then he took a good look upwards and witnessed the awe and majesty of "The Climb". His first good look not weighted down with shopping bags. Now he understood what one of the travel writers meant. It was a warning. "Get Thee Ready!" Obviously, the worst wasn't over yet, that wouldn't come until after they'd conquered the millions of stone steps (seemed like) up to the top of the Fort.

Earlier, she had opined that his dark green shorts looked rather nice with the mint green short sleeve. Of course, that was before both took on a "plastered-to-the-skin look." But she never complained …even when they dripped a bit her way.

Being a DolPhan, she was not as enthused about the Eagles ball cap, however. Perhaps loading him down with packages was her way of demonstrating that fact. He'd thought Raiders fans were rough, but this Miami-type showed an equally tenacious quality. Hours later, though, she finally rewarded her beast of burden for his monumental labors.

"How's the drink?" She smiled across their small indoor table overflowing with plates and saucers and plastic-coated menus. Given his choice, there was no way he would pick an outdoor spot, regardless how lovely the view; perspiration had become full blown sweat. Besides, the inside view presented its own opportunities. The small café was well-appointed, featuring mahogany wood railings separating the dining area from the bar, which was also mahogany. Seemed every wall covered by autographed pictures of celebrities who had visited the establishment. JP wondered whether they received a free meal in exchange. Another plus, inside service was quicker.

"Good. How's yours?" he replied, still a little miffed by her snide comment on his less than adventuresome choice. She wasn't the one sweating under a load few pack mules would easily carry. Her selection --delivered in a hurricane glass-- dwarfed his double shot of Jack Daniels on ice, even after its pink umbrella had been removed and cast aside, the fruit garnish devoured.

"Excellent! Want some?" Now darkened nearly to the color of jade, her grayish-green eyes peered deep into his. Challenging, in a most electric way. They appeared to be promising fulfillment far exceeding previous evening's soul searching. Then their centers sported a much lighter shade of green, tinged with red. Suddenly he wasn't quite as miffed as had been…

"Tol' you don't let yo' lips write a check yo' hips can't cash!"

"Brought travelers checks!"

"More likely credit cards!"

"Whatever! Still spend like cash!" Then she leaned mischievously forward and planted a wet kiss on his lips, her right-hand fingers slipping under the hem of his shorts to brush the inside hairs of his lower thigh.

"That was just a down payment."

"Oh yeah?" he murmured in her ear, nibbling the small opal ring planted there. "In that case, I believe it's time to go."

"Uh, uh! First lunch, then dessert!"

JP nearly bit a hole through his lip to stifle a vindictive instinct to fire back her smart aleck quip with some little jibe of his own, perhaps a simple something like: "Promises, promises" or maybe a "That's what you say now".

But he relented. It was late afternoon, and they were both operating on empty tanks last filled at breakfast. Besides, a pack mule only has so much dignity left. Why waste it making an undignified spectacle in a cat fight. Besides –as everyone knows-- you don't got no pussy, you'll never win in a cat fight …and then you'll never get no pussy.

They left Saint George's after partaking the sumptuous meal, followed by more shopping of course. Valerie seemed never to have met a store or a scene she did not like; one to be shopped, the other photographed; then possibly photoshopped, for all he knew.

He pondered the complexity of her logic as they dove greedily into bowls of Callaloo stew full of meats from conch (that the Grenadians called lambi), joined by crab, chili peppers, garlic, onions and even slices of breadfruit. Somewhere between suppressed burps stirred the mental image of a digitally edited picture on her Facebook page. Him! Bent low, head hanging, tongue out, her burdensome packages on his back while he strained mightily to pull an ox cart she drove. Her right hand held tight the reins to the bit in his teeth while her left cracked a bullwhip on his behind. This far, he had yet to catch her uploading any fluff stuff to the internet, but one never knows these days. If he found it, she'd be toast…

So far it seemed cool though. So far Valerie seemed happy just keeping his loyal slavery a local disclosure. Nothing major newsworthy. She mailed a postcard to her daughter, which would probably arrive after she did, then they headed on a roundabout visit to Grenville on the East Coast to gather a few items for Carlos' party before driving back to L'Anse Aux Épines.

So far, his only issue was that damned camera she flashed this way and that like Zorro's blade slashing "Z's" across the backsides of the sheriff's inept troops. Hopes Sylvia won't see him on Facebook. Even worse, Instagram! She put him on the gram it'll be lights out for him! Sylvia a total Instagram junkie. Probably knows every celebrity on it , maybe half the noncelebrities …the celebrity wannabees!

The FEDEX deliveryman had already climbed back into his truck by the time she opened her door. He never liked to hang around a door more than a moment after he rang a customer's bell, although the vision that popped out of this particular door made him wish just this once he'd taken more time or needed a signature or anything that would have kept him on her stoop a bit longer. Such opportunities he was loathe to miss…

The package –a large envelope—he had slid into a space behind the hedges. No sender information or return address, excepting a PO Box number in Miami, Florida. She wondered if it had come from one of her old college friends. They sometimes used FEDEX to send her business opportunity information. But some inner nagging intimated its subject as JP or about him. He had not called her since he left. But that was nothing new. Usually she initiated their calls. He was so hopeless, half the time he left his cell phone in his car's glove compartment and took off for parts unknown. Other times he would not return her calls even for days after he returned. It was just the way he was. She'd show up at his door and wake him from a two-day sleep-in, sometimes three. Then she'd join him and remember why it was she loved him so much. Apprehensively she opened the envelope.

Sylvia had to admit to herself that he still looked good, very good indeed. It was even dated. So convenient. Well, at least he had been healthy two days ago. Nice scene, casual and tropical. Nice photography too. "Even with that hair-too-short, legs-too-skinny, fake-boobs, no-ass-bitch on his arm!" Her thoughts.

Jealousy flared. Despite her suspicions about the package's sender, she was on the hotline within minutes. It almost had to be that doofus-looking Thompson guy. But regardless who sent it, JP's guilt was obvious. She had to make a connection with Cassie. "Damn him! Mission my ass!"

Island tweaking, booties popping, hot 'n tempting. Oh, the guys had it going too. Not that he really noticed much about them, except checking if they were checking out him. His focus, all things Morano!

Fully lit inside and out, Morano's villa mimicked a beacon in the night for all ships passing. Transforming the scene uber festive rotated floodlights at each corner of the house as well as colored spotlights hung around the huge pool and from nearby trees. Valerie had left him to tend to her duties entertaining guests and coordinating caterers and music and whatever else the party crowd desired. She maybe wasn't so much at microwaving TV dinners at forty thousand feet, but girl could throw a party like nobody's business.

This Saturday night, the normal twice-daily ferry service to Carriacou had another run added; this one detoured south from the Carenage to Morano's island. Others took colorful water taxis from points closer. The ferry took a bit longer, maybe ten or fifteen minutes, but at least everyone aboard arrived dry. Speedboats employed as water taxis were a bit dicier, upping the ante on the possibility of incoming wave spray. But they lived on a tropical island. Such was to be expected. Besides, this was a pool party…

People of every hue and shape gyrated around the pool's concrete apron. There were at least two hundred, maybe three. It was difficult to tell. A few swam and frolicked underwater, others walked the shore with their dates or their prospects. Cases of booze and kegs of chilling beer sat strategically on two sides of the pool and were heavily visited. Most served themselves, the three bartenders they reserved for more eclectic beverages and concoctions. The music was fun and filled with island flavor, as were most of the people.

But Carlos was still despondent. Even all this ribald revelry failed to cheer him. Local politicians came by to make their presence known, in hopes he would remember them come election time when a few well-apportioned contributions could greatly enhance a campaign. Several local females rubbed and pawed him in near-drunken searching for his attention to other favors. One even performed a mini striptease after trailing him into a bathroom. He tried to get into the mood by returning her attentions, all of her being very well-endowed, but he really could not get interested enough to fully explore the toys she offered. He had other toys on his mind…

Back in their place they shared, O'Rourke lay barely aware of the images playing across the TV screen. Relaxation was wonderful thing after so long a day. He saw her before hearing the tiny knock-knock at his bedroom doorway. Pressing the remote's "MUTE" button, he beckoned her to enter, wondering if this already half-unwrapped Greek came bearing gifts, if she brought a need to be resolved. Soon, however, it became obvious that she had not come to make love to him or even to tease. She came with tears that threatened to overwhelm her capability to stem their onslaught.

They hadn't stayed long, barely two hours. Both had agreed to leave early, even though not concerned having a long wait later for water taxi Ubers. Now looked like the party was definitely over for her and that meant for them …and those instincts were on point!

She had a need, but it was a need to be held, to be comforted. She needed a warm embrace and a patient ear, from him and she instinctively knew both would be available. The tale was not very long or arduous, but it had a heart-rending quality whose power took him quite a bit of struggle to overcome. He triumphantly fought down the deep emotional stirrings. She was not as successful…

Soon her tears flowed freely. Her words stuttered, but she pushed them out for both of them to hear. She seemed to need to tell her tale as much as he desired to hear it. "I-I ha-have a little girl. Her name is Caroline. Sh-she's twelve. Handicapped. The umbilical wr-wrapped around her neck. Almost d-died."

Her words gained power with the telling. She began to relax, snuggling deep into his arms, his shirt front drying the tears, helping stem their flow. She looked her big, red-rimmed eyes up into his and continued. "Caroline is so tiny. Barely four-eight. She's slow, but some things she picks up on real quick. She can't read all th-that good. I-I read books to her every night I'm home early. My mother-in-law takes c-care of her when I have to go away. My hus-, err, my Ex, lives in Houston. He left when she was b-born. C-couldn't stand t-to look at her, even though she's really beautiful. One eye is a little f-funny, you know. B-but she's a great kid."

"Comes from havin' a great momma." Trying to lighten the mood. Didn't work! Whole time she talking he thinking, "gotta keep this woman off vodka shooters!"

"Caroline c-called while we were at the party. She j-just wanna say hi an' she loves me." She wore only a white T-shirt and teal panties. He was still in blue jeans, about to pull off the black, short-sleeved shirt and black sneakers when she walked in, not long after they returned from the party. She'd seemed moody the entire boat ride back in the private launch Morano had hired just for their round trip. And it wasn't due to worries about the little, cuddy cabin boats half-drunk captain, although by indications from his steering he barely qualified as first mate. Suddenly she perked, smiling brightly into his warm eyes that titillated her so, hammering at the few barriers remaining between them...

"Bet you dated a lot of women, didn't you? Probably got 'em lined up coast to coast, sittin' by the phone; can't hardly wait for Mister Good Stuff to come 'round again."

Then just as suddenly her effervescence seemed a bit less sparkly; almost as if this subject stepped her one foot deeper inside a lion's den. The fact that the lion appeared friendly helped steady her nerves a bit, but only just so. Such a journey is much less problematic if the lion has recently been fed. She looked for the signs, finding only conflicting indications: "See my smile? See what big teeth I got!"

Each question into his background became another step inside the lion's den. With each subsequent step she wondered all the more fervently, the question straining to escape: "So when's the last time you ate, Mister O'Rourke?"

Couldn't see his expression so good in the dark, that's a problem with dark men, she'd smirked, leaving him a wonder it's purpose. But eventually he drug out an answer for her to digest and also wonder.

"If that's your way of insinuating dating more'n a few women makes me a playboy or somethin', won't agree or disagree. That's your call. You think I'm like your Ex, that's on you, too. Actually, I kinda prefer to think'o every woman as unique. So if we can both agree that's th' case, then number's irrelevant. Let the record reflect th' reality that I have dated individual women on individual days and enjoyed the gift of their time individually."

"What? Oh my God. I said it wrong brother! What I meant is: I bet you bullshitted a lot of women and they waitin' fo' yo' return so they can get some payback by spanking that ass!"

"Spanking is always an acceptable form of greeting." He smiled wide at this bit of clever repartee.

She suddenly realized her near nakedness or, more appropriately, the message it sent to this king of the jungle and rolled out of his embrace, scooting under the covers; effectively blocking his view of hard nipples pushing towards freedom through the thin cotton fabric. Her choice of dress had no play in this event, at least in her mind. She did not intend to turn him on. She had need of a friend. But what about his need? It was with significant trepidation that a tiny voice asked her next question.

"C-can I sleep with you tonight?"

Sunday came bright, sunny and sweet from the smells of spice blooms on warm, tropical breezes. Valerie marched into his room and landed on the bed with a thud, shaking him groggily awake she passed a steaming cup to and fro, under his nostrils, wafting something that smelled like fresh-brewed coffee. "Wake up sleepy head, time to get ready."

"Breakfast? I'll take a pass," his lips mumbled or at least did something along those lines. His eyes remained closed tightly, half undesiring to face the sunshine, half undesiring to face her, even though her mood seemed as sunny as the new day. Maybe it was just a trap she planned to spring, lambasting him with a fury identical to that displayed by Sylvia. His ears still rang a bit from that treat. "Just a few more minutes…"

"Not breakfast. Just Green Mountain blend …and church!"

"You want me to go with you to church? Did I do something wrong? Didn't like my dancing? What is it? What makes you wanna go to some strange church you never been in and worse, drag me along? Yo! This ain't a setup is it? Ain't nobody, like maybe your dad or fav uncle, whoever, standing by cocked and locked to have a shotgun wedding is there? I didn't touch you last night. Don't I get to least try 'fore I gotta buy?"

"It's not really my wish, it's a promise I made. You see my aunt is dying of pancreatic cancer and I…."

"Oh, I'm so sor…" He began, but she shook her head impatiently, grabbing for his fingers which she intertwined with her own to soften the blow. Now he was fully awake, his eyes tracing the serious look on her face, ignoring even the low-cut teddy whose pastel color complemented the green shining from her eyes. Except, suddenly the twin orbs seemed to lose some of their luster and tingeing with reddish hue.

"No, it's okay. She's in so much pain it'll be a blessing now. The hospice helps a little, but she's really hurting. I only hope it's soon. I love her very much and I'll miss her terribly, but I just hate seeing her like that, what she's going through. Anyway, she made me promise to attend church services every Sunday, at least until she passes and that's what I intend to do."

"So she's super religious, huh?"

"Definitely! And I could never figure out why. I mean, she never wavers even though religion hasn't done a whole lot for her, unless you count the good feeling of knowing you'll go to Heaven."

"Yeah, cause you already been to Hell." He whispered the retort softly, but she discerned his thought anyway.

"I agree. I mean, one day back when, she went to her pastor, I won't even describe that fake Reverend Like wannabe reject from the Church of Gimmee All You Got. But she goes to him looking for some solution, some kind of help and he dumped on her."

"Let me guess, 'You'll receive your reward later if you fill up our collection plate now.' That about right?"

"Man, you should be on 'The Psychic Chat Line'."

"Had a familiar ring."

"Anyway, she went to him and said: 'Pastor, I have asked God time and time again, to heal my ailments. I am so much in pain. The cancer is eating my soul. Why won't He come to my aid? I know He is a merciful God. But why won't He answer me?'

'This douche bag gave her his: 'It ain't about your thing; it's about our thing' speech. Talking 'bout: 'God is not only merciful, He is all-knowing. He can see the good inside all of us. He can also see the bad, the evil. The reason why prayers go unanswered is Sin. All the potential blessings we might receive from God's infinite mercy can only be stopped by Sin! God will not be mocked or deceived. As written in Psalm 139: verses 1-4, He knows our every thought. When we are not walking in the Way, when in our hearts we harbor enmity for our brother, when we ask for things with selfish desires, God will not answer your prayer because He does not hear you if you ask selfishly. James 4:3 states that: 'When you ask, you do not receive, because you ask with wrong motives, that you may spend what you get on your pleasures'."

"Reminded me of my Ex, except the preacher could afford better suits, like two grand each an' dozens to choose from. Anyway, the Ex learned his hated ways as an altar boy. Priests beat him regularly with big, wooden paddles anytime he didn't perform the way they wanted. He called them 'Bullies in the Pulpit' …and then he became one like them, quoting scripture while they hurt you, taking out their hatred for all things weak and small. Like God gave them a mandate. One of the reasons I left. I mean I could sympathize, but only so much. I had to go."

"Sounds like someone who became conditioned to the dark side."

"Looked almost just like that preacher too, right down to his big-assed, duck feet."

"Three more reasons to hate him," JP joked, trying to bring down her angst. But he might as well have passed gas in a crowded room. Her button nose wrinkled in the way people do when something smelly sails nearby. Jokes using arithmetic had no chance…

"All I know is, her pastor best be glad I wasn't there when he blamed her pain on her sinning. Now if I'm in the room, I'd be swinging free right about then. Lefts, rights and uppercuts all over his fat head. But she just swallow back her pride and her pain and say: 'Oh, I see pastor. God won't come to my aid if I ask for help, but if I don't ask, then He'll help cause He knows I need help even if I don't ask cause He heard me cause I didn't ask.'"

"Douche bag has the nerve to get indignant on this octogenarian who can barely stand at the time with the aid of a cane. Talking 'bout: 'Are you mocking God sister Beatrice?'"

"Aunt Bea replied, 'I thought I was trying to get an understanding of how I can get help from God, Reverend! It seems you're saying that when a massive wave of pain hits down to my bones and I cry out to my Master to help me endure, then I have been selfish and He won't hear my pain.'"

"Reverend Coin Snatcher says, 'Not true sister. He hears all our pain. But if you ask him to take away your cancer so you can go back to your wicked ways, that would be a sinful thought and He wouldn't listen.'"

"What wicked ways Reverend?' She asks, 'I've been a faithful member of this church for thirty years! I'm here for early Sunday service and regular service. Until my illness progressed, I used to teach the youth group on Wednesdays and rehearse with the choir Tuesdays and Thursdays. I wouldn't have time to sin if I wanted to,' she told this one-track minded reject from Heaven or Bust, Inc. But Mister 'Pius Becomes Us' never heard one word, he just drawled on in that nasally, high-pitched screech of his."

"God works in mysterious ways, sister. First Corinthians, Chapter 1, Verse 27: But God hath chosen the foolish things of the world to confound the wise; and God hath chosen the weak things of the world to confound the things which are mighty. To put it simply Sister Beatrice we cannot know God's Way; we only have to do God's Will."

"I hate that fool. But she stuck with him and his congregation all these years. She's determined that if I keep attending, even though I'm attending a different place, that I'll find some good. Trying to save my soul."

"So you making me go to try and save mine? Sounds very unfair."

"I don't want to go alone. I'm alone enough these days."

"Okay I'll go, but I ain't singing."

"HaHaHa," she giggled and treated him to another jab on his arm. He could see her connecting some serious shots to that preacher's temples. The man would need to be hardy or he'd have little or no chance. But that man's troubles with Valerie that man would need to deal with on his own and on another day. On the other hand, on this day JP would have to deal with a congregation that rose bright and chipper for their 10:15 AM Sunday service which was even earlier than the one he'd last attended back in High Point …not counting his wedding day.

"General, I believe we may have a slight problem on our hands."

"What kind of problem Ben?" Resigned to the fates that seemed always conspiring to add drama to his day, the senior officer sat calmly back in his chair, taking one more look at the figures on the document before closing its folder and glancing up into Peterson's troubled eyes. He could read the man's concern, but that did not necessarily make his problem suitable for elevation.

Generals do not have the same types of problems that Colonels have. In fact, usually the only problem a General has is convincing Colonels to handle their own problems. They need to attend very carefully to this matter. Colonels spend so much of their day playing "Here's the monkey", that Generals are typically caught up in the game at one time or other.

The operative word here is "caught". It is at that time when something magical happens, the General gets caught. And like magic, the Colonel's shoulders are lifted as the monkey leaps from his onto his boss' shoulders. Now the boss has to either fix the problem or pass the monkey off on somebody else, some other unsuspecting soul. But that possibility does not faze the Colonel who is free to head off to the golf course.

Burton was well aware of the philosophy of passing the monkey. He was not buying. He very nearly responded, "What do you mean we?" Accepting the inclusive term "We", transforms a pronoun into an active verb that requires action by the membership.

This General however remained determined to successfully defray joint ownership of the problem, to instead maintain the activity's exclusivity. But they paid him to listen and he could listen without accepting the monkey. Plus, interruptions are part of the job. Allowing the interruption is not the same as co-opting the monkey …is it?

So he sat back, leaving in place the scattered papers and folders littering his brightly polished desk. Message transmission: "I'm busy, so say your stuff and leave quickly and I won't find more stuff for you."

Now all he needed was a "message received notification" on his subordinate's face or demeanor and all would be hunky-dory. There's no monkey passing when they fear possibilities of acquiring more monkeys. So, he wasn't worried about any more stuff being left on his desk …or his shoulders.

Still. Any problem that got him away from this budget issue, even momentarily, could not be all that bad. "Or could it?" Motioning the man to sit, he crowned his fingers and waited. Peterson sat in the right most of the two chairs across the wide desk. Then he got right to the point.

"We just got word that DEA lost two people in Hurricane Eris."

"That storm is really kicking up a ruckus all along the gulf coast. Sorry to hear about those people. Thanks Pete." He had purposely cut Peterson off, brandishing but a modicum of his General Officer powers to indicate in quick fashion that the news flash could have been delivered by email or as a bullet comment for the Monday morning staff briefing. He only intimated this attitude. When dealing with the monkey one must strike quickly to prevent transfer. But he had not stated as much due to the onerous vise tightening in his stomach. Something singsonging in his ears chortled that his Deputy was not finished and that he would end up with a monkey for dinner in place of his wife. He was never more prescient…

"Sir, they were working for us."

"In New Orleans?" again his impatient, abrupt manner was intended to send a signal. "Go away and take that damned monkey with you."

"Miami."

"Are you certain?"

"Pretty much, sir, they were performing surveillance for us when a tree fell on their car."

"Who authorized the surveillance? This is the first I've heard such!" The cryptic pattern of his speech was its own telling. He was struggling with that damned monkey and his Colonel could sense it. But now that his interest was piqued, his impatience took wings of its own and the simian transfer was completed, not unnoticed, but completed. The new ownership he acknowledged and sucked it up as par for the course; no way out of this one. Monkey passers understand that aspect, what they often fail to grasp however, is the reality that once the boss jumps in the pool it means dangerous waters for others already swimming.

Eyes half slits under steel gray brows and teeth tightly clenched around an unlit pipe, the general waited a moment, scarcely a moment before emphasizing his impatience. "Go on, Colonel."

""Thompson!" The single pronouncement escaped in a rush. He braced for the eruption; it was inevitable.

"Thompson! Captain Andy Thompson?" He glared at Peterson who only, meekly nodded once. "What the hell is a geek from Computer Lab doing contracting field agents from another Agency?"

"I think I authorized it."

"Come again?" Fukin' monkey gittin' heavy!

"Sir I think Thompson may have misconstrued something I told him and acted on his own initiative. He decided to keep tabs on O'Rourke's movements to safeguard the classified stuff we gave him."

"Get that skinny little sonofabitch in here!"

"Now, General?"

"Yesterday, Colonel!"

"Yes sir. But before you bring him in, I need to discuss what we're gonna do about O'Rourke. DEA is under the impression that O'Rourke is a potential bad guy. Thompson used the ploy to keep them away from the truth. But DEA might go Injun on him. Scalp him. He could be in grave peril."

"Didn't you say they were only to conduct surveillance and report back?"

"Well, you see, DEA has kinda been keeping tabs on Morano. Loose tabs. You know, his associates, their businesses and locations and such. You recall when they lost one of their field supervisors a few weeks ago. He was last seen alive in Paraguay; the Tri-Border area. A girl he was checking on worked for Morano. Some Venezuelan fishermen found his body just off their coast. The woman has gone to ground. Can't find her. Not even certain of her full name. Connie something."

"What's that got to do with O'Rourke? He's never been to Paraguay or Venezuela." The monkey now had its claws fully dug into Burton's back. He would never get rid of it. But that is the talent of the surreptitious monkey passer. The employee able to slip the monkey from their back onto their boss' back will be home hours before their frustrated senior who has now taken over the task completely.

"The last message he sent was rather intriguing. He paid a visit to Morano's home in Miami to sort out a few areas of concern. Evidently, he ran into someone from the private security force and sort of duked it out. It was too dark for the guard to get a good look, plus his head and face were mostly covered …he says."

"I guess you were right about him being reckless. Understandable, under the circumstances, but no less disturbing. You think we should pull him back for consultation?"

"Well. Things have progressed a bit far afield. O'Rourke is in Grenada."

"Spain?"

"No sir, not Gran-ada. Grey-nay-da," he pronounced. "Caribbean. Down near Venezuela."

"Oh. Never been there. Nice?"

"Very. They call it 'The Island of Spice'. White sand, gentle waters, great coral reefs, nice place to visit. Morano first contracted him to fly him and an Air Force Colonel down to Aruba. Something about the hurricane putting both his pilots out of commission."

"Did they even stopover in Aruba?"

"That's the really intriguing aspect. After they left our airspace, they altered destination to Grenada. Morano owns his own island down there and he's in tight with the locals. So nobody even flinched when he just showed up. In fact he's throwing a party for all the Big Whigs."

"Hmm, that sounds contrived. Can you safely contact O'Rourke? I'd rather not send down any backup. This is still close hold."

"You're really not gonna like this, but Thompson suggested we contact the embassy's Consular Officer for support. You know; comm, surveillance and possibly some logistical support."

"So? You suspect that might be a problem?"

"Well, Consular Ops has been hit especially hard by drawdowns at State in their Foreign Service Officer personnel. Lot of people got so fed up with all the crap going on at State they left in droves."

"Yeah, some of them left skid marks. We have the same fiscal headaches, can't hire the right people, can't promote. The best and the brightest choose the private sector over public service. We're dealing with our issues…"

"Yessir. So are they. Like us they've opted for contractor support. Except State's relying more on foreign nationals to perform functions previously conducted by government folks. Makes sense, I guess. I said as much to Thompson. That's when I found out about the guys in Miami. But I didn't know they were dead until my counterpart at DEA, you know Greg Olsen, anyway he had just found out too. Seems young Mister Thompson has a poker buddy over at DEA who owed him a favor. They just ran the Op between themselves. Olsen called to suggest we use the proper channels next time and to say he's going to use "preventive measures" after he resolves the reason for his men's deaths. One of them was his nephew."

"Damn. We may already have our nuts in a ringer." His right-hand fingers traced a line of stubble growing into a five o'clock shadow. "Well, don't make any further contact with the DEA people. Maybe they'll assume Thompson was just an overzealous Captain trying to make Major. Wait and see if they contact us."

"Yessir. But if O'Rourke's hunch is right and if Morano's group is crooked. We don't know DEA's motivations. They find out, they may go in guns blazing. We may have screwed the pooch. I suggest we scratch the mission, send in someone else."

The reticent General turned his back, leaning down to deliberately retrieve a couple papers scattered during his savage initial reaction; it was either that or ripping out his exec's throat and seemed the better course. Pondering this latest chain of events --including his exec's colorful way of declaring this mission "all fouled up"—he leaned back in his chair, his steel gray eyes focused on the Buffalo Soldier painting as if asking, pleading for some sign. He remembered one of his grizzled veterans – Sergeant Major Griffin—pointedly telling his young Lieutenant Colonel, "Sir, that's why you get paid th' big bucks!"

No two ways around it. Decisions come with the job. "Buck up Cowboy!" He accepted his fates and --with an air of dejected resolution-- turned back to Peterson. The grim look in his eyes was the other man's first clue of what was to be.

"The mission continues. There is no one else."

"You ever sometime just make up some random word and do a search on the internet?" This night they shared the living room sofa, flipping through TV channels, watching but not really listening, the audio muted. Valerie seemed in her most talkative mood since they'd arrived on the island, but it was another blue mood. Maybe it was those solemn services at that church, although she'd seemed to enjoy it all at the time. Maybe. Maybe she was just having Blue Mood Sunday-itis. So he'd decided to lighten her "-itis" somewhat, continuing before she could react: "I do and more often than not it turns out to already exist. Might just be some 'YouTube' video, but it's there. Now does that mean that I've seen it somewhere before or that no matter how crazy I think I am somebody else is crazier?"

"I think it means we're all pre-programmed with a basic set of codes from some centralized data bank and we add our experiences to grow wiser."

"I hate it when you're always on top with all the answers."

"A male chauvinist pig like you would probably hate it when any woman is on top."

"Hey yo, take it down a peg Miss She-Male-Liberal-Half-Chocolate-Chippie! I don't have a problem with direction. Up, down, all around it's okay by me."

"Who you calling a Chippie, Bippie? You not my first John! I'll have you to know I have been highly thought of by John's the world over. They consider me highly skilled and extremely talented, especially when I do my Little Sheba Hoochie-Coochie Dance of the Pharaohs. They pay quite nicely too, a fact you should remember well if you've any intentions of walking in your sleep tonight."

"I thought that was Little Egypt and the Dance of the Pyramids?"

"You remember your way, I'll remember mine."

"Err, okay. I got my dollar bills all ready, let's see that dance! Shake it Sheba, shake it!"

"Dollar bills? Big boy you gonna have to come better than dollar bills you want see some of this act!"

"Oh I got some mo' when it gits ta gittin', know what I mean? Gonna make it rain."

"I know what you say. But piker man, you can't get to getting or gitting without some serious scratch. And I don't mean none of that chicken feed either. Let's see it! Bring it out and it better be big enough to choke a horse!"

"You talking money or something else? Cause it sounds like you want me to whip out something else, something guaranteed to choke a horse."

"Know this; I take cash, credit or debit cards, traveler's checks and sometimes trade. You whip it out; I'll decide whether it's enough. Whatever it is." Both were all in smiles from their flirtation, though neither moved to develop it further. Still, sex talk has its benefits. Thoughts of Morano and his troops faded into the ebony blackness.

From the screen shone a modern movie that they figured must have been sci-fi since it had been shot in the deep south but had only one black in any of the scenes they saw and, according to the "closed captioned" dialog, he was just visiting from New York and gay. No indigenous, heterosexual black men in Alabama? What's that about?

Flipping channels, they found a more believable example of pulp fiction to entertain them. But just barely so. Every one of the principals in this film, representing every race from black to white to Latin to Asian, was wealthy and had servants. Apparently, only the servants missed out on the mega bucks motif.

The movie done and both of them about to turn in, she remarked about that previous movie they'd jokingly labeled as sci-fi. "The guys from The Apple were the people I pitied most cause they acted like they were in a time warp back to the eighties, the eighteen eighties. They could only see New York as beautiful and then only because of all the billboards and advertisements: Buy this piece of junk or that!"

"Got it in for the Big Apple, huh?"

"It's okay. It's just the thought. All those beautiful trees and flowers and unspoiled loveliness and friendly people and they missed a place full of trashy streets where cab drivers aim their yellow missiles at anyone unwary enough to try crossing. An old wise saying is that possessing lots of white men on green sheets of paper will never make you wealthy. Only good health and the love of your family will bring you wealth."

Now JP couldn't resist the urge to chime in, "Speaking of wealth, just so's you know Mickey never considers the one token gay guy in a movie to be representative of other men, who aren't also gay. To Mick, that guy is actually representing gays, 'cause they got their own race. I know, don't say it. He really isn't homophobic, he doesn't hate gays or anything, he's just Mickey."

"Sounds like he is, HaHa."

"Nah, he's just Mickey. Maybe when you meet him…"

"I'll tell him I'm not gay. HaHaHa." She grabbed his hand, pulling him behind her towards his bedroom, verifying that his strategy had actually worked wonderfully well. The location helped quite a bit, also. Grenada is truly a paradisiacal land of spice. And all is extremely nice. It boasts beautiful, powdery, white sand beaches to a sunbather's delight and the surrounding, crystal-clear, aquamarine waters offer pleasures galore to impulsive sea sprites. Grenada enjoys the best of the South Atlantic on its eastern shores and the Caribbean on its western. Paradise was at hand. But not for all. Even in paradise there sometimes come untoward elements bent on disturbing the natural order.

Still, the land of Grenada was not to blame. He himself had stirred this hornet's nest, though at first he assumed his imagination was to blame. He had been on his best behavior since Miami, so who would be out to get him?

He relaxed; he was certain he had brought no attention to himself. That is, with the exception of the phone call from Sylvia and that was just bad luck. And timing. That was all about timing. It happens. Sometimes timing is out of kilter with desire and her timing had come at the wrong time. He could still hear her words, full of anger and accusation. Still remember their tone, their disappointment, their scalding cacophony, a tempest of sound and might.

Her nerve endings were red and raw. Due to destruction from Hurricane Eris she had lost touch with some of her family in New Orleans. Reminded her so much of a similar result of another hurricane that came across Miami then up to the Gulf Coast, one named Katrina. She prayed for a different finale. The suspense was more grating than the last time because even though everyone knew the possibilities, her people still elected to ride it out. They put their trust in God and prayed He see them through just like the last time …even though some didn't make it through the last time.

More. Due to some government conspiracy she had lost touch with her man in whatever place he now called home. Her whole world was crashing in and she liked it not one bit. He had not answered his cell phone lately. Her suspicion was that his failure to answer was intentional, the delivery seemed confirmation. The longer she considered it, the more it seemed valid; suspicion became fact and she let go of every emotion … particularly rage.

Rage usually needs an outlet. Hers was no different. Also inside the package, a slip of paper with a phone number. She decided to try it, but not from home, she would place the call from a number she knew he would accept …his.

"Hi Martha, can I come in?" It was late Sunday night when she finally gave up trying to let go the demons and drove to his home, but his housekeeper loved her like a daughter and she loved her back. Even though this surrogate mother had sort of betrayed her with Miss Ex (who lately seemed determined to be Miss Again).

"Sylvia! Chile, come on in. I'm so glad to see you!" Every inch of her face sparkled, glowing from the light-brown eyes to the tiny nose to the freckles gathered in clusters around her tanned cheeks. The broad smile cast an assurance that she truly meant her greeting. Then again, maybe she was just lonely. "I haven't seen you in a while! Know I missed my soaps Friday. Had to go out an' forgot to put th' Record on. JP know I hate them electronic things. He forgot to do it fo' he left for God knows where! Can I fix you some tea or coffee, you hungry? Did you see…?"

"Oh Martha, I-I'm sorry. I'm just as bad as you. I missed them too. Been out all week, working my butt off and meaning to call him." She cut off the older woman's rapid-fire spiel before it could go too far. She had issues of her own; "All My Children" would have to wait.

Typically, Martha wore a drab scarf over her tiny head and the obligatory apron over her outdated shift dress. She wore the informal uniform rags as a badge of honor even though her master neither required them nor was home for her to fuss around preparing meals for. Obviously that four-eleven, one hundred-three-pound frame didn't seem to do a lot of meal preparing for her own self. At least not as Sylvia saw it.

In fact, Sylvia could never remember her in any other type outfit except for the times they attended some function together or as she headed out to her church services wearing whichever broadbrimmed hat she'd picked for that day. Sylvia had never once even seen the woman's hair. Jealously she wondered if Tina had been given the privilege. Even Martha's Sunday hats came designed for complete coverage. She'd love to steal her away for a shopping spree some day and fix that wardrobe shortcoming, but now she had another theft in mind…

"I keep forgetting. All this news about hurricanes and my family worries. I haven't been hardly able to catch up to anybody. Glad you reminded me. Can I call him from here? Tell you what; I'll come in the living room right after I speak with him. We can catch up. Coffee will be fine."

"Who's the bitch JP? That's the mission, huh? Getting a piece o' ass in Miami!" She got right to the point with him too, sounding more like her best friend Cassie than the woman he dated and she was far from done. "That's why you couldn't tell me nuthin'! That little shit that drove me home let it slip, but I figgered he just wanted ta git wit' me! He was right! I should' a known they wanted you ta…"

"Let me explain Syl…"

"Explain why you all locked up good n' tight wit' a hoochee? Nice picture by the way. What's th' matter, Tina wasn't around? So now you cheatin' both o' us? Well, th' hell with that! I'm through waitin' for you JP. Ya'll brothers all tired anyway! Gotta screw every piece o' ass ain't nailed down!"

"I can't talk right now, Syl." He was trying to dance around a subject which had plagued their relationship for years and his steps were too slow for the beat she was laying down. But Valerie was still within earshot and Valerie was integral to his mission and maybe with his coming out of this mission alive.

This was messed up. She had immediately gotten up off his bed once Sylvia's booming dialog had begun. Funny how women can sense another woman, even if that woman's voice isn't heard. That sixth sense women possess is the real deal. Now she was back in her own room or maybe outside on the lanai. He did not know which, only that she was not happy either. One moment snuggling up to a man she had finally decided to honor with her most intimate glory, the next blown away by his girlfriend's voice screaming out his phone …even if that "out the phone" part was more his imagination than actuality.

It was his own fault for answering the call in the first place. But the number belonged to him and he worried there could exist some emergency. Martha wasn't getting any younger and she was the only family he had left, other than Sylvia, Mickey and recently Tina and possibly a baby that may or may not be on the way with a woman he'd met the night he killed her husband and may have impregnated before the abusive mate found them by accident and tried to kill them and …it just got more complicated each time he ran the nightmarish last few weeks around the inside of his brain.

But when he answered the cell phone, there was no doubt that the emergency consisted of one very pissed off woman. He decided that there was no fixing this. Not from here. Not this night. He would have to try and repair any damage when and if he got back home and when and if he did, he would remember his helpful little friend …Thompson.

He ended her tirade the only way he knew how. He simply hung up, pressing the red "Stop this Shit" button. Then, not wishing to risk another bout of the same, he changed the incoming call notifier setting to "SILENT". Valerie did not come back into the room and he knew better than to go looking for her. Getting chewed out by two women within the same period was not high on his list of desires. He doffed the outer ware, turned off his lights and climbed into the covers and there he lay for the next three hours. No television, no radio, not even a book. Just lay there…

The disturbance occurred as he again struggled to defeat the insomnia which had plagued since news of Tina's fate. Even as a child he was never one for whom sleep came easily, eschewing the ghosts awaiting his passage into dormancy so they could get him and choke him or maybe eat him. He was never certain. He had gotten worse following his best friend

Tony Hellerman's death back in Vietnam and news of Tina's demise had increased this difficulty exponentially.

When the night sounds changed, he blamed the difference on his old ghosts following him all the way down here to haunt him once more. Before, there was only a slight whisper of bay waters slipping ashore. Basically, all was quiet this close to three AM. No loud parties down below or drunken exchanges from kids celebrating their exuberance while heading back to their rooms to play naked twister games. But then the subtle scrapings filtering past the front door, took on ominous proportions. Barely audible, but a definite clicking from metal-to-metal contact. It finally convinced him something was amiss, galvanizing him into immediate defensive posture.

Reacting now. He slipped quietly out of bed and moved, cat-like, in the direction of the noise, knowing he had no time to wake Valerie. Outside his bedroom and into the suite's expanse, he understood the need to get into the kitchen before that door opened. He had no doubt that it soon would open even with the double locks securing it. People don't come out at night just to practice breaking and entry, and they don't attempt it for real unless they know what they're doing. At least nobody he knew…

One other thing he knew, he knew he wished he had a pistol. But he didn't so he would use what he had, meaning the tools given him by God. Fishing around for a kitchen utensil was a non-starter. He chided himself for not having prepared for this eventuality. Bond would have stuck two pistols under pillows, a third in the shower and a K-Bar knife under the end table. Even Axel Foley would have stashed a weapon somewhere in preparation and Foley was mostly laughs and giggles, not serious. What did that say about him?

He could always turn on a light, maybe scare the intruders away. But then he would be jumping at shadows thinking everybody on the island might be the stalking him. He was much too vindictive to let someone think they could cow him. But if there were more than one …and armed? He had Valerie's safety to consider. If they overpowered or killed him, what would become of her? Shiro would have urged him to do the smart thing. But what exactly was the smart thing to do? Situations change smart moves to dumb ones. It might not be smart to leave a backstabber at his back…

"She would have to pick the bed closest to the door," he fumed, waiting in the deadly silence. He would be in better position to waylay the guy or guys from her room. Probably, they would even turn in there first and if they came single file, he could drive one back into the other. A nice surprise, as long as he made short work of the first; punch to the temple, claw hand to the eyes or some sort of "breaking technique". But that was unprofessional, he knew. They'd more likely fan out and launch on signal, doubling their coverage. That's if there were only two…

The kitchen now seemed the wiser choice, even though its opening began a bit further down the hall, leaving more distance to cover. The full-sized refrigerator came first in the appliances lineup. He waited there. Her doors were closed, possibly locked --if he knew pissed off women—but if these were hitmen carrying silenced guns and they just walked in and started shooting through the mullioned glass, her bed stood just beyond. She would have little chance. He actually hoped it was robbers, but if professional hitmen, then what?

He tried to calm his derision. He was making himself crazy. He crept to the edge of the wall near the refrigerator. Forget all this second-guessing. He could not take the chance these were the Merry Men of Sherwood. He would have to do whatever he was going to do and do it violently. The P.I. and Staff Sergeant Haynes came back to his vision, "Kill or be killed!"

The big, black drill instructor vanished just as rapidly as, with an almost imperceptible squeak, the front door opened. Next came sounds of the guy lifting off the chain lock with some sort of hook device or something. O'Rourke's left eye strained out a little past the wall to surreptitiously survey the scene. Light glinted freely off a long, slender object in the intruder's hand. Outside lights played into the room casting a sinister shadow on the tile floor. Poised, crouching low beside the appliance, he let the man enter and listened carefully. No one followed and no other sounds accompanied.

True to O'Rourke's fears, the man stepped to the closed entryway to Valerie's room, reached out his left hand for the knob and raised his right. Springing quickly from his hiding place --an explosive force, a leaping tiger-- O'Rourke smashed viciously into the dark shape, his left shoulder driving the startled assassin sideways into the doorjamb, breaking open the fragile barriers. A single "whoosh" sounded from his quarry as air expelled from lungs crushed between an irresistible force and immovable object. Then he reached his left arm up above, into the area where the man's head should be, and --capitalizing on the trampoline effect provided by their rebounding bodies-- pulled back and down smashing head and shoulders to the hard tile. Next he swept his hands over the immobile form –searching for the weapon—finding it, he flipped it into her bedroom and sprang to the half-opened front doorway. Once there he inspected the outside. Finding nothing he closed the revealing portal, simultaneous to Valerie's startled cry.

She awoke confused and groggy but had the presence of mind to find and turn her lights on, then experienced even more confusion. "What happened? Who is he?" she nervously blurted. "John, what's going on?"

O'Rourke did not answer. He bent to remove the dark ski mask from the man's head, studied his lines then checked for pulse, first at his wrist, then at his throat. Failing recognition and finding no pulse, he rummaged through the bulky pockets. Next he retrieved the pistol from its hiding place in the covers draping the floor. The forty-caliber Glock --complete with silencer screwed onto its threaded barrel-- provided final confirmation of his suspicions. But Valerie was not at all pleased with his cold shoulder.

"I asked you what is happening?" reaffirmed the perplexed female. "You can't go around knocking people out, dragging them into my room and robbing them without at least telling me what's going on!"

"Seems this is one'o the bad guys. Maybe he just came to rob the rich Americans, but I'm thinkin' ol' boy had murder on his mind. Check one, silenced pistol. Two, he likes the early morning scene. Most thieves like to be home 'fore the clubs close. More people on the street to mingle with." O'Rourke finally responded to her demands as he concluded his search, his every fiber filling with dread as remorse pealed for this life taken.

"Who?" she began, then silenced herself, fear filling velvet eyes. She had never seen a dead body, let alone witnessed a body being made dead. The words did not form correctly on her lips. They could not be fully trusted to convey her thoughts.

"Doesn't seem to believe in wallets though, not even a driver's license. What is the world of hitmen coming to?" he joked, trying to hide the anguish.

"A-are y-you sure it's not just a c-coincidence? M-maybe he only wanted to rob us, w-we have been pretty liberal with our sp-spending."

"You mean you have been pretty liberal with our spending! But no. Don't think so. No bag to carry stuff or anything and even robbers have I.D. They prob'ly don't do things that differently in the islands." Their first night he'd conducted a quick check of the State Department and CIA

Factbook web sites to see what dangers called home, this idyllic place, and other stuff they thought American tourists needed know. Other than a few petty thefts here and there, this place didn't have many issues …until now.

"Ha-hadn't we better t-tell somebody, the p-p-police or the Embassy?"

"What kind of pull does your boss have with the police on this island?"

"He-he gets along with them. Why you say?"

"Most cops tend to frown on killings. They lock you up if you're th' ones that live through the event." He said these words while heading back to collect his clothes and his shoes. Over his shoulder he ordered, "Get dressed. I'll put him in the car. Wear pants!"

She did as ordered, though still not convinced. "I still say, do the right thing!"

"Oh yeah, we can call the cops, say: 'Hey Mister po-po, it was him or us. We don't know why anybody wanna murder sweet little innocent folk like us. We even sleeping in separate beds! Know we don't do nuthin' wrong!' We can accept their close-minded, world view judgment: Who's bad, who's good, who's right, who's wrong? We can field their repetitive questions, since they can't figure out why anyone innocent would ever defend themselves instead of calling them first and cringin' in some dark corner hopin' they can finish off their jelly donuts or whatever they prefer down here and get to us in time, provided they don't get lost like we did and we can sit in some pissy-smelling holding cell while they deliberate, handcuffed to a bench or behind our backs or something. We can do that or we can make this thing go away. I vote the latter."

A tightly confining cell in Virginia, in a time not that long before came back to mind. And a dead husband's blood splatter sailed vividly across his memory. The shrieking wail of a fatherless child being born provided background vocals. Then again, if he was the father, it wasn't fatherless, right? That's what she said he was, didn't she? That night of sweet bliss followed closely by a morning on lockdown. If he never repeated that latter, it would be too soon. Unfortunately, Valerie had never experienced such. She still held onto her ideals…

"You got all the answers, right?"

"I got this one. Cops are pretty Neanderthal 'bout stuff like this; at least they are where I come from. It's easier for them to see villains everywhere and jump to conclusions, than to develop some original thought. They rather hold onto what they got than go out an' find somebody new. I just prefer to limit chances of involvement with people who prefer to shoot first and handcuff later. I'm not too thrilled 'bout cuffs neither, an' they love the cuffs."

"Then I guess we best eliminate the obvious by removing the corpus delicti."

"Damn Skippy!" Corpus delicti, aka, DB for dead body, was a definite no-no to the po-po and he meant to disappear this one ASAP.

Luckily no blood smeared the walls or floors. In fact, other than the break between his atlas and axis vertebrae his overall condition had undergone little change. Unfortunately, the resulted tearing of his spinal cord curtailed his body's ability to send signals between brain and lungs, causing death by asphyxiation. But O'Rourke instructed the woman to wipe the area down anyway, just in case, before they drove off to find a burial site.

Twin headlamps illuminated the winding, twisting road as the speeding SUV carried its occupants further inland --northeast, into Grand Etang National Park to one of the highest parts of the island. They'd come back this way on the return trip from Sauteurs, but that was in daylight and in the opposite direction and the scenery was wonderful with fruit and spice trees and lakes and colorful parrots and Cocoa Cafes and much more, not this dark and foreboding scene with a dead body in their tow. Still, he'd thought it through and decided it their best move …this time he did use the GPS map.

The vegetation grew so close it seemed ready to choke off the roadway in sections where tight turns and switchbacks abounded. There were cocoa, mango and tamarind trees rearing high above their heads and coriander, rosemary and lemon balm herbs growing along both sides of their path and they couldn't tell one from another in this gloom. An occasional glimpse of tall sugar cane stalks bunched together was about it for flora recognition class and then only when headed directly towards them before the roadway turned right or left and rose or dove; up, down, all around. All-in-all, it was quite a trip. The headlights barely illuminated most turns in time, ordering him to slow down. When they spoke, out flowed withheld questions she had wanted to ask for some time, until she could withhold back no more…

"Why so fast and so far? We've passed dozens of good places to hide him and the sun will be coming up soon." She was terrified both of his driving and the ghost of their passenger in back.

"I want him far away from the hotel! Don't even want his own friends to find him. Keep 'em guessing" He was calm, though very saddened by this killing. It was one thing to drop bombs or shoot down enemy jets with missiles. Distance alleviated the knowledge that murder was on his hands. In the air war it was more like a game. You did not need to get your hands dirty…

"If he has any friends." she doubted.

"He does."

"You shouldn't have hit him so hard. We could have questioned him and there'd be no doubt."

"Yeah." he quietly concurred, berating his own self for using so much force. But he could not chance giving him time to squeeze off a round. Then Valerie would be the one needing burial. He had no doubts. This was an assassin pure and simple. "Kill or be killed," again approved the Marine Corps mantra to shore up his resolve.

They found a good spot just as first light from the sun began peeking. Night screeches from tiny Mona monkeys still competed with calls from nightbirds that flitted unseen overhead. All were witness to their skullduggery.

Called Mona Guenon, the Mona Monkeys were a specific item on Valerie's list of things to photograph. But she had no chance of spotting the reddish-brown creatures this early before sunrise. Even if she could, the reception might prove less than amicable for murders.

Native to Africa, the monkeys were brought over at the same time African slaves were imported to work the sugar cane plantations, kind of a "two sets of slaves on one trip" deal, although the monkeys had slightly better accommodations. Their name comes from a mixing of Moorish with French. Mona means "long-tailed monkey" in Moorish and guenon is French for "fright". The monkeys were so named because they grimace and bare their teeth when excited or angry. Regardless, at this moment she had other things to frighten her mind…

There they left him, floating face down in a small waterfall-fed pool. It seemed too much to hope that his death would be confused as an accident, that he had slipped and fallen from above, losing his life as well as his identification in the process. But they hoped these things anyway. Actually, the body had fallen for quite a distance, though only after O'Rourke had hiked it to the top of a hilly trail and let it go. But it probably would not matter one way or another. This was no blonde, blue-eyed, white girl from a wealthy American family. He was a black man on an island where over eighty percent of its population is black and death by murder not a common occurrence.

For all practical purposes, the dead man, this would-be-assassin, ceased to be a viable cog in a contest governed by inordinately cardinal principles in which those successful survived and even flourished. In would-be-assassin parlance that means: "Nobody watching and no help, one slip up, you die. So don't slip up! Oooppps, you slipped!"

As an afterthought, he and Valerie brought beachwear as a cover for their early morning trip. After giving the corpse one last swimming lesson, they surveyed their handicraft. She felt less success than he with this final solution.

"Think they'll go for it?"

"It should confuse them," he surmised, "they won't be sure if it's a case of suicide, clumsiness or maybe overactive perverts. Hopefully he won't be noticed for a few days. Hell, maybe whoever finds his corpse will blame its death on the monkeys."

"Luckily we didn't need to rush back and mop up bloodstains." interjected the female, in her pert, overly sarcastic way of reminding him her major contribution. She was not the killer here and was far from thrilled with it all. So far so good though, she'd yet to be arrested and incarcerated in that prison sitting high above Saint George's Carenage. However, now that she had become an accessory --in what some might construe as a crime—incarceration was still a distinct possibility, at least in her mind.

An episode of CSI Miami came to her memory. Horatio Caine peered through his rimless, black Revos or Maui Jims or whatever brand they were, into her face to divine her motive for braining the poor, unarmed porter from behind with a tire iron as he tried to deliver her morning paper. "Ma'am we found fibers from your paper-thin negligee on the murder weapon. Maybe you'd best take it off and hand it over…"

Then again, she remembered that was her CSI bondage fantasy where she portrayed the southern belle pleading her innocence. "Oh Horatio, ah could neh-vah even contemplate such an evil thing! Handcuff me if you must, ah shall not resist. Take me to yo-ah prison, lock me behind closed do-ahs whey-ah no one can see the thangs you will do to my helpless body. Oh Horatio, take me nayow!"

Yeah, she'd need to remember not to confuse the freak with the freaky. Still, she felt guilty for not calling the authorities. Her every fiber wanted to dial their number. But she never did. In truth it had all taken her so completely by surprise she was operating on instinct. She probably should at least have called Carlos. He was good at handling tight situations. But she had somehow fallen into this other man's web, not sure just why, but somehow, she trusted him. Forlorn though they were, her instincts told her to operate on his instincts ...though she was not totally instinctive.

"JP, I don't want you to think I'm totally unappreciative; I mean, he did look like an assassin, you know, silencer and all; it's just that where I grew up, we tended to leave matters like this to the authorities..."

"Same here, except where we're not sure about those authorities, cause Dorothy we not in Kansas anymore." The vision of his father's hanging corpse left no doubts. The vow he made in Vietnam, never to surrender to unknown forces, furthered his resolve. He would not surrender to the police in this place he had never before been who may not be owned by Morano ...but may perhaps be rented. "I'd feel better keeping them out of this. We don't owe this guy tender mercies."

"So you're seeing it that way, huh?"

"Seeing it that way."

"Ok, Mister My-Way-or-the-Highway!"

The solemn pair rode mainly in silence for the balance of their pre-dawn trip --neither desirous of breaking the calm that silence seemed to generate—even their Jeep moved swiftly over the suddenly, less threatening roads as both refreshed in the amazing relief that absence of a corpus delicti imparts. Monday's sunup came rapidly, then soon the tourists and the vendors and the school buses that looked so much like the minibuses --colored red and blue and black and white that shuttled much of the island's population from top to bottom and east to west-- grabbing up children wearing prim and proper schoolhouse uniforms in every color.

They next headed towards Sauteurs Bay where Caribe Indians once committed wholesale suicide rather than submit to slavery under the French. The location was appropriate since both felt their turn was coming. But standing there at Leapers Hill, staring down the one hundred foot cliff to where rocks emerged from the sea, neither desired to reenact the experience. Valerie voiced her opinion that people who feel a need for suicide need to go find someone else to feel.

JP agreed with the lascivious nature of her suggestion, adding his take that it is much better to help the other guys commit the act before they got their turn to help you. His vindictiveness would permit nothing less. In keeping with her salacious suggestion he tossed in a Marines' aphorism come to mind, "You got to bring ass to kick ass!" Not so subtle as hers, but far from a total dis-ass-ter!

Along around midmorning, warm breezes from tropical trade winds rolled scented sensations of fruitful delights their way, enticing visions of epicurean splendor within their pallets, demanding a break to the night fasting, clamoring for succulence to fill empty spaces. So they stopped to partake at a place that seemed somewhat okay, at least better than most (aka, less ramshackle) on this less trendy, northern edge of the Spice Isle, and were rewarded with its welcoming savors and flavors and a cook-slash-owner-slash-magic act who kept them full of warmth and humor. Girlfriend was awesome. She could feed a crowd while wowing a crowd. Low-cut blouses and high cut skirts clad tightly around her wait staff, equally did nothing to harm the genial atmosphere …for the eighty percent male portion of her patrons.

However, the women's contingent seemed equally enjoying the food and the show, Valerie high on that list of only three. They sampled foodstuffs and standards from continents ranging from the American North to the South, the African East to the West as well as the Caribbean up and down and leeward to windward and their sated selves took long to arouse enough to leave the welcoming environs. But eventually they made a reluctant retreat south, intent on returning to their familiar place in this foreign land; stopping from time to time at noted tourist sites they snapped pictures, bought souvenirs and snacked on other delicious edibles. She still filled well the typical American tourist cliché all the drive back, until the warm sun lulled the exhausted female asleep to dream of better times and of better situations where she was not a fugitive felon, even though in this world filled with serious felons her contribution barely reached the level of piker.

"I bet all the stuff you bought today is for Caroline. Twelve years old and probably spoiled something fierce," he laughed, enjoining a matching chortle from her pinkish lips. She appeared totally refreshed after double-napping first during the drive, then climbing from car seat directly to bed upon arrival.

"Like I said, she's a great kid. Hmm, maybe a little spoiled. HaHa. She's got the greatest smile you ever wanna see. Cute little figure too. I can't wait 'til she tries these on."

"She's sounds like a gem. So what's the deal with daddy? I'm seeing a beautiful, intelligent woman here and what guy doesn't want a gorgeous daughter to love. So what if she can't run the marathon! She can still give love. He could still feel the joys of teaching her."

The prospect of a little bundle of joy of his own filled his heart. At the moment he both envied and hated her Ex. The idiot didn't appreciate what he had once had, what he still could have. Again she had come to his room and again she wore only a T-shirt and panties, except this night these were both pastel pink, though no less appealing than the previous night's selection of white and teal.

"Said he was gonna join the Marines."

"Hmmm, did he?"

"Yeah, they would be the ones. Guess it's true what they say about USMC meaning Uncle Sam's Misguided Children."

"Yeah? Maybe so, but I wouldn't blame the whole Corps on account of one jerk. Besides, who ya gonna call when the crap hits th' fan?"

"Good point," she agreed. Her desire for arguing over and done with, she impulsively climbed onto his bed for a snuggle; wrapping him tightly in her arms, her ear pressed against his broad chest. She had grown used to his embrace these recent days. She had grown to enjoy his feel. This night's felt even better; he wore only a pajama bottom. No shirt to stop the flow. However, he suddenly did not seem in like agreement, so she embellished: "Okay, great point!"

"Thank you. Never know when you need that trained killer around." Instantly, he knew that she didn't quite get his jocularity. What she got was the impression of a slap-down and to that perceived negativity she bristled...

"Is that why you killed that burglar?" Her words exasperated. He could see that his joke wasn't the only thing she still didn't get.

"I'm gonna try an' put this into words I think you'll understand," he began. Now it was she who experienced a measure of exasperation. But that bothered him not in the least; in fact, he intended his words and tone just for that purpose. "This is not a Batman movie where bad guys can kill good guys, but good guys only good cause they only try to "catch" the bad guys, even guilt trip if they hurt 'em bad. Uh uh! In this real world, the good guys just try and stay alive."

Lecture over, she suddenly regretted her question.

"I-I forgot you were a Marine. D-din't mean…"

"Yeah, you meant it. Sokay. That was a long time ago. Yeah USMC, Uncle Sam's Misguided Children." She could see a slight glaze to his eyes, as if in recall mode. Then he reverted back to present. "Don't sweat. Like they say: if it's green it's groovy…"

"No, I can't see you as misguided. Not like…"

"We were all a bit misguided. Semper Fi, do or die. Guess that's the way of young warriors full of vim and vigor. The pride, the camaraderie. We'd kill commies fo' mommie, then hit the road an' party til the road hit us…"

He fell silent again. Her eyes searched the lips pinched thin between granite jaws for some sign of remorse. Finding only conviction, she remained silent also. Even the night air outside had stilled; nary a sound save the ocean's goings and comings. Soft wave breaks against the sandy beach the only interruptions as if even the gods deigned hear what he had next to say.

"Vim and vigor. Fighting, fornicating and forgetting." He looked deep into her green eyes, turned hazel. "That's what young men are good at. Except sometimes you don't forget. Sometimes you can't just move on. Comes the day you're no longer on top, top's on you…"

This time his silence, she knew, would remain unbroken. He had turned away to peer off into the television screen, as if reading the lips of its actors. She thought to rise and take her leave. But she still felt the need of a friend. Tonight, even more so. This time with hardly any trepidation she asked her next question.

"Know you heard this before. C-can I sleep with you tonight?"

Against his better judgment, Eisa Abdel-Hakim decided to bring the golden box to Grenada. It was at Carlos' behest, but also for the promise of significant wealth as well as unlimited and exclusive access to the woman. She was a treasure for which he would much endure, but even for such a prize he had refused to even consider taking the treasure to Miami after the run in with the spy outside Morano's home. Too dangerous. Too much risk, despite the potential reward and Eisa had learned at an early age to minimize risk.

It had been he who discovered the Sneak. He went to take a smoke break, combining a walk outside to clear his head of the incessant gibbering from his host with a chance to fill his lungs with the satisfying aroma of his favorite American cigarette, Marlboro. He was used to such practices in America. They were still attempting to legalize Marijuana, but smoking cigarettes was almost a capital crime and not permitted indoors in public places, though he could have lit up inside Morano's home. Although a couple of the guests smoked the occasional Cuban, he was the only one of their group who smoked cigarettes, so he used the excuse to leave their company.

The rain had eased appreciably --though the wind still howled-- but he felt refreshed in the outside air. This was his first hurricane and he reveled in standing tall amongst Allah's rage. His face turned east, towards the dark sky, he uttered a nearly silent prayer to his god. Prayer concluded he paused in the lee created by a corner of the building and lit up using a Zippo lighter he had personally taken off the dead body of an American F-16 pilot. It bore the insignia and colors of the USAF and thus was special to him. This enemy would drop no more bombs on his family.

He recalled how the dead enemy pilot had favored Morano's assistant, the one with the very fine breasts; could nearly have been twins. Americans. What a strange race. Imagine, grown men allowing their women to fly warbirds...

He had thought about asking his host for a date with her –just as a flirtation until Connie returned-- but figured Carlos probably used her himself and would not share. He was like that about quite a few things. Not the best host, but not the worst Eisa had encountered. Saddam held that claim, close after him, his sons.

Carlos was nowhere near their league, though he was a real ninny when it came to world events and customs. He had some favorable skills and he knew well about entertaining, just not much about sharing. Eisa had made up his mind to make the inquiry anyway. The worst Carlos could do is say no. But if he did, perhaps Eisa would take something else …some other treasure the man truly wanted.

But such things could be left for less tumultuous times. There were more important issues at hand and those required resolution before any trivialities or even minor revenges. In retrospect, he decided that it was too bad that the hurricane had showed up …and then the spy.

Didn't bother the least he might never return to Iraq. They'd need time to sort out their mess, made messier by them running around like chickens whose heads had been cutoff in the wake of Saddam's hanging.

Caught up! Just a little. These action by committee fools didn't faze him. He was always a man dynamic enough to plan his own future and chart his own path. Some considered his, a pathway of doom. But those were too limited, their strengths too weak. Those unable to read the future in their own minds are the one's doomed to remain behind …that is, if their behinds survive to have a future.

He left Iraq s few days before the Americans captured Saddam. True, that cargo flight had been more unglamorous and uncomfortable than he'd wished and the small fortune doled out much more expensive than hoped. But it got him to Libya and from there to South America where he stored his wealth …and there brought the golden box.

So he came to Grenada. His first trip to the Spice Island. The promise of endless nights with Connie filled him with such ardor that he would dare even the risk of a double cross by his host. Of course, all that money made this trade a real good thing. Although he doubted such an affront would transpire, he took just-in-case precautions.

The man was too fawning, too weak to challenge one such as he. Only that spy had represented much of a challenge and only then because of Eisa's use of too much alcohol. He vowed that the next time would be different. Had he been clear headed there would be no need of a next time. He would have dispatched the interloper with relative ease. His skills in martial arts were superior to any in the entire Iraqi Army. Deadly superior.

He hoped for another chance at that spy. Just not inside the borders of the United States. The coward would probably call for reinforcements before attempting to face Eisa down again single-handed. But, if he came to South America or even Grenada, then there would come a reckoning…

Eisa flushed the noxious memories of his defeat –justifiable though it was—instead he licked his lips at the thought of tasting the delicious lusciousness of her breasts and her soft lips again. His own woman, his wife, no longer sought to please him. She had become Americanized – South American— and grown fat. She was willful and independent, living for shopping and their two children, not for her husband. He hated her now, wishing he had left her in Iraq …adorned with a pearl necklace from Odai Hussein.

Odai was long dead now, but while alive, he lived for the pleasure of giving his women a pearl necklace --ejaculating on their neck and upper chest, after a blow job—then forcing the girl to lick up all of the pearly white drops of cum; beating her if she missed any. They always missed some…

He did not want to think about either of them. Not now. He needed to be ready for any funny business from Carlos. Not that he expected any; he just needed the focus in case something jumped off …something unnecessary.

He only wished he had not hit Connie so hard that last time together. She must really have hated, perhaps even despised him. He hoped she would have come around by now, but his one understanding of Cuban American's was their fiery temperament. Topping that was her vindictive nature…

He knew instantly that he had made a mistake even though she had remained in his bed. But when she did not return, there had been no doubt. He hoped the peace offering --the diamond earrings set in twenty-four carat gold mounts and surrounded by emeralds—would demonstrate his remorse. Those had set him back a pretty penny –even in Paraguay-- but she was worth it. Connie. She was all he thought about, these days. Even business issues fell well behind in second place. He wondered if he were falling in love.

Valerie slept the sleep of the innocents, her peaceful face turned towards him. A smile so sweet, its innocent beckoning very nearly enticed JP into presenting it another kiss. But time for business was at hand. Given their excitement the night before, he hoped she'd not wake for a while and miss him. The sleep aids he had slipped into her drink should safely do the job. It was, after all, her prescription, stumbled upon while snooping. At least it seemed a good idea at the time and then he was away …off to see the big, bad wolf.

CHAPTER TWENTY-ONE

"So you see my dear, we came looking for Mister Zero, your hero", smirked the smallish, black man as he puffed easily --almost languidly-- upon the slender cigarette. His speech was measured, every word pronounced using precise diction. "Now love, I have a few questions for you to answer. And I just know you will cooperate. Phillip here has oodles of techniques to loosen the tongue.

"Tim. Listen carefully now. I know that you, and I, have had our …difficulties." She was still woozy; her voice slurred the sentence. She had no idea how she came to be in this place, wherever this place was. And where was JP? Her head hurt a little, but not too much. A sensation persisted that she was stuck to the floor inside a deep, dark tunnel and her legs had grown extremely fatigued from her attempts to climb out. Gravity had become her enemy, keeping her down, sapping her strength.

Dressed only in the tank top shirt and panties she had fallen to sleep in, she could feel Timothy's eyes all over her. She did not need to be awake for that. His eyes were ever all over her figure. His lascivious suggestions made her want to gag each time he passed her tiny, little cubbyhole two doors down from Carlos' lavish office. No door, but it did have a small window she could look out to escape the vision of leering lechers. Nothing near her boss' digs with its high windows that spanned nearly the entire length of two walls, its walnut bookcases, plush sectional sofa and polished mahogany desk with matching credenza and chairs. The field hockey squad at her daughter's middle school could have conducted a fairly good practice in those digs, on that thick carpet. They would not need to rearrange much furniture either…

The best she could figure, they must be in a basement somewhere. There was a certain dank smell and it was fairly chilly though no sound of air conditioning. Illumination came from a single lamp behind her, bringing his features out for her full enjoyment, if one called torturous images such things. Maybe they were still in Grenada, maybe Shangri-la; regardless, wherever they were at present you can bet Carlos owned it. She wondered if he also knew what was going on here. A deeper thought surged through her diminished capacity, "what if Carlos had sent the dead guy?"

"If you take me back to my hotel this instant, I won't tell Carlos about any of this," she continued, "but you must take me back now or I will be forced…"

"Wham!" The force of Timothy's backhand sent her flying from the chair. She landed on the floor at the feet of the other man who just looked down at her looking up. This one really smelled. To compensate for his odor, he literally bathed in colognes, not one of them effective. One positive outcome from the submerged senses, she did not gag as she normally did whenever he came near.

One other positive aspect of her stupefaction, the blow did not hurt all that much. But she was totally taken aback by their actions. They must have come to her suite in the dead of night, but why did they want to hurt JP? She felt lost. He should have listened to her idea about reporting to the police. Now it was too late for him, maybe too late for the both of them.

"W-what the hell are you doing Tim?" Her voice nearly screaming, she hoped its message would get across to him or to whoever might wander by, a neighbor, God or somebody, anybody. Shakily she regained her chair seat, but defiant still. "Leave me alone you punk-assed little runt coward. Hitting a woman! Carlos gonna fire yo ass anyway fo' smokin' in his…"

"Wham!" Her head snapped back again, this time from Phillip's blow. But at least she remained in the chair. A minor victory. Her brain reverberated from the shock though she'd become too unfocused to understand that or even appreciate her minor triumph.

Now they saw their error. She was already woozy and all those backhands had the opposite effect of their desire. She would never be able to answer his questions if they beat her to death. Carlos was still peeved at Timothy for accidentally killing the guy on their plane before they got his story. They would need to go a bit more softly with the woman.

"You back with us love? Did that hurt much? Again, no answer. Now you see that is precisely why you should not anger Phillip. He hates women, you see. His mother --rest her soul-- was a horrendous slut. In fact, poor Phillip was often made to sleep in a dark, dusty closet while the whorrish bitch fornicated with any swinging Dick and Johnny possessing the price of a drink or two. He'd hear the sounds, the words those drunken sots said to her; see the things they did to her. Sometimes it lasted throughout the night. Pretty bad for a five-year old kid, eh?"

"He never even knew his father. Probably some drunken sailor. Bitch really liked sailors. In fact, she liked them so much they didn't have to buy half as many drinks as the rest. I'd guess it was the uniform. Regardless, he only knew his Mum and he hated her …right up 'til she died."

Looking into her dilating pupils, Tim worried they'd done permanent damage. Unlike his friend, he liked women best. He might spend an occasional period with some member of the male perspective, but it was women he really preferred. He was a hitter, not a catcher and one day he planned to catch this one. The fact that she might no longer be capable of being caught concerned him greatly, as much as what Carlos would do if she died before talking…

"Rather strange death, it was too." He kept talking, hoping to wake her out of her stupor. "They found the old bag locked in a dark, dusty closet in an old, abandoned building. She must have screamed for days and no one heard. Her body had begun to decompose when a wrecking crew smelled it. Just awful. The rats had a good run at that until even they couldn't take the smell. Oh yes, I almost forgot, there was a man with her. Poor bloke. He had been beaten terribly and then hanged in the closet. His tongue and penis were never found. Gruesome. In fact, I believe he was a sailor."

"Y'know, I appreciate the history lessons." She came back to reality. They hadn't harmed her, too much. But she was still defiant and that, neither of them liked. "I'm sad to hear that Phillip had it so bad coming up. Sad that he had to make himself an orphan also. I'm sure his mommie was proud right up till the end. But…"

"Whap!"

Her conscious waned again, this time evading recapture and she never finished her stinging remarks. Phillip's flashing hand gripped a short piece of rubber hose, which had struck her windpipe, rose high and descended once again, this time towards the closed eyelids. But Timothy angled in --interceding before she could be blinded—and grasping the powerful wrist on its downward travel, he twisted, easily flipping it and owner across the small room …also sending her unconscious form sprawling one way her chair the other.

"The man said not to kill or cripple her. That includes maiming you dolt! Now pick her up!" ordered Timothy, righting the upended chair.

Rising like some behemoth from the depths, he moved menacingly forward. Features flared on the thick-bodied nearly albino as he stepped ponderously over the unconscious woman. Eyes ablaze with unbridled hatred he closed the distance to the unflinching, somewhat bemused Timothy.

"You really don't want to die this quickly, now do you Phillip?" asked the nonchalant black.

"You ain't so tough Tim. I could..."

"Yes, I know love. You could but you won't. After all, how do you think our benefactor would react to the truth about your sexual habits, deviations shall we say? What would you think he might say when told how you acquired your gangland speech patterns from a former lover in cell block twelve? And at a very tender age. Tell me my gay compatriot. What would happen if he knew I used your muscular buttocks for my own bit of sport? That those grossly oversized lips often begged to embrace my throbbing manhood just for the joy it gave you elsewhere. Tell me all this, my dear Phillip and do it from your knees ...I have a need."

"I-I'm sorry Timothy," stammered the suddenly servile giant, slobbering while kneeling to undo his smaller companion's belt, "I-I didn't mean it."

Placated, the black libertine ran his bony fingers through his companion's hair, fondly, as a master to a slave, a king to a subject, a priest to a beguiled orphan. He moaned softly as the unzipped pants drifted downward, the lewdness of the moment enticing a serene smile for his lips as Phillip began the assigned task with his.

He felt powerful at moments like this, a truly amazing accomplishment considering his barely five-foot-six, one hundred-fifty pound stature. But he had learned at an early age to shape situations to suit his needs...

Timothy had barely entered this unconcerned world before his mother deposited her unwanted burden upon the worn doorsteps of a small, Catholic orphanage near her tiny hut in Holetown, Barbados. His cries summoned the aged, overworked nuns to his aid. These brides of Christ were well versed in this particular, disheartening ritual. A hastily scrawled script of paper beseeched their forgiveness, citing her inability to care for this latest charge it proclaimed as Timothy. She named him after Saint Timotheos, the Bishop of Ephesus who was beaten and stoned to death when he tried to halt a pagan procession of idols, ceremonies and songs.

Aside from these lines and a ragged scrap of blanket, the boy was all alone. But his inherited guardians nurtured the scrawny and undernourished young Timothy with carefully prescribed foods and exercise sessions. His weak, frail frame responded more favorably than anyone hoped and the tiny heart began to beat with increased vigor, prompting the orphanage nuns to pray all the more erstwhile that their all-encompassing deity complete this most miraculous of tasks, allowing their favorite charge normal vitality and existence.

His prepubescent period was one of constant battle with life's morbid avenues. Should his tiny frame contact even the most common of childhood maladies his life could be forfeit. Apparently, however, their prayers were somewhat answered, even though Timothy required large amounts of time removed from contact with his fellows, while receiving extravagant portions of the orphanage mothers' attentions …creating other rifts.

Then came a manner of childhood maladies that these good women had never anticipated, having never experiencing such in prior situations. Their young champion began to experience a series of injuries from what he claimed were mishaps such as accidental falls down the long second-story staircase in their children's dormitory's. The period of bad luck lasted slightly more than two weeks, during which time he fell at least once per night.

Finally, they began to suspect foul play at the hands of a few of their older charges, even though young Timothy held stubbornly to his explanation. But even Christian altruism stretches only so far. They sensed a rat in the closet. So they moved him into a room in the Nunnery where his conditional klutziness could be better monitored. Miraculously, his tiny frame suffered not one additional malady. No more bruises, broken fingers or bloodied lips. Even his broken nose healed fairly well, though it would forever remain slightly askew.

A virtual shut-in, Timothy spent long hours ingesting every bit of literature available to him. Determined to shuck his physically weaker self and never again be picked on, he concentrated on developing both his intellect and his prowess. After a few years of study, he mastered the Korean art of Tae Kwon Do Karate that he learned under the tutelage of the parish priest, who had learned the art while living in Seoul, Korea.

The priest grew fond of this small boy who had no other friends, taking him under his wing. During their off hours, after class, they were constantly together, even sharing meals after training. Eventually the priest moved back to Seattle, barely eighteen months after he began Timothy's training, but by then he had started a wildfire. Timothy concentrated nearly every waking moment practicing, either on his own shadow or on any youth ignorant enough to venture by, especially those who had once actively tormented him. His technique came to rival learned experts, which was phenomenal considering much of his latter learning he derived solely from instructional books …more or less aided by tactics practiced on unwilling partners.

However, karate became not his only mastery. Subterfuge numbered among his many talents, seemingly a natural gift. He could lie convincingly without batting an eyelid and the aging nuns (who had always doted on him) he played with a wizardry equivalent to the virtuosic fingers of Frédéric Chopin dancing across his piano …and to insurmountable advantage.

Other orphans found their lives transformed from gay and carefree, to oppressively burdened; from clean and decent to base and adulterated. He manipulated any and all to satisfy the perverted lifestyle he chose; his lascivious lusts instilling mind numbing fear into the hearts of peers, imposing an uncompromising avarice that spread throughout the tiny orphanage unchecked; until one youth --sickened and choked with despair-- summoned sufficient courage to inform the Mother Superior.

The reasons for Tim's departure were hushed so no outsiders would ever discover how one seventeen-year-old boy gained the power to debase twenty-two other youths with assorted acts of sodomy and other violence. Neither did the orphanage reveal that some of the victims not only accepted the acts but eventually began to enjoy; much as Timothy had accepted the same from his mentor before the nuns learned that truth. But unlike the priest, Timothy did not take kindly to being sent away. Also unlike the priest, there was no shuffling off to another location after promising he would never do such a thing again. His dismissal was final.

Certain her troubles were forever gone with Timothy's ouster, the Mother Superior believed this impenitent lad's threats of revenge only hollow speeches, devoid of actual intent. Her beliefs never changed, right up to the moment the shiny blade slashed open her black smock then returned to pierce her heart muscle. They never had the time to change. While the pounding organ ceased its life-long struggle and the blackness set in, she could only reflect on the indignity of the moment.

Mother Superior truly hated dying with her breasts hanging out for all to see. But what she hated much more, the realization she would not take the eternal trip alone …the last words he promised her..

Barbadian authorities conducted an extensive search for the Bajan boy suspected of the gruesome murders. Saint James Parish received a fine-tooth combing from extremely cautious policemen equally desirous of maintaining this dark secret as of finding the dangerous youth. Wide-scale paranoia would surely reign were the news media made aware of a deranged youth running around stabbing nuns, then mounting their severed breasts on religious statuary, along with genitalia castrated from several, small boys. Tourism could suffer severely. The search lasted months, but the slim youth was never found, fading into the shadows like some dark wraith.

She moaned as much for her inability to right herself as for the pain. Struggling against the limbo world seeking to imprison her tortured soul, she stared bleakly through the haze drifting before her red-rimmed eyes at the brightly grinning face of the black as he bent to kiss the airspace near her lips.

"Don't fret, pet, plenty of time for that later. Sorry about dear Phillip. He's a nasty lot when aroused. But he is effective. Shall we talk now?"

"Leave me alone," murmured Valerie, fearful they would beat out of her the truth about their dead assassin. They had to have sent him. "I don't know anything."

"Oh! But you do dear and you will tell all …sooner or later."

O'Rourke lay still, gauging his chances. He had low-creeped through the tangled underbrush of jungle-like vegetation which abounded on three sides of the villa and though he felt safe from discovery, the passage had taken more time than he had at first thought when dreaming up this venture two nights prior.

Truth was, he had not reconnoitered into the trees. Just meandered around the grounds to get a loose feel for this place. Now he could understand just how loose was that feel. The landscaping team had yet to venture out this far and probably never would, except to spray herbicides. He had come out of the east. There was no moon this night, but plenty of starlight in the black sky; overall, not too bad for his purposes, but no help on the side of speedy traverse. Beyond his station, the manicured grounds ran all the way to the spacious pool, broken only by palm trees dotted here and there, completing the picturesque view.

The outside lights were few this evening, nothing remotely as lit up as Saturday. Two stood guard at the rear corners of the house itself and one at each end outside the pool. All four appeared as 1890s-era gas lamps, but these cast bluish rather than warm, yellow light. Underwater lights glowed also, though provided little illumination external to the swim area. The hot tub spa beside the pool remained unlit and silent.

Still, this backyard scene shone too brightly for anyone desiring to close on the house unnoticed. But he was again dressed entirely for skulking, though this night his outfit consisted of a long sleeved, dark blue nylon top --loosely draped over blue jeans-- and sneakers whose color nearly matched. His head was bare and other than the absence of high winds and rain, one other difference from the Miami sortie, this night he came armed.

He skulked forward, circumventing the patches of light as best he could until nearing the villa's southern side. There he stopped momentarily beside a tree, a big palm that offered some measure of screening from prying eyes. Also, this palm appeared less threatening than the Florida variety as it did not greet him with tossed coconuts. About ten yards to go. There was hardly any light emanating from lamps on this end. He hoped that meant that any folks inside were away in some other corner. If not, he was through pussyfooting around anyway.

He made his way safely to the side entry, also constructed as a grand entrance with a small gabled roof supported by twin columns to either side of red brick steps leading to French doors with mullioned, frosted glass sidelights. Purple Bougainvillea growing on each side of the white columns, provided some concealment, but also allowed for hidden security devices. He hoped Valerie's estimation was accurate, that those things had not yet been installed. He also hoped that the lock had not been changed and that her key to the door would still open it …and that she had not discovered its theft.

The thought reminded that the sleeping pills he had slipped in her tea might not keep her under for his entire escapade. But he was rolling the dice this night. The one terrible secret they already shared she would not be quick to tell. Anyone he came across in this place would know him anyway. If they resisted, he vowed to make them wish they had not. There was no desperation within him, only resignation.

He was inside. Nothing audible --nothing he could detect-- had been triggered. Good thing ADT had not visited this place yet. He kept the Glock with its silencer stuck in his belt in the small of his back, rationalizing that his reflexes were more accustomed to employing his own natural gifts rather than those manmade. To strike first is one thing, to shoot first, quite another. A man who pulls a gun better be prepared to use that gun; he was not quite there yet, resolving to use the pistol only at last resort. So best to keep it stashed, otherwise it might slow him somewhat from whatever response was dictated. Trepidation suggested different tactics, but coached instructions from ages before flowed back to him: "Wrestle your way!"

His eyes adjusted to the gloom. There were sounds coming from somewhere else in the house, music television or music box, not certain which. He followed his ears, careful not to alert anyone else's senses with sounds of his own. Lots of furniture and potted plants abounded. Much to traverse without breaking or knocking something over. With each step the sound became closer, but its source not any more certain.

Each corner he approached, and eventually crept past, revealed no one. Perhaps the house was deserted, everybody gone to town. Even Morano's maid only worked days according to his main source, the beauteous "don't call me Val" Valerie. The other source had been Morano himself who had made the observation during the previous night's party, joking that his help would have a lot to do before they returned home after this day's cleanup. His small jibe was aimed at a water taxi driver --who also transported the cleanup crew and had invited himself to the party-- intimating that he would be in no shape to bring the crew back in time for a full day's work. Luckily, O'Rourke just happened to be camped nearby ...or was it luck?

He operated as if the info was genuine, hoping Morano was not setting him up. Now he heard something else. It sounded like, a scream. Where was that television anyway? He passed what appeared the living room. No one there, neither were sounds coming from the second level. He eased past the wide stairway and kept probing. While not huge, this villa was of good size. Valerie never described exactly how big, giving him only a brief picture of its layout. But she had brought a key...

The key she kept in case she needed to have another made up if Carlos lost his. Ever the absent-minded professor, according to her, he often had no idea what he needed to accomplish the things he wished to accomplish. He simply wished them and others made them so. As with most of the services a dutiful assistant provided the boss, it was ever her intention to rush out to the airport and hand him the new key before he flew off with his most recent honey bunny. She considered it part of the job; regardless that some others might consider it the part of kissing ass: "See boss, I am valuable. See how important I am to you?"

He never thought to check for such things until he boarded, she claimed. Actually, he often did not even remember them until the flight crew inquired as part of their checklist. She had ordered extra details added to the preflight, her linkage to places she could only visit through the magic of the telephone or, in this case, of the digital renderings she had studied. The insurance plan and all the various bills she paid monthly for services provided from the main island, she determined without once setting foot here. But she was no less dedicated. She did them for him, but most especially …for Kalliope.

The dream of one day visiting Kalliope she never once bothered to dream. Kalliope was Shangri La, Never Never Land, a place for special people to go. She was not that special and thus, could not go. But she knew about it, knew its background as well as any. Its triumphs and failures.

Its original design called for walls covered with marble and slate roofs, a bullet-proof design that would last forever. However, that design began and died inside the hapless English noble who first dreamed of living out his days here. He believed anything lesser just would not suffice. But like his other grand fancies, this too became too fanciful.

It was not his first flight into Dreamland, he also fancied himself a solicitor of renown repute. But only he so concurred, his law firm fancied him a barrister of second fiddle; fit only to assist a more capable solicitor in defense of their clients. So the challenge took long in coming and once it did, he couldn't win cases his law firm considered slam dunks. Truth be told, Jesus Christ had better chance convincing the Pharisees. He failed miserably.

First the High Court rebuked him, ordering him never again to darken their doors. Then his firm and finally, his entire family (tarnished by his dismal failures) gave him the ol' heave ho. They promptly thanked him with forced retirement and disinheritance, in that order. "We don't want you darkening our doorways either!"

Castigated by all he knew or held dear; he first considered suicide as the solution to his problems, but could not find any method suggested by his less than dutiful wife to be acceptable, considering most either too painful or too hard on the remains. No matter how strongly she encouraged, he could not stomach the idea of his corpse presenting some picture of the macabre to the viewing crowd …if any showed up to bury him.

He denied her ultimatum of killing himself and, before she could do it for him, fled for shores far away. From London he raced to Liverpool, just ahead of the men she paid to help his decision. When her powerful family stretched tentacles there to sever his ties to her, by way of his throat, he jumped ship for Jamaica. But nobody there wanted him either. Soon thereafter --downtrodden and morose, no love, no happiness-- he left the company of all he knew, retiring with his remaining wealth to the bountiful isle of Grenada.

He lived for a time in a small cottage on the mainland, constantly maintaining vigil for the cable from his relatives, begging forgiveness and beseeching his speedy return …it would never arrive at any speed.

Finally, the remorseful, little man set about in search of more appropriate quarters as befitting one of his station. Inwardly acceding to a perceived brilliance he still claimed, as urged on by drinking companions, he divorced the ascetic existence and determined to recapture some portion of his accustomed splendor to the envy of former family and friends alike. He utilized a sizable chunk of his remaining finances to buy a small island just south of the main; there to build a splendorous estate he would name Barrister Hall.

But scarcely had construction begun when his finances began to leech away faster than anticipated. Others could tell that he was a far better dreamer than construction manager and used the advantage. Eventually, he realized that fanciful on paper is one thing; however, in reality it is something else entirely.

He revised his plan for the outer wall materials to incorporate sandstone from the U.S. --rather than marble from Greece-- and in place of the Madagascar Rosewood he opted for locally grown mahogany railings and banisters. There were quite a few other changes to the plan, but none passed muster with the spirited young mistress who had convinced him to build the estate in the first place …as tribute to their love.

He promised her the moon and the stars, beginning with the most lavish castle south of Cornwall. Problem is, promises at night in the heat of passion matter little to accountants in the light of day. He decided on many more changes, hoping still to resurrect some modicum of his initial dream.

However, his blue-eyed vixen was no fan of modicums. Minimalist views she considered surrender to the mundane. She decided his definition of splendorous as woefully deficient and his tastes Spartan; she not only demanded that he complete the original plans, she then rebelled when he balked and eschewed his lusting grasp until he finally capitulated. Back on the scene rolled the Madagascar Rosewood and Greek marble.

In victory, she cheered and rewarded his change of heart with succulent gifting. Her golden locks once more were his to touch. But not even her delights could stay destitution's peril and the avaricious woman decided to move on to greener pastures. She could tolerate his straining at sex, but a straining monetary position would never do. She disappeared as rapidly as his change of fiscal solvency, his coffers bled bone dry …his marble and rosewood gone byby.

Only his inability to impress magistrates surpassed his inept ability at bookkeeping and the enormous financial outlay siphoned all his savings plus a sizeable borrowed sum. Threatened with imprisonment and further disgrace, his pleas unheeded by a family group no longer considering him family; he became even more disheartened.

They say that for every situation there's a solution. They don't say that there's a good solution, but a way to resolve all things. At the end of his road, this former noble and barrister of the English court calmly took out his hand-tooled, silver-inlaid pistol --given in better days, by loving, parents-- and carefully shot himself in the right temple, fearing to the end he might miss and make a mess of things …as usual.

Succeeded to a grieving family, Barrister Hall became a stiletto shoved deep into anguished hearts. They'd played their tough love strategy too tough. Though seemingly inerrant, at least to their thinking, the attempted schooling had escaped its assigned boundaries and fled to another eternity …accompanied by their chastened kinsman's soul.

Mysteriously, and quite unexpected, all the deceased man's debts soon were either paid or just ceased to exist. Even taxes never accrued, evidence that some in his family must have remembered him family. But that was as far as they went, Barrister Hall stood vacant for decades, save for assorted fauna and flora and the occasional beach party. Few persons knew its gruesome history and fewer still knew its general layout. Amongst this latter crowd was John Paul O'Rourke. But at least he had a partial idea…

CHAPTER TWENTY-TWO

O'Rourke's patience never wavered. He listened for any nearby activity while proceeding through the lower rooms. All empty, nearly all darkened. Sans light, excepting that reflected in from a hallway or adjacent room, it became a challenge to avoid tripping hazards since someone of no doubt evil intent had all macabrely filled with furniture and furnishings.

Didn't seem much like a place still undergoing renovation, but what did he know. Finding no one and nothing similar to a cache of stolen goods, at least nothing with a sign proclaiming such, he made for the stairs, about to head up their aged, marble expanse, when he again heard that sound and decided to first check the lower levels before proceeding up.

It sounded like a woman's scream, but he could not be certain over the television playing in the patio room and still couldn't source its location. However, it reminded him of his reason for coming here. Reminded that he had to succeed! He owed her that much. If she was alive, maybe she was here …after all this place he had purchased for her.

Moving stealthily, he discovered the open entry door to a stairway descending down into the stone foundation, then threw caution to the wind and started down. But suddenly a flurry of sound assailed his straining ears and he hurriedly backed out of the stairs and scooted crab-like, back across the wide hall, past the marble steps into the formal dining room.

He wisely anticipated that no one should need come in here. At least he hoped he was being wise; thinking to the kitchen they might go maybe, but dining room? Hopefully, not tonight.

From his hideout he could see a small, lithe man emerge from the top of the steps, turn to his left and head out through the recreation room. Triumphantly, he crept forward to watch Tim progress past the pool table and the arcade games where just the night before dozens of folk played or jested while awaiting their turns. He watched him stop at the wet bar and grab a bottle of cola out of the fridge before proceeding out on the rear patio into the dim, bluish glow from the deck lights. No sooner had he exited; O'Rourke watched a tiny jet of flame appear for a few seconds. The flame extinguished; a glowing cigarette tip attested the man's motivation for the trip.

Then more commotion hailed from the front of the house, sounds of the door opening. Someone, perhaps a couple someone's approached. He backed into the dining room again just as Carlos Morano and another man appeared and also proceeded towards the rear.

Strong chin with piercing, dark, almost hawkish eyes; a swarthy complexion and a head taller than Morano; he strode confidently as if he were the leader of this band, not so the villa's owner. Soon Tim's fire was joined by another glowing tip. O'Rourke crept a little ways down the hall where he could hear their voices through the patio doors left open.

"She talking?"

"Not yet. Keeps blacking out."

"I tol' you don't hurt her. At least not yet."

"We didn't hurt much, just slapped her around a little bit. Otherwise we have been very gentle, like parents. But she just keeps callin' us names, y' know. Can't have much of that now."

"I just need ta know if O'Rourke was workin' fo' th' Feds. But I'm not into torture. Plus th' General wants ta use her befo' she go. You know how he like them big tatas."

"We'll do our best to keep her fresh."

"See that you do."

With that, O'Rourke's rage overcame his patience. He had the feeling the she they mentioned was not the she he initially sought. If that were so, she had to be the one he now rescued. Her life's jeopardy would be his doing that now he must undo. He took the pistol from his back and headed back down the stairs. These were mahogany wood, highly polished and fairly new. But he fretted that they would creak, announcing his approach. Couldn't be helped. He pressed on, crouching low, the weapon at his right side.

Down at the bottom of the fifteen-foot descent he found a large open room. There was not much in the room, a few cardboard packing boxes, some antique lamps and such. It opened out to the right and disappeared around a corner, but it was empty as far as he could see, devoid of human life. Good thing for him, because the entire lower length was exposed, anyone there would have seen his descent. Turning a corner he found another door. Now the sounds on the other side grew even more intriguing, almost familiar. He chanced going in, hoping there weren't too many bad guys inside (he now thought of everyone working for or with Morano a bad guy).

The chair faced directly towards the doorway he crept in through. She arched backward as if seeking to climb out, her hands held above her in a defensive posture. They were midroom in this space half the size of the first he'd come through, this one brightly lit. Hovering above her he could see that same giant of a man he'd first encountered back in Miami. The man faced away, but it was him, O'Rourke knew. His arm was raised, about to strike. There was something in his hand.

Despite Timothy's warning, Phillip was not finished with the woman. He had disliked her for years, considering her to be a haughty, smart-mouthed bitch and he hated her for that and for the offhanded manner which she treated his friend. Whether real or imagined, he construed her treatment of Tim as boorish and impolite --her nose high in the air-- like she was all that. But he also hated her because Timothy desired her.

He was in love with Timothy, but would never tell, because that would pronounce to the world that he was gay. Possessing an innate aversion to labels, he did not even appreciate the word, "gay". He did not like men, per se. He just liked Timothy. Perhaps he was gay, but it was not always so…

Phillip had never known a sire but cared little. Whoever his sire, obviously he had no use for a son, at least not a son like him. So young Phillip decided that he had no need for a sire who did not need him. He could never think of the man as a father. Fathers were men who raised their sons to be men, not just someone who fulfilled the role of sperm donor and nothing more.

Conversely, Phillip always believed that the role he himself fulfilled was that of accident and nothing more. But upon occasion, his juvenile mind might wander about the subject of his sire's identity, usually in a dream where he had real parents who loved and cared about him. Nothing remotely like this real world where his mother not only never talked about his father, never talked about much of anything concerning her son those days. But occasionally he would wonder, while his tortured mind wandered…

The man could have been any of the countless, foul-lipped, putrid-breath dregs who constantly invaded his home, possessively claiming title to the only bed, that normally the young child shared with his mother. They never stayed. Not one of her late-night flings ever greeted the morning sun. In fact each one literally left skid marks after a few moments pummeling this old, wasted rag of a woman, driving their sexual organs deeper and harder into her until she squealed and moaned in the midst of her drunken stupor.

Phillip lay awake, often for hours, in his closet listening to the noise generated by the pretentious lovers beyond the closed door. The dresses or shirts hanging there, he would wrap around his ears to no avail. Three, sometimes four nights a week she would bring "guests" into their one room flat in London's Soho District where they lived. Even the neighborhood kids knew, taunting Phillip in the cruel way kids sometimes pick up from their parents.

"Might as well move over to Chelsea Cloisters ten floors of whores. There's a proper place for her kind!" Everyone knew he was the son of Beatrice. His mother's was the best-known name in that part of town … for a good time.

Her motivations, her demons, the failings that helped mold her into the sad character he knew growing up? Unfortunately, he had been too young to understand. Equally unfortunate was the fact that those motivations were the reason that Phillip's life was lived sans extended family. His world had not only come devoid of the niceties, but also of the necessities most kids take for granted, like grandparents. He had no knowledge of their names. There was only Beatrice.

Phillip couldn't know, but even though totally alone and ostracized, she had been nice when he came roaring into this cold, cruel world. Her son was the product of a forbidden love affair with an American sailor stationed in Scotland. He sailed the underseas in the daring submarines out of Glasgow and they were deeply in love, spending his every Leave together. Her parents disapproved, but the love persisted. Even after learning of her condition, she did not despair. It was no matter. He would soon marry her and take her to American soil to live. To the land of the free where they would raise their coming child. That was the last she ever heard from him.

There had come news of some sort of mid-oceanic mishap, the type of occasional accident one expects when major opposing powers play funny little games with their multi-million-dollar toys. One such accident sent her star-spangled hero's undersea ship to a permanent place at the bottom of the Atlantic, never again to surface with her lover …as well, her salvation.

Bitten by those poisonous fangs of fate, Beatrice had crept inwards. Seeking solace --the tiniest of understanding—instead she was rejected and expelled by her incensed parents. Mater and Pater cared little about the smiling American's demise. Instead they concerned only preventing neighbors in their Marlybone neighborhood from catching on. After all, they lived almost on Baker Street, home of Sherlock Holmes. Scandal would not do. They moved her away to fend for herself, along with that miserable whelp whose birth caused the whole thing.

She never told little Phillip how his grandparents punished what they considered, "her frivolous behavior". She never told him much of anything nurturing. By the time he was old enough to understand, she was already well past caring.

It was as though she also blamed him for being born. She would never buy him gifts, nor celebrate special occasions or even read him stories. He attended school, but never had a permanent friend. They constantly moved to new areas in search of betterment--better surroundings, better jobs, et cetera-- so she said; all the while she stayed hopeful she would find a man to wed and be relieved of this solitary burden …and her anguish.

Eventually succumbing to her most relentless adversary, aka, fate. She began frequenting bars and cheap nightclubs. And inevitably, she soon after began waking up in strange hotels with equally strange men; most she did not recall from the night before. Her memory became dulled by the incessant, alcoholic stupor that robbed all vestiges of chastity. First, she lost her self-respect and then she lost her son.

In fact, the alcoholic trollop very nearly forgot she had a son, a circumstance for which, in retaliation, he no longer considered her family. He seldom ventured from the closet when she came home, no matter that she might be alone. A small incandescent lamp permitted him to read the books he checked out of the library. There was no television, so books were his only method of escaping the drudgery, especially early on. She could sense the quiet, seething hatred, feel the ire and anguish. She knew that one day it would all erupt, but she was usually too soused care.

Phillip tolerated the useless hag until the day of his sixteenth birthday. That was the day she promised to buy him a cake to celebrate his entry into manhood. He recognized her motivation, that she was only giving back a part of that which was his. That she would procure the cake with part of the shoeshine money he worked so hard for after school.

But he looked forward to the event. All the other boys in his school were having parties and sharing the occasion with friends. He just wanted a little of the same, just like the others. He even talked a couple of schoolmates into following him home. They did so despite the trepidation that troubled every step, for fear parents might learn they had entered the domicile of the woman called Beatrice Mattress because she spent so much time there. But both boys secretly hoped Beatrice might show them a favor or two.

Phillip was only too happy to pay for the party. He worked hard helping support them and her habit, never minding the long hours. It was payment enough to escape the putrid odor of vomit often wafting off his drunken bitch of a mother. Their relationship might have endured many more years of her indiscretion had she not only forgotten his birthday cake; she instead spent the money he earned on another of her sailor friends.

The drunken sot did not even apologize when she informed him and his two chums. Her date even ordered them out of the room, spurring the others who burned rubber after receiving some minor pleasure from the sight of the man riding her doggy-style, her naked breasts swaying back and forth and to and fro while she moaned as if this moment constituted her greatest experience …only stopping long enough to slur what she did with his party funds.

But he did not leave. Instead, the youngster exploded into insensate, murderous rage, pouncing upon the coupling pair and beating them senseless with his huge hands. Phillip's few acquaintances had nicknamed him "Baby Huey" for his advanced size and tremendous strength and it was this irresistible force that ran rampant through the tiny flat.

But overall, he was still just a boy. For quite some time he huddled fearfully in his closet before deciding how to proceed. He would be arrested and chained and he did not want to be chained to the child molesters and rapists who populated the prisons. He knew all about them, the books he read warned of them, warned that was where they sent bad kids, even though until now he had never been a bad kid. He had merely lost his temper. A fit of rage, that's all. But no one would believe him or care about him; no one ever cared about him. Not even on his birthday.

They would tell what he had done, not why he had done it. They would say he was a bad kid even though he actually never had been. Resigned, he focused only on his survival. Recalling a scene in a book he once read, he stuffed them both in large burlap sacks before carting the unconscious bodies to an abandoned building two blocks away.

The male he killed then and there, snapping his neck with a powerful twisting motion he'd read about in books. He'd never actually seen it done, didn't even believe it possible. But it was actually easier than he imagined. "Whip! Snap!" and it was done.

However, even though hatred still reigned supreme beneath his square-blocked brow, the boy found himself unable to gather strength enough to destroy his mother. He could not bring himself to do it. However, he was strong enough to leave her to while away her last hours with a most horrible scene for company. He also found strength enough to dump the remains of the lovers' dinner along the floor of their closet coffin before nailing the door shut …the dinner his parent considered more important than his birthday cake.

He hoped any ghetto rats lured by the stench would find it equally pleasing, but not caring if they did. With his large size as a cover, the suddenly much older youth joined the merchant marine, spending two years afloat, shuttling between one foreign port to another before his ship sailed into Miami, Florida.

The grotesque events surrounding his mother's death retreated from his mind over time and had some cheap hooker not made the mistake of pressuring for an extra ten, Phillip might have remained with his seagoing family. He had learned to love the sea, possibly from all the fables and shanty's he'd heard his mother's amorous seadogs ramble. Tales about lusty adventures –nights in Shanghai, porting in Bombay and typhoons off Palau-- were the few positive aspects of their visits.

But the callous greed of a Miami street walker brought a sudden ending to his oceanic career. Actually, it was her near death that brought the ending. Phillip ran. His flight closely resembled that of a frightened Jack Rabbit eluding the coyotes, in this case the coyotes in blue. He ran and hid, lasting nearly three months living on the streets. Unable to get back to sea and with nowhere to go and no one to help, the coyotes with badges eventually found their quarry, setting rabbit runner on another path.

He spent the next ten years reforming behind bars, ten years learning the ignoble fate of a prison inmate. Barely eighteen, his size did not help him. They gang raped the young boy repeatedly; ultimately, he spent most of those ten, long years as a cellblock queen. But he learned what he had to do to survive …and he did it.

And he counted each day. Irony inundated his person, overwhelmingly reminding him and nurturing his hatred of the women whose treachery had mutilated his manhood to the extent to where he now competed with females as sexual rivals. Ruefully, he wished he had slashed the prostitute's throat instead of her face and appendages. One thing he was certain, she would never overcharge again. Now he faced down this other woman. He would teach her also…

O'Rourke could not tell the object he wielded. It could be a knife or a bludgeon. Either way it could do serious damage. He could already see red splotches on her chest from bleeding and her face seemed bruised. Ever a defender of the weak, the sight infuriated him more than he'd ever been. He did not hesitate, his snarling lips sending an audible beckoning through the quiet air.

"Hey ugly!" The giant turned to look; it was his last in this world. The pistol spit once; silenced, but deadly. Surprise creased the gargantuan face, then at first one of the massive tree trunks he used as legs crumbled, then the other, and he fell directly backwards to crash into the tile floor, like a giant redwood after the axes and saws …still hating women.

Instantly O'Rourke was on him, there was no need, but he took the time, checking for a pulse. None. He next ran to Valerie. "You okay?"

"Hi JP," smiling a wane little tribute to her hero. "What kept'cha?"

"Big booty babes blocking th' freeway."

"Can we go now?" She looked tired. Obviously, they had been at her for a while, plus he doubted that the sleeping pills had worn completely off this early. He left her sitting in the chair a while longer as he headed over to a small desk in an adjacent corner. Underneath was a briefcase that caught the corner of his eye.

"What'cha doin' JP? We should probably go now." Her slurred voice came again. He hoped they had not given her any drugs to induce conversation. The combination of some powerful narcotic with the three Ambien CRs he had crushed and dumped into her tea might be seriously harmful, especially since it had been an iced tea of the Texas variety. He could kick himself for mixing them in with all that alcohol Texas Teas are famous for, but that's like bolting your barn doors after your mules got out.

The fact that they belonged to her (a necessary evil she sometimes needed for bouts of insomnia) he could argue, but not with any measure of success. It was irresponsible and could have gotten her killed. Still might, he conceded. Granted, he had not planned on her going out this night or experimenting with other substances, with or without her consent. But he had jeopardized her life. She said it right ...time to go.

"Be right with you Valerie. Just need to check something out."

"What you best check out is th' door before Tiny Tim gets back." Then she smirked at her own joke. "Ha, Tiny Tim. Tiny Timmy, Timmy Tiny, HaHa..."

O'Rourke only half listened to her multiple renditions of "All things Tim". He concentrated on opening the briefcase, all the while wondering if he could really get this lucky. Immediately he "about-faced", realizing that if he really were lucky, Tina would be here also. But he worked on. If this were the government courier's briefcase it would probably be booby trapped to destroy all the contents if opened improperly. That would suit his purposes, but he would have no way to verify that everything was destroyed that needed destroying. Once the thermite bomb --or whatever incendiary device they installed inside this case-- took off, there would only be useless, unrecognizable slag left. Mission Impossible times three. He just needed to proceed as instructed by Peterson and hope he did it right, otherwise, "Poof, up in smoke!"

First the combination 1-5-0-9, next, open the right side catch to the left, then open the left side catch to the right. "Right is left and left is right", he recalled Peterson's words. He only hoped he was on the right side of the case or right would be wrong and he'd be summarily shot for unmitigated stupidity.

But it opened and inside were the most beautiful items he had ever seen outside a fast jet and faster women. The DVDs were still slid into the individual slots of their carry pack. That was all he needed. They could keep the briefcase. He removed the plastic carry pack with the four discs, closed and relocked the briefcase. Setting it back under the table --exactly as he had found it-- he grabbed the woman around her waist, tossed her up and over his left shoulder and headed out the door, weapon held low in his right hand.

The thought struck that Valerie had not complained about his killing the big man as she had about the other. Perhaps it is true what they say that it gets easier after a while, although in this case the apropos phrase more likely concerned hell and a pissed off woman.

But not just women, for he had felt no pangs of remorse, himself. He hoped beyond hope that it would never become so easy that his conscience was not at least a little impacted. But he had not the time for remorse at the moment. Save it for later.

No person, not a sound greeted their departure from the room. Next he stole up the stairs, carrying her like a sack of potatoes. The DVDs he stuffed down the shirt top. Its bottom was securely stuffed in his pants so he felt no apprehension about losing the treasure. He almost giggled that most young men in these modern days probably would need an app in their iPhone to instruct the art of tucking shirts into pants (Android guys still have those skills). Plus, their baggy pants would not hold such a small package anyway. It would probably fall straight out a pants leg … sometimes it's hip to be square.

He let die the humor and refocused. She made no noise. He hoped she would remain this quiet. His humor gene resurrected with wondering: "What if she was asleep, would she snore?"

Technically they had never actually slept together; there seemed always a wall or another woman in between. He did not remember whether she had snorted out a few during the drive back from the north side. But the windows he kept open then to flush out any remaining odor of fresh corpse and turbulent air flowing through the openings probably would drown out a medium-sized snore. But what about a man-sized, wall-shaker? The idea of such ruined any amorous visions of what could have been …he really needed to get a grip on that humor bug.

As he neared the door at the top of the stairs, he tried to push those thoughts from his concentration, silly as they seemed. Then again, if she did not snore those thoughts would remain silly, if she did the repercussions could be serious. But then an erudite quip from a popular ballplayer came to his mind and the silliness began again: "If ifs and buts where candy and mints, we'd all have a Merry Christmas!"

"Thanks guy. One more truism for me to try an' ignore while I try ta git us home." The ballplayer left, but only to be replaced by the steely-eyed visage of Dirty Harry. His trusty forty-four magnum held firm in a tight fist, out issued his gut-tightening challenge: "Go ahead Morano, make my day!"

Through the door now. He needed to shift her slightly to peer around the corner to his left. They were still at the back, but if he crossed over to pass out the side doorway he had entered, there was a good chance someone might see him. But he could not remain where he was now. That would be sure suicide. He had no idea their numbers, at least three for sure, or their firepower, somebody had to be packing. He chanced it, creeping as quickly as he could go quietly. Just then she chose to protest his method of carrying her. "I said let's go, but I didn't mean like a sack o' shit!"

Her statement was not very loud and the men were a decent distance from them, at least forty-five feet, but Timothy had ears nearly as sensitive as a hyena. He called out, "Hey Phillip, where you taking her mate? Get back downstairs!"

But the man never turned. There was little light turned on inside the villa. All he could make out were two, backlit figures, one draped across the other and merged into a shadow that flitted across the hallway before disappearing into the living room …headed toward the side door and outside.

He sprinted from the patio and up the hall, reaching for the weapon hidden in the holster carried at the small of his back. It was also a Glock, but he preferred the forty-five-caliber model. He loved the heft and the huge bullets and its no nonsense action. One never needed worry about an external hammer entangling in one's clothes with a Glock. By the time he rounded the corner it was well out in front of him, at the ready.

"No General, I haven't been able to contact him and yes the DEA still has their folks looking for him too. And sir?"

"Go ahead Ben, what'cha got", asked Burton, wondering if it was another monkey. The furry little creatures tended to multiply immediately after crafty employees figured out the boss was either a soft touch or totally stupid.

"British Intelligence is in on it now too. Somehow, they got wind of the pirated documents. They'd love nothing more than to get their hands on our "Top Secret-No Foreigner" version. O'Rourke is gonna get picked up the moment they find him and if he's found our stuff, the Brit's will take it without so much as a 'by-your-leave'! They'll waggle their chubbies in our face and say, that's what you Yanks get for trespassing our territory!"

"Seems like when it rains it just wets everything," said the older man. "I realize it'll cost us. But they appreciate the embarrassment angle.

Besides, we catch their spies uninvited on our side more than they catch ours."

Peterson wanted no part of British help. They had nearly gummed up the last joint operation in Syria and he did not think a simple "We're sorry" sufficed. But what the hell, this was their territory…

"Get us back in the ball game Ben."

"We'll give it the old college try Burt," answered Peterson as he closed the door behind him. Normally he never used any term --other than General or sir-- when addressing his superior. But he detected a modicum of ease within his boss all of a sudden. These were not normal times and the older man didn't seem to mind the British intervention. Peterson had a feeling he knew something he was not sharing. But then that's why he gets the bigger bucks …isn't it?

Burton watched his executive leave and re-lit his pipe, puffing steadily as he leaned backward in the padded chair. One of the perks. He could smoke even though all government buildings were technically non-smoking areas. But then he did not get the opportunity to leave his office for smoke breaks either. He pondered the situation a moment before swiveling around to stare at the picture outside his window. His view engulfed broad waters where the Anacostia River merged with the mighty Potomac and flowed past on its way out to the Chesapeake Bay.

A few boats headed north on their way to dock, possibly at the Waterfront, just downhill from L' Enfant Plaza. Others headed northwest up the Potomac towards Washington Harbor and the ritzy, millionaire penthouses just downhill from Georgetown. The Washington Monument raised majestic above the white sandstone buildings of the Federal City. Gazing into the cloud-streaked, blue skies, he closed both eyes momentarily --giving silent reverence to his divine leader—and uttered a fervent prayer: "Hope you remember to put us back into the driver's seat too, sir!"

Only slight stirrings of his botanic surroundings by a light breeze answered the question in his head. The pounding in his chest matched cadence with earlier sounds of the feet that were chasing after him. He remained quiet until the chills throbbing along his spinal column ceased and he felt it safe to rise. The night smelled of ginger plants and nutmeg trees that tossed their splendorous, scented offerings high to be carried wafting along the air currents.

Grenada grows more spices per square mile than anywhere else on this planet. Often the sweet scents of nutmeg, cinnamon, ginger and vanilla are blown significant distances about the isle. But to him it was unfortunate that the rules of this game allowed no safeties or ties or room for convictions. Were this so, perhaps he could lie back and appreciate the sweet scents. But at this moment appreciation was no option. There was too much at stake; too much to accomplish; too many debts to repay ... gotta run son!

O'Rourke half carried, half drug the woman with him. He did not have time to waste. He had been hit during their egress, not certain how bad the wound. But he was certain that the wound was bleeding. How much? He could not stop to measure. But the wetness became its own measurement. He pushed the thought away. Grenada's population topped out at around ninety thousand; less people than attend an average USC football game. What were the odds that several of them were chasing him down at this very minute? He had to di di mau. That's Vietnamese for move out fast and he had to di di speedy. They may be at his heel in seconds, loaded down as he was with her dead weight.

One of Timothy's bullets –fired in the general vicinity of his back- - tore into a chair instead, bounced off a metal bracket, then ricocheted out and into him. He didn't know about the ricochet or how deep, he only knew that it hit and it hurt and it bled. It happened as they were nearly outside. Luckily its energy had depleted significantly by the time it deflected into him, ratcheting down its ability to penetrate deeply to where it only creased his ribs ...but he didn't know that either.

He knew the pain and the wet feeling on his left side and hoped he could will himself to carry them both to safety. No sense worrying about how much he leaked or cursing his luck. A few inches higher and it might have caught the back of Valerie's head. But then, a few inches wider and it would have missed them all together. Such is the nature of luck. Sometimes it's good, sometimes not so good, sometimes it's great, sometimes just lousy.

He was just happy his luck had not totally run out. At least he still lived, at least for the moment. He chose not to concern himself with failure. He might be seriously in peril or he may be just scratched. But diagnosis he would remand until later. He just continued on towards the backside of Morano's island where he had beached his ride ...another Zodiac.

He was really beginning to like the little things, renting this particular vehicle at first sight, trusting that it ran well after its engine started immediately. If it started this next time, he'd be moved to love the little, inflatable watercraft. He had choices of some other small runabouts, but the logical part of him rationalized, that he should stick with a winner. "If these things could survive a hurricane…"

But despite the bravado, he hoped again that the blood flowing out was not severe enough to induce a blackout. If so, with her in her present state, neither would ever wake up again. But for now, the wound's only negative aspect seemed a desire to derive pleasure by shooting sensations of pain up his nerve pathways to his brain. Unfortunately his brain interpreted them as sharp slivers that stabbed him repeatedly, over and over and over again, especially when some part of her semiconscious form banged against it or when he moved …so basically it just hurt all the time.

Eventually, though, that condition prompted him to dump the woman onto her own feet. She had become too comfortable riding on his shoulders while remaining half-in-half-out of la-la land. They were out of the brush by then, so the going was easier for people on Queer Street. Only palm trees grew in this section of the sandy soil.

She had also become very heavy and he could not chance fatiguing himself to the point where exhaustion would team up with low blood volume and defeat him. He decided to make her wake and walk or be dragged. She offered only token protest, complying as directed by his guiding hands. Not that it mattered. Her protest meant little to him. Comfort mattered least of all, "Do or die". He had to keep them alive if possible. After that, all that really mattered was getting close to Morano again.

"Plus th' General wants ta use her befo' she go. You know how he likes them big tatas." Morano's words burned. O'Rourke seethed for another chance at the cold-blooded, little puke. He wondered if he had done some similar thing to Tina. Suddenly, he wanted the man's throat between his fingers so badly the anticipation wiped nearly all vestiges of pain from his conscious mind …and right after numero uno would come number two, "Tiny Tim".

He refused to think of this little monster as a Timothy, not just that it took more time than he wanted to spend with thoughts of this man, it was also too formal for one so degenerate. Knowing he had probably done in Tina made his death another goal high on the wish list. Shiro might not approve, but JP O'Rourke did not care anymore. The treatment of Valerie proved their guilt, not to mention the briefcase and now his vindictive nature had need of closure. But first things first…

The Zodiac was right where he had left it, beached on the eastern shore with the flukes of its small, Danforth anchor buried into the wet sand. Depositing her carcass into its bottom close to the bow; he quickly ran to the anchor, yanking it out of its burial and ran back coiling anchor line as he proceeded. The tide had receded somewhat so he had to half-push, half-drag the eight and a half foot boat further out from the beach before starting its engine. Her dead weight did not help one bit. He had to hurry or soon both would be dead weight.

Two high-pitched sounds speeding past announced the arrival of Morano's men. He twisted the throttle handle to its maximum, gunning the engine while simultaneously swinging the lever left, then right, to throw off any sharpshooter. Three more shots dove into the waters on either side, but soon they were out of pistol range and he could straighten his back.

He was not concerned about them chasing him down with their watercraft. His reconnoiter before landing had revealed only two boats docked at the island and they were on the western shore. One, an old, slow motor yacht of near ancient design, appeared as if it would have trouble even starting, let alone chasing down an agile Zodiac. The other, a sleek, modern cruiser, might have been trouble. But he doubted so.

Wasting time disabling them was a nonstarter, so he just popped four rounds into the cabin cruiser, in areas he believed its fuel tanks installed. There were no lights so he figured nobody was home to know; rewarded with three surging streams of liquid, dark in the blackness of this moonless evening, he had felt better about the outcome of any sea chases. It made him feel so much better at the time that he had finally gotten some measure of vengeance, if only on a boat, but it was a really expensive boat and it definitely smelled like diesel fuel "…You kick my dog, I'll shoot your cat".

After holding an easterly course for ten minutes, into the now peaceful sea air, he headed north towards the lights of the island. He needed to get a little closer to figure out the way back home to Prickly Bay. About then, Valerie finally began coming around. Her first action upon waking was to flash him a brave and beautiful smile before leaning over the starboard gunnel and depositing her stomach's prior holdings into the dark sea. Once that mission had completed, she scooped up salty water to wash her face and mouth, then half-slid, half-crawled aft to deposit her head in his lap. A wane smile shone in the starlight as her weary and depleted frame sunk once more into slumber.

She settled peacefully into rest; her stomach may have emptied, but her heart remained full. There was safety here in his arms. He covered her exposed shoulder with a protective palm then turned more to port after spotting the green and red channel buoys marking the inlet's entrance. Now it was time to gather their things and go…

He watched her dynamic profile struggling into the clothes. She was still a bit woozy from the barbiturate concoction poured down her resisting throat on top of the sleeping pills he had foolishly provided. He vowed never again to do such a stupid thing to anyone he cared for, even if he considered the act necessary for their safety. He had very nearly caused her death. He would never have been able to live happily with such remorse.

But she seemed okay now, almost steady on her feet. Coffee helped a good deal, although parts of her were still having their difficulties. Seemingly straining to be rid of the thin, though confining material, the twin globes pushed noticeable indentations forward to signal their dispute. He purposely found another direction to look in order to regain his focus…

He had wanted to type off a private text message to Peterson, but she would not hear of him leaving her alone again --even for a moment—changing with him in the room. So he just typed a few words signaling success and shoved the phone back into the pocket where it normally lived, ignoring the responding tinkle and vibration. He appreciated her apprehension. There seemed to be a whole bunch of folks on this island out for their blood. Now that he had recovered the disks, they needed to go and go quickly. She was a bit too slow for him.

"Come on Valerie. We got's ta di di mau!"

"Huh?" she was not all there yet.

"We gotta go babes. Right now!" She concentrated holding herself steady while finishing her packing. Five feet-seven inches and one hundred-twenty pounds of tottering female, she was too goofy to be rushed at this moment. Frustrated, he ignored her protest at his leaving and ran out and into his room to grab his bags, remembering to get his laptop from the safe. He had barely even turned it on since arriving. Outside. He checked for anyone snooping or lying in ambush. Too tough to tell in the limited lighting of the sidewalk illumination lamps. A few people were walking down toward the beach, but none paid any overt attention to him. So he moved forward.

Opening the Jeep, he stuffed the right side of the rear seat. Then, an afterthought, grabbed a flashlight out of the glove compartment. First he checked the undercarriage, popped the hood and surveyed the engine compartment. Nothing marked "EXPLOSIVES" leapt out at him, so he started the engine. Finally, she stepped out of the doorway and sauntered – still a bit unsteadily, but better than before—over to the SUV. They packed in her two bags and away they went towards the airport.

"What yer thinkin' mate? We take 'em now?

"Let's follow an' see where they go."

"You're th' boss." The Subaru SUV pulled easily out onto the road, No lights. They were nearly a quarter of a mile behind. After moving some distance from the hotel the lights were switched on and they sped up to maintain contact. The other vehicle had disappeared up ahead, but they were confident they would catch up shortly. He accelerated…

It happened so quickly neither man was prepared. As they rounded a corner the headlights suddenly revealed a darkened vehicle parked laterally across the narrow roadway. It was too big to go around; looked like an American SUV, a Jeep. Two ways to go, left down the hillside or right into a tangle of brush and trees …or stop! The driver jammed on his brakes in time to avoid collision, but both knew the outcome of this last resort.

Twice the silenced weapon spitted. Both tires on the Subaru's right suddenly went flat. Another round fired, sending its projectile through the right front passenger window, splattering both occupants with fragments of safety glass which did not cut, but thoroughly aided the confusion.

"Out!" came a threatening call from trees near their right side. "Get out! Now!" Another projectile smashed the right rear glass. Resigned to the fates, both men raised empty hands and climbed outside.

"Hold on mate! We're coming out!"

"If I see your hands you'll survive!"

"Bollocks!"

CHAPTER TWENTY-THREE

Neither spoke as they continued their interrupted travel towards Point Salines. He concentrated on the dark road ahead, while she muddled over thoughts that in one day this man had lost her a good job and turned her into a fugitive now hunted by governments as well as private killers. It was too late to worry what would become of her and her child, there was no going back. But neither could the solution be as simple as his summation that "Life's a bitch and sometimes you marry one!"

They drove through the airport gate and parked the Jeep in one of the rental car spaces. But they did not unpack or turn in the vehicle. Mickey's big hand had crept very close to ten, so the agents had already departed for the day, all gone home or out to some party. Everybody else was trying to have fun while they were trying to stay alive. The terminal building also appeared nearly deserted. A few people came and went, but very few.

"Stay here. If I'm not back in a half hour, take the Jeep to Saint George's, on second thought, head over to Grand Anse. Find an area with a lot of people, a bar or something and wait for my call. If I don't call within an hour, get to the Embassy and call this number. Ask for Colonel Peterson or General Burton. Nobody else. I mean nobody! Got it?"

"Peterson and Burton, got it! Look JP, why can't I come with you? I got that British guy's gun. I can help. I want to help." He looked at her serious face. She had a set to her jaw that left no doubt that she meant what she said. But this was his fight. He did not want anything untoward happening to her. That and the fact that someone needed to keep their gear secure, especially the disks stashed in his computer bag.

"You forgetting Caroline? She already lost a daddy. Please just do as I say." He stroked her chin softly. "Remember, the U.S. Embassy is located on the Lance-aux-Epines Road in Grand Anse. Not sure where exactly, but it can't be too tough to find." A quick kiss and he was gone.

The airport closes at eleven PM sharp. He had to get to the plane before everything shut down. His flight plan was already on file, but no time was entered. He planned to accomplish the latter in quick time. But first to inspect the craft. The few people he met were friendly, but busy preparing to shut down for the night. Most of the businesses and stands had already been locked up, darkened displays pronounced this day's conclusion. None of the skeleton crew bothered him and he reciprocated.

But something was amiss. When he exited the terminal, he saw light emitting from the Lear's cockpit. Outside, a dark figure wearing a dark jumpsuit sat on a stack of chocks piled under the port wing. O'Rourke approached slowly. The man seemed to recognize him and stood up as he neared. The white, Spice Island Air Services patch showed over his left breast pocket. "Trent".

"Hallo JP. What's happenin' mon?"

"How goes it Trent? Workin' late?"

"Yah man! But can't do nuthin' 'til mornin'. Can't get her to start. Meester Morano call up an' say, get my plane ready to go, but I canna do dat now mon. Gonna have to wait 'til dee shop is open to troubleshoot."

"Anybody inside?" O'Rourke's eyes never totally left the man as he checked for any threat of danger. He felt no animosity from the man's persona, but any friend of Morano…

"Yah, dat guy wit' dee hot wife. He in dere. Dey drop him off an' leave when dee bird don't start. Prob'ly close by though. He really wan' go t'nite. Why ain't you drivin'?"

"I'm a little late. Thanks T. I'll go check out th' inside. See if I can figure out th' problem."

"Ain't gonna work, but yer welcome to try."

"Thanks T," he called back before climbing into the cabin. Inside the cockpit, Bill Barnett was scratching his head in derision. Shirtsleeves rolled up, he pushed and pulled at individual circuit breakers without success.

"Leaving without me?"

"Huh? Oh hi JP. No, Carlos wants to fly over to Paraguay for a few days. I told him we'd need two pilots since there's a lot more traffic over there. He said he didn't want to interrupt you an' Val. Guess it's been going pretty good with you too, huh?" he smiled a knowing look. "Me 'n th' wife gonna join him an' some other guy. Anyway, I can get by with just another set of eyes, so I'll make her work the right-side seat. She doesn't mind at all, never been there, but she knows all about the shopping; couldn't hold her back with a mule team," he chuckled. O'Rourke sensed no subterfuge in him.

"Question. What's your relationship with Morano?"

"Oh, he's been a friend for years. If he's vacationing around the time we are, we generally alter our schedules to hang out together. I'm not embarrassed to say it saves me a ton of money and this is so much better than first class on American or Continental."

O'Rourke's tone suddenly deepened. His demeanor reverted back to the cold-blooded killer who had shot Phillip with scarcely a warning. Out came the pistol from under his shirttail. Its muzzle he jammed abruptly into the man's ear, instantly grabbing all attention away from the cockpit ministrations.

"Hey! What gives?"

"I'm short for time and temper Bill! Make no mistake, I can and will use this if I need to." His voice was soft, but tight and focused. "Now tell me, some documents were stolen off your project a few weeks ago…"

"Huh? How did you know…?"

"Focus Bill! Did you pass along information about the details of your meeting to anyone? Did you get word to Morano about…?"

"Hell no!" exploded the Colonel. "I may not be in the jockey seat anymore, but I still know how to maintain security, Goddammit! In my world, somebody dies every time some asshole opens his mouth to the wrong people. That includes those assholes in the press, the AGI Commie Spy and anybody else who ain't in th' loop!"

"So tell me how word got out an' stuff got stolen an' people got killed."

"I don't know!" Barnett stated emphatically. "It wasn't me! I never discuss classified business with any…" Suddenly the blood red complexion changed as liquid drained noticeably from his face.

"Somethin' you remember?" asked O'Rourke. He could easily discern the change in the man even though most of the light streamed down from the two overhead spots. One moment defiant, even with a pistol to his temple, the next shaken and cowed.

"M-my wife! She was insistent that I give her my itinerary. I told her to call my secretary. She wouldn't take no for an answer, kept at me the entire night before the meeting. Said she wanted me home by three. Finally, I told her I'd be at the State Department no later than two-thirty.

But I never told her why, I…"

He paused as if to consider these new details. "I remember wondering whether she was entertaining and wanted to make sure she wouldn't get caught. Yeah, I heard all the rumors, the trysts with this General or that. I never tried to find out the truth because I didn't want to know. I was scared. Afraid to lose her. I have never wanted any other woman, even though I knew I was never her first choice."

O'Rourke could feel the man's anguish. He hated himself for intruding, but he had already done a lot of hateful things since coming to this island. He had killed men and was about to kill more, unless they killed him. He would come to hate himself. But the job was not done. Self-hate could wait for later. He needed to get on with this business. "Morano. You know where he is now?"

"Yeah, they all went over to th' nightclub next door on Bagadi Bay. Probably be there until I can figure out what's wrong with this damned thing." He was talking to the air. O'Rourke was already out the door, racing towards the terminal. The last thing he did was tell Trent to go home and come back in the morning. Then he was truly gone…

She had not left. Appreciating her stubborn streak, if not her sanity, he jumped into the passenger side and ordered, "Drive!"

"Where to oh great and wonderful…?"

"Now! Drive! Terri O'Brien's!" He brought the pistol out and again checked for blockages in the barrel and silencer. The magazine he had swapped with the one spare taken off the hit man, so he was ready to dance, though not very long. She got the message and shifted the transmission into gear, but curiosity ran rampant throughout her being.

"So I guess we'll go after you get a drink at O'Brien's, huh? Ya'll got to be pretty talkative, couple days ago. Now she your kissin' cousin or something?"

"Cute."

"I'm serious JP, what's the deal? I thought you were going to let that sleeping dog lie. Carlos can wait for another time. Why don't we just go back to Miami?" Whether on purpose or by accident, her shapely legs exposed themselves as the short, green dress rode up to reside on her upper thighs, perhaps an automated response that sought to help sell her point of view.

But his was the mission both from the heart and the head. He tried to avoid looking at her at all on the drive over. But, why should a simple drive go smoothly. Seldom had before!

The place was next door to where they'd stayed since Friday and although there was no direct route, he suspected that she "accidentally on purpose" threw in a few wrong turns. Now she was Uie…

Looking into her face one would never suspect such deception. Only light from the instruments illuminated, but he could easily see that she possessed a pixie-like smile and shining eyes that belied her chagrin at his dogged determination. He loved that smile, she was decidedly beautiful, but he had no time to appreciate such wonderful vividness when his goal was to bring wanton destruction and the vindictive blackness of death.

"Turn right! Here! Okay, make your next left. Yeah, down the bottom of the hill." He took over navigation duties. Seeing her intention to stall this thing out. He had to do it. If Morano and his henchman lived, neither he nor she would ever be safe. They would always need to watch behind, perhaps even change names and locations and who knows. People should not need to change their entire lives for the sake of one megalomaniacal little man who desired to rule the world. Better he go and take that other miscreant with him. O'Rourke did not know for certain, but he believed that them probably felt the same way about him.

At over 30 miles per second this Old Man was more powerful than any locomotive and even faster than a Superman. He'd cooked through the Kuiper Belt as if late for dinner and was already past Pluto without so much as a by your leave. Pluto's kids, the moons Hydra and Nix, he gave even less deference. Styx and Kerberos ducked out his mighty way. Charon, the big baby was away from home as usual. But the Old Man still had a very long way to go …and that was the good news!

"What's the latest on our visitor?"

"It's picking up speed."

"Figures. Pull of the sun's gravity does that sorta thing! What's the countdown clock?"

"Figure three years tops. Jupiter may tug it a bit, but might be more slingshot that handbrake."

"Well, we ain't dead yet!" He walked off, head held high. Confidant, apparently.

The younger man admired the guts even though inwardly wondering if they came more because of the advanced years than in spite. That old, he bout ready to meet up with The Maker any day anyway. So what's one or more before?

Meant a lot to him though. A newly wed, he had a whole life ahead of him. They planned on five kids, just like Pluto. .

How could God do this to him? Bad enough God didn't stick up for Pluto. Born on the Dog Planet's anniversary, former planet that is, it was the one thing he'd loved most about the night sky even given it's dwarf size. God coulda made them listen to reason …he a reasonable God!

And now it had been stripped, bitch-slapped down to dwarf-planet status. Man he hated on that Tyson guy!

"Okay Eisa, payment, in full," Morano said, handing over the briefcase. Sorry 'bout the woman. But you still got the other one. I decided I don't need her no' mo. You kin keep her."

They sat in a booth inside the spacious restaurant that metamorphosed into a nightclub full of lively dancers after the kitchen closed down for the night. Large potted plants predominated, some as large as tropical trees, which they were. Their privacy was maintained by a couple such trees as well as the subdued lighting throughout. Music came piped through a sound system connected to the DJ booth. Its flavor was lively and totally Caribbean, predominantly Calypso at the moment, something about a man with a wife who hated his dog or his dog's bone or something similar. He could not tell which, but he was here for business not lip-synching.

"The box you have already loaded in your airplane?"

"Yeah. All ready to go. We'll be taking off soon as Barnett calls." He looked over to where Timothy was sitting with Roda Barnett. Her demeanor was placid, even friendly; much friendlier than in Miami when she learned that she was not invited to fly down in the Lear. "No room in the aircraft," he had told her.

He had not lied. He needed the extra range. Every pound of weight he saved meant more miles he could fly. Especially on the return trip when they loaded up the cargo hold with treasure. But it was more than that. Truth was, Carlos really did not want her on the island. She tended to drink too much and then talk too much. Not a good combination on a clandestine mission. He was happy at first that Bill had agreed to come down alone, pilots being in short supply, but livid when she showed up unannounced. Still, they had kept out of the way.

Now he had Timothy keeping an eye on her to ensure her discretion. Why such an intelligent man remained married to such a ditzy twit, he could not understand. Everybody in the Pentagon had screwed her; even he had diddled her a few times. She was an adequate piece of ass, nothing special. Her main drawback, she was in the way.

People in his way were liability. He wanted to get this transaction over with and get his cargo to the lab in Miami as soon as possible. Once his people figured out its secrets, he would announce to the world his find. Soon he would have the whole world coming to his door. That is if Eisa's suspicions proved true. This transaction could prove to be his largest ever. And it did not cost him all that much in actual dollars and cents. Thank God for the barter system.

Reflecting on the transaction, his conscience was not the least bothered by the knowing that this exchange constituted a major act of treason. His impenitence stemmed not from a festering loathing for the land of his birth, but from an apathetic distaste for its bastions of economic oppression, namely, Corporate America.

"What happened to the woman?"

"She had an accident."

"Unfortunate". Eisa was very unhappy about the loss. But things past can no longer be changed. Still, he had really wanted that woman. "You will permit me the time it takes to inspect the contents; I presume?"

"I doubt if you will be able to open it here. These government briefcases have special locks and…"

Eisa was not listening. He had already started fiddling with a small device held in his hands. It looked like a large penlight. On one end was a connector with a quick disconnect fitting. To this he attached an electrical lead. The other end disappeared into a pouch belted to his right side. Morano wondered at this marvel, but otherwise did not concern himself. If Eisa made a mistake, to him would fall the task of explaining to his customers why the treasure they sought was just so much slag melted to a nightclub's floor.

Morano first met Eisa at a gala ball at the Peruvian Embassy in Brasilia. Introductions labeled him an important businessman from eastern Brazil. No mention of his past posting as a General in Sadaam Hussein's army. But his bearing and demeanor were unmistakable. This was no self-important, opinionated boor meandering about on a delusional quest through gilded passageways that promised him titular ownership to all he could survey.

Well, perhaps he did come off as self-important, just not boorish. His far-off gaze seemed to be surveying the wild prairie below him before launching his cavalry in a vicious onslaught to slice through the heart of an overwhelming force of Mongol invaders. The handshake firm and warm, he showed both his curiosity as well as his preparation by immediately inquiring as to the types of software Morano's company developed.

Following the gala, Morano had an extensive background check run on the curious General. His suspicions were confirmed by a phone call within ten days when contacted personally by the man himself. Eisa desired Morano's attendance at a private party to be held at his South American nightclub. From that time on, the men established a meaningful relationship, even though they had never conducted any business …until now.

Morano's sources could not confirm, so he did not know for certain, but since Eisa Abdel-Hakim was a Sunni Muslim and well entrenched in the local Tri-Borders community, it stood to reason that he would have contacts within al Qaida. Morano would have to be a fool to believe otherwise.

But al Qaida or no, he believed that whatever advantage any entity gained by the use of the STREAMLINE software, there would come no Orwellian cataclysm of epic proportion. For sure the organization was full of angry men who acted crazy most of the time. That made them insidious, definitely to be avoided. So he would never travel to any Muslim country. God didn't make that much money.

They all hide behind their religious dogma which they swear is peace-loving right up to the time they decide it's not. He was never taking the chance they'd get some subliminal message from Allah telling them to kill all infidels within their sight. They were nearly as wacky as those holy-roller bible thumping Jesus-freaks seeding every public southern highway with huge crosses and billboard signs proclaiming their love for Jesus and hatred for everybody else.

But Morano considered al Qaida as more than just people who blew themselves (and everybody around them) to smithereens, although it is just that practice which has garnered the organization worldwide enmity. He focused more on other goals considered high on their agenda, such as to undermine, to imbalance western economics and economic systems.

As-Sahaab, the public relations wing of al Qaida, translates as "Clouds" in English. As-Sahaab produces videos aimed primarily at young, middle class Islamic men. Their tools are western designed, computerized video production devices. But their desire for even more advanced western technology surmounts even the meaning of their name and this evolutionary encryption algorithm is right up their alley. With this tool they could acquire the capability to eavesdrop on all of the secret communications of the "Great Satan" while masking their own. For such a prize they would literally seek to move Heaven to Hell…

Morano understood that whatever they accomplished might undermine worldwide security to the extent that some innocent lives might suffer, but he rationalized that innocent people suffered every day from those most prolific of terrorist groups called national governments. It was to the detriment of those malignant, blood sucking hypocrites he focused his energies …that and getting paid in the process.

However, despite his willingness to forgive some aspects of their modus operandi, Morano refused any direct dealing with al Qaida. He had his demons, but trusting rapacious organizations was a shortcoming with which his people had much too much experience. He was not about to get trapped like his ancestors. He also did his best to keep any word from leaking to Chaco. His cousin's demons were his sensitivities and those were legendary, as well as shortsighted, shortcomings of his own making. Carlos just needed to keep him at bay a while longer…

Chaco's snooping into his affairs was a major hurdle, one he managed to surmount for the most part by misleading his primary source, Rubin Martinez. He accomplished this feat by allowing the mole to "discover" a few less-threatening aspects of an operation targeting a lower level program …one without all the bells and whistles of the STREAMLINE algorithm.

But Rubin persisted. Morano had underestimated his talent not only for ferreting but for separating out the wheat from the chaff and eventually he discovered the planned heist of STREAMLINE itself. But what Rubin was slow to discover was the surveillance assigned to monitor the surveillance he performed. He had to go…

Morano actually disliked the necessity of turning his relative into alligator tucker. Distant or no, he was still family. But still he did not feel any guilt. No remorse. The entire mess would have been avoided had his firm won the contract to produce the end software sets. Instead they only succeeded being selected as a subcontractor to a larger, more established firm. Instead of the billion-dollar windfall he had hoped, came only a few millions, much of that eaten up by overhead generated by the prime contractor's proprietary accounting system interface modules they required all their subs to purchase.

News of the contract award sent him headlong into a tantrum so vehement, every employee within miles ran for cover. He didn't get the award. Worse, the news came not from his contacts at DISA, the Defense Information Systems Agency or the contracting officer, but from a Washington Post reporter fishing to learn how he felt about losing to DIK, Industries. Rubbing a little salt, the reporter's take was that the award made sense, given the reality that DIK also built the hardware component. Supposedly, he just wanted confirmation that Anasazi concurred …just for his records.

Though not picked up by the reporter's ear through the muted telephone, Morano's voice could be heard outside his office door –and probably halfway down Biscayne Boulevard—shouting just how much they had been DIK'd. Of course, he employed more colloquial verbiage. Luckily, it was Valerie –who also doubled as the firm's Public Affairs Officer—who handled their response to the Press. Any public response from Morano would have been unprintable.

The next call, on that subject, came from the DIK, Industries Project Manager assigned to produce the actual software modules. Morano reflected that this guy was not the biggest, just the closest DIK, as the smooth-talking Project Manager expressed his condolences over a selection process he "obviously" had no control. But, to assure Carlos just how important DIK, Industries considered his firm; he wanted Anasazi Miami to build one of the modules; specifically, the interface software that would tie all others together. The PM would provide overall guidance and configuration management.

Unfortunately, Valerie was not around when that call arrived. But she called the PM back two days later to smooth any feathers ruffled by Carlos' vociferous outburst. She assured the DIK man that he had simply been under a lot of pressure and that Anasazi would happily accept the task as soon as contract negotiations could be concluded. What she could neither know nor reveal to the PM was a newly hatched scheme by her vindictive boss to comply with a previous request; a request made through an acquaintance …by an unknown organization.

Eisa may have kept al Qaida ties, however Eisa was definitely not a member of al Qaida. Typical of the Iraqi hierarchy under Saddam, his was a religion of convenience. Prayer was conducted more for show than for communicating with Allah. He was a businessman doing what businessmen had done for thousands of years …benefit from demand and opportunity and survive.

Eisa's primary businesses operated in the Tri-Border area where Argentina meets Paraguay and Brazil, southwest of Sao Paulo, although he also had a small apartment in the capital of Paraguay. The apartment in Asunción, due west about one hundred miles permitted him to get away from home whenever he needed, presumably on business matters. His wife had no desires to actually know what he did while away. She was happy as long as she got her weekly allowance for filling every space and nook of their estate with useless, non-functional "thingamajigs and whatnots".

He owned a five-story department store in Ciudad Del Este that sold merchandise ranging from electronics to textiles, but she would rather shop elsewhere, preferably in Paris --when he allowed it-- seldom ever setting foot in her husband's place. But lucky for them both, many other customers did.

Its first floor enticed the impulsive whims of desirous passersby with piles of Persian and oriental carpets, separated by rows of huge vases and china closets. Floors two and three were filled with orderly rows of tables and shelves full of electronic goods and accessories. Cameras, TVs and computer products from Chinese, Japanese and South Korean manufacturers dominated, plus, of course cell phones. On the fourth floor, baubles galore created instant salivation in the palettes of young people searching for that perfect ring, bangle or necklace. Above the merchandise levels were the business offices and the penthouse suite, respectively.

Each floor had its own color scheme inside and out, beginning with cherry on the first, then orange, lime, lemon and coconut crème on the top level. Locals called it the "Plantation House", humorously wondering why the owner had stopped so short when they needed a banana floor. Some jested that he had moved the grapes across the street…

Almost directly across the wide, four-lane plaza stood another building he owned that garnered him most of his favor in the community and thus his power, also the reason his wife never drove within a mile of the area. Here his business focused on the three most eclectic components of the South American entertainment market: drinking, dancing and prostitution.

Also five-stories, this otherwise unremarkable building --built of cinder blocks painted purplish, with green window frames-- housed his nightclub and brothel. The nightclub encompassed its first two floors and basement and featured colored lights high above and beneath the broad, translucent glass dance floor. Around its deep purple interior were fluorescent, painted images of virile, young dancers frozen in various stages of syncopation. The subterranean basement permitted a more relaxing mood with softer music and soft pillows and comfortable chairs.

Eisa placated local officials with occasional parties –especially Brazilians from across the river-- including gratuitous visits with his girls upstairs. Racism is still a major factor across the river. Brazilians with mixed or white-only ancestry get the best jobs. Blacks get to eke out a minimal existence in the huge slums they call favelas. But all that stops at the bedroom door. Most men's only preference when it comes to a woman is the size of her breasts and how shapely her behind.

He even made an effort to comply with most of their regulations, as long as they did not look too closely. It was necessary, for although both his home on the Rio Paraná and his brothel just north of downtown, were on Paraguayan soil. Ciudad Del Este is treated as a Brazilian suburb.

Brazilian law entitles adults over the age of fourteen to sell sex. The operative term here being "adult", also the profane, stretched liberally in this example to include mere children for the sake of exploitation and, of course, profit.

Many prostitutes—slender and stocky, elegant and haggard, male and female-- all united by their liberal use of eye shadow, fiery-red lipstick, miniskirts and halter tops and push-up bras cruised the downtown areas of the city in search of their daily take from tourististas and military men on furlough. Their take they took from any wishing to partake of what they offered …for many it was all a mistake.

But Eisa's girls all had a roof over their heads and no need to chance being beaten or killed by customers who changed their minds, becoming hostile and unwilling to pay the five to ten dollars for sexual favors. He used doctors to train older, less popular prostitutes to serve as Community Health Agents and supplied condoms to maintain a healthy environment in his stable.

Eisa also forbade his operatives to dabble in any contraband or drug marketing activities in this lush jungle region famous for its porous borders and thriving black markets. There were too many intelligence agencies snooping about for narcotics traffickers and terrorists. Better to leave those endeavors to others more capable, more dedicated. And there were plenty of those among the over twenty thousand shops, stalls, tin shacks and mini malls crammed into fifteen blocks: selling everything under the hot, humid sun.

Ciudad Del Este's neighborhoods included Little Asia, with its thousands of Taiwanese, mainland Chinese and Koreans and its Middle Eastern collection of over twenty-five thousand Arabs of Syrian and Lebanese descent. Across the Friendship Bridge in the Brazilian resort of Foz do Iguacu were another twelve thousand Arabs.

Many of the Brazilians earned their finances in Ciudad del Este's contraband center as merchants, workers and as Sacoleiros or ambulatory merchants, door-to-door salesmen, if you will.

Twenty thousand or so Sacoleiros crossed the bridge daily between the two countries, often more than once to circumvent Brazil's import limits of three hundred dollars per trip. Add to these, groups like the Nigerian and Russian mafias, the Hong Kong Triads and al Qaida and along come members from other groups like the CIA, the Mosad, the Argentinean SAID and Ciudad del Este's population of two hundred thousand becomes a veritable tide, surging and ebbing, controlled by the clock.

For Eisa, this new world had surpassed anything he had ever felt for his home country. All those idiots seeking death in the service of Allah should take a shorter, less bloody trip west to inspect this land of milk and honey. Here they might find that the Heaven they prayed for had already been provided on Earth. At hand were luxurious waterfalls and lush trees full of fruits and sweet nuts and colorful birds and animals for the taking and women for every pleasure. Here their only requirement was a quick mind and a willingness to pursue readily available opportunities. Supply and demand presented a wealth of such opportunities. Here, Paradise was already at hand…

This latest demand came from one such clandestine organization, some considered terrorist; the opportunity came from another link he maintained with a man desirous of a treasure that Eisa would not otherwise part with. But the reward was too great to forgo. All Eisa needed do was play the role of facilitator and he would be paid millions of dollars that his shopaholic, bitch of a wife could spend for the remainder of her days. As a bonus, Eisa would also receive a very special and most beautiful woman with which to toy. Women he had plenty in his employ, but none like the one Carlos had promised to him. Those he commanded were well-used by the time they reached womanhood. But not Connie, he remembered her taste…

And then there came another woman. When this woman arrived she did so with conditions. The first condition being her own condition. Unconscious. More than that, she was a different kind of woman. Regal, elegant, the accolades rolled easily off the tongue wherever she roamed. Beautiful and sleek like a lioness in her prime, but not Connie as promised. That was another condition; Connie had an assignment and would not arrive until later. However, he could amuse himself with this prize in the meantime, as long as he did not get too amusing …weary is the head that wears the crown.

Morano had not been present to witness the lustful gleam in his friend's eye. Knowing the man well, he did not need to see. He knew that unlike himself, Eisa did not accept the word No! At least not from women, but he would hold off a bit for him …until he decided what to do about her.

But this one already did say no. She refused to eat any food, threatening to starve herself down to a pile of bones if they did not let her go. The old woman tasked to keep her healthy was worried. At this rate, she would die of starvation and then the old woman would lose her job. It was a good job. But what could she do? She could not beat her or drug her. Obviously, she could not threaten not to feed her. But at least the woman took water. So at least she would not die of dehydration.

She had been here nearly a month now. But for the last five days she had refused any solid nourishment, insisting that she would only drink bottled water with the seal unbroken. The old woman had ordered the guard to bring vitamin water, hoping to spur her appetite while at the same time keeping her just a bit healthier.

None of the twenty-four other girls her boss owned had it nearly this good; the old woman reflected. Staring out the window to where the others lived, she imagined twenty-four other faces who would love to be in her shoes. Most were castaways, primarily from the dregs of Brazilian society. These poor barely educated souls – who came in all colors and races and whose labors made their patron rich-- resided in the five-story building just across the plaza at "Las Chicas". Their lot in life was to be remanded to the status of putas; prostitutes to service whomever and whenever … and, however.

Prostitution goes back quite a ways in Brazil, originating soon after the Portuguese came and enslaved the territory. They came to this vast land primarily for the sugar cane, leaving their women and families behind. Behind was also left their morality or, at least, such as they once practiced. Society in their rear with their families and friends, they found little need for civilities …and assumed the mantle of wild animals.

First, they enslaved the indigenous population. But the native tribes did poorly as slaves. They ran off, rebelled and died from European diseases. Productivity suffered, which could never be tolerated. So, they looked elsewhere and out of Africa they imported another type of slave. These were better able to withstand the poxes and pestilences common amongst people conditioned to unsanitary practices from men without souls. Moreover, these slaves couldn't run very far, because they had no place to go.

They imported males they could work and females they could work over and work them over they did. Plantation owners and their overseers raped African slaves as they wished, treating all slaves with intolerable indifference –little food, horrendous toil for untold hours, whippings, torture and even murder-- until they died …and they died in droves.

To the malignant Portuguese, African slaves were an inexhaustible resource, as were the ships that brought them over. The cramped, wooden ships were filthy after months of passage with chained slaves stacked against each other like cordwood, unable to relieve themselves except on themselves or at their own feet. The stench coming up from the holds was unbearable; down in the holds it was positively inhuman. Most ships were abandoned or burned after only one passage. Many slaves did not last a good deal longer, if they survived the trip at all.

Generally desiring strong laborers for the fields and the mines, the Portuguese brought few slave women; but the women who were forced to come were treated just as cruelly as the men. Often, they would try to abort childbirth rather than raise children under such destitute and miserable conditions.

Their strength is legendary and to be applauded. However, the fact they deny reproductive rights belong even to women raped by sadistic miscreants, many religious snobs these days would clamor for their arrest. They'd lock them up for violating the rights of an unborn fetus …only their god gets to do stuff like that!

The Catholic Church not only condoned the horrid treatment but justified it as a method of spreading the faith. Catholic priests –full of sumptuous foods and drink-- taught starving slaves that the trials and tribulations in this life would be rewarded by great happiness in the next; that only their physical half was enslaved, not the half containing their souls …dropped this on their way out to happy hour.

The Church never campaigned against the institution of slavery; neither did its priests forgo those sumptuous meals, delectable wines and comfortable dwellings to test their theories about which half was enslaved. In other words, to the church it was okay to work people to death as long as they were first baptized …and, as long as plantation owners used their slaves to build a church here and there.

But later, as much of the population moved to more urban settings, things changed. Suddenly it was not quite as easy as simply ordering your slave to submit or snatching a wayward female up behind a barn. Suddenly, white men had to pay for services from the descendants of slaves …know them southern hemisphere KKKs hated that!.

Now the descendants of slaves maintain a profession in a land where they once had few options. Though they still have not many…

Brazil today concentrates the lion's share of its wealth in a relatively small, almost totally white segment of the population, sort of like much of the western world. But here, much of the population lives in poverty and the life expectancy for non-whites is dismally low …as before suggested, they still have not many options.

Educational opportunities are also few and far between for the poor slum dwellers, too many of whom live on the streets, including children. For many women seeking independence, their only salvation comes from between their legs. But for most of these, that goal of independence is only just a dream…

They came thin and fat, old and young to Eisa. But they were mostly appealing to look at, not like runway models who are all thin; though pridefully, even the heavier girls brag that they have flesh that men like … and a great many truly do.

None is under sixteen, allowing an extra cushion in anticipation of future changes being forced on the Brazilian government by the United Nations. Brazil has created the National Policy of Combating Peoples Traffic to align with the United Nations Fund for Population Activities and has already cracked down on sexual exploitation of minors under fourteen (aka, can't employ them in brothels, but on the street –go for it).

It's all window dressing, as if these tokens are measures to feel proud. Still, their patron saw this and UNFPA praise for the Brazilian government's crackdown as certain proof of more changes in prostitution regulations. He wanted no excuses for raids by overzealous politicians seeking reelection. It's the only time politicians show zeal for anything other than campaign funding …for which there is always time.

To the old woman, this irascible girl was very lucky to be treated so special. The owner had yet to even touch her, even though his eyes more than affirmed the desire. She could recall the time when men looked at her as he did this strange one. She suspected that the girl was brought here against her will to be his concubine and expected that she would eventually come around. Everyone before always did …though none had ever refused to eat like this one.

Then she had an epiphany. There is always someone or something lower on the totem pole. Calling up one of the young runners --one of the street kids who ran errands for the girls-- she sent him out to buy a Coati. The next morning, the irascible captive awoke to find a small cage in her room along with the usual tray of food. Inside the cage was a small animal that she had never before seen. About the size of a kitten, but it looked almost like a raccoon. It had an upturned, black nose and a long bushy tail ringed almost exactly like the more familiar raccoons she watched skulking through the forest at UC Irvine. Soft noises emanating from its mouth sounded like a tiny baby crying in its sleep. Her heart was lost in a moment.

"What is it?" she asked in a tiny voice that demonstrated just how weak she had become from lack of nutrition. But to the old woman, her voice was about the most wonderful sound she had ever heard. If her charge did not survive, neither would her position here; perhaps neither would she.

Relief flooded in, although she did not show her emotion.

"W-what kind of animal is it?" she asked again. Her big, brown eyes glowed softer than the old woman had remembered …and just a little sadder, perhaps.

"Es un Coati, señora." She could see in this refined woman no virginal young girl. So she addressed her as such, though very respectful, almost reverential. "Eets like un, como se dice, a raccoon! Eets muy infirm, sick. Muy pequeño. Little. Ah, hmm, very little."

Her English was stumbling, halting. She decided not to risk defeat owing to inadequate language skills. Handing a small bottle to the captive, she urged, "Alimente por favor. Please to feed."

But the woman did not move to take the bottle. She merely turned to face the window, lying back on the spacious bed that was easily twice the size of any across the street. The old woman shook her graying head, then turned and walked to the door. One knock and it opened to allow her passage. One last look and the other had not moved. The old woman clucked her tongue and headed away, wondering what to do next. She was already envisioning her death as the door closed behind. He would probably just take away her job, not her life. Small matter. It amounted to the same thing…

But when the door opened the next morning, to her amazement, both the tray and the bottle were empty. On the bed lay the little Coati, snuggled tight up against the sleeping woman. The old woman did not utter a sound, just deposited the breakfast she had brought on the cocktail table near the window and left. She felt as if a heavy stone had been lifted from her heart. Her hog-nosed racoon had done its thing.

For Tina, the stone had also lifted somewhat. They had knocked her unconscious and taken her, but by some strange turn of events, she again had her blue gris-gris bag. Waking to find the Coati's company was nice, but the sight of her gris-gris lying beside its cage was almost a God send. Strange because it had disappeared way back in the seventies before she moved out of their quarters on El Toro. Way back before she lost her baby and then her husband …way back before she lost her mind.

She had lost her mojo when it disappeared. Her good luck charm from the time she turned thirteen. It had given her confidence to marry the young man of her dreams, even though neither had the proverbial "pot to piss in". Didn't matter, she believed in its power to protect her as well as her chosen one. So she threw caution to the wind…

Tentatively she touched its blue muslin cloth to verify its reality and was reassured by a familiarity she thought never again to feel. The only gris-gris charm she had ever owned, hers again. She never wanted one of the pink bags used for vanity or a green bag used by gamblers to increase their chances or even a red bag to enhance her love life, even though JP had always joked how she had snared his heart that way. Truth was she let him think that way to keep him in line. The New Orleans shop woman who sold her the bag hinted that men are far less likely to stray when worried they could be turned into a gelding by one simple incantation. She took the lesson, though she never used the other bags.

JP knew the lesson. But with him it was just a humorous anecdote to entertain friends. He didn't believe in evil incantations, evil spirits, any spirits, at least none he'd revealed. As far as superstitions, he'd never revealed any of those either.

She had decorative bags of many colors that she hung from a hook on her bedroom door, but none of these were set up to work magic. Without the stuff that goes inside they might as well be paper bags. She had plenty of decorative replicas, but this was her only actual, ready to rock, gris-gris bag.

It's pronounced greegree, kind of a voodoo amulet thingie and this one is used to ward off evil. Where it had come from after all these years and how it had come here, she had no clue. But it gave her confidence. Maybe it would even keep her alive, even though it hadn't stopped them from capturing her, taking it and bringing both of them here. She wondered where here was, this place.

Sunlight streamed in through the wide windows to give its dark blue a lustrous sheen. Irreplaceable due to its one-of-a-kind content, she had never considered getting another when it disappeared. Neither did she ever consider it lost. She would never have done such a thing with something so precious to her, something whose loss initiated an avalanche culminating in others of far greater worth.

It looked the same as she had remembered, no fading or shrinkage. Three inches long by two inches wide and tied at the top with a string of white cotton to contain the magical formula of dried agrimony and star anise herbs, plus a small vial of camphor oil and a bracelet, which she quickly dove slender fingers to the bottom of the six inch deep enclosure to retrieve.

Expertly, she slipped it over a slim left wrist that still ached as though having been restricted from movement for an extended period. The pain seemed to ease instantly …better by measures.

It definitely lifted her spirits, this loose chain alternating opal, amber and turquoise gemstones around a single, elongated bead stone of etched Tibetan agate quartz, called dzi (Tibetan for splendor). Surrounded by the reddish opal, sky blue turquoise and golden amber, its black and white patterns made the tubular dzi stone appear carved with mystical runes, promising that she still had some of her power.

Anointing the bag with exactly nine drops of oil, she grimaced, reflecting that it was too bad she didn't have a purple-blue candle. Others called the color indigo, but she preferred purple blue. Either description, its magic would enhance the protective power of her beloved gris-gris bag, then she might be able to escape. She decided to eat food again to increase her strength for when the time came. Still, a purple blue candle would be a nice addition. Even a tube of incense could amplify her power to escape this place …wherever this place was.

Down inside her fingers fished again, finding two finger-length samples of hair wound together and not just any hair, these had been held together and simultaneously clipped by her trembling fingers as her husband filled her full of his complete measure. She crumbled a few herbs and sprinkled them on the hair locks before reestablishing their position in a bottom corner of the bag. This she hoped would help him find her again. She prayed he had not given up on her …unknowing; another who watched would never give up either.

He smiled inwardly at her delight upon waking to the token gift. It came as part of the bargain transferring title of her to him. He did not quite understand the significance of the little blue bag of trinkets, only that belief in its magic should make her less troublesome …and less troublesome is always a desirable trait in slaves.

He had watched her obvious joy through the magic of the CCD camera planted in her room's air vent. One day soon he would collect on the debt she owed for his humane treatment. But she would have to wait until he completed this task.

Eisa aimed the laser-cutting beam carefully, first drilling a series of holes into the top side of the briefcase to neutralize the incendiaries, then turning it upright, he began cutting through the two metal locks. These proved a bit tougher, so he reached down to the pouch at his waist and turned a small knob, increasing the power pumped to the laser and thus the intensity of the beam. He had to work faster now; his battery pack had reduced capacity at this higher level.

Within minutes, both locks were sliced through and he laid the briefcase again on its side. About to turn off the laser power and disconnect the power feed, he changed his mind and left it ready to operate. Morano's first lie might not be the only one. He returned the pen to the pouch but kept it in a ready state.

When Morano's henchmen arrived at his nightclub office carrying the woman, she wore the earrings he had given Connie, the diamonds set in twenty-four carat gold mounts and surrounded by tiny emeralds. At first he feared that she had rejected his gift and given them away. But now he realized that Morano had killed her and given them to this woman they brought to him for safekeeping. Even more noticeable, when the henchmen were gone so were the earrings. What game was this man playing? Was he sending some arcane message of power? Regardless, he now knew for certain he could no longer trust a common thief like Morano. Anyone low-mannered enough to steal trinkets from a friend merely to break their spirit had no honor and required close watch. Better yet, they should be eliminated as soon as no longer useful. Morano's usage was nearing its end.

Now taking a breath, as if fearing the possibility that his information on the incendiaries' locations might also be flawed, he carefully lifted the upper edge, averting his eyes just in case. But the hours spent in his lessons were rewarded. No greeting flash spelled his undoing. Now to see if there was additional treachery…

The case lay open, but no elation embraced the two. Morano's reaction was one of incredulity. Eisa's expression never changed. But his nearly subliminal signal, a tiniest squinting of the lids around his dark eyes, was received by the swarthy man sitting across the aisle, even in the darkened nightclub. His hand snaked to the pistol in his belt and out it flashed, only to leave his hand and fly halfway across the room, landing with a dull thud on the table between a man and woman leaning across from either side to whisper love messages. The ominous black barrel pointing towards the fellow's flower print shirt was obviously not the indication he had sought from her…

Morano also had an associate attuned to his signaling devices. Timothy's antennae had jangled an alert even before the other man began his movement. He did not quite understand what had transpired, being too far away to actually see inside the case. But the danger bell rang hard and flat inside him. Once the man sitting across from him and the inebriated wife --aka, drunken bimbo-- made his move, Timothy's own bony fingers exploded into instant action. His left hand slapped the other's pistol away as his right pulled the Glock. But he did not lift it, instead he fired under the table into the man's stomach and out through his backbone.

Only those sitting nearby heard the gun's report, loud and compelling above the Reggae beat. A woman screamed as Eisa's bodyguard's body flew back up over his seat back and tumbled onto her, the force knocking both down. She continued to shriek and wail, trying to rise. She made it up, but he would never rise again…

Roda sat frozen in place, the cocktail glass held inches from her ruby lips. But Timothy was already moving, striding up and nearly away from her to better protect his boss. His head on a swivel, he noticed Eisa's right hand move up and back, set to trigger the laser into Morano's face. Without hesitating he fired again. Eisa's head snapped back –a widening hole opened where once had been unibrow-- and he too flew backwards, tumbling over into a potted tree trunk behind him before sagging back down and coming to rest in the corner of his booth. Morano had not even flinched.

A tinkling of glass alerted and he swung to his left, firing almost instantly. Tim had already marked him as a threat, probably a bodyguard. The swarthy, "Middle Eastern meets Madison Avenue" look a dead giveaway. Another man at the end of his chain. Next life be faster!

This one sported manicured nails, neatly trimmed beard, long-black hair pulled back into a ponytail. Add to that a surprised look frozen on his face paying tribute to the better man. He took a few steps back, then fell heavily; a small hole reddening in the center of his chest. Tim's head remained on a swivel. Finding no other danger, he reached automatically down to grasp the woman's wrist to pull her after him, but she was not there.

Perplexed, he forced his eyes away from surveilling the room and down to where she had been sitting. But now her body lay sagged into the corner of the booth, a small spot in her forehead spreading an ever-enlarging dark pattern across her once beautiful face.

Timothy's face showed no expression. He waited until his employer stood, then followed him through the front door. All around, people huddled under tables or behind any barrier they felt would safely shield them from these purveyors of instant death.

"Can you believe that? There wasn't nuthin' in that case; just a few incendiaries, no disks." Morano stated this as matter-of-factly as if he were discussing a curious account in a newspaper headline.

"O'Rourke!" Spat Timothy.

"Yeah, that's how I figger. He's probably on the shuttle to Barbados by now. But if I see him again…"

Timothy ripped his weapon up and fired, but the shadow was gone. He then pushed Carlos sideways in time for the projectile to pass between them, embedding deep into the wall beside the door. Now he fired rapidly, the staccato sounding nearly like a machine gun. "Kapow, pow, pow, pow, pow."

Empty. He automatically ejected one magazine, slapping in another. But his target had vanished. Timothy sprinted forward at the ready, his fervor for this most desirous of kills fueling him. But incredibly, his employer called him back. He was halfway around to the back of the building when he heard the call.

At first he thought O'Rourke had doubled back and now endangered the man he was paid to protect. He raced back, but soon realized that Morano's motivations were singular and egoistic. He only wanted to get away, alive.

CHAPTER TWENTY-FOUR

Timothy smoldered in the boat's cockpit. He was livid with rage at the deadly enemy who had so suddenly destroyed their carefully laid plans, destroyed his friend and came close to destroying him. Visions of the giant man's corpse lying in its own blood pool resurrected themselves to feed his enmity. Never to be confused with any of the world's more appealing appearances, his final features now mirrored characteristics of the macabre thanks to O'Rourke's unkind intervention.

The forty caliber bullet that ended his life had entered just below Phillip's lower lip; drilling through yellowish, front teeth –that Timothy had always counseled him to bleach-- shattering much of the prodigious mandible before severing his spinal cord and exiting near the base of the block shaped skull; making a huge mess, though Phillip never knew any of it.

But despite his ire, Timothy admitted to himself that it had been a good shot. Phillip's massive size would have absorbed rounds to his torso long enough for him to close with and destroy most enemies. If it had been any other victim he might even have applauded it. But it happened to his only real friend and he determined to wreak a terrible vengeance upon his killer.

He initially ignored Carlos' urgent commands to follow him out to the boat. There was no way he wanted to leave the job unfinished now. The bloodlust was in him, piqued by an overwhelming desire for revenge. He tempted to turn on his employer. But, even in his rage he could compose himself enough to remember that there was no profit in that. One day though there might be…

Eventually, numbly, he capitulated to the order and ran after the cowardly one towards the dock. In his mind he felt himself crawling like a sand crab on hands and knees. He tossed occasional glances back over his shoulder in the direction he had last seen the man trading rounds with Eisa's last bodyguard. This one had remained near the boat and came racing when he heard the exchange outside.

Certain that he'd foolishly choose to follow them in an attempt to complete his terror, he half hoped O'Rourke would win. The idea that another might steal the pleasure of revenge nearly overwhelmed his obedience. He could lie in a dark shadow and ambush the vermin. It would be a piece of cake. But, alas, "Carlos the Pussy" was scared shitless and wanted to run away like the bitch he was. So he had no choice but to wuss out too.

Inside he railed against the decision to leave. However, Timothy also realized that there might be law enforcement types on the way. Rather than take that chance, he reluctantly decided it better to flee for now. Hatred seethed inside his eye lids. Narrowing to tiny slits, they saw clearly two things he knew for certain. He hated O'Rourke even more and now he hated Carlos nearly as much. He vowed that eventually he would kill at least one of them, hopefully both…

They ran to where Eisa's cruiser tugged gently against its dock lines at the end of the pier, past dozens of other boats they could have taken if need required. With most ignition components exposed under open dashboards, boats aren't all that difficult to steal. However, it does take a bit of time and even though a longer distance to run, the keys would be standing by and ready to fire up both engines on the brand new cruiser Eisa had driven over from Sao Paulo. Big and powerful and brand new, its length beckoned in the harsh illumination cast by nearby dock lights …and Eisa certainly had no more use for it.

His aircraft non-functioning, Morano's plan was to take the cruiser and head to Venezuela. There he would remain for a while. The President was not a friend, but he would welcome anyone escaping from American assassins. El Presidente still simmered over the memory of the United States invasion of Grenada that had eliminated the influence of his good friend, Fidel Castro …along with many of his troops.

As soon as he paid a few fines, he was certain that his Lear Jet would be released. He would have his pilots fly down commercial, get the jet, then pick him up. There was no going back to the States anymore, but he was still very rich and he still owned an island. Perhaps he would lay low in Venezuela for a while. A few years should suffice. He would take one step at a time.

Suddenly he noticed the fuel gauges. Both barely above empty. This boat was not going anywhere far. He reformulated his plan. He would return to his island and transfer to his old sixty-six-foot dive boat, the Mona Lea. She was old, slow and made of mahogany wood, but had full tanks and reconditioned engines. He could make any point in the South Atlantic. Already out to sea, they had to turn around immediately or paddle. The cruiser's low fuel gages strongly recommended against trips of any longer duration. But they did not have far to go. He spun the wheel.

The sporadic shots ceased. O'Rourke chanced standing again. Creeping cautiously, he eventually found the other man. He was face down, his pulse slow and feeling nearly nonexistent under O'Rourke's fingers. Two of his shots had hit their mark. The unlucky fellow's chest was torn open. He kicked the man's weapon away, sending the M-16 clattering across the parking lot into a ditch. Then he ran towards the spot where he had left Valerie.

At first he did not find her. He found the Jeep, but not her. He panicked, thinking that they had her again, cursing himself for not slapping her silly until she drove away as he had commanded. She was so stubborn. Then he saw her…

The arm moved freely. Blood caked the hair above her right ear and another tiny dribble lined a small tear in her sleeve, but nothing major seemed damaged. The tiny, brass-coated, five-point-five-six-millimeter projectile had ricocheted off the concrete and gone through the sleeve before slightly brushing the skin on the side of her head. She had been extremely lucky, another few centimeters and he shuddered to think what might have happened. "Thank you so much, Lady Luck".

"Dammit! Didn't I tell you to…?"

"Please don't shout JP. My head is killing me."

"Okay. I won't shout. But you should have stayed by the car."

"I thought you needed me," still stubborn.

"I needed you to stay by the car!"

"You're starting to shout again." That musical voice is unfair. He knew of no defense against it. And those liquid eyes. No defense indeed.

"Okay. This is th' deal. I just saw Morano and his sidekick take off on one of the boats that was docked at his pier earlier. He might be trying to leave the country."

"Let him go. Who needs him?"

"I need him! Remember, he's got a lot of money. He can send a hitter to your door, anytime. Your kid doesn't need that. I don't need that. We're th' only people left alive to testify. If he ever wants to come home, he gotta git us first."

"Cut the crap JP. It's not about me or my daughter; it's about your wife!" The musical voice had been replaced. Now her words came hard and edgy.

"Huh? What…?"

"Yeah! Tim told me everything! You're crusading around on a mission to avenge your dead wife. Right? Well avenge on! Kill everybody who even looked at her! Kill 'em all!"

"Val…"

"Don't call me Val!" Now she was shouting. "Don't you ever call me V-V-Val! You were just bullshitting me with all that fake, brother-got-a-sensitive-side romance! All you want is to get some payback!"

"She's part of the equation, no doubt." His voice came to her softly, torturously. She was my first love and something drove her away. I guess it was Vietnam. It killed a lot of things. We haven't been much more than good friends for years Valerie. Even if Morano hadn't killed her, we would still only be friends. I came looking to find the truth and maybe to find a way to set it right. But now I got two reasons not to fail. I failed my father; I failed a couple guys close to me in th' Nam an' I failed Tina. But I don't ever want to fail anybody close to me again."

That said, he turned her face up and kissed her lips. They were hard and unyielding, but soon softened and returned his kiss. He let go and turned away, walking at first slowly, then with more spring. "I got something to do. You get to the hospital and get looked after. I'll be back."

"JP!" The voice sounded tortured. "JP, where you going? He's gone. Leave it go!"

"He's not goin' far. I popped a few holes in that boat's fuel tanks. He'll have to go back for the other one. I'll be waiting."

"She's not dead!"

His feet nearly slid out from under him, so quickly did the stride halt. "Huh? What? Who?"

"Tina's not dead!" She stared at the pavement. Sirens were fast approaching. "Tim told me. Carlos kidnapped her, sent her to that Iraqi guy's place in Paraguay. They put another woman in her place an' blew up th' car so it would look like her. He was actually boasting, trying to get me to tell where you were hiding. Ha! He thought you were hiding from him all the time you were coming for him. I was hoping you would come for me. Then I just hoped you'd come anyway…"

He listened incredulously as her voice weakened and trailed off. Then he started again. This time he sprinted towards the boats docked in front of the nightclub. He heard nothing else. Had he been able to hear her small, subliminal question he would have answered a resounding, "Yes!"

But she had already realized the answer and thus had no need to voice it. She merely turned and walked to the Jeep, knowing the truth. Yes! He was about to steal a boat…

Timothy acted quicker than his employer, diving sideways and rolling onto the sand, while pulling his weapon to fire back. Carlos went down also, but in a heap. Timothy feared he had been killed. He had not seen where Carlos fell, concentrating on evading an inopportune death while offering his own violent destruction in the general direction of the source. He had squeezed off two, hasty shots before realizing his target had gone.

Two more bullets tore through the night air in the frantic search and destroy mission he launched. However, their intentions went unrequited. He checked his weapon, only three rounds in the magazine, one in the chamber, he was out of mags. His position rather untenable. He lay half-hidden behind a small rise in the beach sand. He started crawling, pistol out in front in search of a target. Eventually he made his way to the bole of a palm tree and stood up. But two bullets thudded into the tree and he went down again before vainly firing back. The other man's weapon was silenced so it was difficult to make out his location. He cursed that advantage.

Suddenly he heard one of the Mona Lea's engines roar to life. Carlos was not dead after all. Timothy instinctively knew he had little time. Carlos being Carlos –narcissistic by an order of magnitude-- would soon leave without him. He stood straight up, hands high in the air and stepped out from behind the tree. He made a presentation of throwing his pistol away. Down to one round, it would not help much anyway. Now he relied on the other man's need for face-to-face, up-close-and-personal killing.

Anybody could kill with a weapon. But when the only weapon available was the open hand, what then?

"Over here." The whispered voice stunned. He had no idea that this man had gotten behind him. If he had not risen when he had, this man would now be standing over his dead body, several holes leaking life fuels out onto the sand. But he was still alive and where there's life, there's chance.

O'Rourke's weapon plopped when it struck the sand, far enough away that his adversary would have trouble finding it, as would he. But that fact had little importance. This contest they'd continue at much closer range. He closed quickly.

On the boat, Carlos Morano switched his engines off. He was no longer apprehensive. O'Rourke had just made the biggest mistake of his life and would soon pay with his life, of that he felt certain. Timothy was a worthy adversary for a Karate master. He made short work of men possessing twice his size. Even Capoeira masters of Brazil proved no match for his lightning speed and decisive strikes. He would catch them in mid-leap and render their technique useless. O'Rourke was a dead man.

The two styles approached, Shotokan "the house of waving pines" versus Taekwondo "the way of hand and foot". Deadly art from Japan and Korea, respectively, now came together in the form of two gladiators. There would be neither referees nor one-minute breaks with rest and water bottles. This was to the death and until came death, the contest would continue. On they came, two modern day gladiators engaged in ancient blood sport, in the ultimate game of Fuk-Fuk, each man believing his the biggest dick and both with valid reason to believe so; moreover, both had the motivation of revenge spurring them …though one still harbored the tiniest hope of a rescue.

"Miss me JP?" Hooded eyes, showing barely a sliver of her true self, watched him casually from their corners. But the slight sign of a smirk on those painted lips told him she knew the answer before she asked. He wanted to find her no matter who stood in the way. More kami figures assaulted his consciousness. He could see Henry urging him to be the man and Shiro, stern but approving. This guy presented just one more roadblock. He needed to transform into a road grader. "Okay Mister Billy Bad Ass, meet Johnnie Red Dog," he thought; then, just as quickly, realized he may just have grabbed a tiger by the tail.

Timothy's feet were the fastest O'Rourke had ever seen. They came at him with blinding speed, continual and untiring. Low, spinning back kicks followed high front snap kicks in series and combinations; leaping side thrusts that he barely avoided, roundhouse kicks that led to more spinning back kicks followed up by more side thrust kicks shot his way from every possible angle. Their explosive power nearly overwhelmed, seeking to shatter ribs, shoulder blades or kneecaps. Raging fury fueled each blow. Death stalked this beach, this night. To go down was to never rise again …ever.

For a moment he wanted to retrieve his pistol and finish this off at longer range, but only for a moment. He had his own rages. The blood lust had risen in him to levels above stratospheric dimension and would not soon decline. First must come the healing powers of retribution. To his consciousness came Shiro's patient teaching: "Karate is like hot water, you must give it heat constantly or it will again become cold water."

Hands, forearms, feet and an occasional shoulder became weapons as well as blocking tools. Smaller and quicker, his adversary had a speed advantage even in the soft sand and he used it well. With every strike he sought concentration of his power. Focus points. His style reminded so much of another's. Yes, focus points.

Barely five-nine; Shiro was much too small to challenge larger guys one on one, blow for blow and, unless you're the Hulk, there's always somebody bigger. So he urged JP to concentrate focusing his power on their weaknesses; strikes to the solar plexus, joints and temple, his favorite.

Now that same strategy came full at him, excepting this time like a double-odd shotgun loaded with lethal intent. This was all about crazy. Rather than the counterpuncher, this guy seemed to consider his size the bigger amongst them, his tools the greater. He came head on, loaded for bear. Small men argue that "the bigger they come, the harder they fall"; now this small man fully intended to prove that argument.

"Papa will whup! So take care when rousing papa." But obviously, he had a different take on this game of "Who's Your Daddy?" Quite obviously. But size adds its own quality …especially when honed by a master's touch.

"Transform yourself according to your opponent," Shiro's counsel commanded. Out of the dark recesses came hard lessons learned over a lifetime. O'Rourke employed his greater strength and weight, countering forceful kicks and claw hand slashes to his eyes and throat with feints, pivots and wrist blocks. But never did he become the bull and rush massively forward, contributing his momentum to further assist the other. Shiro spoke again to him: "Think your arms and legs as swords."

Timothy's defense was nearly as capable as his offensive component, though not quite as spectacular. He thrilled at the destruction caused by spinning jump kicks to the face and leaping axe kicks to the collarbone, mixing in the occasional back fist to the temple or side thrust to a knee. He preferred to fight from distance, where a larger opponent would have less success weighing him down with superior bulk. His game is to fight, not to wrestle.

He came in again, perhaps pressing a bit, impatient with his inability thus far to strike down this neophyte. A savage roundhouse kick sought the ribs; missing he instantly transitioned into a spinning back kick, followed up by leaping front kick. None was successful. Realization. Perhaps this man was not the neophyte he had considered. But he continued to press, circling then attacking again and again. His quarry, for the most part, remained defensive. An approach that Timothy considered cowardly and would never have chosen.

He noticed a glistening in the moonlight. Even against his dark shirt, the stain on his side shone, coming from some form of liquid soaking through the man's shirt. Indicating the presence of some wound, perhaps? Timothy feigned an overhand left cross, then skipped to his right side and shot a side kick into his adversary's ribs, right about where the stain originated. He was rewarded with sounds of a thud, followed by an "Ooph!"

Unfortunately for him, the back fist he followed with missed its mark. But at least he experienced the minor satisfaction of extracting a cry of pain for his efforts. Maybe he had even cracked a rib. He hoped so; those could be extremely painful, making breathing that much more difficult. He followed the back fist with another axe kick; leaping high, his right leg snaked out in front and above his head, then he whipped it down onto the area of the man's left shoulder blade. You find a weakness; you exploit the weakness you found. But you must be aware, that every perceived weakness is not always …weak.

"Do not think that you have to win; rather think that you do not have to lose." These words of comfort became lost in the flurry of movement and combat. Most of the pain dissipated rapidly, but it still hurt well enough, as in a whole bunch.

"Thanks Shiro. That really helps," he thought as he spun away from the back hand. Luckily he had been moving, anticipating, and the kick only glanced. Otherwise he was certain he would be in serious difficulty, perhaps he was already. He had let go the "ki yah" to harden his muscles and help defeat the incoming blow, but he was getting tired. It was time to end this affair while he still had stamina remaining. All this activity was pretty hard on an old man. Young men are full of energy, strength and endurance. But old men are full of wisdom, guile and craftiness, which all mean about the same thing …sneaky.

He watched Timothy's leap as if it were slow motion. Again he had anticipated such a move. Timothy seemed to like aerials. Perhaps he had become attuned to the murderer's mind. Perhaps the killing he had done these past days –he no longer recalled exactly how many—had transformed him into one of them.

The story they told Valerie, he still tried to believe. But why had he not found her? Tina must be dead. After all, this was the fourth time they tried to kill him. What did he ever do to them that they knew about? His only connection here was his role as the Ex. They were even going to kill Valerie. These are just rabid monsters pillaging their way through life. The realization came on him the moment that assassin entered their suite, silenced pistol in hand. He knew it, but still repressed it. Now he would no longer. These are unfeeling killers. They had killed her and now they would die. Simple as that.

The foot arced high in the air, almost to the clouds before beginning its journey back toward Earth, a hammer to smite ruin upon any it found and its target, him. A quick skip-step forward and he launched his left shoulder into the other's groin during its decent, an extremely painful strike. But he was far from satisfied. His right arm snaked up to brace the waist, pulling him backwards and down.

Timothy had no chance at all. His head shot back from the agony of O'Rourke's groin strike and added to the momentum. "Crack!" The sound was akin to that from a dead tree branch put upon by too much weight. But in this case, this sound came from Timothy's neck being put upon by too much man.

Timothy's lifeless form lay crunched into the sand. JP did not look back, just started sprinting towards the boat. Tired. His lungs ached as if singed by liquid fire. But no time for rest. He needed to sprint as never before. He needed to outrace a boat.

Now panicked, Morano started his engines again. The unanticipated scene clutched at his throat as he ran to undo the dock line tied to the bow. But he pushed away the terror, employing logic in an attempt to calm himself. He would be well away before the man could run all the way down the beach to the dock, it said. Carl Lewis in his prime could not have caught up. There were at least two hundred yards of soft sand for him to cross, if he could run at all in his condition. Timothy had represented himself quite well. Just not quite well enough.

He undid the bowline. The amidships and aft lines he had undone at the dock before climbing aboard, to save time. He was just climbing back up to the Fly bridge when both engines sputtered to a stop. Then he did panic. He scuttled out the cockpit and around the deck trying to figure out what to do next. All the while death came closer. The man seemed to be gliding over the starlit sand --scarcely touching its surface, let alone wallowing within. He had to get away.

No time to find an operator's manual, he searched through all of the stories he had ever heard Scubaman telling him about the boat trips, the problems with maintenance and more. He himself was not proficient with any of his vehicles. He could not fly the plane, could barely drive the boat and seldom even drove his own car. He had grown soft, too soft. Now he was about to pay the ultimate price…

Then he recalled. The fuel petcocks! They always turn them off to prevent diesel oil from ruining seals. Some kinda nonsense like that. Still didn't understand the technical gobbledygook, still didn't care. Just fix it!

He ran to the engine compartment and opened the twin hatch covers –lifting them both outward toward the respective gunnels. Both petcocks were mounted on a stanchion, center forward of the twin, Detroit Diesels. He flipped both to the open position and ran back to the flybridge. After a few, tense seconds --perhaps ten or twelve—both motors sputtered to life and he threw both transmissions forward, followed by full throttles. The old lady slipped slowly away from her berth, rumbling a bit with the slightest protest and Morano felt a sense of triumph as well as safety. He headed directly out to sea, making a beeline for the coast of Venezuela. Let them come to Venezuela for him he wanted to shout into the winds flowing past.

He flipped the radar's control switch, firing up the Furuno and setting it to twenty-mile search. There were no navigational hazards in this direction. Even "Kick 'em Jenny", the underwater volcano, was too far north. As long as he steered due west there should be no problems with any eruptions. Then he remembered another story from the Scubaman. He kept an old Colt forty-five caliber pistol under the Fly bridge dashboard in case somebody fished a shark on board. He reached under the cover and found the box. Opening it, he turned back to pop off a couple of shots at O'Rourke, left high and dry and in fitful rage on the beach. To his horror, O'Rourke was not to be seen. He was no longer on the beach.

Morano turned back to his controls. He had to get away before O'Rourke caught up to him. He might have a speedboat. The Mona –as Scubaman affectionately called her—was only good for around twenty-five miles per hour top end. He had to get away. His fear gave flight to his boat. She seemed to be traveling faster than indicated on the speedometer. Perhaps there was a trailing wind pushing him. Every knot counted. He had to get away.

Suddenly a sound. But from where? He whirled with the pistol out, apprehensively aware of another knot, the knot in his throat threatening to choke him. How did he get aboard? Where the hell is he?

There he is. Carlos could not see his quarry. But instinct told him exactly where to look. At his elevation, he had a good angle from which to view the aft deck. All the deck lights were lit, bathing the entire rear area in their harsh, pale glow. O'Rourke had to be hiding amidst three fifty-gallon oil drums, full of diesel fuel and lashed to the starboard side about midway back. There was not much space to fit in there but that had to be where.

The extra fuel he had ordered aboard for longer duration journeys. In a more adventurous moment he once toyed with the idea of voyaging over to South Africa, around the Cape of Good Hope and into the Indian Ocean, perhaps sailing around the world. It had been Tina's idea. But her ideas no longer applied.

"Come out, come out wherever you are!" Morano cursed his stupidity. In his haste he had neglected to bring the aft and amidships springer lines aboard. That must have been how he came aboard, climbing one of those. But he could fix that problem once and for all. He spoke loudly, vainly attempting to rise above the throaty roar of the engines through the open engine covers. Then he turned back and pulled the throttles down midway to cruising speed. "I know where you are. See the big gun? Come you out or be you target!"

Nothing. "Kapow! Pow! Pow!" Three shots exploded from the pistol.

Three streams of oil spurted from holes drilled into the drums. Two of the streams christened O'Rourke with their flow. He was being soaked. He contemplated heading over the low railing but thought better of swimming that far at night …on purpose.

Unappreciative of the man's rhyming, as well as this situation, O'Rourke did as he was told, standing up, but not fully leaving the security of his barrel hideaway. Not that there was much security here, Morano already demonstrated he was idiotic enough to shoot into barrels of diesel fuel close to his engine compartment. One never knows the motivations of egotistical madmen.

The pistol was aimed in his general direction, but not directly at him, a fact which somewhat emboldened. He would take the chance, anticipating that the man's penchant for megalomania surpassed his desire for quick destruction. Since Morano knew he had the only firearm and thus could kill whenever he felt like killing, chances were he'd spend a little time savoring his superior position. As long as he believed it so. O'Rourke decided to humor Mista Masta Blasta and his hand cannon. It wasn't like he had any really great choices. Besides, he hated diesel fuel bathing…

Welcome aboard Mister O'Rourke. Yes indeed. And please be careful as you step. I neglected ta close th' hatches. My bad. You could slip and get all hurt up and we most definitely don't want that now do we? You could git your side bleeding again."

O'Rourke did as beckoned. He had become careless, now he was a prisoner, at least for the moment. His hell-for-leather dash had brought him to the dock just as the boat began chugging out of its berth. His dash speed got him there a bit too late, but he dove for one of the lines hanging from deck cleats on the starboard side. It took a while, fighting the air and water rushing aft into his face. But eventually he made his way aboard, only to slip on a small screwdriver the crew had left behind …and now was about to get shot in his behind.

"As you say Carlos, we meet again. Jus' th' two of us."

"Yeah, but this time I got th' upper hand. You ta be commended, though. Single-handed you brought my whole shit to a grinding halt. It's gonna take me a while ta put it all back together."

"Doubt if you'll have that chance."

"O'Rourke I doubt if you'll have time to care." They had traveled some distance from shore. The auto navigator, Morano set on a course of two-six-five, slightly south of due west, to Venezuela. He put one eye peeled to sea and one on his hostage. Satisfied that he had no other company, he climbed carefully down the ladder to face the man. He was not the least bit sad that O'Rourke had to die. He just wished things had not progressed so far and so costly. But he could bring everything back up to speed; make it all right again.

"I know this all about Tina. Guess I don't blame you fa' being pissed. But I loved her too. I did everything fo' her an' she sneaked me behind my back."

"So you killed her an' put th' whole world in jeopardy, jus' cause she had trouble making up her mind? What kinda self-centered, egotistical, amoral, arrogant, nihilistic sonofabitch are you?" He ran out of superlatives, so interjected a well-used colloquialism to round out the spiel. Mickey was the one for superlatives. He could chant them to the beat of Eminem or Kanye rap lyrics if necessary. But O'Rourke still had ways to get his message across. He just needed to find the best way…

"Hey! I didn't want it ta be like this! I had plans fo' us. She screwed them up!"

"Well your horse didn't come in! Face facts Morano! You blew it!" Even in the face of the pistol, O'Rourke's voice steadily rose, his lips had pulled back --exposing the clenched teeth-- his nostrils flared and he leaned forward on his feet. The oily smell covering his body and soaked into his clothes did not help his disposition.

"Back!" ordered Carlos. "Back up or die! I didn't want you floating up anywhere close by, but I'll shoot you now and dump your body later! Besides Homes, you smell like shit."

He smiled as O'Rourke eased back a step. It was the same toothy smile that Stephanie hated; the one that always fell short of his eyes. "It wasn't just her. Yeah she really pissed me off. I was too good to her an' she pulled that shit. What the hell was she looking for?"

"Maybe somebody whose mama's children had lived…"

"Cute. Guess there's no moving ahead for some people." Said Morano reflectively and then he flew along a different tangent altogether. "But she wasn't the only one, cause so did th' Government. Yeah, they always shortin' us minorities. They blowin' smoke up my ass every time I bid on a contract. Naw, they pay lip service, but they always line up wit' the big guys, th' DIKs, 'n th' Boeings, 'n Lockheeds. Even if we got th' best product they give the bid to them, so they come to us ta do th' work. I'm tired o' that!"

O'Rourke looked down to his feet. There was much truth in Morano's statement. He had seen it too often before. "Yeah man. I feel you. Lotta bullshit in that political jungle. Friends o' mine going through th' same crap."

Morano looked as if he had just been slapped. He stared at the man, not expecting any agreement to be capable between them. Especially since each believed the other a monster. His voice came softer this time, barely perceptible over the engine noise. "Yeah, I know I blew it. I really blew it. But man, that last hit. Got that phone call. Lost it. Couldn't stop myself. Chaco tried ta stop me, ducked him. Rubin tried, killed him 'n Connie. I just lost it."

Momentarily, but only just, O'Rourke had felt the tiniest sympathy for the man. Everyone has their passions. Sometimes passions become demons. But he felt only a tiniest bit of sympathy. All the harm caused came flooding back to wash out any vestiges of sorrow. He had to get a bit closer.

"Well, th' Government got their secret codes an' stuff back, so they probably won't be lookin' too hard. I guess you can buy off these local guys, besides, they still pissed at th' U.S. fo' invading back in 'eighty-three."

"Yup! Ol' Tiger Grendle over in Saint John hates the U.S. Marines. Some Force Recons captured the ganja he had grown 'n stored in garbage bags. They didn't let him keep any of it. He suspects they smoked it before they left. He pissed they didn't at least share." Carlos smirked with that last part.

"Hey, you know the drill. Uncle Sam's Misguided Children." They both laughed. More like a short chuckle.

Serious again, Morano spoke. "Y'know, Tina in Paraguay. She ain't dead."

"So I heard." Suddenly he regained a toehold on believing it himself. Holding out hope wasn't going to improve this situation though. He had inched closer, maybe a foot or two. Even when Morano ordered him back, he only appeared to back up, shuffling feet to the rear without actually moving that way. A combination rope-a-dope and moonwalk. But he was still too far away. "Why there?"

"Couldn't kill her, man. She put th' same spell on me she put on you. But I sent her to live in a whorehouse. I mean she made me mad, man! I been chasin' her since she was carryin' yo' kid. Even put some stuff in her soup ta make her abort. She blamed it on you. You don't come down on me in th' Nam, I wouldn't a done it. I sent a guy ta pay you a visit th' other night. Ain't seen 'em since. Guess you got him too." He said these things as matter of factly as if he were repeating a weather report. But now his eyes had regained their hard edge. He too had been flushed back to the fore by the realities.

"Morano, you'll never live to see another sunrise. You could never kill me." These words radiated and surged within his mental self. But none even approached his lips.

Outwardly he remained calmed even as the fire heated him near to boiling. His eyes were devoid of all expression. Instead, he chastised: "The difference between me and you is I don't compare myself to you or anybody else. I only compare myself to my own expectations. This is about life, not Monopoly. How well you go is on you."

Ten feet away. It had been not the most impressive of bitch slaps, but he needed the distraction more than the words. He was about out of time. He had to move now; Morano had only told these things to send to the grave with him. He was about to kill.

Perceptions could not have been more accurate. Across the boat's deck, Morano had tired of this gamesmanship. He realized that even though he admired this man, he truly hated him. He would endure him no longer. Raising the weapon, he fired. But O'Rourke was already moving before the hammer fell.

In karate "there is no first attack." It was Shiro's most important lesson. He had been manipulating the other man for his own purposes, attacking his mind to influence this outcome, inching ever so steadily closer.

Him! That's who this guy was! He finally placed him! It came back, clear as day. The form of a young drug pusher in Marine Jungle Utilities, squirming, about to die at his hands, but surviving under the threat of assured destruction should he ever again come selling around his airbase. He had totally forgotten 'til now. So that was what this was all about! This malignant monster stole his woman and his child over some bullshit! He should have locked him up back then. If he had, maybe things would never have come to all this. Too late. Can't go back, can't second guess. If this was his time, he was taking this asshole with him. But how to do it? He inched another few millimeters…

Scared, nervous men make poorer marksmen than calm, composed men. Fear turns the mind to jelly. But he doubted he could rattle Morano sufficiently while he held the weapon. This man had come up both from the streets and the Marines. Killing would not overly faze one such as he, especially since he believed he held the advantage. Perhaps he believed he held too much advantage which could shift the advantage. So he had engaged him in conversation –no threats or braggadocio—first expressing anger, he then exhibited understanding, even a semblance of camaraderie. "There is no first attack!"

"Deceive the sky to cross the ocean." This time the advice stretched across twenty-five hundred years from the Chinese academian, Sun Tzu who counseled in his Thirty-Six Strategies, or proverbs, that: "Moving about in the darkness and shadows, occupying isolated places or hiding behind screens will only attract suspicious attention. To lower an enemy's guard you must act in the open and hide your true intentions under the guise of common every day activities."

Advantages are often greater in one's mind than in reality. O'Rourke also held a weapon of his own. In his left hand he held the small screwdriver he had found lying near the barrels. Actually, it had found him first, causing the stumble that alerted Morano. Otherwise this contest could have been concluded differently. He figured it owed him. He palmed it, hiding its presence, its shank pointed up against the inside of his wrist.

"Kill with a borrowed knife," suggests Sun Tzu stratagem number three. As Morano fired, O'Rourke leaped sideways. As he leaped, his hand came up to his chest and then flashed out toward the target as if tossing a Frisbee. "Whap!" Its wooden handle caught Morano's forehead with full force, stunning him for a moment. In that moment, O'Rourke was upon him. Anticipation possessed him, now would come retribution …however, anticipation sometimes fails to fully anticipate.

Morano's calm resolve had dissipated with lightning speed. In its place strode a battered and bruised nervous disorder and he knew fear. Blindly he fired again and missed again. His vision still clouded. Then he cried out in pain as he was thrust backwards and his right wrist twisted cruelly.

O'Rourke had rolled headfirst across his shoulder to his hip to avoid the deadly projectile which whined past. In one smooth motion he was back on his feet and leaping catlike, this time forward, and he was on Morano. Driving his shoulder into the man's ribcage, he slammed him into the cabin door. His left hand clutched the barrel of the forty-five and jammed it up and back, until it fell.

Morano grunted in pain from the blow. He let go of the pistol but was not about to relinquish his hold on life this easy. He clawed savagely --intent on blinding his tormentor-- all the while growling like a cornered wolf. Using a fear-spawned inner strength, he hurled himself and O'Rourke through the already battered, cabin door and over a chart table.

Hanging on with tenacious determination, he rolled, kicked and bit. Some inner instinct warned that he would die soon, unless O'Rourke died sooner. The gun had fallen somewhere along the deck and there was little chance of ever recovering it in the dark shadows. He had to hold the man down. But it was like holding down a Bengal tiger.

O'Rourke smashed an elbow into Morano's face, kicked both feet into his chest and sprung to his feet. He was genuinely surprised at the man's toughness. The slowly rocking boat action didn't hurt his balance, but these close quarters would not do. He had to get some room. He backed towards the door and Morano lunged again, but this time all he grabbed was air. O'Rourke blocked the outstretched arms with his left forearm and snapped a sharp ridge-hand into the base of Morano's skull with the leading edge of his right. The blow's effectiveness was attenuated by its target's forward motion, but it did send him through the door with increased velocity.

Morano was lucky, any slower and his brain stem might never have withstood the strike. He tripped over the sill and sprawled out onto the rear deck. But was quickly back to his feet, wild-eyed and ferocious. The fear within had given wings to his fearlessness. If he was going to die today, so be it, but he would not go willingly or alone.

O'Rourke moved in to deliver a back-knuckle strike and stepped directly on Carlos' lost pistol, stumbling momentarily. Carlos saw his chance. Plowing forward, he drove O'Rourke back, against the boat's railing. O'Rourke twisted to slip him past ...too late.

Both men plunged over into the dark, cool waters and separated. Carlos panicked. Swimming after his slowly disappearing boat, he strained every muscle in the vain attempt. He was in near frenzy, spurred on by a heightened inner instinct for survival. But his last tool to ensure such was floating away. He had to catch it. He screamed in frustration, but still swam on. His two knots per hour, full out, versus its ten knots was no contest.

Treading water while attempting to get his bearings, O'Rourke listened to Morano's half-crazed ranting and tempted to call to him. Fighting the sea was like fighting God. Totally unwinnable, totally stupid! But he changed his mind. He really cared little about Carlos Morano's future dealings with God. Actually, his only cares concerning the man's future was a preference that he had none. He thought about stripping his shoes and pants to make it easier to swim, even though such was contrary to Marine Corps doctrine for survival at sea, figuring he did not have all that far to go. But doctrine is the Corps' bible for a reason.

Drown Proofing is designed primarily to keep you alive in the middle of the ocean. To be declared drown proofed, fully-clad Marine boots were required to remain in the pool forty-five minutes without touching anything but water (no bottoms or sides), then swim one hundred-eighty yards carrying a rifle, then tread water five minutes using only feet for propulsion and another five with hands and feet. All that in a swimming pool filled with fresh water. He was only a few miles offshore, by his calculations, and this was salt water.

It would be much easier to swim without the extras, especially the sneakers, but they served other purposes. Never knew when some jellyfish might come dancing by, looking to sting dinner and found O'Rourke. Too tough to eat, but not too tough to shoot full of venom, yeah, he'd stay clothed for a while. Suddenly another sound assailed his ears; a large splash from somewhere close, by something big; something was coming in …and fast.

He took one deep breath, curled his body in a loose ball and relaxed every fiber as best he could, attempting to present a hole in the water and, if that did not work, to prepare himself for coming doom. The thought of sneaking one last prayer to a deity was not in him. He only hoped that he had done enough good things in this life so that he would not return as a slug or a worm in the next.

Silently and unmoving, maintaining his blob float –straight out of drown proofing class-- he felt water currents strike as the thing passed underneath. He heard the inner voice of fear, fear of the unseen, the unknown. His lungs ached and his body complained of this poor treatment; still, he remained coiled. Untimely movement might well spell death.

Whatever was nosing around might only be a dolphin, but it might also be a shark or a big barracuda. So he bobbed along just below the surface until his aching lungs demanded replenishment. He hoped his wound did not take that opportunity to bleed. Lucky for him it did not …not so lucky for some others.

It detected sound vibrations emanating from a large splash. Possibly nothing, but maybe food. Then came the erratic vibrations from something splashing along the surface. Evidently something was in trouble. Better chance that it was food.

Traces of blood, trailing from some wounded creature, beckoned. Following its sensitive nose, the animal moved forward, propelled by powerful sweeps of a superbly crafted tail, upper and lower sections nearly identical in size and shape.

It could not see, but it really did not need to see. It had other superb tools to find its meals. Its path shifted left, then right, then left again. Its inherent devices triangulated back to the source of the disturbance. Two, three, four powerful sweeps of its tail propelled it straight towards its quarry. Definitely food. Now nothing else registered. It sensed something as it passed directly underneath, but it was something which smelled foul, not at all tempting. It might be food, but it did not act like food. No movement, very unappealing.

Sensors registered their distaste as O'Rourke's shoe brushed by its leathery hide as it swept past. Perhaps if nothing else was available it would take a bite just to be certain. But this thing did not seem appealing. Besides, there was a more favorable source ahead; a source that beat the water into a frenzy, indicating its helplessness. It was overpoweringly irresistible…

Carlos stopped swimming. His boat was gone now, might as well turn around and make it back to land. He was over five miles from the nearest land and his ribs ached like hell. He felt certain they would not bleed too much. Perhaps a minor cut or abrasion from some corner of some part of his boat, at least not enough to attract any night feeders. But he had to get to shore.

Now he had neither a boat or a plane. What else would go wrong this night? But he comforted himself. All was not bad. He would send people to get his boat back (somebody's Coast Guard would surely pick it up) and more importantly, he would get his airplane back, too. The golden box remained secure in his plane and soon he would be so much richer ...so much more powerful, too.

Stroking easily for the distant shore, he smiled. The lights of Kalliope looked out to sea to beckon home its master as the virgin bride from her wedding bed. They were a welcome sight even from so far away. They seemed to say to him: "Come on home master. It's all waiting for you" He happily stroked for the distant shores. His place.

Perhaps delusional, perhaps not. Was it such a reach? Couldn't a man's home welcome his approach, remembering all he had done to bring it to life?

Truly, it was all waiting for him. He would have many more wonderful adventures there. And one other thing he would have, he would have the last laugh on O'Rourke. One day when he least expected it ...and that was no delusion!

He determined to end the man's existence as soon as he finalized negotiations with his "friends". In fact, he'd get them to do the job. Soon he'd avenge all debts owed, past and present. O'Rourke would be dead; Tina would have no one else, she'd have to come back to him. He wasn't delusional or irrational, he reasoned, stroking all the more powerfully through ocean swells. No, not delusional by a long shot, he was determined.

He had heard the legends over the many years his aunts and uncles had taught the heritage of their ancestors, listening to the tales of Chicomecoatl the Aztec goddess of nourishment and plenty. However, he took the lesson of the Mother one step further than did Chaco. Chicomecoatl was not the wimpy Awitelin Tsta worshipped by his cousin. She did not take crap lying down. You do her wrong, you pay serious penalty. Chicomecoatl was a tough chick. She demanded blood sacrifices and she got them. Decapitation her favored way to take you home.

He felt her pain from mankind's polluting and destroying. Sadly, he recalled images shot from satellites high in space: rivers dark with pollution spilling out into the seas far from man's dwellings. And other rivers, these composed primarily of plastic waste matter, snaking hundreds of miles across the middle of nowhere close to anywhere called dry land.

Man's madness had usurped international boundaries until every man's backyard had become every other man's toilet. There seemed no chance at all that the Earth Mother could survive the inevitability. One day she must fall to this poisonous onslaught. Not an apocalypse produced by some god of the Hebrews or the predictions of ancient Mayans, but death by her own uncaring children bent upon conquest and profit.

Again from a differing perspective of his elder cousin, he saw the solution in Earth Mother's lesson of old. Blood sacrifice. It made perfect sense, balanced perfectly the old with the new. Soon he would bring the old to make good the new…

The worst things in today's world he attributed as a result of over population. A blind man could see it. If he looked. Too many people led to greater crime and pollution and would eventually lead to an ultimate conflagration where nations battled over the remaining table scraps and then destroyed our world trying to steal the last scoop. Estimates already speculate we'll need another entire earth in a few decades just to satisfy China. They can't feed all their one and a half billion people now. With thirty-four children born each minute, soon it'll be two billion …and they have nuclear weapons.

He despised pro-life advocates, always demanding every pregnancy give birth. They didn't get it. He saw the current trends of illegal alien flow from the southern lands as proof the time was near. They can't live at home, got nowhere else to go …and he had a plan to resolve the problem.

Chaco would never understand. Their relationship had devolved to one akin to Judas and Jesus, at least as he believed. Like most others, Carlos believed Judas betrayed Jesus because he lost faith. However, unlike most, Carlos sided with those theologists who believed that loss not necessarily Judas' fault, the result from his lord showing him too little of the kingdom to come. Either that or he saw too much of his lord's purpose and that purpose showed less than Judas felt was needed.

Judas, they say, searched for the messiah of the Old Testament. He searched for and hoped for a messiah who would lead the Hebrews in revolt against their Roman oppressors, who would cast those ruthless jackals down from their role as conquerors …to lick the very sandaled feet of those they once enslaved.

These latter apologists say Judas felt betrayed by a master who wanted to love his enemies; a master who first told his disciples to buy swords, then to save them for some other time. This lord didn't want to fight. He was no warrior. This man was a lover. He preached love, not conquer. So Judas lost faith in his lord, then lost his lord and then lost himself. So it was with him and Chaco. Chaco sided with the enemy…

Morano had explored his options, initially thinking maybe to enlist the aid of tyrants seeking solution to their population woes. The legend of this Ark of the Covenant includes a telling how whole grains of crop were mutated when stored nearby. Every animal that ate those grains remained barren for a number of years. Every woman who ate the flesh of any of those animals or drank their milk was also made barren. To his manner of thinking, no problem! They'd then fulfill their most useful function … items of pleasure.

He could take the Ark to China, use its mystical force to alter the chemical makeup of soy products used by pregnant women worldwide. By the time people recognize, it'll be too late. Auto-aborted fetuses by the gross. At least one generation down. Pissed off right-to-lifers? Who cares? Get the usual Chinese apology, "Oops, my bad".

He could go to sub-Saharan Africa, maybe Sudan or someplace like where feeding hungry mouths had become over burdensome. No one would even know, much less care, that people unable to feed themselves suddenly weren't having more mouths they couldn't feed.

Then it had come to him, a vision out of the blue. He knew what he'd do. He wasn't gonna do this haphazardly; he wasn't gonna trust no red Chinese; black Africans or white Russians or anybody else having their own agenda. He was gonna blow it up, simple as that.

Legend has it that this Ark caused Philistine and Mesopotamian women to miscarry the entire time it remained in their possessions even without tainting their food. First captured by the Philistines, then recaptured years later when they forgot its first lessons (unlike Nebuchadnezzar's folk who got the message first time straight). The Ark has a tendency to show its displeasure by doing bad things to the people for whom it wasn't intended. Even his late Iraqi general had seen evidence of its power when childbirth dropped precipitously in his corner of Paraguay, soon after he brought it there. That part he swore was no legend, but fact and it did kill a host of his troops after all. Roasted and toasted.

But the joker in the deck and what most concerned Morano were legends concerning this Ark's indestructibility. Legend also had it that, try as they could, neither the Philistines nor the Mesopotamians could find a way to destroy the Ark. Burning fires, heavy hammer blows, chisels, nothing did the job. It was just too powerful and beyond them. Of course, they didn't possess the resources available today. Perhaps the thing is magic, but legends can seem overwhelming.

Still, he felt confident. There are ways to kill anything. Supposedly the Ark is the original power generator of unprecedented magnitude. If he could generate a powerful enough explosion, blowing it to bits, this thing was sure to magnify its effect. Isn't that what power does? He could envision a gigantic mushroom cloud looking like God had just nuked earth, hurling its nasty little fragments thousands of feet in the air, into the prevailing jet stream winds. It could shower the entire planet with Ark fragments, getting into the water, the animal feed, you name it. It should have the same effect as on those biblical folk.

Problem was how to generate an explosion big enough to turn this mystical contraption into a divine wind. Then he saw it, on TV news, doing its best imitation of a scourge from God ...Kilauea.

Two thousand degrees of boiling lava. If that wouldn't do it, he'd have to steal a thermonuclear warhead from somewhere or maybe buy one off the black market. But he knew this was an all or nothing shot. No getting it back once it went in. Delivery was no problem. They fill it up with a powerful explosive, pack it inside and out, maybe in some kind of container, drop it in from a helicopter, right down the maw, and fly like the wind. Get maybe a good ten minutes, maybe twenty. That's what he'd tell the crew he paid to do the deed. They need not know the real purpose. Just drop it and go. Twenty-five to thirty minutes, then kaboom! So what if the helicopter died.

It should work. He'd have his engineers run simulations, check wind vectors and optimum seasonal conditions and such. They wouldn't need to know why. Hawaii is a perfect location; low-level trade winds out of the northeast would get to Malaysia and Kona winds from the southeast would reach China and Japan, the jet stream up high blowing west to east would carry across the American continent to Europe, even Russia. Gonna probably blow up a good chunk of Hawaii's Big Island but couldn't be helped. But it should do the trick. Instant universal birth control. Man, what a lovely thought.

He even considered the geologic ramifications. That big crack south of Kilauea they call the Hilina Slump might let go and drop a big chunk of island into the Pacific. That would indeed be bad news. Back in 1975, a chunk around forty miles long dropped eleven feet into the Pacific generating a seven-point-two magnitude earthquake and a forty-eight-foot-high tsunami that beat the crap out of the other islands. But if all forty-eight hundred square miles go, the estimated quake and megatsunami could top magnitude nine and one thousand feet tall and travel six hundred miles an hour straight at Frisco and Baja and Australia, Tokyo and Shanghai. It would take out every patch of low-lying shore for thousands of miles in nearly every direction, flooding the LA Basin out to the Santa Ana Mountains. You name it; the Pacific Rim would have a very bad day. Everybody be swimming.

A memory, long repressed, swam to surface in his consciousness. Two people, both young and in love. She died of a mysterious poison, taking their unborn child. He very nearly joined her for a glorious meeting in the afterlife before Chaco found him, had his stomach pumped and his name changed so his life could begin anew. Your classic bait 'n switch. Now he is free to revenge his murdered family ...and they'll never see it coming!

Sorry mommies, not trying to hurt you, just them spoiled-ass brat kids you was about to have. But if you gotta go too, you gotta go. Suddenly brilliance seemed his retinue, following close behind to favor each idea. He felt erudite, vivid and omnipotent, deciding to sell his west coast properties just in case. Another brilliant thought: he wouldn't have O'Rourke killed. He let him return to his California home. It would be so perfect. Wondering, he surmised O'Rourke's last thoughts while watching that onrushing wall of water from his beachfront patio, knowing he couldn't do a thing about it except bend over, touch his toes and kiss his ass goodbye.

As for those power mad corporate raiders now cheating America and the world, he'd get them too. Soon they would all go running for the hills once all their secret deals and crimes were laid bare. He didn't need the government's software. His company developed it anyway, he'd cut all pretenses and just sell it to the highest bidders (there would be many, he anticipated). Besides, there was no going back to Florida, not after all this. He had everything he needed here. No need to go back. Anyone who thought WikiLeaks was big time before, had no clue. He'd personally provide them enough ammo to last years, perhaps decades. He'd be bigger than the Walker Spy Ring, except he would never get caught like those amateurish scrubs. And his "friends"? Well, suffice to say, they had other plans for the American way of life. Too bad!

Also, much too bad his aunt was no longer around to see his shine, only his gloom! She'd been his favorite til then!

"Hijos de un Dios Perdido", the old woman told him. "You don't come from nothing, don't know for nothing. You are Children of a Lost God!"

Stunned, he read the cragged, ancient lips pronouncing first in Spanish, then English, as if he were incapable of such a simple translation. That wasn't even the stunning part. How could she see him such? All he had done for her, all his sacrifices. How she think she got the house she now lived in?

"One day you will wish you took more time to listen and to learn. But that day is not this day. This day hijo you and your pandilleros, your gangster wannabes, remain en los brazos del Diablo, in the arms of the devil! No good will ever come from you!"

Looking back those many years, her words still stung. More so because he could never prove to her how wrong she had been.

Tradition. Nothing like it for old people. They can't get enough of it. For him though, it's crack-assed boring as hell.

Ancestors didn't know better. They tech sucked, so religion was the course of the day, every day.

Crack'o dawn. Here come God on his chariot'o fire. Sky turns blue 'n gold, God did it. Gee thanks God, ain't he great. Sky dark midday, funnel clouding a twister. Oh shit! Who fukked up and forgot to thank God when it was blue?

"Eenie meanie minie mo! Must be dat gimpy one, Antelope Joe! What' cha mean he wasn't in town? Kill dat dumb sum'bitch anyway! An bring me his big-ass wifie! Dat teach him to forget God! Know what? Make dat the rule an' make sure ev'rybody know 'bout it! In fact, make dat our new religion! Yeah, an since I invented it, I gits finders fees, make dat founders fees. Also, member ta break me off a piece'a ev'ry penny ya'll make to pay for our brand new invention! We'll call it tithing! Got a nice ring to it!"

The old ways he left for the old days, buried deep in the past where they belonged. Same with bronze-age religions. No time for them neither. No matter what his Tia believed. She see him now, she'd know the deal. She'd know what was real. If only she could see him now. But nope that won't do, can't be. Her traditions like her religion may as well rot deep in the cold, dank earth beside her, with all the other useless ghosts. He needed neither. His was a different path.

They'd be unstoppable. They'd know every time any agency was targeting their operations as soon as those agencies decided who to target. They'd stay two steps ahead. Retribution would be the order of the day.

Big business and their cohorts in government would learn the error of their thieving, conniving ways when it all started blowing up around them. Soon they'd need so much of the army to guard their domestic offices, wouldn't be anybody left to send out pillaging and plundering other shores.

Once highrise casinos in Vegas and AC began crashing into rubble piles and with half of Manhattan, Chicago and LA smoking and in ruin, all those bullshit corporate slogans and tag lines would-be dead-on arrival. Who'd care which one of them you can trust according to them? For the little guys, soon everything would be gravy. He smiled to himself and remembered: "He who laughs last, laughs best." And he planned to have that last laugh …at least that's how he planned.

Morano's last thoughts erupted in searing pain. He screamed once as twin jaws--each equipped with rows of razor-sharp, serrated teeth--closed on him, tearing half his side away. Moments later they struck his chest--collapsing it. Carlos did not feel that portion separate to slide down the creature's maw. He was already dead. Thoughts of conquest, of precious art treasures from antiquity, of revenge, even of love for another man's woman sank with the remaining few scraps --where once had been a human-- down to the coral reef.

"Wow! It sucks to be you!" O'Rourke flippantly jested. But he was in no position to gloat, he could be next. He swam slowly and easily as far away from that area as he could. The idea was to mimic a hole in the water, no splashes, barely a ripple. Then, after an hour or so, he removed his trousers and tied knots in the legs. Cupping air into them he then rested his tired chin on the crouch. Commencing a lazy scissors kick he pushed his makeshift Mae West towards shore, to where the lights of Grenada beckoned but seemed years away. Ten minutes later he heard another splash --powerful and close-- and ceased moving, wondering if the thing that nearly broke his leg when it passed and proceeded on to finish Carlos had returned for a little ham to go with the turkey.

The lights did not seem to get any closer. Maybe the current was pushing further out to sea, out to where the big fish were waiting for their dinner bell. Suddenly, the sea behind him erupted, blossoming into a brilliant chiaroscuro of colors, primarily dominated by reds, yellows and oranges. The leaking diesel finally found a sufficient heat source. Now the Mona Lea had gone to join her master.

Eventually though he made it to shore. He was right back on Morano's Island or what used to be Morano's Island, Morano being fish food and all. He did not know exactly which part he had landed on, but any land would do. His waterlogged body sagged into the sand, too fatigued to move further.

It seemed like hours before he felt like standing. By then the rising sun heating the sand around him coaxed his eyes awake. But his tortured eyes refused to function correctly. Real life scenes did not register in their sensory mechanisms, instead were only mirages, visions of things past.

He blinked, but there was that mirage again. He sat up. The vision smiled, then began running and squealing. No mirage, Valerie. He got to his feet and walked towards the rapidly closing woman. She was definitely the best mirage he had seen, ever.

"JP! I been looking all over for you! Where's Carlos? What happened to Tim?" Seeing his condition, she looked even more concerned. "You all right? C'mon. Let me fix you up!"

Vibrant sunlight streamed through the cockpit windshield as the plush jet climbed higher over an impossibly beautiful Grenadian landscape. Green everywhere. It surrounded houses, large and small, as well as lakes and streams and waterfalls and paradise everywhere and everything except where sand beaches met turquoise waters. It was wonderful.

Valerie came forward with a cup of steaming coffee for him. Trent sat in the back, taking advantage of the free air fare as an opportunity to visit a relative in Florida. He thought about the distraught Colonel who stayed behind to tend to his wife's remains and remembered that things could have been a lot worse. O'Rourke suddenly felt good to be alive. They banked once and zoomed out over the blue-green sea, destination, Miami. There were still a few loose ends to tie up…

The DIA was content. Their secrets all returned via the Embassy. The compromises had been resolved; in fact, eliminated. The case was closed …as they saw it. General Burton and Colonel Peterson now spent the lion's share of their workdays briefing higher powers at DoD, State, Commerce and a few other interested government departments. Lucky for them, word had not leaked outside Spice Island locals or they would no doubt have the British hounding them for an After-Action Report …or whatever formal note of apology Her Majesty's minions now prefer.

O'Rourke, they thanked for his service and then they ordered (requested) his return to headquarters so that he could be properly appreciated. They would look into Morano's claim about the whorehouse.

It would take time through diplomatic channels. But insisted they would get right on it.

"They'd get right on it."

He was not happy. Her fate still in doubt. He hated to leave this in the hands of government folk worried about diplomatic channels. He had to concur with Mickey's assertion that "The government could screw up a wet dream!" Mickey did not say "screw", but JP remanded the use of such language to specific occasions, not for everyday use ...one never knew which government agency was listening.

His mission had been as much about her as it was about the theft. Even Valerie knew it and said it! No sense denying. But that still didn't make it feasible.

He needed a closer look inside Morano's digs to find his own way towards speeding her freedom. The reminder that Morano no longer had use of them only a minor comfort at the moment. His primary interest in that man had always been his link to someone special. He hoped there would be something: paperwork, an email, anything linking the Iraqi to a Paraguayan address. How many freaking whorehouses they got down there anyway?

This time he used the ferry. Officially he was Morano's pilot so his name was already added to the guest list of a man who would never take another flight or throw another fling. The house looked deserted. Two knocks without reply convinced him and his impatience spurred him, so he used his jacket to stifle the sound as he broke a small windowpane in a rear door and made his own way inside. It was nearly dark outside, but he did not turn on a light right away. He first wanted to take a reconnoiter, just in case the dead man still protected the place with guards.

He padded slowly inward. Each room appeared the same, dark and empty. He remained cautious but emboldened by the quiet. Everywhere was quiet. The silence only disturbed by the occasional whisper of air conditioning cycling on in response to programmed, thermostatic commands. He startled at a sudden movement on his right. Fight or flight mode! But quickly recognized that the curtain's impetus, for its engaging dance, came from a turning ceiling fan. "Don't shit your pants Marine!"

Chastened by his timidity he proceeded upstairs. His entry into a large bedroom found much the same, pitch black, no sign of life. He figured he was inside the master bedroom, now he needed to find the computer desk which Valerie felt certain would hold whatever hardcopy information Morano might have stored pertaining to business associates.

Now his only concern was not tripping over a spare from Morano's urine stash. Again, the chuckle escaped, unheeded. Now he felt secure enough to feel for a light switch on the adjacent wall. But suddenly, almost imperceptivity, another whisper encroached. This time his conditioned reflex to turn and face another phantom threat was a bit too slow and relaxed …and that was the last he knew.

CHAPTER TWENTY-FIVE

The lights were fully on when he awoke, his hands tied securely behind him. But he remained still, unmoving, neither changing breathing rhythm nor uttering the moan his head's aching advocated. He waited for his vision to clear while peering through slits in his partly opened eyes. His body lay on its side atop bed covers. His face was half buried in the soft cotton fabric so that only his left eye had full view.

Somewhere a television was broadcasting a football game. Roaring crowd noise greeted his unburied ear. The smell of food enticed his nostrils. Involuntarily his nose wrinkled. Then a soft padding approached from an angle outside his limited vision and his body stiffened, anticipating another blow …or worse.

"Looks like ol' sleeping beauty is back wit' us," came a rough voice that somehow sounded familiar. "Last time we did a dance you seemed heavier JP!"

O'Rourke lifted his head, craning his neck back to face his tormentor standing above and just beyond the bed's periphery. A huge shape loomed. At first the shadowy splotch in the center of his slowly clearing vision hid the face tied to a somewhat familiar voice. Then he saw him. His face had grown a bit more craggy with the years, his hair now more salt than pepper, but otherwise he looked pretty much the same. "Martinez?"

"Es mio!"

"Angel?"

"Hi JP. Long time no see. Sorry I hadda clock you man. You okay?"

Angel sounded genuinely concerned. O'Rourke remembered how he had looked so apologetic when Mickey had talked him and Billy Ray (meaning bribed) into throwing him into a shower with a bar of soap. But he had also looked determined. Much the same as now.

"I'll live. I guess," he added. What you hit me with, the right or the left?" Angel's right-handed swats were legendary amongst the El Toro and Chu Lai fraternity. He had sent more sailors and doggies to the dispensary than Johnnie Walker.

"Right!"

"Yeah, that figures. You wanna tell me why you hit me?"

"You wanna tell me why you broke into Carlos' house?" O'Rourke tempted a smart-alecked rejoinder that he had come back to retrieve a pair of sunglasses he had left behind at a party but thought better of it. Martinez could easily snap his neck if so inclined. Still, he figured he was going to die here so what was the caution all about anyway?

"Looking for your wife, Mister O'Rourke." This voice was softer and came from the doorway. He recognized the small, gray-haired man he had seen through the window the night he first spied on Morano. It seemed so long ago, an eternity. The older man's sentence was neither spoken as conjecture nor question. It was stated as a matter of fact. "She's not here."

Martinez had gone back to his seat on a powder-blue lazy boy chair that his bulk nearly made disappear. Feet stretched out on a matching ottoman were covered by a pair of the largest sneakers O'Rourke could ever remember seeing this close up. Shaquille O'Neal's size twenty-twos could not have been much larger. His ham-sized hands were proceeding to shove the remainder of a huge po' boy sandwich into his open maw, while his eyes had returned to watch the sports contest on the LCD television screen mounted across the room on an otherwise bare wall. Focused on the large screen, he ignored O'Rourke altogether. His job, for the moment was done.

O'Rourke focused back on the smallish, gray-haired man. The face was at once all-knowing and sad. He walked with the aid of an elegant, wooden cane whose curved handle fit neatly in his delicate right hand. O'Rourke studied the man's dark eyes and wizened face for a moment before responding to his comment. This was not necessarily the visage of a ruthless destroyer of helpless women. But he exhibited an inner strength that seemingly would enable him to achieve whatever task he considered necessary.

O'Rourke sensed no fear in this tiny frame. But neither did he perceive onerous threat. His aura calmed. He did not totally relax, but neither did he evidence outward hostility. Not quite a façade, more a realization. His voice came strong and unwavering, certain, though unchallenging. "I guess you don't have her either."

"No. I don't know what happened to her. I am afraid she may be, dead." This last pronouncement was spoken as delicately as he could deliver. He felt the pain even before the words commenced. But there was little he could do to turn back time. Better to get it all out in the open. "I'm afraid my cousin might have reacted grotesquely to some perceived disloyalty on her part. I do not condone his actions, whatever they may have been."

O'Rourke's spirit sagged measurably. Even the lack of feeling due to the tight bonds around his wrists was forgotten for a time. No more fond memories of times past, playing games in the dark with neighborhood girls in big, pink bows and white, patent leather slippers who smelled as delectable as ripe persimmons. No more sweet kisses, soft caresses and warm embraces. Morano had lied to him and he had been too late for her. It was just like Vietnam all over again. He had failed like he failed his father Henry and best friend Tony.

He studied the patterned colors of a painting on the wall behind Martinez' head, deigning not to look at the man uttering words so painful, so full of agonizing horror that they bore deep inside to rip away the thin veneer of hope with which he had covered his heart. He would never dream sweet dreams again. Obviously Morano had lied about Paraguay, but what purpose?

"If I have those ropes removed, will you do anything rash?" The words called him back to the tormentor. What displayed in his eyes, in his revealed countenance, said more than any words his lips could have formed. The little man's nod was barely perceptible, but Martinez instantly was at O'Rourke's back, undoing the thin, though strong bonds.

Both watched for a few seconds while their "guest" rubbed feeling back into wrists and fingers. The sound on the television had long ago been muted. Seemingly they could hear each of his sinews crying out as blood once again pumped back into starving tissues. Then the smaller man turned and walked from the bedroom. "Come with me."

Chaco was in quandary. The government transmissions he intercepted all pointed to the middle east region as the danger zone. Perhaps China or the Himalayas. It would all be wiped out, whole populations destroyed. The area generating most of today's current conflicts would generate no more. Gone would be the filthy air, water and land polluters. Gone would be the radical zealots all trying to kill and die for their deity. They'd all disappear in an instant. No more strife and persecution and intolerance and blatant hatred over somebody else's interpretation of instructions given their ancestors by space aliens eons back when.

It would be so easy to just sit back and let it happen, just do nothing and watch fate play its hand. It wouldn't require him to lose his soul in the manner of his recently deceased cousin. Carlos had planned to use the Ark's powers to inflict terrible blights and plagues upon the world and the world was much better off without him.

But his situation was different. All he needed do was nothing. But could he? There was the question, his quandary. Could he sit on the sideline and do nothing? At first, he did just that …nothing.

In the beginning, he had been paralyzed with inactivity. He first gave instructions for his people that they would only watch and wait. No action other than observing. It was as if he were awaiting divine intervention or at the very least, inspiration. He'd stay his decision until a later time. But then along came a man who refused to sit on the sideline, in for a penny or a pound. Admiration swelled him further with each report. He became literally fascinated by the chess game between cousin and challenger. Then came end game and checkmate. Suddenly Chaco was in for the pound.

The fact of the matter, he reasoned, there are crazies and fanatics and zealots everywhere you look. You focus all your energies on killing them all off, you got time for nothing else on your hands. Plus, once you unleash the four horsemen, who can tell how far they'll choose to ride? Their gallop might even consume our side, maybe even the entire earth. No. He could see the importance of getting off the sideline. Better to go down swinging.

O'Rourke followed him downstairs and into the patio room, aware of Martinez a few steps behind him. He tempted to turn and launch furious assault at the looming giant but ignored the impulse. That could prove a fool's errand. This was a very large man. To defeat one such as him, an adversary would need to bring a picnic basket; in Devil Dog parlance that's because it's an all-day job. Besides, he had always respected and liked Angel Martinez, who Mickey had nicknamed "Thumper".

No. He would pay out this string a little further to see how far it went. Morano's cousin seemed to have something more in mind that his demise. So why not listen. Couldn't hurt. Could it? Looking outside, he remembered that last time he came here. On the outside looking in through the rainy wet. He could not be certain if he were safer this time or that, at least he knew how to get out of here alive …that time.

"Something to drink? You hungry?" asked the suddenly hospitable little man. As if on cue, there came music, sweet and low piped over the sound system. "Heyyy senorita. Every time I look in your eyes, I can see you smiling."

He wondered whether it was an auto program or if someone else was in the house. One thing for certain; if it was Carlos, he was leaving in a hurry. He'd had quite enough of ghosts.

The older man sat easily down into a sofa chair and motioned for O'Rourke to sit across from him. Then he grabbed up a remote control and switched on the television. Its screen displayed a frozen scene that appeared to have been waiting for an audience. "Hey, foxy lady, come and give me all the love you have inside ya!"

About the frozen TV image he had no clue, but he recognized the song off the Galaxy album by War. Somebody had good taste in this place. Another rustling sound and he turned his head in time to see…

"Valerie!"

Chaco now put on his imaginary educator's hat –one crowned with the virtues of patience and repetition—and turned back to his captive student. "At first we perceived the stranger to be just another denizen of the Kuiper Belt. That's a cloud of icy space rocks and debris orbiting our sun out beyond Neptune between thirty to fifty astronomical units or thirty to fifty times farther from our sun than earth, some estimate it might even extend out one hundred AU."

JP mentally prepared himself for another lecture. It seemed he had experienced more of these --"I'll talk, you'll listen"—sessions recently than he had his entire last year of college.

"Pluto and Charon had been the largest known members of this belt and considered by many astronomers to be merely large asteroids, not a planet with a captured moon." If Chaco noticed any discomfort in his pupil, he kept it to himself. "The fact that Pluto and Charon orbited each other in kind of a celestial folk dance, further confirmed this idea for many earthbound, so-called "experts".

"I'm assuming there's a point to all this." JP's demeanor was one of the curious, not the contemptuous. Alex merely treated him with a humorous glance. Chaco acted as if he had never even spoken.

"Then higher resolution telescopes, like the Keck in Hawaii and the

Hubble Space Telescope enabled a new discovery. Larger objects like Planet X emerged from the Kuiper Belt morass to suggest that our solar system had at least ten planets, not the nine that most earthlings had been taught from grade school."

In O'Rourke's mind the man's lecture style had devolved to a level approaching condescending. His midget karate students would have bolted from such low-level dribble; then again those were all very bright kids. He wondered if he'd ever see them again, some inner voice warned that possibilities might bounce between slim and none …though not necessarily because of anything these people might do.

Still, he hoped gray hair man would get on with it. Not only did he already possess a modicum of knowledge on this subject, he also already knew that he did not appreciate the style in which it was currently being presented. Only he still did not know what to do about it or how any of this was relevant …but it couldn't be good.

Screaming out in frustration would only generate more frustration, and possibly another knock on the head from the big Mexican. He understood perfectly most of what the man was talking about –mostly. An episode he had once watched on the Discovery Channel helped fill in the gray areas. In that particular documentary, Discovery contributors berated the Dog Planet's unique orbit, its unusual one hundred twenty-two-degree rotational axis and its small size, only fourteen hundred miles or so diameter. Those facts proved too much for the anti-Pluto crowd to endure. So they shitcanned it down to dwarf planet, pissing off a shitload of his karate kids.

Pluto, they decided, could be nothing more than a large asteroid or comet, a Kuiper Belt Object as these hundreds of thousands of trans-Neptunians are termed. But then this man said much of these same things …and kept saying them.

"Okay," JP decided, "now this guy had become downright rude and abusive. If he didn't come through the same "teacher college for the insecure" as Peterson, it must at least have been a sister school."

Though the term "trans-Neptunians" was new to him, every school kid knows the story about the decision to reclassify Pluto as just another KBO and just about every school kid was really pissed off when the "know-it-alls" did reclassify Pluto as just another KBO. He wanted dearly to articulate as much to this "know-it-all" with some additional comment about the man's family, beginning with his mother. But something held his tongue …though long in coming; whatever he lead up to couldn't be good.

"They moved to strip Pluto of its lofty status as planetary body," continued Chaco in his best imitation of the erudite professor, "and just like that, they remand it to the bowels of asteroid hell. Along with Pluto went Xena, uh, that's the name they gave Planet X."

Now Chaco pauses, studying O'Rourke to discern whether any of this was reaching him, withholding additional comment about the "Warrior Princess" who inspired the name. For the first time he perceived his miscalculation, this was not one of the semiliterate street thugs in the Barrio. This man was educated, experienced, one who understood technology and a man of the sky. He had forgotten himself, treating this man, who was now his guest, like an eighth grader, consistent with the educational apex of many in the East LA Barrio. He would need to modify his approach.

Chaco had never agreed with the rationale, or the idea of mere men assuming the mantle of deity, unilaterally determining their contrived calculations to be absolute truth. But who could refute their claims? Man has named the farthest reaches of the cosmos. Every point of light available through the optics of his telescopes has been ordained with some name and number. Every galaxy and each discernable star within, every globular cluster and even the unknown phenomena like dark matter and black holes men have named. Their dates of origin, their speed of travel through the universe, their chemical construct and all this accomplished from the comfort of mankind's earthbound seats.

It's not as though he was hating on them and their ways. Some cultures give a name to every unique thing they can define, while others just lump inconsequential things, as if to say "why bother". His way leaned more towards the latter. As a point of fact, Chaco had yet to even name his observatory. He thought about giving it some title appropriate to his southwestern backdrop or maybe to its cosmological focus, but to him it did not need a name, its function would suffice.

He was not interested in starting a web site and employing his observatory to name celestial objects so far away they probably aren't in existence anymore, just so he could report his findings to somebody even less important. Immortality was never his purpose. He just needed a connection with the night sky. Perhaps one day he would let Hilda's sons name it. But not just yet. He had no wish to be like white men, marking their names on every rock they could find on earth and in the sky as if claiming each for whatever fame and fortune they might garner. "I saw it first!"

What was the point? He could never be stressed by the enormity of the universe, just the beauty of it. While other men are interested in developing equations to prove out theories concerning the size of objects on the other side of the galaxy, his interests lay in developing disease resistant plants to feed the starving on this side. While others devote their energies entirely to academic pursuits, his energies are channeled into the pursuit of useable products of more immediate utility. He has little patience for pie-in-the-sky endeavor.

After all, other than God, how many witnesses are available to disprove or prove the Big Bang theory?" he once asked friends. For him, be it WAG (wild ass guess) or SWAG (scientific wild ass guess) don't make much difference without actual, up close observation.

"And just what frame of reference would these watchers employ to determine how fast the universe expanded from its initial soccer ball size to the limitless expanses we contemplate today? And what if the ball was not like a soccer ball, but a basketball or tennis ball or even the marble size some others tout, does that really matter? Why don't they simply agree it was really, really small and expanded really, really fast? Now let's figure out how to get off fossil fuels."

He summed it up to arrogance. But more than that, though he attributes arrogance as the most often repeated of men's failures, he recognizes the need for some to be dreamers to help others be doers. He knew in this current situation mankind would need a bit of both to survive. Too much of either and the result could be, garbage in, garbage out …and all would be trashed.

But eventually, he eased back down to reality. His foundational workup completed; Chaco got to his point. "JP you remember that movie *Armageddon*?"

"Comet 'bout to destroy earth. Team of guys fumble 'n bumble their way to blowin' it up, savin' mankind. That about it?"

"Exactly. Well this time, we need to be the fumbler-bumblers."

"Uh, you saying we gotta learn how ta drill oil wells and go up in a Space Shuttle?"

"I'm saying there's a comet on a collision path to our planet and if we don't find a way to prevent it, earth might just be toast."

O'Rourke's lips pursed, but the whistle got locked inside. He could not make his whistler work. He decided instead to remain silent. This was no joke. Chaco was deadly serious. He reflected back to his childhood days. Sunday School lessons espoused "The Rapture" when all those "Saved" would meet in the sky and celebrate with "The Lord", while all those who remained sinners would be cast down into a pit of fiery brimstone. Hell, damnation, eternal torture and agony …End of Days.

Chaco was speaking, but O'Rourke's ability to follow precisely had jumped ship. He only caught bits and pieces. Time was about to end. All the things he had not yet done he might not ever do. He closed his eyes.

Flashing, stroboscopic scenes blazed in wanton fury beneath his eyelids. Visions of a scorched and barren rock which had once been a vibrant, verdant Earth dominated; its blue skies all gone; its great cities all charred and dank and dark and sullen. How much time did they have? His math skills were on siesta, not a chance of them working out any equation. Chaco's stated figures …two years at the outside?

What to do now? Call up everyone he knew to say goodbye? Or should he steal Morano's airplane and just go visiting? Make his dead ass pay for the gas.

He hadn't seen Bev in years. How 'bout a trip to Bermuda? He could introduce her to Sylvia. They should get along fine. What's there to be jealous over? The world's about to end …love somebody while time still exists.

He'd bring his best friend, certain that Mickey would be up for the trip. What did the business matter for anyway? In fact, they'd take everybody, tour the whole world; just give the old girl one more look see. One more time around. He'd even go back to 'Nam, something he swore he'd never do. Lots of guys did it. Vietnam Vets went back all the time and made their peace with the people and the land they had once razed nearly to oblivion just to forsake another people's ideology. We lost tens of thousands of ours and hundreds of thousands of theirs, just because our side refused to understand their side …and vice versa.

The toughest part was figuring out how he'd tell his karate kids, his pupils. They probably wondering where he at this very moment. He'd already missed half a dozen classes. He missed them too, those eager, bright-eyed faces that flashed from intense concentration to instant glee the moment they achieved a difficult task; a hip toss here, an error-free kata there.

How do you tell a tiny child that they will never grow old? What words will assuage their grief, their abject terror at the thought of being rended and torn and crushed beyond recognition, then burned to a cinder. "Shoot yourselves in the head now kids. That's what I plan to do! Yeah! Me. Big brave John Paul O'Rourke, gonna go out like a faggot!"

Another thought. Speaking of kids, there was a chance he had a kid of his own coming on the way. What was it Jeanne had said? A little girl? Imagine him with a little girl. Too bad she would never have the chance to grow up. He needed to get in touch with Jeanne to see how she was doing these days. It had been awhile since she visited him in his jail cell. He had hoped their next meeting would be less …formal.

And what about the child? He'd never had one before. What kind of time would she or even he have to experience this life before he or she was blown to bits along with the rest of us. That's if he or she was even coming? There was no guarantee. She could have been mistaken, her emotions ruling her head, she so wanted a child to love in the loveless world she had endured. Jeannie.

But what if? What time would he have to hold her or him and tell them all the things fathers tell their children about and teach them about all the things fathers taught their children about? This was so screwed up!

Visions. Hugs and kisses by the dozens. A trusting face smiling up into his. Images flowed. Tiny arms clung tight in his protective embrace at the zoo, in the park, on the beach; even while looping up and down the Silver Bullet at Knots Berry Farm. But now they'd never happen. There was no time…

"Got a question JP, it's very personal. You tell me if it's too personal."

"This coming from the guy who just told me to bend over, touch my toes and kiss my ass goodbye? I don't think you can get much more personal than that."

"Yeah, I see your point. But this concerns your view of religion."

"That's easy, I don't have one."

"Everybody has a religion JP, even if they don't believe they do.

Atheism is a religion. Oh, you'll hear arguments against, but in its most simplistic definition, religion is merely a system of faith and worship. People who believe there is no God are just as faithful to their belief system as people who believe there is. What I'm interested in are your views and especially your motivations."

The man seemed as sincere as he had moments before while revealing his knowledge of an incoming space object about to destroy our existence. His face said so as did his demeanor. There was no subterfuge, only business.

"I believe in God. I just don't believe in the kind of God that wants me to kill everybody who doesn't believe. I don't believe we live to do God's bidding, but that God lives to do ours."

"So you believe God lives inside us rather than in Heaven?"

"I'm not sure I believe in a heaven or a hell, but yeah I look inside myself to find that power that moves me."

"Guess you're not Catholic then."

"Nor Baptist. I consider my beliefs more common sense than religious. In a way it's a kinda combination of Baptist, Buddhist and Shinto religions, without the rituals and praying to invisible deities and definitely no chanting."

"No worshipping snake gods, huh?"

"Nah, not my thing. Don't get it twisted; I got no problem with the idea of space aliens with higher intelligence and technology. I just got a problem worshipping them as gods. Obviously, other people don't seem to have that problem. But that's their problem."

"I agree. They tend to worship anybody with a video on MTV or BET."

"Exactly. Just 'cause they can do stuff I can't do, I'm not gonna do knee drops ...or kiss ass." Neither of them mentioned politicians or talk show hosts.

"Good answer, Mister O'Rourke. You'll do. You'll do just fine." He had turned and walked, more like limped, slowly for the stairs leading to the sleeping quarters.

"Huh? Not following." He suddenly felt lost again. But Chaco never paused a step, his aged framed holding firmly to the cane with one hand, the stair railing with the other.

"We'll discuss it in the morning. G'night." His soft voice faded, still sounding assured …very assured.

These and other raging thoughts eventually shook him out of the land of dreams and he awoke with a start. It took a few seconds before he realized where he was. Chaco had convinced him to sleep in one of the guest bedrooms rather than a hotel. It seemed the best for all concerned, especially after he and Martinez had spent the wee hours sampling some of Morano's best stock while getting reacquainted …you die, we drink your booze.

The 94 proof "Single Barrel" Jack Daniels Whiskey went quickly and rather well, for two. Chaco and Valerie left early, saving the majority of their livers for some wistful future they still hoped would come. Then again, they had no need of reunion celebrations –only the two Devil Dogs-- and celebrate they did, remembering all those past and those still present. But Jack's quality was wasted on the pair who rapidly dispensed with sipping and simply slurped it all down noisily in good Jarhead form; not quite toasting …but definitely getting toasted.

Like most of the world's whiskey drinkers, they preferred Jack Daniels. But this night almost any fermented mixture of corn, rye, barley and water would have worked for these two. The years of aging through four seasonal cycles each year in the Lynchburg, Tennessee warehouse could have been reduced by two-thirds, even more. The casks might as well have been stored in a Newark, New Jersey back alley bar and poured into "A/C or Bust" shot glasses. They were well past caring how often the whiskey leeched into and out of the charcoal wood barrels to give it the legendary smoothness and wonderful aromatic characteristics. After the first hour or so they were well past observations of characteristics.

Eclectic refinements, like the hand-labeled barrel number they noticed not the slightest. Neither of these men was ever going to share tasting notes with other connoisseurs about which barrel from which it came and what year. Though both did approve the way its toasted oak flavor captured their taste buds, neither was sufficiently versed to differentiate the fruit drawn from this barrel's wood over any other they might sample at some future time. If such a future time existed for them and their kind. For now, if a bottle be near enough, it be dear enough, pedigree be damned.

Not long after the last drops of Jack left, they replaced it with a two hundred-year old Richard Hennessy Cognac. Already well past hammered, this one they sipped slowly, until about half was gone; both men seeking to uncover its secret. At over three grand a pop, Morano was no doubt saving it for some special occasion, but neither of them took more than a few moments to admire its delightful color or the artfully etched figures on its elegant, Baccarat Crystal. They did, however, admire its rich bouquet ... though not nearly enough to purchase it.

What they also admired were his tastes, you had to give it to him. Neither had liked the man personally. Each of them felt somewhat appeased by knowledge that he was swept to his reward by a brutality more violent than either of them would ever have committed. Just deserts perhaps, as repayment for some of the brutality he had fostered on others. But this night they toasted to his taste in booze, purposely spilling a few drops for those who could not be present on this occasion ...some due to a timely demise.

Slumber came easy after all that. But morning wakeup was another thing entirely. He hovered in and out of semi-consciousness for what seemed an eternity, unable to fall back asleep or proceed forward to full awake. In this dream state his control held no power. He merely danced to the tune being played; this one to a decidedly female flavor, though not necessarily docile or demure, just all about females...

Idiots, zealots and fools! Valerie swore she suffered none of these, avoided them like the plague. Her conviction stared him down, as if daring rebuttal. But if so, what the heck was she doing hanging around this Morano character? It made him wonder, though he still dared not voice dispute, even were this out-of-his-control dream state to permit such. But there definitely was more to her than met the eye. Once you think you know a woman you find out, it's not so much...

Still, she was far from finished with him; her memory piqued, her essence arousing him once more. Back came the Spice Isle into his dream path, post Morano. Three days and nights they "recovered" from their ordeal, both showing bruises and a few small cuts, but otherwise little worse for the wear. She attended to his aches and he to hers.

Unlike their first few days in this paradise, time dashed by a bit too quickly, though in blissful harmony. No more stress from onerous threats or demanding phone calls, instead they rose late and turned-in early. They took catamaran cruises to offshore reefs and snorkeled hand-in-hand in the brilliant waters over colorful corals and schools of gaily decorated tropical fishes.

They swam alone, though in the company of others from their party cruise, seemingly in their own little world, oblivious to any and all and at night they clung tightly to each other until drained of all energies. Coffee-brown nipples thrust alluringly upward from their coffee-with-cream colored background to demand his every attention. Even an occasional freckle seemed to beckon for his attending …and so he did.

The feelings titillated, lingering long after his eye shutters blinked open, the memory pleasing. Those were his first thoughts upon fully waking. But he had no answer to the question, so he eventually forced himself upright. Just when he thought he knew her. Women, what a difficult gender! Or could they even be their own species? Men from Mars, women from somewhere else. At least she was home safe and out of whatever this was he was now in and whoever he was now in it with; these idiots, zealots or fools…

But her memory was not quite done with him. The taste of sweet essence thrilled and titillated. Soft moans welcomed practiced caresses from thick, ebony lips and soft nibbles from bared, white teeth. Gentle thrusts, commencing of a tentative nature, threatened impalement. Strong fingers reacted to cup his bottom, signaling the end of teasing time. Deep, throaty groanings replied to even deeper thrusts, every part of her belonged to him and him to her. That time had been so wondrous and so fulfilling and healing …until after, with Peterson's message that Tina had still not been found.

Playtime had ended; fantasy came crashing down all around him, feelings of guilt reemerged. Again he had taken his eye off the mark. Packing hurriedly, they flew back homeward …back to reality

If you need something done right, do it yourself. His body had refreshed. However, the good feelings dissipated in the image of her helpless gaze staring, accusing, wondering when he would find the interest to come rescue her. The cursed message assured him it was only a matter of time, but now an old instinctive distrust for all things bureaucracy resurfaced. He needed to get back into this game. He needed to find her himself.

But all that had happened before knowledge of this new peril. If he believed Chaco, finding Tina would not matter even if he got lucky and somehow stumbled across her location. There'd be no place for him to bring her back to …there'd be no place for anyone.

Tina's image faded again, into his last few days spent mainly in Valerie's arms. In turn, that memory sailed straight into the maelstrom of Sylvia's; her heated accusations providing background lyrics. Perhaps he fit her profile of a slut more than he cared admit. Maybe. True, he never promised fidelity or nurtured hopes of matrimony or even a future together, only the gift of the free spirit whom one can never own. But he had loved her, still did, and ideas of settling down with her had tempted him. But one first burned is twice shy around fires! Maybe too late for that settling thing. Maybe now it was too late for everything …but where life reigns, hope attains.

Later, showered and shaved, he dressed quickly and headed toward the kitchen where the most wonderful aroma emanated. Martinez sat on a stool at the center island and shoved a huge fork load of eggs and potatoes into his cavernous maw. He nodded at O'Rourke, finishing what passed for chewing in a millisecond or so before greeting. "Morning JP. How's that head? You ain't up ta partyin' like back in th' day, huh?"

"Thought I hung in there okay. Though I do remember somebody couldn't hang onto his queen."

"I was rusty. Last time I worry about that thick scull of yours," he laughed, remembering the butt-whipping he took in the half-dozen games of chess they played while enjoying Morano's booze.

"I just took a bottle o' Tylenol. I'll be fine amigo. Where's Chaco?" He took another look at Martinez plate as another forkful disappeared down the two-chews-per-insertion macerator. He hoped the big man had saved a little. Just then an elderly woman entered the far door leading to the living room. She smiled as if relieved that he had finally awakened.

"Good Morning Mister JP." She sounded Spanish, maybe Cuban, but her English was very clear, no slurs or broken vowels. "May I get you some eggs and sausage or bacon? Or I can make you an omelet or waffles?"

"Whatever everybody else is having is fine. And I'm just JP. Not Mister. Okay? And you are?"

"Oh yeah. JP this is Carmen. She's the housekeeper and the best cook this side of New Mexico. I'm not too hungry today Carmen. You can give him the eggs and sausage I didn't get to." Martinez lifted his plate up from the gray granite surface and held it out towards the housekeeper-slash-cook. "But I'll be needing that bacon."

She smiled at him and quickly scooped the remaining four strips onto his plate. "Coffee JP?"

"Yes please."

Four eggs over easy and more bacon and sausage patties than his cholesterol-hating doctor would have recommended, he finished his breakfast and left the kitchen, tossing Carmen a huge grin after she pointed out the few hash brown potatoes he had missed. He found the big man in the living room draped across a huge divan that suddenly appeared tiny.

"So what you think amigo?"

"Which? About the Government's plan to blow up half the world wit' nukes or Chaco's plan ta blow up th' problem with magic?"

"Yeah, nuff said." Martinez sat back watching the Military Channel. Nothing in his demeanor indicated the slightest concern with the coming conflagration. His only interest appeared to be the TV screen where P-51 Mustangs tore through the skies over Nazi Germany dispatching Messerschmitts and Focke-Wulfs in this current offering. O'Rourke's heart swelled with the pride it always felt when he witnessed fellow aviators fighting life and death battles against his country's enemies. He was still a sucker for "Mom's apple pie".

On this occasion that was especially so, for these fellow aviators were the Tuskegee Airmen. More than mere aviators, these men were his uncles. He remembered listening wide-eyed and trembling as Mister Collins regaled his fourth-grade class with tales of their exploits in the air over Italy and Germany.

On the screen, Lieutenant General Ben O. Davis Jr. —who had commanded the Tuskegee Airmen as a Colonel—is promoted to the rank of General by President Clinton, the fourth star long overdue. All the brothers arrayed around the thin, wrinkled, retired war hero, stand proud in their red jackets with a Tuskegee patch on the breast pocket. Even Clinton is given a jacket and helped into it by the brother airmen at the ceremony. JP has to fight hard to stay the tears welling in his soft brown eyes. It was an honor long in coming, but no less deserved. He hopes no one asks him a question at this moment. The thick frog in his throat will prevent any dignified vocal answer.

One of the retired aviators describes the action that occurred during their longest mission, escorting bombers fifteen hundred miles to Berlin. In order to extend their Mustang's range, they coopted ground crews to hijack a train carrying U.S. Army supplies, including drop tanks. That escapade went down in Tuskegee laurels as "The Great Train Robbery". It also spelled doom for many a German pilot, including the three ME-262 jet fighters shot down despite the Messerschmitt's more than one hundred miles per hour speed advantage over the American's Mustangs. They received a Presidential Unit Citation for the Berlin Mission, but the accomplishment for which the group is most proud is that they never lost a single bomber to an enemy fighter during their entire campaign.

JP often wondered whether southern rednecks would rather the all-black unit had lost at least one bomber to the Nazi fliers just for the sake of pride. Sadly, he knew the answer. He also knew they weren't all southern.

These same sorts were responsible for completely shutting down Philadelphia's transit system, to keep blacks out during the height of World War Two, resulting in the loss of valuable goods and commodities manufacture from the city supplying more of these than any other. Production decreased to less than one-third in ships, electronics, weapons, food and materials used to manufacture aircraft. The crisis became so critical, Army troops –led by a no-nonsense Major General—were called in to quell the strike and put down potential riots in what was called "The Battle of Philadelphia". The strikers' saw the hiring of black transit workers more a threat to their ideals of racial superiority than Hitler and Tojo.

It seemed logical to him that these people would rather lose an eye than see themselves rescued by those whose abilities and accomplishments they had for so long denigrated. Moreover, he knew that there are people to this day who have either never heard of the Tuskegee Experiment or ignore the fact what they did. It is akin to post-war Germans and anti-Semitics denying that the Holocaust ever occurred. Bigotry must indeed be a powerful motivator if it leads people to cut off their noses to spite their own faces …too bad that statement is only figurative!

But for the men from Tuskegee there was no denying the message upon their return to the U.S. They disembarked their ship and were promptly greeted by signs instructing the blacks to one side and whites to another. Some experienced even worse humbling as they were still prohibited from entering the officer's club's and segregated latrines even though German POWs could. Men who had fought and bled for this country were treated with contempt while the people who had ravaged and raped half the world were given every convenience and respect. Small wonder few other countries trust America if that is how they treat their own people. Then he remembered that America was about to go away and idly wondered how'd Roger Redneck feel about being saved from that by minorities …probably cancel Christmas!

O'Rourke felt somewhat akin to a ping-pong ball. He had been bounced back and forth by more people than he cared to remember, first the DIA, then the CIA. Although this latter acronym he made up to cover Chaco's Intel Agents and now included himself in that group.

He didn't much go in for joining. But now a convert, along with Valerie, speaking of who he'd finagled into feeding him information on all things Carlos. Wasn't too tough, she was happy to oblige since she might never get to see him again. But somebody else would and to O'Rourke's surprise, "Trent?"

"Hallo JP. How's it goin' mon? Good to see you again." Trent's bright, toothy smile was the same as O'Rourke remembered.

"Hi Trent. You going with us?"

"Yah mon. I go wit' de box."

"What box?"

"De box you brought back wit' you. Man you flyboys never know what you got packed less I tell ya. Dat's why Carlos don't want Mista Barnett wifie onboard. He need save de weight an' space fo' de box. It heavy mon. Even more than her luggage, which is a lot. Dis' little plane, Y'know."

"So that's why you wouldn't leave when I told you to go home."

"Right as rain mon. Gotta make sure it all go well. Guess it don' go too well fo' some o' th' others though," he smiled. With Trent, JP got the notion that everything was good as long as the sun came up.

"Oh well. Hop aboard and let's boogie."

"I heard dat, mon!"

Now he was again at the controls of the Lear Jet, this time heading for some one-hole town in New Mexico, chasing the nooning sun. Valerie remained in Miami. Saddened, he also wondered if he would ever see her again …wondering whether he should even try.

Nobody mentioned and he never inquired, if it was she who had dropped the dime on him, warning Chaco of his coming. He questioned to his heart whether sleeping with a dime store is a good thing or should "snitches get stitches"!

Women are a strange breed, he reminded himself. They'll love you more than life but still kill you just as dead. He'd sweat these minor details with her later, if later came. But now he looked forward to seeing New Mexico. He actually missed the desert. One did not have to drive far from his California home to see yucca and mesquite and piñon. He was anxious to get out west again.

He had not been to that state since he and Tina drove out to El Toro following his graduation from flight school. That was a long time ago. Another age, when they were happier and with fewer worries because they were still only children, innocent and full of vigor; sailing gaily forth into the wide, wonderful world of what was to come.

Children are invulnerable. Each is shielded by a force field that wards off all evil, converting sadness into silly, little clown puppets that they can stick on their hand to frighten other children. But only for a very few moments. Soon they are all back at play, the thought of fear well to the back of their capricious minds. However, add a few passing years tainted with tragedy –a lost friend here, a divorce there—and suddenly the child is all grown up. Suddenly the cloak of invincibility has fallen away and the world is not so wonderful. Suddenly it has eroded, shrunk down to a barely breathable space.

CHAPTER TWENTY-SIX

Silver City has a quaint charm that sells itself to most ordinary visitors. Those who are paying attention that is. So far O'Rourke fit in with most ordinary visitors, but at least he paid attention, although primarily from a reflexive need to know more than one way out of anyplace he visited. Otherwise, a feeling of claustrophobia would begin slowly pecking away at his comfort level.

The land appeared bleached in some areas, sunburned in others. The people appeared laid-back. Any frenetic, schizoid types were probably transplants from somewhere else and to be avoided. Perhaps that's the reason he was so easily swayed by Chaco. Both the graying little man as well as his giant bodyguard exuded a calm, casual demeanor that was about as captivating as any he had faced. He was smitten by their manner and their message. But buying this plan, still a work in progress.

The weather was predictable for this time of year; cool early mornings, warming nicely by midday and pushing high by mid-afternoon. Reminded him of winter in Yuma, Arizona where you put on layers under your jacket in the early morning, begin peeling down to T-shirt and shorts by mid-morning and be swimming in Senator Wash reservoir afternoons. But this wasn't quite there. The lakes here are a lot higher above sea level, so not nearly as warm.

They had landed just south of the city at the Grant County Airport and driven straight to Chaco's vineyard, following closely the pickup truck carrying the golden box. JP sat in the second-row right seat, but kept his head turning left and right …taking it all in.

As they drove out of the gravel, parking lot they passed buildings belonging to an aerial firebase for the Gila National Forest. There weren't many large trees around the airport, not much taller than the nearby stands of cholla cactus—but he could appreciate these aerial firemen's dilemma. Only a relative few tens of miles to the North ran the huge Gila National Forest; full of sixty-foot high pine trees growing up ten and eleven thousand foot high mountains and all along the winding turns, hairpin switchbacks and horseshoes that comprised the few roads braving this breath taking scenic beauty where one thousand to five thousand foot drops down into bottomless, rocky ravines were common. Often, air presented the only way to any fire through this wilderness dotted here and there with tiny communities of hardy folk, many of whom ranched cattle.

JP could understand why people flying missions such as these were labeled heroes. Snuffing out forest fires with air-dropped water bombs and chemicals seemed an almost impossible task while dancing heavily laden aircraft through roiling updrafts created by hellish, threatening heat. He could only recall lighting such fires with napalm and five hundred-pound bombs and two-point-five rockets and other useless things he wished he could forget.

North they drove, up Route 180, under the typical big sky found in this part of the country. From horizon to horizon there was this beautiful deep blue blemished with but a single golden orb which fearlessly held sway, perceiving no threat which required its ducking behind sheltering clouds. No matter, there were seldom any clouds with which to perform such a feat and even on those occasions their numbers as well as volume would seldom suffice.

Devoid of any discernable attributes other than dirt covered brown grasses and sandstone rock, the flat, grassy plain turned into the small town whose outlying homes seemed more of the mobile variety. But soon these gave way to more conventional dwellings and businesses. The air smelled fresh and free, if free could be considered a smell.

Angelic cherubs, their porcelain chubbies ignominiously deposited onto yellow sand --that fulfilled the role of sidewalks in these parts—lined the entrance of an equally ignominious gas 'n go fill up spot where street vendors hawked everything from extra-large sized confederate flags to beach towels imprinted with the image of Tupac Shakur. His take on this local variation: "wherever you go some things always remain the same … business is business".

Rows of grape vines stretched as far as he could see along this parcel of landscape divided by shade trees, all surrounded by wire fencing to bar entry to two and possibly four-legged denizens. There was minimal activity this time of year; all fruit had been plundered from its locations between the green leaves. A few workers were visible, performing maintenance rituals on the plants and soil. As they drew closer, he spied a single forklift carting large, oaken barrels into the open bay door of a large warehouse. Chaco explained that these contained wine and were being moved down the ramp into the cellar for storage. Then, after Martinez drove the Lincoln Navigator to the only house on the property, he bid them goodbye, got out of the vehicle and softly closed its door before limping with his cane towards the front door of the home.

Chaco neither looked back nor offered a goodbye before leaving. Possibly he anticipated his guest's confusion given this latest wrinkle. But he wasn't the only one with more questions than answers. He would trust Alex Martinez to handle that end. Trent and two other men who worked for Chaco had already driven past the house, heading out among the vines.

"Hope you don't mind slumming it fer a few, JP. Chaco let us know when he ready."

"I got a choice, big man?" He decided it best not to move to the front seat just yet.

"There's a couple nice hotels round town. I used ta stay in this one downtown that's owned by the sweetest lady you ever met. Name's Nancy. An older place, kinda quaint, but clean an' quiet. Good breakfast there too. Walking distance ta nice restaurants 'n art houses 'n such. Silver City famous fo' its art galleries. You want, I kin drive you back an' pick you up in a couple days or so. Plus, we got Uber an' Lyft!"

Martinez seemed especially proud of their modern transport systems, but whether he had taken any offense to the suggestion of house arrest, the big Mexican-American never once indicated. His matter-of-fact attitude suggested that any way O'Rourke desired was fine by him…

The big man pointed off to the northeast at a flat-roofed, single-story, Santa Fe-style ranch home sitting atop a nearby hill which he called "my place". Its white walls and chrome lawn furniture before a huge patio door all gleamed radiantly in the brilliant sunlight, inviting viewers to stop in, sit a spell. As the raven flies, Martinez' home was only a good stone's throw from the vineyard. But those of us without wings would need to follow the hard-packed dirt road winding up, down and around several hills and shallow valleys in between …which wasn't an issue at the moment anyway.

The giant chauffeur was merely giving a guided tour, aka, showing off. He drove back down the dirt road to the highway and headed east. Along the entire desert landscape they were shepherded by three different types of cactus, narrow leaf yucca, four-wing saltbush grasses (now turning from green to yellow) and ubiquitous Mormon Tea plants whose leafy bushes waved back at them in the stiff, swirling breezes.

Along with these joined the occasional pinion pine tree. Occasionally one of these took up blocking positions to guard scenic views from the unworthy, but otherwise one could see near forever out here; horizon to blue horizon, not a tall building in sight …nor a cloud.

He did not speak, just hummed a little tune that O'Rourke could not catch and watched the nose of his Navigator gobble up the miles back to Silver City. Suddenly, he stopped and pointed out a green sign whose white lettering proclaimed the spot as the Continental Divide and the elevation over six thousand feet. He thought about performing more of the tour guide role but balked at explaining how rain waters flowed west to the Pacific on the side they currently sat and east to the Atlantic on the other side. Such minutia might be received as a bit too condescending. Marine officers could get a bit testy when provoked, even former Marine officers. He decided to ease on the tour guide reins. Instead, he looked back into the noncommittal gaze directed his way and said, "I ain't gonna bite Compadre, you kin sit up here."

"Thought you'd never ask amigo, even though I don't mind being chauffeured." JP flashed his most winning smile, at least he flashed what he hoped was a winning smile. "Where we going?"

Dinner! I'm hungry an' th' woman ain't home just yet."

"Good! I hoped all that grumblin' was comin' from yo' belly. Cause if you was fartin' I wasn't even gonna be happy!" He climbed into the front seat and cinched up his seat belt before closing the door.

"Now I know you ain't about ta be talkin' 'bout smelly! I seem ta recall that time in Chu Lai…"

"Man you don't forget nuthin, do you?"

"Not as bad as my nose hurt carrying yo' heavy ass to th' showers, err, sir!" He emphasized the salutation in a way that caused both men to throw back their heads in raucous laughter.

"Hey! You ain't gotta call me sir, my daddy married my momma!" JP tossed the phrase back at Martinez and then both began to giggle again. A lot of military officers never heard the enlisted men under them hurl that same rejoinder at any unfortunates who mistakenly addressed them as "sir". People who could work with their hands did not need such civilities. "Hey you, shithead", would work just as well for many.

Martinez drove them to a steakhouse south of town that came complete with a bar, dance floors on two levels and a liquor store. It had a rustic look outside that blended well with its insides. The music was lively as were several of the patrons who ran up to hug Martinez like he was their long, lost kin. The people were friendly, the service speedy and the steaks thick and flavorful. JP had a great time. The Jack Daniels they poured heavy-handed, adding to the feeling…

Nights here were dark, very dark. Outside the downtown area proper, few streetlamps added to the illumination provided by a beautiful, full moon and luxurious starlight. He could surmise that it took a bit of getting used to this part of America, though it obviously didn't take forever, as Martinez seemed to have no problems at all negotiating through the inky shroud.

His big brown eyes must have acquired some sort of night vision-like qualities over his years of living here, O'Rourke considered. The man aimed the SUV unerringly through streets both broad and narrow. Mainly it was the turns which impressed JP, especially the left ones. He could make out no discernable markings either in the roadway itself or on the median or shoulders, but Martinez always turned onto some blackened street which had no remarkable features until they were actually within its confines when only then its neighborhood was revealed.

Angel was a country-western fan. Willie Nelson's "Always on my mind" played softly through the Navigator's speakers, pulling JP back into a land of long ago. "Maybe I didn't treat you, quite as good as I should have. Maybe I didn't love you, quite as often as I could have…"

The haunting strains wafted across a vision of Tina's startling beauty, reminding that maybe he hadn't loved her the way she needed. He had left her for another, the cockpit of a lightning-fast fighter jet whose beauty he also loved dearly. He had left her alone and vulnerable. He had failed her like he had failed so many others. This time he could not fail. In silence he vowed that this time he would not fail, no matter what the price. "Little things I should have said and done; I just never took the time. You were always on my mind…"

Willie's voice faded as he came back to the present and the presence of his host. All the while, Martinez pointed out this landmark or that, oblivious to his guest's time in mental walkabout, obviously very proud of this place where he had grown up before heading out to answer Uncle Sam's beckoning. To JP it came off a bit like magic. He was amazed…

He found the guest room in Martinez home to be spacious and comfortable. In fact he was finding everything about these folk comfortable. Martinez was not married, intimating that making a woman that unhappy for that long would be a sin before God. But he did have a live-in girlfriend named Frieda who was extremely friendly and fairly beautiful, in a southwestern sort of way. She had good lines of curvature, oodles of long, dark hair that had just begun to gray along its right side where it exited her forehead and a quick, becalming smile that warmed her guest even more than the westerning sun.

This was no China Doll. Her hands showed their years as did a few spider wrinkles radiating around her eye sockets in a fashion typical of folk that pronounced their heritage as southwestern by way of sun worship. But only the slightest few and those very fine lines, far overshadowed by the brilliance dominating an impish gaze cast from jet black pupils whose clarity caused in him wonder whether within possessed clairvoyant properties that could see right through him to unwind his twisted heart strings.

The guest room had its own small, en suite bath but neither of these was designed for women, at least most women JP knew. There were few accoutrements –no frilly curtains, doilies or piles of throw cushions --and only two small mirrors. Sylvia would have bolted for the door.

A narrow strip attached to the wall adjacent the doorway acted as the full-length version, as long as the door remained closed. The bathroom's peeking-back-at-cha was much smaller and barely provided coverage down to his upper torso. Some might term the space as Spartan, but it was functional for its primary purposes …crapping and sleeping.

There were few distractions inside these spaces, not even a television to entertain the viewer until long after bedtime. In fact, the entire home seemed set up with one primary purpose …fellowship.

There was only one television in the whole place, the living room. It had access to hundreds of channels for display on its large flat screen but allowed no nonsense about individuality here. Television viewing went by committee in this house. No one person domineered the selection criteria. The loner inside JP became thoroughly impressed by this aspect of family. It brought his memory back to the time when he and Tina could only afford one TV set. Now-a-days, if he wanted to watch a show she found no interest in, Sylvia would simply pick up and head to the TV in another room. Actually, she'd probably make him head to another room…

He woke up in a sweat. An enveloping darkness clinging around him perpetuated the nightmarish scenario that had invaded, rousting him out of a perfectly useful sleep. The spectre was back. It had to be because --even though he could see no visible trace-- in the bedroom's blackness he could feel its presence. It only came in the dark. It waited until exposure was least likely, then alerted his senses with the knowing that something different, something very different floated there in the dark; just outside his ability to see, just outside his ability to grasp …just like all those times before.

After all these years and barely a peep, it was back to bother his dreams or maybe it was a they and they were back. He could not discern whether one or a hundred and one disembodied entities had just assailed his unprotected, slumbering state. He could not even discern its intent, whether to actually do harm or merely warn him about something onerous at hand. Its presence during its last visit seemed peaceful, almost quiescent, that last time in Thailand before he flew Mickey into the sights of those NVA guns, literally down the barrels …before Mickey became crippled for life.

The nightmares had left him after that tragedy, perhaps gleefully joyous at his grief, perhaps sobering at the repetitive similarity or maybe because the test was over. Like a biblical Job, maybe they had decided he had taken enough. Whether he had passed or failed, he did not know, the spirit wraiths simply stopped haunting his dreams for a time. Obviously that time had ended.

It seemed this or these things always made their presence felt during times of discord. Did they come back now because of Tina's plight, to guide or warn him? Sometimes he felt a sort of ESP about things about to happen, nothing precise enough to win the Powerball Lottery, but usually good enough to steer him left where minefields plagued his right. It might help keep egg off his face – "Don't kiss her on the first date, she hates that" or "Kiss her now, she likes that"-- but these were different. Were they indeed the kami-spirits of his departed family and friends blaming him for his inability to protect them or did they just hang around in some vain effort to remain on this side? If they knew his future it would have been nice if they'd tell him. "Say something beyatch!"

All these many years into his advanced days, he had grown so used to the freedom from this entity. Free --he had believed himself-- from this wraith that first began terrorizing his pre-pubescent child-self, emerging on dark nights from inside his bedroom closet shortly after the country club kitchen fire that took his mother's love ...and scarred him for life!

After a malevolent lynch party murdered his father, leaving him so totally and so terribly an orphan, its reemergence heralded an even lengthier period embedded within the traumatic nightmares brought glaringly into his bedroom nightly. Rejoice had greeted its subsequent departure and hope had stirred that it would never again return...

But it or they came back shortly after his best friend Tony succumbed in his arms --a bloodied, smoldering carcass ripped apart by rocket delivered incendiary explosions-- and now again after Tina's reported demise --crushed and burned to a crisp by Morano's minions-- the entity has again reared its presence into his sleep state, still refusing his attempts to spy its form. In a moment or two it would be gone, he knew, leaving barely a whisper of sibilant sound as it jetted away outside his sensory limits, back to its side of the multiverse or from wherever it came ...like it always did.

It would leave him still clueless, most likely mirthfully laughing at his feeble tries to decipher its meaning. "Spectres and spooks be damned, weren't tragedies supposed to stop after three?"

No answer to his muttered question. It still wouldn't speak. Frustration welled up at the thought that he might never know whatever this thing was that seemed to enjoy tormenting him from its camouflaged hideout in the gloom. It, or its kind, had followed him from North Carolina to South Vietnam and now to New Mexico. This presence, this mute thing he decided must be a coward, scared to show itself.

"Be gone spirits from another world!" He didn't say it, but he almost did. Were he projecting his dramatic best as some brain half-dead, B-grade actor in a D-grade horror movie or on some fake-reality TV show he would have said it. But the words remained within. He didn't think Martinez would have appreciated him scaring the neighborhood silly with a lot of midnight shouting and screaming ...and cussing.

The thing probably wouldn't care anyway. If he adhered to his father Henry's belief system he'd be tempted to believe it the Holy Ghost trying to convince his unredeemed self of his own sinfulness and to get right with God before he had to face God. Henry and Aunt Maude had done their best to convince him in their faith, but in him those roots had never taken hold.

Where they saw religion, he saw only tradition. What they regarded as faith, he decreed as blind obedience. His look into their world uncovered too many dichotomous contradictions between concepts lauded by the religiously ordained or retained, whatever they claimed. They preached one thing in public while practicing another behind closed doors. Faith it might be, but he had not the faith in him to follow anyone blindly. The fact that ministers could be ordained online (pick a web site) without ever meeting in person those who ordained them he saw as more proof to his principle.

From his childhood days he had studied people of his family's faith. He still watched an occasional Sunday morning evangelist preaching the Gospel. He watched them both for the entertainment value as well as to see what new age concepts they'd come up with in this new age and listened carefully to these purportedly, devout Christians. He would never whole heartedly put them down as people, at least most of them. Despite his protests of denial he even attended church on occasion, mainly for weddings and funerals, but there indeed was the occasional Sunday service visit. In fact, the prior New Year's Eve he had passed up a night of ribald party going and attended "Watch Night Service" at a friend's church in New Jersey.

He had never visited the tiny township of Willingboro before. Just across the Delaware River from Philadelphia's northern suburbs. It turned out to be, he felt, one of his most enjoyable New Year's Eves ever, the lack of a next day hangover even more a plus.

Alpha Baptist they called the single-story modern architecture and congregation led by a charismatic young preacher who stirred the faith-filled pot, churning out pourings of love and wholesome good feeling. The choir singers were pretty good too. In fact, there were three of them, beginning with young children, then a women's and finally a men's choir. So enjoyable, he nearly suggested they should make a DVD, but decided they might already have and that such common knowledge he should have already known. So he wussed and kept the question inside …and still wondered to this day.

But from those in this flock he never noticed any hidden deception. Their message was clear and unsullied by disdainful remarks belittling deeds of other groups. Not like so many historic examples, not even like so many popular televangelists who never seemed to live the lives they preached.

He had watched very closely, some of those icons to the Godhead, as they extolled virtues of love but practiced hate towards others outside their faith. They say they want to embrace Jesus, who was always Jew, but decry most things Jewish, in hypocrisy anew.

Ultimately they strive to recreate the Crusades, kick the Islamic peoples out of Jerusalem, destroy the Al-Aqsa Mosque and rebuild the Hebrew temple so that Christ can return and initiate the Millennium. They want these things dearly and even though they may not openly lobby for violent reconstruction, many pray for its occurrence. From his perspective these folk were no better than people from the other religious groups they hated and looked down upon. They see their religion as the only true religion and themselves the only true believers. In this, they were one in the same.

"Ya'll are God's children." They preach, "He loves you and wants you to do His work on this earth in preparation for His kingdom in Heaven! Turn away from the dark path followed by the weak in spirit! Only the pure of heart, those saved by the blood of the Lamb, those who believe in Jesus, will see the Kingdom! Do not listen to false prophets seeking to turn you away! Vote for Senator Dickwad. He'll stop the illegal aliens from stealing your jobs and moving into your neighborhoods and marrying your daughters! He'll fight government takeover of your right to bear automatic assault weapons. His close association with the gun industry and the military-industrialist contributors to his finances assures he understands their needs. Also important, he'll ensure your right to be dropped by whichever healthcare provider wants to drop you without any competition from some government-sponsored providers! I have personal assurances from the senator and his staff. You support him; he'll support them and me, I mean us. In fact I got a six-figure honorarium for this presentation, so you know he supports our cause."

Every side seemed to warn against paying attention to false prophets. O'Rourke was most confused about which prophets were false. The ones telling that the others were false or the ones they told about. If every religion is based upon worshippers' faith, literally "blind allegiance", to concepts derived from people long dead who believed thunder was God's voice and lightning a sign he was pissed, maybe the best religious concepts are actually a compilation from all religions, a bit of these added to a bit of those to get something that worked. To him it made no sense to learn from the unlearned whose primary world view anticipated a god more into slavery than benevolence. 'Do as I say or die, bitch!"

What if the Bible's portrayal in Genesis was true and God purposely divided and scattered people around the world in order to challenge them to grow and survive in that adversity? What if it is truly the synergy of mankind's beliefs that will light our path to enlightenment and thus to God? From the earliest of times, men have fought each other in the name of their parochial religious beliefs and deities. And best not be the outsider! Anyone developing an original thought --including members of their own family, tribe, group or nation—was and often still is, harshly dealt with.

Hebrews under Moses used torture and ritual execution (aka, murder) to cull the ranks of doubters and those they perceived less than devout. "You guys wearing those pukie looking, vulture-shit, colored robes are sinners and blasphemers! You only exulted: 'Thank you o Lord for your mercy and kindness!' You should have said, 'Thank you o Lord for your mercy, goodness, benevolence and kindness!' Obviously, you worship the demon ha-Satan! Somebody tie these people up! We gonna cut off their heads, piss down their necks, then have a weenie roast!"

In the Dark Ages the Catholic Church used torture and ritual execution (aka, murder) to cull the ranks of doubters and those they perceived less than devout. "Yes, God has instructed us to collect ninety-six percent of your earnings as revenue for the Church. Why are you concerned brothers? Have you been praying for acceptance as we instructed? Hmmm, it appears you haven't. Soldiers! Seize these blasphemers and sharpen the axes … and light a fire!"

Even today, Islamic radicals use torture and ritual execution (yup, still talking, murder) to cull the ranks of doubters and those they perceive less than devout. "Allah forbids radical thinking Bin Zulli! You want to free your female to go about as she pleases? Wearing any type clothes she wants? Are you crazy? That is a sacrilege! Zamir! Omar, Ali, hold down this Satan worshipper 'til I can cut off his filthy head! Oh yeah and light a fire!"

To him, these folk just don't get it? We're all in a circle, an orbit, a pattern that would continue until mankind grew up to where we are no longer children of God, but people of God. At least that was his theory. Unfortunately, suddenly if we don't grow up soon, we may never have another chance. If this coming thing; if this planet buster ever hits earth; right, wrong or in between, we're all gonna get flushed alongside our religions. Won't be any more need to hate the neighbor's practice of praying on a different day. Mankind will cease to exist; there won't ever be another day. Maybe that's what some of these self-absorbed, self-righteous, sanctimonious people want. But if they thought about it, maybe they'd see their coming extinction as something nature considers a radical form of evolution. "You've been trashing my planet much too long. Die Bitches! I'm starting over! No, ain't no boats this time! Ain't no Noah, neither!"

Two evenings later, they got the call and he drove with Martinez back to Chaco's ranch house. He roughly had a working knowledge of the project, though wonder still filled his every fiber. But he kept his silence well after they exited the vehicle's plush leather and were ushered into the home by a beautiful woman whose bloodline appeared flavored with both Spanish and Native American. Arched eyebrows over obsidian eyes topped high cheekbones and full lips painted dark red that tantalized with neither a smile nor frown against the ruddy complexion. Dark tresses fell down her back well below the hip pockets of the worn jeans that she fit extremely well.

Though the black hair had acquired a crop of gray that announced her advancing years, it did nothing to detract from her overall appearance. In O'Rourke's eyes she could have been closely related to Frieda, maybe an older sister. But he chose not to venture the query. Maybe if he saw them together after he had downed a few tongue looseners. She spoke not a word, just opened the door and waved them both inside. Then she was gone.

The home had a rustic, southwestern quality tailor-made for this neighborhood. Plants and paintings of plants hung all about. O'Rourke had no knowledge of most of them, but he did recognize several types of cactus and fern that grew from large pots strategically positioned beside couches and chairs. Other paintings of desert animals and birds and flowing streams hung about on whitewashed walls underneath the thick, dark, wood beams supporting the roof. Native American figurines and Mexican pottery adorned end tables and colorful rugs covered the flooring underneath. He appreciated the warmth even without any flames searing the logs piled high within the large fireplace situated midroom.

They entered the solarium as the sun was beginning to set and beautiful reds and yellows adorned tall peaks touching the western quarter of the sky. Chaco greeted them and bade them sit. A pitcher of lemonade and glasses sat on a nearby table to quench any thirsty palates. O'Rourke boldly poured himself a glass and offered to serve the others. Seated comfortably, each man sipped silently for a while. When there was any, conversation centered on sports, football mainly. Martinez was a total Oakland Raiders junkie, no matter if they move or not. Vegas, smegas! Still his Raiders! He and JP bantered back and forth about this week's upcoming games, until the phone rang. Chaco limped over and answered the call. "Okay gentlemen. Let's go."

Single file they followed Chaco's lead over a well-worn path through low sage and yucca up the hilly terrain to a small structure with a dome on top. The sound of three ATV engines snarling and popping echoed from the nearby boulders and cliff faces and startled jackrabbits and roadrunners into full flight to escape the unwelcome din. Shadow figures emerged in the dim light of dusk, only to retreat. When the vehicle lights and switches were turned off, peace was again restored and all things settled back to normal.

Once inside the steel door, he removed his amber goggles, staring awkwardly into the confines to adjust his bearings. The room was barely as large as Chaco's living room and not nearly as well furnished. JP humorously wondered if there would be room for Martinez and began to feel claustrophobic.

In its center a large telescope dominated, pointed skyward into the starry night. The black cylinder was not nearly as impressive as those found in major observatories, but it seemed pretty good-sized to him. There was one small wooden desk in the far corner, one table and a few chairs and that was about the extent, other than a placard over the door which read: "Observe always that everything is the result of a change, and get used to thinking that there is nothing Nature loves so well as to change existing forms and to make new ones like them." Meditations. iv. 36. –Marcus Aurelius.

Two men worked at the desk, studying the displays of side-by-side laptop computers. Across the room, the small table held another pair of laptops and a stack of papers. Underneath was a small, white refrigerator humming along while it fulfilled its destiny as beer cooler or perhaps some scientific purpose. JP preferred to envision its job in his own way and after their dusty ride up here a cold one would go down very nice. Another hum, along with the temperate climate inside, indicated the air conditioner was also at work. Noticing their visitors, the men left their work and came forward. Both were dressed in blue jeans and long-sleeved sweatshirts, one blue, the other brown. Trent and the others were not in sight.

"Mister O'Rourke, this is Doctor Tomas van Oldstein and my assistant, Herman. Doctor van Oldstein is a professor at Western New Mexico University downtown by way of South Africa and has consented to help us out on this matter." Obviously, JP was the "odd duck" here; everyone else seemed familiar with one another. He shook their hands in turn.

Mister Brown, aka Herman, looked very young; perhaps early twenties with his bronze-complexioned tan and movie star quality good looks chiseled seemingly from a desert granite block. He sported long dark-hair with a hawkish nose that would have made Geronimo proud and he was tall –at least six-four—and would have been even taller if some doctor had straightened out his bowlegs at birth.

Mister Blue–O'Rourke preferred to think of him as the Professor—topped out significantly shorter and looked more like Mister Rogers in an innocuous, almost bland sort of way. JP half expected him to break out a keyboard and lead them in a song about looking and listening carefully while a projector flashed images of the starry night universe across the top of the dome in Technicolor and Sensuround. He even sported a similar hairstyle to the television icon; mostly all gray, sprinkled white, with a small face, pink complexion and blue eyes; but instead of the trademark sweater over a shirt and tie, he wore a blue sweatshirt ...so much for similarities.

"Hallo, welkom, welkom Mister O'Rourke. It ist you wee haf to t'ank for bringing dee Ark here. Baie Dankie, thank you, thank you! You are most welkom."

"I think you mean Trent."

"Yah, him too. Now we must get back to work."

The Professor was all business. He bustled about clicking this and switching that and adjusting other devices. They appeared to be power circuits and CCD camera controls. On one computer screen a dark, oblong shape hung suspended against an even darker background, its backlit edges tinged here and there by the hint of a yellowish glow. It almost looked like a black-on-black presentation with the center black a bit less black than its surroundings. It held his attention even with its vague definition. A curiosity indeed…

Going with Chaco's tale from their first meeting (when they knocked him out, he ruefully recalled), O'Rourke surmised that evidently this computer tied into some classified NASA feed with the software Morano had somehow acquired access to before he went the whole nine yards. Nobody knows where originated the phrase, but suffice to say that with Morano's intentions it totally matched its meaning of "all the way".

The ebony image appeared static, unmoving, but O'Rourke figured that it must be the comet and if so, it was probably moving pretty fast; impossible to tell over such vast distances. It did not look all that sinister or even intriguing; neither surrounded by a blossoming corona nor a trailing tail. But those conditions would change the closer it approached our sun and would not matter at all when it crashed into our fragile sphere …other than the very last thing you see!

While the Professor worked, he kept up a steady dialog in his guttural voice, though primarily with himself. O'Rourke struggled to follow some of his phrases, spoken in a mixture of his native Afrikaans and English that sounded oddly Germanic. Oddly that is until he recalled that the Afrikaans language is West Germanic in origin. Made sense even though descended from eighteenth century Dutch.

But this professor's mannerisms seemed descended only from the scientific field. He stood rather than sat before the computer, fingers flying seemingly unmindful back and forth across its keys, though enough of his attention he directed to his audience to preclude them feeling totally as intruders.

"Many historians and scholars speculated dee Hebrew Ark waas built wit some type auf alien technology waat give power dat hurl electric fire. Maybe. Arks were common ceremonial objects to ancient Egypt, you know. King Tut waas buried wit en Ark in his tomb en Egyptian Ark builders carved dee image auf Egyptian deity on top auf dere Arks. Possessing dee magical skills auf Egyptian priests, Moses waas well aware auf dese attributes, yah. He also learned his warrior skills from dee Egyptians, did dey ever regret dat, I tell you!"

"But unlike its Egyptian counterparts, dee Hebrew Ark ticked en sparked en flew, as if by magic …or by God." He nearly whispered these words, almost reverently. "If touched by dee wrong people, it killed by incineration. Totsiens! See you later! Nothing left! If opened inappropriately, it caused dreadful diseases. Dere may have been a radioactive component to some auf dee materials stored inside. We don't open it here today, no! Haha!" he jested, flipping a switch that caused the overhead shutter to close.

"Did you ever open it?" Questioned O'Rourke, curiosity peaking.

"Never. Wee must learn how first."

"Perhaps it has fused due to heat generation caused by a huge voltage output." Chaco interjected.

"Maybe, maybe," said the doctor, reclaiming his role as teacher of this class. "Maybe as simple as some hidden mechanism wee don't see yet. So far, nothing."

Now devoid of starlight, the darkness inside became even darker. But the dialog never ceased…

"Wee will study, wee will learn." His pronunciation of the word we stretched to sound as if drawn out in some formal ceremony for some monarch or archbishop or somebody. O'Rourke couldn't help feeling them both out of place. Well, one of them for sure…

"Een mine, err, one auf my old colleagues believed it like large capacitor. You know, gold outside, inside, sandwiching Acacia wood frame. I won't go over dee physics auf capacitance or energy transmission. But from dee biblical accounts, if you believe so, it was tremendous. Anyway, wee believe diss Ark can also be used in charge pump circuits as dee energy storage element to generate tremendously higher voltages dan dee input voltage. Normal charge pump circuits are capable auf high efficiencies, sometimes as high as ninety-five percent while being electrically simple circuits. Dat means for every watt of power wee apply, wee get about dee same when comes out, then multiplies when added to additional input charges. Diss thing has some unknown properties dat might dwarf dat figure by orders of magnitude. Wee can only guess how it does dat but you put in maybe fifty volts, you get out maybe fifty thousand, maybe more. Ek verstaan nie, I don't unnerstand. But significantly higher."

He kept working, but redirected his commentary, "So JP, wat you t'ink? You know deese type things? Waarvandaan kom U? Frum where you come?"

JP almost did not perceive that the man now asked him questions, so focused was he on the lecture about the arcane apparatus. Thoughts flew throughout his being faster than light speed, nearly drowning out every other consideration. "Huh? Oh, ah, born in North Carolina, High Point. I grew up in Philly."

Although he perceived no marginalization in the man's voice, no underlying dig at his ancestry, he never fully appreciated questions such as this. It wasn't due to some overly active suspicious side that saw hate mongers wherever he looked. Even were they so, he had always believed in his ability to win over even the most jaded of bigots …or to kick the living shit out of them if the first technique failed.

But he found no shame in his heritage. Typical of many of this nation's African Americans, his blood --mixed with African, Cherokee and European lines-- was as confused as were his jumbled thoughts at this moment. But his jumbled bloodlines flowed from parental goings and comings and their parents and on and on back through history. Nobody among them started out trying to get a John O'Rourke, just to get laid. He came along simply because they came and since some of them tended to like mates of dissimilar background, he's more mutt than thoroughbred … but that's not a negative as he sees it.

He never actually envied people capable of tracing their lineage back thousands of years down a single racial branch or even further. Those who focused on such issues seemed to pride their fortune at being Asian or European or African, whatever. But selective breeding he viewed as a more limiting than a strengthening attribute. He preferred familial lineage to racial, who they came from rather that what they came from. But rather than ignite some brush fire, he preferred to leave that subject for those more impressed by such measurements.

In a more jocular setting, normal response to a question regarding his origin might be "Earth". Had the questioner requested his nationality or race, the answer may have been "Terran". South Africans had their own issues. But this man being of foreign stock probably understood little about America's trials and tribulations over racial biases. So he answered the man honestly, as if he'd even heard about High Point, North Carolina.

"Oh Ja, dee furniture capital. Very nice. We figure diss more apparent in der dark." With that said, and after totally humbling the black man, he grabbed a remote control and hit a couple buttons. On the wall behind the table, a flat-screen monitor flared to life, instantly revealing the image of a mystical creation JP had only before seen in artistic renderings or in science fiction or religious movies …which amount to the same thing.

There in all its resplendent glory the Ark of the Covenant poised on a raised cement platform unmoving, neither glowing, sparking, flying or any of those magical things it was famous for doing. The wide-screen television presentation split into two images. The right side image showed a large boulder. On the left, four electrical cables clamped to each of the Ark's golden feet. Another led up to a small device mounted on a tripod set up beside the Ark. All the cables trailed out of sight off the screen. He wondered but said nothing.

Any misgivings O'Rourke may have harbored about the biblical story disappeared in an instant with the fantastic object's appearance. He quickly closed his agape jaws before any of the others in the room took notice. The only sound came from Martinez tiny, uttered: "Oh my God".

All eyes glued to the beauty of the shining gold instrument from a biblical age beyond their ken. Two Cherubim angels atop its cover, the mercy seat, seemed purposeful and remorseless. Grim faces with unfurled wings pointed in towards each other, these seemed in direct contrast to the otherwise quiet beauty of the gleaming treasure, as well as in direct contrast to his own image of the cute and cuddly cherubic figurines and paintings a youthful John O'Rourke had first studied at Philadelphia's Franklin Museum.

These Cherubim were anything but cuddly. But he kept the question that formed inside his mind from reaching his straining lips. Obviously none of the others appeared to notice the dichotomy, so he refused to speak out his dilemma with that contrast. They'd never know his stupidity if he didn't broadcast. "Open mouth, insert foot!"

Now the images merged into one and zoomed out to encompass the Ark as well as the landscape out to and just beyond a nearby rock ledge, perhaps one hundred yards away. The Professor flipped another switch on the power panel on the wall above the laptop and a louder humming commenced. Without a word he reached to the computer's keyboard and tapped the "ENTER" key. Instantly arcs of electrical energy leaped out from the Ark of the Covenant's two winged angels toward a nearby rock ledge where the single, large boulder sat perched as if it had endured time immemorial in that same place. "CRACK! BOOM!" And the boulder was no more.

"Holy Jesus!" Martinez again. He could say such things, and often did, as he was still religious. Although, this time, O'Rourke very nearly supplied a supportive, "Amen Brother!" The Professor flipped his controls back to off, then, turned to his audience and waited. Demonstrations are so much more effective than lectures, he knew. His audience would now hear his every word.

"Unfortunately, dat is dee best we can do right now. We need to build better connectors. We gotta have aiming devices. We can steer dee beam direction manually over short distance, by changing direction of trigger pulse, but not across hundred thousand miles of space. En power! Wee must have more power! Much more power!" The Professor touched a key on the laptop, then used its arrow keys to pan the camera across the Ark. Smoke curled up from the power cables. The tripod lay on its side, some distance away, as if swatted by the hand of a giant. "You see? Dee connectors all fried. Dee circuit breaker only t'ing save our generator. Too much feedback, inefficient radiation. Need better every' ting. We must either deflect or totally obliterate dee comet or we will not survive! Either dat or we unmake it…"

Now he had his own questions, at first ignoring the obvious one about whatever "unmaking" meant. "Doctor, how is this thing gonna deflect something as massive as a thirty-mile wide comet? And what if it just breaks the rock into a whole bunch of little pieces?"

"Wal you see, it's possible The Ark iss antimatter reactor, een theory, err, one theory is to use dee Ark to power big ol' deflector device en push dee rock away so it sail past. If so, here we don' let out right away. We just keep pumping in until we reach threshold en soon it go away. But we must get more data en dee comet's composition. Is it soft or hard in der core? Den we know where to focus our energies, I t'ink! If soft core, den we let fly en it go zoom!"

His right hand thrust out before him. For a moment, JP wondered if he was performing a NAZI salute. He half-expected a snapping together of heels followed by an exaggerated, "Heil Hitler". But these things did not happen and he put away his paranoia for the moment. Besides, there was still that hard core aspect the doctor had yet to disclose.

"You mentioned it might be hard composition. What do we do then?" He wasn't sure he wanted to hear the answer, but he was sure he wouldn't like it. Hairs standing attention at the nape of his neck confirmed all that.

"Wal, you see comets en asteroids comprised of mixed hard en soft materials more prone to fly apart if hit with laser or nuclear explosion. Diss beam we send up, if wrong polarity or power could make dat type comet fly apart. Den wee got trouble. Lots of incoming. So we need better way to deal wit' dem…

"Since we don't yet know what it's made of, we will plan for worse case and proceed from there." Chaco seemed genuinely motivated to clarify any misconceptions in his guest's understanding of this project. JP wondered why, remembering the gentle method the older man had employed back at Morano's villa. Even though he knew this person to whom he spoke to be his cousin's destroyer…

"Everyone always worry 'bout the size of t'ings, how big t'ings are. It's really a matter of how deep we look inside t'ings. You look inside yourselves to find your God..."

JP startled out of the trance from where he had devolved, seeking escape from "Lectures 'R Us". He'd had so many of late. But now this guy was speaking directly to his very makeup, he could sense it so. How did this mad scientist know where he sought his understanding of God? Now he'd have to pay a bit more attention to figure this all out. Unfortunately, that meant listening to another lecture. So he listened and tried not to get too lost...

"In places like CERN near Geneva en Fermilab near Chicago dey look for dee God particle, dee boson, which is billion times smaller than atom or so theory goes. Of course dee atom waas theory hundred years ago. But dee Higgs boson particle dey believe is dee fabric, dee building block for all matter. We not so certain yet, but I t'ink this Ark has some elemental power dat causes dat fabric to unwind in way we don't yet understand."

"You mean it's like a disintegrator ray or something outta Buck Rogers?" Martinez said what O'Rourke was thinking.

"It might be some form of antimatter. Doctor van Oldstein has conducted a series of experiments. But there are more to come." Chaco chose to voice his opinion. Even in dispute, his words remained soft as if intended to soothe rather than disturb these ignorant people barely able to walk while chewing bubble gum. At least those were O'Rourke's thoughts in consideration of his malaise. Chaco never indicated anything of the sort, always the teacher.

"You know antimatter mixed with matter will cause the most powerful of explosions, nearly total annihilation of each other, more powerful than atomic weapons and much more efficient. We're not sure, but whatever it is, you saw one example of the results."

"Not sure what I saw." Martinez was only sure he was ill at ease with whatever it was.

"Dee subatomic world is where wee find our answers." O'Rourke had gotten used to the doctor's guttural phrases. Didn't sound anything like Mister Rogers. But at least now he could clearly understand most.

"Wee haf discovered properties in diss Ark which behave like particle accelerator. However, instead of around circular path like at CERN or Fermi, somehow they flow through diss rectangular box much like photons through the sun's photosphere --inside, outside, up en down en up en all time slamming into each other-- pumping higher en higher en higher energies en frequencies until release. Tremendous efficiencies. Not so sure how it all happens, not yet. But it has demonstrated ability to cause unmaking of dat fabric binding things together. Wat it did to boulder. Makes sense, you see. God makes. God's box unmakes."

"Because it makes bosons, right?" Martinez had now warmed up to this game of "befuddle my noodle".

"Dee boson is a force-carrying particle. As en particle accelerator dee Ark creates force-carrying particles. It stands to reason diss Ark from God generates dee God particle. So, because matter can neither be created nor destroyed, just changed in form en structure, we feel diss Ark might pull matter apart down to its constituent bosons which are tens of billion times tinier than dee former mass, converting in a way that appears to disintegrate dee composition. First you haf big, den infinitely small."

The doctor stayed on his theories (which to the laymen among them seemed to be all over the spectrum), while Chaco stayed on his. O'Rourke smiled inwardly at the thought of competing theories even in so small a group. Anytime you get more than one scientist in a room, you're going to end up with more than one approach to theory, sometimes even with only one scientist in a room. It wasn't quite a Rodney King moment. No need yet to ponder his classic: "Can we all just get along?" No knock down drag outs here. Just a dueling of competing theories that probably didn't matter all that much since the differences seemed more semantic than substantive. Scientists have long theorized about antimatter but have never been able to duplicate more than microscopic amounts of something they believe might be and might not be. But now that they got their super-duper, new gazillion-dollar toy in Switzerland they might any day now create more … provided they can stop blowing up large sections of the device every time they run it up to full power.

Theoretical antimatter versus theoretical bosons; both so minute and so elusive neither them nor their effects can be fully proven to exist. O'Rourke's impulse was to pat both men's shoulders and promise them everything would be all right. Like a friend assuring his buddy it was okay he didn't get to start at quarterback.

"Don't sweat Phil; consider this only a minor distraction, a character builder. You can play at wide-receiver and still get to score." Besides, he considered, distractions can be constructive. Then the other shoe dropped and he remembered they can easily prove destructive. But he forced these negative thoughts away and refocused on Mister Rogers' long lost twin…

"As with other high power generators, dere is een electrical field component dat radiates outward en can cause great harm if not properly shielded. Dee Iraqi lost quite a few of his soldiers when dey exposed it unwisely to light rays."

"So you're saying you only need the sun to set this thing off?" O'Rourke decided to hold off questions about "the Iraqi", thinking maybe such would make him sound too unawares to register any legitimate comment. They might make him go into the corner and wear a dunce cap. By the professor's tone this Iraqi person was someone familiar …at least to them.

However, dunce cap or not, he found the professor's summation too simplistic. It sounded like one of those movie scenes where a mystical object sits quiet and alone in a dark, dusty hole in the ground until uncovered by the heroic, white hunter and his voluptuous companion whose every movement promises erotic thrills and passion galore, but who never needs more than a few batted lashes in his direction (and the audience's) to achieve all her desires. Once uncovered, the emerald-crusted, golden amulet causes a mighty earthquake that crushes all in the immediate vicinity, including the heroic, white hunter who gives his last to save the fair lass and is forever entombed along with the golden amulet, returned to its hole in the ground.

JP finally shook visions of the seductress and her raven tresses from his mind enough to refocus on the matter at hand. The professor's summation he found too simplistic even though it did seem to jibe with biblical accounts that the Ark's handlers always kept it covered except when they took it into battle and it destroyed their enemies with bolts of lightning or fire or whatever. Must have been some sight to behold, he decided. Small wonder those later kings like Saul and David grew afraid to consult something so volatile. Probably scared them shitless, especially if they figured God was pissed at them for all the raping, pillaging and plundering they did cause they wanted to while saying it was for the glory of God …as usual.

"Light energy is dee same as any other electromagnetic radiation, just in dee visible spectrum. Our Ark responds to electromagnetic energy. A single flashlight could start dee pumping action," said the professor.

O'Rourke thought of him almost entirely this way now that his lectures had grown longer. "Now it wouldn't be nearly enough to destroy boulder like we just demonstrated. But it could build to sufficient power level to kill. Depending how long you trained flashlight beam on it. But we have discovered dat it reacts differently to different types power. Direct current input seems to cause generation of some kind of force ray, like repulsor rays in comic books. HaHaHa, we used car battery for dat test this morning. Alternating current, on other hand, well you saw dat result yourselves."

Chaco had not given up his side of the argument either. "Say we decide it's best to try and use the Ark's ability to disintegrate or unmake the subatomic particles that compose the comet. It's not a given, not by a long shot. We'll need to focus a beam of energy; say it's comprised of positrons…"

Spying the blank looks on two members of his audience, Chaco further elaborated: "Positrons are like electrons only they belong to antimatter. Like positive electrons. From the time our beam makes first contact, positron-electron collisions will begin annihilating each other at a sub-molecular level, literally like tiny lasers zapping each other into nothingness. So our beam has to be at least as wide as the rock and we'll need to maintain it until every bit is destroyed. What isn't hit by the beam will keep coming, so we want to get it all the first time cause power drain is gonna be humongous." In O'Rourke's current vision, an image of a half-destroyed comet hurtled into earth's atmosphere while technicians scrambled to connect other power sources to a shiny, golden Ark that had greedily just sucked all others dry.

"Now, say we can only accomplish this feat within, oh maybe two-three hundred miles, as it's about to enter our atmosphere," continued Chaco. "Gonna get real dicey, gonna wet some pants with this thing looming larger and larger an' sporting a huge plume and tail. Be visible day and night as it first looks like a star, then another moon and then…"

His voice fell off momentarily before continuing. "All that corona plume will make it tough to focus our beam and even tougher to track its movement. The harder it is to focus and track, the closer we gotta let it get before engaging. And the shorter our range, the closer we'll have to be sited near wherever it's gonna hit. Any power wasted might be our doom, so we gotta get our measurements exact, down to minimum tolerance."

"Hmm, I'd say it's gonna do more than wet some pants," chuckled Martinez.

Snatching his opportunity, the Professor chimed back in. "…and there will be no second chance. No time to figger out mistake en correct. Now wee might be able to deflect it at about thousand miles, possibly more. So dat's consideration. But in order to either push aside or disintegrate thirty mile wide space object traveling close to seventy thousand kilometers per hour, wee gone need enough power to light up Albuquerque."

"Wow! That is some serious power," exclaimed O'Rourke. Except now he wondered why they wanted him here. Obviously, he was no physicist. Maybe they just felt "the more the merrier". Whatever, but even his untrained eyes could see they had some significant hurdles, like how did you get that kind of power out here? He said as much…

"Wee rather be taking Ark to place dat already has power available", answered the professor. "Problem is, wee have to conduct further tests, determine best way to couple to Ark, perhaps some kind of enclosure, as well as best types of power for our purposes. Even then, wee can't just walk into facility and ask to hook into dere power grid with our one of a kind magical gift from God. Dey will pronounce us crazy, declare it fake and kick us out on our asses. Wee actually took little bit chance tonight. Coulda been embarrassing. Diss t'ing don't always work as advertised. Can't chance dat wit' big whigs."

"Ah! So, after you conduct your physical and simulated tests and figure out what you need and how much. Then you bring out the heavies and show them, right? Then they jump on board and give you funds, facilities, females and anything else you want that begins with 'F'."

His joke totally missed his audience, not even a snicker from Martinez. But it didn't matter, for the "F" word he anticipated those captains of industry giving would be followed by the word "You" and would come after they stomped all over Chaco's invitation, this plan and any other logically-derived solutions he presented to their jaded view screen filters tuned only for money-making opportunities. Where Chaco saw logical, they would see loco. Any plan whose operation might jeopardize those opportunities, by possibly damaging a multibillion-dollar power system, for example, wasn't likely to fly even if they thought they might die. Money has powers rivaling the possibility of doom, especially when doom is only a possibility.

This philosophy of rational self-interest rejects altruistic goals and ideals and points to the achievement of man's own happiness as the highest moral purpose of his life. Evidenced by mega-millionaires fighting tooth and nail against minimum wage laws or social entitlements, while simultaneously demanding favorable taxes and military intervention against threats to their profit making. This pattern has so pervaded society, we accept our politicians being paid shills of corporate lobbyists with barely a whimper or a whine. O'Rourke could see no way, shape or form that these dollar-as-the-bottom-line plutocrats would risk any or all for the benefit of mankind. No way. Wasn't gonna happen. However, he didn't always see very clearly…

"Actually, we're gonna take it to them." O'Rourke took a good look into Chaco's unblinking, coal-black eyes. They said he should trust their vision. They said he knew what needed doing and obviously had no choice. They said he should stop playing games.

So he did. No more wisecracks. He now knew why they wanted him. Bus driver. A subconscious thought stirred to tease his hubris at just how far the mighty had fallen; from supersonic space ace to middle of the road cargo hauler.

"What a world, what a world." His vanity lamented, but only for a moment before realization asserted, "What matters a job title? If they fail, all will soon be melting just like that Wicked Witch of the West."

Another thought, this one almost a plea: "Where was Dorothy when you needed her?"

Resigned to his fate, he merely looked back into Chaco's dark orbs and obediently nodded his acceptance. What else could he do? Both of them aware that simple solutions such as Dorothy used to save Oz could not solve this riddle, would not save mankind, not this time …no matter how ruby her slippers or big her glass of water.

"Don't need to tell you that we must keep this to ourselves, JP. If anyone finds out we'll need an army to keep all the religious nuts away. The Government will probably just take it away from us and sit on it with all the other secrets they're sittin on." They walked in the cool night air. The others remained inside; even Martinez --who felt certain his boss had nothing to fear from O'Rourke-- and being very curious about the Ark, was more than happy to leave them in their own company.

"I understand what you're saying Chaco. Just not sure you got this right."

"Think about it, JP. The Government's trying to keep a tight lid on this. They aren't gonna be real happy that we know. And when they figure out that we stole the program that allows us to break into their message traffic, our corpses will never see the light of day. At the very least we'll be locked away somewhere deep. They're running scared, that's why they're planning to explode a whole bunch of nuclear missiles around the comet after it enters our atmosphere. They're gonna pollute the whole world with radioactive fallout. I don't care if some idiot has developed a theory. It's an unproven theory. It's bogus. I can feel it."

"Yeah, I don't see how that'll work either, forces countering forces and nullifying each other without the explosion, slash implosion tearing half our world away. Doesn't seem like it got legs. So how does the whole scientific community let something like this just walk all over them? They should be screaming from the rafters."

"Number one, they're all scared out of their skulls. They have been brainstorming ideas back and forth for years about ways to defeat incoming comets and asteroids and still don't have anything near ready. Maybe some solution will present itself five to seven years or more likely, 2025. But this thing is on its way now and we need a solution quick, fast and in a hurry!"

"I still think it might be best to tell somebody. How can we assume we are the only ones qualified to save the world? Even Superman joined the Justice League." His joke landed like a flat balloon. He did not bother to add that even the great James Bond got help from "Q" (as well as any beautiful woman nearby). It would not have mattered; Chaco was a rock.

"Probl'y half the people in our country believe in 'The Rapture' or 'Paradise'. They have been waiting to die ever since they were born. A lot of them work for me. Dumbassed wetbacks. It's one of the most divisive concepts ever invented. I emphasize, invented. It makes Christians and Muslims look down their noses on everybody else in the world and say, 'We going to Heaven, you ain't!' Those people will not like us trying to stop this."

"But do you think you can develop all those things the Professor wants?"

"We started working on them when we found out Eisa had the Ark."

"Who's Eisa?"

"You met him the night you came over to Fisher Island uninvited. He's the Iraqi general Doctor van Oldstein just mentioned."

"Oh, the chain smoker swathed in too much cologne. Smelled him coming. You figured that was me, huh?"

"I figured. You gave him a pretty tough time, Y'know."

"Well, if it's any consolation, he gave me a pretty tough time too. Took a week before the smell wore off. My nose still has flashbacks…"

"I didn't like you much back then," continued the smaller man, ignoring the levity. "I almost had him convinced to bring the Ark to me. After that night he got scared. Wouldn't admit it, but he was scared shitless. That's when Carlos took over. Scared people go back to where they feel safest. He knew Carlos longest. But I figured Carlos might keep it. Try to sell it to the highest bidder. He never bought into the idea of Armageddon, convinced himself that he could ride out the storm like the Government is planning to do. Drinking your own piss makes you all kinds of crazy."

"But you don't?"

"Drink piss?"

"Believe the Government!"

"I think they've made mistakes before."

"I agree. But I think you won't succeed either. Not without a lotta help."

"I got some other people coming. You'd be surprised, there's lots of people who don't think much of the Government's capability to resolve this in a way what's most valuable will live through. Even if we build shelters deep underground and fill them with stores of foods and hydroponic gardens and energy sources. What's most valuable is Mother Earth. It will most likely take her hundreds of years to recover. We don't think she wants that. Mankind has done enough harm."

"Well, if you're taking Trent, make him wash up first. That boy got a hellacious BO." Another joke that bombed, he may as well have squirted the little man with a water pistol. Something about tree huggers, no sense of humor.

"Trent is just one. Trent was going to snatch the Ark before Carlos got away if he could. If he couldn't, well, let's say my cousin was expendable. But after Carlos didn't come back from you chasing him, we figured it would be much easier for you to bring it back. You being a Government man…"

O'Rourke studied the small man before him, reminded again that it's not the size of a ship, but its motion in the ocean that matters. He had begun to admire his grit and determination. Here was a force to be reckoned with no matter what his height. This person would never blindly accept a government censure or some religiously-inspired folly, not without a significant fight. It was more than that stubborn set to his square jaw.

JP thought back to all those teachings his adolescent self valiantly tried to absorb in the little brick church (as well as those that came later in life) and all the investigation his adult self had invested in his search for enlightenment, only to find the finger pointed back towards that same self. The awakening. The answer finally awoke in him to reveal its ultimate truth even to one as hardheaded as he. In its message he finally understood that every individual held responsibility for his or her own discovery. To each of us is given the ability to find our own pathway to "enlightenment", to sort out things good from evil, necessary from unnecessary and erudite from base.

It was there for him all the while he searched for it. It waited until he had matured enough to understand its message. Perhaps it was the same with this Ark. Perhaps it too had waited until we as a people had matured sufficiently and perhaps we had …as a people.

"All things are revealed to you through the prism of your soul," had preached the old pastor. He always wondered what that meant, until he finally understood what that meant. "You want to find yourself, don't look to her or him, look within!"

What he learned from all his chasing about was akin to the dog that discovers it is only chasing its own tail. Why depend on others to tell you about yourself? They don't know you. They may not even know themselves. Sometimes you must follow your own instincts; sometimes you must follow your own nose …even if it leads you through some smelly places.

And JP had traveled some smelly roads, though he didn't consider all of those all that bad. At least he picked them. He figured it could have been so much worse to travel a shitty path picked out by someone else. There are people picked out by other people blowing up themselves every day because the other people said so. Now that fit perfectly his definition of a smelly road …aka, a really shitty path!

Even shittier, people who can barely add prime numbers climb on soap boxes and scream across television sets in dispute of the very mathematicians whose formulas helped develop those television sets, as well as the cell phones their throngs of devout followers employ to send belittling text messages and photos to their social engineering databases like Twitter and Facebook, whose technology also derived from mathematicians. Equally ridiculous he finds the followers of religious doctrine written by men who gave us their ideas about worshipping God, while peeing and dumping raw sewage into the very water they drank from and then blamed resulting outbreaks of disease and pestilence on demons. Yeah, the devil definitely in them! Today, they'd blame the Government for forcing them to buy health plans to defeat the possibility of an outbreak …since that's God's job.

That is not to say that O'Rourke believes that none of the ancient wisdom is valid, he just believes that none of the ancient wisdom is always valid, i.e., infallible. To his eyes it is unfortunate that too many of our present day leaders tend to follow, lock-step, the logic and guidance of camel drivers and sheep herders from ancient times who –if they could write-- wrote about the only things they thought they knew.

They knew that if they drank fermented milk they'd see images of God. They knew that when the wind blew and the rain fell, there often came thunder and lightning from the sky where God lived. They knew God lived in the sky because everybody had worshipped sky gods, like the moon and sun and planets, since time began.

When the lightning struck a rock or tree and split it in two, they knew God was telling them something in his booming voice that rolled across the heavens and then they drank that fermented milk and figured out exactly what God's thunderous voice meant. Then other men took what they wrote down and translated it into a more modern format that made them look good and didn't piss off the emperor who paid them to build him a bible. And now we take and reinterpret their poorly written, poorly translated (often conflicting) passages and use it as Gospel today. "Blind Faith?"

He had always wondered how those ancient men could be taken serious after they blamed pestilence and disease on God's punishment, when they themselves were the actual cause and still are in most cases. Men cut down all the trees, knowing that trees clean the air of carbon dioxide, then wonder why carbon dioxide levels are rising. They build houses below sea level, then rail against the hurricane that floods them.

Fundamentalist Christians believe strongly that restoration of the Temple in Jerusalem will bring back Jesus Christ and they wish this no matter what holocaust is ultimately caused. All because a Christian man, who hated Rome and its emperor named Nero, wrote a coded text that said he hated Rome and Nero the Beast who was persecuting Christians. We have life imitating art and it ain't pretty.

When John of Patmos spelled out the name of the beast in Revelations, he used Gematria or number symbolism to come up with the number "666", which in Hebrew equates to "Nero Caesar". Later Christians have since reinterpreted this number as a symbol of the Anti-Christ and applied it to represent everyone from early day Popes, through Martin Luther and Adolph Hitler and on to present-day Presidents. O'Rourke knew all these things. What he did not know was how to convince Chaco that he was now acting as those foolish Christians had, that he needed to follow a different path.

"So, you believe this device, which might be the Ark of the Covenant, can either destroy the comet or deflect it. Then why not approach the Government on the down low, like in a classified manner and get the help you're gonna need? They got the resources and all of them aren't dummies. I have personally met some very fine folks who are government." All the while he preached these things, he wondered if he was being genuine or just desperate…

"JP, these people you wanting us to trust have no honor. They're people who have recreated their God in the gold they worship just like the Conquistadores. My ancestors called them "Children of a Lost God". Yes, we might find the few honorable men left and they could take the Ark and spend their usual two to four years fighting amongst each other about the cost to make it go and who should get the contract and then studying how it works for another ten, then write up some operator manuals at an eighth grade reading level so that any of their people could turn on whatever design they come up with. They'd probably be ready to go by say, twenty-thirty-five. But we don't have those years, we don't have two. We gotta get this thing up and running or we're gonna lose, big time!"

What he held back was his belief that white men always want everything they see, especially when what they see is made of pure gold. His mother's people had always expressed wonder and amazement at the white man's insatiable appetite for gold, for land and especially for land containing gold. He tried in vain to make the man see, but O'Rourke remained bulldog stubborn.

"So who's this we? So far I've seen one guy who talks to himself in one language and answers in another, but…"

"Professor, err, Doctor van Oldstein was born in Geneva. He worked twenty-six years as a physicist at the University of Oslo, the largest university in all Scandinavia and one of the most prestigious. Thirty-six thousand students, bigger than Harvard and Yale combined. He moved to South Africa a few years back and has worked there since."

"I'm convinced if you're convinced. Why'd he leave Norway?"

"Personal reasons Mister O'Rourke." The Professor had come outside for a cigarette and now was right behind them. Both men were amazed at how silently he moved and made mental notes to be a little more aware next time.

"Personal like in, mind your business personal?"

"I blew up science lab conducting experiments, antimatter power generation. Two assistants injured, one serious. She not walk again, ever." Those last words were spoken in anguish and the man turned to walk back down the path the way he had come but hesitated momentarily before speaking again.

"You here dee biblical legend about dee walled city of Jericho, right?" asked the scientist, before answering his own self. "Yah, you do. You got Joshua leading seven priests carrying ram's horns or shofar, en behind dem more priests carrying dee Ark of dee Covenant. Once every six days dey march 'round dee entire city, den on dee seventh day, dee seven priests blew loud on dere shofar en dee walls come tumbling down. Wal we t'ink dey do dis t'ings so dee Ark collect solar power, get powerful, den on seventh day; after one more turn around dee town, when God's device full of power en might, dey stand behind it en blow dem horns toward Jericho. Hebrew believe in dee power of seven. It sacred to dem. So all dat sound energy trigger all dee power of dat Ark straight at dem stone walls en Kapow! Dem walls come tumbling down."

"Of course you understand that sound is just a lower scale electromagnetic frequency range". "But it makes sense that the ancients could have used it as a trigger for the Ark's stored up power. Obviously, they didn't have power amps like we do today."

"Yup, we're so advanced we're still trying to figure out how to duplicate what they did way back when." JP couldn't resist poking a tiny little hole in Chaco's logic. But it was just a teeny, tiny hole and then he was done with smart alecking. Even more after the South African turned and abruptly walked away, a cloud of tobacco smoke following his progress.

The moon was just rising, catching up to Venus, already high in the sky. Neither spoke for a few seconds. Chaco could tell what JP was thinking. "Now you ask, how can we trust the future of the world on the Nutty Professor? Right? I trust him. I met him during a class lecture at UCLA. I still get over there from time to time. We have corresponded since. He lives in Pretoria now. Gone native. Has an African wife, Zulu tribe. If this thing misses the target area by a few degrees it could hit them, it could hit us. Either way it's going to make one hell of a mess."

"Exactly what I mean! Hell is coming to earth any way you slice it. Ya'll wanna go on your own and build some kinda 'ain't never before been built' power device for some ain't never been seen since antiquity mystical gift from God. Antimatter! God particles! That's your focus. That's why you brought the Professor in even though those scientists who still live in Geneva are trying to develop the same stuff with multi-billion dollar machines bigger than this corner of New Mexico and power out the ying-yang. Not saying they're right and you're wrong. Just sayin'…"

"The people at CERN have a different focus JP."

"Focus-pocus! I watch Discovery Channel. I remember a show they did on that 'God Particle', that Higgs Boson the prof, err Doctor was lecturing, err, talking about, if it exists."

"It's true that they're involved in a search for the ultra-tiny. But those six thousand scientists they employ are pretty much all focused on recreating the Big Bang. So they want to win Nobel awards for figuring out what happened at the beginning. We're looking along a different path."

"I read that the Large Hadron Collider at CERN cost over ten billion dollars to construct its seventeen mile circuit that runs under Switzerland and France and is capable of using seven trillion volts of electricity. All I can say is that sure would relieve any power aches you got."

"It's not that simple!" Chaco's voice seemed a bit more strained. Perhaps he had achieved threshold and now frustration had begun takeover. O'Rourke didn't concern himself with Chaco's comfort zone. A little girl's bright smile floated into his mind's eye. There were more important issues at stake. Egos could go to Hell …or some other useless place.

"So if you build your anti-matter repulsor-slash-unmaker power source and golly gee-whiz steering mechanism an' it doesn't blow up this corner of New Mexico, or whatever place you move it to, you'll pop it off through the Ark at this comet when it gets into range, right? Until then it'll just be computer simulations or desert rocks. If it works great! We win! En if it don't, poof, we lose!" He mimicked the Professor, hoping the white-haired older man had already left earshot, but not overly concerned had he not. The heat of this moment flushed all sense of propriety --exit Emily Post, reemerge Devil Dog—final metamorphosis stage-three, cold-blooded. His drill instructors would truly be proud …as would Colonel Peterson.

But if any of this retro-Marine resurgence measured sufficiently to command attention within his cognitive faculties, his outward appearance never once waivered; another aspect which would have engendered pride in those who had helped shape him. His business sense was all business. Cosmetic things, such as menacing glares and chest poundings and such niceties were immaterial and would not be employed. The old training resurfaced as the calculating warrior. Things germane to this issue evolved and clashed and clanged about in rapid-fire pace just beneath a placid countenance that gave no overt clue to the turmoil. Along which path lay the demon? Should he follow the leader or seek his own counsel? Which leader? Trust the government weenies or this meek, but determined man before him? What to do?

He resisted the temptation to toss up a coin and let its imaginary flop decide --tails, stay the course, heads, call his Uncle. No, this was much too involved for any stochastic remedies. A heads up flop would leave no choice but a "kill or be killed" approach. It would be the only way to steal back the device; take all these people out and call DIA. Peterson would love that.

Chagrin began a mindless jaunt through his every, inner fiber, though remaining unregistered on the surface. But somehow Chaco must have perceived some nearly imperceptible message. His one good eye fixed O'Rourke with a knowing stare whose gleam shone unmistakably across to the black man now that the full moon rising eastward provided assistance to the dim starlight.

"Don't do it JP," his soft voice both pleading and powerful at the same moment. "All for one or all will fail. I understand your dilemma, you've been institutionalized most of your life, first government, then corporate. It's difficult to fight the establishment. They've got the numbers, the expertise, right? Do you really believe that one man can't make a difference? If not one then how about two? The power input-to-output ratio is one concern, threshold is another. We'll need to test it to see how much it can take. But we have other experts on the way. We'll make it work, by the Mother!"

"Let's say this thing is just a gaudy power amplifier that was built by people who possessed some kind of advanced knowledge. We'll call it, magic. An' let's say it was ultimately designed for times like this. Those being the case, it shouldn't need stuff the old timers couldn't provide, should it?"

"Possibly. This Ark produces a form of elemental power that we have only begun to study. Some might term it as magic; I choose to believe it science. We do not know exactly how it does what it does, we may never know. What we do know are the results we get from channeling relatively small charges of current through it. We feel certain it can save our planet."

"You think it maybe was left to us by some far-seeing ancient people." His statement came out gently, not quite an accusation ending in, "And you're nuts!"

"Years ago I found petroglyphs in a cave that depicted an event similar to what we are about to face. Fire raining down from the sky out of a star pattern similar to the Orion Nebula. The scene showed a comet and burning fields of corn and I named it Orion Rain. I believe my Puebloan ancestors were leaving a message for the future, for their descendants, maybe even for me. My mother's people were skilled astronomers. I'd like to take you to see what they did in Chaco Canyon up north of here … if we get the chance."

This tailing statement came almost as a whisper, as if chance was a commodity over which he had little control, as if he sensed his impending death, possibly at the hands of the man to whom he spoke. But he showed neither fear nor the desire to flee or call for help. Instead he gathered strength back into his vocal cords and continued.

"We have experts in hieroglyphics and hieratic Egyptian script on the way also. It's gonna get crowded." He winked, even though its effect was lost in the shadows. He did not worry whether the other perceived his joke, just plodded on with the explanation. "We found some ancient writings in the Ark that appear to be instructions. Some on papyrus some chiseled into stone. The ideograms we feel confident we have solved, but we've yet to decipher most of the hieratic symbols; they appear to be in some arcane code. But we're confident…"

"Where have I heard that before? Oh yeah, that's what they said in Vietnam. 'We know how the gooks think; we'll bomb 'em back to the Stone Age.' Hell, those guys lived in th' Stone Age! They said it again before they took us into Afghanistan. I once looked up the meaning of the word 'expert' to try and make sense of it since so many so-called experts seem to be either plain fools or opinionated assholes that get everybody else dead. The word means to try, to test, a person wise through experience. Well, I now have a different opinion. I'm reminded that 'ex' means used to be or used to have. You know, ex-boss, ex-wife, ex-Catholic. So I kinda look at experts as people who used to know. In fact, Plato urged rulers to tell their people 'The Noble Lie' to keep them passive and content, without the risk of upheaval and unrest. So experts are often not only unknowing, but untruthful. So excuse my manners but I don't jump up and clap at the mention of experts."

"I trust these people. They're highly…"

"Chaco, you're making the same mistake all those jerks you hate made." JP could not get off the soapbox. He was too far along to be redirected easily. "Man you gotta be inclusive, not the other way around. Any idiot can exclude. We got a zillion tons o' Kryptonite 'bout ta rain down on our heads an' you tryna play Superman. Even if your ancestors were warning you personally, suppose those inscriptions, those hieroglyphics, hieratics, whatever, what if they only mean bring everybody to th' dance?"

"And how do you propose that we do that?"

"Why not just email that video and the findings of what we know to everybody we know? Like the Israelis, they won't be too happy with that thing comin' their way. No matter what their Christian and Islamic brethren might prefer, they don't wanna speed up Armageddon. They can help and how 'bout Doc's government? They gotta have some smart people. I know it took a while before they figured out how ta do away wit' apartheid, took quite a while, but they did. You're bringing your folks, but what about the real deal? The Egyptians probably got some people with ideas about how to read this ancient writing. Let's not keep this thing under wraps. We need all the players!"

"They'll never let us keep it."

"So? Look, you checked up on me, well I checked up on you. You aren't into heirlooms and keepsakes. Who cares who keeps the Ark? We gotta care about who gonna keep us! I remember reading about a guy who was standing in a rowboat, pointing at the guy at the other end and sayin', 'Hey fella, your end's sinking!' The way we gotta look at it Chaco, is if one of us goes down, we all go down! One world!"

"I think it's taking a big chance, a hellova chance. I gotta think it over."

"You think it's strange that all those old civilizations failed and died out Chaco? When the guys who built the pyramids left, didn't nobody know how they did their thing. When your Anasazi people in Chaco Canyon left, nobody knew their secrets. Yeah, like I said, I checked up on you too. They could forecast seasons based on the stars and align their observatories to catch the changes in equinoxes. What was their problem? Territorial! Exclusivity! aka, racism. If mankind gonna keep on that path, the next group to come along will be startin' all over again cause we'll have passed on, been smashed to smithereens, takin' our secrets with us. We gotta do better than all them old folks Chaco. Every time I see people on their knees beggin' God to help them with this bill or save them from that problem or th' other, I'm about ta puke! I believe that even if God is looking at those people when they doin' their trained seal impressions, God just sighs and walks away, thinkin' 'Ya'll still don't get it'! That's cause I believe God gave mankind all we need to survive. Now all we gotta do is find a way with all our tools and talent. I know it sounds kinda like I'm on a soapbox 'n all. But I gotta hammer this point! We are a race of people --not of religions, tribes, nationalities or colors—but people, we all are part of this! We won't make it alone. This is the midnight hour that the old church folks been talking about, except it's the time for mankind to either shit or shine! I propose we go for the shine!" Finally he quieted, standing down from his soapbox, all but argued out. But help was coming…

"JP got it right Chaco," Martinez' rumbling voice came out of nowhere, shaking JP momentarily. He had really gotten caught in the moment, high up on that soap box. A humorous thought suggested he could have gotten snuck up on by anyone of a dozen jealous husbands; wouldn't have had a clue 'til it too late. He smiled back at the big man who took that as his cue to continue.

"Gotta get past that predator mentality, thinking everything along territorial lines. We need to get as many resources together on this as possible. We got people out there who can dream up ways ta make a bullfrog croak crickets."

Back in the day, Martinez' one-liners had become well known and oft-repeated across myriad realms and time zones. Some had been incorporated into Marine Corps lore as legendary witticisms employed in motivational speeches to the troops, primarily by drill instructors chewing out those same troops. "A genius is person that can figger out how ta make a bullfrog croak crickets. However you shit maggots ain't got th' sense ta make popcorn pop! Left foot first, numb nuts!"

Martinez appeared dead serious, calm, maybe even stoic, in the poor light. Both the others could see he still had more saying to say. So they allowed him his way. Normally he stuck to his famous (some said infamous) one-liners. However, tonight he morphed temporarily. In place of his slowly worded quips --that cut to the quick-- a more erudite, long-winded version of this gentle giant.

"Y'know, I was watching some little cartoon a few days ago an' the heroes were tryin' ta move a giant mirror so it wouldn't deflect a super-hot heat wave onto a small town. It weighed around a hundred thousand pounds, so moving it wouldn't be easy. These guys tried ta blow it up, pull it down, you name it. Sun was about to rise and everybody in town would soon be roasted 'n toasted. The heroes were all desperate, going crazy, runnin' around like spastic chickens chasing jumpin' bugs. Whole time I'm wondering, why don't they just cover it up? One big tarp and problem solved. All I'm tryin' ta' say is keep it simple. Sometimes a little kiss is all you need."

Chaco smiled weakly at Martinez' mention of the K-I-S-S principle, admonishing his lofty ideas and imploring him to: "keep it simple stupid". But it was JP's characterization of his motivations as racist that really shook him, causing instantaneous reflection. Was he acting just like the white men he despised for their mendacity, their underhanded dealings with others? Was he? His mind surged into reverse; his thoughts chronicling Anasazi hiring practices; his internal mechanism searching for any memory related to decision mechanisms prompting selection of one candidate over another. He couldn't recall. When was the last time he'd hired a person of Negro ancestry? He remembered some Asians, some whites and obviously some Latinos, but who was the last black person he had promoted? There were some, he knew, probably not many. When was the last time? The young kids always say: "once a racist, always a racist."

Perhaps these two were right, perhaps he was jousting at windmills, seeing ghostly phantasms behind each tree and making up excuses to support his own prejudices. He looked up and west into a deepening night sky that still resisted any evidence of the moonlight peeking above hills on the eastern flank to his rear, as if searching for some celestial sign.

An exploding star would be very appreciated about now. None apparent in the obsidian tapestry, he focused his one good eye on Sirius, the Dog Star. The interloper coming to finish them all was already well past another cosmic hound, the Dog Planet, Pluto and sniffing the bait. He himself could not see its ebony mass of ice and stone, but he knew it had already spied his home and now made steadily, unerringly for it.

He prayed again to the Mother Earth that she was guiding his decisions. He did not desire to be left alone with a decision whose import could affect his entire race, the human race. Despite JP's assurance that God was only a spectator, Chaco desired divine assistance or, at the very least, divine guidance. But he considered what this passionate new friend had asserted. If God is indeed inside each of them, it was they who must make this work. He looked to the two men …still unconvinced, but not quite like before.

JP caught the look and reminded him, "Every day starts good, Chaco. Maybe your ancestors only got it part right. Maybe we're all children of a lost god. What I do know is that humanity is all about teamwork. Everybody can't be quarterback."

"Yeah," chimed Martinez, "now let's figure a way that we don't hurt nuthin' we might need later."

And then he was gone, just as quickly as he'd come, leaving them to digest his words, his meaning. JP still felt somewhat amazed at the big man's speed and stealth. It seemed he'd barely blinked and then no more Martinez. It was probably a good thing he hadn't attempted any attacks on that man mountain, could have ended ugly, very ugly. But now he was left alone with this much smaller, though no less determined man.

"Yeah, few men could stand up to him. Most haven't a prayer of succeeding," whispered Chaco. Now JP stared even more keenly at the older man. It seemed as if he had become a mind reader. How else could he know? He was probably correct in his assessment that he wouldn't have a prayer; he hadn't specified; however both knew to whom he referred. Regardless, it was the word itself which snatched him backwards, dredging old memories from the cobwebs of his inner workings, his mindsight, into clairvoyance.

"Let's go see it." Barely a whisper.

"Kay. Know I'm curious."

A few minutes later they stood before the gleaming Ark of the Covenant.

It sat alone on its concrete platform illuminated only by moonlight. They could see that all foot connectors had been melted away.

"We've tried a few different kinds of power connectors. So far, without satisfactory results.

"See that!"

"It be okay, we figure it out." He looked back over his shoulder. Trent. "Not too close! We techs wear protective suits when working. Found out the hard way even tricky with those."

"I figured." He pointed at the man's white coveralls. "How's New Mexico treating you man?"

"Ayebegoo! Little chilly, nothin' bad!" Removing his right glove, he shook O'Rourke's hand, flashed his award winning smile, then went silent, allowing the other two to continue their convo.

Another presence, this one seemed familiar, though not any of the men here tonight. Instinctively he knew it, even though he never knew it. The moon was high now. Its light beams inducing a faint glow in the device. A whisper emanated, a call commanding…

Before either of the other men could grab onto his outstretched arm his left hand touched against the Ark, as if magnetically attached. Next his right and then the golden glow surrounded him. Instantly the sound spiked higher, not unbearably, just noticeably.

"Oh, shit! JP what you doing mon?" Trent rushed forward to save his friend, hoping his heavy electrician's protective suit would suffice even without the glove he'd no time to slip back on. But Chaco's slight body slid between them. "Chaco?"

"Wait Trent!" His calm command perplexed the other. But he instantly obeyed. Both turned to see. One confident, the other fearful. But O'Rourke was still alive, the palms of his hands still affixed to the device as if magnetically glued. But he didn't burn up, electrocute, not even char. It was amazing …at least to Trent.

O'Rourke's head was lifted to the sky. Eyes closed, he appeared to meditate, as if releasing all his cares and fears into the cosmos. No words, at least none verbal that their ears could detect. But instinctively Chaco knew. He'd trusted his Earth Mother and somehow he knew.

O'Rourke knew only that he had finally come round circle to meet all his boogeyman tormentors. Except they weren't tormentors. They were his protectors, mamma, daddy, Aunt Maude, Tony and …Shiro!

"Some say that prayer changes things", spoke Shiro's soft voice. "Others say that prayer changes people and people change things. Prayer is like a form of meditation which focuses the mind inward. We see clearly when we look deep inside ourselves. There we find God."

It was a lesson from the past. None of the phantasms spoke words to him, just radiated love. And something more …pride!

"I saw them all." He spoke softly, scarcely believing himself. "They showed me what we gotta do to beat this thing. We can do it!" Trent had run to get a first aid kit, certain there would at least be burns. But Chaco just studied his face intently, uncertain why he'd known, just somehow he knew JP would not be harmed. Probably anyone else would be coal dust or ashes right now, but somehow he knew.

"Chaco you ever get the feeling there's something pulling you, something very different; something you can't quite understand or explain?"

"I always have. It's like a message in another language. I always attribute it to my mother's people; like they're watching me, maybe even coaching me. If not them, maybe it's Awitelin Tsta whom they worship as the Earth Mother Goddess. Either way, I always feel inadequate; like I'm undeserving of their attention." His small voice trailed away even smaller "…since I haven't done anything to deserve it."

"Yeah, I get that too. Bottom line, it's about choices. What you choose and how you choose them is important. Sometimes we breakdown what ultimately contributes to our successes and failures as Lady Luck. It takes a bit of all three. Sometimes one may play the greater role; however, it still takes the three, perhaps fine-tuned to feature one above the others, but still the three. They say you gotta buy your ticket and take your chance. They're probably right. But you gotta buy that ticket to find out."

"So you want to choose a course and hope luck is waiting?"

"I prefer to believe that regardless whether we call it luck or fortune it will favor us to make the best choice because we are either lucky or qualified or both. We choose what we choose based on what we know and believe and if lucky we get it right. We get it right, we win."

"So, if I said I hope you're right, you'd be okay with that?

"Funny, but maybe not so far from truth. I remember an author once comparing the choice of writing with farming, owning a deli or driving a truck. His point was that self-employment of any kind is often just as bad a deal, just as tragic, just as full of misplaced hopes and accidents that can pitch a well-meaning and diligent person into fortune or into poverty. Whatever your choice, if you get the luck, it's fortune and fame. If not, maybe poverty and ruin. Make your choice Chaco. We'll deal with it, whatever it is."

Chaco didn't reply. Instead he turned his face up, towards the moonshine, eyes closed, feeling its pale light rather than seeing. The spoken words came clearly, though without introduction.

"What, is a reality? Whom, does it consume? When, in our knowing, will realities claim our doom? Is it as simple as a whistle or the plaintive song of the lonely lark? Can we ever know its meaning, if we ever fear the dark?

Is it simple as our looking close or a second look from we? Can discovery prove more wondersome when we fail to even see? Just one more little, tiny thought to render us obsessed; reality among us, must surely be possessed. For do ever really any other positives abound, devoid opposing seeking chance to gather hither round?

Exist without our opposites? Can such a state be won? Is good so good it can remain once bad abandons, gone? Yet whimsical, though fearingful, this thought escape from sensible and practically delightfully, we fanciful the questionfull. Is reality a state of mind that we create within our time?

And what about the times before or times have yet to come? Is all about those nether states philosophy undone? Can reality exist without us playing true our part? Our conscious contribution, are we really all so smart?

Does the sound of mountains tumbling down even sound if we can't hear it? Is it manifest that its only best with our presence there to cheer it? We seek our way to find our God, to show us all we are. But could really be, the reality, is that we live in God, because God lives in we?"

Chaco's poem ended and for a few moments neither of them broke the silence until JP whistled softly, "Wheeww. Deep. I'm not sure I know what that all means, but I think I really like it."

"I call it 'Where God Lives'. It's kind of old. From back in my UCLA days. Somehow it just popped into my mind. Kinda seemed apropos."

"Yeah, kinda does."

"So you really believe you saw your folks?"

"I really do! Spooky, ain't it! I could sense Shiro reminding me, 'It is mind over matter JP. Without mind, what does it matter?'"

"Sounds like a very wise man. Wish I'd have met him."

"Me too."

Then both men fell silent once again. The poetry filling the void. It did seem appropriate. As he replayed its words, at that moment he could feel the presence of everything around him or so he felt. In his mindsight he could sense them all in this reality: the night crawlers scurrying at his feet, the black man standing resolute at his back, a gentle night breeze flowing lazily past tinged with fragrance lifted from desert cacti blooms and the earth mother smiling her grace. She seemed at peace with him, confident that he would choose wisely; perhaps because he possessed those qualifications, those skills that his new friend had just mentioned. Perhaps because he knew good counsel when it came his way…

Their assuredness nurtured and emboldened him. Perhaps divine assistance had come after all, maybe in a different manner than he sought. But who's to say what's divine? In that instant his clouded vision suddenly cleared remarkably permitting even his long useless right eye to witness the glowing revelation being spun in the starlit heavens. The ultimate reality. Time without end. As his ancestors had once gazed up into the ebony background and seen grizzly bears battling mountain lions, he now saw the answer his questioning heart had sought.

He could not explain it, it just appeared to him. The mystery unraveled; as if mystical words and phrases, formed by the celestial host, he could now decipher. His eyes still closed tightly, he could see all and all became apparent to him; its meaning flowing into his head, his heart: "Look inside you! See inside yourself!"

His eyes opened and the blindness which had tried to overwhelm him had gone. He felt very different as he turned back to face his friend. "We earthlings all believe we are special, and we are." He began, pausing to offer a wan smile.

"In the grand scheme, we occupy a meaningless, obscure planet that constitutes the third rock from an obscure sun in an obscure corner of an obscure galaxy. No different than many, many other places throughout this universe I'm sure. However, what is different, millions of years ago something not so obscure transpires. Poof! We have life. It is diverse and rich and fruitful and ubiquitous. We have everything, all the tools we need to make it chicken salad. Our only task is to ensure it doesn't end up chicken shit!"

He paused again, reflecting on another thought, which had erupted in searing reality, before explaining: "God is not lost, JP. Never has been. That's the reality. Man just needs to open his heart and there he will find God. Why this is so? Who knows the mind of God? It just is!"

As if in response, a song began playing over the night sounds. It was the same song that had nurtured a broken little boy who had nearly lost his battle with a desert tree, so many years before. Then he realized the Mother was still with him, had never left. He could feel her warmth, her wisdom. She was singing to him the old song she had sung dozens of years before: "COME TOGETHER, RIGHT NOW, OVER ME…"   FIN

"For now we see through a glass, darkly; but then face to face: now I know in part; but then shall I know even as also I am known." (1 Corinthians 13:12)KJV

Where God Lives

"What, is a reality? Whom, does it consume? When, in our knowing, will realities claim our doom? Is it as simple as a whistle or the plaintive song of the lonely lark? Can we ever know its meaning, if we ever fear the dark?

Is it simple as our looking close or a second look from we? Can discovery prove more wondersome when we fail to even see? Just one more little, tiny thought to render us obsessed; reality among us, must surely be possessed. For do ever really any other positives abound, devoid opposing seeking chance to gather hither round?

Exist without our opposites? Can such a state be won? Is good so good it can remain once bad abandons, gone? Yet whimsical, though fearingful, this thought escape from sensible and practically delightfully, we fanciful the questionfull. Is reality a state of mind that we create within our time?

And what about the times before or times have yet to come? Is all about those nether states philosophy undone? Can reality exist without us playing true our part? Our conscious contribution, are we really all so smart?

Does the sound of mountains tumbling down even sound if we can't hear it? Is it manifest that its only best with our presence there to cheer it? We seek our way to find our God, to show us all we are. But could really be, the reality, is that we live in God, because God lives in we?"